Buddha-Messiahs, Vol. 1
Yeshu, Essene Jesus *of the* Gnostic Nazoreans

Davied Asia Israel

Contents

¯ 0 ¯
Introduction

THE ORIGINAL JESUS, or Yeshu as he was called in his native tongue of Aramaic, taught what is now a greatly unknown system of enlightenment and purification that some have called Gnosticism, but which more correctly is called *"Nazirutha"*. Nazirutha is an Aramaic term whose closest western equivalent is "enlightenment". The concept is related to the Bonpo[1] Buddhist idea of enlightened Buddhahood, but the means and methods are quite different. This system of Nazirutha once taught by Yeshu of the Nazoreans has now been replaced by a false form of worship begun by Paul called Christianity. This Christianity represents the teachings of this Paul, not Jesus, and bears little semblance to the original message of the Nazorean Messiah. This book attempts to present these original teachings of Yeshu as discoverable in the ancient but now obscure Aramaic scrolls and other ancient documents. We will contrast these teachings, which will appear novel or even heretical to many, with the standard doctrines and prejudices of orthodox and protestant Christianity so that the reader may judge for themselves the validity of the Gnostic view of Yeshu, or Jesus, the Buddha-Messiah of the Nazoreans.

The world and teachings of Jesus the Nazorean, Yeshu's "Secret of the Holy Plan", have been misunderstood by the modern world that have made the mistake of viewing him from a Judeo-Christian worldview, rather than the truer Bonpo-Buddhist. False ideas and fantastic tales abound and taint the truth of whom and what became known as Jesus of Nazareth. Few have been open minded enough to consider the

---

[1] The origin of the Bön lineage is traced to a Persian Buddha named Tönpa Shenrab Miwo, rather than to Buddha Shakyamuni of India. Bonpo Buddhism teaches Dzogchen.

evidence of the other Jesus - the real Yeshu of the Nazoreans. As we previously claimed, the traditions that have come down through Christendom are greatly fantasized. Among these fantasies and false traditions are the myths of the conception, birth, childhood, teachings, and resurrection of Jesus. These accounts found in the New Testament are greatly flawed, greatly exaggerated, and wholly off the mark when it comes to the truth of Yeshu and his birth, upbringing, message and ascension. It is provable, for instance, that Jesus was not born of a virgin, or as a Jew, nor did he grow up reading the Old Testament. Ancient records indicate Jesus belonged to a different group of people who had different Gods and scriptures from those of the Jews. Nor did Jesus reform the Jewish religion or even invent one of his own. Jesus was born into and raised within an ancient spiritual tradition that was the foundation of his later teachings. This ancient spiritual tradition was known as the Nazorean sect, and for this reason Jesus was called "Jesus the Nazorean". His death was not a blood atonement for sin, nor was he resurrected in his physical body. All these matters are myths that obscure the real and authentic teachings and works of the Gnostic Savior.

In this book we will explore what it meant to be born and raised a Nazorean, and ancient Syrian sect with closer ties to central Asian Buddhism than to Judaism. We will use original Essene scrolls to explain the Nazorean teachings and traditions and detail how Jesus fit into this system and how his identity and teachings were eventually altered and expanded by certain brilliant but deluded people to form a religion totally different from what he originally taught and stood for. Some of the information in this book may appear disturbing to some, for the Essene Nazorean Christ is not the same as the Romanized Jesus propagated by the New Testament and modern Christianity.

Original Gnostic Nazoreanism was composed of family and friends of Yeshu who knew him well and understood perfectly his mission and life. Like the Central Asian Bonpo faith, Nazoreans passed down their teachings within family lineages of married practitioners. Members of Pauline Christianity were not so well informed or connected and they made many calculated misrepresentations to further their own ends. Original Gnostic Christianity certainly had a deeper and better understanding of the real historical Jesus before the cover-up and falsification of the record by the Pauline school.

In addition, we will explore to some degree the Nazorean office of Messiah which differs drastically from that of the Jews or Greco-Roman Christians. In Nazoreanism the office of Messiah (Mashiah) is filled by both Yeshu and his female counterpart who form a cosmic duo who set in motion the events that resulted in the incarnation of heavenly souls in the physical bodies of this world. This same cosmic couple also established the machinery that makes escape from the material universe possible. We will touch upon these principles briefly in this book and will concentrate mainly on Yeshu, the male aspect of Christ, deferring exploration of the feminine aspect of Christ to the companion of this book which focuses on Miryai, or Miryam of Magdala.

Correctly identifying the Essene Nazorean culture and backdrop of Christ's life and teachings is an important component of identifying the true tradition, as is identification of the correct historical record. We shall delve into these matters in later chapters. We reiterate that Jesus WAS NOT a Jew or a believer in the Law of Moses! The New Testament IS NOT an accurate portrayal of His life. Yeshu was vegetarian and taught a unique form of Nazorean Gnosis called Nazirutha. It is important to understand that this gnosis, or Nazirutha, is not intellectual understanding of dry facts, figures and concepts, nor is it the ability to debate, argue or rationally speak about spiritual matters. It is not book knowledge, but spiritual wisdom and illumination gained from personal mystical experiences. It is firsthand knowledge of Deities, angels and heavenly worlds acquired by profound dreams, koan insights, revelations, appearances, theophany experiences, or even pure understanding coming into the heart in the form of whispered truths or life altering images. It is not something that can be taught, only experienced. The Nazorean Way of Yeshu was designed to heighten the possibility of these personal mystical experiences and lead the seeker into personal acquaintance with Deity. Yeshu taught how to do this in great detail.

Sources

Many ancient Aramaic texts of the Nazoreans have been preserved. These ancient scrolls were copied and recopied hundreds of times until fairly faithful renditions survived. In these source documents we read claims that the Nazorean faith goes back to the first significant couple – Adam and Havah, and is periodically renewed and refreshed by a series of restorative couples and messengers of light. They contain stories of prophets and prophetesses not found in Jewish writings, like Ram and Rud, Shabai and others. They also contain writings and tales of messengers of light that share common names with characters in the Old Testament but have different stories and teachings associated with them. In Nazorean texts we read of Shem, Noah, and others, but the stories and teachings are different. For instance Noah's son, and not Noah, is the main character of the story. He is called Shum bar Nu and his wife is called Nhuraita. We also read of some names that show up in the New Testament, like John the Baptist, Mary, and even Yeshu or Jesus. But again, the stories are very different. When we read of John the Baptist for instance, his Aramaic name of Yuhana is used. We learn that he was taught by a Nazorean named Anush, that he had two wives names Anhar and Qintat, and that he baptized Yeshu on numerous occasions and taught truths not found in the bible. Previous to Anush the leader of the Nazoreans was a prophet called Bihram. After Yeshu, and after his brother James and his brother Shimeon ruled over the Nazoreans, other great prophets arose. These include Elchasai, Yexai, Mani and others. This alternant history found in alternant texts is unknown for the most part among Roman Christians who usurped the name and identity of Yeshu for their own ends and rewrote history as they wished. But the authentic texts and traditions have survived. We will elucidate these to some degree in this book.

Although our main intent is to elucidate the life of Yeshu from ancient Aramaic and Coptic sources, we would be remiss if we did not also mention other secondary information that supports these ancient documents, such as the Christian heresiologists who wrote condemnations of the Gnostics but nevertheless preserved much information about them in the process. Occasionally these ancient Roman Christian writers, like Epiphanius or Clement, will make a useful comment or two on Gnosticism, mostly to ridicule or degrade it in the eyes of those they wrote their propaganda for. This has helped to preserve some useful information that might have otherwise been lost.

Other sources of note are the Essene readings by Edgar Cayce, and the Suddie readings facilitated by Dolores Cannon. Both these sources result from information received while the subjects were under deep hypnotic trance. Edgar Cayce (1877–1945) was an American psychic who channeled answers to questions on subjects such as health, astrology, reincarnation, and Essenes while in hypnotic trance. The Suddie Readings are dialogues between modern Past-Life Regressionist Dolores Cannon and Suddie, a member of a Qumran Essene community, alive around the time of Christ, speaking through a hypnotized subject. This type of information gathering is not inharmonious with practices of the ancient Nazorean Essenes, since they too were keen on dreams, portents, and revelations flowing from altered states of consciousness. The Bible, which is against most things Nazorean, is also against hypnotic regressions, spiritual mediums, and other communication with the dead or discarnate, but for Gnostics the only issue is the purity of the information, not the manner in which it is gathered. Despite the acceptability of this type of practice among the Gnostics, one needs to be very careful not to confuse it with historical documents. Historical documents too have their problems of authenticity, but they rest on a different foundation. The Cayce readings have the benefit of being numerous and extensive, and have a well proven track record of accuracy in many fields of knowledge. Also, their Essene and Jesus material was given well before many of the modern discoveries have verified much of their information. These Cayce readings fill in details, but do not alter the basic construct created by close attention to details in the ancient Gnostic scrolls. Cayce was once asked:

> "Is Gnosticism the closest type of Christianity to that which is given through his source?"

He answered:

> "This is a parallel, and was the commonly accepted one until there began to be set rules in which there were attempts to take short cuts. And there are none in Christianity." [2]

---

[2] Cayce Reading 5749-14

Modern Christianity represents a false short cut to salvation, and as Cayce said, there are no shortcuts. Gnosticism, on the other hand, represents the true but more difficult path to enlightenment and divinity.

The Suddie material functions in a similar light to the Cayce Readings, and is amazing in its harmony with subtle details in Gnostic Nazorean philosophy. It backs up or details many matters set forth or alluded to in Gnostic manuscripts seemingly unknown to those who channeled the material. It portrays Qumran as an Essene community and purports to tell us that both Yeshu and Yuhana spent time there during their education. There is nothing in these two accounts that conflict with the theology in the more solid sacred scrolls of antiquity, which is amazing when one considers just how different the Nazorean and Essene world view is in comparison to Judaism or modern Christianity. A complete list of sources used in reconstructing this account of the secret and public life of Yeshu the Nazorean can be found in appendix one at the end of this book.

This book is the first of a three volume series on the enlightened Savior Prophets of the Gnostics. The three volumes are:

- ❖ "Buddha-Messiahs, Vol. 1: Yeshu, Essene Jesus of the Gnostic Nazoreans";
- ❖ "Buddha-Messiahs, Vol. II: Miryai, the Mysteries of Mary Magdalene";
- ❖ "Buddha-Messiahs, Vol. III: Mani, Christian Buddha and Taoist Sage".

˜ 1 ˜
PRE-EXISTENCE OF Yeshu

Yeshu as Only-Begotten

YESHU THE NAZOREAN, like all Nazoreans, was born to Heavenly Parents[3], in a spirit filled Light Land above. Unlike other Pearls[4], Yeshu had a special connection and understanding of his Parents that allowed him to take the lead in all important spiritual endeavors both then and now. He was called *Mana*, or Mind, in the Order's ancient scrolls. Mainstream Christianity accepts the pre-existence of Jesus, but usually sees him as unique in this pre-earth life existence. Gnosticism that developed out of older Nazorean Essenism understood Yeshu to be only the first among many pre-existent spirits; they also understood that he had a female spiritual counterpart, a syzygy[5] or twin. His female counterpart is called *Dmuta* in Aramaic, meaning image, and *Kushta*, meaning Truth. When asked about Miryam, or Mary, the mother of Yeshu, the Sleeping Prophet replied:

> "In the beginning Mary was the twin-soul of the Master in the entrance into the earth! . . . They were one SOUL so far as the earth is concerned; because [else] she would not be incarnated in flesh, you see." [6]

---

[3] Nazoreans worshipped both a Heavenly Father as well as Heavenly Mother, calling them the Great Life (*Hiya Rba*). These are Kuntuzangpo (*the All Good*) and Kuntuzangmo(*All Good Woman*) of the Bonpos.

[4] Pearl is a Nazorean term used to denote a pure soul from heaven.

[5] Syzygy is a kind of unity, especially through coordination or alignment, most commonly used in the astronomical sense. From the Late Latin syzygia, "conjunction," from the Greek σύζυγος (syzygos), "yoked together."

[6] Edgar Cayce Readings, Text Of Reading 5749-8

Because of Their special understanding and depth of Gnosis and acquaintance with the Primal Parents, Yeshu and Miryam[7] are the archetypes of perfection and the role model for all developing Nazoreans. This ancient summary of Valentinian beliefs expresses such this way:

> "There is a perfect pre-existence, Aeon, a dwelling in the invisible and unnamable elevations; this is Pre-Beginning and Forefather and Depth. It is uncontainable and invisible, eternal and ungenerated, in quiet deep solitude for infinite aeons. With it is Thought, which is also called Grace and Silence. Depth thought of emitting itself, a beginning of all. Like a seed, this thought from Depth was placed into Silence, like a womb. Silence received this seed and bore Mind. Mind resembled and was equal to it that had created him.

> "Mind alone comprehends the magnitude of his Father; he is called Only-Begotten and Father and Beginning of All. Along with him, Truth was emitted; this makes the first Four, the root.[8]

God Incarnate

Orthodox Christians worship a male Trinity called the Father, Son and Holy Ghost. They derived this Trinity from the older Nazorean one which included both Gods and Goddesses. The Christians simply removed the Goddesses from their list of Gods. Christians and Nazoreans were in agreement that the second male member of this Trinity was born on earth as

---

[7] Mariam (Virgin Mary) is considered a Goddess incarnate among Nazoreans. Her purity stands on its own merits and is not the sole result of the efforts of Yeshu. According to Yeshu in the Pistis Sophia Codex, Mary the Mother and Magdalene both were earthly emanations of the Virgin Of Light above. They, like Yeshu, came to earth as Messengers of light from that Good Realm above to teach, not die for, humanity. As a product of Nazorean eugenics, the Maiden was conceived, gestated, and raised in holiness according to the ancient patterns established by Elijah, Elisha, Samuel and other instigators of the Bnia-Amin Eugenics program at Carmel. In this teaching, not only Miryam, but many others for many generations had been immaculately conceived and reared according to ancient Essene laws of purity and purpose.

[8] Robert M. Grant, Gnosticism, pp.163-181.

Yeshu, or Jesus. They differed in their understanding of this incarnation, however. Christians claimed Jesus had a divine body while on earth while Nazoreans denied this. Nazoreans saw Yeshu's soul as divine but considered his divinity latent while he was incarnated in a body of flesh and bones. We will delve into this matter more in future chapters.

Yeshu's Primeval Crucifixion

Orthodox Roman Christians think that the most important thing that their Jesus did was be crucified. For Gnostics, the earthly crucifixion was not the greatest thing Yeshu, or Jesus, did. For Gnostics the grandeur of Yeshu was whilst he was not incarnate on earth. They saw Yeshu as achieving a primeval sacrifice on a Cross of Light way before the earth was inhabited, and tended to interpret his manner of death while on earth as but a poor and unnecessary shadow of this primeval sacrifice.

Orthodox Christians can be a bit vague when it comes to describing just how their Jesus and his blood affected redemption through death on the cross, and why a loving God would require such a barbaric act. Gnostics, on the other hand, were very detailed and precise in their views. We won't delve into this lengthy exegesis of the available Gnostic texts that detail the reasons for and the manners in which this extension on the primeval cross of light occurred, and of the resultant spiritual wars that ensued as a result. For those accustomed to the blood atonement fable, the Gnostic concept can seem particularly mystical and phantasmagorical.

To understand the Gnostic version of the crucifixion, it is necessary to understand that all related things, and all related souls, are connected in a very deep and very real way. Much of the work of perfection consists in coming to understand the depth of this common unity. A basic premise of Gnosticism is that we can be affected by what others do through our very real but invisible connection to them, and they to us. In The Prophet, by the Lebanese poet Kahlil Gibran, this idea is expressed:

> "Oftentimes have I heard you speak of one who commits a wrong as though he were not one of you, but a stranger unto you and an intruder upon your world. But I say that even as the holy and the righteous cannot rise beyond the highest which is in each one of you, so the wicked and the weak cannot fall lower than the lowest which is in you also. And as a single leaf turns not yellow but with the silent knowledge of the whole tree, So the wrong-doer cannot do wrong without the hidden will of you all. [9]

In the writings of Paul there is evidence of this Nazorean principle as well:

> "For just as we have many members in one body and all the members do not have the same function, so we, who are many, are one body in Christ..."[10]

This invisible bond is what makes it possible for a redeemer like Yeshu to affect our soul, but it is also that which makes the state of our soul affect him. Thus in Gnosticism you cannot have a pure redeemer atoning for sinful humanity as a whole, for there is no common unity of their souls. Only by being part of the family of Yeshu, part of his "soul", can we be affected by what he does and he by us. And we can become part of the family of Yeshu only by being like him, at least to a degree, and by passing through the initiatory ceremonies which accomplish this rebirth and adoption. Even Greco-Roman Christianity has echoes of this:

---

[9] The Prophet, by Kahlil Gibran, On Crime & Punishment
[10] Romans 12:3-8, Paul

"For even as the body is one and yet has many members, and all the members of the body, though they are many, are one body, so also is Christ. For by one Spirit we were all baptized into one body, whether Jews or Greeks, whether slaves or free, and we were all made to drink of one Spirit." [11]

In Nazorean soteriology [12] it is understood that Yeshu, and his female counterpart, are part of a group of souls who left heaven aeons and aeons ago. This group of pearls, or souls, is called the "Living Soul". After departing heaven, this group of souls became ever more engrossed and mixed into the material universe, and ever more dense in their consciousness. The final result was our entrapment here on earth in a physical body that deadens and benumbs the vitality and wakefulness of our spiritual souls. This descent into materiality, or the "mixture", is what is meant by the crucifixion on the Universal Cross. All true Gnostic Essenes considered themselves a part of this wave of souls that was crucified in pre-earth times, but they considered Yeshu and his counterpart as the main crucified one since he led the descent as well as the ascent again out of matter into pure spirit. The Sleeping Prophet Edgar Cayce, when speaking of why Mary Magdalene departed heaven in the beginning, had this to say:

"Each soul is a portion of its Maker, with those attributes of the divine; and when manifested in materiality it is with the attributes necessary for the awareness in that environ. The soul was among those that found it necessary that there be those experiences or sojourns in the earth that there might be an application in material forces of the divine influences in the experience of the soul; to justify, purify self as a companion of

---

[11] 1 Corinthians 12:12-17, Paul

[12] The term soteriology is a branch of theology that deals with the study of salvation. In Christian systematic theology it is used to refer to the study of the biblical doctrine of salvation. In Nazoreanism it refers to the Gnostic doctrine of salvation.

one to dwell in the presence of divinity, and in the realm of that which would be one with the influences in the lives of individuals that will make for the becoming aware of the consciousness of the Christ-life healing, purifying, the drosses of materiality." [13]

This spiritual "awareness" that is possible to achieve while in the material universe is "Nazirutha". This Nazirutha is what Yeshu and Miryai taught so effectively.

So in Yeshu all Essenes were crucified primevaly, and in Yeshu and Miryam all the righteous shall re-ascend, or spiritually resurrect, through possession of Nazirutha. In this way Yeshu is the "Living Soul" that was bled out into the universe upon the cosmic crucifixion and primordial sacrifice of the Yeshu and Miryam – the Primal Man and Woman. The resulting "Living Soul", stretched throughout matter on or as a Light Cross, and has since been captive of the archons[14] of unholiness and trapped in this material universe far from our true spiritual home. She is reclaimed through alms and rites of redemption that regather the scattered particles of light (*ziwane*)[15]. Pearl souls, as coagulated and crystalline ziwane, are also gathered in, purified, and made perfect once more.

"The Eucharist is Yeshu. For in Aramaic they call him farisatha — this is, the outspread. For Yeshu came to crucify the world.[16]

Yeshu was crucified before the foundations of the world. The symbol of this is mentioned in an ancient Nazorean scroll:

---

[13] Text Of Reading 295-9

[14] Archon, in Greek, means "authority," and comes from the same root as "arch," as in "archangel." In Gnostic belief, Archons were planetary rulers and guardians of the spiritual planes. The archons were associated with the seven visible planets, and perceived as predatory beings who suck life out of souls.

[15] "Five luminous ones whom they term Ziwane." Ephrem, Hypatius

[16] Gospel Of Philip 57

'I stretched out my hands and sanctified my Lord; for the extension of my hands is his sign'[17]

An example of Yeshu personally teaching concerning the Cross of Light, or Buddha nature, can be found in the eighth book of the Pistis Sophia, an ancient Manichaean text dated to the 3rd century or earlier. In it we read of the Light Cross:

> "And you have received your parts from the power which the last helper had breathed into the mixture, this which is mixed with all the invisible ones and all the archons and all the aeons. In a word, it is mixed with the world of destruction, namely the mixture.

> This (power) which, from the beginning, I brought out of myself, I cast into the first ordinance. And the first ordinance cast a part of it into the great light. And the great light cast a part of what it received into the five helpers[18], and the last helper took a part from what it received and cast it into the mixture. And (the part) has come to be in all who are in the mixture, as I have just said to you." [19]

With this essence cast into the mixture came a multitude of souls destined for trials and tribulations. When Yeshu led the descent into the mixture so many aeons ago, he did so in the role of Hibil.

Yeshu as Hibil

Perhaps the most important thing Yeshu ever said while he was on earth was: "I am Hibil-Ziwa, I have come from the

---

[17] Odes Of St. Solomon 27:1-2

[18] The Five Helpers of Yeshu, Miryai, and Mani are the Five Buddhas of Buddhism, Bonpoism and Manichaeism and the Five Lights of Gnostic literature. They represent the 29°, 28°, 27°, 26°, and 25° of Nazirutha. They are the embodiments of the five Living Elements, the Od-nga, or Five Pure Lights, of Bon which come forth out of the Ma, Bu, and Tsal.

[19] Pistis Sophia, Ch 8

heights."[20] These were significant words to Nazoreans of that day and are not found in the Roman Bible. For Nazoreans, Hibil is the great cosmic savior, the one who set in motion the whole plan of redemption. Without Hibil, all souls are trapped inside the light land in a perpetual state of naiveté, or outside of the Light Land in a perpetual state of impurity and unconsciousness. Hibil makes it possible for us to gather together our scattered spiritual components and return to the Living Ones above. As the orthodox looked to the crucifixion of the flesh of Jesus, so Nazoreans looked to the crucifixion of his soul before the foundations of the earth were laid. Yeshu's work of salvation had already been accomplished before he incarnated as the son of Miryam. Why then did he come? He came to comfort, to teach, to dwell amongst those he loved, thus was he called Amin-il, or God with Us, and Beni-Amun or Son of God. He did not come to die for us; he came to reassure and nurture us and to lead us ever closer to enlightenment and liberation. In The Ginza Rba, the Great Treasury, which was the bible of the ancient Nazoreans, we read of Yeshu:

> "His name is Amun-el (Emmanuel, Amun God) and he called himself Y'su Mashiana (Yeshu the Messiah). He appears to you and says to you: 'Come and stand beside me and you shall not be burned. . . . .He says: ' I am Alaha (God), and the Son of Alaha (God). I have been sent here by my Father'. And he further says to you: 'I am the first Messenger, I am Hibil-Ziwa, I have come from the heights."[21]

The phrase "He appears to you and says to you: 'Come and stand beside me and you shall not be burned. . ." are again not in the Roman Bible. They sound similar, however, to words of Yeshu to John the Baptist at his baptism, as recorded by Ephraim of Syria:

---

[20] Ginza Rba, The Great Treasury
[21] Ginza Rba, The Great Treasury

"I have revealed to Thee My Will; what questionest thou?—
Draw near, baptize me, and thou shalt not be burned.--The
bridechamber is ready; keep me not back--from the wedding-
feast that has been made ready." [22]

Descent of Yeshu

Yeshu and Miryam were the first to descend out of the pure
Light Land or Bridal Chamber above. They led all other Pearls
out of perfection into the great school house of the outer
materialistic universes. Their fall seeded Their light essence
throughout all the material worlds. This is the spiritual
crucifixion of the Primal Pair on the Cross of Light. The
symbol for this is the leaven in the sacramental bread. This
diffused the light everywhere and made the need for things
here to be organized in a way that this trapped and scattered
light could be reclaimed and regathered back to its original
home and source above. This trapped and scattered light is the
Living Soul of which each person who has heard the Call of
Life is a part. This is the one mystical soul which includes all
Pearls and Perfect ones that originally descended with Yeshu
and Miryam, and who now have the opportunity to reascend
back to Them and to their Heavenly Parents above.

In the Essene texts preserved by the Mandai we read of the
world of darkness to which these innocent souls descended,
led by Hibil, who is Yeshu. These texts are very ancient and
are in the form of a "myth" or "mythos" designed to be
memorized and passed on orally to children. They contain
great truths thinly veiled by symbols and archetypal beings.
These are the stories and teachings that Yeshu would have
grown up hearing. When he was older he would have been

---

[22] Ephraim of Syria, Epiphany Hymns

taught their allegorical and mystical meaning. We here break into the myth in its description of certain beings of darkness:

"Ruha was the daughter of Hagh and his wife Magh in the world of Darkness. It was Hibil Ziwa who brought her out of the World of Darkness of which Akrun is the ruler. With him are Gaf and Gafan, who are male and female, Hagh and Magh of whom I have just spoken, Sargi and Sargani, also male and female, and Ashdum, who had Ruha for consort. The lion, scorpion, and hornet are their symbols.

But I will tell you how Ruha came to the upper worlds. Once the melki and the 'uthri, twelve thousand of them, wished to see Melek Ziwa (the Light King), the great god of all, for each had a question to ask about the created world, such as 'Why are the trees green?' 'Why does this happen, and why that?' and so on. Each one of them had a question. They mounted vehicles like ships that moved by electricity and they rose from Awathur until they reached the highest heaven. When they had attained the highest heaven, a blinding light fell upon them, and they could not gaze, but fell on their faces.

Only Hibil Ziwa, who was with them, remained upright. Now with Melek Ziwa are two mighty spirits called Shishlam Rabba, the Road-Opener, and Yawar Rabba. Hibil Ziwa begged Shishlam Rabba to open him a road through the barring light so that he might approach Melek Ziwa, Lord of All Things, and Melek Ziwa gave Shishlam Rabba permission, saying, 'Go, bring Hibil Ziwa to me!' The others could not approach, but remained prostrate; but the answers to their questions came into their minds without the asking. Moreover, when the 'uthri and melki yearned to see the Lord of All, they beheld in their minds a Countenance of Light, which was the likeness of God, whose other name is Parsufa Rabba ad 'Iqara (Great Countenance of Glory). This is his secret Name, which none but the initiated know. I have declared this sacred name to you! When they saw this vision, the melki and the 'uthri began to pray and worship. As for Hibil-Ziwa, who had approached nearer than they, he received such sovereign power that whatever he sought, he obtained. [23]

We are next told how Yeshu, in his roll of Hibil Ziwa, was commissioned to lead the angels into the worlds of darkness and how he was promised that he would not be abandoned there. Being trapped in a state of stupor and dullness is the greatest danger of descent into the mixture:

"In the Name of Living Vastness, may hallowed Light be glorified! Beyond, in the fruits of glory, in the farm of light, in the house of completion, in you o garden of the ether, which building [. . . . . .], in you o garden of Adam, is proclaimed the "Call of Life" which the Vast One utters. Parables, Parables it utters in glory, words it utters in glory, words in a (heavenly) voice utters it and reveals the secrets, which are had between father and son.

As this dwelling yet did not exist, when this was [. . . . . .], when sun and moon were not yet there and traversing the world, when they were not yet there there burned already the glory in its container. In their coverings the regulations were hidden, hidden and kept in their books. The storms protect silence and sit in the deserts of the world. The father, the clear brilliance, the light, clear radiation, the master of the greatness, stands and upholds in the house of the completion. The Vast One spoke to the First, his son: My son, come, be my messenger, come, be my carrier, come, be my carrier and press for me the rebellious low earth. Go into the world of darkness, in which darkness there is no ray of light, to the place of the lions, to the seat Of the requiring leopards, to the place of the dragons, to the seat of the perishable Demons, to the place of the veiled Lilith and Astarte, to the place of the water brooks and the blazing tar pits. Then the First spoke to the Vast Ones, his Parents: If I descend down there, who will bring me up again? When I fall, who will catch me? Who will hold my soul together when I fall into the burning water? Who will create for me a purification when I fall into the murky water? Who will create for me a crown, which front curls

---

[23] The Mandaeans Of Iraq And Iran By E.S. Drower Leiden: Brill 1962 (Reprint Of 1937) Page 88

of glory, and place it again on my head? If the evil ones keep me imprisoned in their stronghold, who will be for me a Redeemer? Whereupon the Vast One answered the First, their son: You ask, if you descend, who will carry you up, if you fall, who will catch you; who will hold together your soul that she does not fall into the burning water? I will create for you a purification, so that you do not succumb to the murky water. I will create for you a crown, with front curls of glory, and put such on your head. If the evil ones throw you into their prison, I will be for you a Redeemer. Stand fast on the names of Life, fold up the front curls of glory, and robe yourself. Go into the suffering worlds and go into the worlds of darkness, in which darkness there exists no rays of light. He is encircled by lions, he is surrounded by perverse demons, dragons surround him, and veiled Liliths and Astarte's encircle him, and surrounding him are rivers and pools of tar. When the strength was gone from me as one who is not a disciple, the call of the disciple brings and causes the man, his helper, to appear. Then the Great Master spoke to him: How did I sin against you that you sent me here, that you sent me into the depth, which is completely full of stench, and in which nobody is at ease? When Nsab heard this of me, he sent a staff, he gave speech and hearing to me, and spoke to me: Kill the lions with it, kill with it the requiring leopards, kill with it the dragons, kill with it the perishable demons, kill with it the Liliths and Astares which are hidden. Drain with it the water brooks and the blazing tar pits. I called loud to the house of the Life which sent to me strength and glory. Whereupon I executed in sequence the works which my Parents had given me. I squashed down the darkness and elevated the light. Without errors I ascended upward, and lacking and wrong was not in me. Life is transcendent and victorious, and victorious are those that have gone forth! [24]

When Hibil Ziwa was commissioned to lead the angels into the worlds of darkness and reclaim some of the scattered light that existed there in the form of Ruha and Zahariel, he went to them and proclaimed:

---

[24] Doctrine Of Kings 66

"He told the melki, 'I am going to descend, and to build a world called Olma ad eHshukha' (World of Darkness, i.e. the physical world). He descended, and went lower and lower and lower, for years and years, until he reached Akrun T'ura ad Besera (Krun, Mountain of Flesh) in the depths of creation. The whole visible world rests on this king of darkness, and his shape is that of a huge louse. When he saw Hibil Ziwa, Akrun said, 'Why hast thou come to our realm? How didst thou travel hither? Now I will swallow thee up!' and he opened his mouth wide. The throat of Akrun is vast, and it has such power of suction that everything is drawn into it. Now Melek Ziwa had sent two powerful spirits to protect Hibil Ziwa, for in the realm of spirits one is more powerful than another, and these fought beside Hibil Ziwa. When Akrun wished to shake Hibil Ziwa from his place and swallow him, these thrust a light like a sword into the throat of Akrun, and the latter feared, knowing that a mightier than he had come and that the power of Hibil Ziwa was from the King of the Light of Day. For Ziwa means the pure light of the day, while Anhura means the light of the moon. When Hibil Ziwa saw that Akrun, Lord of Darkness, was thus smitten, he said, 'This is the work of Melek Ziwa!' and he commanded Akrun, saying, 'I have come to take Ruha. Let Ashdum, her spouse, give her up.' Now Ruha is the breath of life in the created world, and our breath is from her. Then the powers of darkness gave Ruha to Hibil Ziwa, and, at that time, she was pregnant. With her, Hibil Ziwa took a talisman, a seal, upon which were depicted the likeness of Gaf and the scorpion Had. This was to protect Ruha when she set out on her journey to the upper worlds. Ruha asked Hibil Ziwa, 'Whither takest thou me?' He showed her the path. Now, Ruha had a sister, named Zahariel. When she beheld Hibil Ziwa, Zahariel loved him, and, as nothing was hidden from him, he knew that she yearned for him. So he took her also, with Ruha. She bore him a son, Pthahil. So Pthahil, who takes souls to be weighed and sends his spirits to fetch souls from their bodies, is the child of both Light and Darkness. [25]

[25] The Mandaeans Of Iraq And Iran By E.S. Drower Leiden: Brill 1962 (Reprint Of 1937) Page 88

From Zahariel, Hibil created Pthahil who was to help organize and create the earth, create its inhabitants and fascilitate the harvest of souls when they died.

"The son of Hibil Ziwa, Pthahil, by order of his father opened the sky, cooled the earth, loosed fountains and rivers, founded mountains, made fish and birds, flowers with their seeds, and animals for Adam and his descendents. Awathur (Abathur) and his son (i.e. Pthahil) looked at their own bodies and thought of them and so produced the body of Adam Paghra (the physical Adam). From Adam's rib was taken Hawa his wife. Exactly as there was an Adam Paghra and a Hawa Paghra, there was an Adam Kasia and a Hawa Kasia (Occult Adam and Eve). These and their progeny peopled the world of Mshuni Kushta. Adam had six children, three boys and three girls. The names of the three boys were Adam, Shitel, and Anush. Adam son of Adam took a wife from amongst the children of darkness, for the world was inhabited before the creation of Adam by shiviahi (shibiahia), children of blackness and darkness. From this union sprang children of darkness, those of humanity who are not Mandai. The Mandai are the children of Adam Paghra and Hawa Kasia. The other two sons of Adam, Shitel and Anush followed the teaching, which Hibil Ziwa gave their father. Hibil Ziwa taught Adam the secrets of life, gave him the holy book, and instructed him in the arts of agriculture and writing." [26]

Thus was the Gnostic plan of redemption explained to Yeshu as a child and by him and others to the children after them. These teachings not only explained how we got here, but also, how we can escape. The actors in these dramas also represent metaphysical concepts which are grasped only by the initiated. For example, in the earthly life of Yeshu, Miryam (*Ruha)* and Miryai (*Zahariel*) represent the lower portions of our souls which are rescued by Yeshu's program of light.

---

[26] The Mandaeans Of Iraq And Iran By E.S. Drower Leiden: Brill 1962 (Reprint Of 1937) Page 88

Purification of Yeshu

Yeshu (*Hibil*) and Miryam (*Ruha*) after uncountable years in the lower worlds of darkness, cried out in a series of prayers seven times each day. These prayers were heard and two great light Beings, called the Living Spirit and Mother of Life, came to their rescue. They were lifted up out of the darkness and purified by multiple baptisms and other Gnostic rites of redemption. This ascension and purification of the Primal Pair is the pattern which all fallen Pearls must duplicate if they wish to return home to heaven. An ancient scroll, preserving the method of this purification, exists still. This scroll contains detailed information about how to execute a Great Baptism. It also has, within its 66 pages, an account of the situation that created the necessity for such a rite. Part of this story is as follows:

> "Yawar went on until he reached the King. Seeing that luminous appearance, Hibil-Ziwa was afraid and fell on his face. Then the King grasped him with his right hand and addressed a speech to Hibil, whose quaking and trembling fled from him. He said to him: Fear not, Hibil-Ziwa, for not one of the Uthras can cause thy strength which I instilled into thee, to fall away from thee. For I endowed thee with this power, so that all the mighty spirits of Darkness should fear thee, and that thou mayest tread them underfoot and inspire fear in all the worlds of the Children of Darkness. Then the King of all worlds of light took him into his inner Abode of light and baptized him in 360 Jordans, sealed him with 360 seals of light, clothed him in 360 robes of light, transferred to him 360 monasteries and bestowed on him 360 Rivers and streams. . . "[27]

Yeshu was then blessed with this great blessing:

---

[27] Diwan Masbuta d Hibil-Ziwa

"And He spoke to the great Radiance and Light that is mightier than all worlds, the Eldest of all the worlds of Light, before whom none existed, to him who is the Great Presence of Glory which emanated from Himself. And he said to him: Lay thy hands on Hibil-Ziwa, seal him and arm him and establish him and say to him: Thou art an offshoot of the Life, thou art the First and the Last, thou art the predestinate being that was destined to be. Act and achieve! The Great Life hath Called thee; all that thou doest shall succeed, and in these thy deeds there shall be naught that is lacking or deficient! Invest him with the Great Mystery, the strength of which is great and mightier than all worlds. And the Kings took Kushta with him and each conferred on him some of his own glory. They gave him seven coverings and sealed him with a first seal, its name, a secret name, was graven thereon. [28]

Yeshu's work was not yet done, for he is again sent down into the darkness:

"And they said to Hibil-Ziwa: Why dost thou rest, great Hibil-Ziwa, sweet and gracious one? Arise, go, travel to the world of darkness, because one, the eldest son whom Gaf begot, seeketh to strive against the world to which he can lay no claim. What sayeth thou? So Manda and his brethren went to the world of darkness. They descended world after world till they reached the world of Krun, the Great Mountain of Flesh." After accomplishing his task in the worlds of darkness, which are our worlds, Hibil again began to ascend, world upon world. When he and his companions "reached the world of Gaf, and Hibil uttered his mind and expressed his wisdom and said: How can we rise up towards my Parents, when these creatures that I brought are not like Us, nor is their appearance radiant like that of the Uthras, the children of light? My Parents will not now desire to have them in Their Presence! When Hibil-Ziwa said this, the Great Life was cognizant of that which occupied his mind. Then Hibil-Ziwa offered up sublime and worthy

---

[28] Diwan Masbuta d Hibil-Ziwa

devotional prayers, and he worships and praised the King of
Light and said: May there be sent for me, Hibil-Ziwa, by the
mercy of the Living Ones, a Messenger from the Great Life since
it was by your will that I went to the place of darkness. Then
said the Great Primal Mana (Heavenly Father)to the First great
Occult Drop (Heavenly Mother): Our son mourned in the
darkness and hath not the strength to rise! Summon his father,
Manda dHiya, in Order that he may send him strength, so that
he may arise and come from the darkness and be raised up to
our presence. So word came to Manda dHiya: Arise, write a
letter of truth and furnish it with a seal and send it to Hibil-
Ziwa." After receiving the Letter of Truth and ascending
partway, the foes of darkness again seized Hibil and his
companions, necessitating further intervention by his Heavenly
Parents above. The Great Occult First Drop said: "The King that
has visited thee saith that we should read a Requiem-Mass like
unto that mystery that we sent to thee." So 60 Temple Workers
assembled and performed a Masqita Mass for Him and his
companions, and they were able to escape the clutches of
darkness. [29]

After a lengthy explanation of just how to accomplish a Great
baptism, Hibil-Ziwa gives this promise:

"Everyone that is baptized with my baptism, Hibil-Ziwa's, shall
be set up beside me and shall resemble me, and they shall dwell
in my world, Hibil-Ziwa's." [30]

This purification and ascent of Yeshu, or Hibil, set in motion a
scenario whereby other entrapped souls could also be purified
and ascend. This whole idea of the descent and ascent of Hibil
is the whole rational for Nazorean baptism. The principles
involved are important if one wishes to understand the true
roll of Yeshu and just what he accomplished while on earth.
This is alluded to in the Gospel of Philip:

---

[29] Diwan Masbuta d Hibil-Ziwa
[30] Diwan Masbuta d Hibil-Ziwa

"Before Christ some came forth. They are no longer able to enter into whence they came, and they are no longer able to exit from whither they went. Yet the Christ came. Those who had gone in he brought out, and those who had gone out he brought in."[31]

Before Yeshu and Miryam incarnated in the Mount Carmel and Yerushalom regions two thousand years ago, souls had been sojourning in these lower worlds and heavens for millions of years. All members of the "Living Soul" had lost their way and forgotten their previous glory and home in the Bridal Chamber above. They were trapped. Yeshu and Miryam showed that it was possible for a spirit, defiled by entanglements in lower worlds of darkness, to be purified and return upward to the Light Land once again. This initial ascent and restoration of Yeshu and counterpart set the stage for others to ascend up as well. Once humanity was created and souls were entrapped in human bodies, the original ascent of the Primal Pair made it possible for souls on earth to achieve the same. Before this could be done, Yeshu and counterpart had to enlighten humankind, restore the truth, the true people and the true rituals and understanding that made such possible. These "true people" are the Nazoreans.

"There was another people and these blessed ones are referred to as the "chosen people of the living God" and "the true man" and "the Son of man" and "the seed of the Son of man." In the world it is called "this true people". Where they are, there are the sons of the bridal chamber." [32]

Ascent of Yeshu

---

[31] Gospel of Philip 75
[32] Gospel of Philip

Lady Drower in her book The Mandaeans of Iraq and Iran writes of an ancient ceremony that preserved the account of Hibil's ascent:

> "The 18th day of Taura is the Dehwa Hnina or Little Feast, sometimes called the Dehwa (Dihba) Turma. The feast lasts for three days and baptisms should take place and the dead be remembered by lofani or ritual meals for dead. Dehwa Hnina celebrates the return of Hibil Ziwa from the underworlds to the worlds of light"[33]

With the return of Hibil, Ruha and Zahariel comes the hope and promise of the return of all fellow members of the Living Soul of Yeshu, Miryam and Miryai. These are the Nazoreans, whether living two thousand years ago or now incarnate. Before one can qualify for ascent, however, the stain and pollution of millions of years of life in a dark material universe must be purified. The reverberation of darkness that stains the spirit and the soul must be bleached out by certain mystical methods that characterize societies focused on such matters. They are meaningless for worldly individuals who are not focused on spiritual realities. They are all important, however, for those who wish to shake off the dust and filth of a million years of stupor.

Adam Created

Jews and Christians believe that Adam was created by their God and then rebelled and fell. Nazoreans believed humanity fell from heaven and then had their bodies created by lesser beings unconnected with the Highest Gods. In Nazorean lore, humanity was created by imperfect beings seeking to pattern their creation after archetypes in heaven. They did not have the power to infuse their creations with soul, and so it is said

---

[33] The Mandaeans Of Iraq And Iran By E.S. Drower Leiden: Brill 1962 (Reprint Of 1937) Page 88

that Yeshu came down and whispered into their ears and assisted them to animate their bodies with soul. He did this so souls could eventually escape the darkened universe.

> "Ruha and Pthahil tried to make Adam and, when they had finished, he was like a man, but moved about on all fours, had a face like an ape, and made noises like a sheep. They were puzzled and went to the House of Life and told them of their failure, and the House of Life said, We will send Hibil Ziwa. Hibil Ziwa came, and the Soul was in his hands. When the Soul saw Adam, she was horrified, and said, 'What! Must I dwell in this flesh and blood, this house of uncleanness?' And she refused. Hibil Ziwa said, 'Dost thou refuse the order of the House of Life?' She said, 'I will accept on one condition only, and that is that everything that is in the world of light shall be in this world-flowers, trees, light, ajar (pure air), running water (yardna), baptisms, priests, and everything as it is up there.'

> Hibil Ziwa returned and told them (the House of Life) and brought back a letter ('*ngirtha*). It would not open, but spoke, and promised that the House of Life would give all that the Soul had asked. So the Soul (*Nishimta*) entered the body of Adam and he stood erect and talked, and Hibil Ziwa taught him reading and writing, how to marry, how to bury the dead. . . and all knowledge. [34]

Gnostic ideas about the first man certainly differ from those of their Jewish and Christian antagonists. Even later offshoots of these Nazoreans, like the Mandaeans and Sabians, had similar legends. The Jewish writer Maimonides, who died in 1204 AD, writes that these Sabians[35] believed in Adam, but the god of Adam was Sin:

> "Adam was in their belief a human being born from male and female, like the rest of mankind—he was only distinguished

---

[34] The Mandaeans of Iraq and Iran By E.S. Drower Clarendon Press, Oxford, 1937
[35] Sabeans means Baptists, and can refer to Elchasaites, Mandaeans, or others of similar persuasion.

from his fellow men by being a prophet sent by the moon. He accordingly called men to worship of the moon and he wrote several works on agriculture... The Sabeans contend that Seth differed from his father Adam, as regard the worship of the moon... Adam they said left the torrid zone near India and entered the region of Babylon bringing leaves and branches...[36]

Essenes looked to Seth and his wife Norea, rather than the earthly Adam, as the most spiritual of early mankind. The story of travel from India is just a remnant of ancient migrations out of Africa made by nascent humanity. Once humanity evolved sufficiently, Yeshu once again took control of their destiny.

Yeshu as Enlightener

Gnostics see Yeshu, as well as his feminine counterpart, as a prime player in the ongoing struggle to enlighten and wake up mankind. Essenes postulated multiple incarnations of Yeshu upon the earth, as well as manifold spiritual appearances to bequeath gnosis to various prophets and priestesses on earth. This always bothered Roman Christianity who could not fathom multiple incarnations for their Jesus. They wanted to pretend that life on earth was a one time affair. They wanted shortcuts and there are none. Nazoreans also saw Yeshu involved in post earth life happenings and future events as well. There was no doctrine or prophecy in Nazirutha that forbade Yeshu from incarnating again in the future. In the Greek Bible, however, there is a false warning meant to prevent anyone from seeking after him where he could be found, such as the deserts[37] or river beds where the

---

36 Maimonides, Guide for the Perplexed
37 Thomas 78: "Yeshu said, "Why have you come out into the desert? To see a reed shaken by the wind? And to see a man clothed in fine garments like your kings and your great men? Upon them are the fine garments, and they are unable to discern the truth."

Essenes lived or in inner meditation chambers where gnosis is found. This false warning goes like this:

> "So if anyone tells you: 'There he [the Messiah] is, out in the desert,' do not go out; or: 'Here he is, in the inner rooms,' do not believe it. For as lightning that comes from the east is visible even in the west, so will be the coming of the Son of Man."[38]

The verse sounds a bit like the beginning verses of Thomas where Yeshu says to not seek the kingdom in the sky or sea, but within. Here we have the within put off to some nebulous outside future event. This false verse and view has confused many in the western world and has helped then ignore important first steps toward enlightenment. Those who seek Yeshu with all their hearts must seek him among small mystical groups in rural and deserted places, and must seek to deepen their connection to him through turning inward in inner chambers of the heart. Yet it is also true that the Son of Man must enter the inner heart and mind of each of us like a lightning flash. With this flash also comes the thunder of the awakened kundalini. Yeshu, and Miryai and Mani after him, sound the Call of Life to awaken slumbering souls to remembrance. Not all awaken, but those who do are allowed to return on high if they are endowed with the proper Naziruthian credentials and certificates that impress themselves on the inner souls. These Naziruthian credentials and certificates are the mysteries and rites left to us by Yeshu. They are a detailed step by step program designed to poise us to eventually receive instantaneous Naziruthian enlightenment. Blessed are the Pearls who find them and again find their way home.

Yeshu Teaches Adam

---

[38] Matthew 24:26-27

This descent of souls into the material worlds that we have been talking about happened way before the creation of the physical earth or physical humanity. Once this physicality had been established, however, and once we had souls encased in a stinking stump of a body, we once again encounter Yeshu being instrumental in the rescue of these trapped and fallen souls. This begins with the symbolic, but not actual, first of humanity.

In the ancient Aramaic scrolls we learn that Yeshu and Miryam, in Their roll as Yeshu-Ziwa and the Hour of Life, came to Adam and Eve in the Garden and informed them of their heavenly origins and of the not so grand spirituality of the person attempting to be their God in the lower worlds. Yeshu explained to Adam about how He, Yeshu, had been scattered throughout the material worlds and how His Living Soul suffered terribly therein and longed for salvation. Yeshu and Miryam were the first Apostles and Messengers of Life sent to humanity, and in Their name many other Apostles have followed Their example. Many of these Messengers of that Good Realm have even incarnated on earth, taken on a stinking stump body of flesh, and have uttered the Call of Life to all who would listen.

"The Christ came! Some indeed he ransomed, yet others he rescued, yet for others he atoned. He ransomed the alienated, he brought them to himself. And he rescued those who came to him. These he set as pledges in his will. Not only when he appeared did he voluntarily lay down his soul, but since the day of the world's coming-to-be he placed his soul. Then at the time he desired he came earliest to reclaim her, since she was placed among the pledges. She had come to be under the bandits and they had taken her captive, yet he rescued her. He atoned for both the good and the evil in the world.[39]

Adam Awakens

In a Manichaean fragment we read:

> "Then Adam examined himself and recognized who he was, and (Yeshu) showed him the Fathers on high, and (revealed to him) regarding his own self, all that into which he (Yeshu) had been cast - into the teeth of leopard(s) and the teeth of elephant(s), swallowed by voracious ones and absorbed by gulping ones, consumed by dogs, mixed and imprisoned in all that exists, bound in the stench of Darkness." [40]

Mani says that Yeshu raised Adam up and made him taste of the Tree of Life.

> "Then Adam cried out and wept, and raised his voice loudly like a lion that roars and tears (prey). He cast (himself down) and beat (his breast) and said, 'Woe, woe to the one who formed my body, and to the one who bound my soul, and to the rebels who have enslaved me."[41]

One of the first foundational principles of Gnosticism is when one understands that they have been trapped and deceived by those they may have worshipped as God. Each true Gnostic must experience for themselves the cry: 'Woe, woe to the one who formed my body, and to the one who bound my soul, and to the rebels who have enslaved me."

Humanity Evolves

---

[39] Gospel Of Philip 8
[40] Theodore bar Konai, LLber Scholiorum (ed. Scher) 317-18
[41] Theodore bar Konai, LLber Scholiorum (ed. Scher) 317-18

According to Nazorean teachings, humanity evolved in two very separate and distinct lines. One dark line dominated by souls from the worlds of darkness, and another smaller one animated by light sparks, or ziwane, from the bridal chamber above. The true lineage is said to have descended through four dispensational pairs.

First, Seth and Norea, who are said to have lived around 443,367 B.C. and to have been the children of Adam and Hava (Eve). Around 227,367 BC a second couple were said to have survived destruction by 'sword and plague', named Ram and Rud. Geneticists believe that circa 144,000 BC an ancestral human population of about 2000 individuals, who lived somewhere in Africa began to split up before populating the world. According to Gnosticism, these, and all human flesh, arose from evolution influenced by dark deities. Gnostics felt that a portion of these humanlike beings were also animated by divine sparks from heaven above.

Scientists tell of worldwide effects of a super-volcano exploding in Sumatra about 70,000 BC. causing the entire earth to be covered in thick clouds:

> "An estimated 75 per cent of the northern hemisphere's plants are thought to have died. Six years of this dramatic cooling triggered a thousand-year ice age causing a volcanic winter but most importantly it all but eradicated the human race, such as it was at the time, from the face of the planet.... The geologist explained about the Lake Toba super volcano eruption some 75 000 years ago and the scientists were able to make the connection between the Lake Toba Super volcano eruption and the cataclysmic reduction in variety of the human DNA, estimated to have occurred some ± 70 000 ago as well! An so it was established that the Lake Toba Super volcano eruption was responsible for the volcanic winter, that lasted for an estimated 1000 thousand years, and which lead to the near annihilation of

the entire human race and the modification of the human DNA today."[42]

Yeshu apparently knew of this event some two thousand years before its rediscovery by modern scientists. According to ancient Nazorean scrolls, about 71,367 BC a second disaster resulted in the perishing of most of the human family through fire (super-volcano). A second pair survived, Shurbai and Sharhabi'il. Studies based on mitochondria suggest that a small group of a couple hundred descendants of an "Eve" who survived severe heat and drought migrated eastward out of Africa about this time and became the ancestors of all non African humans. In Gnosticism this group is symbolized as Shurbai and Sharhabi'il.

Sam and Anhar, the children of Nuh (Noah) & Anhuraita, would be the next couple commissioned to preserve the race of light from destruction by water. This flood was probably the catastrophic and rapid rising of the Black Sea level in the early Holocene. From these two flood survivors would eventually come the Nazorean and Essene sects of Palestine. The other sects were thought to have derived from the children of Adam son of Adam and Ruha.

These stories of divine lineages helped explain to Nazoreans the divine origins of their people. The main value of a lineage was always its spiritual culture, not its genes, and Nazoreans were not racists. They invited all colors and genders of people to participate in their Mysteries. In the modern era there is no one pure or better race since the pure culture has dissipated. Higher souls, no longer able to incarnate into a relatively pristine culture, are forced to accept bodies in a variety of diverse races and fallen cultures. This is both a blessing as well as a curse. Like Miryai born amidst the Jews, all returning

---

[42] Super Volcanoes by Nicholas Richards

Essenes must seek until they find. Yeshu, however, had the option of being born into a highly evolved culture known as the Nazorean Essene.

˜ 2 ˜
SECTS IN IST CENTURY PALESTINE

Sectarian Cultures

FOR AN INDEPTH understanding of Yeshu it is necessary to understand the world and sect in which he lived. Unlike modern sects, ancient sects were not just belief systems; they were often also cultures or subcultures within their greater world. They oft had specific dress, diets, religious scriptures, and often their own Gods or Goddesses. When we speak of the seven ancient sects of Palestine, we are really speaking of seven ancient cultures and subcultures. To known the sect of someone was to know who their God or Goddess was, what they ate, what they revered as scripture, their ethics, and a whole host of other factors.

Modern Christianity, assuming that Jesus had been born and raised as a Jew, has made all sorts of assumptions of his early life, lifestyle and belief systems. Many of these conclusions have been the opposite of the truth. This misunderstanding has been compounded by the New Testament writings, which have often supported this mistaken idea of a Jewish childhood. These New Testament accounts are flawed, however, for Yeshu never was a member of the Sadducees, Scribes, Pharisees, Hemerobaptists, or Herodians. He was, of course, a Nazorean! To truly appreciate Yeshu the Nazorean, it is important to know what he, as a Nazorean, did and stood for. These details are not in the New Testament story books which transform Yeshu the Gnostic Nazorean into Jesus the Greco-Roman God.

Two Currents

There were two very distinct currents of thought and culture in ancient Israel. The pure current of the Essenes and Nazoreans who worshipped a "Living God"; and the muddy current of the Jews who worshipped "Jehovah", a God of death and destruction.

Nazoreans worshipped a Heavenly Father and Mother and call Them "Hiya" which means "Life" or "the Living Ones", for it is Their life-force that animates all things. Essenes worshipped this Life by offering to Them the Firstfruits of fields and orchards on bloodless altars, for They were thought to delight in living ziwane[43] in foods and bounty of the Earthly Mother, and in hearts that sincerely love them.

In contrast to this adoration of life, growth and fertility, the Jews worshipped a male God of death that demands animal sacrifice, destruction and the blood of innocent victims. Yeshu the Nazorean condemned this animal slaughter when He said:

> "I am come to do away with sacrifices, and if you cease not sacrificing, the wrath of God will not cease from you." [44]

Yeshu also condemned the bloody Jewish God behind the sacrifices when He said:

> "If God were your father, ye would love me: for I proceeded forth and came from God; neither came I of myself, but He sent me... Ye are of your father the devil, and the lusts of your father

---

[43] Ziwane is an Aramaic term that refers to spiritual light trapped in material objects such as food.
[44] Epiphanius, Panarion 30.16,4-5

ye will do. He was a murderer from the beginning, and abode not in the truth, because there is no truth in him. When he speaketh a lie he speaketh of his own: for he is a liar, and the father of it!" [45]

These things may surprise since many believe that Yeshu the Nazorean worshipped the non-Nazorean God of the Jews and was sent by him, but this is not so. Yeshu was sent by the Living Nazorean God called "Hiya", or "Life". He was not sent by Yahweh, Jehovah, or Elohim. These loving Nazorean Parents in Heaven never demanded a bloody sacrifice of Their son on a cross, nor were They behind the so called Jewish "Law of Moses" nor did They inspire the so called Jewish prophets found in the Old Testament. There is an ancient Nazorean saying preserved in ancient scrolls which says: "Nazirutha is older than Judaism!" The ancient historian Epiphanius called the Nazoreans "rebels" because they did not believe in his bloody bible. They had good reason to reject it however.

The pure current of life was represented by the Essenes, or Essene Nazoreans. The muddy current of death was represented by the Pharisees and Sadducees and their subgroups like the Herodians, Scribes, and Hemerobaptists. There was always animosity betwixt these two groups of very diverse Judeans. Eventually the Pharisee sect of Judaism would dominate and wean itself from many bloody practices like animal sacrifice; yet modern Rabbinical Judaism still contains many remnants of its ancient origins. It also contains many doctrines borrowed from Essene Nazoreans, and therefore represents a mixture of both light and darkness.

The Sects

---

[45] John 8:42,44

Many have made the mistake of thinking that Palestine was entirely "Jewish" in the times of Yeshu the Nazorean, and that he (Yeshu) was raised as a "Jew". In the Talmud Rabbi Jonathan says: "there had arisen 24 parties of heretics". He blames these for causing the destruction of Jerusalem in 70 A.D. There were in reality many diverse groups in and around Palestine, as reflected in the Rabbi's comments, and Yeshu belonged to the Sect that rejected the Jewish Law of Moses, the Jerusalem Temple, and the Old Testament Scriptures.

Three Sects

Epiphanius, a Roman Christian historian writing in 375 A.D., mentions seven Jewish sects of which the Nazoreans are but one. The ancient historian Josephus simplified these and tells us of these 3 sects at the time of Christ:

> "For there are three philosophical sects among the Jews. The followers of the first of whom are the Pharisees; of the second the Sadducees, and the third sect, who pretends to a severer discipline, are called Essenes." [46]

These Pharisees are now Rabbinical Judaism and the Sadducees are Karaite Judaism. Essenes no longer exist despite their considerable contribution to later Kabballistic Judaism, modern Mandaeans, and to a lesser extent Sufi and Shiite Islam, Taoism and Mahayana Buddhism. Josephus elaborates on this third Essene Philosophy by saying:

> "Moreover, there is another Order of Essenes who agree with the rest as to their way of living and customs and laws but differ from them in the point of marriage." [47]

---

[46] Wars of the Jews by Josephus
[47] Wars of the Jews by Josephus

" ... in white veils, they then bath their bodies in cold water. And after this purification is over ..." "These men are despisers of riches and so very communicative as raises our admiration." "They are also among them who undertake to foretell things to come, by reading the holy books, and using several sort of purifications, and being perpetually conversant in the discourses of the prophets and it is but seldom that they miss in their predictions." [48]

" ... many of these Essenes have, by their excellent virtue, been thought worthy of this knowledge of Divine revelations."[49]

The only surviving remnants of these Essenes are the Mandaeans of southern Iran and Iraq, but these represent a break off branch that did not directly accept Yeshu despite their preservation and use of his Nazorean scrolls and culture.

Seven Sects

The ancient Christian historian Epiphanius, in his Panarion, speaks in more detail than Josephus of the Judean sects, saying that there are seven in all. These are not different sects from the three mentioned by Josephus, just a different more detailed grouping of the ancient sects. Epiphanius names them:

Sadducees, Scribes, Pharisees, Hemerobaptists, Ossaeans, Nasaraeans and Herodians."[50]

The Pharisee philosophy of Josephus includes the sects of Pharisee, Scribes, and the Hermeobaptists mentioned by Epiphanius. His Sadducee philosophy contains the sects of Sadducee and Herodian mentioned by Epiphanius. Josephus'

[48] Extracts From Josephus' Wars, Ii, Viii, About Essenes
[49] In Ant., Xv, X, 5:
[50] Panarion 1:19

Essene philosophy includes two of Epiphanius' sects - the Ossaeans and the Nazoreans. It should be noted that the Nasorean sect that Yeshu belonged to was not really "Jewish" in the modern sense of the word. The use of "Jewish" and "Jew" by these historians is best understood to mean "Judeans" or inhabitants of the Palestine area. The various sects of the "Jews" were often very different in race, religion, and culture and the Nazoreans were known to accept gentiles into their Order.

Pharisees, Scribes, & Hemerobaptists

The Christian Epiphanius, in his Panarion, speaks:

> "Pharisees, meaning "men set apart," whose life was the most extreme, and who, if you please, were more highly regarded than the others. They believed in the resurrection of the dead as the Scribes did, and agreed that there are such things as angels and the Holy Ghost. And they had a different way of life: periods of continence, and celibacy; fasting twice a week; and cleansings of vessels, platters and goblets, (as the Scribes did); payment of tithes and first-fruits; constant prayer; the styles of dress which were characteristic of a self-chosen religion and consisted of the shawl, the robes or rather tunics, the width of the "phylacteries," or borders of purple material, fringes, and tassels on the corners of the shawl. Things of this sort were signs of their periods of continence. And they also introduced the ideas of destiny and fate. [51]

> Scribes, who were lawyers and repeaters of the traditions of their elders. Because of their further, self-chosen religion they observed customs which they had not learned through the Law but had formulated for themselves-ways of showing reverence to the ordinance of the legislation. [52]

---

[51] Panarion
[52] Panarion

Hemerobaptists. These were Jews in all respects, but claimed that no one can obtain eternal life without being baptized every day. [53]

The term Hemerobaptists means daily baptizers. Nazoreans were known to daily ritualistically immerse themselves in water, but this sect called Hemerobaptists are linked with the Scribes and Pharisees because their other practices and philosophies were more closely linked with these Scribes and Pharisees. The Pharisees are the only one of these Jewish sects to survive. They did this by forming a pact with Rome, thus creating Rabbinical Judaism.

Sadducees & Herodians

Sadducees, meaning "most righteous," who were descended from the Samaritans, as well as from a priest named Zadok. They denied the resurrection of the dead and did not recognize the existence of angels or spirits. In all other respects they were Jews. [54]

Herodians, who were Jews in all respects, but thought that Herod was Christ, and awarded the honor and name of Christ to him. [55]

Sadducees and Herodians' were the two branches of the Sadducees mentioned in Talmudic and Karaite sources, one supporting the status quo and the other rejecting it. Thus we have political Herodians and Sadducees vying for control over the Jerusalem Temple and taxes, and Hemerobaptists, Scribes and Pharisees vying for control over the people and synagogues.

---

[53] Panarion
[54] Panarion
[55] Panarion

Despite their many differences, these five sects shared a common acceptance of the Books of Moses and the Jewish prophets, whilst the Nazoreans and Essenes rejected them. The Sadducees, Scribes, Pharisees, Hemerobaptists, and Herodians, because of their common belief in the Jewish Old Testament, all worshipped Jehovah and all believed in offering bloody animal sacrifices to Him. The Ossaeans and Nasaraeans, on the other hand, rejected the Old Testament, did not worship Yahweh, and did not believe in offering, killing or eating animals. The division between these two groups of sects was great. The writers of the New Testament did not always understand these differences, and so the distinction between them is blurred in mainstream Christianity, fostering an erroneous view of Yeshu and his life and times. Yet even in the mainstream bible we have:

"He shall be called a Nasorene!"[56]

Dead Sea Scrolls not Essene

The Dead Sea Scrolls found near the ancient site of Qumran are products of very religious, but for the most part very non Essene writers. Dead Sea Scroll texts like the War Scroll and Temple scroll that advocate animal slaughter could not be written by a vegetarian people like the Nazoreans or Essenes. Some of the focus of the scrolls, however, was shared amongst many of the sects, including the Essenes, such as astrology, community and monastic rules, mystical commentary of texts, etc.

The scrolls themselves declare their authors to be the Sons of Zadok, or Sadducees. Sadducee is the Greek form of this Hebrew name of Zadok. A few modern authors have

---

[56] Matthew 2:23

attempted to develop a relationship between these Dead Sea
Scroll documents and the early Nazoreans and Christians, but
radio carbon dating has confirmed that the Dead Sea scrolls
predate Yeshu and his companions by more than a century. It
is possible that Qumran was an Essene or Nazorean
community, since it is in the area where ancient historians say
these two sects lived, but even if Qumran were Essene, the
texts found there are not. They were probably hidden there in
the mass frantic exodus that occurred out of Jerusalem as the
Romans invaded in the circa 70 AD war. As the Romans
approached from all directions except the area of Qumran, the
fleeing inhabitants would have been forced to flee in this
direction. They would have brought their libraries with them
to avoid their destruction by the Romans, and would have
been motivated to hide them for safe keeping before they
crossed the Jordan River during their flight. The destruction of
the Zealots on Masada a short time later is probably why the
owners never returned to recover their scrolls. Some Dead Sea
Scroll like fragments were actually found at Masada. Some of
those near Qumran were found in ancient times by Kairite
Jews, with a substantial horde recovered and made popular in
modern times. Their contents do not shed much light on the
practices of the Nazoreans and they do not represent the type
of material that Yeshu would have spent much time studying.
Yeshu even condemned one of their beliefs in his Sermon on
the Mount:

> "You have heard that it was said,' You shall love your
> neighbor, and hate your enemy.' But I tell you, love your
> enemies, bless those who curse you, do good to those who
> hate you, and pray for those who mistreat you and persecute
> you." [57]

---

[57] Matthew 5:44

There is no command to hate your enemies in the Old Testament or rabbinic literature, but in *The Rule of the Community* from the Dead Sea Scrolls there are several commands to "hate" the children of darkness. Yeshu rejected this hate and the Dead Sea Scrolls that espoused it.

Nasaraeans & Ossaeanes

We now give Epiphanius' information about the most important remaining two of the seven sects:

> "The Nasaraeans - they were Jews by nationality - originally from Gileaditis, Bashanitis and the Transjordan . . .They acknowledged Moses and believed that he had received laws - not this law, however, but some other. And so, they were Jews who kept all the Jewish observances, but they would not offer sacrifice or eat meat. They considered it unlawful to eat meat or make sacrifices with it. They claim that these Books are fictions, and that none of these customs were instituted by the fathers. This was the difference between the Nasaraeans and the others. . ."[58]

Epiphanius seeks to convince us that:

> "Nasaraeans, meaning, "rebels," who forbid all flesh-eating, and do not eat living things at all. They have the holy names of patriarchs which are in the Pentateuch, up through Moses and Joshua the son of Nun, and they believe in them - I mean Abraham, Isaac, Jacob, and the earliest ones, and Moses himself, and Aaron, and Joshua. But they hold that the scriptures of the Pentateuch were not written by Moses, and maintain that they have others."

Of course the word Nasaraean does not mean "rebel", this is just a slight employed by Epiphanius to denigrate his religious

---

[58] Panarion 1:18

rival. Nasaraean means keeper of the covenant, or keeper of the mysteries, in Aramaic. Epiphanius loved to twist the meaning of names to downgrade his enemies. In an ironic twist, it is said that the Jews used to twist the meaning of Epiphanius' own name, since he shared it with a king they hated. They changed Epiphanius to Epimanius which meant "fool" or "lunatic". [59] From a Nazorean perspective Epimanius was indeed a fool who mocked and distorted all things sacred. It is unfortunate that we must depend on him for so much detail on the ancient Essene sects.

As "Epimanius" states, Nazoreans did indeed have the names of the Patriarchs, but they were not always the same, and the stories were different. For instance, Adam and Eve did not birth a Cain, Abel, and Seth like the bible story, but they had Adam the son of Adam, Sethil, and Anush. They also had other Patriarchs and Matriarchs not in the Bible, like Ram and Rud, Shurbai and Sharhabi'il, Sam and Anhar, etc. Moses was not the Moses of the Jews, nor was the Nazorean Law of Moses the same as the Jewish Law of Moses. These traditions were shared by both Nazoreans and Essenes:

> "After this (Nasaraean) sect in turn comes another closely connected with them, called the Ossaeanes. These are Jews like the former . . . originally came from Nabataea, Ituraea, Moabitis and Arielis, the lands beyond the basin of what sacred scripture called the Salt Sea. . . Though it is different from the other six of these seven sects, it causes schism only by forbidding the books of Moses like the Nasaraeans. [60]

Another historian, Eusebius, writes that original followers of Yeshu were the Nazoreans and the Essenes (Iessaeians):

---

[59] Humphrey Prideaux, The Old and New Testament Connected in the History of the Jews, Vol. II, pp. 106, 107
[60] Panarion

"They did not give themselves the name of Christ, or that of Jesus, but they called themselves Nazoreans. All Christians were called Nazoreans once. For a short time they were also given the name Iessaeians, before the disciples in Antioch began to be called Christians. And they were called Iessaeians because of Jesse, it seems to me, since David was from Jesse, and by lineage Mary was of the seed of David, fulfilling the Holy Scriptures according to the Old Testament when the Lord said to David[61], "From the fruit of your loins will I set upon your throne".[62]

Epiphanius is wrong in his conjecture of the term Iessaeian being related to Jesse. Iessaeians is simply a misspelling of the Aramaic term Essenes, which means healer. Epiphanius also mentions the Essenes under the name of Ossenes, whom he gives as one of the seven sects:

"Ossenes, meaning "boldest." They kept all the observances as the Law directs. But they also made use of other scriptures after the Law, though rejecting most of the prophets that came after it. "[63]

The linking of the Ossaeans (Essenes) with the Nasaraeans allows us to deduce that the two Essene branches, spoken of by Josephus, were the Ossaeans and Nasaraeans. At least one side branch of Ossaeans were, at least temporarily, more open to limited celibacy. (Historical descriptions of these celibate Essenes can be found in Appendix 4) Nasaraeans, and most other Essenes always insisting on marriage for all. The Nasaraeans are the northern branch of Essenes based on Mount Carmel and in Galilee, with smaller temples and enclaves elsewhere. Of the two groups of Essenes, the Ossaean Essenes and the Nazorean Essenes, it was the northern Nazorean Essene group that the promises were made:

---

[61] Psalm 131:11
[62] Epiphanius, Panarion 29, 1,2-4
[63] Panarion

"He (Messiah) shall be called a Nasorean."[64]

Epiphanius groups the Ossaeans and Nazoreans together because they were so similar. They both refused to use the Old Testament of the Jews. Later, after Yeshu, these two sects actually merge into one sect. This was a result of an Ossaean prophetic figure accepted by both the Ossaeans and the Nasaraeans. This was Elxai, or Elchasai, who has given his name to the ancient Elchasaite sect. Epiphanius is one of our sources on this Ossaean prophet named Elchasai, who is said to have insisted on matrimony and introduced into their oaths and worship certain substances.

> "The man called Elxai joined them later, in the reign of the emperor Trajan, after the Savior's incarnation . . . He wrote a book by prophecy. . . By designating Salt, Water, Earth, Bread, Heaven Aether, and Wind as objects for them to swear by in worship. But again he designates seven other witnesses. . . Sky, Water, Holy Spirits, Angels of Prayer, the Olive, Salt and the Earth. He has no use for celibacy, detests continence and insists on matrimony. . . he confesses Christ by name . . He bans burnt offerings and sacrifices, as something foreign to God and never offered to Him on the authority of the fathers and Law . . . he rejects the Jewish custom of eating meat and the rest, and the altar. . . "

> Four sects. . . have made use of him. Of those that came after him, Ebionites and Nazoraeans. Of those that came before his time and during it, the Osseaens and the Nasaraeans." [65]

Elchasai was not the first to mention these substances, just the first to be well known in Christian circles. Yeshu had taught of them before him. Epiphanius tells us that the Osseaens and Nazoreans, after 101 AD, were known as Ebionites and Nazoreans. As we mentioned before, the other five sects of

---

[64] Matthew 2:23
[65] Panarion 1:19

Pharisees, Scribes, Hemerobaptists; Sadducees and Herodians merged into Rabbinical and Karaite Judaism. Since the identity and beliefs of the Nazoreans and Essenes are so critical to correctly understanding the message of Yeshu, we will speak of them a bit more.

Philo on Essenes

Another first hand report concerning the Essenes comes from the Jewish philosopher of the Egyptian dispersion, Philo of Alexandria, who lived between 30 B.C. and 40 A.D. His writings about the Essenes come from two works, 'Quod omnis probus Fiber sit' and 'Apologia pro Judais.' The second work was lost but quotes are preserved in Eusebius' 'Praeparatio Evangilica.' We are not told which branch of Essenes Philo is commenting on, but similarity in lifestyle probably existed amongst all branches. Philo writes:

> "They do not offer animal sacrifice, judging it more fitting to render their minds truly holy. They flee the cities and live in villages where clean air and clean social life abound. They either work in the fields or in crafts that contribute to peace. They do not hoard silver and gold and do not acquire great landholdings; procuring for themselves only what is necessary for life. Thus they live without goods and without property, not by misfortune, but out of preference. They do not make armaments of any kind. They do not keep slaves and detest slavery. They avoid wholesale and retail commerce, believing that such activity excites one to cupidity. With respect to philosophy, they dismiss logic but have an extremely high regard for virtue. They honor the Sabbath with great respect over the other days of the week. They have an internal rule which all learn, together with rules on piety, holiness, justice and the knowledge of good and bad. These they make use of in the form of triple definitions, rules regarding the love of God, the love of virtue, and the love of men. They believe God causes all good but cannot be the cause of any evil. They honor virtue by foregoing all riches,

glory and pleasure. Further, they are convinced they must be modest, quiet, obedient to the rule, simple, frugal and without mirth. Their life style is communal. They have a common purse. Their salaries they deposit before them all, in the midst of them, to be put to the common employment of those who wish to make use of it. They do not neglect the sick on the pretext that they can produce nothing. With the common purse there is plenty from which to treat all illnesses. They lavish great respect on the elderly. With them they are very generous and surround them with a thousand attentions. They practice virtue like a gymnastic exercise, seeing the accomplishment of praiseworthy deeds as the means by which a man ensures absolute freedom for himself."

Josephus on Essenes

Another writer contemporary with the Essenes was Flavius Josephus, the famous Jewish historian and priest-general at the time of the Jewish war. His descriptions are found in 'The Jewish War' written between 70 and 75 A.D., and 'Jewish Antiquities.' written before his death in 100 A.D. Josephus, in his second account, tells us that the Essenes were farmers who offered produce on their altars, rather than animals like the Jews of that day:

"The Essenes declare that souls are immortal and consider it necessary to struggle to obtain the reward of righteousness. They send offerings to the Temple, but offer no sacrifices since the purifications to which they are accustomed are different. For this reason, they refrain from entering into the common enclosure, but offer sacrifice among themselves. They are holy men and completely given up to agricultural labor."

Eusebius

Eusebius, Bishop of Caesarea, writing around A.D. 300, seems to be referring to the Essenes when he writes:

"Even in our day, there are still those whose only guide is Deity; ones who live by the true reason of nature, not only themselves free but filling their neighbors with he spirit of freedom. They are not very numerous indeed, but that is not strange, for the highest nobility is ever rare; and then these ones have turned aside from the vulgar herd to devote themselves to a contemplation of nature's verities. They pray, if it were possible, that they may reform our fallen lives; but if they cannot, owing to the tide of evils and wrongs which surge up in cities, they flee away, lest they too be swept off their feet by the force of the current. And we, if we had a true zeal for self-improvement, would have to track them to their places of retreat, and, halting as supplicants before them, would beseech them to come to us and tame our life grown too fierce and wild; preaching instead of war and slavery and untold ills, their Gospel of Peace and freedom, and all the fullness of other blessings."

"𝔥e shall be called a Nazorean" [66]

It is interesting that the prophecy recorded about Christ in the gospel called Matthew can not be found in the Old Testament. "He shall be called a Nasorene!" in Matthew 2:23 is nowhere to be found in it. There is a verse that speaks of a Nazor, or branch, coming out of the stem of Jesse, but nothing that says someone will be called a Nazorean or even a Nazor, or "branch".

The compiler of Matthew goes to great lengths to portray Jesus as a fulfillment of Jewish expectation and prophecy; and it would be amazing if he or she made the blunder of inserting a quote not found in the texts. Yet the anonymous author or authors of expanded Matthew did indeed make at least one such blunder, for they misquoted a prophecy:

---

[66] Christian Bible, Matthew 2:23

"So cavalier is Matthew with his 'quotations' from the prophets that he even wrongly attributes one quote: in referring to Judas's "thirty pieces of silver" (27.3,10) he maintains that the prophecy of 'Jeremiah' had been fulfilled – and yet it is 'Zechariah' (11.12-13) who used the phrase! [67]

Jerome, who died in 420 AD, wrote:

"To these (citations in which Matthew follows not the Septuagint but the Hebrew original text) belong the two: "Out of Egypt have I called my son" and "For he shall be called a Nazaraean." [68]

Apparently this quote was once in the Jewish scriptures, but was later edited out because of its use by Christians. As amazing as it sounds, there are many examples of this type of deletion by the rabbis, various lines being deleted from Jeremiah and other Jewish scriptures for just this very reason. Medieval documents exist that threaten punishment on anyone among the Jews who publishes older versions of texts containing prophecies used by Christianity.

Implications

The Nazorean canon and the Jewish canon were distinct. Each group observed something they both called the Law of Moses, but this was not a common law shared by both. The Law of Moses for the 5 Jewish sects was defined by the Old Testament Scrolls and the Old Testament Prophets. The Law of Moses for the Nazoreans and Essenes was defined by the Nazorean and Essene scrolls. These texts, and religions, were so different, and the Laws of Moses based on these distinct canons were so different, it is unfortunate that they both referred to their practices by the same name. There is, of course, a good reason

[67] Kenneth Humphreys
[68] Jerome, De Viris Inlustribus 3

for this which we shall go into in greater detail later. The simple answer is that the Nazoreans had the original simple Nazorean Law of Moses and their scrolls of light long before the Jewish version came along. The Jewish version of the Law, along with the Jewish Old Testament, came along long after the Nazorean one was well established. That is why the Nazoreans had an ancient saying that says: "Nazoreanism is older than Judaism." They made statements like this because they believed that the Judaic religion and scriptures were actually of a late date, pseudipigraphic forgeries, fostered upon the people of Judea by the Persians when they were in control of the Jerusalem area in the fifth century BC. They went on to say that the Torah of Moses was actually written by someone called Tavish, and that the Jews pretended to find it hidden in the Temple when they returned from Persian exile when in reality they had brought the new creation with them. The Nazorean scrolls even tell us that the Jewish priests were aware of the true author of the Torah, for they informed the father of John the Baptist that he was a descendant of his:

"The man who has inscribed the Torah, named the great Tavish, has arisen from your ancestry."[69]

Another account has more detail:

"The Jews were of the children of Ruha and Adam. Their great men were the children of Ruha; Moses was Kiwan, and Abraham was Shamish. They traveled and traveled until they came to 'Ur shalam (Jerusalem), which they called "Uhra shalam', 'The-road-is-complete'. They wanted books and Melka d Anhura said, 'A book must be written that does not make trouble for the Mandai', and they sent one of the melki-T'awus Melka (I.e. Peacock King) to write the Torat (Old Testament)." [70]

---

[69] Mandaean Book of John the Baptist.
[70] The Mandaeans of Iraq and Iran By E.S. Drower Clarendon Press, Oxford,1937 (Reprint Leiden:E.J. Brill 1962) page 257-258 Narrator: a priest (Drower gives no name)

Nazoreans, who never left Palestine, had a continual tradition and history going back for centuries. They knew that the supposed priests on the payroll of Persia were introducing a totally novel and new religion and set of writings when they read the Torah for the first time to the crowds of Jerusalem in 445 BC. They also knew that the stories about Old Testament heroes and prophets were being made up as well, despite the Persians use of names recognized by the Nazoreans. Epiphanius tells us of the Nazoreans:

> "They have the holy names of patriarchs which are in the Pentateuch, up through Moses and Joshua the son of Nun, and they believe in them - I mean Abraham, Isaac, Jacob, and the earliest ones, and Moses himself, and Aaron, and Joshua. But they hold that the scriptures of the Pentateuch were not written by Moses, and maintain that they have others."

The beliefs of the Nazorean Essenes, or Naassenes, are spoken of by another hostile historian named Hippolytus. Extracts from Book V of his Refutation of all Heresies tells us the following:

> "What the assertions are of the Naasseni, who style themselves Gnostics (*Mandai*), and that they advance those opinions which the Philosophers of the Greeks previously propounded, as well as those who have handed down mystical (rites), The priests, then, and champions of the system, have been first those who have been called Naasseni, being so denominated from the Hebrew language, for the serpent is called naas (in Hebrew). Subsequently, however, they have styled themselves Gnostics, alleging that they alone have sounded the depths of knowledge. [71]

---

[71] Hippolytus. Extracts from Book V of his Refutation of all Heresies

It should be noted that Naasseni is possibly a compound word derived from the union of the term Nazorean and Essene, echoing the fact that the Essenes and Nazoreans became one sect after the teachings of Elchasai about 100 AD. The Naasseni, being anti-torah, did not necessarily reject their association with snakes however, for they knew that thru word puns their name could be so understood. In ancient times the serpent was seen as an aspect of the Mother Goddess, and was identified with health, wisdom and healing. They also did not object to this symbol since they saw the snake in the Eden story as being an allegory of Yeshu who taught Adam and Eve to reject the false commands of the false god Yahweh and instead seek for gnosis from the tree of Knowledge. This was a common belief among all Gnostics whose origin goes back to the Nazoreans:

> "These (Naasseni), then, according to the system advanced by them, magnify, (as the originating cause) of all things else, a man and a son of man. These are the heads of very numerous discourses which (the Naassene) asserts James the brother of the Lord handed down to Mariamme.. . . . For the promise of washing is not any other, according to them, than the introduction of him that is washed in, according to them, life-giving water, and anointed with ineffable ointment (than his introduction) into unfading bliss." [72]

Hippolytus speaks here of James, the brother of Yeshu, as taking over leadership of the Nazoreans after his death, and then turning it over to Mariamme, who is Miryai, or Mary Magdalene the sought for one. He also writes:

> ". . . And concerning this (nature) they hand down an explicit passage, occurring in the Gospel inscribed according to Thomas, expressing themselves thus: "He who seeks me, will find me in

---

[72] Extracted From Book V Of Refutation Of All Heresies By Hippolytus

children from seven years old; for there concealed, I shall in the fourteenth age be made manifest." . . . . "[73]

Hippolytus tells us here that the Gospel of Thomas, which exists today and which does indeed contain this quote in the beginning, was used by the Nazorean Essenes. We shall quote this entire gospel in a later chapter.

Thus is a portion of the fragment of Naassene philosophy preserved by Hippolytus. In it we learn that the Nazoreans were not afraid to make use of and identify with ancient controversial symbols like the serpent, nor were they hesitant to interpret scriptural passages in a very mystical and tantric manner. It might be a little tedious to go into the details of just what they meant by these ideas, but it should be plain from reading the full fragment that this sect had a very evolved metaphysical philosophy that they received from Yeshu, through his successor James, and thence from Miryai of Magdala. Some of these traditions and teachings were even older than Yeshu, going back to Yeshu's predecessors like Yuhana, Anush, Bihram and others.

The precious Ginza that Yeshu read warns us against accepting the Old Testament prophets:

> "I now, the resounding Messenger, say to you: Listen not on the speech of the lying prophets who pretend to be true seers and who claim for themselves a likeness to the three Uthras who have gone forth in the world. Your radiance is no radiance, your mantel is no true mantel. Some from them are vested in garments of darkness, bedecked with robes of darkness, and your odor is odious and rotten." [74]

---

[73] Extracted From Book V Of Refutation Of All Heresies By Hippolytus
[74] Ginza Rba

All ancient Nazorean Essenes looked with great suspicion on
the authenticity of the New, as well as the Old Testaments.
Their position on the Bible was summed up by the Gnostic
Bishop Faustus about 400 A.D. Faustus tells us that the New
Testament is not pure and that one should be careful what one
receives from it. He warns that it was not written by either
Christ or His Apostles, but nameless men many years later:

> "We have proved again and again, the writings are not the
> production of Christ or of His apostles, but a compilation of
> rumors and beliefs, made, long after their departure, by some
> obscure semi-Jews, not in harmony even with one another, and
> published by them under the name of the apostles, or of those
> considered the followers of the apostles, so as to give the
> appearance of apostolic authority to all these blunders and
> falsehoods." [75]

From Manichaean sources we know that early true followers
of Yeshu did not accept the New Testament as authentic. The
following quote from an Arabic manuscript points out the
origin of these dubious texts in a manner consistent with the
position of the Nazorean Essenes.

> "And the Romans said: "Go, fetch your companions, and bring
> your Book ." The Christians went to their companions, informed
> them of what had taken place between them and the Romans
> and said to them: "Bring the Gospel, and stand up so that we
> should go to them." But these companions said to them: "You
> have done ill. We are not permitted to let the Romans pollute the
> Gospel. In giving a favorable answer to the Romans, you have
> accordingly departed from the religion. We are therefore no
> longer permitted to associate with you; on the contrary, we are
> obliged to declare that there is nothing in common between us
> and you;" and they prevented their taking possession of the
> Gospel or gaining access to it. In consequence a violent quarrel
> broke out between the two groups. Those mentioned in the first

[75] Faustus, Contra Faustus Manicheun

place went back to the Romans and said to them: "Help us against these companions of ours before helping us against the Jews, and take away from them on our behalf our Book." Thereupon the companions of whom they had spoken fled the country. And the Romans wrote concerning them to their governors in the districts of Mosul and in the Jazirat al-Arab. Accordingly, a search was made for them; some were caught and burned, others were killed.

"As for those who had given a favorable answer to the Romans they came together and took counsel as to how to replace the Gospel, seeing that it was lost to them. Thus the opinion that a Gospel should be composed was established among them. They said: "the Torah consists only of narratives concerning the births of the prophets and of the histories of their lives. We are going to construct a Gospel according to this pattern.

"Everyone among us is going to call to mind that which he remembers of the words of the Gospel and of the things about which the Christians (Nazoreans?) talked among themselves when speaking of Christ." Accordingly, some people wrote a Gospel. After them came others who wrote another Gospel. In this manner a certain number of Gospels were written. However a great part of what was contained in the original was missing in them. There were among them men, one after another, who knew many things that were contained in the true Gospel, but with a view to establishing their dominion, they refrained from communicating them. In all this there was no mention of the cross or of the crucifix. According to them there were eighty Gospels. However, their number constantly diminished and became less, until only four Gospels were left which are due to four individuals. Every one of them composed in his time a Gospel. Then another came after him, saw that the Gospel composed by his predecessor was imperfect, and composed another which according to him was more correct, nearer to correction than the Gospel of the others." [76]

---

[76] The Establishment Of Proofs . . . By 'Abd Al-Jabbar

The following quote from the same source on the falsification of the record of the New Testament is in full accord with ancient Nazorean beliefs:

"As for the prodigies and miracles which as the Christians claim (were worked) by him, all this is baseless. He himself did not claim (to have worked) them. Nor is there in his time or in the generation which followed any disciple who claimed (that Jesus had worked miracles). This was first claimed only a very long time after his death and after the death of his (direct) disciples; similarly the Christians have claimed that the Jew Paul (has worked miracles and this) in spite of his being known for his tricks, his lying and his baseness; they have done the same for George and for Father Mark, and they do the same at all times with regard to their monks and nuns. All this is baseless.'[77]

Roots of Nazoreanism

"Nazoreanism is older than Judaism." [78]

Nazoreans claim that "Nazoreanism is older than Judaism." They believed that the Judaism they knew, as promoted by the five Jewish Sects, was less than 500 years old at the time of Yeshu. They rejected the 5 books of Moses as being forgeries of a man called Tavish. They, and Yeshu, rejected the book of Kings and Chronicles, and the prophets like Isaiah, Jeremiah, Ezekiel and others. They believed that a few historical facts and truths had been woven into these books when they were created by the returning exiles, but that the bulk of their message and meaning were flawed. They did not accept the Priesthood claims of the Jerusalem Jews and they certainly did not accept the animal slaughter that took place in the Jerusalem temple. They did not worship the bloodthirsty

---

[77] The Establishment Of Proofs . . . By 'Abd Al-Jabbar
[78] Mandaean saying reported by E.S. Drower

Jehovah, or Yahweh, worshipped by the Jews and honored in these false books.

The Judaism known to the modern world is rabbinical Judaism. It did not exist in ancient Palestine but was created by the Pharisee sect after the destruction of Jerusalem in 70 AD. To its credit it has abandoned animal sacrifice and looks allegorically upon commandments to do so in its scriptures. Ancient Nazoreans would have approved of this allegorical interpretation but would still reject their use of the Old Testament canon and worship of Yahweh. The Cabbalistic tradition in Judaism, which gained strength in the middle ages, is much closer to Nazoreanism than it is to Judaism. This is because much of the doctrine and philosophies of the Jewish Kabballistic tradition actually come from Nazorean scrolls and traditions. Over time this tradition, since it developed within Rabbinical Judaism, found clever ways to graft its foreign ideas onto this Jewish tradition. Kabballistic books, like the Zohar, even try to portray themselves as commentaries on the first four books of Moses, but the correlation is weak and the systems do not agree. The concepts and ideas of the Kabballahh are just too close to the Nazorean philosophy to ever be harmonized with Judaism proper despite the mental gymnastics of Cabbalists.

Kabballah

The light and truth of ancient Nazorean Essenes was wisely seeded all over the Middle East by these ancient brothers and sisters. Encampments were made in many lands which affected many schools of religious thought. The original Essene speculations and doctrines of Deity espoused by Liliuk and Lalaitha in the 9th century B.C. and preserved by the Nazoreans eventually show up in Jewish Kabballistic schools in the middle ages. Many of these teachings were even codified in such Jewish Kabballistic texts like the Zohar, Bahir, Yetzirah and others. These Kabballistic echoes of original Nazirutha doctrines were written in Aramaic, the language of the original School of the Prophets on Mt Carmel. They contain much of the original truths, but these truths are ingeniously wedded onto corrupt Biblical texts as supposed commentaries.

The Kabballistic Tree of Life, preserved in mystical Judaism, is a true carry over from original Nazirutha teachings. Nazoreans did not use the same names of Deity that Jews place on the different Sephiroth of that Tree, however, for Nazoreans worship different Gods than the Jews, but the basic concept is the same in both systems. Nazoreanism is the secret doctrine borrowed by the Jews, but it has not been preserved purely by them and contains many things out of harmony with the basic Naziruthian world view.

The ancient historian Josephus mentions that the Essenes imparted the names of angels to initiates, together with other Kabballistic mysteries:

> "He (the initiate) swears to communicate the doctrines to no one in any other way than as he received them himself and that he will abstain from plagiarizing, and will equally preserve the books belonging to their sect and the names of the angels." [79]

The Nazorean Essenes were the wellspring of what the world now knows as the Kabballah. It has always been looked upon as a sin for a Mandai (Nazorean Gnostic) to reveal the names of the Malkia (angels) to a non-Nazorean. Nevertheless, many many centuries ago these secrets were acquired by Jewish Nazorean hybrid break offs of the main Nazirutha current, and were eventually transmitted to secret Rabbinical Jewish

---

[79] The Jewish War, Book 2, Chapter 8

groups who secretly taught an ever Judaized form of the original Nazorean gnosis. These were transmitted to writings such as the Zohar and Sephir Yetzirah and eventually became known to the western occult world.

In our day the Judaized names of the Nazorean emanations can be bought in almost any mall, but they are greatly removed from the pure Qabbalah once taught by Yeshu and Miryai in the hallowed caves and temples on ancient Mount Carmel. Since we dwell in the information age "when all things are revealed on the housetops", as prophesied by Yeshu, it seems appropriate to disregard many of the ancient taboos about secrecy and openly discuss the mysteries of Nazirutha with those who have an interest in them. We shall do this more fully, however, in the companion volumes to this book which focus on Miryai and Mani.

Sleeping Prophet

In the spiritual life readings of the American born seer Edgar Cayce, uttered in deep hypnotic trance, we find collaborating testimony on the existence of Essene Nazoreans:

> "Q) Were the Essenes called at various times and places Nazarites, School of the Prophets, Hasidees, Therapeutae, Nazoreans, and were they a branch of the Great White Brotherhood, starting in Egypt and taking as members Gentiles and Jews alike?
> (A) In general, yes. Specifically, not altogether. They were known at times as some of these; or the Nazarites were a branch or a THOUGHT of same, see? Just as in the present one would say that any denomination by name is a branch of the Christian-Protestant faith, see?

> "There purpose was of the first foundations of the prophets as established, or as understood from the period of the prophets, by

Elijah; and propagated and studied through the things begun by
Samuel. The movement was not an Egyptian one, though
adopted by those in another period, or an earlier period, and
made a part of the whole movement. They took Jews and
Gentiles alike as members. The Essenes were a group of
individuals sincere in their purpose and yet not orthodox as to
the rabbis of that particular period....that taught the mysteries of
man and his relationships to those forces as might manifest from
within and without. . . . the Essenes . . . were students of what ye
would call astrology, numerology, phrenology, and those phases
of study of the return of individuals - or reincarnation. These led
to a proclaiming that a certain period was a cycle; and these had
been the studies then of Aristotle, Enos, Mathesa, Judas, and
those that were in the care or supervision of the school - as you
would term in the present. These having been persecuted by
those leaders, Sadducees (who taught) there was no resurrection
- or there is no reincarnation, which is what resurrection meant
in those periods."

Enos, said to be a supervisor of the school, is apparently the
same as an Anush mentioned in the ancient Aramaic Book of
John who supervises the education of Yuhana for his first 22
years. The Aramaic scroll says that Enos (Anush) took John to
Mount Parwan where little ones on holy drinks are reared up:

"When Anush the treasurer heard this he took the child and
brought it to Parwan the white mountain, to Mount Parwan on
which sucklings and little ones on holy drinks are reared up.
There I abode until I was two and twenty years old. I learned
there the whole of my wisdom and made fully my own the
whole of my discourse."

The brief Roman Christian version of this is: "the child grew,
and was strengthened in spirit; and was in the deserts, until
the day of his manifestation to Israel"[80] This is probably all the
authors of Luke knew about the situation.

---

[80] Luke I, 80

Nazorean Gods

The Nazoreans had several systems of conceptualizing their Gods and Goddesses. They used a male female balanced Trinity but also worshipped a fourfold God[81] called the "Life, Light, Power and Wisdom". The Fourfold God is actually four groups of god-goddess pairs. The first three pairs are the Gnostic version of the Christian Trinity which includes three Goddesses to their male counterparts. Our Heavenly Parents make up the first Pair, Yeshu and Miryam make up the second, and Mani and Miryai make up the third. This fourfold God was known as the Ogdoad[82] of Valentinian Gnosticism.

There are four Peaceful Deities, or Four Transcendent Lords, spoken of in Central Asia Bon[83] Buddhism. These are led by a goddess called "the Mother" (Yum[84]), followed by three male deities known as "the God" (Lha[85]), "the Procreator" (Sipa[86]), and "the Teacher" (Tönpa[87]). These four Peaceful Deities come forth out of primal parents known to the Bonpos and Nyingmas as Kuntuzangpo (All Good Father) and Kuntuzangmo (All Good Mother). These are the same beings worshipped by Yeshu under the name of the Great Life (*Hiya Rba*), or the Palmtree (*Sindirka*) and Wellspring (*Aina*). They were also known in Gnosticism by the titles Father of Light and Mother of Life, as well as Deep and Silence. Yeshu's twin-

---

[81] LIFE is an acronym describing this Four Fold Deity.

[82] A group of the first 8 Gods of the 32 membered Pleroma.

[83] The teachings of Bon were revealed by Tonpa Shenrab. Their origins is said to have been to the west and north of western Tibet, brought by white robed Priests from Persian lands. Both the Jain and the Bon religion use the swastika, and no doubt go back to the same source - the swastika using Yuezhi "Moon People" . Both Bonpos and Jains trace their origins to Mt. Kailish in western Tibet. Mt. Kailish was an ancient hub of a type of Buddhism that eventually became Ch'an, Mahayana and Vajrayana. Its multi-Buddha worship is in stark contrast to the atheistic branch of Indian Buddhism promoted by Siddhartha.

[84] Sherab Jyamma (Chamma) who is the Prajnaparamita or Perfection of Wisdom.

[85] Shenlha Odkar, the Sambhogakaya Buddha, or God of Compassion.

[86] Sangpo Bumtri, the Creator and Procreator Deity called Sidpa (with Chulcam rGyalmo)

[87] Buddha Shenrab Miwo, the Nirmanakaya Buddha or World Teacher (with Hoza Gyelmed)

soul is Sherab Chamma, the Perfection of Wisdom, in the Bon Pantheon. The cosmic Yeshu himself is identical to Shenlha Odkar, the Sambhogakaya Buddha, or God of Compassion of the Bonpos. Mani and Miryai, the Gnostic Logos and Will, make up the third pair of peaceful deities known in Bon as Sangpo Bumtri the Creator and his syzygy Chulcam Gyalmo.

The Bon concept of four Jewels[88], which was also taught by the Gnostic prophet Mani, is related to these Deities.

Maligned Sect

Yeshu grew up in a Goddess worshipping sect of Palestine that was both hated and misunderstood by most of the other sects of the area. He grew up in a sect that did not worship Yahweh, did not accept the Jewish Law of Moses or Jewish prophets, and which abhorred animal sacrifice and meat eating. Mass conversions of Jews to Nazoreanism, as a result of the teachings of Yuhana (John the Baptist), Yeshu, and his disciples caused additional strife. What Yuhana began, Yeshu and his brother Jacob (James the Just) concluded. Ancient Aramaic scrolls tell us that from these two sons of Mary 360 priests were ordained. 360 white robed and long haired Gnostic baptizing and initiating priests and priestesses can stir up a lot of controversy in a land divided with such strong sectarian divisions. The scrolls go on to say that almost all of these were martyred by the Jews who hated all things Gnostic. Some did escape, however, fleeing northward into Syria. These fleeing initiates formed the backbone of future vegetarian Gnostic communities. Eventually these fleeing Nazorean Essenes settled in northern Syria and in lower Iraq from whence the original gnosis continued to flow along with and beside the ancient Euphrates River.

---

[88] These became the Buddha, Dharma, Sangha and Lama of Tibetan Buddhism.

The historian Pliny, by the year 70 AD, speaks of a people he refers to in his Natural History as "Nazerini" in northern Syria.[89] In the second century a Hellenistic author named Lucian of Samosata also encountered Nazoreans along the Euphrates River and wrote:

> 'These prayed to the rising sun, baptizing themselves at dawn. They ate nothing but wild fruit, milk and honey."

Nazoreans, according to their Gospel of Philip found in the Nag Hammadhi library, claim that their native tongue is Syrian. This would have made them quite at home in both northern and southern Syria, as well as along the lower Euphrates River in Iraq, not to mention Galilee in northern Palestine. All these areas spoke a form of Aramaic known as Syriac. Aramaic was also spoken among the common people in Judea, but it was a different dialect of Aramaic. That is why one reads in the flawed gospels of the strange sounding Galileans accent that Peter had. This small tidbit of truth managed to survive the misunderstandings and falsifications that went into creating these bible texts.

The Syriac dialect of Aramaic that linked the Nazoreans of Galilee with northern Syria and southern Iraq was a result of an ancient affiliation between these groups that goes back to the Assyrian invasion of Palestine around 722 BC. At this time many people of northern Syria are said to have immigrated into northern Palestine. This may account for many of the differences between the dialects and religion of the Galileans and the Judeans. These differences were accentuated with the return of the exiles and fabrication and fostering of the new fake Laws and Scriptures on the Judeans by Persian duped Ezra and Nehemiah. Before Ezra and his new law, the beliefs and practices of the am-aretz, or people of the land in the

---

[89] Natural History 5.81

Judean hills and those in the fertile land of Galilee would have
been much more in synch. After the resettling of Judea by
Persian refugees around 520 BC, many of the similarities
would diminish. On the surface some remained, for the new
Persian propagandists used traditional Jewish names and
stories when they wrote their texts, but they changed the
stories and the laws to fit with Persian beliefs of animal
sacrifice, worship of a solar Jehovah like deity and other
matters approved of by Cyrus. This is why the Nazoreans
were known to "have the holy names of patriarchs which are
in the Pentateuch, up through Moses and Joshua the son of
Nun, and they believe in them - I mean Abraham, Isaac, Jacob,
and the earliest ones, and Moses himself, and Aaron, and
Joshua. But they hold that the scriptures of the Pentateuch
were not written by Moses, and maintain that they have
others." If there is any doubt as to the involvement of the
Persian king Cyrus in the creation of the Jewish state and
religion, one need only consider a passage in Cyrus' Old
Testament where he is called the Messiah:

> """Thus saith the Lord...that hath said of Cyrus: 'He is My
> shepherd, and shall perform all My pleasure, even saying of
> Jerusalem, 'She shall be built', and to the Temple, 'Thy
> foundation shall be laid'." Thus saith the Lord to His Anointed
> [Hebrew: Messiah] to Cyrus whose right hand I have holden to
> subdue nations before him....'I will go before thee and make the
> crooked places straight...'" [90]

This religion of Cyrus in Jerusalem continued to be practiced
by the Jews until 334 BC.. When Alexander the Great
conquered Judea in that year, he further altered the landscape
of the capital city and its beliefs established previously by
Cyrus. A great influx of all things Greek happened at this time
to both the Temple and its adherents. Throughout all these

[90] Isaiah 44:28-45:2

changes the humble Nazoreans continued to worship the Great Date Palm and Wellspring, the Hidden Living God and Goddess, or Great Life, and continued the ancient practices, rituals and teachings that characterize their faith. The Nazoreans continued worshipping in their ancient temple on Mount Carmel, and continued their spiritual eugenics program that they hoped would help birth more pure souls amongst them.

¯ 3 ¯
MOUNT CARMEL TEMPLE

3 Brothers on Carmel

THE ARAMAIC NAME of John the Baptist is Yuhana, and we learn from his book that when he died his death was reported to the Nazorean central Temple on Mt Carmel:

> "Yuhana has left his body, his brothers make proclamations, his brothers proclaim unto him on the Mount, on Mount Carmel. They took the Letter and brought it to the Mount, to Mount Carmel. They read out the Letter to them and explain to them the writing, - to Yaqif (James) Beni-Amin (Yeshu) and Shumel (Samuel/Shimeon). They assemble on Mount Carmel." [91]

So in this ancient Aramaic scroll we have reference to the death of Yuhana being reported to three named Beni-Amin, Yaqif and Shimeon. These are the Aramaic names of Yeshu (Son of Amin[92] or Beni-Amin), and Yeshu's two brothers James (Yaqif) and Shimeon (Shumel). All three brothers are connected with the sacred Mount of Carmel and with the temple there and would eventually lead the Nazorean Sect. At

---

[91] Sidra Dyahya (Book Of John)/Drashe Dmalke (Discourses Of Kings) 26
[92] Amin, or Amun, was one name of the Nazorean's Highest God. Beni meant "son of".

the death of such an important Nazorean as Yuhana, it was protocol that such be reported to the central Temple and to those who preside there. These three sons of Miryam[93] and Yoseph are the ones to which the death of Yuhana is reported to. The first of these brothers, Yeshu, is immediately appointed successor to Yuhana. After Yeshu's death in 30 AD. the second brother James (Yaqif) will assume leadership. When Yaqif is killed in 64 AD. the third brother Shumel will succeed him. Shumel himself was reportedly martyred in the reign of Trajan (98-117 AD), bringing to a close the presidency of these three sons of Miryam. They, with their female counterparts, presided over the Naziruthian system of enlightenment and purification for more than 70 years. Their home and seat of authority was the Temple at Carmel.

Pythagoras on Carmel

Independent proof of an ancient Temple on Mount Carmel is proven by an ancient text called the Life of Pythagoras by Iamblichus, written before 333 AD. History has preserved for us this link between Pythagoras and the Mount Carmel Essenes:

> "In Phoenicia he (Pythagoras) conversed with the prophets who were the descendants of Moses the physiologist, and with many others, as well as the local hierophants . . . . After gaining all he could from the Phoenician Mysteries, he found that they had originated from the sacred rites of Egypt, forming as it were an Egyptian colony. . . . On the Phoenician coast under Mount Carmel, where, in the Temple on the peak, Pythagoras for the most part had dwelt in solitude . . . Mount Carmel, which they knew to be more sacred than other mountains, and quite inaccessible to the vulgar..." [94]

---

[93] "Virgin" Mary
[94] Life of Pythagoras by Iamblichus

We learn from this ancient quote that Pythagoras, the father of mathematics and founder of the Pythagorean School, was actually initiated by Nazorean Essenes on Mt Carmel. Mount Carmel, in the times of Yeshu, was actually a part of Phoenicia rather than Judea. We know from other ancient documents that both Essenes and Pythagoreans shared many things in common. Both were vegetarian, both wore white, and both were deeply immersed in Kabballistic studies. Pythagoras was nicknamed "the long haired one" which further links him with the northern Nasarene Essenes who were all Nazarites (long hairs). Carmel is found in writings dated to the reigns of the Egyptian pharaohs Thutmose II, Ramses II and Ramses III where it appears under the name *Rosh Qidshu*, meaning "First and Holiest". This term seems to denote that the mountain was seen as a prime holy place even in those ancient times.

Ancient Eugenics

The purpose of eugenic engineering is "to produce individuals whose capacities go beyond the normal."[95] Many ancient societies attempted to do this, and we find admonitions in this regard in the teachings of Pythagoras, Plato, and other ancient philosophers. Temples throughout the ancient world were particularly prone to practice some form of eugenics, or selective breeding, and the Nazoreans were no exception. An example of ancient eugenics would be the priestesses within the Babylonian Temple cultus:

> "Virgin-birth was the responsibility of the Ishtar priestesses, who conducted fertility rites, prophesied and performed elaborate rituals in the temples throughout Babylon. ... The role of the Ishtar priestess was to act as both mother to the

---

[95] Agar, Nicholas. Designing Babies: Morally Permissible Ways to Modify the Human Genome. Bioethics 9(1): 1-15, January 1995.

prospective man's child and minister to the child's divine needs." [96]

The writer goes on to say that "Holy Virgin" was the title of these priestesses of Ishtar and Asherah:

"The title didn't mean physical virginity; it meant simply "unmarried." .....The Hebrews called the children of these priestesses bathur, which meant literally "virgin-born" ..."[97]

Even the Catholics say of the "Virgin Mary" that:

"She was a consecrated Temple virgin as was an acceptable custom of the times." [98]

They also elaborate:

"The legend of Mary's life in the Temple (from age 3 through 12) is presented in the Pseudo-Gospel of Matthew, and is based on the Proto-Evangelium of James. According to the latter Mary one day, although already betrothed to Joseph and living in his house, was called to the temple with other maidens and given wool to weave a new curtain for the temple. While spinning this purple wool at home, she was visited by the angel of the Annunciation. Thus, spinning is one of the typical activities in representations of Mary's Annunciation, pregnancy and Joseph's doubt. Weaving is more typical for Mary's activities as Temple Virgin, and is frequently combined with representations of an angel bringing food or the presence of Mary's companions." [99]

Nazoreans did not write or accept the Pseudo-Gospel of Matthew or the Proto-Evangelium of James. They did, however, concur that Mary was a temple virgin, but had a

---

[96] The Virgin Birth and Childhood Mysteries of Jesus, James Still
[97] The Virgin Birth and Childhood Mysteries of Jesus, James Still
[98] ScriptureCatholic.com
[99] http://www.udayton.edu/mary/questions/yq2/yq299.html

different idea than the Catholics about which Temple she served in and what it meant to be a "virgin".

Carmel Eugenics Program

Since neither Mary nor Yeshu were associated with the Jewish temple, but were Nazoreans, we must look to the Nazorean culture for answers. Accounts of this Nazorean's Vestal Virgin program and other special endeavors to create a more spiritual race can be found in the Cayce readings. We are told in these that a prophetess named Anna, using astrology and numerology, chose the maidens that made up this special Mount Carmel Temple Order of the Nazoreans:

"Anna lived in the promised land preceding and just following the entrance of the Prince of Peace into the earth. And she was a member of an organization which attempted, through the mysteries of the sages, to interpret time and place according to astrology and numerology. Her interpretations were much sought after by the leaders in the group. However, because some individuals were inclined to interpret and apply the knowledge for material benefits, difficulties arose between Anna and the leaders of the Essenes. She was not in the Temple, but she chose the twelve maidens who were to be channels that might know truth so thoroughly that they could be moved by the Holy Spirit. Anna was the waiting maid with Elizabeth and Mary when they were heavy with child. This was during the activities which brought the Prince of Peace, the Christ, Jesus, into the earth. At their meeting when they had both become aware of what was to occur, she blessed them and made the prophecies as to what would be the material experience of each in the earth. She helped the maidens prepare and consecrate their lives during their periods of expectancy. Hence, she was known as a seeress and prophetess."

Anna chose the twelve maidens, but one called Eloise was said to have presided over them in the role of Matriarch:

"Eloise then was in the capacity as one of the holy women who ministered in the Temple service and in the preparation of those who dedicated their lives for individual activity during that sojourn. The entity was then what would be termed in the present in some organizations as a Sister Superior, as an Officer, as it were, in those of the Essenes and their preparations. Hence, we find the entity, then, giving, ministering, encouraging, making for the greater activities; and making for those encouraging experiences oft in the lives of the disciples; coming into contact with the master oft in the ways between Bethany, Galilee, Jerusalem. For, as indicated, the entity kept the School on the way above Emmaus to the way that goeth down toward Jericho and towards the northernmost coast from Jerusalem. The entity blessed many of those who came to seek to know the teachings, the ways, the mysteries, the understandings; for the entity had been trained in the schools of those that were the prophets and prophetesses, and the entity was indeed a prophetess in those experiences - thus gained throughout."

There were two dedicated quorums on Carmel, a quorum of 12 "maidens" and one of 12 "males" composed of special children like Yuhana and Yeshu who were being groomed for Buddhahood. The Cayce readings tell us that these chosen ones were dedicated:

"By all those who chose to give those that were perfect in body and in mind for the service...each as a representative of the twelve in the various phases that had been, or that had made up, Israel - or man."

Their purpose, according to Cayce, was that:

"Each should give their bodies and there is a necessity for training, even as there was a training in that experience of the twelve girls, in the fitness of their bodies, and of their fathers and mothers. In the present this is called eugenics, which is the preparation for the entrance of souls that make the earth better in material and spiritual ways."

We are told that they experienced:

> "Training as to physical exercise, first; training as to mental exercises as related to chastity, purity, love, patience, endurance. All of these by what would be termed by many in the present as persecutions, but as tests for physical and mental strength; and this under the supervision of those that cared for the nourishments by the protection of the food values. These were the manners and the way they were trained, directed, protected."

We are told that this eugenics program was established by Elijah and had been going on since his day.

> "Some four and twenty years before the advent of that entity, that soul entrance into the material plane called Jesus, we find Phinehas and Alkatma making those activities among those of the depleted group of the prophets in Mount Carmel, begun by Samuel, Elisha, Elijah, Saul and those during those experiences. Because of the divisions that had arisen among the people into sects, as the Pharisee, the Sadducee and their divisions, there had arisen the Essenes..."[100]

Around 872 BC significant events were transpiring in both east and west. In eastern lands Parsva[101], the 23 Jain Buddha, was born and would go on to attain liberation on Parsvan, or Parsva*natha* mountain, and about this same time in the west Elijah (*Liliuk*) and Lulaitha establish the School of the Prophets

---

[100] Cayce Reading on 1472.

[101] Historical Jainism begins with the enlightened liberation by Parsva (877-777 BC) in the Parasanatha Hills (in Bihar). He was the son of the king of Varanasi (Benaras) in India. Parsva renounced the worlds at the age of thirty and after a season of meditation and austerity he attained enlightenment. Thereafter he preached his message and gathered followers around him. He died at the age of 100, about 250 years before the time of the next famouse Jain Buddha - Mahavira. He taught four of the five great moral precepts of Jainism, non-violence, truthfulness, non- stealing and non-acquisitiveness. Parsva and older Jainism/Buddhism did not teach the vow of sexual restraint which was added 250 years later by Mahavira and Siddhartha. From a Gnostic standpoint, Parsva has greater authority than Mahavira, and the Svetambara branch the more ancient and correct, since they wear white, accept woman as equals and acknowledge a female in the list of 24 buddhas. The nude Digambara sect probably originated from the followers of Gosala who was a companion of Mahavira.

on or near Parvan, the White Mountain where pure children are raised. The similarities between Parsva and Liliuk are not accidental. Both established monasteries at the same time on holy mountains, one on Parsvan and the other on Parvan, and both created legitimate schools based on principles of enlightenment. Neither one of these "buddhas" created their religions themselves, they simply reorganized and restructured more ancient systems then prevalent. Both of these numinous streams herald back to a common source of enlightenment and a common spring of gnosis whose ancient figurehead was one Shenrab Miwo. Shenrab, like the three brothers Yeshu, James and Simeon on Carmel, and like Hibil, Sethil and Anush in Nazorean eschatology, was a member of a three brother team:

> "In past ages there were three brothers, Tonpa Shenrab Dagpa, Salba and Shepa, who studied the Bön doctrines in the heaven named Sridpa Yesang; under the Bön Sage Bumtri. When their studies were completed, they visited the God of Compassion, Shenlha Odkar, and asked him how they could help the living beings submerged in the misery and sorrow of suffering. He advised them to act as guides to mankind in three successive ages of the world. To follow his advice the eldest brother, Dagpa completed his work in the past world age. The second brother, Salba took the name Shenrab and became the teacher and guide of the present world age. The youngest brother, Shepa will come to teach in the next world age." [102]

Shenrab reformed the primitive Indo-European faith of Europe and Asia and laid the foundation for all schools of enlightenment from Eastern Lands, such as the Tibetan Nyingma, the Chinese Cha'an, the Indian Jain and Buddhist Faiths, as well as many others. His remarkable achievements

---

[102] Excerpted from a publication by Triten Norbutse & Yungdrung Bön Monastic Center

and teachings have been erroneously associated with other later teachers.

Yeshu and his brothers appear to have been the result of almost nine centuries of eugenics breeding, over 50 generations of vegan giving birth to vegan amidst intense spiritual and physical training. The first Matriarch of this Carmel school was the female companion of Liliuk (Elijah), known as Lulaitha, who in Nazorean tradition is understood to be the divine being who presides over pregnancy and childbirth. Elijah was called the Tishbite. Some translate this term as a town but the word means "foreigner", denoting that Elijah was not from Judea. Gnostics of Carmel later would refer to themselves as "foreigners" or "strangers" in a strange land, and the Jews called them "strangers" when they swore that none of them would ever walk in Jerusalem again. All these things indicating that the Nazoreans were not Jewish in their origins, but from father north which explains why Galileans spoke Syriac while the rest of Israel spoke another dialect of Aramaic and Hebrew. This contributed to the animosity between the two peoples.

Temple Training

We are told that Mariam, the mother of Yeshu was among this group of twelve maidens in the Carmel Temple:

> "Q. How old was Mary at the time she was chosen?
> A. Four, and as ye would call, between twelve and thirteen when designated as the one chosen by the angel on the stair." [103]

Joseph was apparently among the 12 male consecrates of this Carmel Temple, perhaps from the previous generation of eugenic births, and appears to have been the actual physical

---

[103] Edgar Cayce's Story of Jesus

father of Yeshu and proxy for the "Great Life". He was chosen for this service by divination and revelation:

"Thus the lot fell upon Joseph, though he was a much older man compared to the age ordinarily attributed to Mary in the period. Thus there followed the regular ritual in the temple." [104]

Joseph and Mary, sealed as one in ancient Temple Marriage rites, conceived Yeshu in an especially pure or Immaculate Conception. This does not mean conception without sexuality, but conception as a result of spiritual sexuality as spoken of in the Nazorean Gospel of Philip:

"Those who are separated will unite ... and will be filled. Every one who will enter the bridal chamber will kindle the light, for ... just as in the marriages which are ... happen at night. That fire ... only at night, and is put out. But the mysteries of that marriage are perfected rather in the day and the light. Neither that day nor its light ever sets."

Cayce continues, telling us that these twenty-four special priests and priestesses of the Nazorean Temple are the very foundation of the Church:

"Thus in Carmel - where there were the priests of this (Essene) faith - there were the (temple) maidens chosen who were dedicated to this purpose, this office, this service . . . That was the beginning, that was the foundation of what ye term The Church." [105]

So Nazoreanism, as well as its corrupt offshoot Christianity, began on Carmel. We are told a little about the Temple Altar there where they worshipped each morning:

---

[104] Edgar Cayce's Story of Jesus
[105] Cayce 5749-6

"The Temple steps - or those that led to the altar, were called the Temple steps. These were those upon which the sun shone as it arose of a morning when there were the first periods of the chosen maidens going to the altar for prayer; as well as for the burning of incense. [106]

Lest we confuse this Essene Temple on Carmel with another, the question was asked:

"Q. Was this the orthodox Jewish Temple or the Essene Temple? A. The Essenes, to be sure. Because of the adherence to those visions as proclaimed by Zacharias in the orthodox temple, he was slain even with his hands upon the horns of the altar. Hence, those as were being here protected were in Carmel, while Zacharias was in the temple in Jerusalem."

"Q. "Where was the wedding of Mary and Joseph?" A. "In the Temple there at Carmel." [107]

And again we are told:

"Josie was close to Mary when the selection was indicated by the shadow or the angel on the stair, at that period of consecration in the Temple. This was not the Temple in Jerusalem, but the Temple where those who were consecrated worshipped, or a School - as it might be termed - for those who might be channels. This was part of that group of Essenes who, headed by Judy, made those interpretations of those activities from the Egyptian experience - as the Temple beautiful, and the service of the Temple of Sacrifice. Hence it was in this consecrated place where this selection was made. Then when there was the fulfilling of those periods when Mary was espoused to Joseph and was to give birth to the Savior, the Messiah, the Prince of Peace, the Way, the Truth, the Light, soon after this birth there was the issuing of the orders first by Judy that there should be someone selected to be with the parents during their sojourn in Egypt.

---

[106] Edgar Cayce's Story of Jesus
[107] Cayce 5749-8

Thus the entity Josie was selected or chosen by those of the Brotherhood..."[108]

Conceived of the Holy Spirit

The New Testament accounts of Mary's conception say such was a result of the Holy Spirit, and this Holy Spirit is symbolized by a dove. G.R.S. Mead, in his Gnostic John the Baptizer book tells us that:

> "...among the Mandaeans there was a class of the perfect called doves." [109]

Misunderstandings of a special quorum of temple workers called "doves", who may have been involved in the Nazorean eugenics program, may have resulted in the confusion about Mary's conception. Yuhana the Baptist is called the "dove" in some writings, which may indicate that he and Yeshu also participated in the eugenics program on Carmel before their ministries:

> "The Dove . . . which is John the Baptist." [110]

Because Mariam, or Mary, had every stage of her conception presided over by wise individuals being influenced by the Holy Spirit, it is appropriate to say that Mariam conceived under the influence of this Holy Spirit. In addition, her training from infancy upward had taught her how to open herself and be overshadowed by this Spirit in all her activities, including sexual intimacy. The wisdom of the spirit of Life guiding her and her guides to insure as perfect of a conception and birth as humanly possible for that time period. In later

---

[108] Edgar Cayce's Story of Jesus
[109] G.R.S. Mead, in his Gnostic John the Baptizer
[110] G.R.S. Mead, in his Gnostic John the Baptizer

Kabballistic jargon this would be known as being overshadowed by the Shekinah.

> "For the Kabbalist the ultimate sacrament is the sexual act, carefully organized and sustained as the most perfect mystical trance. Over the marriage bed hovers the Shekinah. Kabbalism also includes, of course, a group of divinatory and magical practices, manipulations of the alphabet and the text of the Pentateuch, magic spells and rites. All of these elements go back to very early days — to the beginnings of Israel in Palestine.... [111]

Actually, they go back to the Nazoreans and Mount Carmel and are independent of the Pentateuch which the Nazoreans rejected.

False Tales & Misunderstanding

Much of the misunderstandings concerning Yeshu and his birth are a result of the four gospels that claim to tell his definitive story in the New Testament. These books, written or altered from hearsay and rumor by the uninitiated, do not do justice to the hidden truth. There may be bits of truth in them, for many true stories circulated with the false, but as a whole they are unreliable as historical witnesses. The first Greek "gospel" was Mark, who was reportedly an interpreter for Peter. He is reported to have written down some of the things he remembered Peter saying about Yeshu. The Sleeping Seer Cayce said that at least the original draft letter of Mark was written in collaboration with Peter and Barnabas in 59 AD. Either Mark, or those after him, must have included much additional matter to this letter at a later date, for Peter would not have said many of the things reported in its final expanded rendition. The last chapter of the Gospel of Mark, which contains the physical resurrection story, does not exist

---

[111] Introduction to A.E. Waite's The Holy Kabala

in the earliest copies of Mark and was added some time later. This shows how the text evolved over time. Other portions of Mark were also certainly added over time, making the account more and more miraculous and more and more in line with stories loved by the Roman people brought up on tales of Greek and Roman mythology. Luke followed Mark, and Matthew followed Luke. Each time one of these editions surfaced, the gospel of John was altered to keep up with it. With each new "gospel", and with each new edition of each of these "gospels", new material was added that took them farther and farther from the truth. They are particularly inaccurate when it comes to the birth and childhood of Yeshu. These accounts were written a long time after the events by people who were not well informed about them. They were well informed about Roman Savior myths however, and these helped them fill in the details the way that they wished they had occurred.

Virgin Birth Controversy

The anonymous author or expander of Matthew maintains that 'Isaiah' had prophesied that Jesus would be born of a virgin:

> "Behold, a virgin will be with child, and will bring forth a son, and they will call his name Emmanuel..."[112]

Matthew's source for his quote is Isaiah 7.14 is the Greek Septuagint translated in Alexandria in the 3rd century BC. It mistakenly translated 'almah' (young woman) into the Greek 'parthenos' (virgin). The Hebrew original has: 'Hinneh ha-almah harah ve-yeldeth ben ve-karath shem-o immanuel.' Correctly translated, the verse reads:

---

[112] Matthew 1:23

'Behold, the young woman has conceived — and bears a son and calls his name Immanuel.'

Nazoreans spoke Syriac, a form of Aramaic. The word "almah" in Aramaic also means virgin, maid, and young girl. Confusion over the meaning of this term seems to have led to mistranslations of the Isaiah quote about a virgin conceiving, and in the matter of Yeshu's conception. The Roman Christians, ever influenced by their Roman mythology, were quick to assume Yeshu had experienced just such a birth. This misunderstanding was probably fueled by the virginity and celibacy of Miryam whilst serving in the Carmel temple prior to her pure conception. Some later writings, such as the fake Protovegilion of James went so far as to claim perpetual virginity for her even after becoming pregnant. As Rome developed this myth ever further, the wiser Nazoreans of Palestine became more and more outspoken about their firsthand knowledge of these matters. They were continually derided for believing that Yeshu was conceived naturally and that Joseph was his biological father. There were, interestingly, some Jewish stories about virgin births, beginning with Philo Judaeus of Alexandria (20B.C.E.-50C.E.):

"Tamar, when she became pregnant of divine seeds, and did not know who it was who had sown them ..." [113]

"For when she [Hannah] had become pregnant, having received the divine seed ..." [114]

"the angels of God went in unto the daughters of men, and they bore children unto them." [115]

---

[113] On the Change of Names, XXIII
[114] On the unchangeableness of God, ch. II
[115] On the unchangeableness of God, ch. I

All the people who had known Yeshu, or were descended from those who knew him, universally contended that Yeshu's father was Joseph and that he was not born of a virgin, but from a "maiden". The mistranslation of the Aramaic term for maiden was the original inspiration behind the Virgin Mary stories. This initial confusion was fueled by the Roman Christians familiarity with popular God myths that spoke of virgin births and by ideas circulating in Hellenistic Judaism. There are many of these:

> "Famous children born of a virgin include: Buddha (China), Krishna (India), Zoroaster (Persia), Adonis (Babylon), and Mithra (Syria). Among the Greeks it was even more common. For example, Alexander the Great was believed to have been conceived from a celestial thunderbolt, or to have been the result of a union between Philip's wife Olympias and the God Jupiter who took the form of a serpent. Perseus, the Greek hero who decapitated Medusa, was born of a virgin named Danae, by the God Zeus who came to her in a golden shower. Even Plato was said to be born of the union of a virgin (Amphictione) and a God (Apollo), and only after his birth did Ariston, Amphictione's husband, have sex with her. More relevant to Jesus' time, Romulus and Remus, the founders of Rome, were born of a Vestal Virgin whose father was the God of War, Mars. The Roman emperor Octavian was born from the union of his mother, Atia, and the God Apollo. The Egyptian goddess Isis gave birth to Horus despite the fact that her husband, Osiris had his phallus cut off by his brother Seth. Thus, virgin conceptions were quite popular at the time, although this was only in "pagan" worlds, not in the Jewish world."[116]

Thus non Aramaic speaking peoples from far away lands came up with another version of Yeshu's birth that fit their own personal bias and traditions. When they became dominant they used their power to persecute the original followers of Yeshu who knew the truth of his origins and

---

[116] http://www.jesuspolice.com/common_error.php?id=7

maintained his humanity. Rabbi Trypho writing in 155 to the Christian Justin in Rome said:

> "You should blush at telling the same stories as [the Greeks]…If you do not want people to say you are as mad as the Greeks, you must stop speaking [about the virgin birth]."[117]

A careful reading of the NT Gospels reveals original wording that implies the Joseph was indeed the father of Yeshu, so these changes must have happened over time. In the Nazorean Gospel of Philip we read:

> "Some said, "Mary conceived by the Holy Spirit." They are in error. They do not know what they are saying. When did a woman ever conceive by a woman? Mary is the virgin whom no power defiled. She is a great anathema to the Hebrews, who are the apostles and the apostolic men. This virgin whom no power defiled [...] the powers defile themselves. And the Lord would not have said "My Father who is in Heaven"[118], unless he had had another father, but he would have said simply "My father".

Irenaeus insisted that to deny Jesus was born of a virgin was to destroy God's "plan for salvation":

> "Their interpretation is false, who dare to explain the Scripture thus: Behold a girl (instead of a virgin) shall conceive and bear a son. This is how the Ebionites say that Jesus is Joseph's natural son. In saying this they destroy God's tremendous plan for salvation…"[119]

Pope Benedict, in 1969, made a succinct point in harmony with Ebionite ideas and Nazirutha. He broke with the insistence of Irenaeus that: "In saying this they destroy God's tremendous plan for salvation". He said:

---

[117] Rabbi Trypho writing in 155 to St. Justin in Rome
[118] Mt 16:17
[119] Irenaeus, Against Heresies, III 21.1

"According to the faith of the Church, the Sonship of Jesus does not rest on the fact that Jesus had no human father: the doctrine of Jesus' divinity would not be affected if Jesus had been the product of a normal human marriage..." [120]

The Ebionites under James the Righteous understood well the true nature of the maidenly birth:

"Those who belong to the heresy of the Ebionites affirm that Christ was born of Joseph and Mary and suppose him to be a mere man." [121]

Aramaic Hints of Polygamy

Since we are explaining the parentage of Yeshu according to Aramaic sources rather than hearsay Greco-Roman traditions, we will go one step further and also explain the fuller story of the family Yeshu grew up in.

The Aramaic scholar, Dr. Lamas, in his commentary on the Gospels contends that the wording therein seems to denote in the Aramaic that Joseph was a polygamist and had more than one wife. This is certainly possible and even probable since this was a form of marriage honored by the Nazoreans and insisted upon for all Ganzibras, or High Priests, in the Nazorean faith. Lamas writes:

"The reference to Mary [in the genealogy of Matthew 1: JS] is to show that Jesus was born of her and not of the other wives of Joseph. Whenever a reference is made to a particular son, the name of the mother is mentioned throughout the Scriptures. Whenever a king's name is mentioned his mother's name is also mentioned to distinguish her from the other wives of the king. If

Joseph had no other wives except Mary, the word "awed" would have been used in the case of Joseph as in other instances. The sixteenth verse would then read "Joseph begat Jesus", but as Mary's name is mentioned the word "etteled" is substituted for the word awled to indicate that Mary was the mother of Jesus. Even today in many eastern countries where polygamy is still practiced, whenever a son is mentioned, reference is made to his mother as the one who gave birth to him. [122]

In the writings of Anastasius of Antioch we also find mention of Joseph's many wives:

"Anastasius of Antioch cites the lost writings of Epiphanius to claim that Salome was Joseph's wife. In which case, he would have been married to both Mary and Salome at the same time. . . . Jerome tells us that Escha was Joseph's first wife (the daughter of Haggi, brother of Zachariah, father of John the Baptist)..."[123]

Of course this type of lifestyle, highly frowned upon by the Romans known for championing monogamy, was hushed up by the early Roman Church fathers. It was not at all unusual for northern Israel and many other oriental lands at the time. If Yeshu's mother did indeed have sister wives, then Yeshu would have grown up with many mothers all adoring him and bequeathing to him their own unique virtues and insights. Nazoreans, as a long standing Goddess worshipping cult, included many great Matriarchs and prophetesses overflowing with hidden knowledge and spiritual gifts among their enclave. These gifted priestesses would have greatly enhanced Yeshu's upbringing and deepened his sense of the divine feminine.

Toledoth Yeshu

---

[122] Gospel Light, Harper & Row, P. 5-7
[123] Salome: Matron Saint Of Midwives

Since we are mentioning obscure reports on the parentage of Yeshu, we will not omit the Toledoth Yeshu which is a derogatory version of the life of Yeshu of very limited worth, growing out of the response of the Jewish community to mainstream Christianity. This slanderous work concentrates on Yeshu's supposed inferior conception and of his supposed theft of the magic name of God from the Jewish Temple. It also contains legends concerning the corrupting influence of either a Simon Keha (Peter) or a Shaul (Paul) who supposedly worked for the Jewish government to separate the Nazoreans from their synagogues. The slanderous tradition is mentioned in 197-198 A.D by the Bishop of Carthage. Who mocks the Jewish stories by saying:

> "This is your carpenter's son, your harlot's son; your Sabbath-breaker, your Samaritan, your demon-possessed! This is He whom ye bought from Judas; He who was struck with reed and fists, dishonoured with spittle, and given a draught of gall and vinegar! This He whom His disciples have stolen away secretly, that it may be said He has risen, or the gardener abstracted that his lettuces might not be damaged by the crowds of visitors." [124]

Toledoth Yeshu is mostly superstition and slur but does mention Yeshu having 310 disciples. This 310 number is very close to the 360 disciples mentioned in true Aramaic scrolls for both Yeshu and his brother James. These same Nazorean scrolls also say that Yeshu was known as Immanuel (amin-il) and possibly Sons Amin (Beni-Amin) as well. One text says that 360 priests came forth from Jacob (James) and Beni-Amin (Sons Amin, i.e. Yeshu)

In the Toledoth, Yeshu is called the bastard son of Pandira. Around 375 A.D. Epiphanius stated in the genealogy of Jesus, that Joseph was the son of a certain Jacob whose surname was

---

[124] "De Spect.," Xxx.

Pandira or Panther.[125] Much of this goes back to confusion resulting from more than one individual known as Yeshu:

> "The Toledot Yeshu stories generally show a confounding of the Talmud accounts of the individuals titled Yeshu, ben-Stada and ben-Pandera with the Greek myth of Pandareus, Gospel elements about Jesus and elements resembling the account of Simon Magus in the Acts of Peter, all conflated into a single character called Yeshu. The stories typically understand the name Yeshu to be the acronym yemach shemo vezichro but justify its usage by claiming that it is wordplay on his real name Joshua."[126]

Generational Breeding

The Nazoreans worshipped both God and Goddess in sacred groves, high places, before stone altars, within caves and in constructed tents and shrines on this holy mountain of Carmel, and had been doing so for almost nine centuries. Part of the Temple Priests and Maidens duties were to weave veils, or curtains, for these holy places, to burn incense and to pray at certain fixed periods of the day. They also studied intensely and performed rituals of purification and redemption. Time and activities were carefully regulated by the movements of moon, sun and stars. The diet was vegetarian and women, as well as men, held positions of leadership and honor. Of course their main duty was to create children born "perfect in their generation", and they successfully accomplished this generation after generation after generation. Only those perfect in body were allowed to participate and their unions were regulated by astrology. From these enclaves of faithful pure ones, or Regions of the Faithful, came wave after wave of children destined for holy marriage themselves.

---

[125] Haer.," Lxxvii. 7
[126] From Wikipedia, the free encyclopedia

"Thereon they fashioned for Yahya (John the Baptist) a wife out of thee, thou "Region of the Faithful". From the first conception were Handan and Sharrath born. From the middle conception were Birham and Rhimath-Haya born. From the last conception were Nsab, Sam, Anhar-Ziwa and Sharrath born."[127]

The astrological timings of this "Region of the Faithful" apparently resulted in several groups of birth each year. Yahya's main wife Anhar appears to have been born in a third wave of births. Yeshu, Yuhana, and others would have been born within these waves of conception, as would most of their mates. Although there was apparently one maiden for each month out of the year, certain months would have been determined as inauspicious for conception, resulting in several maidens beings impregnated at certain auspicious times. Whenever an auspicious time for conception was determined by the stars, as many of the twelve maidens as possible would have been impregnated. If the above list of three conceptions represents one year's births, it would appear that only eight of the twelve maidens were impregnated in that year. It is reasonable to assume that at any given time there were not just twelve maidens in the Carmel Temple, but twelve who were ready for conception in any given year. Younger quorums of virgin maidens would have been in preparation to take their places as soon as the newly wedded generation graduated through conception. As a result of all these eugenics activities, it is easy to understand how misinformed people could come up with the Virgin birth stories associated with Yeshu of the Mount Carmel Nazoreans.

~ 4 ~
BIRTH OF A NAZOREAN

---

[127] Sidra Dyahya (Book Of John)/Drashe Dmalke (Discourses Of Kings)

Early Non-Christian Writings

SOME HAVE QUESTIONED the very existence of Yeshu as a historical figure, but there are ancient neutral records that indicate his presence on earth. There are a few references to the life or following of Yeshu in various Roman histories and one in Josephus. There are also references in later Jewish and Mandaic records. These references, although few, are absolute proof for the historical reality of Yeshu of the Nazoreans and of his birth among men. We will quote them here and would note that some of these quotes refer to the Roman Christians of Paul, not true Nazoreans:

Cornelius Tacitus, who lived from 55 to 117 A.D., wrote about persistent reports of Christian "abominations":

> "...to get rid of the report, Nero fastened the guilt and inflicted the most exquisite tortures on a class hated for their abominations, called Christians by the populace. Christus, from whom the name had its origin, suffered the extreme penalty during the reign of Tiberius at the hand of one of our procurators, Pontius Pilatus, and a most mischievous superstition, thus checked for the moment, again broke out not only in Judea, the first source of the evil, but even in Rome where all things hideous and shameful from every part of the world find their centre and become popular.[128]

Gaius Suetonius Tranquillus (c. 69 to 140 A.D.) was a contemporary of Tacitus who wrote of riots which broke out in a large Jewish community in Rome in 49 A.D. Of course true Nazoreans were not riotous, but peace loving. Paul's Christians in Rome, however, were of a different nature:

---

[128] Chronicle of Cornelius Tacitus

"Because the Jews at Rome caused continuous disturbances at the instigation of Chrestus, he [Claudius] expelled them from the city."[129]

In Josephus' book, Antiquities of the Jews, there is a passage about Christ. The version circulating in the western world has been tampered with by Christians to make it sound like Josephus endorsed Christ. In an obscure Arabic translation of Josephus, however, we have the original neutral words of Josephus without the Christian interpolations:

"At this time, there was a wise man who was called Jesus. His conduct was good and was known to be virtuous. And many people from among the Jews and other nations became his disciples. Pilate condemned him to be crucified and to die. But those who had become his disciples did not abandon his discipleship. They reported that he had appeared to them three days after his crucifixion, and that he was alive accordingly he was perhaps the Messiah, concerning whom the prophets have recounted wonders." [130]

The Babylonian Talmud includes a section in which Jesus is mentioned by the Jews to have been hanged from a stake on the eve of the Passover.

"On the eve of the Passover Yeshu was hanged. For forty days before the execution took place, a herald went forth and cried, "He is going forth to be stoned because he has practiced sorcery and enticed Israel to apostasy. Any one who can say anything in his favor, let him come forward and plead on his behalf." But since nothing was brought forward in his favor, he was hanged on the eve of the Passover."[131]

---

[129] Gaius Suetonius Tranquillus
[130] Arabic summary, presumably of Antiquities 18.63. From Agapios' Kitab al-'Unwan ("Book of the Title," 10th c.)
[131] The Babylonian Talmud, Vol. Iii, Sanhedrin, 43a, P. 281

Pliny the younger was a Roman author who at one time served as governor of Bithynia in Asia Minor. He tortured two deaconesses and wrote to the emperor concerning the information he had gathered thereby. He states that they ate only vegetarian or innocent food and met before dawn:

> "They were in the habit of meeting on a certain fixed day before it was light, when they sang in alternate verses of a hymn to Christ, as to a god, and bound themselves by a solemn oath, not to any wicked deeds, but never to commit any fraud, theft or adultery, never to falsify their word, nor deny a trust when they should be called upon to deliver it up after which it was their custom to separate, and then reassemble to partake of food - but food of an ordinary and innocent kind."[132]

Although not numerous, these historical accounts bear witness to the fact that Yeshu did indeed live and die in first century Palestine and that his early followers were vegetarians.

Yeshu as Firstborn

Yeshu was the firstborn son of Yoseph and Miryam. The siblings of Yeshu are said to have been first Yeshu, and then Jacob (James)[133], Judas (Judas Thomas), Shimeon (Simon), Jose (Joseph) and at least two daughters – one who was named Salome.

The Sleeping Prophet readings state that Mary and Joseph together had James some ten years after Yeshu was born, followed by the daughter and Jude in succession. These same readings also say that Yeshu performed the marriage ceremony of his Greek educated sister Ruth to a Roman man.

---

[132] The Tenth Book Of Pliny's Letters
[133] Two rather strained quotes from the normally accurate First and Second Apocalypse of James from the Nag Hammadhi, which seem on the surface to say that James was not a real brother, are probably an interpolation or corruption from a later hand. Their context seems contrived. We will not quote them here.

The Reading does not say that Shimeon and Jose and another daughter were not born to them as well, but their absence from this list implies it to some degree. Shimeon, Jose, and the other daughter were, no doubt, the children of Yoseph from his other wives – Salome and Escha.

Yeshu's Siblings

"Isn't his mother's name Mary and aren't his brothers James, Joseph, Judas, and Simon? Aren't all his sisters here with us? ..."[134]

The other brother, Shimeon bar Cleophas, was called either brother or cousin of Yeshu in various early writings by non Nazoreans, and it is he who succeeded James to the leadership of the Nazoreans after James was martyred in 64 AD. Shimeon himself was reportedly martyred in the reign of Trajan (98-117 AD). The conflicting accounts of his relationship to Yeshu, some saying brother and others saying cousins, are the result of the accounts being written by strangers far removed from the center of events in Palestine. The complexity of Nazorean marriage laws and relative titles were not easily understood by Roman's far removed from Mount Carmel. It is possible, however, to be both the brother and the cousin of someone in a polygamous setting.

There are many dialogues between Yeshu and Salome within Gnostic texts, but this is probably not the sister of Yeshu, but another woman by this name since Yeshu speaks of occupying her bed:

---

[134] Mt13:55b-56a

"Yeshu said, "Two will rest on a bed: the one will die, and the other will live." Salome said, "Who are you, man, that you ... have come up on my bed and eaten from my table?" [135]

Salome, like Mary, was a common name in first century Palestine and Yeshu's second mother as well as sister was known by this name. He had a mother and sister by the same name of Miryam as well. A full quarter of all female funeral boxes from that period have some form of the name Mary on them, and in the Nazorean Gospel of Philip we read:

"There were three Mariams who walked with the Lord at all times: his mother and sister and the Magdalene, she who is called his mate. Thus his Mother, Sister and Mate are called 'Mariam'." [136]

Yeshu had a good relationship with his family, despite this being downplayed in the Greek Gospels for political reasons:

"Considering the prominent place that Jesus' family held in the Jewish Christian sect that emerged following his death, one has to conclude that he had a good relationship with his family. His mother and brothers all worked together to continue his ministry, and after their deaths, the leadership of the Jerusalem church remained in the hands of his grand nephews. Moreover, during his ministry, there are several clues that indicate his family was actively involved prior to his death. For example, his mother Mary initiates the first of Jesus' "acts of power" (turning water into wine) at the Cana wedding (John 2) and his mother and brothers join Jesus and his disciples for several days in Capernaum (John 2:12). Moreover, It's his brothers who encourage him to display his miracles in public (John 7:5), and his brother James is considered one of the apostles to whom the risen Jesus appears (1 Cor 7; 1 Gal 18). Looking at all the evidence, pro and con, Butz (2005) concludes: "on balance there

---

[135] Gospel of Thomas 61
[136] Gospel Of Philip

is more evidence to support a positive role for Jesus' family in his ministry than a negative one (p. 39)." [137]

Wilson (1992) has theorized that the negative relationship between Jesus and his family was placed in the Gospels (especially in the Gospel of Mark) to dissuade early Christians from following the Jesus cult that was administered by Jesus' family. Wilson says: "…it would not be surprising if other parts of the church, particularly the Gentiles, liked telling stories about Jesus as a man who had no sympathy or support from his family (p. 86)." Butz (2005) is more succinct: "…by the time Mark was writing in the late 60s, the Gentile churches outside of Israel were beginning to resent the authority wielded by Jerusalem where James and the apostles were leaders, thus providing the motive for Mark's antifamily stance… (p. 44)." Other prominent scholars agree (e.g., Crosson, 1973; Mack, 1988; Painter. 1999). [138]

In the writings of Anastasius of Antioch we find mention of Yeshu's siblings. Here is one authors attempt to reconcile the overlapping information:

"Anastasius of Antioch cites the lost writings of Epiphanius to claim that Salome was Joseph's wife. In which case, he would have been married to both Mary and Salome at the same time, although the argument can be made that his marriage to Mary was symbolic only. Distilling from the early records, we find five sons identified with Joseph: James, Simon, Jude, Joses, and Jesus. There were also five daughters: Lysia, Lydia, Salome, Mary, and Anna. . . Anastasius tells us that Mary, the sister of Jesus, married Clopas, her uncle (an accepted custom in ancient Israel) which clarifies the confusion of John 19:25, which identifies her as Mary's sister (sister-in-law). It is almost certain this Mary was the daughter of Salome and named after the beloved Holy Virgin. This leaves the daughters, Anna and Salome, to be identified. These two were most likely Mary's daughters: Salome after her namesake, and Anna, named after Mary's mother. This

---

[137] http://www.jesuspolice.com/
[138] http://www.jesuspolice.com/

a reasonable deduction from the records, but not explicitly stated (Salome could have been the mother of these girls).[139]

Jerome, who died at Bethlehem in 420, also claimed that Yoseph had six children with a woman named Escha. Jerome was not against marriage but he did promote celibacy: "I praise marriage, but it is because they give me virgins."[140] Here is the author of Salome: Matron Saint of Midwives speculation on Escha and Simeon:

"Jerome tells us that Escha was Joseph's first wife (the daughter of Haggi, brother of Zachariah, father of John the Baptist) and bore the four brothers and two daughters, most of whom would have been grown by the time of our Lord's birth. Simeon, however, was the son of Clopas, the younger brother of Joseph who assumed the levirate position, as I said, after Joseph's death. In which case, Simeon would not have been Escha's son and also would have been younger than Jesus. He would have had to have been the son of either Mary or Salome. Or, perhaps, he was the son of Mary, Jesus' sister. [141]

Bethlehem Story

The whole Bethlehem account is of little import to the Gnostic worldview but it has become a major facet of the modern conception of Jesus. Some critical scholars have discounted the Bethlehem story in the New Testament as too convenient, and something that one would think would have been added into the story when all the Old Testament quotes were placed in the Greek Gospels. These gospel accounts make Bethlehem sound like an accident, since the stories make it clear that Joseph had no other reason for being in this locale except to register for taxes. Yet both the Cayce Essene Readings and the Suddie Readings associate Bethlehem with Yeshu's birth.

---

[139] Salome: Matron Of Midwives
[140] Jerome's Letter XXII to Eustochium, section 20
[141] Salome: Matron Of Midwives

It is reasonable that the eugenics program of Mt Carmel that went to all the trouble of infusing the royal Davidic line into their genetics might have chosen to go one step further and allow, or even insure, that their "heir to the throne" was born in the place traditionally expected. It is fair to say that the Nazoreans had no desire to mingle in the politics of Rome, but they no doubt would have relished a replacement for the corrupt kingship of the Herods by getting one of their own on the throne. Lust for kingship is incongruent with the very essence of Gnosticism. Yet they may have thought it wise to fulfill some prophecy in the Nazorean records and to relieve the great suffering that ensued from the corrupt kings. They would not have been trying to fulfill a prophecy in the Jewish record or impress the Jews, but both Jewish and Nazorean records may have contained a similar prophecy concerning Bethlehem. As Joseph was indeed of the Davidic line, which seems irrefutable considering the great risk his grandsons took before the Emperor for admitting such, he also may have had a nostalgic wish to have his firstborn son born in the Bethlehem of his ancestors. There may very well have been a type of census at that time which required Joseph's presence in Bethlehem, as indicated by biblical lore. Bethlehem was also very near the place that Miryam would have stayed with Elizabeth, making the journey a short one. One writer says:

"In 2 BC Augustus was given the highest honor that could be bestowed on any Roman - that of Pater Patriaeï. It is said that a decree went out from Augustus that required the entire Roman people to register their approval of Augustus receiving this title, before it could be bestowed upon him. This oath took place in the late summer and early fall of 3 BC and was required of all Roman citizens and others of distinguished rank among the client kingdoms associated with Rome. This universal census of allegiance to Augustus was demanded of those who claimed any kind of authority within the Empire. It was also required of any person, most notably the Jewish communities, who could trace their ancestry back to the great Jewish royal families. Jesus parents, Mary and Joseph, both being descendants of King David, fell into this category. They, among others, were required to swear an oath that neither they, nor any of their offspring would usurp the throne. It was Jewish custom that, during such a census, each travel to the city of their ancestry. In the case of Mary and Joseph, this city was the city of David - Bethlehem."[142]

The biblical Matthew is untrustworthy, but in 2:22-23b we read of Joseph that:

"But when he heard that Archelaus was reigning in Judea in place of his father Herod, he was afraid to go there."

Joseph seems to consider Judea his first choice to return to, as he would for his former home, but opts for Nazareth over Bethlehem since Archelaus did not preside over Galilee. It should also be noted that the original Bethlehem prophecy in Matthew is misquoted there. The original prophecy is about a ruler from the clan of Bethlehem, not the town:

""But thou, Bethlehem Ephrathah who is little among the clans of Judah, yet out of thee shall he come forth unto me that is to be a ruler in Israel."[143]

'Bethlehem Ephrathah' here refers to the clan who are descendants from a man called Bethlehem, the son of Caleb's second wife Ephrathah referred to in 1 Chronicles. Apparently Joseph was of this clan, and maybe even owner of a house in a Nazorean region of Bethlehem. Yeshu was probably born into the clan as well as in the vicinity of Bethlehem despite his conception and connections on Mount Carmel.

---

142 The Star Of Bethlehem: An Astronomical And Historical Perspective By Susan S. Carroll
143 Massoretic (Hebrew) text of Micah 5.2

Seed of David

Yeshu's brother Judas was said to have had two sons, Zoker and James. Hegesippus tells us that they were both arrested and brought before the Roman emperor Domitian on charges of being of the royal line of David which was considered a threat by the Romans. They confessed they were, which is something they never would have done unless totally committed to telling the truth always. No one would have lied about being roayl since it most likely would result in their death by Rome. The Emperor considered them no threat to the Empire after he noticed their poverty and callused hands from doing field work, and so released them unharmed. This small event proves, in a way the fabricated gospel genealogies can not, that Yeshu really was of the royal line of King David. They also show that the Nazorean conceptions of kingship did not exclude farm work. There are other rumors that the genealogies that showed up in the Roman Gospels were being circulated by the family of Yeshu after they fled to Pella just before the War. This is possible.

> "Now there still survived of the family of the Lord grandsons of Judas, who was said to have been his brother according to the flesh, and they were related as being of the family of David. These the officers brought to Domitian Caesar, for like Herod, he was afraid of the coming of the Christ [= "Messiah"]. He asked them if they were of the house of David and they admitted it. Then he asked them how much property they had, or how much money they controlled, and they said that all they possessed was nine thousand denarii between them, the half belonging to each, and they said that they did not possess this in money but that it was the valuation of only thirty-nine plethra [= about a quarter of an acre] of ground on which they paid taxes and lived on it by their own work." They then showed him the hardness of their bodies, and the tough skin which had been embossed on their hands from their incessant work. They were asked concerning

the Christ ["Messiah"] and his kingdom, its nature, origin, and time of appearance, and explained that it was neither of the world nor earthly, but heavenly and angelic, and it would be at the end of the world, when he would come in glory to judge the living and the dead and to reward every man according to his deeds. At this Domitian did not condemn them at all, but despised them as simple folk, released them, and decreed an end to the persecution. But when they were released they were the leaders of the churches, both for their testimony and for their relation to the Lord, and remained alive in the peace which ensued until Trajan"[144].

Eusibius tells us that Hegesippus wrote:

"They came forward and presided over every church as witnesses and members of the Lord's family."

Oesposyni

The relatives of Yeshu came to be known as the *"Desposyni"*[145]. Julius Africanus (170-245 AD) spoke of two villages associated with the Desposyni, or family of Yeshu. He names them as Nazara (Truth) and Cochaba (Star) and thinks they were in Judea. Epiphanius, however, thought that Chochaba was in Syria near Damascus. Some ancient accounts do indeed place a town by this, or a similar name, near Damascus as well as east of Galilee in Batanaia. Some locate a small village named Kakab a few miles north of present Nazareth. Although Josephus does not mention Nazareth in his lists of towns in Galilee, he does refer to over 195 small hamlets which he has

---

[144] Ecclesiastical History 3:19-20
[145] The Desposyni (from Greek δεσπόσυνος (desposunos) "of or belonging to the master or lord") was a sacred name reserved only for Yeshu's blood relatives. In Ebionite belief, the Desposyni included his mother Mary, his father Joseph, and his sisters and brothers and all their descendants.

not named.[146] The wondrous Gospel of Philip mentions Nazara:

> "The apostles who were before us had these names for him: "Jesus, the Nazorean, Messiah", that is, "Jesus, the Nazorean, the Christ". The last name is "Christ", the first is "Jesus", that in the middle is "the Nazorean". "Messiah" has two meanings, both "the Christ" and "the measured". "Jesus" in Hebrew is "the redemption". "Nazara" is "the Truth". "The Nazorean" then, is "the Truth". "Christ" [...] has been measured. "The Nazorean" and "Jesus" are they who have been measured."

From this text we learn that "Nazara", the root of Nazorean, means "truth" and that "the Nazorean" means "he who reveals what is hidden." The Nazoreans, or Nazoraii in the original Syriac, means then "the people of the truth" or "the people who reveal the hidden truth" or simply - "this true people". Yeshu was not from Nazareth, but possibly from Nazara and definitely from the Nazoreans. Eusebius speaks of 15 of these Desposyni, or Relatives of Yeshu, who sat on the Bishop's throne in Jerusalem until the second great Jewish revolt of 132-136 AD. He lists these as: 1. James the so-called brother of the Lord, 2. Symeon 3. Justus 4. Zacchaeus 5. Tobias 6. Benjamin 7. John 8. Matthias 9. Philip 10. Seneca 11. Justus 12. Levi 13. Ephres 14. Joseph 15. Judas

The first two are Yeshu's immediate brothers and the rest his relatives. After the last Judas the Greco-Roman church put its own non Nazorean bishop into Jerusalem and the true lineage was exiled and faded out of western Christian history except for their one attempt to persuade Pope Sylvester to restore them their rights in 318 A.D. The history of the Desposyni is important because it conflicts so drastically with the party line of the Christians who maintain that Peter and Paul in Rome

---

[146] Galilean Towns Named In The Talmund Are 63, In Josephus' Works There Are45, But In His Life 45, He Says "There Are Two Hundred And Forty Cities And Villages In Galilee".

constituted the early authoritative lineage. In the Desposyni the claims to Apostolic Authority of the Church of Rome dry up, leaving Protestants and all other break offs of the Mother Church of Rome in a precarious position. Built on a false foundation, they have tried to set matters strait by going around Catholicity but find themselves again based on yet another false foundation – the fabricated Greek Gospels and letters of Paul. Only by going directly to the source of Nazorean and Ebionite origins, is the truth disclosed.

Birthday

Early Gnostics of the Palestine area were known to have celebrated the birthday and baptism date of Yeshu on January sixth. They accused the Romans of moving this date backward to December 25 so that it would coincide with a Roman festival called Saturnalia. The modern 12 days of Christmas goes back to this period when many kept a semblance of the original date by counting the 12 days that led up to it. January 6th is also the date celebrated by the Eastern orthodox churches. It is interesting that the Cayce Readings on Yeshu's birthday also say January sixth:

> "The arrival was in the evening, - not as counted from the Roman time, nor that declared to Moses by God when the second Passover was to be kept, nor that same time which was in common usage even in that land, but what would NOW represent January sixth. Just as the midnight hour came, there was the birth of the Master."

The year of his birth has also been controversial and is usually based on the death date of Herod. It is commonly thought that Herod the King died in 4 BC, but there is compelling evidence that he actually died near January 10, of 1 BC.[147] There are

---

[147] The Star Of Bethlehem: An Astronomical And Historical Perspective By Susan S. Carroll

reports that Herod had arranged for the slaughter of a great many Jews upon his death so that the nation would be in mourning during his funeral. Flight to Egypt, even if born just a few days before Herod's death would have been prudent for someone known to be of the royal line. The Mandaean custom of fasting the day after Yuhana's birthday in remembrance of the slain children indicates a long standing ancient tradition of this event in Nazorean circles.

Placement of Herod's death in 1 B.C. allows us to accept the ancient tradition that Jesus was born in 2 B.C. The four earliest Christian writers who report the date of Jesus' birth are Irenaeus (late second century), Clement of Alexandria (about A.D. 200), Tertullian (early third century), and Africanus (early third century).[148]

Africanus specifies the date in terms that can be understood as 3/2 B.C. [149] Both Irenaeus and Tertullian assign Jesus' birth to the forty-first year of Augustus. If this date presumes that the reign of Augustus began when he was elevated to consulship in August 43 B.C., the year intended is 2 B.C. Tertullian conveniently confirms this conclusion by adding that Christ's birth was 28 years after the death of Cleopatra and fifteen years before the death of Augustus. Cleopatra died in August 30 B.C., and Augustus died in August A.D. 14[150], giving us the circa 2 BC date once again.

Clement of Alexandria wrote:

---

[148] Irenaeus Against Heresies 3.21.3; Clement Of Alexandria Miscellanies 1.21; Tertullian An Answer To The Jews 8; Africanus Chronography 1, 16.3, 18.4.

[149] Jack Finegan, Handbook Of Biblical Chronology, 142-144.

[150] S. A. Cook, F. E. Adcock, And M. P. Charlesworth, Eds., The Augustan Empire, 44 B.C.-A.D. 70, Vol. 10 Cambridge Ancient History, 112; Finegan, 270

"From the birth of Christ, therefore, to the death of Commodus are, in all, a hundred and ninety-four years, one month, thirteen days"[151]

Konradin Ferrari d'Occhieppo has demonstrated that the date which Clement of Alexandria furnishes for the birth of Jesus is equivalent to 6 January 2 B.C.[152] The Roman emperor died on 31 December A.D. 192. [153] This yields a date of 6 January 2 B.C. [154] using an Egyptian year of 365 days.

If Yeshu was born just after midnight, as Cayce says, then he was a Capricorn with a Virgo moon and a Libra ascendant. The sixth of January 2 B.C. was a Wednesday, 3 Shevat 3759 on the Jew's calendar. The 1st of Shevat is the New Year for the Mandaean remnants of the ancient Nazoreans and is called Dihba Rba, the Great Feast. Festivities would last two weeks. This is just a couple days before the birth date of Yeshu on 3 Shevat and was perhaps influenced by it.

The 1st of Shevat is also the New Year for trees according to the Jewish School of Shammai, whilst the School of Hillel said 15 Shevat. Judaism observes it by the eating of nuts and fruits, and donating funds to plant trees in Israel. Sephardic Kabbalists had a Tu Bishvat Seder, created in 16th century Safed, which used four glasses of different colored wine, and certain fruits used to symbolize the four Kaballistic worlds. This concept of four Kaballistic worlds came from the Nazoreans. Perhaps the Tu Bishvat Seder did as well.

Ephraem the Syrian (c. 306-373 C.E.) was not a friend to Gnostic Nazoreans, but he was a renowned poet who, in his

---

[151] Clement 1.21.

[152] Konradin Ferrari D'occhieppo, Der Stern Der Weisen: Geschichte Oder Legende? 2d Ed. (Wien: Verlag Herold, 1977), 147

[153] S. A. Cook, F. E. Adcock, And M. P. Charlesworth, Eds., The Imperial Peace, A.D. 70-192, Vol. 11, The Cambridge Ancient History, 383.

[154] D'occhieppo, 147.

Hymns on the Nativity, mentions the birthday of Yeshu according to the Syrian tradition:

> "Yodh" stands at the beginning of Your name (Yeshu) It stands at the tenth in the month of April. On the tenth You entered the womb. Your conception was in a symbol of the perfect number The number ten is complete; on the tenth of April You entered the womb. The number six is also perfect; on the sixth of January Your birth gave joy to the six directions. . . . The conception of John took place in October in which darkness dwells. Your conception took place in April when the light rules over darkness and subdues it." [155]

The date that he mentions for conception, the 10th of April 3 BC, was a Wednesday, the 24th of Nisan, 3758. This 24th day of the lunar month of Nisan was not a day in which it was forbidden to conceive children under Nazorean Law, as would have been, for example, the 29th which was a dark moon. If Yeshu was conceived upon this day, it would have only been after careful scrutiny of the heavenly bodies by the conception astrologers of the Mount Carmel Temple Order. They would have planned this conception time for decades in advance and carefully guided Miryam toward it.

Star Story

Star legends are part and parcel of modern Jesus nativity stories. As for stellar activity, there was a lot happening at the time of Yeshu and Yuhana's birth.

On September 10 or 11, 3 B.C. the Jewish New Year began, and on September 11, 3 B.C. there was a rare close conjunction of Jupiter with Regulus, indicating something unusual was going to happen that year. Jupiter (Tzedec/Righteousness) is the

---

[155] Hymns on the Nativity 27:2-3, 18:

planet of kings and Regulas the star of kings. There was also a world wide census going on at this time that could have required Joseph's presence in Bethlehem.

This planet Jupiter and star Regulas stayed close together throughout January and another conjunction repeated itself in February and again in May of 2 B.C. Finally, on June 17, 2 B.C., Jupiter and Venus appeared to touch. There was also a very bright Jupiter/Venus conjunction on August 12, 3 BC (1 Elul, 3758) in the constellation Cancer. This would have occurred shortly after the birth of Yuhana.

With a birth date of date of 6 January 2 B.C., Yeshu would have been born near the February 2 B.C. conjunction of Jupiter with Regulus, having been conceived the previous April. He would also have been born in the auspicious year begun by a conjunction of the planet and star of kings. These events were significant enough for ancient astrologers to account for the Star of Bethlehem stories.

Stable Story

Nazoreans believed that souls do not permanently come into the fetus until it was five months old. They believed that special midwife angels named Zahariel and Lulaitha assisted the Nazorean woman. They also taught that conception, birth, and death were situations when the participants should avoid unnecessary contact with others. This led to a custom of having a birthing mother isolated to some degree from the day to day activities of the household. Nazorean woman traditionally had a special place they went to birth their children, some even using stables, sheds and barns for this. Nazorean mothers oft had a special stable like place prepared before hand for birth. Nazorean mother's then marked off a corner with a semi-circle of pebbles, called the *misra as glali* and covered it with soft straw or cloth. Miryam would have done this in accordance with the customs of her people, even if she gave birth in a stable cave in the countryside.

After the child Yeshu was born he was rubbed down with consecrated olive oil and salt, like all Nazorean newborns, and his mother would have immersed herself three times in the river, or have warmed water mixed with fresh water poured over her since it was the cold month of January. After changing into dry clothes, Miryam would have been incensed and would have put the iron seal ring and talisman called a *skandola* on her right little finger. After Yeshu's birth an oil lamp would have been lit and would been kept burning for three days as was customary at both birth and death of a Nazorean.

Circumcision

Nazoreans do not customarily circumcise their children on the eighth day, or any day. This tradition of no circumcision goes back at least as far as Yeshu, who said in the Gospel of Thomas:

> "His disciples asked: Is circumcision of use? He said: if it were useful, your father would of begotten you circumcised out of your mother. But the real circumcision of the Spirit has always been useful and nothing but useful."

Nazoreans, at least after this proclamation of Yeshu, and the later Elchasaites, never cut the flesh off their children's genitalia. This was a barbaric Jewish custom that goes back to ancient Egypt. Modern Mandaeans have preserved the legend that neither Yeshu nor Yuhana were ever circumcised. They say:

"But Prophet Moses never suffered himself to be circumcised, neither did the prophet Jesus, for Jesus was of our sect, and they do not allow mutilations". [156]

Nazoreans, like all people in Palestine, were sometimes referred to as "of the circumcision" in early Christian writings. When anti-Nazorean writers of the third and fourth century wrote scathing attacks on the Gnostic Nazoreans and other sects from this area, they often referred to them with this term. The Hellenistic Jews converted by Roman Christianity were of course circumcised, as were many in Palestine. Some of these Hellenistic Jewish converts eventually broke off and promoted a mix of Jewish and Christian observances. One of these in the third century even called itself the Nazarenes, but they had different laws, scriptures and customs from the original Gnostic Nazoreans. Epiphanius and other early Christian historians try to differentiate between the two types, but sometimes confusion resulted. Eventually all the Jewish Christians were lumped together and called Torah observing and circumcised. This was a misnomer for true Nazoreans.

Many cultures that do not practice circumcision have the custom of pulling back the foreskin of their male infant children periodically so that it does not attach itself and cause problems. Some even have ceremonies that insure that this is done. These pulling back rather than cutting ceremonies are sometimes referred to as circumcision although they technically are not. The circumcision of Yeshu reported in the Cayce Readings could have been just such a circumcision, and would only be literal if it was Yeshu himself who outlawed this unnecessary practice. The extent in which cutting circumcision was practiced before Yeshu's ban among the

---

[156] from Mandaeans of Iraq & Iran, pg 260

Nazoreans is not known. There is certainly no need to continue this barbaric custom in the modern world.

Carmel Temple Purification

Nazoreans, like their Jewish antagonists and other ancient cultures of the Mediterranean, had their own version of purification after the blood and ordeals of childbirth. For the mother, a triple immersion is done on the third, and again on the seventh, tenth, fifteenth, twentieth, and twenty-eight day after birth. The pebbles that surrounded her are changed on the third day when fresh myrtle powder is put on the baby's navel and the skandola seal is pressed onto the navel as the Priest or Priestess says, as in the case of Yeshu:

> "In the name of the Great Life, Health and Purity, sealing and protection and the great safeguard of soundness be Yeshu bar Miryamme, by this image and mystery of Ptahil. And the name of Life and the name of Manda d Hiya are pronounced on thee."

The surrounding pebbles are removed after the baptism on the seventh day. Ancient purification rites associated with birth no doubt evolved due to the fact that so many mothers and children died during this ordeal in ancient times. Nazorean and Jewish purification rites were not particularly radical in the ancient world. Here, for example, are the requirements for the Temple of Athena at Pergamon:

> "Whoever wishes to visit the temple of the goddess [Athene Nikephorus], whether a resident of the city or anyone else, must refrain from intercourse with his wife (or husband) that day, from intercourse with another than his wife (or husband) for the preceding two days, and must complete the required lustrations. The same prohibition applies to contact with the dead and with the delivery of a woman in childbirth. But if he has come from the funeral rites or from the burial, he shall purify [sprinkle]

himself and enter by the door where the holy water stoups are, and he shall be clean that same day.[157]

The Rules of Purity for a Priestess of Demeter were also strict:

"The priestess must be pure from the following: She must in no way come in contact with anything filthy; she must not participate in a meal for the dead; she must not touch a grave; she must not enter a house where a woman has given birth to a child, whether a live birth or a still one, during the preceding three days; nor during the three days following a burial shall she enter the house in which someone has died; and she must not eat carrion."[158]

Naming Rituals

Ancient Nazoreans like Yeshu were given both a worldly (*luqav*) name and a spiritual "Malwasha" name. A "Malwasha" was anciently determined by the rising sign and other horoscope configurations. A hint of this ancient practice was preserved among the Mandaean descendants of the Dosithean break off of the ancient Nazorean order:

"When an infant is to be named, the priest takes the Zodiacal sign of the month in which its birth occurred, counts from it round the Zodiacal circle, and calculates from it the sign of the hour. The sign of the day does not matter. From the numerical value which results, they subtract the value of the mother's name. " [159]

A spiritual name is an important part of becoming a fully spiritual person. The new name becomes a focal point in the subconscious for a new and more pure spiritual personality to

---

[157] Temple of Athena at Pergamon, Dittenberger, Sylloge (2nd), 566, 2-9. Very old law, probably still in force in Hellenistic period.
[158] Rules of Purity for Priestess of Demeter (at Cos)
[159] Mandaeans Of Iraq And Iran, E.S. Drower, Leiden, 1962

develop. A Malwasha name also helps one overcome the more negative influences of the zodiac and the archons that control mankind through such. All Nazoreans have traditionally been expected to discover their spiritual name and use such in all spiritual ritual work. An official "Malwasha" Name within the Nazorean Order was considered indispensable since certain proxy work for the dead, and other practices, are determined by similarity in horoscope and name of the various participating parties. Ancient Nazoreans often had many spiritual names. It is of interest that Yeshu was also known as Yeshu Mahiana, Amin-il, Beni-Amin, and Hibil-Ziwa among the Nazoreans.

> "His name is Amun-el and he called himself Y'su Mahiana. He says: ' I am Alaha (Amin), and the Son of Alaha (Bnai-Amin). ... I am Hibil-Ziwa".[160]

The name Yeshu and Emmanuel showed up in the bible gospels as well:

> "And she shall bring forth a son, and thou shalt call his name Yeshu: for he shall save his people from their sins. Now all this was done, that it might be fulfilled which was spoken of the Lord by the prophet, saying, Behold, a virgin shall be with child, and shall bring forth a son, and they shall call his name Emmanuel, which being interpreted is, God with us."[161]

The name Yeshu is not derived from a shortening of the Hebrew Yehoshua or Jehoshuah. His name was Yeshu, or Yeshua. It has the meaning of redeemer and savior in Hebrew and meant "star" in Aramaic. The Talmudic spelling of his name is Yesu (Yeshu), not Yeshua. The Syriac and Mandaic also have Yeshu, pronounced as Yeshoo.

---

[160] Ginza Rba, The Great Treasury
[161] Matthew 1:21-23

"The Apostles who preceded us called him thus: Yeshu the Nazirite Messiah, that is Yeshu the Nazirite Christ. The last name is the Christ, the first is Yeshu, the middle is the [Nazirite]. Messiah has two significations: both anointed and also measurement. Yeshu in Aramaic is the Atonement. Nazara is the truth, therefore the Nazirite is the true. Christ is the measurement, the [Nazirite] and Yeshu are the measured."[162]

In the Pistis Sophia Yeshu has a secret name of Aberamentho.

Yeshu was of course also called the Nazorean, denoting his association with the Nazorean sect of ancient Palestine. This was a hated and small sect at that time, and to be known as a Nazorean was not without consequences.

In the Gospel of Philip from the Nag it says:

"No Jew was ever born to Greek parents as long as the world has existed. And, as a Christian people, we ourselves do not descend from the Jews. There was another people and these blessed ones are referred to as the "chosen people of the living God" and "the true man" and "the Son of man" and "the seed of the Son of man." In the world it is called "this true people". Where they are, there are the sons of the bridal chamber."

Infant Baptism of Yeshu

Infant baptism and anointing has always been a part of the Nazorean Path. A newborn Nazorean baby, along with its mother, is baptized together on the 30th day of life for a male, and 32nd if female. In the Cayce readings this is echoed:

"(Q) How long did the holy family remain in Bethlehem?

---

162 Gospel of Philip 51

(A) Until the time of purification was passed. Twenty-nine days, as ye would count suns today." [163]

Nazorean woman were purified after childbirth by six separate immersions, the last being on the twenty-eight day after birth. Cayce is apparently referring to Miryam's purification, rather than Yeshu's. A joint baptism of Yeshu and Miryam would also have taken place on the thirtieth day. Nazoreans counted "suns" from dusk, rather than dawn, thus the 29 as we "count suns today" could have been after the 30 day joint immersion. The corresponding Jewish rite was 40 days for a male, 80 for a female. But then, neither Miryam nor Yeshu were Jewish.

There is an Ein Eitam spring and Solomon's pools less than two miles south-east of Bethlehem which is the ancient source of purification water for Jerusalem. Such a short journey would still have been considered within "Bethlehem", or the Bethlehem locale since there were no "city limits" at the time as we know them today.

At this first immersion the infant is immersed thrice, signed across the forehead thrice, given three sips, and has a crown of myrtle put on his or her head. This was all done to Yeshu at the appropriate time. After this, he was taken to an altar and his father Yoseph said:

> "Health and purity are thine, O Angels and Archangels and Shekinahs, and flowing waters and streams and all the monasteries of the worlds of light." [164]

---

[163] Text Of Cayce Reading 1152-3
[164] The Mandaeans Of Iraq And Iran By E.S. Drower Leiden: Brill 1962 (Reprint Of 1937)

Yeshu was then anointed with olive oil and symbolically given masticated sacramental bread and water from the lips of his mother in a lengthy ritual too detailed to reproduce here.

Customs

It is perhaps difficult for many to conceive of Nazorean life two thousand years ago, and so a few words on their habits may prove informative.

Yeshu the Nazorean, and other children of his sect, wore special off-white linen clothing whenever they were not out in the world traveling. Laymen and woman wore five pieces of clothing, and the priests and priestesses wore an additional two to make a total of seven. Before being ordained as a Tarmidaya, or priest, Yeshu wore a long linen shirt (*sadra*) which was six cubits long with a small pocket on the right breast. Yeshu wore this over loose pants which he called *dasha*. These pants had a drawstring (*takka*) with one unsown end that was tied over the sewn one, representing the God and Goddess above. Yeshu had a cubit wide cloth (*burzinqa*) to use as a thrice wound turban which he wore with one end hanging down over his left shoulder unless tucked up to cover the mouth of one officiating in the Priesthood. A woman would wear this same piece of cloth a bit different, as a shawl over the head. Yeshu also wore a long thin stole (*nasifa*) with the left side worn shorter than the right. The fifth piece of clothing that Yeshu and all Nazoreans wore was a tubular belt (*himiana*) woven of sixty threads with one end tasseled and tied in a special symbolic manner about the waste. The two diverse ends once again representing the male female mystery of the Palmtree and Wellspring above.

When Yeshu passed through the long and arduous process of becoming a priest, he received two additional items: A tubular

headband called a crown (*tangha*) and a gold ring worn on the
right little finger upon which was engraved "In the Name of
the Dazzling Brilliance (*Shum Yawar Ziwa*). We may conjecture
that Priestesses wore a silver one on their left little finger
engraved with "In the Name of the Treasury of Life" (*Shum
Simat Hiya*). Priesthood holders also had staffs made from
special woods, olive for priests, and willow for priestesses.
The long thin stole (*nasifa*) is used to secure this staff in the
river at baptisms, and to veil the hand for the special handgrip
of truth that is given afterward.

Other items were used as well. A wreath (*klila*) of fresh leaves,
grape or myrtle, was used during most rituals, and some
priests had banners that were hung upon folding wooden
crosses representing the ancient cross of light.

The association of Nazoreans with grapes is an ancient
tradition, and young initiates were called "Young Vines". The
reference to being a grape vine was an ancient tradition
among the Nazoreans. The Grapevine was used as a symbol
not only of the individual consecrated to Deity, but also of the
community as a whole. We find this in both the Pharisee Bible
as well as Mandaean writings. It also meant someone with
long uncut hair:

'I am the true vine and my Father is the husbandman' [165]

Nazorean children who had ever had their hair cut were
barred from entering the Priesthood. This tradition was
preserved for many centuries among the Nestorian Christians
as well. True Nazorean Nazarites were required to grow their
hair out long, but they were not forbidden to partake of
products of the grape vine like the false Nazarites found in the

---

[165] Yeshu John xv

Pharisee bible. Modern Mandaean remnants of the ancient Nazoreans still use grapes in their sacramental drink like their ancient Nazorean forbearers. This practice prevailed among Christian Nazoreans as well, as evidenced by the ancient custom of using wine in the sacrament. Many ancient Nazorean hymns use the vine as a metaphor. Here is an example:

> "There is a vine for Sethil and a tree for Anus: Sethil hath a vine yonder in thee, Land of the true, Laden with reward, laden with oblation and laden with Enlightenment (*Nasirutha*). The tendrils that curl at the leaf-ends Bore prayers, hymns and sublime recitations. When I arose in my place I made a request that was great; I asked that a tall ladder be given me That I might place it against the Vine for ascent, That against the Vine for ascent I might place it And might mount into my Vine, Might wax great and grasp its foliage, Might eat, be refreshed by its shade And enjoy its leafiness, Might twine me a wreath of its tendrils and place it upon my head.[166]

If the fruit of the vine were forbidden to true Nazarites, it would not be used as a symbol of Nazirutha enlightenment and eventual eternal reward in the pure land of Msunia Kushta.

The false Nazarite vow found in the Pharisee bible is recorded in Numbers 6:2-21 This text, rejected by the Nazoreans according to Epiphanius, does not mention any Nazarites before Samson, yet it is evident that they existed before the "time of Moses". The false vow of a Jewish Nazarite involved these three things:

> 1) Abstinence from wine, grapes, raisins and grape vinegar. This was not required of true Nazoreans.

---

[166] The Canonical Prayerbook of the Mandaeans (Leiden: Brill, 1959). ES Drower

2) Refraining from cutting the hair off the head during the whole period of the continuance of the vow. This was a life long requirement for Nazoreans.

3) Avoidance of contact with the dead. Nazoreans had special purification rites when this occurred.

When the period of the continuance of the false Jewish vow came to an end, the Jewish Nazarite had to present himself at the door of the sanctuary with 1. a male lamb of the first year for a burnt-offering, 2. a ewe lamb of the first year for a sin-offering, and 3. a ram for a peace-offering. After these sacrifices were offered by the priest, the Jewish Nazarite cut off his hair at the door and threw it into the fire under the peace-offering. Such practices were abhorrent to vegetarian Nazoreans who would never kill an animal or quit their Nazarite vows. Jewish Nazarite vows were short by contrast, and lasted only thirty, and at most one hundred, days. Samson is the only one recorded in the false Pharisee bible to observe a Nazarite vow longer than this limited time. In his story there it is significant that abstinence from the grape is not mentioned as part of the secret to his strength. The addition of a prohibition toward the grape may have crept into the Jewish bible as a political stance against the grape eating true Nazarites and possibly as a result of the Rechabite influence.

The Rechabites were the descendants of Rechab through Jonadab or Jehonadab. They belonged to the Kenites, who accompanied the children of Israel into Palestine, and dwelt among them. The main body of the Kenites dwelt in cities, and adopted settled habits of life[167] but Jehonadab forbade his descendants to drink wine or to live in cities. They were commanded to lead always a nomad life.

---

[167] 1Sa 30:29

True Essene Nazorean Nazirites were not nomadic, but settled in villages and monasteries where they grew and partook of the fruits of the grape vine. At least one ancient author, however, thought that the branch of Essenes in Egypt were founded by Rechabites.

Nazorean Economy

The ancient economy of the Palestine region was primarily agrarian.

> "Production in Palestine centered on the labor of the peasant household to produce essential foods. The principal products included grain (wheat, barley, millet and rice), vegetables (onions, garlic, leeks, squashes, cabbages, radishes and beets), fruits (olives, grapes, figs and dates), legumes (lentils and beans), spices (salt, pepper and ginger), and meat (fish, cows, oxen, lambs, goats; cf. Klausner 1975 [1930]:180-86; Hamel 1990 [1983]:8-56). The peasant's diet consisted mainly of bread and salt, along with olives, oil, onions and perhaps some grapes (Hamel 1990 [1983]: 34-35)." [168]

Some trade routes did go through the region.

> "Long-distance luxury items from East Africa, Arabia, India and the Far East would also pass through Palestine following the usual trade routes." [169]

Palestine did have some exports:

> "The principal exports from Palestine were olive oil (cf. Josephus, *B.J.* 2.591; *Vita* 74-76), dates, opobalsam and spices." [170]

---

[168] The Economy of First-Century Palestine: State of the Scholarly Discussion, Philip A. Harland (Concordia University, Montreal)
[169] The Economy of First-Century Palestine: State of the Scholarly Discussion, Philip A. Harland (Concordia University, Montreal)
[170] The Economy of First-Century Palestine: State of the Scholarly Discussion, Philip A. Harland (Concordia University, Montreal)

We know from an ancient royal letter that the tax burden to Nazoreans and other am-ha-aretz was heavy. There was a salt tax, crown tax, grain tax: one-third of the produce, tax on fruit and nut trees: one-half the produce, poll tax, tithe, tribute, and imposts/duties [171] Nazoreans, after having half of their date and olive crop confiscated by the government, would have been able to send surplus olive oil and dates to Egypt in exchange for high quality papyrus to be used in their massive literary efforts. 2% to 5% of these would have been further taxed as they crossed each Roman tax district border. This heavy taxation encouraged the Nazoreans to be as self sufficient as possible. And of course, the Nazoreans, like the Essenes, shared their wealth, or shared their poverty, equally:

Both the Jewish philosopher Philo and the Jewish historian Josephus speak of this common ownership of property:

> "Riches they despise, and their community of goods is truly admirable; you will not find one among them distinguished by greater opulence than another. They have a law that new members on admission to the sect shall confiscate their property to the order, with the result that you will nowhere see either abject poverty or inordinate wealth; the individual's possessions join the common stock and all, like brothers, enjoy a single patrimony." [172]

Nazoreans, who practiced a shared economy, would have been able to grow their own flax to make the off white linen clothing they were known for. With each soul having but one or two sets of undyed clothing, this was well within their ability. Their potters would have made the utensils they needed for storage and cooking. Shared fields, orchards and

---

[171] letter from Demetrius (c. 152 BCE) listing the following taxes he was willing to suspend (1 Macc 10:29-31; 11:34-36; Josephus, Ant. 13.49-51)
[172] Josephus, Jewish War, trans. H. Thackeray and R. Marcus, Loeb Classical Library (1988), 2.122.

vineyards, after taxation, would have been enjoyed jointly. Nazorean carpenters and combined labor would have made the erection of simple adobe, stone and timber dwellings a short public event. Artisans in wood, copper, fiber, thread, glass, and pottery would have created the few needed personal items, like wooden combs, craftsman's tools, or oil lamps; as well as the public items needed by such a society such as baskets for harvesting, storage jars for oil and wine, etc. Life was simple but good.

Priesthood Training

Nazorean priests began training early, even as young as the age of three. They were allowed to assist older priests and priestesses, usually their own mother or father, in the role of an acolyte. The Aramaic Priesthood title for this helper or deacon office is Ashganda. Yeshu would have been trained in this same manner. He would never have been allowed to cut his hair, and he would have begun learning ritual liturgy and prayers by heart at an early age. By his teenage years he would have been expected to memorize the entire Book of Souls liturgical scroll and to have been very familiar with other Nazorean scrolls. He would not have read the Torah, but the Ginza. He would not have sung the Jewish psalms, but the Nazorean Qulasta hymns. He would not have prayed to Yahweh, but to the Great Life, to Sindirka the Palmtree and Aina the Wellspring.

Before any major life change, ritual cleanliness through baptism was a requisite in the Nazorean faith, The Baptism of Yeshu at 3 would have been indicative of Yeshu's preparation to enter Priesthood training as a Shganda. Ancient scrolls confirm that Yeshu was indeed baptized at this age and we do know that he trained for priesthood since he later baptized his disciples. Unlike some protestant Christian groups, Nazoreans did not believe someone could just go out and baptize. A very special consecration process had to be gone through first.

Flight to Egypt

The Beleaguered Bible speaks of a flight to Egypt, as do the regression readings. In the past life readings of Cayce we are told about the flight to Egypt of the infant Yeshu and of his early training:

> "The period of sojourn in Egypt was in and about, or close to, what was then Alexandria. Joseph and Mary were not idle, during that period of sojourn, but those records - that had been a part of those activities preserved in portions of the libraries there - were a part of the work that had been designated for the entity. And the interest in same was reported to the Brotherhood in the Judean country... Those same records from which the men of the East said and gave, By those records we have seen his star. These pertaining, then, to what you would call today astrological forecasts, as well as those records which had been compiled and gathered by all of those of that period pertaining to the coming of the Messiah. These had been part of the records from those in Carmel, in the early experiences, as of those given by Elijah, who was the forerunner..."

> "Q. Were there any others besides Josie who were associated with the training or early education of Jesus?
> A. Sofa was one of the women educated to service in the Temple...the entity was chosen by - what would be, what is termed in the Qabbalah - the moving of the symbols on the vesture of the priest...to be the attendant or the nurse to the babe when there was the birth then of John... "

The moving symbols were the 24 letters of the Syriac alphabet, two per stone, engraved on the breastplate. Certain letters reflected themselves in a urim and thummin stone, spelling out words not unlike a modern ouija board. In later Jewish propaganda, Yeshu was credited with doing miracles by magic which he learned in Egypt. Apparently knowledge of Yeshu having been in Egypt, not as an infant but as a young man, was prevalent, and the Nazoreans were known for practicing white magic. Both Cayce and Suddie Readings mention a return to Egypt for further education. When asked where Yeshu went on his travels with Yoseph of Aramethia, Suddie answered:

> "Where did he not go? He traveled all over most of the world as we know it. It is said that Joseph, his uncle, went with him."[173]

When asked why he traveled, Suddie said:

> "To learn of the people. It was told that they traded, which they did. But they also did a lot of learning and speaking to people and finding out their views on things and life." [174]

Yesseans of Egypt

A group of Nazorean like Essenes dwelt in Egypt near the great library of Alexandria, and were known as Issaeans. Epiphanius identifies these Issaeans with the Essenes, for he tells the "studious reader" ("Haer.," xxix. 5), that if he would know more about them, he will find it in the memoirs of Philo, and especially in the book which that famous Alexandrian had entitled "Concerning the Issaei". Epiphanius goes on to outline Philo's treatise "On the Contemplative Life.". Philo calls the community and monasteries on the southern shore of Lake Mareotis, south of Alexandria, the Therapeuts, and mentions other related communities. He says that he had already written of these "Essaei who lived in Palestine and Arabia. He mentions that these Essaei (Essene) communities there were

---

[173] Jesus and the Essenes, pg 222
[174] Jesus and the Essenes, pg 224

not as impressive to him as the ones in Egypt.[175] An abbot
Nilas thought these Essenes were followers of Rechab:

> "Apart from this, however, it is by no means improbable that the
> name Issaei was not original with Epiphanius, for Abbot Nilus,
> the renowned ascetic of Sinai, who had previously enjoyed a
> high reputation at Constantinople, and retired to one of the
> famous monasteries of the mysterious region of Sinai and Serbal
> in 390, and died in 430, speaks of the Issaei and says that they
> were the Jewish philosophers and ascetics who were originally
> followers of the Rechabite Jonadab. [176]

> "The Therapeuts have been recognized throughout the centuries
> as identical with the earliest Christian Church of Egypt. They
> were known to Philo at the very latest as early as 25 A.D., [177]

Philo's fuller account of the Egyptian Essenes, quoted in
Appendix 4, describes a beautiful but non Nazorean culture
that sounds more like a Catholic celibate monastery than a
Nazorean coed encampment. Philo is no doubt describing a
branch of the Essenes which did not insist on marriage, or
allow wine drinking, as did the Nazoreans of Yeshu. This
would not have prevented Yeshu from visiting and interacting
with them, however.

Yeshu's Education

Nazorean Essenes and some of their Essene cousins took their
education seriously, and we read in Philo's account of the
Egyptian Essenes that each one had a small library and shrine
attached to their hut. This implies universal literacy in a time
when few could read or write. Essenes were distinguished by
their ability to read, and they had the best books in the world

---

[175] Did Jesus Live 100 B.C.? By G. R. S. Mead
[176] Did Jesus Live 100 B.C.? By G. R. S. Mead
[177] Did Jesus Live 100 B.C.? By G. R. S. Mead

collected from the Far East via the Silk Road and also manuscripts copied from the great library in Alexandria. Nazoreans also emphasized education, and were exceptionally literate for the times. They had group schools as well as private tutors.

In the Cayce readings we are told that a female Essene leader named Judy, 24 years Yeshu's senior, presided over his personal instruction. Cayce says:

> "Hence not only the manners of the recording but also the traditions of Egypt, the traditions from India, the conditions and traditions from many of the Persian lands and from many of the borders about same, became a part of the studies and the seeking of the entity Judy early in the attempts to make, keep, and preserve such records."[178]

So in addition to studying ancient Essene Scrolls like the Ginza Rba, Qulasta, Diwan Abathur and others, Yeshu apparently had access to the Zarathustrian Avesta, Bonpo and Buddhist texts, Taoist texts, as well as those from the Library of Alexandria in Egypt. He would not have spent the bulk of his time studying Ezra's Torah or other Jewish writings which the Nazoreans considered corrupt and pseudipigraphic. Josephus writes of the Essenes:

> "There are also those among them who undertake to foretell things to come, by reading the holy books, and using several sorts of purifications, and being perpetually conversant in the discourses of the prophets; and it is but seldom that they miss in their predictions."

Yeshu was trained in Gnostic theology amongst the Essene Nazoreans:

---

[178] Edgar Cayce On The Dead Sea Scrolls, Pg 126

"For in those days there were more and more of the leaders of the people in Carmel - the original place where the School of the Prophets was established during Elijah's time and that of Samuel - these were called the Essenes; and those that were students of what ye would call astrology, numerology, phrenology, and those phases of study of the return of individuals - or reincarnation."[179]

Yeshu would have continued his studies, even after his official installment as a full Tarmidaya capable of performing baptisms, lay weddings, and Mass ceremonies for the dead. Full authority to perform all Nazorean rites, such as last anointing, would not have been given to Yeshu until later. A Nazorean would have to preside at a funeral before becoming a Ganzibra. Additional initiations would have given him the right to perform these and other rituals also.

Yeshu's Baptisms

The Mandaean remnants of the ancient Nazoreans have a tradition that Yeshu was baptized more than once, which of course he was since he grew up in a sect and cult which practiced daily washings and weekly and yearly baptisms. The Mandaean tradition told by Adam to Siouffi in 1875 mentions one at age twelve, and in Abraham Ecchellensis we read of one at fourteen. Actual accounts of conversations and events at Yeshu's more significant Baptisms are preserved in ancient Aramaic scrolls. We will quote many of these in full in later chapters. One form of these washings consisted on a triple self immersion. Basil, Bishop of Caesarea, once said in 360 AD:

"By three immersions, the great mystery of baptism is accomplished." [180]

---

[179] From The Cayce Readings
[180] Baronius' Annals, V.; .Bingham's Antiq., B. XI., ch. 11.

Training for Priesthood

Along with his studies, Yeshu was trained to officiate as a Priest for ritual work. This is absolutely certain. Yeshu functioned as a Priest (*Tarmidaya*) and a High Priest (*Ganzibra*). It was customary for this initiation to be given soon after puberty. Yeshu would not have delayed in this matter and probably went through it somewhere around his twelfth birthday. If Yeshu traveled to India when he was thirteen as Cayce insisted, his handlers would have insisted that he complete this process before his departure.

Nazorean candidates for priestly orders could be either male or female, and so Yeshu encountered both sexes in his training. It should be noted that unlike the Catholic heresy, Nazorean Priests had to marry:

> "For priests and priestesses may marry; indeed, marriage is obligatory." [181]

Yeshu's initial preparation took nine days and eight nights, and started out in a householders hut covered with blue cloth denoting its lay status. Yeshu then reciting the entire Book of Souls from memory as other priests and priestesses checked it against a written copy for accuracy. The next day Yeshu recited this lengthy baptismal ritual once again between two large banner draped crosses before being led into another white roofed building called the monastery (*shkinta*). Once Yeshu entered the monastery, the other hut was destroyed. He was then ordained and spent one week of sleepless study and instruction before coming out to perform a baptism on his initiating Rabai. Yeshu, as a new priest and non celibate monk then spent 60 days in isolated retreat baptizing himself thrice

---

[181] Gnostic John the Baptizer: by G. R. S. Mead

daily and saying the required hymns at each office of the hours. After the sixty days he performed an eight hour Mass (*Masquita*) which sealed his new office upon him and made him a full Essene Nazorean Elder, or Tarmidaya. This training was not easy, and it is reported that only 360 were ordained before the Essenes and Nazoreans abandoned Israel for northern Jordan and Syria in 64 AD.

Distant Enclaves

Besides staying and studying with the Therapeutae of Egypt, Yeshu traveled widely. We know that the Nazoreans and Essenes were spread out over several countries since Pliny, by the year 70 AD, speaks of the "Nazerini" in northern Syria[182] and Lucian of Samosata also ran into them there along the Euphrates river whence he wrote: "'These prayed to the rising sun, baptizing themselves at dawn. They ate nothing but wild fruit, milk and honey." The Syrian dialect of Aramaic, which the Nazoreans confessed to speak in the Gospel of Philip, extended out from Syria into southern Iraq and northern Galilean Israel, and this is just where we find reports of Nazoreans during the days of Yeshu and afterwards. Areas east of the Jordan River, in present Jordan, as well as parts of Egypt also arise in regards to Nazoreans and their offshoots. From these reports we can conclude that various enclaves of the Nazorean sect were spread over a large area. It is reasonable to assume communication and travel between these various centers, as well as exchange of goods, information and sacred scrolls as is reported in the Cayce Readings.

The town of Capernaum which Yeshu seems to have been so associated with is actually on a major caravan route that

---

[182] Natural History 5.81

would have connected this town with major religious centers along the Silk Road. Open minded truth loving Nazoreans in Capernaum would have found it possible to connect with many Bonpo, Buddhist, Taoist, Jain, Zarathustrian, and other religious philosophies that are known to have flowed along this Silk Road with the commodities. It is reasonable to assume that Yeshu encountered such and recognized truth wherever he found it.

The visit of the Magi from Persians lands is indicative of some link with communities in the Babylon area. The well organized and administrated Nazorean sect would have sent officials to these various outlining communities from time to time. Yeshu would have advanced quickly through the various levels of the Nazorean organization, and it would not be unusual for officers in his position to be sent on missions to distant lands. There are quite a few rumors and legends of Yeshu having traveled eastward to the land of the Persians and even Indians. Although not conclusive, it appears that Yeshu probably traveled to India as an official representative of the Nazorean Order. The extensive communication and trade between various Nazorean communities and semi-Nazorean communities throughout the world would have given the Nazoreans access to an unusually large collection of scriptural writings, herbs, medicinal information, and even seeds and foods not commonly available to the more locally centric village dwellers. The Sleeping Prophet readings and Suddi Readings speak of such travels.

Silk Road Travels

Cayce, in his Readings on Yeshu and his life, tells us of his travels:

"...first India, then Persia, then Egypt, for "my son shall be called from Egypt" Then a portion of the sojourn with the forerunner that was first proclaimed in the region about Jordan; and then the return to Capernaum, the city of the beginning of the ministry. Then in Canaan and Galilee. In the studies that were a portion of the preparation, these included first those that were the foundations of that given as law. Hence from law in the great initiate must come love, mercy, peace, that there may be the fulfilling wholly of that purpose to which, of which, he was called." (Q.) From what period and how long did he remain in India? (A.) From thirteen to sixteen. One year in travel and in Persia; the greater portion being in the Egyptian. In this, the greater part will be seen in the records that are set in the pyramid there, for here were the initiates taught." (Q.) Under whom did he study in India? (A.) Kshjiar (Q.) Under whom in Persia? (A.) Junner. (Q.) In Egypt? (A.) Zar

(Q.) Outline the teachings that were received in India? (A.) Those cleansings of the body as related to the preparation for strength in the physical as well as in the mental man. In the travels and in Persia, the unison of forces as related to those teachings of that given in those of Zu and Ra. In Egypt, that which has been the basis of all the teachings of those of the Temple, and the after actions of the crucifying self in relationships to ideals that made for the abilities of carrying on that called to be done."

"(Q.) In which pyramids are the records of Christ? (A.) That yet to be uncovered."

Cayce, in his Readings, says that Yeshu's mentor Judy arranged for him to go on these long distance sojourns as part of his education.

"Q. "How closely was Judy, the head of the Essenes, associated with Jesus in His Palestine sojourn?"
A. "For a portion of the experience the entity Judy was the teacher. How close? So close that the very heart and purposes were proclaimed as to those things that were traditions! For the

entity sent Him to Persia, to Egypt, yea to India, that there might be completed the more perfect knowledge of the material ways in the activities of Him who became the Way, the Truth!" [183]

Christianity has developed the myth of an uneducated untraveled peasant boy of a humble carpenter suddenly turning into a great teacher and leader. It is more reasonable to suppose that an organized multi-national Order intent on spirituality and education would see that the products of its eugenics program received the best education and experience possible so as to maximize their potential. There may also have been a decision to keep whereabouts of Yeshu, and other prodigies, unknown through travel because of the hostile forces that sought them out. This is one of the reasons given for the flight to Egypt in the New Testament accounts. Cayce was asked:

> "Can any more details be given as to the training of the child (Jesus)?" Cayce answered: " Only those that covered that period from six years to about sixteen, which were in keeping with the tenets of the brotherhood as well as that training in the law – which was the Jewish or Mosaic law in that period."[184]

It is to be remembered that the Essenes had a different Law of Moses than the one presently known.

If Cayce's time table is correct, Yeshu was in India and Persia from age 13 to 17, and in Egypt for 4 years, 6 months and three days, or until he was almost 22. 22 was the age given for Yuhana's graduation from his studies, and it is likely that both he and Yeshu received similar training. Yuhana may have begun teaching at this time, at age 22, which was about seven years before the most likely year of his death. The Mandaean remnants of the Nazoreans say that Yuhana actually taught for

[183] Cayce 1471
[184] Edgar Cayce On The Dead Sea Scrolls, Pg 140

42 years, but Mandaean's are recognized for having a propensity to multiply numbers by their sacred number six[185]. Seven years is a reasonable amount of time for Yuhana to have gained the popularity and fame that is afforded his memory. It appears that Yeshu did not become active publicly until his thirtieth year, and contrary to modern legend, only taught for one year.[186]

While in India Yeshu would have encountered various forms of Buddhism which he would have already been familiar. Among these were the Jains and the followers of Siddhartha[187] who most know as "the Buddha". Siddhartha is oft seen as a reformer of Hinduism who came up with Buddhism all on his own in the sixth century BC. This is similar to the Christian idea of Jesus being a Jewish reformer who started his own religion. Both of these views are wrong. Siddhartha was a lax reformer of older Jain Buddhism that predated him. He was no doubt an excellent teacher, but his success and popularity were not always due to his wonderful new teachings, since most of these were not unique to him and had already been spread about by his Jain predecessors like Mahavira and Parsva. Part of Siddhartha's fame and popularity was due to his having once been rich and royal, and because of his many contacts with the powerful segment of society who made living life as a "beggar" quite easy. He also promised enlightenment for less of an investment than the other sects, which gave him appeal with the masses. His watered down

---

[185] "Mandaean Love For The Number Six And Its Multiples, Used To Define All That Is Mandaean..." The Mandaeans, Edmondo Lupieri, Pg 148

[186] According To Peter In The Clementine Recognitions.

[187] Gautama Buddha (563-483 BC.) was the junior contemporary of Mahāvīra. We possess no authentic accounts of his life and teachings. Having taught for forty-five years from his supposed enlightenment to his death, Gautama supposedly left behind a large compendium of oral teachings that were memorized by various of his disciples, yet none of his teachings were written down until several hundred years later. There is much controversy on just what is authentic in these supposed teachings. The Gnostic prophet Mani taught that these teachings were not preserved in purity and contain error. Mrs. Rhys Davis, and other scholars, have observed that "Buddha" found his two teachers Alara and Uddaka at Vaisali and started his religious life as a Jain.

disciplines also appealed to lazy monks who didn't want to follow the more strict Jain programs of discipline and vegetarianism. His followers were known for their lax approach by other Buddhists of the time. This lax approach may explain why his form of Buddhism became so popular among royal supporters in foreign lands. Siddhartha became a figurehead to which many diverse forms of older Buddhism were associated.

Frightened by what they considered Buddhist heresies, a council of conservative Buddhist monks was convened at the Mauryan capital of Patna during the third century BC to purify the doctrine. This is similar to the Christian Council of Nicene where orthodox Bishops condemned Gnostic ones. What arose were the teachings of Theravada Buddhism which would undergo little change at the time Yeshu encountered them firsthand. With his Gnostic background he would not have been very impressed by their lax diets and lifestyles, nor with their celibacy and begging.

Yeshu knew that the roots of Buddhism go back beyond Siddhartha's alterations of Jainism, and back beyond the beginnings of Parshva's and Mahavira's historical Jainism. He knew that they even go back beyond the first Mt. Kailish Buddhas recognized by both the Jains of India and by the Bonpos of Tibet. Buddhism is a very ancient religion which the Bonpos tell us came from Persian speaking lands west of Tibet. Ancient buddhas like Shenrab taught the dharma centuries before it flourished in the ancient kingdom of Zhang-zhung. One should reject the notion that Mahayana Buddhism grew out of a redefining of Siddhartha's Hinayana or Theravadic Buddhism. Mahayana[188] developed in the Kushan empire of

---

[188] "Mahayana, in contrast to the Theravada school of Buddhism, can be characterized by:
Universalism, in that everyone will become a Buddha; Enlightened wisdom as the main focus of realization; Compassion through the transferal of merit; Salvation - as opposed to liberation - supported

northern India in the first few centuries after Yeshu from older forms of Buddhism. These older forms of Buddhism have their true origins among the Yuezhi, or "Moon People". Yuezhi" was the ancient Chinese name for five tribes of easternmost Indo-Europeans who spoke the Tocharian language. They lived in the arid grasslands of the Tarim Basin in modern-day Xinjiang, until they were driven west around 160 BC. They resettled in northern India, Uzbekistan, Afghanistan, and Pakistan and eventually became the Kushan empire. This group of people were easily distinguished from others by their height, blue eyes, and light skin. These blond and red long haired Caucasoids practiced an ancient proto-indo-european religion which is at the root of western Gnosticism and central Asian Bonpo Buddhism. Yeshu would have interacted with them.

¯ 5 ¯
yeshu's diet

Food Laws

IN THE MODERN world a choice of diet, whether it be vegan, vegetarian or omnivore, is considered a matter of personal preference having little, if anything, to do with spirituality. Essenes in the days of Yeshu looked at the subject a bit differently and considered vegetarianism an eternal law, and were willing to separate from anyone who put meat to their mouths. This adamant attitude is poignantly manifest in the controversy between Peter and Paul. Paul insisted that being vegetarian was a personal choice and hinted that those who chose it were actually spiritually weak - "the weak man eats

---

by a rich cosmography, including celestial realms and powers, with a spectrum of bodhisattvas, both human and seemingly godlike, who can assist followers."

only vegetables"[189]. Peter, in behalf of James, insisted that Nazoreans not even share a dining table with anyone who ate meat:

> "For the demons would never have had power over you, had not you first supped with their prince. For thus from the beginning was a law laid by God, the Creator of all things, on each of the two princes, him of the right hand and him of the left, that neither should have power over any one whom they might wish to benefit or to hurt, unless first he had sat down at the same table with them."[190]

For Peter, it was a matter of conforming to eternal laws laid down before the foundations of the world. To breech this law was to invite possession by inferior and dark forces. Neither Peter, nor anyone else who had personally been taught by Yeshu, was willing to compromise on this point. This lack of compromise resulted in the split between Paul's Greco Roman Christianity and the Aramaic speaking followers of Yeshu. Modern Christians have long forgotten the intensity and attention that this issue once commanded.

Darkness in Food

Nazorean Essenes felt the foods and drinks available on earth were of diverse kinds, some leading to awareness and others leading to deeper drunkenness and unconsciousness. Thus Nazorean Essenes always insisted on a pure plant diet consisting of grains, legumes, produce and root crops. But even these types of food contain only a degree of light and must be eaten in conjunction with other practices that insure that we are not lulled to sleep by the spirit of the world. Essene scrolls warn that the powers of the world have arrayed

---

[189] Romans 14:2
[190] From the Homilies of Clement

a tempting party, a cleverly disguised orgiastic feast, designed
to dull the senses and enslave the Children of Light:

> 'Ruha and the planets began to forge plans and said: "We will
> entrap Adam and catch him and detain him with us in the earth-
> sphere. When he eats and drinks, we will entrap the world. We
> will practice embracing in the world and found a community in
> the world. We will entrap him with horns and flutes, so that he
> may not break away from us . . We will seduce the tribe of Life
> and cut it off with us in the world . . ." [191]

> "Arise, let us make a celebration: arise, let us make a drinking
> feast, Let us practice the mysteries of love and seduce the whole
> world!" . . . The Call of Life we will silence, we will cast strife
> into the House, which shall not be settles in all eternity. We will
> kill the Stranger. We will make Adam our adherent and see who
> then will be his deliverer . . We will confound his society, the
> society that the Stranger has founded, so that he may have no
> share in the world. The whole House shall be ours alone . . What
> has the Stranger done in the House, that he should found
> himself a Order therein?" They took the head of the tribe and
> practiced on him the magic of love and of lust, through which all
> the worlds are inflamed. They practice on him seduction, by
> which all the worlds are seduced. They practice on him the
> magic of drunkenness, by which all the worlds are made
> drunken. . . The worlds are made drunk by it and turn their faces
> to the Suf-Sea." [192]

Nazoreans used wine and produce in their sacraments, and
encouraged love, the creation of children and festivals full of
music, dancing and life. But these are not the same as the
allures of the world mentioned above. Nazoreans were taught
to eschew meat eating, not only because it dulls the spiritual
senses, but also because it uncompassionately causes the death
of other living creatures. Nazoreans were taught to eschew

---

[191] Ginza Rba
[192] Ginza Rba

drugs, getting drunk or even drinking with materialistic people, and other mind altering practices of the world, because these lead to unconscious worldly behavior and open one up to spirits and influences and friendships that are not good and which eventually lead one away from the Path of Life. Spiritual souls who eat, drink and associate with worldly companions eventually sacrifice their spirituality. Nazoreans were taught to eschew the lust driven mating practices of the world, from her one night stands all the way up to her elaborate marriage ceremonies, for these were seen as a method of the Seven and Twelve to entrap man in lower forms of union independent of true love and devotion to Deity. Indeed, Nazoreans were taught to reject everything impure and imperfect in the world and to get as far away from its noise as is possible, for the noise of the world drowns out the subtle Call of Life.

Ancient Nazoreans, who had the luxury of well evolved communities, were encouraged to feast only within the confines of the Holy Order, to eat only food and drink consecrated on her holy altars, to drink only wine offered up in her holy sacraments, and to marry only those who share the same spiritual vision and aspiration for purity and eternal life. These are ideals, of course, that are only practical when functioning Nazorean communities exist. If, while on earth, we make decisions and so position ourselves to eat, drink and procreate only according to Essene ideals, then we are spared much of the heart ache and distraction that comes through the world's false counterparts to these spiritualized Nazorean practices. Such wise practices lead toward the eventual transcendence of the influences of the matter of the world and do not lead to further entanglement in it.

"He who thus possesses gnosis . . .is like a person, who, having been intoxicated, becomes sober and having come to himself reaffirms that which is essentially his own." [193]

This leads to an eventual sobering from the wine of the world and a type of drunkenness in the Great Life:

"Form the Lord's Spring came Speaking Water is abundance to my lips. I drank and was drunken with the water of Everlasting Life, yet my drunkenness was not that of ignorance, but I turned away from vanity."[194]

Diet of the Nazoreans

Nazoreans and their successors were very strict vegetarians, as Epiphanius tells us. Nazoreans were later called Elchasaites after 100 AD, and Manichaeans later on. Manichaeans were known for their strict vegan diet and extended fasting. Elchasaites also had special food laws and food categorization principles inherited from their ancestors within the true flow of gnosis.

Yeshu the Nazorean would have eaten a totally vegetarian diet based on the changing seasons and harvests periods of Mt Carmel and Galilee, or the area of his travels when abroad. No meat, pork, poultry, fish or eggs would have touched his, or any Nazorean's lips. Certain foreign foods would also have been available to Carmelites from the Silk Road trade route that had opened in 105 BC and which was connected to Capernaum.

This seasonal schedule is reflected in the Gezer Calendar, a 10th century BCE inscription excavated at Tel Gezer in Israel:

---

[193] Gospel of Truth
[194] Ode X1.6-8

"two months of sowing; two months of late sowing; one month of hoeing weeds; one month of barley harvesting; one month of harvesting and measuring (wheat); two months of cutting grapes." [195]

It is said that grain constituted over fifty percent of the average person's total caloric intake in ancient Judea, followed by legumes lentils, olive oil, and fruit, especially dried figs. The crops known to have been available were: Wheat, emer, millet, barley, squash, pumpkins, watermelon, cucumbers; legumes, lentils, chick-peas, grapes, raisins, figs, olives, apricots, dates, citron, jujube, pears, plums, peaches, quince, cherries, pomegranates; onions, leeks, garlic, shallots; almonds, pinenuts, pistachio nuts, walnuts, sesame, cinnamon, spices; lettuce, chicory, cress, sorrel, dandelion, cabbage, brassilicas; radishes, beets greens and roots, turnip greens and roots, grape sugar and honey. These are the foods Yeshu was nourished upon, each in their season.

Peter, the great Apostle of Yeshu, tells us his exact traveling diet in the Clementine literature. Peter says that when on the road:

"I use only bread and olives, and rarely vegetables; and that this is my only coat and cloak which I wear; and I have no need of any of them, nor of aught else: for even in these I abound."

The great Apostle Mani said in the third century that:

"...sacrifices and eating meat were forbidden by (Christ) to everybody...and that (Christ) has declared to have nothing in common with Abraham, Aaron, Joshua, David and all those who approve of the sacrificing of animals, of causing them pain, of eating meat and other things."

---

[195] Gezer Calendar, a 10th century BCE

This statement, by a prophet in direct line to Yeshu through Elchasai, explicitly states that Yeshu had nothing to do with Abraham and David. Augustine tells us that Manichaeans also did not eat fish, milk, or eggs:

> "They do not eat meat either, on the grounds that the divine substance has fled from the dead or slain bodies, and what little remains there is of such quality and quantity that it does not merit being purified in the stomachs of the elect. They do not even eat eggs, claiming that they too die when they are broken, and it is not fitting to feed on any dead bodies...Moreover, they do not use milk for food..." [196]

A form of the Manichaean diet was lived by Yeshu and those who lived before him on Carmel.

The spiritual Readings of Edgar Cayce are quoted extensively in this work, and in some of these he appears to advocate a non vegetarian diet. A careful perusal of his work, however, reveals that he only suggested such a diet for those who were not yet ready for fuller truth. For those who were ready, he said:

> "Let the diet be only vegetable forces. Do not lower the plane of development by animal vibrations." [197]

This seems to have also been the position of Yeshu. Cayce also wrote of the diet designed to nourish the vines and doves of the eugenics Temple program. We are told that they experienced:

> "Training as to physical exercise, first; training as to mental exercises . . . under the supervision of those that cared for the

[196] Augustine, De Haer 46:103-113, Faustum 16
[197] Reading 1010 This Psychic Reading Given By Edgar Cayce At The Tutwiler Hotel, Birmingham, Alabama, This 24th Day Of November, 1922.

nourishments by the protection of the food values. These were the manners and the way they were trained, directed, protected."

"Q. "Were they put on a special diet?"
A. "No wine, no fermented drink ever given. Special foods, yes. These were kept balanced according to that which had been first set by Aran and Ra Ta."[198]

The "no wine, no fermented drinks" applied only to the young Temple children being prepared for conception. Adult Nazoreans did indeed drink wine. The falsified New Testament contains false accounts of Yeshu eating the Passover "sacrifice" which was really a lamb bar-b-q, but the records of the vegetarian Nazoreans who really knew what Yeshu did and ate have him saying:

"Where will you have us prepare the Passover?" And him to answer to that: "Do I desire with desire at this Passover to eat flesh with you?"[199]

"I am come to do away with sacrifices, and if you cease not sacrificing, the wrath of God will not cease from you."[200]

The flawed New Testament account of the life of Jesus has him also eating fish on numerous occasions. This is a tradition that conflicts with the Fisher parable and with later detailed diet practices of Yeshu's Manichaean followers. Much of that which found its way into the imperfect "gospel" documents was later passed off as original eye witness testimony of the original Apostles. In reality these Biblical documents are later forgeries loosely based on more true Nazorean traditions. The forgers were meat eaters and so they wrote these allowances into their texts as if they were uttered from the mouth of the meat eschewing Yeshu. This ploy has confused many

---

[198] Cayce 5749-7
[199] Epiphanius, Panarion 30.22.4
[200] Yeshu Quote In Epiphanius, Panarion 30.16,4-5

generations of true seekers after the perfect lifestyle. Truer and more original Aramaic scrolls contain the original parables of the Fisher of Men which was reworked and abridged to form the later New Testament account. This original Fisher parable is contained in the 36th through 39th chapters of the Fisher of Souls section of the ancient Nazorean Prophets scroll. In the first of these four instructive chapters we read of Yeshu the fisher:

"For there is the call of the fisher, the fisher who eats no fish (is a vegan)." [201]

In a later verse of this same chapter Yeshu says:

"But I made answer unto them: O ye fishers, who lap up your filth, no fisher am I who fishes for fish, and I was not formed for an eater of filth (non vegan). A fisher am I of souls who bear witness to Life." [202]

In a later verse of chapter 38 we are further told that:

"Thou art, say they onto him, a… fisher, thou who hast caught no fish of the marsh."[203]

The New Testament encouragement to eat fish and lamb is a false tradition. We know that it is false because we possess an account of the effect that the preaching of the Nazorean John the Baptist had on eradicating all kinds of inferior behavior in Judea, including fish eating:

"Before my voice and the voice of my proclamations…the fishers fish not in Jerusalem."[204]

---

[201] Nazorean Prophets 36
[202] Nazorean Prophets 36
[203] Nazorean Prophets 38
[204] Doctrine Of Kings 21

Original Nazorean Christians were vegans who eschewed all such defiled food which caused harm and pain to innocent creatures and ill health to humans. Of course fish, fowl and meat can provide nourishment for people with an impoverished diet, but they are of no benefit to a well nourished vegetarian with a balanced healthy diet and lifestyle. The diet of the Nazorean Essenes was a true reflection of the compassionate and healthy lifestyle taught and practiced by the original and historical Jesus.

Lucian of Samosata did write that some Nazoreans he met in northern Syria: "ate nothing but wild fruit, milk and honey." But if this was a common practice, it had entirely been done away with by the days of Mani in the late 200's. There are also two references to fish eating in the Cayce accounts, and again, if some Nazoreans did indeed eat fish, by Mani's day they did not. As an argument for veganism even in Yeshu's day, we have the testimony of two verses in the ancient Aramaic parable of the Fisher and the testimony of Pliny the younger who tortured two deaconesses to find that the Nazoreans:

"... reassemble to partake of food - but food of an ordinary and innocent kind."[205]

Food Blessing

"Harmlessness" in regards to diet is the traditional vegetarian stance of the Ancient Nazoreans, of whom it is written:

"The Nazoreans . . . would not offer sacrifice or eat meat.."[206]

---

[205] The Tenth Book Of Pliny's Letters
[206] Epipahius. Panarion 1:18

In addition to eating innocent food, Yeshu and his sect always blessed their food and drink. Yuhana the Baptist warned all:

> "Those who smell the aroma of Life (*Living Foods*) and over it do not express the names of Life (*food blessing*), will be dragged to the account in the house of the Abathur."

This insistence on blessing food was a result of a belief that food contained both positive and negative elements, which in turn affected the moods and mentality of those who ate it. They believed that certain foods contained more light, others more darkness, but that all food contained a relative amount of undesirable qualities that only prayer could begin to mitigate. They did not think praying changed the nature of the food, but they believed it helped them poise themselves spiritually to deal with its innate darkness. When blessing their food, Nazorean would sing this prayer which recognized the solar (yang/Yawar) and lunar (yin/Simat) essence of food:

"Shuma Hiya Nirmala Tabta Yawar, u Simat Hiya; Amen!"

This means: "The name of Life is pronounced over thee, O life giving Nourishment of Yawar-Ziwa and Simat-Hiya. Amen"

Later, after Yeshu and Miryam were recognized as incarnations of very high light beings it became appropriate to change this prayer to: "Shuma Hiya Nir-ma-la Tab-ta Yeshu, u Miryam; A-men!" meaning "The name of Life is pronounced over thee, O life giving Nourishment of Yeshu-Ziwa and Miryam-Noorah.

Fear of Meat

Many of the early Roman Christian fathers followed a vegetarian diet for a while due to the influence of the original disciples. Their writings indicate that flesh eating was not officially mandated by the Early Church, until the 4th Century, when the Emperor Constantine decided that Christianity would eat meat. This soon became the official Creed of the "Holy Roman Empire" and its Christian church. Vegetarian Christians had to practice in secret or risk being put to death for heresy. It is even said by some that Constantine poured molten lead down the throats of vegetarians, if they were caught.[207] People were tested as to their loyalties by forcing them to eat a chunk of meat in the fifth century:

> "A priest who is an abstainer from flesh, let him merely taste it and so let him abstain. But if he will not taste even the vegetables cooked with the meat let him be deposed." [208]

The whole Roman Christian church was tested in this way and purged of covert Nazoreans.

Earliest Christian vegetarian practices are beautifully outlined by Peter in the Clementine Homilies from the first century. In these Nazoreans versions of the Acts of the Apostles we read of the importance of a compassionate diet to early followers of Yeshu. In the Homilies Peter is very clear that eating meat puts one under the dominion of dark forces:

> "The unnatural eating of the Flesh of Animals is as polluting as the Heathen Worship of Devils, with its Sacrifices and its impure Feasts, man becomes a fellow eater with Devils".

> "For the demons would never have had power over you, had not you first supped with their prince. For thus from the beginning was a law laid by God, the Creator of all things, on each of the two princes, him of the right hand and him of the left, that

---

[207] Stevenrosen's: Food For The Spirit 1987
[208] The Council Of Ancyra, Epitome Of Canon Xiv

neither should have power over any one whom they might wish to benefit or to hurt, unless first he had sat down at the same table with them."

"Since, on the other hand, you are oppressed by strange sufferings inflicted by demons, on your removal from the body you shall have your souls also punished for ever; not indeed by God's inflicting vengeance, but because such is the judgment of evil deeds. For the demons, having power by means of the food given to them, are admitted into your bodies by your own hands; and lying hid there for a long time, they become blended with your souls. And through the carelessness of those who think not, or even wish not, to help themselves, upon the dissolution of their bodies, their souls being united to the demon, are of necessity borne by it into whatever places it pleases."

Peter tries to explain why demons inhabit humans:

"But the reason why the demons delight in entering into men's bodies is this. Being spirits, and having desires after meats and drinks, and sexual pleasures, but not being able to partake of these by reason of their being spirits, and wanting organs fitted for their enjoyment, they enter into the bodies of men, in order that, getting organs to minister to them, they may obtain the things that they wish, whether it be meat, by means of men's teeth, or sexual pleasure, by means of men's members. Hence, in order to the putting of demons to flight, the most useful help is abstinence, and fasting, and suffering of affliction. For if they enter into men's bodies for the sake of sharing pleasures, it is manifest that they are put to flight by suffering. But inasmuch as some, being of a more malignant kind, remain by the body that is undergoing punishment, though they are punished with it, therefore it is needful to have recourse to God by prayers and petitions, refraining from every occasion of impurity, that the hand of God may touch him for his cure, as being pure and faithful

"Therefore the demons themselves, knowing the amount of faith of those of whom they take possession, measure their stay proportionately. Wherefore they stay permanently with the unbelieving, tarry for a while with the weak in faith; but with those who thoroughly believe, and who do good, they cannot remain even for a moment. For the soul being turned by faith, as it were, into the nature of water, quenches the demon as a spark of fire. The labor, therefore, of every one is to be solicitous about the putting to flight of his own demon. For, being mixed up with men's souls, they suggest to every one's mind desires after what things they please, in order that he may neglect his salvation."

Peter, coming from a tradition that practiced bathing in flowing water every morning at dawn, elaborates on the way this reverence for Living water helps quench darkness:

"But in the present life, washing in a flowing river, or fountain, or even in the sea, with the thrice-blessed invocation, you shall not only be able to drive away the spirits which lurk in you; but yourselves no longer sinning, and undoubtingly believing God, you shall drive out evil spirits and dire demons, with terrible diseases, from others."

Peter here sums up the importance of not sitting down to a table that has dead meat being served. This practice was practical when there was a whole culture of vegans to associate with:

"This then we would have you know, that unless any one of his own accord give himself over as a slave to demons, as I said before, the demon has no power against him. Choosing, therefore, to worship one God, and refraining from the table of demons, and undertaking chastity with philanthropy and righteousness, and being baptized with the thrice-blessed invocation for the remission of sins, and devoting yourselves as much as you can to the perfection of purity, you can escape everlasting punishment, and be constituted heirs of eternal blessings."

Nazoreans & Wine

The early Nazorean Christians drank alcohol, but never unto drunkenness. Preserved wine is mentioned in the Qulasta hymns in a very positive fashion and in the ancient Aramaic Nazorean Prophets scroll we read:

> "Do not drink immoderately and do not forget your Lord from your thoughts."[209]

This early Nazorean text would not admonish one to not over drink if there had been a ban on all drinking. The verse is very exacting, admonishing us not to over drink! We are also warned in the Ginza Scroll that over drinking puts us into the power of the hostile planets:

> "They practice on him the magic of drunkenness, by which all the worlds are made drunken. . . The worlds are made drunk by it and turn their faces to the Suf-Sea." [210]

Some later Gnostics and Jewish Christians were known to have abstained from wine, but this appears to have been a later alteration to the original tradition. It may also be partly based on the fact that Catholics only used wine in their public masses, but the Aramaic Yeshu followers used only water in theirs. They did, however, use the grape in their Masqithas, and these masqithas were the original inspiration for the Catholic masses. That is why the Catholic Mass has this name based on the longer Aramaic word and includes wine.

Reduced wine was used in first century Palestine as a sweetener as well as a preservative, and ancient techniques

---

[209] Nazorean Prophets 67
[210] Nazorean Ginza Rba

were known that allowed grape juice to remain unfermented all year:

> "If you want to have grape juice all year, put must in an amphora and seal the cork with pitch. Submerge in the fish-pond. Take out after 30 days. It will remain unfermented all year."[211]

We could also quote the passage in the Gospel of John that has Jesus turning water into wine, but this is not an authentic event, but rather one taken from a pagan legend of Dionysus, the Greek god of wine. In the pre-Christian Dionysus version of this miracle, priests at Dionysus' wedding to Ariadne bring vessels of water to a building, which is sealed and later opened only to find that the water has been turned to wine. This story was copied into the Gospel of John in an attempt to make Jesus outshine Dionysus. The miracle did not occur.

Fasting and Feasts

Nazoreans have an ancient saying in the Ginza Rba that says:

> "I say to you, my chosen, I instruct you, my faithful: Fast the great fast (*sauma*), which is not a fasting from the eating and drinking of the world. Fast with your eyes from (immodest) winking, and do not see or practice evil. Fast with your ears from eavesdropping at doors which do not belong to you. Fast with your mouths from wanton lies and do not love falsehood and deceit. Fast with your hearts from wicked thoughts, and do not harbor malice, jealousy, and dissension in your hearts... Fast with your hands from committing murder and do not commit robbery. Fast with your body from the married woman who does not belong to you. Fast with your knees from prostrations before Satan and do not kneel before images of deception. Fast with your feet from going craftily after something that does not

---

[211] Cato on Farming, 120

belong to you. Fast this great fast and do not break it until you depart from your body."

This is the true fast, the spiritual fast, but Nazoreans also practiced physical fasting. The Valentinian leader Ptolemaus, in his Letter to Flora, explains the tradition held in his day:

"Among us external fasting is also observed, since it can be advantageous to the soul if it is done reasonably, not for imitating others or from habit or because of a special day appointed for this purpose. It is also observed so that those who are not yet able to keep the true fast may have a reminder of it from the external fast." [212]

Nazoreans, ever intent on achieving balance in all things, also had many feasts to compliment their many fast periods. These fasts and feasts were regulated by the Nazorean liturgical calendar which was lunar based. Fasting on the day before feasts, on the lunar Sabbaths, which are the seventh, fourteenth, twenty-first and twenty-eighth of the lunar month, is an excellent way to walk in harmony with the ancient rhythm of the Nazoreans. The beauty and strength that lies hidden in fasting is beautifully spoken of by the Sufi mystic Rumi:

"There's hidden sweetness in the stomach's emptiness. We are lutes, no more, no less If the soundbox is stuffed full of anything, no music. If the brain and the belly are burning clean with fasting, every moment a new song comes out of the fire. The fog clears, and new energy makes you run up the steps in front of you. Be emptier and cry like reed instruments cry. Emptier, write secrets with the reed pen. When you're full of food and drink, an ugly metal statue sits where your spirit should. When you fast, good habits gather like friends who want to help. Fasting is Solomon's ring. Don't give it to some illusion and lose your power, but even if you have, if you've lost all will and control,

[212] Ptolemaus, Letter to Flora

they come back when you fast, like soldiers appearing out of the ground, pennants flying above them. A table descends to your tents, the Lord's table. Expect to see it when you fast, this table spread with other food, better than the broth of cabbages.[213]

ˉ 6 ˉ
yeshu's cOIRyAI

cOIRyAI ARchetype

THE OBVIOUS PLACE for the soul mate of Yeshu to incarnate was within the eugenics program of the Mount Carmel Temple of Nazorean Essenes. It appears that she did indeed do this, but as Yeshu's mother rather than spouse. This forced Yeshu to marry someone else who had not been his twin soul in heaven. This was not a problem for Nazoreans, however, who understood the variety of relationships that exist between various interlinked souls in numerous earthly lives. It is not always important to link up with and marry one's twin soul. One of the facets of multiple incarnations is the opportunity to develop close bonds with others as well as our fellow twin soul. Most of the fruit of this eugenics program did indeed find most of their mates therein, but Yeshu married at least one woman from outside. So why did Yeshu not exclusively marry young vines from Carmel? Birth placement is not by accident, but by design, especially when it involves someone as important as Miryai. So why did she incarnate in a culture antagonist to that of her future mate Yeshu?

---

[213] Poem by Maulana Rumi Fasting

Judaism, especially Sadducean Judaism of the high Priests, was indeed hostile to Nazoreanism. There were both Nazorean Essenes and Sadducees living in Miryai's home town of Bethany and nearby Jerusalem, but they did not interact or get along. Yet Miryai, also known as Miryam and Mary of Magdala, did indeed incarnate among the Sadducee elite. By divine design she was blessed to be born near Nazoreans and in a locale frequented by her future beloved, but for her formative years she knew only an elite' form of Judaism.

The apparent reason for this event was to show forth a previous cosmic event when Yeshu, as Hibil-Ziwa, entered a dark land to rescue Miryai, as Zahariel, and take her back home into the light. We have recounted this legend in the first chapter. This is the allegorical scenario that repeats itself again and again in the lives of Yeshu and Miryai and is a type of the redemption of our own soul when we hear and hearken to the Call of Life as Miryai and Miryam did.

Miryai the Jew

The fact that Miryai was raised a Jew and yet still managed to outshine her fellow Nazoreans after her conversion manifests both her innate intelligence and endowment, but also the prowess of the Jews of her day to train young prodigies. Despite her innate spiritual endowment, without a fostering childhood she would not have developed to her full potential. Despite their pact with death, Judaism has excelled in intellectual prowess. Ashkenasai Jews as a group score the highest in the world in IQ tests, and Judaism as a whole is known for its intellectuals, its doctors, scientists, and scholars. Miryai, the future bride of Yeshu, was born into the more intelligent of this already exceptional gene pool, and it is said that she out shown them all. Her conversion to Nazoreanism was preceded by years of intense study, memorization, and training. Her conversion was also prefaced by a short period of decadence. At her abandonment of Judaism and decadence, her mother reminded her that

"A thousand stand there and two thousand sit there. They submit themselves to thee, as a eunuch-made slave, and they give ear to thy word in Jerusalem."[214]

Torah Fame

Miryai was born many times before and after her incarnation in first century Palestine. In her incarnation with Christ, Miryai d-Magdala (Mary of Magdala, or Mary Magdalene) was born outside the veil of Nazirutha amongst the Jews and raised in the High Priest's home. Miryai tells us in her personal autobiography:

"Miryai am I, of the Kings of Judaism, a daughter, a daughter of Jerusalem's mighty rulers. They have given me birth: the priests brought me up. In the fold of their robe they carried me up into the dark house, into the temple. Adonai laid a charge on my hands and on my two arms."[215]

We know, from ancient scrolls of the Order that Miryai's father, the High Priest Elizer, was a very influential member in the Jewish world, and that his daughter Miryai taught in the school, and lectured to thousands at a time. As the well funded and well supported daughter of the High Priest, this size of crowd is plausible. When pleading with her to return to Judaism, her mother reminds her of this:

[214] Sidra dYahya, Book of John the Baptist from Mandaic Doctrines of Kings
[215] Sidra dYahya, Book of John the Baptist from Mandaic Doctrines of Kings

"Rememberest thou not, Miryai, that the Torah lay on thy lap? Thou didst open it, read therein and knewest what stands in it. The outer keys lay in thy hands, and the inner thou didst put in chains. All the priests and priests sons came and kissed thy hand. Far whom thou wouldst, thou didst open the door, whom thou wouldst not, must turn and go hack to his seat. A thousand stand there and two thousand sit there. They submit themselves to thee, as a eunuch-made slave, and they give ear to thy word in Jerusalem."[216]

Sadducees read only the five books of Moses and their "Book of Decrees" - a criminal code. Miryai's great intelligence, fame, and grasp of Torah would have caused her father to hope to use her to bolster his own political aspirations through marriage, but Miryai had other plans which would come to anger him greatly. She would later show equal if not greater skill in grasping the Nazorean texts and teachings of her mentor Yeshu, and would eventually rise to be lineage holder of the Nazoreans during the tenure of James the Just. Even after her conversion to Nazoreanism, there are still records of Jews coming to her to receive light and knowledge, even as the other Nazorean Apostles did.

Mary Magdalene's father Elizer was one of the most important and one of the richest persons in the entire region. He would not have been happy with a Nazorean Temple and its devotees in his Jerusalem and neighboring villages, nor would they have been thrilled with his local Jewish animal slaughter cult. We are told by Miryai that her parents repeatedly warned her to stay far away from the vegan Nazoreans whom the Jews hated so much:

"My father went to the house of the people, my mother went to the temple. My father went out and said to me, and my mother went out and charged me: "Miryai, close thy inner doors and

---

bolt the bar. See that thou goest not forth into the main streets and that the Lord's sunshine fall not upon thee." [217]

Apparently the threat of the Nazoreans was felt to be very real by the Jewish leadership.

Nazorean Temple

Miryai did not heed her parent's warnings. She writes in her scroll:

> "But I, Miryai, listened not to what my mother did tell me, and hardened not with the ear to what my father did charge me. I opened the inner doors and the outer let I stand open. Out went I into the main streets and the Lord's sunshine fell upon me. To the Jewish Synagogue (*bit 'ama*, the house of the people) would I not go, but my way bore me onto the Nazorean Temple (*Bit Mshkana*). I went thither and found my brothers and sisters standing there, and giving forth doctrines." [218]

Miryai, rejecting the "dark house which benefits no one", sought refuge in the Nazoreans Temple of Light where both men and woman wore white clothing and headbands, and studied Nazorean scrolls together. Thus we have white robed vegan Nazoreans in the region of the Jewish Temple and slaughterhouse, and a Nazorean Temple and School of the Prophets near to a Jewish school and place of worship! The risk of being caught for a whole incarnation in a dark spiritual culture was overcome, and the innate draw to her true home and family prevailed.

Conversion

---

[217] Sidra dYahya, Book of John the Baptist from Mandaic Doctrines of Kings
[218] Sidra dYahya, Book of John the Baptist from Mandaic Doctrines of Kings

Because the Nazorean's had different ideas about sexual and marital purity, they were accused by the Jews of having loose morals. This resulted in a general slander of the Nazoreans as adulterers and their converts as being morally lax. This was an unfair accusation, especially from the hypocritical and corrupt Sadducee elite', but a useful one for scaring away would be converts from investigating the sublime teachings. After Mary Magdalene converts from Judaism to Nazoreanism, her former Jewish family and admirers accuse her of abandoning their faith, becoming a loose woman, and becoming a Nazorean only because she has fallen in love with the head of the Nazoreans.

> "All the Jews gathered together, the teachers, the great and the little; they came together and spake of Miryai: "She ran away from the priests, fell in love with a man, and they took hold of each other's hands."[219]

In her scroll Miryai goes on to explain that she did not convert to Nazoreanism because she fell in love with its leader, but because she knew it to be the true religion. She writes that her father taunted her with these accusations:

> "Come, look on Miryai, who has left Jewry and gone to make love with her lord. Come, look on Miryai, who has left off colored raiment and gone to make love with her lord. She forsook gold and silver and went to make love with her lord. She forsook the phylacteries and went to make love with the man with the head-band." [220]

Nazoreans wore only white, avoided jewelry and other outward displays of wealth, and wore silk headbands denoting their priestly status. Miryai answered her father and responds:

---

[219] Sidra dYahya, Book of John the Baptist from Mandaic Doctrines of Kings
[220] Sidra dYahya, Book of John the Baptist from Mandaic Doctrines of Kings

"Far lies it from me to love him whom I have hated. Far lies it from me to hate him whom I have loved. Nay, far from me lies it to hate my Lord, the Life's Gnosis (Yeshu/Manda dHiya), who is for me in the world a support, a support is he in the world for me and a helper in the Light's region." [221]

She goes on to curse the corrupt and controlling Jewish cult, saying:

"Dust in the mouth of the Jews, ashes in the mouth of all of the priests! May the dung that is under the feet of the horses, come on the high ones and Jerusalem's mighty rulers." [222]

Zatan Oath

Mary Magdalene's own autobiography informs us as to the real reason Yeshu was crucified. The Jews were mad at Yeshu because he stole the heart of their precious progeny. They swore to crucify him for this and destroy the Nazorean sect:

"We will slay them and make Miryai scorned in Jerusalem. A stake (*Cross*) will we set up for the man who has ruined Miryai and led her away. There shall be no day in the world when a stranger enters Jerusalem." [223]

Gnostic Nazoreans were called strangers by the Jews, for they seemed like they were from another planet to the earthbound Jews. The Stranger is that Envoy of the Living Ones who does not belong here. He or she is an alien who has crossed over the border of worlds and entered this universe to rescue the Seed of Life. The Spirit of the Worlds warns the Seven Rulers of the Seven Planets:

---

[221] Sidra dYahya, Book of John the Baptist from Mandaic Doctrines of Kings
[222] Sidra dYahya, Book of John the Baptist from Mandaic Doctrines of Kings
[223] Sidra dYahya, Book of John the Baptist from Mandaic Doctrines of Kings

"The Man does not belong to us, and his speech is not your speech. He has no connection with you . . . His speech comes from without."[224]

Call of Life

Miryai responded to the Call of Life and left her Judaism and later decadence for the Nazorean faith. Unlike worldly souls who hate "the strangers", pure souls are said to respond positively to the Call of Life:

"Adam felt love for the Strange Man whose speech is alien, estranged from the world." [225]

Through this Call the lost children of the Diaspora are collected into a Holy Order, and enclaves of strange souls form in the world. This troubles the powers of this universe, and the Gods of this universe, and they say:

"What has the Stranger done in the House, that he could establish himself an Order therein?" [226]

"We will kill the Stranger . . . We will confound his Order, so that he may have no share in the world. The whole House shall be ours." [227]

Another one of the scrolls speaks about the advent of Yeshu the Word (*Malala*) in these material universes:

"When the Word appeared, the Word which is in the hearts of those who pronounce It – and it was not only a sound, but It had taken on a body as well – a great confusion reigned among the

[224] Ginza Rba, the Great Treasury
[225] Ginza Rba, the Great Treasury
[226] Ginza Rba, the Great Treasury
[227] Ginza Rba, the Great Treasury

vessels, for some had been emptied, others filled; some were provided for, others were overthrown; some were sanctified, still others were broken to pieces. All the spaces were shaken and confused, for they had no fixity nor stability. "Error" was agitated, not knowing what it should do. It was afflicted, and lamented and worried because it knew nothing. Since the Gnosis, which is the perdition of Error and all its emanations, approached it, Error became empty, there be nothing more in it."[228]

Thus the Gnosis of Life incarnates into the dungeon of the worlds, "to clothe itself in the affliction of the world", and voluntarily enter exile and imprisonment for the sake of liberating those still enmeshed in the web of the Seven. Miryai recognized this and came to him.

In the sinking phase of cosmic history, beings of light descended down to lower worlds to become forgetful therein and to experience the opposite of Life so that they could eventually reaccept that Life completely. Miryai's incarnation among the Jews and her decadent period was a type of this cosmic event. The descent of the Envoy is of a different nature, for the Envoy comes not to forget as in the first phase, but to remembered and to cause all the sleeping Seed of the Living Ones to awaken and begin the journey homeward. This is why Yeshu was born in the enlightened Nazorean sect. The coming together of Yeshu and Miryai is a cosmic symbol of the union of the Messengers of Life with those who heed their call.

"One Call comes and instructs about all calls. One speech comes and instructs about all speech. One beloved Son comes, who was formed from the worlds of splendor . . . His image is kept safe in its place. He comes with the illumination of life, with the

---

[228] Gospel of Truth

command which his father imparts. He comes in the garment of living fire and betakes himself into thy world." [229]

Yokabar and Kushta are titles of Yeshu and Miryam. They together bring the Nazirutha Light to enlighten believing humankind. Yeshu brings the Ziwa-Splendor (a masculine form of light) and Miryam brings the N'hurah-Luminosity (the female form of light), and through these two types of light the "new man" or "new woman" is created:

> "We are Yokabar-Kushta, who has gone forth from our Parent's House and come hither. We have come hither with hidden Ziwa-Splendor and with N'hurah-Luminosity without end." [230]

Connected with "The Call" is the promise of rebirth through the Ziwa-N'hurah light of Yeshu-Miryam. It is They who come with the Seals that unlock the imprisoned sparks of light and seal them up unto Eternal Life:

> "For his sake send me, Father! Holding the Seals will I descend, Through all the worlds will I take my way, All the mysteries will I unlock, The forms of the gods will I make manifest, The secrets of the Sacred Way, Known as Nazirutha, I will transmit." [231]

Thus the Gnosis of Life, the First Man-Woman, forces a passage way through the labyrinth of worlds and opens up a conduit of escape:

> "In the Name of Them who came, in the Name of Them who come, and in the Name of Them who is to be brought forth. In the Name of the Strange Man who forced Their way through the worlds, split the firmament and revealed Themselves." [232]

---

[229] Ginza Rba, the Great Treasury
[230] Ginza Rba, the Great Treasury
[231] Naassene Psalm of the Soul
[232] Ginza Rba, the Great Treasury

Contrasts

Mary Magdalene's life changed drastically when she left the opulent world of her powerful father to marry his counterpart in the Nazorean world - the High Priest Yeshu dMiryam (Jesus son of Mary). She gave up the rich colorful clothes of a High Priest's daughter to adorn herself in simple off-white clothing of a Nazorean priestess. She left behind all her jewelry for the simple ring of a Nazorean Initiate. She abandoned animal sacrifice and Jewish paraphernalia to keep an all plant diet and lifestyle. Her father says:

> "Came, look on Miryai, who has left off colored raiment and gone to make love with her lord. She forsook gold and silver and went to make love with her lord. She forsook the phylacteries and went to make love with the man with the head-band." [233]

According to the Sleeping Prophet, Miryai found Yeshu in her twenty third year after a time spent promiscuously. Cayce said that Mary Magdalene was a:

> "...courtesan that was active in the experiences both of those that were in the capacity of the Roman officers, Roman peoples, and those that were of the native lands and country."[234]

The Sadducee elite' of the period were quite corrupt, including the High Priest and his household that Miryai had grown up in. They were known for their lust of luxury and pomp and their denial of angels, spirits, the soul, reincarnation and afterlife judgment. This led them to engage in all sorts of immoral and hypocritical behavior. Rich, affluent, hypocritical and compromised by corrupt dealing with both rich Roman officers and rich Jewish officials, they nevertheless had the pretense of religiosity. The Talmud records that in Yeshu and

---

[233] Sidra dYahya, Book of John the Baptist from Mandaic Doctrines of Kings
[234] Text Of Reading 295-8

Miryai's time the high priest bought the office from the government and the position was changed every year. Being the High Priest's daughter was not a blessing for Miryai. It would be wrong to see Miryai as abandoning a chaste pure and religious life as an orthodox Jew only to abandon herself headlong into a world of corruption. Miryai was raised in such corruption – an unholy mix of power, decadence and false piety. Miryai's activity with Roman officers was simply an outgrowth of her corrupt surroundings. Her crime, in the eyes of her father, was prostituting herself for her own benefit rather than his. He wanted to use her to further his own political and economical ends. The spiritual state of Miryai's parents and the rich Sadducee elite' in charge of the lucrative animal slaughter cult of Jerusalem was certainly not a pure one. Sadducees are thought to have been a small hated minority in ancient Israel numbering not more than 3000 of the rich and powerful.

Miryai Marries

Miryai's early studiousness, lapse into lasciviousness, and conversion to Nazorean purity bears witness to the elasticity of the human soul. Miryai is the archetype of us all who must abandon our dark past to embrace the shimmering light. Miryai became a constant companion of Yeshu. They settled at the mouth of the Frash river which was probably the Siah River in Wadi Esiah canyon on the western slopes of Mount Carmel, where the main Nazorean Temple and monastery was located. Miryai tells us this in her scroll:

> "She ran away from the priests, fell in lore with a man, and they took hold of each other's bands. Hold of each other's hands they took, went forth and settled at the mouth of Frash."

We are told more of their relationship in later Nag texts which say:

"There were three Mariams who walked with the Lord at all times: his mother and [his] sister and the Magdalene, she who is called his mate. Thus his (true) Mother, Sister and Mate is (also) called 'Mariam'." [235]

"And the Mate of the [Christ] is Mariam Magdalene. The [Lord loved] Mariam more than [all the other] Disciples, [and he] kissed her often on her [mouth. He embraced] the other women also, yet they said to him: Why do thou love [her] more than all of us? The Savior replied, he said to them: Why do I not love you as I do her?" [236]

After the death of Yeshu, both Miryam and Miryai lived together in the household of Yuhana Zebedee:

"With the joining of the mother of the Christ with John's household (which was composed then of Mary Magdalene and Elois, or the sister of Mary that was the mother of James and John), these journeyed then to what would be called their SUMMER home - or that portion on the lake of Gennesaret where the activities of those that came and went were supervised by those of the whole household. The period of life of Mary (that is, of Mary the sister of Lazarus) was some twenty and two years; she being twenty-three years old when the Christ cleansed her from the seven devils: Avarice, hate, self-indulgence, and those of the kindred selfishness; hopelessness and blasphemy." [237]

Essene Women

---

[235] Gospel Of Philip
[236] Gospel Of Philip
[237] Text Of Reading 295-8

Nazoreans saw a male female balance in all things. Because of
this sense of male-female balance, Nazoreans found it easy to
comprehend the concept of a Heavenly Mother as well as
Father, and a Female Messiah figure as well as a male. This
outlook lent itself to full appreciation and respect for female
Nazoreans, and their acceptance into roles of authority and
Priest(ess)hood. The archetypes of all female perfection are
summed up in the figures of Miryam and Miryai of Magdala
whom Yeshu called the "woman who knows all".

In the spiritual past life readings of Cayce, there is reference to
woman leaders among the Essene Nazoreans. In commenting
on one of them named Duene he said:

> "Before that the entity was in the land of promise, during those
> periods when there were the holy women set as the heads of the
> church, or as counselors; not as deaconesses, not as those today
> considered as sisters of mercy or sisters superior, but rather
> those who took the veil that there might be the better
> preparations of self to be offered AS channels through which
> greater blessings might come, and greater abilities for teaching.
> They were those who separated themselves from their families,
> their homes, that they might become as channels of blessings to
> others."[238]

On another he said:

> "Yes, the entity gained, or obtained, a record of that as had been
> gathered by the keeper of records from Carmel. Before that we
> find the entity lived in the earth during those periods when there
> were the activities just previous to the advent of the Holy One
> into the earth's experience, among those peoples of that group
> then called the Essenes. The entity was active among those in
> aiding to gather the data from the various teachers of the varied
> lands for the interpretation of that for that particular group.

---

[238] Text Of Reading 2308-1

Then the entity was very close to one Anna, in the temple service. For it was of the same household, of the same activity, yet varying somewhat in the manner of their presentations. Yet when the ministry began in the latter days of the entity's experience in and about that portion of Bethany and a part of Jerusalem, there became much of that the entity had given, the entity gave, that became as a part of that to those who looked for the activities of the minister, the teacher, the Holy One. For the entity then was a prophetess as well as among those, as it might be said, who were the recorders or who kept the records of those peoples. For the entity then was in that capacity as one of the holy women who ministered in the temple service and in the preparation of those who dedicated their lives for individual activity during the sojourn. The entity was then what would be termed in the present, in some organizations, as a Sister Superior, or an officer as it were in those of the Essenes and their preparations. Hence we find the entity then giving, giving, ministering, encouraging, making for the greater activities; and making for those encouraging experiences oft in the lives of the Disciples; coming in contact with the Master oft in the ways between Bethany, Galilee, Jerusalem. For, as indicated, the entity kept the school on the way above Emmaus to the way that "goeth down towards Jericho" and towards the northernmost coast from Jerusalem. The name then was Eloise, and the entity blessed many of those who came to seek to know the teachings, the ways, the mysteries, the understandings; for the entity had been trained in the schools of those that were of the prophets and prophetesses, and the entity was indeed a prophetess in those experiences - thus gained throughout."[239]

Miryai as Priestess

Miryai began her teaching career in a hypocritical Jewish world of parchment, indigo and meat, but ended it in the sincere white Nazorean world of papyrus and produce. She fully functioned as a Nazorean Priestess and was eventually

---

[239] Cayce Reading 1391-1, Par. R10

recognized as an incarnation of their heavenly Goddess - the "Maiden of Light ".

In the Gospel of Mary and Pistis Sophia she is recognized by Yeshu and the other apostles as the most understanding of them all. In the Pistis Sophia codex she is said to tower, along with one other, over all the other disciples. The term "tower" is wordplay on her epitaph of Magdala, meaning tower:

> "Where I shall be, there will be also my twelve ministers, But Maria Magdalene and John the Virgin will tower over all my disciples and over all men who shall receive the Mysteries of the Ineffable. And they will be on my right and on my left. And I am they, and they are I." [240]

After the death of Yeshu we are told that James the Lord's Brother became Yeshu's successor!

> "Jesus said to them: Wherever you have come, you will go to James the righteous for whose sake heaven and earth came into being." [241]

Yet James did not preside alone, but with others. Miryai was among this elect group. We are not told her exact status in relationship to James, but we are told that she went to live with John the Beloved as the death of Yeshu. She would not have been celibate: "For priests and priestesses may marry; indeed, marriage is obligatory."[242] Eventually she was recognized as the official repository of all the mysteries of the Nazoreans. From James the leadership, and all the secret scrolls, went to Miryai or Mariamme as she is sometimes called:

---

[240] Pistis Sophia, p193
[241] Gospel of Thomas
[242] Gnostic John the Baptizer: by G. R. S. Mead

"These are the titles of very numerous discourses which (the Naassenes) asserts James the brother of the Lord handed down to Mariamne (Miryai)" [243]

The fact that James had to hand down the secret scrolls to Miryai, rather than Yeshu doing so, tells us a little on why the twenty year old James was made the Rishama of the Nazoreans, rather than the twenty-three year old convert Miryai. Miryai, since she was raised in another faith, needed time to absorb the secrets and mysteries of Nazirutha. Eventually both James and Miryai taught the deep secrets of Nazirutha which they alone had received from Yeshu. They represented the true lineage of light in contrast to the false Pauline Churchanity that was on the rise in the west during the latter part of both their lives:

> "The priests, then, and champions of the system, have been first those who have been called Naasseni, ...alleging that they alone have sounded the depths of knowledge." [244]

Miryai died about a decade before James, after twenty two years teaching among the Nazoreans. She, and her beloved John, would incarnate again and again toward the perfection of their fellow Nazoreans.

Miryai as Goddess

The Gnostic Mary Magdalene, or Mary of Bethany, is constantly called the blessed one, the one who knows the all, and an incarnation of the Maiden of Light by Yeshu. She is also known as the sought for one:

---

[243] The Refutations Of All Heresies By Hippolytus (Book V Section Ii)
[244] - The Refutations Of All Heresies By Hippolytus (Book V Section I)

"...which is begotten above, where, he says, is Mariam the sought-for one..." [245]

The Maiden or Virgin of Light is a Nazorean Heavenly Goddess archetype spoken of extensively in the Pistis Sophia. She was recognized as the Maiden of Light, the female counterpart to the Third Messenger of Manichaean lore. Miryai is the "Little Sophia" mentioned in the Gospel of Philip, and the Aeon called "Life" in Valentinian mythos. In Her role as bride and mate to Yeshu, Nazoreans saw in Her their hope for full reconciliation with the All-Parents above through the saving gnosis that She, Yeshu, and others dispense jointly to all seeking gnostikoi Nazoreans.

> "The Treasury am I, Life's Treasury. A King for the Nazoraeans became I. I became a King for the Nazoraeans, who through my Name find praise and assurance. Praise and assurance they find through my Name, and on my Name they mount up and behold the Light's region."

Miryai Slandered

Roman Christianity, in an attempt to de-emphasize the importance of woman, sought to overly focus on Mary of Bethany's indiscriminant youth. They sought to downplay her role in early Nazoreanism. They also removed all vestiges of female Goddesses in their attempt to recast the Nazorean worldview into their own flawed system. Miryai became only Mary the reformed slut and Mariam (Virgin Mary) became the immaculate virgin. Although they sought to de-emphasize the roll of Miryai in the Gospel message, they failed to fully tarnish her image. In the imperfect and reworked New Testament she is still portrayed as the first witness to the resurrection. Wise ones should seek to return to the pristine

---

[245] -The Refutations Of All Heresies By Hippolytus (Book V Section lii)

image of the historical Miryai and Mariam and to a true understanding of just what the resurrection was.

The Barren One

There have been some modern speculation on possible children between Mary Magdala and Yeshu, yet she seems to have had an ancient epitaph of "the barren one". In the Nazorean Gospel of Philip we read:

> "The wisdom which humans call barren is the Mother of the Angels. And the Mate of the [Christ] is Mariam Magdalene. The [Lord loved] Mariam more than [all the other] Disciples, [and he] kissed her often on her [mouth. He embraced] the other women also, yet they said to him: Why do thou love [her] more than all of us? The Savior replied, he said to them: Why do I not love you as I do her?"

The portrait of Mary Magdalene painted in the Romanized Gospels of the New Testament, and in Catholic legend and myth, is but a weak and adulterated version of the true Miryai who may be worship jointly with Yeshu and Miryam. A more accurate picture of the personality and activities of this female Savioress can be gained by a study of references to Her in surviving Nazorean texts preserved by the Mandaeans, in the Nag Hammadhi Library, and in the Pistis Sophia codex. By deepening our understanding of this very important and pivotal Goddess in the involution and evolution of the universe, we broaden our appreciation for the feminine aspect of Creation, for our Heavenly Mother and all Goddesses above, and for the spiritual women who have or who now bless us with their presence on earth.

An indepth study of the life and times of Miryai can be found in the second volume to this series, entitled: "Buddha-Messiahs, Vol. II: Miryai, the Mysteries of Mary Magdalene".

- 7 -
NAZOREAN MARRIAGE

Jewish Resentment

THERE WAS QUITE A BIT of hostility between the five Jewish sects and the two Gnostic Nazorean Essenes ones. The Jews did not like the Gnostics saying that "Nazoreanism is older than Judaism.", and they especially resented the way the pun loving Nazoreans would slightly misspell Judaism so that it became the word "abortions" in Aramaic. To the Jews, the Nazoreans were everything they hated and feared. Not only did the Nazoreans claim to be older and wiser than the Torah loving Jews, but they had many records and traditions that proved it. No matter how hard they tried to cover it up, the more astute among the Jews knew of the fabrication of their religion in the fifth century BC when the Persians introduced animal sacrificing into Palestine with the return of the exiles under Cyrus. The condemnation ploy of these Persian sponsored texts had not worked well. All the admonitions that these Persian sponsored writers had put into the mouth of their made up prophets had not succeeded in ridding the land of the older and more ancient traditions that revered the Queen of Heaven and other Gods and Goddesses condemned in the new fake Torah texts. When these texts were created, every ill that had ever befallen Israel was blamed on their departure from the Persian Law of Moses. But this law did not even exist in the time period portrayed in these texts.

The simple original oral law was still being kept by the
Nazoreans and Essenes, and the worship of the original Gods
and Goddesses of this Law was still observed as well. The
Jews of the five sects hated this reality and had grown great in
their zeal for their Yahweh and his laws. Despite their late
arrival, they felt superior to those who still observed the old
ways. They felt richer, smarter, and more powerful than those
who eschewed the cities for a higher quality life in small
spiritual communities. This hostility grew more acute during
the days of Yuhana the Baptists great popularity, and was not
helped any when the star Jewish prodigy, Miryai by name,
abandoned her Jewish roots and embraced Nazoreanism. Her
High Priest father Eleazar was furious about this, but even
more furious was one Zatan, known as the pillar. He spread
malicious slander about Miryai and helped fuel the rising
tensions. The oath that some Jews took, to crucify the husband
of Miryai that had stolen her from them, was no doubt fueled
by jealousy of jilted suitors who were disappointed that the
brilliant Miryai had chosen a goddess worshipping Nazorean
over them, even if he did have royal Davidic blood in his
veins. When Miryai was first caught visiting the Nazorean
temple, her parents accused her of being a slut. Miryai denied
this vehemently, but was not believed because of her own
discriminate past and the bad reputation the Nazoreans had in
Jewry as a consequence of their quite different marriage and
mating laws. As Goddess loving people, the Nazoreans had
preserved many of the ancient practices of the land that had
been newly prohibited against in the new Persian mandates.
Although not licentious like the Romans with their orgies and
prostitutes, they nevertheless practiced various forms of
marriage that were condemned in certain puritanical and
hypocritical Jewish circles, as well as most Roman and Greek
circles. These accusations by Zatan against Miryai would
survive down through the ages to fuel the idea that Mary
Magdalene was nothing more than a prostitute out of whom

went seven devils. She may have had seven spirits cast forth from her due to a wild stage she went through, but in the end she became the Apostle to the Apostles and the heir to all the mysteries of the recondite Nazoreans.

Cultic Sexuality

The Nazorean eugenics program, with twelve maidens set aside to conceive prophets according to astrological and other occult factors was a controversial matter, even in ancient times. The additional worship of the Goddess, coupled with many other ancient practices associated with ancient Israel, Canaan and Babylon, no doubt fueled prejudice against the Nazoreans by the more conservative religious establishment of the Second Temple who were convinced that the Nazoreans were still practicing at least some of the things that they themselves had given up. In the Sleeping Prophet material there is a little information about the pre-Christ phase of the Nazoreans. The "need for the gratifying of the bodily forces" that the early Nazoreans are said to have participated in was said to be for the purpose of increasing the depth of physical and spiritual relationships:

> "For, the entity was among those of the Grecian land who journeyed there with those who were of the faith and sect known as the Nazoreans. Not those who later became followers of Jesus of Nazareth, but those that held to the needs for the GRATIFYING of the bodily forces that there might be the greater expression in the material as well as the spiritual relationships. For, literal were the concepts of that sect as to doing to others as others would do to you; not as ye would that men should do to you, do ye even so to them." [246]

---

[246] Text Of Reading 2329-1

Ancient Israel was known to have participated in many cultic sexual practices that were common to almost all ancient temples and high places. These practices continued many centuries after the Jews claimed that their Law of Moses was established in the land in 1280 BCE. Rather than admit the truth that their Law of Moses had not existed in such ancient times, the Jews pretended that it had existed but had been overshadowed by an evil force for over eight centuries until 444 BC. According to Rabbinic tradition this pretended dominant evil force was called the "instinct of idolatry". According to Rabbinic tradition, this "instinct of idolatry" was not eradicated until well after the influx of peoples from Persia which began in 539 BC. A Talmud account states it continued to live in the Temple itself, where it had always lived, until Nehemiah's 445 BC reforms. After this time the new Jewish sects created by the Persians began blaming all Israel's past woes on this "instinct". They then encoded this blame in newly created biblical books which they postdated to an earlier time. They labeled the ancient religion of Judea, both its good and bad forms, as something evil and then claimed that their new Persian one was in fact the older ancient one they sought to destroy. After they gained control of the Temple, they even claimed and that the willingness of the Judeans to cast it out of their Temple worship was rewarded by a Tablet of Truth falling down from heaven.

This Tablet of Truth was none other than the Persian created Law of Moses that Tavish or Ezra wrote under the direction of King Cyrus and read to the Israelites for the first time in 444 BC. The legend of this Tablet states that the spirit of idolatry actually exited the holy of holies chamber of the Temple, indicating that the temple itself was its ancient center previous to 445BC.

In Nazorean tradition preserved by the Mandai, the author of the Old Testament is said to be Tavish. Yet it is Ezra who is credited, by Jewish tradition, with the compilation (but not authorship) of the books of the Old Testament. Tavish may be a title of Ezra, or perhaps the inspiration behind Ezra's work.

In the ancient apocryphal account of 2nd Esdras, or 4th Ezra, the books of the Old Testament are not only said to be put together by Ezra, but actually "channeled", or written by him! If this account is not historically accurate, it is at least allegorically correct in its assertion that some redactor, about the time of Ezra, wrote down a hodge podge of religious traditions and cultic practices and called it the "Law of Moses" In this account Ezra laments that there is no existing Law, for all copies of it have been burnt or destroyed upon his return to the land of Palestine. His solution to this situation is to simply write a new one. Ezra had not been raised with the Law, for he and all his generation had grown up in exile in Babylon where animals were sacrificed as a form of worship. Had his generation possessed copies of the true Law during their exile, Ezra would not have said that no copies had survived. With no firsthand knowledge of the ancient Law of Moses, or because he rejected the original oral one in favor of a new Persian inspired law, Ezra was forced to write a new and different Law based on his own experiences in exile. Ezra called this new law the "Law of Moses" and pretended it was actually an old law. Ezra's "new law" was no doubt based partially on older oral tradition, and perhaps even included scraps of earlier written material, but its main core of animal sacrifice was most certainly not part of the original Law of Moses. Here is Ezra's account of his channeled writing that so much of the world has gullibly accepted:

> "For the world lies in darkness, and its inhabitants are without light. For thy law has been burned, and so no one knows the things which have been done or will be done by thee. If then I

have found favor before thee, send the Holy Spirit into me, and I will write everything that has happened in the world from the beginning, the things which were written in thy law, that men may be able to find the path, and that those who wish to live in the last days may live." He answered me and said, "Go and gather the people, and tell them not to seek you for forty days. But prepare for yourself many writing tablets, and take with you Sarea, Dabria, Selemia, Ethanus, and Asiel -- these five, because they are trained to write rapidly; and you shall come here, and I will light in your heart the lamp of understanding, which shall not be put out until what you are about to write is finished. And when you have finished, some things you shall make public, and some you shall deliver in secret to the wise; tomorrow at this hour you shall begin to write." [247]

With these reforms and changes brought about by the Persian henchmen and their pseudipigraphic forgeries, there came a disdain and condemnation toward all the people of the land (am ha-aretz) and all the Nazoreans who kept a higher and more refined version of these ancient practices alive. Some of these reforms were no doubt needed, for many corruptions and abuses of sacred sexuality no doubt occurred in Israel, as they had in other lands. Among the Nazoreans, however, a pure form was preserved in their sacred Mount Carmel Temple.

Nazorean Disdain

There is some indication of Jewish disdain for Essenes found in the Nazorean scroll of Yuhana (John the Baptist) when Miryai if forced to face and refute some of these charges at the time of her conversion. The term used is "Zubia", which the scholar Pallis defines as referring specifically to ancient sexual temple rites. This term is found in the Mandaean Book of John

---

[247] Apocrypha Account of 4 Ezra 14,15

the Baptist in three places. Pallis, in his Mandaean Studies, comments that when:

> "... Miryai refutes the Jewish accusations of adultery, exclaiming: "lAn AtuAt AnA dnipkit lzubiA"; that this does not refer to some casual erotic intrigue is evident."

He also comments on another passage dealing with similar issues:

> ...it is evident that to the Mandaeans the chief point was to refute the Jewish accusations of unchaste cults. To me, then, there is no doubt that zubia was widely spread among the Mandaeans, for the defense against accusations from abroad that we find in the Mandaean writings is a sure proof . .." [248]

We are not suggesting here that the ancient Nazorean-Mandaeans were sacrificed their chastity to the Nazorean Goddess with strangers, like Herodotus said the Babylonian daughters did to Mylitta. What we are suggesting is that twelve temple maidens, or vines, were set apart as Priestesses to the Goddess and charged with the honor of conceiving children perfect in their generation with very select and well regulated male counterparts. They were probably closer to the Vestal Virgins of Rome than to the Qadashim prostitutes of the ancient Jerusalem temple. In the Readings we are told that the "wedding of Mary and Joseph" was "In the Temple there at Carmel." [249] The Jewish misunderstanding of these things, and their own checkered past and hypocritical present, caused them to accuse the Nazoreans of engaging in an unchaste sex cult. All Gnostics have faced these same accusations down through history. They became especially numerous when Roman Christianity came to influence, and still continue to this day.

---

[248] Pallis in Mandaean Studies, p14-17
[249] Cayce 5749-8)

Monogamy vs. Polygamy

In the Cayce Readings the subject of monogamy vs. polygamy is addressed, and this has some relevance to the Carmel Eugenics program and the relationship of Miryai to Yeshu. Because this is such a controversial subject to many westerners, this reading from Cayce seems warranted:

> (Q) Is monogamy the best form of home relationship?
> (A) Let the teachings be rather toward the spiritual intent. Whether it's monogamy, polygamy, or what not, let it be the answering of the spiritual WITHIN the individual!

> Q) Would it be better for a woman, who desires to marry, to be one of two or more wives to a man in a home rather than to remain unmarried?
> (A) This is again a matter of PRINCIPLE; or the urge within such conditions must be conformative to that set as the ideal.
> In the education of individuals as regarding sex relationships, as in every other educational activity, there must be a standard or a rule to go by or an ideal state that has its inception not in the emotions of a physical body but from the spiritual ideal which has been set, which was set and given to man in his relation to the Creative Forces.

Most modern westerners consider themselves enlightened in comparison to other cultures who endorse polygamy, but for the most part westerners do not do much better, entering a string of serial relationships based on "the emotions of a physical body", failing in common practice to uphold their myth of the monogamous couple. The Christian bias against polygamy goes back to its early days. Justin Martyr (c160) rebuked the Jews when he said:

> "You imprudent and blind masters even until this time permit each man to have four or five wives."

Both Greek and Roman societies at the time of Yeshu tended to practice monogamy and denounce multiple spouses, as did the Dead Sea Scroll Sect and school of Hillel. The school of Shammai, however, along with most of the remaining residents and sects of Palestine accepted polygamy. Josephus spoke of polygamy and concubines among the aristocracy and Herod the Great was known to have had ten wives. The Nazoreans of Yeshu were known to have practiced polygamy and to have even required it of their higher Priesthood officers. The practice of allowing woman, as well as men, to have more than one spouse was where the Nazoreans got into disputes with the other sects.

Polyandry among Nazoreans

The most poignant and well documented account of polygamy among Nazoreans is that of Yuhana (John the Baptist). He married both Anhar and Qintat and had at least eight children. The lifestyle of Yuhana and Yeshu would have been very close, if not identical. In his book we read of his struggle to marry his first wife Anhar:

"Yahya (John) proclaims in evenings the nights, Yuhana (John) on the night's eves. Yahya proclaims in the nights and speaks. (The heavenly) wheels and chariots quaked. Sun and Moon weep, and the eyes of Ruha shed tears. He says: Yahya, thou art like to a scorched mountain, which brings forth no grapes in this world. Thou art like to a dried up stream, on whose banks no plants are raised. Thou hast become a, land without a lord, a house without worth.

A false prophet hast thou become, who hast left no one to remember thy name. Who will provide thee with provision, who with victuals, and who will follow to the grave after thee?

When Yahya heard this, a tear gathered in his eye; a tear in his eye gathered, and he spake: It would be pleasant to take a wife, and delightful for me to have children. But what if I take a woman, and then comes sleep, desire for her seizes me and I neglect my night-prayer? What if desire wakes in me, and I forget my Lord out of my mind? What if desire wakes in me, and I neglect my prayer every time? When Yahya said this, there came a Letter (communication) from the House of Abathur: Yahya take a wife and found a family, and see that thou dost not let this world come to an end. On the night of Monday and on the night of Tuesday go to thy first bedding. On the night of Wednesday and on the night of Thursday devote thyself to thy hallowed praying. On the night of Friday and on the night of Saturday go to thy first bedding. On the night of Habshabba (first weekday) and yea on Day's Eve devote thyself to thy hallowed praying. On Habshabba take three and leave three, take three and leave three. See that thou dost not let the world come to an end. Thereon they fashioned for Yahya a wife out of thee, thou "Region of the Faithful". From the first conception were Handan and Sharrath born. From the middle conception were Birham and Rhimath-Haya born. From the last conception were Nsab, Sam, Anhar-Ziwa and Sharrath born. These three conceptions took place in thee, thou ruins, Jerusalem."[250]

This "Region of the Faithful" may refer to the Carmel eugenics program where brides for prophetic men were birthed and trained.

Among ancient religious leaders and Apostles of Light there are many instances of multiple marriage partners. Zardoz (Zarathustra) had three wives, Shenrab Miwo, the original Buddha had six spouses[251], Yuhana was married to two woman named Anhar & Qinta, and Yeshu was said to have been married to Miryai among others. One writer in the early

---

[250] Sidra dYahya, Book of John the Baptist from Mandaic Doctrines of Kings

[251] Hoza Gyelmed, dPo bza thang mo, gSas bza ngan ring, Phywa bza gung drug, Kong bza khriicam, and rgya bza phrul bsgyur.

1800's, who may have had access to a more complete copy of Celsus' arguments that is not now available, wrote:

> "The grand reason why the gentiles and philosophers of his school persecuted Jesus Christ was because he had so many wives; there were Elizabeth and Mary and a host of others that followed him." [252]

We know that the great Vajrayana master Padmasambhava had many mates and that his female counterpart, Yeshay Tsogyal, who was probably a reincarnation of Miryai, had more than one partner as is customary for advanced female adepts in the Tibetan tradition. There were many others.

There is no such thing in Nazoreanism as a celibate Angel, God, or Redeemer. A Nazorean oral tradition states:

> "If a man has no wife, there will be no paradise for him hereafter and no paradise on earth". [253]

It is also an ancient Nazorean custom for those in the Priesthood to have more than one mate:

> "A man may marry as many wives as his means allow..." [254]

E.S. Drower also observed that among modern Mandaean remnants of the ancient Nazoreans, around 1935, multiple marriages were still quite common. She states:

> "I have noticed, however, that most priests have had at one time two or more wives." [255]

Roman Love of Monogamy

[252] Jedidiah Grant, Journal of Discourses
[253] from Mandaeans of Iraq & Iran, pg 59
[254] from Mandaeans of Iraq & Iran, pg 59
[255] from Mandaeans of Iraq & Iran, pg 59

Plurality of wives was not an issue among Nazoreans and some other Jewish sects of Palestine, but for Romans who are credited for championing monogamy in the ancient world, it was a serious issue.

It is said that Romulus, the founder of Rome, was the leader of a band of outlaws who captured some Sabian woman who came to the river to bathe and wash clothes. After they enslaved these women, they made a law against any man having too many wives while others had none at all. It was called monogamy as is the first instance of any such law to enforce that system of marriage. When Rome became powerful they continued to promote this practice. Since the Roman government was officially an advocate of monogamy, the Roman Christians who leaned on her for support were forced to adopt this practice as well. Nazoreans, unbound by any pact with Rome, continued their ancient practices. Two early Roman writers, Tertullian (c207) and Methodius (c290) both expressed the growing Roman Church's abhorrence of polygamy.

Most western views on marriage are derived from the Roman, via Roman Christianity. It is of interest that Romans were known as advocates of celibacy and monogamy, but practitioners of drunken orgies, state sponsored brothels, and other sexually promiscuous practices.

Nazorean Celibacy Stance

Romans and Roman Christians held celibacy in high esteem and considered all natural acts of the body to be dirty to one degree or another. Essenes only thought the natural acts deplorable when they were not under the control of the mind and higher instincts. Nazoreans were opposed to celibacy and believed that anyone born childless would pass through purgatorial worlds, rest a while in the Light Land, and then be reincarnated on earth to try again. This attitude is also reflected in the oral tradition preserved by the Mandaean remnants of the ancient Nazoreans, and by Cayce readings on the Essenes which say:

> "Q) Did I take the vows of celibacy?
> (A) They didn't take the vows of celibacy! Not to have children during those periods was considered to be ones not thought of by God!"[256]

The Mandaeans remnants of the Nazoreans have preserved the ancient Nazorean stance on celibacy. They worshipped "Life" and had no patience for life long celibacy. They considered human sexuality a holy and a natural affair:

> "Sex to the pious Mandaean is the holiest mystery of life and it is enjoined upon him to regard it as such and to pronounce the most sacred name, 'the great Life', before performing a sexual act. Continence is praised but celibacy is an unnatural and unholy state, condemned in the GR, especially in polemical passages referring to monasteries and convents." [257]

Ancient Rome had a system of special temple vows of celibacy for a group of virgins known as the "Vestal Virgins". After a period of celibacy and tending the sacred temple fire, they were allowed to marry. This system was operational even in the days of Yeshu. The founding fathers of Rome were said to have been born from one of these virgins. Originally there had been two, and then four and eventually six virgins served in the temple. Other ancient nations and peoples had similar systems, including the Nazoreans. The Vestal Virgins of the

---

[256] Text Of Reading 2175-6
[257] The Secret Adam by Drower, p 10

Nazorean Temple on Mount Carmel were twelve in number, and were called "vines".

> "I ascended thee, Mount Carmel, Thee I ascended, Mount Carmel. Twelve vines awaited me: They saw me, the vines beheld me! When they saw me the vines waxed great, Their foliage they spread out." [258]

As mentioned before, their purpose was to preserve certain bloodlines and to conceive special souls who could be raised as prophets and prophetesses.

3 Year Trial

Josephus speaks of the Nazorean Essene three year trial marriages practices when he writes:

> "Moreover, there is another order of Essenes, who agree with the rest as to their way of living, and customs, and laws, but differ from them in the point of marriage, as thinking that by not marrying they cut off the principal part of human life, which is the prospect of succession; nay, rather, that if all men should be of the same opinion, the whole race of mankind would fail. However, they try their spouses for three years; and if they find that they have their natural purgations thrice, as trials that they are likely to be fruitful, they then actually marry them. But they do not use to accompany with their wives when they are with child, as a demonstration that they do not marry out of regard to pleasure, but for the sake of posterity."[259]

Nazorean Essenes had three year probationary betrothal-marriages because once married, they seldom divorced. They used astrology to help determine suitable companions, and the three year trial to insure that a perfect match had occurred.

[258] The Canonical Prayerbook of the Mandaeans (Leiden: Brill, 1959). ES Drower
[260] Josephus (Wars 2)

This great care in forming a marriage must be understood in the context of Nazorean culture. In a society where such great unity existed among all members, marriage was seen as an arrangement to bring children into the world. It was not seen like a nuclear family, for the whole group helped rear and support the children, as the African proverb states: "It takes a whole village to raise a child." Nazoreans, "having all things in common", had a different understanding than do many moderns on the institution of marriage. Marriage was a child conceiving instrument that was not connected to other issues like love, sex, money, and shelter as it is in the modern dysfunctional world. It was a spiritual calling to engage in a sacred activity according to rules of eugenics, done for the sake of the future of the people, not personal indulgence or fulfillment. Sexuality could be personal, but conception was a political act of the Voluntas Communis, or common will of the monastery.

Weddings

In the Readings we are told that the "wedding of Mary and Joseph" was "In the Temple there at Carmel."[260] This was a special type of marriage, but all Nazorean marriages had similar elements. They were always conducted using the couple's spiritual names (*Malwasha*). The couple's astrology charts would have been compared and the stars studied for an auspicious time for the ceremony. Both couples were baptized twice by someone who themselves had been twice immersed. The ceremony itself was conducted on the first day of the week (*Habshaba*). The ceremony is always conducted in white temple clothes (*rasta*) and within a temple (*mandi*) with the use of white veils hung from ropes of red and green. Eight small clay tablets marked with circles divided by a cross and four

[260] Cayce 5749-8

dots in each quadrant are also used for the sacramental food. Two altar trays are also used, one with fruits and nuts and the other with a pitcher of water.

The first phase of the ceremony is the blessing of a basket containing both their clothes, then the investing of the bridegroom with an iron blade and talisman and the bride with a red stoned ring on her right little finger, and a green on her left. They then have their hands washed and they are blessed before the bridegroom is led into the bridal chamber whilst a clay pot is broken over a millstone. A ritual meal in memory of departed ancestors (*Zidka Brikha*) is then performed and the bride and groom break and eat a special consecrated bread roll filled with fruit.

Other ceremonies and prayers ensue, including the donning of myrtle wreaths intertwined with white thread and smeared with saffron, and the ceremonial drinking of seven bowls of wine (*hamra*) before the couple is placed back to back and their heads are knocked together three times. Marriage hymns are sung and eventually the Ganzibra priest waves his staff over them three times, ending the wedding. The honeymoon lasts at least one week and is followed by special baptisms and prayers. Nazorean marriage rituals are patterned after the cosmic marriage of Shishlam Rba and Ezlat and to a lesser extent on those of Hibil-Ziwa and Zahariel, and have many beautiful blessings and songs that are too lengthy to include here. Yeshu would have participated in all these rites despite Roman Paulinity's unfounded conviction that he was a celibate. Even their fabricated scriptures do not say Yeshu was unmarried. It is curious that Christianity conceives of their Jesus being celibate without a shred of Biblical support to base it on.

Sex Drive Origins

Roman Christians and many of their offshoots consider the sexual drive to be an evil thing. They seem to view it as a necessary evil whose only purpose is to create children. The Nazorean felt differently. Peter tells us:

> "And let them inculcate marriage not only upon the young, but also upon those advanced in years, lest burning lust bring a plague upon the Church by reason of whoredom or adultery. For, above every other sin, the wickedness of adultery is hated by God, because it not only destroys the person himself who sins, but those also who eat and associate with him. For it is like the madness of a dog, because it has the nature of communicating its own madness. For the sake of chastity, therefore, let not only the elders, but even all, hasten to accomplish marriage. For the sin of him who commits adultery necessarily comes upon all. Therefore, to urge the brethren to be chaste, this is the first charity. For it is the healing of the soul. For the nourishment of the body is rest." [261]

Peter is very clear that this is not just a way to deal with an evil urge, for in the following he tells us that the sexual urge is healthy and good when reasonably controlled, and this same view is held in the ancient Qulasta hymns that Yeshu sung:

> For lust has, by the will of Him who created all things well, been made to arise within the living being, that, led by it to intercourse, he may increase humanity, from a selection of which a multitude of superior beings arise who are fit for eternal life."

> "But if it were not for lust, no one would trouble himself with intercourse with his wife; but now, for the sake of pleasure, and, as it were, gratifying himself, man carries out His will. Now, if a man uses lust for lawful marriage, he does not act impiously; but

---

[261] Clementine Homilies

if he rushes to adultery, he acts impiously, and he is punished because he makes a bad use of a good ordinance." [262]

Peter next explains that the urge is not evil, only its misuse:

"Wherefore God is not evil, who has rightly placed lust within man, that there may be a continuance of life, but they are most impious who have used the good of lust badly. The same considerations apply to anger also, that if one uses it righteously, as is within his power, he is pious; but going beyond measure, and taking judgment to himself, he is impious." [263]

Nazorean Sexuality

Because the subject of sexuality is so highly charged, and because prejudice against it has been so strong in Christian circles, it may be wise to explain in detail the ancient Essene attitude toward it.

Sexuality, according to Nazorean doctrine, is a natural and normal urge whose ultimate source is the highest heaven, as stated by Qulasta 213. These urges are to be understood as affecting five diverse levels. All acts, including intimate ones, should be understood in regards to how they affect the Flesh (*Pagra*), the Instincts (*Napsha*), the Emotions (*Ruha*), the Mind (*Mana*), and the Spirit (*Nishimta*). Sexuality, according to Yeshu's Order, can be either a positive or negative experience depending on the motivations and conditions in which it is carried out. As a Gnostic, rather than Judeo-Christian, branch of Christianity, Nazorean Essenes has a positive but careful attitude toward sexuality. They taught that the wise use of the sexual urges may increase ones spirituality and closeness to Heavenly Parents and Their children here on earth, but they

---

[262] Clementine Homilies

[263] Clementine Homilies

also recognizes that sexuality, when abused and misused, leads to alienation from Deity, others, and even oneself.

Sexuality is a powerful tool that should be understood and used only with the utmost care and responsibility. It is expressed most appropriately and perfectly in Holy Order marriage, but other expressions are not necessarily evil and sinful if they do not involve deceit or irresponsible behavior. Yeshu taught that sexuality, in and of itself, is neither good nor evil. How it is used, and how it affects oneself and others is the criteria for judging its harm or helpfulness. Gnostics never condemned loving intimacy to the same extent as is found in normative Judeo-Christian traditions. The Order did, however, severely frown on expressions of sexuality that cause hurt, pain, disease, breakup of marriages, unwanted pregnancies, deceit and betrayal. There can never be any excuse for such consequences for we are ultimately responsible for how our actions affect ourselves and others. Indiscriminate and unwise sexuality can affect the five levels of being in the following way:

- Flesh (*Pagra*) - In unwise sexuality the flesh experiences short lived pleasure but possibly contracts fatal or debilitating diseases in the process. Unwanted pregnancy may result leading to hardship, resort to abortions, or family or social ostracization.
- Instincts (*Napsha*) - In unwise sexuality the sexual appetite and desire for unwholesome sexual contact is increased, and the instincts are conditioned and habitualized to self indulgence and possibly self destructive behavior. Repulsion and unrational hatred can also result.
- Emotions (*Ruha*) - In unwise sexuality the emotional capacity to love and bond in an enduring and beautiful manner is short circuited, and through continual engagement in lower forms of sexuality the heart grows cold and incapable of experiencing true love and affection. Others may become simply sex objects devoid of personality. Human interaction

can become predatorial and devoid of human warmth and caring.

- Mind (*Mana*) - In unwise sexuality the mind fails to find companionship and eventually tends to shut down and let the lower instincts take over more and more.
- Spirit (*Nishimta*) - In unwise sexuality the purity of the Pearl Soul is severely tainted and the gulf between the spirit and its Heavenly parents grows more and more faint. Alienation from others practicing more compassionate and caring behavior can increase. Guilt can riddle the person and cause despair.

Compassionate and wise sexuality can affect these five levels in the following way:

- Flesh (*Pagra*) - In wise sexuality the flesh experiences revitalizing pleasure which leads to vibrant health and possible wanted and wise pregnancy which perpetuates ones genes and provides opportunity for service and character building through rewarding family life.
- Instincts (*Napsha*) - In wise sexuality the sexual appetite and desire for wholesome sexual contact is increased, and the instincts are conditioned and habitualized to positive and caring expression. The repeated expressions of desire within marital intimacy builds mutual bonds of trust and concern.
- Emotions (*Ruha*) - In wise sexuality the emotional capacity to love and bond in an enduring and beautiful manner is developed, and through continual engagement in loving forms of sexuality the heart grows warmer and ever more capable of experiencing true love and affection. Family unity increases and the backdrop for caring home life increases.
- Mind (*Mana*) - In wise sexuality the mind finds comradely and companionship which eventually transcends limitations of the flesh and lower instincts, setting the stage for a more eternal bond of love and companionship.
- Spirit (*Nishimta*) - In wise sexuality the purity of the Pearl Soul is enhanced and the unity and harmony between opposites grows more and more profound, and the eternal

spirit moves ever closer to merger with the Living Soul that
transcends all duality.

Three of the thirty two points of the Manichaean Confession
address the misuse of sexuality:

> IX. If, O Great Life, we have sinned in any way against the
> Living Self by dishonoring the marriage bonds between
> Listeners, or the Sealings between married Monastics, or if we
> have weakened a holy union between any two souls or tempted
> them to separation or be unfaithful to their vows, and if we have
> weakened the unity of any quorum, or brought disharmony to
> any monastery or household in any fashion - then we now, O
> Great Life, pray to be forgiven.
> XVIII. If, O Great Life, we have sinned in any way to keep the
> dark and light separate, if we have mixed with the wrong type of
> people, or mixed low desires with higher ideals, or if we have
> created a wedge between good people or weakened the
> solidarity of the pure - then we now, O Great Life, pray to be
> forgiven.
> XXXI. If, O Great Life, we have sinned in any way against Yeshu
> the Sun God and Miryai the Moon Goddess, or have sought to
> misuse the allure of their light to improperly seduce or captivate
> others, or have mismanaged the attraction between male and
> female in any shape or fashion - then we now, O Great Life, pray
> to be forgiven.

Ɱultiple Ɱarriage Partners

The rational for this practice lies in the fact that Nazoreans do
not marry the body, but the soul of another, Since Nazoreans
have lived many lives on earth, they have also married many
times during those various incarnations. Nazoreans do not
marry another only until death, as the common modern
marriage formula states: "until death do they part". Nazoreans
seek to marry for eternity on a deep and enduring soul level.
Granted, marriage may begin only on the physical level, but if

it does not progress more deeply to encompass the Napsha, Ruha, and Nishimta levels, it is considered a dead marriage by Nazoreans. If, however, a bond of love and unity develop between two souls on these deeper levels, it cannot be severed by demise of the flesh. It transcends death and continues into other lives. Since we have lived many lives and may have many souls mates as a consequence, our present incarnation may entail a reuniting with one or more of our former partners. If this happens then a deep knowing and familiarity may arise upon meeting such a one, or shortly thereafter.

Ones former marriage partner may be in a different body, but their soul is the same. In light of this situation a person may be married to many others, on a deeper and more real soul level, even though they are not aware of such in their present incarnation. Their lack of knowledge does not negate the fact of their spiritual bond with another or others. Thus many may be polygamous without even knowing it. If these individuals are encountered in ones present life, and one abides within the Nazorean Covenant that acknowledges such situations, then it is not forbidden for one to acknowledge this fact. It is forbidden, however, to engage in physical intimacies with such a one without consent of ones present spouse. Marriage on a deeper soul level does not give one the right to be physical with them unless ones present physical mate, or mates, is in full support of such. If ones physical spouse okays the reunion of a long lost spouse, it cannot be adultery. This concept is explained in the Suddi revelations which say:

> "Adultery would be to lie with another and not openly with approval. If it were something that had been discussed between the two, and it was decided upon, then this would be acceptable. The whole idea of adultery was very strange. For did not Abraham have two wives? Therefore, if it was not accepted by Sarah that he have another wife, would he not also be an adulterer?"

A reunion with a former spouse would be wrong if entered into on a physical level without full approval, as Suddi also states:

> "To hide this, to seek to make a fool out of the other party. Adultery is, in the case where everyone knows but the one who is being hurt the most. If it is discussed and openly agreed upon, this cannot be adultery. This is just a different type of sharing. It has also been misrepresented for many, many years." [264]

Are such multiple relationships practical? Usually not, for only very advanced and mature souls can transcend the instinctual urges of jealousy and possessiveness upon which worldly marriages operate. Those who feel called to these special types of spiritual bonding are forced to rise above their lower instincts and abide in a state of continual compassion, patience and awareness that is beyond the normal range of more base souls.

The ancient Essenes did not condemn those who sought to enter into such unusual expressions of love under the proper circumstances, but the Order did warn its members to only do so after great amounts of prayer and reflection and only with the total approval of all who are involved or who have a stake in such relationships. For those who are filled with the wisdom of Miryam and the compassion of Yeshu, such relationships can generate a form of divine and holy love beyond the reach of those who only know more worldly forms of union. Such unions are best pursued among Monastics who have many tools at their disposal that enable them to transcend their lower nature and more base instincts. All others should be extremely hesitant to even consider such unusual forms of marriage.

---

[264] Suddi Revelations

Sexuality among Gnostics

Here are the views of two great second-century A.D. Gnostic teachers, Valentinus and Basilides, on Marriage. Taken from Book 3 of the *Stomateis* of Clement of Alexandria:

> "The sect of Valentinus justify physical union from heaven from divine emanations, and approve of marriage. The followers of Basilides say that when the apostles enquired whether it was not better to refrain from marriage, the Lord answered, "It is not everyone who can accept this saying: some are eunuchs from birth, others from necessity." They explain the saying something as follows. Some men have from birth a physical aversion in relation to women. They follow their physical make-up and do well not to marry. These, they say, are the eunuchs from birth."[265]

The Roman Christian Clement goes on to accuse the Basilides of being promiscuous, and then gives his own false views, saying:

> "I must tell you our people's view of the matter. We bless abstention from sexual intercourse and those to whom it comes as a gift of God. We admire monogamy and respect for one marriage and one only. We say that we ought to share in suffering and "bear one another's burdens," for fear that anyone who thinks he is standing firmly should in fact fall. It is about second marriages that the Apostle says, "If you are on fire, get married." [266]

Nazoreans and their Gnostic descendants continued many ancient marriage practices. Iranaeus (c180), like Clement after him, also condemned some Gnostics for these practices when he said:

---

[265] Book 3 of the *Stomateis* of Clement of Alexandria

[266] Book 3 of the *Stomateis* of Clement of Alexandria

"Others again, following upon Basilides and Carpocrates, have introduced promiscuous intercourse and a plurality of wives."

He accused them of introducing something that in reality had existed long before them.

Christians have long pretended to have some sort of moral high ground in regards to sexuality and have been quick to accuse the Gnostic sects of impropriety. Much of these accusations are misconstrued or outright false but at the heart of the matter there was a very real difference between Christians and Nazoreans. Both engaged in intimacies, but Christians considered their own to be vile whereas Nazoreans considered theirs to be a holy form of worship of the Goddess above. This was the real problem that the Christians had with the Gnostics – the spiritualization of the sexual urge.

- 8 -
Yuhana the Baptist

Pre-Life of Yuhana

BOTH YESHU AND Yuhana dMasbuta were known as "Nazoreans". They were called Nazoreans because the customs and practices of the Nazoreans were a significant part of their message and teachings. By carefully studying ancient historians, modern anthropologists and seers who have spoken of these Nazoreans, we can reconstruct many ancient Nazorean customs and traditions which formed such a significant part of the original message of Yeshu and Yuhana.

According to the sleeping seer, the Nazorean Order was revitalized by the teachings of Yuhana, or John the Baptist. It is probable that Yuhana taught for seven years before his death, baptizing Yeshu for the final time just before he, Yuhana, was beheaded by Herod. Yuhana was one of the heads of the Nazorean Order and spent most of his time in Bethany Beyond Jordan, which is a few miles north of Qumran in ancient Israel.

A teaching of Yeshu of the reincarnation of Yuhana can be found in the seventh book of the Pistis Sophia (an ancient Manichaean text dated to the 3rd century or earlier). In it we read:

"Now it happened that when I came into the midst of the archons of the aeons, I looked down at the world of mankind, at the command of the First Mystery. I found Elisabeth, the mother of John the Baptist , before she had conceived him and I cast into her a power which I had received from the Little Jao , the Good, who is in the Midst, so that he should be able to preach before me, and prepare my way and baptize with water of forgiveness . Now that power was in the body of John. And again, in place of the soul of the archons which he was due to receive, I found the soul of the prophet Elias in the aeons of the sphere; and I took it in and I took his soul again; I brought it to the Virgin of the Light, and she gave it to her paralemptors. They brought it to the sphere of the archons, and they cast it into the womb of Elisabeth. But the power of the Little Jao, he of the Midst, and the soul of the prophet Elias were bound in the body of John the Baptist. You doubted now at the time when I spoke to you because John said : 'I am not the Christ' and you said to me : 'It is written in the scripture : when the Christ shall come, there will come Elias before him and he will prepare his way'. But when you said this to me, I said to you : 'Elias has indeed come and he has prepared all things, as it is written : And they did to him as they pleased. And when I knew that you did not understand what I said to you concerning the soul of Elias, which was bound in John the Baptist, I answered you openly in speech, face to face, saying : 'If it pleases you to accept John the Baptist, he is Elias of whom I have said that he will come'".[267]

Liliuk

Edgar Cayce tells us that the Essenes on Mount Carmel were begun by Elijah who is generally dated to the ninth century BC. The name Liliuk shows up in some ancient Nazorean texts as an Order, or person, on Mt Carmel proficient at interpreting dreams. We feel this is a reference to the founder of the Essenoi movement in Palestine who is called Elijah in the Jewish Bible. In commenting on this mentioning of "Liliuk" in the Mandaean Book of John the Baptist, Mead writes:

> "This is most probably Elijah (the Eliyahū of the O.T.); I owe this illuminating conjecture to Dr. M. Gaster. Is there here also a hidden reference to an existing 'School of the Prophets'? [268]

It seems wise to shy away from using the name Elijah, since Liliuk seems to have been his original name according to Mandaic texts. The story of Elijah in the Bible also contains a bloodthirsty element which we doubt Liliuk, the original inspiration of the story, had. We feel it likely that the writers of the Old Testament simply reworked a general Liliuk oral tradition, changing his name to make it appear the God (El) he worshipped (i) was Jah (jah)[269], and attributing to him the slaughter of the prophets of Baal. It is interesting that even though they have him killing Baalites, which Liliuk would not have done even if he disagreed with them, it amazingly has him leaving the Priestesses of Ashereah alone, thus showing his toleration, if not outright acceptance, of their presence on

---

[267] Pistis Sophia, Ch 7
[268] Gnostic John the Baptizer: Selections from the Mandæan John-Book by G. R. S. Mead
[269] El + i + jah = Elijah

Carmel. It is even possible to conjecture that his wives were priestesses of Asherah who assisted him in establishing the eugenics program on Mount Carmel.

This Elijah, or Liliuk, is associated with two springs in the Levant – one on Carmel in Wadi Siah, and another in Bethany Beyond Jordan. Both these locales are associated with the Nazoreans and with both Yeshu and Yuhana. Liliuk seems to have founded communities in both these locations. Eventually a Nazorean Monastery developed in both locales.

Lulaitha

We know, from ancient Nazorean texts, that Yuhana was married to Anhar and Qintat when he incarnated 2000 years ago. We also know, from these same records, that Yeshu said that Yuhana was an incarnation of Liliuk, or Elijah from almost 900 years before. In his previous incarnation as Liliuk, Yuhana would have been accompanied by Anhar and possibly Qintat. There is no mention of a name for the female companions of Elijah preserved in history, but Nazoreanism preserved the tradition of one Lulaitha who is associated with midwifery and child nurturing. With the Carmel emphasis on eugenics, and with its origins with Liliuk and his female companion or companions, it is reasonable to suppose that this Lulaitha name associated with midwifery goes all the way back to the very origins of the Order and to at least one of Liliuk's female companions.

The names of both Liliuk and Lulaitha are based on the LIL formula that is traceable as far back as Summer. Lilith and Allah and Allat are all based on this same Semitic root of LIL. Many names in later Nazorean and Jewish writings end with "il", again referring to the ancient Semitic concept of El, or Alaha, meaning God. Elohim is one popular name of Deity that survived with positive associations in Jewish writings. The name Lilith, however, came to represent everything evil and disgusting in Jewish folklore. In ancient Nazorean texts, however, she is often depicted as a helpful midwife. It is this nurturing aspect of Lilith or Lulaitha that Nazoreans venerate and not the baby stealing Lilith demon of later Jewish folklore. This attempt to demonize the image of Lilith was perhaps an attempt to demonize all ancient Goddess adoring cultures, Nazoreans included. It should be understood that the references to Lilith in Nazorean scrolls are in no way a condoning of the new age attitude of honoring one's "dark side". Nazirutha teaches subjection and control of the baser instincts, dark side, and drives within humanity.

As adopting midwives and nurses of consecrated Temple children, the office of Lilith, or Lulaitha, in Nazoreanism were despised by the Jewish sect. If any child ever came up missing in Jewish circles, the Nazoreans were the first to be accused for possibly stealing children for their eugenics program. Of course the peace loving respectful Nazorean midwives would never do such things, but over time hatred fermented this crude suspicion into a belief that even when a child dies, it must have been black magic on the part of Nazoreans who made it happen. Some of this misunderstanding is understandable, since the term Lilith was a very ancient one associated with dark forces in some circles, but the real reason was rivalry and xenophobia, or the fear or demonization of other peoples and creeds. The Greeks accused the Jews of it, the Romans accused the Christians, and Christians accused the Jews and the Nazoreans. A supposedly Christian group called the "Minunei" was even accused of eating Jewish children:

> "They kill a Jewish child, they take his blood, they cook it in bread and they proffer it to them as food." [270]

---

[270] Ginza Rba 9.1

There is a lot of nonsense in ancient records that must be sifted through to arrive at the truth.

Birth of Yuhana

In the 16 chapters of the ancient Aramaic Book of John one can read the original Nazorean version of this great prophet and his prophetess companions. It begins with prophetic dreams and celestial portents surrounding his birth and a prophecy delivered by Liliuk that John will destroy the Torah, or fake Jewish Law –

> "Woe unto you, Mistress Torah, for Yuhana shall be born in Jerusalem."

This, of course, upsets the Jewish priests and they went to Yuhana's mother to try to convince her to raise him Jewish. They knew she would raise him a Nazorean instead when she said that she would give him the name the Great Life had given him. The Great Life (*Hiya Rba*) was the God and Goddess of the Nazoreans that the Yahweh worshipping Jews hated:

> "the name Yahya-Yuhana will I give him, the name which Life's own self has given unto him."

They then plotted to kill him, but Anush rescued him and took him away to the school of the prophets, to Mount Parwan where little ones on holy drinks are reared up. It is said in Nazorean oral legends that Yuhana was raised there by Lulaitha:

"Anush 'Uthra sent a woman named Sofan Lulaitha to tend him."[271]

We would interpret this to mean that Yuhana was raised by Sofan, one of the Temple Priestesses (Lulaitha) descended from the foundress of Carmel. Yuhana tells us that:

"There I abode until I was two and twenty years old. I learned there the whole of my wisdom and made fully my own the whole of my discourse. They clothed me with vestures of glory and veiled me with cloud-veils. They wound round me a girdle of water, a girdle which shone beyond measure and glistened."[272]

The High Priest mentioned in the text is called Elizar, and there was indeed a Eleazar ben Boethus who served as High Priest from 4-3 BC., as well as an Elizer head priest in Magdala.

In the ancient Nazorean Book of Yuhana we read more about the Jews anger about John's birth, for he had been predicted by his father to overthrow their false Torah:

"When the Jews heard this they were filled with wicked anger against her and said: What weapon shall we make ready for a certain one and his mother that he be slain by our hand? When Anush the treasurer heard this he took the child and brought it to Parwan the white mountain, to Mount Parwan on which sucklings and little ones on holy drinks are reared up. There I abode until I was two and twenty years old. I learned there the whole of my wisdom and made fully my own the whole of my discourse. They clothed me with vestures of glory and veiled me with cloud-veils. They wound round me a girdle of water, a girdle which shone beyond measure and glistened. They set me within a cloud, a cloud of splendor, and in the seventh hour of a

---

[271] The Mandaeans of Iraq and Iran By E.S. Drower Clarendon Press, Oxford,1937
[272] Doctrine Of Kings 32

Habshabba (first weekday) they brought me to the Jerusalem region.

Anush, who took and instructed Yuhana, was a leader of the Nazoreans according to other accounts. His title "the treasurer" denotes his high rank. This term Treasurer (*Ginzi*) means something akin to an archbishop and the treasury referred to is a treasury of truth, a secret library over which he has charge.

Parwan the White Mountain is probably the Mount Hermon region in southern Syria where the peaks are known by the name of White Mountains and are a striking white color. This is an area known to have had Nazoreans in it, and it was an area frequented by Yeshu according to flawed biblical accounts. Mount Carmel, also rather white, is at the southwestern extremity of this area and could be considered a part of the White Mountains.

The gospel of Luke says Yuhana was 6 months older than Yeshu, and this seems echoed in Suddie and Cayce readings. This gives a date around July 6, 3 BC for his birth. The Mandaeans celebrate it on the first day of Sagittarius, with a fast the next day for those children who were slain by Herod, but their calendar has long since lost track with the seasons. According to Hippolytus the ancestors of Yuhana and Yeshu's mothers were from the Bethlehem area, and this seems likely since Miryam gave birth there according to tradition:

"Hippolytus wrote that a Mathan had three daughters: Mary, Soba, and Ann. Mary, the oldest, married a man of Bethlehem and was the mother of Salome; Soba married at Bethlehem also, but a "son of Levi", by whom she had Elizabeth; Ann wedded a Galilean (Joachim) and bore Mary, the Mother of God. Thus Salome, Elizabeth, and the Blessed Virgin were first cousins, and

Elizabeth, "of the daughters of Aaron" on her father's side, was, on her mother's side, the cousin of Mary.[273]

Yuhana's Ministry

In Luke 3:1-4 a very specific year is put forward for Yuhana:

> "In the fifteenth year of the reign of Tiberius Caesar - when Pontius Pilate was governor of Judea, Herod tetrarch of Galilee, his brother Philip of Iturea and Traconitis, and Lysanias tetrarch of Abilene - during the high priesthood of Annas and Caiaphas, the word of God came to John [the Baptist] son of Zechariah in the desert. He went into all the country around the Jordan, preaching a baptism of repentance for the forgiveness of sin."

"In the fifteenth year of the reign of Tiberius" would indicate that John would have started the Bethany portion of his ministry in the winter/spring of 29 C.E., which is the time of Yeshu's baptism on or near January 6, 29 BC. Yuhana probably began teaching almost seven years earlier, shortly after he graduated from the Carmel School at age 22.

Yuhana's Baptism Site

There is a two kilometer long wadi, or canyon, that begins at the Ain Kharrar Spring of Wadi Kharrar in Jordan. That is most likely the site of an ancient Nazorean Shkinta, or monastic community, begun by Liliuk and continually occupied up until the time of Yuhana and Yeshu. The Kharrar stream flows some two kilometers west toward the Jordan River just above where it empties into the Dead Sea and creates lush vegetation and animal sanctuaries. This Canyon, rather than the Jordan River itself, is the probable Essene site where Yuhana was baptizing in the days of Yeshu:

---

[273] In Nicephor., li, lii

"These things took place in Bethany beyond the Jordan, where John was baptizing"[274]

This was also the place where Yeshu oft took refuge from hostile Jewish leaders:

"went away again across the Jordan to the place where John at first baptized..."

This Nazorean community appears to have brought in an abundance of water from other areas, as evidenced from extensive aqueducts systems, for use in baptismal and agricultural activities. Although the spring is sufficient for drinking water, the ancient inhabitants obviously desired an over abundance of flowing water for their natural and spiritual endeavors. Three large rectangular pools exist on Elijah's Hill within the monastery walls and pottery shards from the first century confirm that these baptismal pools were not of later construction.

Message of Yuhana

In this Aramaic John we are told that Yuhana's preaching against the Jewish Torah resulted in its decline and disappearance, as well as the decline of harlotry, consumerism and consumption of fish. Colored clothing and vanity also evaporate.

"Before my voice and the voice of my proclamations the Torah disappeared in Jerusalem. Before the voice of my discourse the readers read no more in Jerusalem. The wantons cease from their lewdness, and the women go not forth to the.. . . . Hither to me come the brides in their wreaths, and their tears flow down to

---

[274] John 1:28; 10:40

the earth. The child in the womb of his mother heard my voice and did weep. The merchants trade not in Judea and the fishers fish not in Jerusalem. The women of Israel dress not in dresses of color, the brides wear no gold and the ladies no jewels. Women and men look no more at their face in a mirror.[275]

White clothing, non fish eating vegetarianism, chastity, simplicity, sobriety and Gnostic writings rather than Jewish ones are all principles of the Nazorean Way which Yuhana successfully espoused. He says again to the Jews who love their Torah:

"When the soul strips off the body, on Judgment-Day, what will you do? O thou distracted, jumbled-up world in ruin! Thy men die, and thy false scriptures are closed."

The teachings of Yuhana were the teachings of Yeshu; they both belonged to the same sect and adhered to the same Nazorean laws. In the following we are told the gist of the Nazorean version of the Law of Moses. It is written that Yuhana cried aloud, called and spoke:

"The Great Vast Light looks proportionally at defilements. Everyone, which is defiled in indecency, becomes found in a narrow place in the fire. Everyone, which is defiled in theft, will be bound on those dark mountains. Everyone, which is defiled with the woman of another, will have the fire to be the judge, until his spirit ceases. Everyone, which is defiled with a widowed woman, will be bound on that dark mountains. Everyone, which is defiled with a bride, will be struck on dual engines and his eyes will not fall satisfied on Abathur. Everyone, which leaves a woman and takes another, will be struck with a fire shaft. A woman, which is driven by indecency, will be at a furnace block and she will not look with satisfaction on the house. Everyone, that to fortune-tellers and lying Chaldaeans

---

[275] Doctrine Of Kings 21

goes, on devices will be struck. Everyone, which gets drunk on wine and drinks amidst bass drums and songs and sleeps around in debauchery, with combs of chains will be combed, and such will not look with satisfaction at Abathur. Everyone, which goes to as entertainer and she becomes Pregnant by seed sowed dishonestly, then takes a medicine and into the excrement throws the abortion, digs then a pit and buries it, and steps with their heels on it; the eyes of the child of looking after the mother, but the mother does not regard the child; the child dies then in the excrement, and the mother does not cry about it; such will be taken to account will be dragged into that watchtower of the greedy, furious, mute and deaf dogs. It will be pulled to the rack, their eyes on Abathur will not look with satisfaction, and their name will be wiped out from the house of Life. Everyone, which approaches his wife and does not wash himself with water, will find his home in the body of Leviathan. A woman, who does not wash herself with water, receives blow upon blow. The pure name will curse her, and the guardian of the light will trouble her with a ceaseless dissolution, and her name will be wiped out from the house of the Life. Men, who sleep on that first day on which their wives wash themselves with water of the impurity and menstruation, will cause one to be found in the black clouds of the darkness. Everyone one charges interest and compound interest on gold and silver will be found on those mountains, which are dark mountains. Everyone who loves gold and silver and that does not do good with it, a double death will they die and are imprisoned. Those who smell the aroma of Life (Living Foods) and over it do not express the names of Life (*food blessing*), will be dragged to the account in the house of the Abathur. Everyone, which does ugly works, will be hung by the sword and the sword of the planets. Everyone which will seize and tinge hands and feet and their shape alter, which his maleness has determined, with his hands shall fan the coals and with his lips the fire. Such requires death but cannot not die; the Life does not approach them, He lets it die and does not release it from agony, in order to climb and look at the place of the light. Because of the baptism, which one in the Yardna receive, one is not condemned to remain in the dwelling of the sinner. One who dresses and covers themselves and which loves colored things, in darkness and with coverings of the darkness is such arrayed and to such a ones feet is put fire. Darkness goes before them, and darkness follows them, and bad spirits and demons form their company. Because such a one loved colored stuff, they will be lashed in the watchtowers until their spirit stops. I say and explain to you souls of the righteously established religious ones which testify of Life: commit no ugly work, so that you may not sink into the place of darkness. Life is transcendent and victorious, and victorious are those that have gone forth!

Be you warned from me, my brothers, of actions, which are hateful and not worthwhile. Be you warned from me, my disciples! Be peaceful and modest. Love Habshabba (*first weekday*) and honor the Day's Eve. Pray and offer alms, which are worth more than woman and child. Tithes and alms are required on the way, like the hand which is sufficient for the mouth.

Yeshu would have taught these same Nazorean doctrines and would have lived a similar lifestyle to that of Yuhana's.

CDaRRiages

Yuhana, according to ancient Nazoreanism, was married to two women named Anhar & Qinta. The following passages from his book speak of his struggle to marry:

"Yahya proclaims in evenings the nights, Yuhana on the night's eves. Yahya proclaims in the nights and speaks. (*The heavenly*) wheels and chariots quaked. Sun and Moon weep, and the eyes of Ruha shed tears. He says: Yahya, thou art like to a scorched mountain, which brings forth no grapes in this world. Thou art like to a dried up stream, on whose banks no plants are raised. Thou hast become a, land without a lord, a house without worth. A false prophet hast thou become, who hast left no one to remember thy name. Who will provide thee with provision, who with victuals, and who will follow to the grave after thee? When

Yahya heard this, a tear gathered in his eye; a tear in his eye gathered, and he spake: It would be pleasant to take a wife, and delightful for me to have children. But what if I take a woman, and then comes sleep, desire for her seizes me and I neglect my night-prayer? What if desire wakes in me, and I forget my Lord out of my mind? What if desire wakes in me, and I neglect my prayer every time?

When Yahya said this, there came a Letter (*communication*) from the House of Abathur: Yahya take a wife and found a family, and see that thou dost not let this world come to an end. On the night of Monday and on the night of Tuesday go to thy first bedding. On the night of Wednesday and on the night of Thursday devote thyself to thy hallowed praying. On the night of Friday and on the night of Saturday go to thy first bedding. On the night of Habshabba (*first weekday*) and yea on Day's Eve devote thyself to thy hallowed praying. On Habshabba take three and leave three, take three and leave three. See that thou dost not let the world come to an end. Thereon they fashioned for Yahya a wife out of thee, thou Region of the Faithful.[276]

Status

Yuhana and his spiritual status are downplayed in the New Testament gospels, yet he is mentioned before Yeshu. The somewhat derogatory remarks made concerning him, such as the least in the kingdom is greater than he, is not commiserate with Nazorean tradition. In Nazirutha, Yuhana is seen as a great being of light. He is considered the head of the fifth spiritual dispensation on earth. His predecessors being Adam, Ram, Shurbai, Shum and their female counterparts. We read:

"I have not forgotten my night-prayer, not forgotten the wondrous Yardna. I have not forgotten my baptizing, not forgotten my pure sign. I have not forgotten Habshabba, and the

[276] Doctrine Of Kings 31

Day's evening has not condemned me. I have not forgotten Shilmai and Nidbai, who dwell in the House of the Mighty. They clear me and let me ascend; they know no fault, no defect in me.

When Yahya said this, the Living Ones rejoiced over him greatly. The Seven sent him their greeting and the Twelve made obeisance before him. They said to him: Of all these words which thou hast spoken, thou hast not said a single one falsely. Delightful and fair is thy voice, and none is equal to thee. Fair is thy discourse in thy mouth and precious is thy speech, which has been bestowed upon thee. The vesture which First Life did give unto Adam, the man, the vesture which First Life did give unto Ram, the Man, the vesture which First Life did give unto Shurbai, the Man, the vesture First Life did give unto Shum bar Nuh (*Shem son of Noah*) has He given now unto thee. He hath given it thee, O Yahya, that thou mayest ascend, and with thee may those descend [. . . . . .] The house of the defect (*thy body*) will be left behind in the desert. Everyone who shall be found sinless, will ascend unto thee, in the Region of Light, he who is not found sinless, will be called to account in the guard-houses.[277]

Baptism of Yeshu

There are three accounts of various baptisms of Yeshu in ancient Mandaic scrolls. In the Scroll of Yuhana we have an interesting account of the baptism of Yeshu, but it appears to be a conflated account containing historical material on Yeshu and traditional formulas for baptism intermingled with later polemics against Paul and his Roman Christianity. The banter and exaggeration displayed in this text is typical of the literary style of the book as a whole and was not meant to be taken too literally.

---

[277] Doctrine Of Kings 19

"Yahya (*John*) proclaims in the nights, Yuhana (*John*) on the night's eves. Yahya proclaims in the nights. Glory rises over the worlds. Who commanded Yeshu, who commanded Yeshu Messiah, son of Miryam, who commanded Yeshu, so that he went to the shores of the Yardna (*Flowing*) and said: Yahya, baptize me with thy baptism and also utter over me the Name thou art wanting to utter. I will show myself as thy disciple, I will remember thee then in my writings: If I attest not myself as thy disciple, then wipe out my name from thy book. Thereon Yahya answered Yeshu Messiah in Jerusalem: Hast thou lied to the Jews and deceived the priests? Hast thou cut off seed from the men and from the women bearing and being pregnant? The Sabbath, which Moses made binding, hast thou relaxed in Jerusalem? Hast thou lied unto them with horns or spread abroad disgrace with the shofar?

Thereon Yeshu Messiah answered Yahya in Jerusalem: If I have lied to the Jews, may the blazing fire consume me. If I have deceived the priests, a double death will I die. If I have cut off their seed from the men, may I not cross over the Suf Sea (*Great Abyss*). If I have cut off from the women birth and being pregnant, then in truth a judge is raised up before me. If I have relaxed the Sabbath may the blazing fires consume me. If I have lied to the Jews, I will tread on thorns and thistles. If I have spread disgrace abroad with horn-blowing, may my eyes then not light on Abathur. So baptize me then with thy baptizing, and utter over me the Name thou art willing to utter. If I show myself as thy disciple, I will remember thee then in my writing; if I attest not myself as thy disciple, then wipe out my name from thy book.

Then spake, Yahya to Yeshu Messiah in Jerusalem: A stammer becomes not a scholar, a blind man writes no letter. A desolate house mounts not to the height, and a widow becomes not a virgin. Foul water becomes not tasty, and a stone does not with oil soften. Thereon Yeshu Messiah made answer to Yahya in Jerusalem: A stammer a scholar does become, a blind man writes a letter. A desolate house mounts unto the height, and a widow becomes virgin. Foul water becomes tasty, and a stone with oil softens. Thereupon spake Yahya unto Yeshu Messiah in Jerusalem: If thou then givest me illustration for this, thou art a wise Messiah! Thereon Yeshu Messiah made answer to Yahya in Jerusalem: A stammerer a scholar becomes: a child who comes from the bearer, blooms and grows big. Through wages and alms he comes on high, he comes on high through wages and alms and ascends and beholds the Lights region. A blind man who writes letter: A villain who becomes virtuous. He abandoned wantonness and abandoned theft and reached unto faith in Great Life. A desolate house who ascends again to the height: one of position who has become humble. He quitted his palace and quitted his pride and built a house on the seashore. A house he built on the seashore, and into it opened two doors, so that he might bring in unto him whoever lay down there in misery, to him he opened the door and took him within to himself. If he would eat, he laid for him a table with Truth. If he would drink, he mixed for him wine cups with truth. If he would lie down, be spread a bed for him in Truth. If he would depart, he led him forth on the way of Truth. He led him forth on the way of Truth and of faith, and then he ascends and beholds the Lights region. A woman who a virgin becomes: a woman who already in youth has been widowed. She kept her shame closed, and sat there till her children were grown. If she passes over, her face does not pale in her husbands presence. Foul water that is made tasty: a girl wanton who has got back her honor. she went up a hamlet and she went down a hamlet without taking her veil from her face. A stone with oil softens - a heretic who has come down from the mountain. He abandoned magic and sorcery and made confession to Great Life. He found a fatherless and filled him full and filled full the widows pockets. Therefore baptize me, O Yahya, with thy baptizing and utter over me the Name thou art willing to utter. If I show myself as thy disciple, I will remember thee in my writing: if I attest not myself as thy disciple then wipe out my name from thy book. Thou wilt for thy sins be called to account and I for my sins will be called to account.

After Yeshu says this, the text says that "there came a letter out of the House of Abathur" telling Yuhana to lead Yeshu down into the Yardna and baptize him and lead him up again to the shore and there set him. The text then continues with a condemnation of Paul and his form of Christianity. Paul is called Messiah Paulis:

"Afterwards Ruha made herself like a dove and threw a cross over the Yardna and made its water change into various colors (*heresies*). O Yardna, she says, thou sanctifiest me and thou sanctifiest my seven son. The Yardna in which Messiah Paulis was baptized have I made into a "cesspool" (*dead religion*). The bread which Messiah Paulis (*Pauline Christians*) receive have I made into "sacrament" (*false sacrament*). The drink which Messiah Paulis receives, have I made into a "supper" (*false eucharist*). The headband which Messiah Paulis receives, have I made into a "priesthood" (*priestcraft*). The staff which Messiah Paulis receives, have I made into a "dung-stick" (*Bishop's Crosier*). Gnosis of Life speaks: Let me warn you, my brothers, let me warn you, my beloved! Let me warn you, my brothers, against the [....]who are like unto the cross. They lay it on the walls; then stand there and bow down to the woodblock. Let me warn you, my brothers, of the god (*Roman theology*), which the carpenters have joined together. If the carpenter has joined together the god, who then has joined together the carpenter? [278]

We have this fragment on Yeshu's immersion from the Gospel of the Nazoreans:

"Behold, the mother of the Lord and his brethren said to him: John the Baptist baptizes unto the remission of sins, let us go and be baptized by him. But he said to them: Wherein have I sinned that I should go and be baptized by him? Unless what I have said is ignorance (a sin of ignorance). [279]

Demise

---

[278] Doctrine Of Kings 30
[279] Jerome, Adversus Pelagianos 3.2

Yuhana's death was duly reported to the Nazorean central Temple on Mt Carmel:

> "Yuhana has left his body, his brothers make proclamations, his brothers proclaim unto him on the Mount, on Mount Carmel. They took the Letter and brought it to the Mount, to Mount Carmel. They read out the Letter to them and explain to them the writing, - to Yaqif (James) Beni-Amin (Yeshu) and Shumel (Samuel/Shimeon). They assemble on Mount Carmel." [280]

Josephus writes:

> "Now some of the Jews thought that the destruction of Herod's army came from God, and was a very just punishment for what he did against John called the Baptist [the dipper]. For Herod had him killed, although he was a good man and had urged the Jews to exert themselves to virtue, both as to justice toward one another and reverence towards God, and having done so join together in washing. For immersion in water, it was clear to him, could not be used for the forgiveness of sins, but as a sanctification of the body, and only if the soul was already thoroughly purified by right actions. And when others massed about him, for they were very greatly moved by his words, Herod, who feared that such strong influence over the people might carry to a revolt -- for they seemed ready to do any thing he should advise -- believed it much better to move now than later have it raise a rebellion and engage him in actions he would regret. And so John, out of Herod's suspiciousness, was sent in chains to Machaerus, the fort previously mentioned, and there put to death; but it was the opinion of the Jews that out of retribution for John God willed the destruction of the army so as to afflict Herod. [281]

The date of John the Baptist's death is put on 29 August in the Roman Christian liturgical calendars. His widows Anhar and

---

[280] Sidra Dyahya (Book Of John)/Drashe Dmalke (Discourses Of Kings) 26
[281] Antiquities 18.5.2 116-119

Qintat, as well as their eight children would have been taken care of completely by the Nazorean shared wealth system. At the Baptist's death, Yeshu immediately became the focus of attention for the more serious followers and disciples of Yuhana, although one Samaritan branch of the Order did rebel and break off under Dositheus (Doshtai).

˜ 9 ˜
yeshu's sucession

Yeshu Succeeds Yuhana

AT THE DEATH of Yuhana his acknowledged successor in the public arena was Yeshu. When Yeshu assumed leadership, he continued the ritual regime of his predecessor, including baptism. In the New Testament account in John 4:1-3 it says:

> "Now when Jesus learned that the Pharisees had heard that Jesus was making and baptizing more disciples than John (although Jesus himself did not baptize, but only his disciples), he left Judea and departed again for Galilee.

This makes it sound like Yeshu himself was not performing rituals, but the "Jesus himself baptized not, but his disciples" is a later gloss proved by its absence in at least two ancient texts where we read instead:

> "Because not only was our Lord baptizing, but his disciples.[282]

> "Jesus was not alone who baptized, but the disciples also baptized."[283]

---

[282] Jn 4:2 Sinaitic
[283] From A Medieval Persian Manuscript, As Published In The London Polyglot Of 1657 (Walton's Polyglot),

Yeshu could not have officiated as a priest during certain periods, as mandated by ancient Tarmidaya law, such as when one of his wives was menstruating. During these periods Yeshu would not have been personally baptizing. Yeshu continued to honor his crown and function as a Priest whenever needed. He was assisted by other Priests and Priestesses. Most, if not all, of his earliest followers would have had the privilege of being baptized personally by him on numerous occasions.

Since Yeshu was born on 6 January 2 B.C and was baptized when about 30 in 29 AD, he apparently took over Yuhana's leadership responsibility about 3 ½ months after his birthday in 29 AD, at the time of Passover. Yeshu's temptation in the wilderness, as reported by biblical hearsay, is probably redolent of this lapse period between his famous immersion and his ministry commencement.

Epiphanios of Salamis (315-403) in anti-heretical polemics records an ancient tradition on the baptismal date of Yeshu:

> "[Jesus] was baptized on what is for the Egyptians the twelfth of Athyr (and for the Romans) the eight of November, meaning sixty full days before Epiphany, which is the day of His birth in the flesh." [284]

If this information is correct, Yeshu was baptized about 5 ½ months before Passover. Monday April 18 was the first Passover day for 29 AD and the most likely date for the beginning of Yeshu public ministry probably inaugurated by another less dramatic baptism (*Maswetta*) at daybreak.

Nazorean Baptism

---

[284] Haer. 51.16, Holl, 270.1-3

The central Rite of Nazirutha, or the Nazorean Gnosis of Yeshu and Miryam, is Mystical Immersion (*Maswetta*) in the Waters of Life. Consecrated, pure and flowing water is not only a symbol of Life and of the sacred rebirthing Womb Waters of the Mother of Life, but is considered Life in and of itself. The pure flowing waters of the earth are considered sacred and imbued with the Life force of the Holy Ones because Yeshu (*Hibil-Ziwa*) infused the dark earthly waters with "Living Water" when the foundations of time were laid. The sacred Scrolls say that Hibil-Ziwa brought Living Waters and laid it round the earth in a circle, and set a measurer there who measured the waters and poured living water therein. And that:

> "When the Living Water entered the turbid water, the Living Water lamented and wept." [285]

A Nazorean oral tradition states:

> "The water of this world is divided into nine mithkal; eight of earthly water, and one of water of life to strengthen the body of man. It is only the earthly part of the water and bread which passes out of the human body as excrement and urine, the heavenly part remains in it to give it life." [286]

In Naziruthian Immersion Rites these Life infused waters are fully submersed in as well as drunk. They bequeath health and wholeness, protection against negative forces, and the promise of everlasting Life through forging a deeper connection with the Living Ones above. The Living Water within the turbid water washes clean the living soul within the turbid flesh, each to its own, being effectual on several levels simultaneously. Initiation into the Nazorean Path is initiation into familiarization and association with these divine living

---

[285] Sidra Dyahya (Book Of John)/Drashe Dmalke (Discourses Of Kings)
[286] The Mandaeans Of Iraq And Iran By E.S. Drower Leiden: Brill 1962 (Reprint Of 1937)

elements which infuse physical creation. The purpose of all Sacramental Rites within Nazirutha is to ingather and draw these living elements of Yeshu and Miryam into the deeper layers of the soul where they can be woven into a garment of light capable of ascending upward at death. Their salvic process is two fold: These living elements add to and increase the consciousness of the initiate, making the goal of enlightenment and inner purity more real. They also allow the individual to participate in the more universal salvic process of redeeming the light elements of Yeshu and Miryam out of the world and preparing them to return upward to higher worlds of light.

To understand the Nazorean Path, it is imperative that one understand this principle of how living light elements infuse material creation and need to be extracted from that creation and returned to their source.

"There is liquid in water, there is fire in Chrism." [287]

As our personal souls are trapped in imperfect physical flesh, so the greater soul of Yeshu and Miryam is trapped in imperfect physical matter. Both need redemption and can be "saved" simultaneously, since both are intricately intertwined and are drawn together through the sacred Mysteries of Miryam.

Through Sacramental Rites on the Nazorean Path, the lifeless fluid (*tahma*) is separated from the living fluid (*mia hiya*) and the living soul (*Nishimta*) is separated from the stinking stump (*Ostuna*), creating a state of ritual purity. Our sacred Scrolls say:

---

[287] Gospel of Philip 28

"The purity, then, which was spoken about, is that which comes through knowledge (Naziruthian Gnosis), a separation of light from darkness, of death from life, and living waters from turbid." [288]

When we go down into the living waters of Mystical Immersion, we die unto the world which Yeshu called a corpse, and we are reborn into the world of light, sacramentally through the image. For it is written: "Yeshu says:

"Whoever has recognized the system has found a corpse--and whoever has found a corpse, of him the system is not worthy." [289] and

"By perfecting the water of Baptism, Yeshu poured death away. Because of this, we indeed go down into the water yet we do not go down unto death, in order that we not be poured away into the spirit of the world." [290]

Each immersion is meant to be a death of the old self benumbed by the flesh, and a reincarnation of the higher soul (*Nishimta*) in a water woven body of light:

"The living water is a body. It is appropriate that we be clothed with the Living Person. Because of this, when he comes to go down into the water he undresses himself in order that he may be clothed with that." [291]

The ceremonial and liturgical nature of Nazorean Baptism is designed to bring out the innate presence of the living water within the turbid water. Such is also designed to bring to the fore the hidden higher (*Nishimta*) spirit secreted within lower

---

[288] Mani, Cologne Codex
[289] Gospel of Thomas 56
[290] Gospel of Philip 115
[291] Gospel of Philip 107

states of consciousness so that the two may meet, face to face, and become one.

This union of higher spirit with living water in formal Mystical Immersion represents the first of thirty-two degrees of Nazirutha which Yeshu referred to in the Pistis Sophia. It is reflected in two lesser expressions of heavenly washing – the daily and the weekly absolutions. The daily cleansing is called the Signing (*Rushma*) and the weekly one is called the Submersion (*Tamasha*). Both are instrumental in solidifying and preserving the greater purification of the great Mystical Immersion (*Maswetta*).

The daily Signing (*Rushma*) is a little like the Moslem purification (*Tawaddu'*). It is a personal rite that does not require the presence of the Priest(ess)hood. The Priest(ess)hood is also not required to perform the Tamasha which consists of a triple submersion associated with the seventh day conclusion to the week. The fuller Maswetta baptism is reserved for certain occasions that fall on the first feast day of each week, called *Hab-Shaba*. All three washings are done in the name of the Nazorean Trinity and include reference to all six pairs of Nazorean Deities.

Nazorean Altars

Fresh Myrtle twigs were used anciently to make Baptismal wreaths. This myrtle symbolized the healing that can incur through this Ritual because in the ancient Aramaic tongue of the Nazoreans, the word for Myrtle is similar to the word for Being Healed. Other sacred substances and symbols were also utilized. A sacred Banner (*Drabsha*) was erected on a wooden cross near the flowing water, and a small altar (*Quintha*) was set up, upon which were a: Ritual table (*Tariana*); bottle for sacramental water (*Qania*); Fire-Saucer (*Brihi*); a terra-cotta cube for holding incense (*Qauqa*). The altar (*Quintha*) is for the Chalice (*Keptha*) for Libations (*Naquta*) and bread & fresh fruits offerings, or alms (*Qurbana*), all intricate parts of sacramental rites. Without the giving of Alms there can be no purification for one seeking immersion. So interwoven is this idea of Alms and Immersion that the two cannot be separated and both are considered part of the first foundational degree of Nazirutha. Thus the Scrolls say:

> "The first duty of the Listener which he does is . . . Almsgiving. [292]

> The Alms is this, that he must make an offering of food through the Righteous and piously give it to them. [293]

> The Alms will be reckoned to his good. . . .[294]

Alms have traditionally been interpreted to be fresh food and drink offerings when feasible or currency when this is not possible. The modern Mandaean remnants of the Nazoreans leave a certain amount of money on the bank of the river whenever they are baptized and Catholic priests are given a fee for saying Mass. Both these facts are traceable back to the time when food offerings were given in Nazorean Ritual work – not for the priests, but collected by the Priesthood for the temple. The Ginza warns that priests should not personally accept money for ritual work as the Catholics do.

Food offerings are important because they contain a certain degree of the Life Force which the ritual is designed to extract and accumulate within the higher soul (*Nishimta*). The Life within fresh and organically grown produce is thought to be added to the Life within the Baptismal water, each helping to

---

[292] Kephalia 192: 29 31
[293] Kephalia 193:2 3
[294] Kephalia 233: 16 19

nourish the higher soul within the initiate and to help that initiate participate in the great redemption of the Light of Christ crucified in matter. The association of Alms with purification in water also has to do with the fact that both are concerned with embracing Life and rejecting death, the death associated with non vegan diets of the world. Mani of blessed memory once said that one element of righteousness consists of:

> "...the purity of the mouth: he must cleanse his mouth from all flesh and blood . . ." [295]

By stressing the need to offer firstfruits of the field and orchard on Holy Altars, Nazoreans were encouraged to engage in organic gardening as a means of sustenance as well as livelihood. By this endeavor they participate daily in the great redemptive work of liberating entrapped light from field and garden and collecting it within the souls of the righteous, preparatory to their ascent upward into Worlds of Light. Not all Nazoreans could embrace a lifestyle entailing gardening, but all could and must embrace a nonharming all plant based diet. By keeping to an all plant diet, Nazoreans reject the cycle of death associated with worldly foods, for the flesh and dairy foods of the world cannot be offered on holy Naziruthian Altars. They are contaminated with the vibrations of death that cannot be used in weaving the light robe of the righteous. Not only can such death derived foods not be offered on holy Nazorean Altars, such foods also cannot be offered to the bodily temple of a Naziruthian initiate. Only the body of souls nourished on an all plant diet can enter the sacred waters of Nazirutha, for such waters are Waters of Life and not death.

> "In this world they who wear garments (of cloth) are more valuable than the garments. In the Sovereignty of the Heavens

---

the garments (of imagery) are more valuable than those to whom they have been given by means of water and fire, which purify the entire place." [296]

This verse is talking about the outer physical body woven of earthly elements and how that earthly sheath is inferior to the spiritual body (*Nishimta*) within it. When it says that the garments of the Sovereignty of Heaven will be greater than those who put them on, it refers to the eternal light elements that are woven into a robe, or bodily form of righteousness, for the spirit (*Nishimta*) to wear in the eternities. It is a Nazorean teaching that the collection and creation of this eternal perfect body begins in rituals such as Immersion (*maswetta*) that are designed to gather in light particles and weave them into eternal cloth.

The first part of the Path of Purity, entered into by Mystical Immersion (*Maswetta*), concerns itself with appreciating and respecting all living things and their ultimate source – the Living Ones above. Without a respect for all Life there can be no advancement on the Path of Peace, for Life is a manifestation of the Great Life - the Hidden Living Ones above. Because this foundational principle is so important, the Heavens have ordained that all who begin to walk Their Holy Path do so with a submissive gesture that honors this Great Life and which entails an oath to respect all living things and to avoid harming them whenever possible. This beginning gesture is a ceremonial and mystical immersion beneath clean, pure and flowing waters which is done in a special way and at a special time. This mystical immersion is meant to represent our abandonment of the world of death and our birth into the world of Life.

Great Baptism

[296] Gospel of Philip 26

The Nazorean Path has a very special immersion ceremony that represents formal initiation into the Path of Peace. It is very different from the baptism rites of other Christian groups. It is also a very ancient rite which Nazoreans claim to be older than other types of Christian baptism known in the world. Certain principles are associated with this special rite. Certain commitments are also required of each person who seeks to dedicate their life to the Great Life through such a process. These principles and commitments concern themselves with respecting all living things and inflicting the least amount of harm to them through daily life. By submitting to the ceremonial initiation of the Nazorean Path, baptismal initiates agree to surrender their individual lives to the Nazorean Trinity of Amin-Hiya, Manda d-Hiya, and Mani-Hiya above and to forsake their old habits and lifestyles. One agrees to respect the Nazorean Path of Life and to do what they can to prepare to progress further within it.

Ancient Nazoreans who practiced these Cleansing purifications ate an all plant based diet and adamantly refused to eat any type of dead creature. It is for this reason that a person should not enter the Nazorean Path through mystical immersion unless they are ready to simultaneously take a vow never to eat animal flesh or products again. This vow is part of the Baptismal liturgy. When we eat the dead bodies of once living creatures, we participate in the cycle of death that all true Nazoreans eschewed. The importance of this principle cannot be stressed enough and a commitment to abide by this principle is necessary before taking refuge in the Living Amin, Manda and Mani.

Respect for Life

In this first Naziruthian Degree the Order initiate was required to openly and formally manifest their respect for Life and the Living Ones by showing their willingness to live a compassionate and responsible life that inflicts a minimum level of pain and damage to the planet. This could only be completely done by growing ones own food and by donating a portion of such food to those unable to grow such themselves. Newly Baptized Nazoreans did not vow to do so however, but only vow to eat an all plant diet from that day forward.

The first five degrees of the Naziruthian Path address the necessities of daily life, creating a solid and practical foundation for deeper inner work on the subtle planes and within the subtle body. The vows associated with these first five foundational degrees are based on the utterances of Manda d-Hiya and Mani-Hiya, blessed be Their names. In the ancient texts we read:

> The Lord [did] everything sacramentally: Baptism and Chrism and Eucharist and Atonement and [Holy] Bridal-Chamber. [297]

> The first duty of the Listener which he does is Fasting, Prayer and Almsgiving.[298]

> The Alms is this, that he must make an offering of food through the Righteous (monastics), and piously give it to them. [299]

> The Alms will be reckoned to his good, the Fast that he has kept, the cloth that he has put upon the monastics; and thereby they daily share a communion with them in their fasting and their good deeds. [300]

---

[297] Gospel of Philip 73
[298] Kephalia 192: 29 31
[299] Kephalia 193:2 3
[300] Mani, Kephalia 233: 16 19

Ritual initiation was considered extremely important in the Nazorean Way. This is reflected in the statement that:

> "No one will be able to see himself either in water or in a mirror without light. Nor again will thou be able to see thyself in the light without water or a mirror. Therefore it is appropriate to baptize in both--in the light and the water. Yet the light is the Chrism. "[301]

The importance of ritual is also spoken of in verse 72 of this same Sacred Scroll:

> "The truth does not come unto the system naked, but rather it comes in symbols with imagery. The world will not receive it in any other fashion. There is a rebirth (or upbirth) together with a reborn (or upborn) imagery. It is truly appropriate to be reborn (or upborn) thru the imagery. What is the resurrection with its imagery?--it is appropriate to arise thru the imagery. The Bridal-Chamber with its imagery?--it is appropriate to come into the truth. This is the restoration. It is appropriate to be begotten not only of the words 'the Father with the Son with the Holy Spirit', but also to be begotten of them themselves. Whoever is not begotten of them will have the name also taken from him. Yet one receives them in the Chrism which comes in the power of the cross, which the Apostles call: the right with the left. For this-one is no longer a Christic but rather a Christ." [302]

The Living Ones, as Gardeners of our tiny seedlings, gather together the five light elements, separating them from the darkened ones, in the first five foundational degrees. Of this cultivation of the soul it is said:

> "Cultivation in the world is thru four modes--(crops) are gathered into the barn thru earth and water and wind and light. And the cultivation by God is likewise thru four: trust and hope

---

[301] Gospel of Philip 81
[302] Gospel of Philip 72

and love and recognition. Our earth is trust in which we take root, the water is hope thru which we are nourished, the wind is love thru which we grow, yet the light is recognition thru which we ripen. [...]"[303]

Those who take refuge in the Gnostic Trinity take refuge in the Life and the Great Life. They renounce death and all activities that cause needles death.

"[Those who] go down into the water do not go down to death, for he atoned for those who are [fulfilled] in his name. For he said: [Thus] we must fulfill all righteousness." [304]

We are warned:

"If anyone goes down into the water and comes back up without having received, but says 'I'm a Christic', he has taken the name on loan. Yet if he receives the Holy Spirit, he has the gift of the name. He who has received a gift is not deprived of it, but he who takes a loan has it demanded from him." [305]

When the ritual is internalized, however, we are told that immortality will eventually ensue:

"God is a dyer. Just as the good pigments which are called true then label the things which have been permanently dyed in them, so it is also with those whom God colors. Because his hues are imperishable, (those who are tinted) become immortal thru his coloring. Yet God immerses whomever he baptizes in an inundation of waters. "[306]

Thus are born the Daughters and Sons of Amin:

---

[303] Gospel of Philip 122
[304] Gospel of Philip 96
[305] Gospel of Philip 63
[306] Gospel of Philip 47

"The soul (Ruha) and the spirit (Nishimta) of the Son (and daughter) of the Bridal-Chamber come forth [in] water and fire with light. The fire is the Chrism (Misha), the light is the fire. I do not mean this fire that has no form, but rather the other-- whose form is white and which is made of beautiful light and which bestows splendor." [307]

It is important to receive these ceremonial initiations whilst earthbound, so that one can begin their transformation into Life and toward the Great Living Ones:

"Those who say that they will first die and then arise are confused. If they do not first receive the resurrection while they live, they will receive nothing when they die. Thus it is said also of Baptism in stating that Baptism is great, for those who receive it shall live." [308]

Through the wondrous rites of Nazirutha, Nazoreans have the promise of liberation from all illusion:

"Ideally did the Lord say: Some have entered the Sovereignty of the Heavens laughing, and they came forth [from the world rejoicing]. The Christic [...] who went down into the water immediately came forth as lord over everything, because [he not only considered] (this world) a farce but also [disdained it for] the Sovereignty of the Heavens. [...] If he disparages it and scorns it as a farce, he will come forth laughing." [309]

Submission

So many things were deigned to occur in the first Naziruthian degree, on various levels and in various ways – some conscious and some unconscious. On the conscious part of the initiate there should be a threefold submission to the Great

---

[307] Gospel of Philip 71
[308] Gospel of Philip 97
[309] Gospel of Philip 103

Life on the level of the Body, Speech and Mind. The body submits to physical Submersion beneath flowing water, with speech the initiate vows to live a harmless compassionate life and keep to an all plant diet, and with the mind the initiate resolves to live a pure dedicated life. This dedicated life is one of acceptant service to the Nazorean Triple Refuge which consists of the Holy Living Ones above, Their saving program of Naziruthian teachings and texts, and Their Family of Truth congregate on the earth.

On a subtle and perhaps unnoticed level the Light Mind affects our individual mind, the words of the liturgy affect our subconscious, and the Law of Light enters into the sincere submitting soul and separates the light elements of the Nishimta soul from the dark elements of the dark flesh, establishing portals for the living elements within the sanctified substances of the water, oil, bread and other elements to enter and strengthen the Nishimta soul.

> "When any Messenger of the Light appears in the world to teach and convert the host of living beings in order to save them from their sufferings, he (or she) begins by bringing the sound of the wonderful Law down through the gate of their ears. Then he enters the Ancient Dwelling and, using the great magic prayers, imprisons the swarm of venomous serpents and all the wild beasts, no longer leaving them free. Next, armed with the Axe of Wisdom, he cuts and fells the poison tree and uproots their Stumps, as well as all the other impure plants. At the same time he has the Palace Hall cleansed and splendidly adorned, and a seat placed there for (the throne of) the Law; afterwards he sits down in it. . . When he has entered the Old Town and destroyed the hateful foes, he must quickly separate the two Forces, the Light and the Darkness, and no longer let them mingle. [310]

---

[310] CMOUNT 18-19

These were the mysteries that Yeshu promulgated when he took over the Baptismal work of his friend Yuhana.

Dosithius Schism

Dositheus was a Samaritan Heresiarch who broke from the legitimate Nazorean Stream headed by Yeshu after the death of John. The Clementine literature speaks of this Dosithius being the teacher of Simon Magus. In the Recognitions of Clement we read:

"For after that John the Baptist was killed, as you yourself also know, when Dositheus had broached his heresy, with thirty other chief disciples, and one woman, who was called Luna--whence also these thirty appear to have been appointed with reference to the number of the days, according to the course of the moon--this Simon ambitious of evil glory, as we have said, goes to Dositheus, and pretending friendship, entreats him, that if any one of those thirty should die, he should straightway substitute him in room of the dead: for it was contrary to their rule either to exceed the fixed number, or to admit any one who was unknown, or not yet proved; whence also the rest, desiring to become worthy of the place and number, are eager in every way to please, according to the institutions of their sect each one of those who aspire after admittance into the number, hoping that he may be deemed worthy to be put into the place of the deceased, when, as we have said, any one dies. Therefore Dositheus, being greatly urged by this man, introduced Simon when a vacancy occurred among the number. Meantime, at the outset, as soon as he was reckoned among the thirty disciples of Dositheus, he began to depreciate Dositheus himself, saying that he did not teach purely or perfectly, and that this was the result not of ill intention, but of ignorance. But Dositheus, when he perceived that Simon was depreciating him, fearing lest his reputation among men might be obscured (for he himself was supposed to be the Standing One), moved with rage, when they met as usual at the school, seized a rod, and began to beat

Simon; hut suddenly the rod seemed to pass through his body, as if it had been smoke. On which Dositheus, being astonished, says to him, 'Tell me if thou art the Standing One, that I may adore thee.' And when Simon answered that he was, then Dositheus, perceiving that he himself was not the Standing One, fell down and worshipped him, and gave up his own place as chief to Simon, ordering all the rank of thirty men to obey him; himself taking the inferior place which Simon formerly occupied. Not long after this he died.[311]

Origen states that "Dositheus the Samaritan, after the time of Jesus, wished to persuade the Samaritans that he himself was the Messias prophesied by Moses"[312]

In a desire to be the leader of his own sect, Dositheos rejected Yeshu after Yuhana's death and set up his own school from whence came Simon Magus and the later Mandaeans who were known as Dositheans by certain Arab historians several centuries later. This explains why the Mandaeans of Mohammed's time redacted the older Nazorean texts and interpolated into them certain criticisms of Yeshu and Mohammed like their founder Dositheos had done.

Epiphanius tells us that the Dositheans were a sect which began in the time of the Maccabees and called God only Elohim not Yehovah or Lord. They rejected the normal dates of festivals, insisted that every month had thirty days and that members should bathe every day. Epiphanius wrote that Dositheus finally retired to a cave and there practiced such severe asceticism as to bring his life to a voluntary end. There was indeed a Dosithius at the time of the Maccabees, but this was a different one from the disciple of Yuhana. A fourteenth century Arab source confirms Epiphanius, but adds that this

---

[311] Recognitions Of Clement
[312] Contra Celsum, Vi, Ii

sect lived near Jerusalem and was prosecuted by the High Priest.

Simon-Helen Echo

Yeshu and Miryai ascended to leadership over the legitimate branch of the Nazoreans, and their example inspired other duplicate Orders to emulate them. Simon is often credited with being the first of the heretics, but this is not accurate. Simon was the successor to Dosithius however. Justin tells us that this Simon traveled together with a woman named Helena, whom he declared to be the "First Intelligence," he himself claiming to be the first manifestation of the hidden power of God.[313] He calls himself the manifested power of the great hidden Deity ("Hel Kisai", or "Elkesai"[314]) and "the one who will abide forever"[315] His spouse Helena (Selene, "the Moon") is the mother Wisdom, one with the highest Deity, who came down to earth under that name.[316] These of course are Nazorean ideas fulfilled in Yeshu, Miriam and Miryai.

It is said that Helen had originally been a prostitute, which adds to the similarities between her and Mary of Bethany:

> "While teaching in the Phoenician city of Tyre, the divine Simon beheld a courtesan on the roof of a brothel. Her name was Helena, and he recognized her immediately as the current incarnation of Ennoia, His First Thought, the Holy Spirit, the Mother of All. She was the Lost Sheep, forced by her progeny the angels to wander through the centuries from vessel to vessel (including that of Helen of Troy), until she ended up at the brothel in Tyre. He purchased her from her master and she became his constant companion during his travels and teachings.

---

[313] Apologia," I. 26, 56
[314] Recognitions," I. 72, Ii. 37
[315] Recognitions," Ii. 7, Iii. 11; "Homilies," Ii. 24
[316] Recognitions," Ii. 8-9, 39; "Homilies," Ii. 23

Their reunion represented the beginning of the redemption of the world, and was the model for the process of salvation to Simon's followers."

A fragment of Simon's "The Great Announcement" has been preserved wherein he speaks of he "Standing One" who he claimed to be: "This is He who has stood, standeth, and shall stand, a male-female power, after the likeness of the pre-existing Boundless Power, which has neither beginning nor end, but exists in oneness. It was from this Boundless Power that Thought, which had previously been hidden in oneness..."[317]

Peter, in the Clementine teachings condemns these teachings of Simon and flatly states that Simon is not the "Standing One":

"For if it belongs to the Son, who arranged heaven and earth, to reveal His unrevealed Father to whomsoever He wishes, you are, as I said, acting most impiously in revealing Him to those to whom He has not revealed Him."

"And Simon said: "But he himself wishes me to reveal him." And Peter said: "You do not understand what I mean, Simon. But listen and understand. When it is said that the Son will reveal Him to whom He wishes, it is meant that such an one is to learn of Him not by instruction, but by revelation only. For it is revelation when that which lies secretly veiled in all the hearts of men is revealed unveiled by His God's own will without any utterance. And thus knowledge comes to one, not because he has been instructed, but because he has understood. And yet the person who understands it cannot demonstrate it to another, since he did not himself receive it by instruction; nor can he reveal it, since he is not himself the Son, unless he maintains that he is himself the Son. But you are not the standing Son. For if you were the Son, assuredly you would know those who are

[317] A Fragment Of The Apophasis Megalê Of Simon Magus

worthy of such a revelation. But you do not know them. For if you knew them, you would do as they do who know[318]

The standing one, or column, is an ancient concept of Nazirutha that implies a perfect being that draws souls upward to heaven. The concept is spoken of even by Ephrem the Syrian:

"Baptism without understanding--is a treasure full yet empty;-- since he that receives it is poor in it,--for he understands not-- how great are its riches into which he enters and dwells.--For great is the gift within it,--though the mean man perceives not-- that he is exalted even as it. Open wide your minds and see, my brethren,--the secret column in the air, whose base is fixed from the midst of the water--unto the door of the Highest Place, like the ladder that Jacob saw.--Lo! by it came down the light unto Baptism,--and by it the soul goes up to Heaven,--that in one love we may be mingled." [319]

Dosithius to Zazai

Zazai d-Gawazta, son of Hawa, flourished in 272 AD: This is the date associated with the most famous of the earliest Mandaean copyists, although a woman named Lama daughter of Qidra is the earliest-named copyist in Mandaeism. She lived earlier than Zazai of Gawazta. These ancient scribes are the true founders of modern Mandaeanism, being the main link between them and earlier Dositheans that resulted from a break off branch of Nazoreanism during the first century A.D. These Dosithean are mentioned in several Bahai writings under the name of Sabians (*baptizers*):

"...when after the martyrdom of the son of Zachariah some of his followers did not turn to the Manifestation of the All-Merciful,

---

[318] Clementine Homilies
[319] Ephraim The Syrian, Fifteen Hymns For The Feast Of The Epiphany.

that is Jesus and strayed from the way of the Unity of God. They still dwell on earth and are known by some as the Sabeans." [320]

Lama daughter of Qidra is the earliest-named copyist of the Left Ginza. Zazai is the earliest copyist of the: The Thousand and Twelve Questions, Alma Risaia Zuta, Diwan Masbuta d-Hibil Ziwa, Qolasta, and he is mentioned in the Abahatan Qadmaiia. The language of these works represents a fully developed Babylonian-Aramaic idiom and a poetic skill that has never been matched or surpassed in any later Mandaean literature. The classical period ends with the redaction of the Ginza in the first Muslim century.

After Zazai came the copyist Ramuai son of Qaimat from Tib who seems to have redacted many earlier writings and possibly interpolated the negative remarks therein concerning Christ. This period is known as the Post Classical Mandaic. There is evidence that there is still the classical Mandaic being spoken but already the written literature show the introduction of Arab words and Islamic influences after 639 AD. The Ginza was once again redacted during this time. Mahammed ben Is'haq en-Nedim, in his "Fihrist", written in 987-988 A.D., tells us that the Mogtasilah, or Baptists, were then very numerous in the marsh districts between the Arabian Desert and the Tigris and Euphrates. Their head, he says, was called el'Hasai'h (Elchasai), and he was the original founder of their confession. This el'Hasai'h had a disciple called Schimun. The Mandaeans must therefore be, if the Islamic historians are correct, a blend of the Dositheans and the Elchasaites. This accounts for their numerous scrolls containing anonymously rendered teachings of Yeshu which would have come down to them from the Elchasaite side of their lineage.

[320] Directives from the Guardian by Shoji Effendi (pages 51 & 52)

Later Alterations

The wonderful scrolls of early Nazoreanism have been faithfully preserved down through the centuries, except for very slight alterations that are easily detected. Because the texts were preserved by a group whose dominant branch had followed Yuhana the Baptist but not Yeshu, there was a tendency to alter references to Yeshu within them. These alterations are few, late, and tend to be sloppily executed, making restoration of the original text fairly easy. Occasionally one finds interpolations that refer to Islam and Byzantine Christianity which are obviously from a late hand. The Baptism of Yeshu is one place that alterations occurred. There are two versions of this event in the scrolls, one positive account where the name of Yeshu has been changed to Manda dHiya, and another of a mixed nature which we quoted before. When compared them it is obvious that they speak of the same event. In the version we quoted before, the altered text has:

> "When Yeshu Messiah said this there came a letter out of the House of Abathur: Yahya baptize the "deceiver" in the Yardna. Lead him down into the Yardna and baptize him and lead him up again to the shore and there set him."

Following this is the paragraph which mentions Messiah Paulis and Roman Christian practices. The name Yeshu Messiah has been changed to "the deceiver" in the verse above in a lame attempt to show Yeshu in a negative light. They failed, however, to change the most important part of the text that has a divine revelation coming down out of heaven commanding that Yeshu be baptized. Why would the heavens want Yeshu baptized if he were a deceiver? This question has always haunted those who accept Yuhana as a great prophet, but reject Yeshu. They shift the blame for this to Abathur in the heavens, but why would a divine being command it? This baptism is also a problem for the Roman Christians, who wonder why Jesus would need to be baptized by the lesser John for sins that he did not have. The Mandaean remnants of the Dositheans also found it necessary to criticize and misinterpret the miraculous events that some saw at the baptism, but they failed to do this very effectively since they preserved other accounts of these events shown in a positive manner.

The positive account, where Yeshu is addressed under his heavenly title of Manda dHiya to cover up his real identity, is found in the Ginza Rba 5:4. It reads:

> "The radiance of Manda dHiya spread over the Jordan."

In the other more negative and doctored account in the Book of Yuhana we find:

> "Afterwards Ruha made herself like a dove and threw a cross over the Yardna and made its water change into various colors. O Yardna, she says, thou sanctifiest me and thou sanctifiest my seven sons."

Manda dHiya was a saving deity, whereas Ruha was usually seen as the spirit of the world and mother of the seven planets which were considered evil. The Mandaeans also called Ruha the Holy Spirit of the Christians which they viewed as a negative thing. So in one account we have the miraculous display on the water attributed to a high being of light, and in the other attributed to a false holy spirit. Here is the positive account of Yeshu's immersion:

> "Manda d-Hiya went to Yuhana Masbana and spoke to him: "Now then, Yuhana, baptize me with your baptism, with which you baptize, and utter over me something of that name that you

take care of pronouncing." Then spoke Yuhana to Manda dHiya: "My belly is hungry for food and my body is thirsty for drink. I gather herbs and I observe silence. I yearn for peace, but the souls oppress me. Now the morning is about to arrive, come, later I will baptize you."

Then Manda dHiya stood, he raised his eyes to that place which is completely glorious, which is completely light, and afterward spoke greatly in prayer, that very largely was not small. He spoke: I petition a request to the First Life, the Second Life, the Third, and equally to Yufin Yufafin, to Sam, the well guarded Uthrai, to the place that is completely life, the great building which is completely healing, to Usar Hiya and all the plantings of light, to the creations of life, and to all the created plantings of Life. With your approval I offer up one very large and not a small request. At this hour, in which I am, please set me over the twelve hours of the day and the twelve hours of the night, over those twenty-four hours that they be made to be less than they are. The of cycle of the day and those that night, the cycle of the night and those of the day. Sleep and slumber of the eyes of the Yuhana come. May he be as if he has slumbered, and let his soul be refreshed in your glory so that I can speak with him of the baptism, with which he is known to baptize, in this very hour in which we are. Manda dHiya goes and comes from that place, which is completely radiance, from that place which is completely light, and from that place which is over the hours of the day and those twelve hours of the night, and they granted him his request, that the hours become like one hour, the cycles of the day were taken away; and they became those the night. The wheels of the night became switched; and they became those of the day. It became evening, it became mornings, it became evening, it became day.

Sleep and slumber came over the eyes of the Yuhana . He slumbered and slept, then being awake he sat up, sneezing, and put his right hand over his eyes and rubbed the sleep from the eyes. Then Manda dHiya spoke, saying: Greeting to you, master Yuhana , great father, greatly honored. To Manda dHiya Yuhana spoke and said: Come in peace, small boy, whom I ordered already yesterday to Jordan - today I will not deceive you. Then Manda dHiya spoke to Yuhana: Now then, Yuhana, baptizes me with your baptism with which you baptize, and utter over me something of the name, which you always utter. Whereupon Yuhana answered Manda dHiya, forty-two years have I been baptizing people in the water, and still nobody has ever called me to the Jordan. Now I have been called by you to the Jordan, o small boy of three years and one day

Then said Manda dHiya to Yuhana: What is your baptism like, with which you baptize? Whereupon Yuhana spoke to Manda dHiya: I throw human being into the Jordan like sheep before the shepherd. I draw about her with my staff water and speak the name of the Living Ones. Then Manda dHiya asked Yuhana the Baptizer: What names do you utter in the baptism which you baptize? Then all the disciples opened their mouth like one and spoke to Yuhana: For forty-two years you have carried out baptisms, and never have you been called to the Jordan except by this small boy. Do not fail to note his words which he has spoken. The disciples urged Yuhana, then Yuhana rose, rose to Jordan, entered the freely flowing Jordan, spread his hands out to receive Manda dHiya, and spoke to him, saying: Come, come, small boy of three years and one day, least among his brothers but great among his fathers, who is small, but whose speeches are great. Whereupon went Manda dHiya to Yuhana in the Jordan. When the Jordan saw Manda dHiya, it rose up and jumped up toward his presence and leaped forth from its banks. Yuhana stood with water over his first opening and under the last opening between. Between water and water he swims and has not much strength to swim. Manda dHiya saw Yuhana and was worried about him. The radiance of Manda dHiya spread over the Jordan, and as the Jordan saw the radiance of Manda dHiya, it turned itself back, and Yuhana was left on dry land. Manda dHiya went near then to Yuhana and spoke to him: baptize me with your pure baptism and speak over me something of the name which you are accustom to utter. Whereupon spoke Yuhana to Manda dHiya: A thousand times a thousand people to the Jordan do I let descend, and I baptized ten thousand times ten thousand souls in the water. Yet one like unto you my hand has yet to take. Now explain to me; how do I baptize you? Then Manda dHiya spoke to Yuhana: as far as the water, go also, and I want to go with you. Baptizing me with your pure baptism, with which you tend to baptize, and speak about me something of the name, which you to tend to utter. So Yuhana went back down to the water from the dry land, and Manda dHiya went with him. The radiance of the Manda dHiya was over Jordan and its banks. The fish opened their mouth from the sea, the birds on the two banks of the cosmic sea. They praised Manda dHiya and spoke to him: Blessed art you, Manda dHiya, blessed be the place from which you came, and praised and strengthened is the great place to which you go. When the voice of the fish from the sea and the birds from the two banks of the cosmic sea entered into the ear of Yuhana, he knew that it was Manda dHiya who went with him. Then Yuhana spoke to Manda dHiya: You are the one in whose name I baptize with the living baptism. And he asked him: In whose name do you baptize? Whereupon Yuhana answered Manda dHiya: In the name of the one who has been revealed to me, in the name of the predestined, of he who is destined to come, as in the name of the Mana well guarded, who has to reveal himself. Now place upon me now your hand of Truth, your great right hand of healings, and speak over me your names, for I am the planting which you planted. In your name will be strengthened the first and the last. Whereupon spoke Manda dHiya to Yuhana: If I place mine hand on you, you will separate from your body. Then Yuhana spoke to Manda dHiya: Since I have seen you, I now want to be here no longer. Do not cause me to be cursed to be far from you, far from the place from whence you have come. Arm me and give me instruction for the great place where you are going. Reveal to me the Mysteries of the kings benevolent, over the great fruit of the light, over the foundations and fruit of the earth, to know upon what they are set, and the foundations of the water, those from which the living fire spreads, where the Life lives, to know who is the pre eminent and greater than the other." [321]

Yeshu's Reforms

---

[321] Ginza Rba 5:4, Translated By Davied Israel

Yuhana is credited in Nazorean oral tradition for lessening the rules a bit, and from changing the daily prayer requirements from 5 times a day down to three. Yeshu is also said to have simplified the purity laws as well, too much according to the Dosithean remnants of southern Iraq. It is important to remember, however, that Yeshu said that he came to fulfill the Nazorean law. What Yeshu relaxed were laws that were not part of the pure legislation. Over time there is a tendency for religions to add more and more prayers, practices and rites. Eventually these become a burden rather than a help in maintaining a spiritual focus. Prophets must periodically restore lost truths as well as weed the garden from too much of a good thing. Yeshu apparently did this and there are other Gnostic records that have Yeshu warning his disciples not to lay down too many rules.

7 Women

In the Apocalypse of James from the Nag we read:

> James said: . . . Yet another thing I ask of you: who are the seven women who have been your disciples? And behold all women bless you. I also am amazed how powerless vessels have become strong by a perception which is in them."

In this same Apocalypse four woman are named:

> "When you speak these words of this perception, encourage these four: Salome and Mariam and Martha and Arsinoe ..."

There is definitely something unusual about this group of "seven women". Since 360 to 365 disciples were known to have been ordained by Yeshu and his brother James (*Jacob*), it is certain that a lot more than 7 of them were woman, for they were culled mostly from the Nazorean and Ossaean sect which gave equality to woman. Of the hundred plus priestesses, these seven held the status of spouses to Yeshu, or some other prestigious relationship that has caused James to single them out.

It should be mentioned also that Yeshu, as a product of the special eugenics breeding program of Carmel, would have been expected to contribute his genes back into this special gene pool to insure a continuance of his line. Since its ancient inception, this eugenics program would have always recognized that the best candidates for its programs were the result of previous births within it. Occasionally new blood would be infused therein from fresh dedications of children deemed worthy, but the backbone of the program would have always been the products of its previous labors. With exceptional candidates, multiple spouses would have insured the greatest influx of higher genetics into the program.

Parable of the Bridegroom

In the New Testament there is a parable attributed to Yeshu called the parable of the ten virgins. This is an unlikely parable of monogamous Roman Christians to have invented since they were so opposed to the polygamist marriage systems of Palestine. The very fact that this parable exists indicates that it was given and circulated among people who were not offended by someone having ten brides. Thus it shows indirectly that the earliest Nazorean Christians were not monogamous. It may also indicate Yeshu's eugenic activities at the Carmel Temple where he was said to have been at the death of Yuhana.

"They read out the Letter to them and explain to them the writing, - to Yaqif (James) Beni-Amin (Yeshu) and Shumel (Samuel/Shimeon). They assemble on Mount Carmel." [322]

Polygamy & Ganzibras

When Peter says "Now, if a man uses lust for lawful marriage, he does not act impiously", he is referring to the marriages considered lawful for the Nazorean Sect. These go beyond the Roman monogamy.

A High Priest (*Ganzibra*) in the Nazorean Sect was consecrated to his or her office by another High Priest assisted by two normal priests (*Tarmidaya*), and two Acolytes (*Shgandi*). This consecration could only occur when last rites (*Ingirtha*) were given to someone almost dead. When Yeshu, and also Miryai, became a Ganzibra they did so by presiding at a funeral of another and by performing a polygamous wedding 49 days later. In ancient Mandaean records there is record of two female Ganzibras, besides Miryai, called Hava and Anhar, and one female ethnarch around 700 AD named Hayuna daughter of Tihwia.

When Yeshu presided over last rites, he did this with date juice and oil which he pressed himself, put into a tiny clay vial and sealed with clay stamped with the impression of his ring upon his little right finger. Yeshu placed this vial in the small pocket on the white death shirt of the departing, and said all the appropriate prayers and hymns which were associated with it and which were said at specific times for the next 49 days. For the first three days after the death Yeshu would have maintained a sleepless vigil, and the Nazorean Book of the Dead would have been read constantly. After the third day he, as a Ganzibra elect, stayed in retreat for 45 days while the

---

[322] Book Of John The Baptist 26

departed soul ascends through the purgatorial worlds with his message to Abathur at the Gates of Light. On the forty-ninth day since death Yeshu performed, according to Naziruthian law, a marriage for a priest or priestess so that he could claim the fullness of his office. It is said in Nazorean oral tradition that there is always some priest willing to marry another wife in a polygamist marriage for the sake of his colleague's advancement, but if no priests are found who are willing to enter into such a marriage, the Ganzibra must remain in isolated retreat until someone is. If the opportunity never arises, the Ganzibra must live out his days alone and isolated until the day of his or her death. There are no reports of this ever having been necessary.

Promise of Life

Nazoreanism teaches union, not celibacy, and encourages each person to be multifaceted. For men, spouses must manifest the archetype of the Mother of Life, whilst simultaneously being a spiritual sister as well as spouse. Brides see in their fellow male counterparts a manifestation of the threefold Living Soul, who is as Father, brother and son to them. We see this reflected in the Apocryphon of John which has:

> "Straightway, while I was contemplating these things, behold, the heavens opened and the whole creation which is below heaven shone, and the world was shaken. I was afraid, and behold I saw in the light a youth who stood by me. While I looked at him, he became like an old man. And he changed his likeness (again), becoming like a servant. There was not a plurality before me, but there was a likeness with multiple forms in the light, and the likenesses appeared through each other, and the likeness had three forms. He said to me, "John, John, why do you doubt, or why are you afraid? You are not unfamiliar with this image, are you? - that is, do not be timid! - I am the one who

is with all of you always. I am the Father, I am the Mother, I am the Son. I am the undefiled and incorruptible one."

We also see this concept in Thunder and the Perfect Mind which has:

"I am the wife and the virgin. I am the mother and the daughter."

Such concepts are no doubt strange for one who has yet to absorb the truth of the oneness of the Living Soul. Until one transcends the duality and limitation of personal ego existence, such magnanimity of outlook is probably quite foreign. Miryai is the mate of Yeshu on several levels. All Nazorean teachers tend to marry, oft a multitude of times. For in spiritual nuptials is found the fulfillment of many promises, and as Yeshu said in Thomas:

"When you make the two into one, and when you make the inner like the outer and the outer like the inner, and the upper like the lower, and when you make male and female into a single one, so that the male will not be male nor the female be female, when you make eyes in place of an eye, a hand in place of a hand, a foot in place of a foot, an image in place of an image, then you will enter [the kingdom]."

˜ 10 ˜
ACCEPTABLE YEAR

One Year Ministry

CHRISTIANS FOCUS ON what they think is the miraculous birth and supernatural death and resurrection of Jesus, and to a lesser degree on the teachings. Gnostics did not focus on either the birth or death of Yeshu, but on what he taught and what he represented. Within the Christian camp many falsehoods and erroneous beliefs have been perpetuated. One of these myths is the tradition that Jesus taught for three full years. Peter, however, tells us in the Clementine literature that Yeshu only taught for one year:

> "'Why did our teacher abide and discourse a whole year to those who were awake?'[323]

The length of Yeshu's ministry has been hotly debated in scholarly circles over the years, since the pseudo-gospels found in the New Testament, especially John, do seem to indicate at least three years. Peter, who declared it to have been only one year, would have authoritatively known. Other early writers agreed:

> "The year of my redemption"[324], appear to have induced Clement of Alexandria, Julius Africanus, Philastrius, Hilarion, and two or three other patristic writers to allow only one year for the public life. This latter opinion has found advocates among certain recent students: von Soden, for instance, defends it in Cheyne's "Encyclopaedia Biblica"."[325]

Even Ephraim of Syria, in his hymns for Epiphany, resonates the thirtieth year death of Yeshu:

> "In the year that is the thirtieth let them give thanks with us;--the dead that have lived through His dying,--the living that were converted in His Crucifixion,--and the height and the depth that have been reconciled in Him! Blessed be He and His Father! [326]

Also, the people called the "Docetae", according to Catholic heresiologists, say:

---

[323] - From The Clementine Homilies
[324] Isaiah 34:8; 63:4
[325] From "Chronology Of The Life Of Jesus Christ", Catholic Encyclopedia:
[326] Ephraim of Syria, Epiphany Hymns

"From the thirty Aeons, therefore, (the Son) assumed thirty forms. And for this reason that eternal One existed for thirty years on the earth, because each AEon was in a peculiar manner manifested during (his own) year."[327]

They, however, that they may establish their false opinion regarding that which is written, "to proclaim the acceptable year of the Lord," maintain that He preached for one year only, and then suffered in the twelfth month.[328]

Yeshu probably began his public ministry at this Aries full moon period. The Astronomical Aries New Moon Conjunction in 29 AD occurred on Saturday, April 2, at 7 p.m. First evening of a visible crescent was on Monday April 4; and so the 14th day of Nisan (Passover) began on Sunday, April 17 and continued till dusk on Monday April 18. So Monday April 18 was the first Passover day for 29 AD and the most likely date for the beginning of the acceptable year of the lord. Yeshu was probably baptized at dawn on this day in living water in preparation for his last year on earth.

The earliest textual account of observance is found in the late second century Epistula Apostolorum. In it we read that the earliest followers of Yeshu stayed up all night on the eve of his death to celebrate a "Dukrana" (Memorial wake) and Lofani (Agape meal), a practice in harmony with ancient Yessean Jubilee observance but one at variance with common Jewish practice. We know form the following quote
that the orthodox Christian interpretation of the Acceptable Year varied from that maintained by the truer Gnostics:

"Moreover, they affirm that He suffered in the twelfth month, so that He continued to preach for one year after His baptism; and

---

[327] The Refutation Of All Heresies, Viii, I
[328] Irenaeus, Against Heresies, Book Ii

they endeavour to establish this point out of the prophet, being
truly blind, inasmuch as they affirm they have found out the
mysteries of Bythus, yet not understanding that which is called
by Isaiah the acceptable year of the Lord, nor the day of
retribution." [329]

Acceptable Year

The concept of the Acceptable Year goes back to the very
dawn of historical "Christianity" and was espoused by both
Gnostic and Orthodox camps. Paul speaks of adherence to
some sort of Passover and Pentecost festivals in his first letter
to the Corinthians, indicating early observance of liturgical
seasons amongst Nazoreans when he was still part of their
group.

Since we know that the Nazorean sect rejected the Jewish bible
and much of what is understood to be Jewish, we may assume
that the Nazorean version of Passover and Pentecost was not
Jewish in nature. This is confirmed by the snippet found in the
Gospel of the Nazoreans and criticized by Epiphanius:

> "But they abandon the proper sequence of the words and
> pervert the saying, as is plain to all from the readings attached,
> and have let the disciples say: "Where will you have us prepare
> the Passover?" And him to answer to that: "Do I desire with
> desire at this Passover to eat flesh with you?" [330]

The Nazorean version of these feasts was not perverted nor
rooted in the Old Testament festivals, but in an older more
ancient tradition that predated these forged documents. While
some similarities may have existed due to the Bible's
dependence on older indigenous holydays, there were major
differences even beyond the obvious fact that vegetarian

---

329 Irenæus, Against Heresies: Book I, Chapter XXII
330 Epiphanius, Panarion 30.22,4

Nazoreans would never kill a Passover lamb. Whereas Rabbinical Judaism has only two firstfruits festivals of Passover and Pentecost, the Dead Sea Scrolls also mention a Festival of New Wine, a Festival of New Oil, and a Wood Festival. We know from Philo that the Essenes kept a fifty day festival every fifty days.

> "...Once every seven weeks they assemble for their supreme festival, which the number 50 has had assigned to it, robed in white and with looks of serious joy. [331]

Yeshu's Nazoreans would have had two more than the five mentioned in the Sadducee scrolls for a total of seven a year. These ancient seven seasons are the root source for the later liturgical seasons of the Catholics and Church of the East.

The Christian interpretation of the concept of an acceptable year entails a series of symbolic events leading up to one all important event – the shedding of blood. The Gnostic school understood the Year as a reoccurring year long series of initiations that allow the participant to deepen their gnosis of the universe and the cosmic dramas that have transpired within it. This liturgical march through the seasons has survived in the Christian camp to some degree, most notably in the liturgical calendar and seasons used therein. The roots of these concepts go back to earliest Nazoreanism, but over time the original Gnostic interpretation of them was lost and replaced by Jewish and Roman concepts.

Liturgical Year

This thirtieth and last year of Yeshu's earthly sojourn was called the acceptable year of the lord and among Nazoreans it

---

[331] (From Therapeutae In Hastings Encyclopedia).

referred to a year long liturgical period where all fasts, feasts, readings, rites and ceremonies have been executed perfectly. The whole year becomes an extended symbolic ritual that encapsulates the entire history and future of humankind, from their origins in the highest light worlds to their descent into the deepest darkness, their purification, redemption and ascension up to the pleromatic light worlds once again. This is the "Year" that Yeshu and Miryam accomplished. The present liturgical year of the Orthodox and Catholics is a dim recognition, as is the yearly cycle of readings, fasts and feasts observed in various monastic institutions. None of these large institutions have correctly preserved the ancient pattern. Of these major religions, the Aramaic speaking Assyrian Church of the East has best preserved the ancient liturgical year observed by the Nazoreans. In their liturgical calendar can still be found echoes of the original seven week seasons of the Essenes. There is no other logical source for these traditions in the Aramaic speaking churches except even more ancient Nazorean customs.

With several overlapping calendars[332], it can be confusing to pen down the exact beginning and ending dates for the "acceptable year" of Yeshu. The fact, however, that Yeshu died on Nisan 14 on the day before Passover, and began his spiritual ascent 36 or so hours later at the time of the full moon of Aries, weighs heavily in favor of the full moon of Aries being the beginning and end of the "acceptable year". This seems in accord with the ancient liturgical calendar of the earlier Nazoreans as passed on to the Christians and observed by them at the Aries full moon until Rome changed the date of

---

[332] Ancient Palestine had several calendar years, the civil from Tishri 1, the spiritual from Nisan 1, and the New Year for trees from Daula 1. The Mandaean calendar officially begins on Daula 1, but their 5 Parwanaia days proceed Tishri 1, and their number of months puts Nisan as month one, indicating that they, and their ancient Nazorean ancestors, observed several overlapping calendars and new years days as well. With Yeshu's birthday on Shevat 3, a Shevat 1 New Year among the Mandai may be a remembrance of this since they are descended from both the Dositheans as well as the Yeshu loving Elchasaites. It is also the New Year for Trees according to the Jewish Shammai School.

this festival to be the first Sunday after this full moon instead of the full moon itself. The "Jewish Christians", as they called them, continued to celebrate this date at the full moon of Aries despite what weekday it fell on. This shows an ancient adherence to some sort of lunar calendar and precedence of the lunar over the fixed week when both are being used concurrently.

> "In Asia Minor most people kept the fourteenth day of the moon, disregarding the sabbath: yet they never separated from those who did otherwise, until Victor, bishop of Rome, influenced by too ardent a zeal, fulminated a sentence of excommunication against the Quartodecimans in Asia. Wherefore also Irenæus, bishop of Lyons in France, severely censured Victor by letter for his immoderate heat; telling him that although the ancients differed in their celebration of Easter, they did not desist from intercommunion. Also that Polycarp, bishop of Smyrna, who afterwards suffered martyrdom under Gordian, continued to communicate with Anicetus bishop of Rome, although he himself, according to the usage of his native Smyrna, kept Easter on the fourteenth day of the moon, as Eusebius attests in the fifth book of his Ecclesiastical History. [333]

This same author writes for us on the liturgical season that proceeds Passover. Although the season is seven lunar weeks long, only six of them are before Easter. The remaining week runs concurrently with Passover week. The Nazoreans kept to a strict vegan fast regime throughout the period preceding the death and ascension date of Yeshu:

> "The fasts before Easter will be found to be differently observed among different people. Those at Rome fast three successive weeks before Easter, excepting Saturdays and Sundays. Those in Illyrica and all over Greece and Alexandria observe a fast of six weeks, which they term 'The forty days' fast.' Others commencing their fast from the seventh week before Easter, and

---

[333] The Ecclesiastical History of Socrates Scholasticus. Book V, Chapter XXII

fasting three five days only, and that at intervals, yet call that time 'The forty days' fast.' It is indeed surprising to me that thus differing in the number of days, they should both give it one common appellation; but some assign one reason for it, and others another, according to their several fancies. One can see also a disagreement about the manner of abstinence from food, as well as about the number of days. Some wholly abstain from things that have life: others feed on fish only of all living creatures: many together with fish, eat fowl also, saying that according to Moses, these were likewise made out of the waters. Some abstain from eggs, and all kinds of fruits: others partake of dry bread only; still others eat not even this: while others having fasted till the ninth hour, afterwards take any sort of food without distinction. And among various nations there are other usages, for which innumerable reasons are assigned. Since however no one can produce a written command as an authority, it is evident that the apostles left each one to his own free will in the matter, to the end that each might perform what is good not by constraint or necessity. Such is the difference in the churches on the subject of fasts. [334]

The historian Josephus tells us that at least one important calendar cycle, the 7-weeks count, did indeed begin, at least according to some, on this same day of Yeshu's ascension - the day after the 1st full phase of the Aries Moon[335]. This made each week of this week of weeks correspond with one of the quarter phases of the Moon – thus the lunar week. It is important that Yeshu began his ascension on this date in 30 AD as well, doubling its significance in the eyes of the Nazoreans who had known him well.

There were also some Jewish groups who started the count of seven weeks one week later, on the 22 of Nisan. [336] This too

---

[334] The Ecclesiastical History of Socrates Scholasticus. Book V, Chapter XXII

[335] Antiquities, Book 3, Chapter 10

[336] Iain Ruairidh mac Mhanainn B&oacuted writes in "Principles of Samaritan Halachah", Leiden: E.J.Brill, 1989, p. 332-3 has: "A striking incidence of ... the verse that is inexplicably vague or ambiguous, is Lev. 23:11, 15, which give the method of calculating the time of Pentecost each year. As is well known, the

yields a system of lunar weeks. The ancient confusion concerning these dates is easily resolved. Starting with the full moon of Aries, one counts around the zodiac wheel in seven lunar week increments. Because there are only 48 lunar weeks in the year, the last and 49th week of this series must overlap the first week, ending one week after the full moon of Aries. Thus the acceptable year of the lord actually runs one year and one week. In the life of Yeshu, this last overlapping week concerned itself with the after death experiences of the Nazorean Mashiah. These included rescuing souls out of the dark bardo of Gehennna in his role as Habshabba, appearing to his wife Miryai and brother James [337], and appearing one week later to his brother Judas Thomas[338], and other such events.

Lunar Week

We have alluded above to a liturgical week or lunar week. This differs from a fixed week in that it is determined by the phase of the moon, not a continual count of seven days. In the lunar week system the first day of any lunar week is always the beginning of a quarter of the moon cycle. The new, quarter, full and last quarter of the moon start each lunar week. The day or two of the dark moon when the moon does not shine are not counted as lunar weekdays. They are skipped over and serve as down times when one withdraws, fasts, and reviews the events of the last month.

---

expression "morrow after the Sabbath" has been used to support four different and incompatible ways of calculating the date. The Rabbanites and Dositheans take the word "Sabbath" to mean the first day of the Passover week; the Falashas, the translators of the Peshitta, and apparently the author of IV Ezra, take it to mean the whole Passover week; the Karaites, Boethusians, and all Samaritans except the Dositheans take it to mean the Sabbath day that falls somewhere in the Passover week; the author of the Book of Jubilees and the Qumran sect take it to mean the first Sabbath day after the Passover week. The verses will support all these opinions."
[337] 1Co 15:7
[338] John 20:26 A week later his disciples were in the house again, and Thomas was with them. Though the doors were locked, Jesus came and stood among them and said, "Peace be with you!"

Most theologians and some scholars assume that all of Jewish
society, at the time of Yeshu, was practicing the fixed seven-
day week which was the same as the modern fixed seven-day
week. This is probably true although it is a mistake to
automatically assume the ancient followers of Yeshu kept only
a modern week consisting of Sunday, Monday, Tuesday,
Wednesday, Thursday, Friday and Saturday. At least one of
their dating systems, the liturgical year, appears to have been
a lunar system based on seven lunar weeks. We know this
because of the controversy that arose later with Rome which
wanted to abandon this system to some degree and to divorce
itself from most lunar based calendar systems used in Judea.

We know, however, from ancient documents and artifacts that
ancient Rome, Palestine, Babylon and other Semite cultures of
the near east observed a lunar week in antiquity.

"... the Babylonian sabattu and the Hebrew sabbath, sprang
from a common [Semite] source.... this calendar has been aptly
designated as the pentecontad calendar because of the
significant role which the number 50 played in it. Its basic unit of
time-reckoning was the week of seven days. Its secondary time
unit was the period of fifty days, consisting of seven weeks - i.e.
seven times seven days - plus one additional day, a day which
stood outside the week and which was known and celebrated as
'atsrah', a festival of conclusion or termination - termination, of
course, of the pentecontad or fifty-day period. The year of this
calendar consisted of seven pentecontads ..."[339]

"The Babylonian ... seven-day week...this was the 7th, 14th, 21st,
and 28th days of every month"[340]

[339] Interpreters Dictionary: Sabbaths
[340] Hastings Encyclopedia: Sabbath: Babylonian

The global change to a seven day fixed week was begun by Judeans but is credited to Egyptians in the first century and made popular by the power and influence of Rome.

> "Early Romans subdivided time by using the epoch of the Calends, and by determining the times of the Ides and the Nones. The practice of counting the 7 planetary days didn't begin to catch-on until about the beginning part of the second century. The usage of the week among the Romans in the third century is attested to by Dio Cassius (c. 200-220 CE) who wrote: "The dedication of the days to the seven stars which are called planets was established by Egyptians, and it spread also to all men not so very long ago... [This dedication now] prevails everywhere..."[341]

Many scholars think that the modern concept of the week began in the first century, although there is not unanimous agreement on this point.

> "Since the earliest evidence for the existence of the planetary week [i.e. the modern week named after the seven planets] is to be dated toward the end of the first century A.D." [342]

This does not seem correct, however, for there is proof of a seven day fixed week in Judea. In Judea the fixed week was indeed older than the first century AD since some of the Sadducee Dead Sea Scrolls, such as 4Q325, 4Q326, 4Q327, and 4Q394, contain fixed week calendar systems. Yet these same Dead Sea Scroll fragments also preserve a luni-solar calendar, along with new and dark moons which are unnecessary if they only kept the purely solar calendar of 364 days. One scroll dated by radiocarbon technique is an astrology text called Phases of the Moon. It tested between 164 BCE and 93 BCE, thus showing the antiquity of these documents. They seem to

---

[341] Dio Cassius, Historia 37,18
[342] W. Rordorf

show a diversity of calendar systems in use by the Sadducees of the period, including a fixed week system that may have gone back as far as the influx of ideas in 445 BC when so many of the more ancient customs were changed by the Persian influence. Before 445 BC an exclusive lunar week may have been observed throughout Palestine. The Universal Jewish Encyclopedia states:

> "The New Moon is still, and the Sabbath originally was, dependent upon the lunar cycle." [343]

> The idea of the week, as a subdivision of the month, seems to have arisen in Babylonia, where each lunar month was divided into four parts, corresponding to the four phases of the moon. The first week of each month began with the new moon, so that, as the lunar month was one or two days more than four periods of seven days, these additional days were not reckoned at all. Every seventh day (sabbatum) was regarded as an unlucky day [an obvious corruption of God's meaning for the day]. This method of reckoning time spread westward through Syria and Palestine, and was adopted by the Israelites, probably after they settled in Palestine. With the development of the importance of the Sabbath as a day of consecration and the emphasis laid upon the significant number seven, the week became more and more DIVORCED from its lunar connection...[344]

After the 445 BC reform of the Jewish sect the Nazoreans of Galilee continued using the lunar week since they were not influenced by these 445 BC changes. This custom even prevailed in first century Nazorean circles and even later amongst Ebionites and Elchasaites.

The Jewish philosopher Philo Judaeus (c. 25 BC - 45 AD) tells us that in Yeshu's day Judea was keeping a fixed week:

[343] Universal Jewish Encyclopedia, pg 410
[344] Universal Jewish Encyclopedia, Volume 10, 1943. Article, "Week," p.482

"The fourth commandment [of the Ten Commandments] has reference to the sacred 7th day, that it may be observed in a sacred and holy manner. Now some regions keep a holy festival once in the month cycle, counting from [or by] the new Moon as a day [or days] sacred to God; but the region of Judea keeps every 7th day regularly, after each interval of 6 days..." [345]

We would not deny knowledge, experimentation, or even use of other alternant systems among later Nazorean Essenes, but maintain that the official liturgical yearly calendar of Yeshu and the Beni-Amin was luni-solar in nature. This is proven by the Easter date controversy that ensued later. The Nazorean remnants were known for preferring the lunar date over the Sunday date for its celebration. Although they may have kept fixed week days like Sunday to regulate their prayer hymns, they certainly observed lunar periods as well to determine major annual festivals. This dual calendar system came about, in part, from the Nazorean love of male female balance in all things. The lunar calendar being a "noorah" system, the solar a "ziwa" system, and the fixed week possibly being as a marriage of the two.

As long as the Nazorean's held power over their own in Jerusalem, all Roman practices and customs, including that of the consecutive fixed week being used to date annual festivals, were held at bay within Gnostic circles. The eventual propagation of this Roman Week in Christian circles, begun by Bishop Sixtus (c.a. A.D. 116-c.a. 126), probably did not occur until the complete ascendancy of the Roman Church over the original Essene-Nazoreans culture in western areas. This momentum continually gained strength until its climax in 135 A.D. when the central Nazorean leadership, and Jerusalem Bishopric, was replaced with non-Essene leadership

---

[345] Philo, The Decalogue, Xx, Paraphrased From The Yonge Translation

sympathetic to the interests and culture of Rome. When the Roman church finally gained enough political power to outlaw lunar week observance for festival timing, she did not hesitate to do so. The Nazorean Ebionites and Elchasaites kept to their own customs, despite the changes in the larger Christian offshoot sect.

Sabbath vs. Habshabba

"Except ye make the sabbath a real sabbath, ye shall not see the Father." [346]

Not only did the ancient Nazoreans observe a lunar based week in at least one of their calendars, they also kept a sacred day on the first rather than the seventh day of their fixed week. This put them at odds with the Jews of Judea and explains the controversies surrounding Yeshu and Sabbath observance preserved in the biblical accounts. The scriptural basis for observance of a Nazorean Holy Day is found in the Nazorean Prophets, or Doctrine of Kings text, chapter 34, which preserves an address of Miryai's mother to Her when she abandoned Judaism and joined in with Yeshu. Miryai's mother elucidates the difference in holy day observance with the following comment:

"Work does she on Sabbath (Seventh Day), on Habshabba (First Day) she keeps her hands still. Miryai has cast aside straightway the Law (Mosaic) that the Seven have laid upon us."

These two verses point out a very significant calendar difference between the religions of death and of Life. The seventh day is at the end of the lunar or fixed week - a time when the life force of the week is worn down and about to die. It is a fitting time for those who worship death to celebrate for

---

[346] Gospel of Thomas

it comes at the end, or demise of the week. It is also to be noted that Nazoreans worked on the seventh day, but refrained on the first day of Habshabba. Habshabba is an Aramaic word for the first day of the week, the beginning of the week when its essence is strong and fresh. Habshabba day probably refers to the first day of the fixed week rather than the beginning of the lunar week that began on the first, eighth, fifteenth and twenty-second days of the lunar month.

The Shawui Calendar and celebration of habshabba at the beginning of the fixed week was probably used by all the original disciples of Yeshu and Miryai. Its observance was no doubt strengthened when Yeshu began his spiritual ascent on this day.

Friday, March 24 was the first visible crescent of the Aries lunar month and the beginning of Nisan for the Jews who waited till they could observe the actual new moon before they declared the month begun. Fourteen days later, on Thursday April 6th, the 14th of Nisan began at sundown. The death date for Yeshu therefore corresponds to the next late afternoon of Friday on the 7th of April 30 AD. This means that he "arose" on the fixed week day of "Sunday" in accord with Christian tradition. In the Epistle of Barnabas we have this first day of the week called:

"the beginning of another world" [347]

Epistle of Barnabas also says:

"Wherefore also we keep the eighth day for rejoicing, in the which also Jesus rose from the dead and having been manifested ascended into the heavens".[348]

---

[347] Epistle of Barnabas xv
[348] Epistle of Barnabas xv

The Aramaic names for the days of the week that Yeshu would have known and used are:

Habshabba, had̲ bə-šabbā or had (Shamesh) = 1st day of the week
Trin or tarēn (Sin) = 2nd day of the week
Thlatha or talātā (Nirgah) = 3rd day of the week
Arba (Nbu) = 4th day of the week
Hamsha or haṃēšā (Bel) = 5th day of the week
Rahatia or arūbtā (Libat) = 6th day of the week
Shafta or šabbəṭā (Kiwan) = 7th day of the week [349]

Daily Watches

Watches is an ancient term referring to blocks of time set aside for prayer. For most Nazoreans these were three – one in the morning, at midday, and at eventide. For Priestesses and Priests there are usually seven a day, but sometimes more or less. Here is one of the prayers from the morning prayer service:

"In the Name of the Great Life! Up, up! ye Elect righteous ones, Rise up, ye perfected and believing ones! Rise, worship and praise the Great Life! And praise the great king Šislam-Rba, And praise the Occult Tanna and Ham-Ziwa, And praise the great Yawar and 'Zlat the great, And praise Simat-Hiia, From whom all worlds came into being; And praise the Wellspring and Datepalm From Whom the Father of 'uthras came into being. I worship and praise that lofty and great King of light, the Compassionate One Who is full of loving-kindness." [350]

---

[349] Mandaeans of Iraq and Iran, Leiden, 1962, http://www.geonames.de/days.html
[350] The Canonical Prayerbook of the Mandaeans (Leiden: Brill, 1959). ES Drower

The Aramaic names for the prayer watches of each day that Yeshu would have known and used are preserved in the Syrian orthodox tradition that still uses Syriac:

> Evening or *ramsho* prayer (Vespers),
>> Drawing of Veil or *Sootoro* prayer (Compline)
> Midnight or *lilyo* prayer, The Midnight prayer consists of three qawme 'watches'. (Nocturns)
>> Dawn prayer
> Morning or *saphro* prayer (Matins/Prime),
>> 3rd Hour or *tloth sho`in* prayer (Terce, 9 a.m.)
> 6th Hour or *sheth sho`in* prayer (Sext, noon)
>> 9th Hour or *tsha` sho`in* prayer (Nones, 3 p.m.) [351]

Mor Gregarius informs us that the Syriac Ascetics added another prayer- the Eighth which is called Dawn Prayers. Laymen in this Syriac tradition, however, "not being able to keep the seven times of prayer, pray in the morning, at noon and in the evening."[352] This is founded on the ancient Nazorean tradition.

There are set Nazorean hymns and responses that are meant to be sung at these three main prayer watches of the day – morning, noon, and evening. Priests and Priestesses were required to memorize these and Yeshu would have known them well.

After a few hundred years, the Manichaean branch of the Nazoreans was still keeping the watches. The author of the Fihrist, an-Nadim, speaks of the obligation of the followers of Mani to daily offer "four or seven prayers (salawat)". He writes:

> "The Ordinance of Prayer: Four or Seven

---

[351] The Syrian Orthodox Church website
[352] http://www.soc-wus.org/worship/prayer.html

"It is that a man shall rise and wash himself with water, which is either running or not. Then he shall face the supreme brightness while standing, and then bow down, saying while in prostration, "Blessed be our guide the Paraclete, the Apostle of Light, blessed be his guardian angels and praised be his shining hosts." This he says while he prostrates himself. Then he shall arise, for he must not tarry in his prostration, but stand erect. After that he shall say in a second prostration, "Praise be to thee O, thou shining one, Mani our guide, source of light and branch of the living, the great tree all of which gives healing." Then during the third prostration he shall say, "I bow down and render praise with a pure heart and a trueful tongue to the great deity, father of the lights and their substance; praised and blessed art thou, and thy greatness in its entirety, as well as to those blessed ones who know thee and whom thou hast called upon. Let the praised among thy hosts glorify thee, thy justice, thy word, thy greatness, and thy favor, for verily thou art a deity who is altogether Truth, Life, and Righteousness." Then during the fourth prostration he shall say, "I render praise and bow down to all of the deities and to all of the light shining angels and to all of the lights and all of the hosts which have sprung from the Great Deity." Then during the fifth prostration he shall say, "I bow down and give praise to the great hosts and to the shining deities, who by their wisdom have pierced and driven out the darkness, subduing it." Then he shall say during the sixth, "I bow down and offer praise to the Father of Greatness, the mighty and shining, who has come from those who have knowledge. " and in this same manner until the twelfth prostration. If he completes ten prayers, he starts another prayer in which there is praise; it is unnecessary for us to record it."[353]

In the Scroll of the Nazorean Prophets it mentions that there are 101 beads of prayer.

"The Mystery of the bead (prayer knots) is to say one and to hear a hundred and one." [354]

---

[353] Fihrist page 790
[354] Drashe Dmalke (Discourses Of Kings)

This is reference to an ancient Nazorean mala source and precursor to the 100 knot prayer ropes erroneously attributed to Pachomius in the fourth century to count the number of prayers and prostrations done each day. This in turn evolved into the Catholic rosary.

Week of Weeks

The acceptable year was defined by 7 liturgical seasons, each with 7 lunar weeks. Overlapping this lunar year was the constant reoccurring seven day fixed week cycle that had nothing to do with the phases of the moon. The imperfect biblical Book of Acts has early Nazoreans correctly keeping Pentecost, which means 50 day festival:

"And in the day of the Pentecost being fulfilled, they were all with one accord at the same place..." [355].

Daily prayer hymns and responses rotated themselves through the fixed week. Harvesting and Feasts, however, were calculated on the different lunar phase liturgical calendar. Philo Judaeus wrote of this link:

"... he ordered that the finest wheaten flour mixed with oil be offered and wine in stipulated amounts for drink-offerings. The reason is that even these are brought to maturity by the orbits of the Moon in the annual seasons, especially as the Moon helps to ripen fruits; wheat and wine and oil... Don't the fruits of cultivated crops and trees grow and come to maturity through the orbits of the Moon... ?" [356]

---

[355] Acts, Chapter 2
[356] The Special Laws, Part 2

Records indicate that ancient Judea had first fruits festivals on seven lunar week intervals that coincided with certain harvest. Passover dealt with Barley, seven lunar weeks later was Pentecost and the new wheat harvest. These were followed seven weeks later by a new grape Jubilee and a new olive Jubilee. These Jubilee periods were said to be fifty days each, but in actuality they were only 49 since the first and the last day overlapped.

> "..You shall count--seven COMPLETE Sabbaths from the day of your bringing the sheaf of the wave offering. You shall count until the morrow of the seventh Sabbath. You shall count fifty days. You shall bring a new grain-offering...it is the feast of Weeks and the feast of Firstfruits, an eternal memorial... 2. You shall count seven weeks from the day when you bring the new grain-offering... seven FULL Sabbaths shall elapse until you have counted fifty days to the morrow of the seventh Sabbath. You shall bring new wine for a drink-offering... 3. You shall count from that day for the new wine offering seven weeks, seven times (seven days), forty-nine days; there shall be seven FULL Sabbaths; until the morrow of the seventh Sabbath you shall count fifty days. You shall then offer new oil..."..[357]

Gregory Nazianzen, about 381 AD, records the fact that the fiftieth Jubilee day is outside of the normal day count, making it the eighth day of the seven day week as well as the first of the next:

> "For seven being multiplied by seven generates fifty all but one day, which we [Christians] borrow from the world to come, at once the Eighth and the first, or rather one and indestructible. For the present sabbatism of our souls can find its cessation there, that a portion [of Sabbath time] may be given to seven and also to eight..." [358]

---

[357] Temple Scroll, 'The Complete Dead Sea Scrolls In English', by Geza Vermes
[358] Oration XLI: On Pentecost, II

Whether using a fixed or a lunar week system, the Jubilee day was an overlapping day. A fiftieth Jubilee day on a fixed week calendar like the Therapeutai would not fall in the same season year after year. A fiftieth Jubilee day on a lunar week calendar would fall in the same harvest season each year. A modern Palestinian version of the ancient Pentecontad calendar, similar to the Nestorian one, has 365 days:

> "Passover Week (7 days), Pentecost (50 days), Festival of Elijah (50 days), Festival of the Cross (50 days), Tabernacles Week (8 days), Festival of St. George (50 days), Christmas (50 days), Lent (50 days)." [359]

This is not the original Nazorean luni-solar calendar, however.

Clement of Alexandria writing in the 2nd century in 'The Stromata' tells us that in "*Peter's Preaching*" Peter warned that one should not worship as the Jews who base their festivals on the visible sighting of the moon. Since we know early Nazoreans did keep festivals based on the lunar phases and were excellent astrologers, we may infer from this passage that Peter was not condemning lunar calendars but preferred astrological calculation to determine the new moon rather than visible sightings. He warns:

> "Neither worship as the Jews; for they, thinking that they only know God, do not know Him, adoring as they do angels and archangels, the month and the moon. And if the moon be not visible, they do not hold the Sabbath, which is called the first; nor do they hold the new moon, nor the feast of unleavened bread, nor the feast, nor the great day."[360]

---

[359] Morgenstern, Julian, "The Chanukkah Festival and the Calendar of Ancient Israel," part VI, Section A of which is entitled, "The Pentecontad Calendar in the Ancient Semitic World," Hebrew Union College Annual (Cincinnati, Ohio: Hebrew Union College, 1948), vol. 21, pp 365 - 374.
[360] The Stromata, Or Miscellanies, Book 6, Chapter 5

The Book of Sirach, or the Wisdom of Joshua the son of Sirach, is a book in the Apocrypha written in Hebrew at Jerusalem c. 180 BC by Jesus ben Sirach. In it he writes

> "He made the moon also to serve in her season for a declaration of times, and a sign of the world. From the moon is the sign of feasts, a light that decreaseth in her perfection."[361]

Echoes of the ancient Nazorean Essene calendar were preserved in the ancient Nestorian liturgical calendar which tried to maintain the seven week seasons:

> "The year is divided into periods of about seven weeks each, called Shawu'i; these are Advent (called Subara, "Annunciation"), Ephiphany, Lent, Easter, the Apostles, Summer, "Elias and the Cross", "Moses", and the "Dedication" (Qudash idta). "Moses" and the "Dedication" have only four weeks each.. [362]

The modern Assyrian Church of the East has preserved the Syriac-Aramaic names of the seven week seasons that were once observed by Yeshu and other Nazoreans. These are given as:

Raising (*Qyamta*), Ascension (*Kaalu D'Sulaaqa*)
Apostles (*Shleeheh*)
Summer (*Qaita*), Newness (*Nusardil*) Elijah (*Elia*)
Cross (*Sleewa*), Moses (*Moshe*), Church Consecration (*Qoodash Aiyta*)
Annuciation (Soubra)
Birth (*Yalda*), Epiphany (*Denha*)
Fast (*Sauma*)

---

361 Sirach Chapter 43:6-7
362 East Syrian Rite, From Wikipedia

These loosely equate with the western Catholic liturgical seasons of Triduum/Paschaltide, Pentecost, Ordinary Time, Ordinary Time, Advent, Christmas, and Lent.

They also equate with certain harvest periods and first fruit dedication of that harvest before consumption. This in turn was given mystical significance. For instance, the controversy about eating wheat rather than Barley that got Mani in so much trouble with the Elchasaite had to do with the spiritual significance of the various grains.

"Passover season was the time period during which the first ripened of two different grains or seeds were gathered and presented in the Temple. These were the barley seed and wheat seed. Symbolically these represent the masculine spora and the feminine sperma. (The Greek word sperma was derived from the name of an ancient feminine Greek goddess who could change any grain into wheat.) . . . .

The barley seed represents these masculine saints with the spirit of Christ while the wheat seed represents feminine souls of the faithful in Christ Jesus, which eventually will be derived from believing Israel and believing Gentiles. According to the Encyclopedia Britannica and Webster's Dictionary, cultivatable wheat was first discovered by the Egyptians in the land of Canaan, while barley, on the other hand, grew throughout the world. Yeast or leaven was acquired from barley seed which was crushed and added to water to produce malt. It is the yeast from barley malt that is needed to raise the wheat flour from ground wheat seed to obtain the full loaf of bread. (The sporadic action of the yeast's cell division causes the gases that make the wheat dough to rise.) [363]

[363] The Mark of the Cross by Steve Santini

The Zohar calls the time between Passover and Pentecost the "courting days of the bridegroom Israel with the bride Torah." [364]

These ancient seven seasons had certain themes that can be at least partially recaptured by indepth study of certain scrolls during certain seasons:

Raising (*Qyamta*): Post-Resurrection Teachings (i.e. Pistis Sophia)
Apostles (*Shleeheh*): Preaching scrolls (i.e. Clementine Homilies)
Summer (*Qaita*): Qabballistic texts (i.e. Zohar, Bahir, Yetzirah)
Cross (*Sleewa*): Archon teachings (i.e. Ginza, Apostasis of the Archons)
Annuciation (*Soubra*): Prophetic (i.e. Doctrine of Priestly Kings)
Birth (*Yalda*): Secret texts (i.e. Nag Hammadhi)
Fast (*Sauma*): Silk Road sutras (i.e. Manichaean, Nestorian, Zen)

Therapeutae Calendar

The Jewish/Greek writer Philo, who lived in the first century AD during the time in which proto-Nazoreans still observed the true calendar, graphically described the usage of a seven-weeks calendar (with fiftieth day) among the Therapeutae and Therapeutridae of Egypt. Epiphanius later reports these to be Nazoreans which cannot be wholly correct since their stance on marriage conflicts with the Nazorean insistence upon such. They were in reality Issaei, or Essenes Rechabites, as Nilas tells us:

"they were the Jewish philosophers and ascetics who were originally followers of the Rechabite Jonadab." [365]

---

[364] Pentecost, Jewish Encyclopedia.com

[365] Did Jesus Live 100 B.C.? By G. R. S. Mead

Of the Therapeutae or the Healers of Egypt, we read:

> "The seventh day is...for relaxation... Once every seven weeks [a]
> supreme festival [is celebrated], which the number 50 has had
> assigned to it... [The 50th] a banquet... [is celebrated] with
> hyssop... being added out of reverence for the holy table of
> offering in the sacred vestibule of the Temple, to signify that the
> Therapeutae are too humble to emulate the unleavened bread
> reserved for the priests[366]

The Therapeutae of Egypt were not exactly the same Essene
sect as that of Yeshu, but they had similar calendars. Eusebius
of Caesarea in the third century implies that early Christians
continued this tradition:

> "[*Philo Judaeus wrote of*] a mode of life which has been preserved
> to the present time by us alone [*or by the Christians alone*],
> recording especially the vigils kept in connection with the great
> festival [*or the great festival celebrated on the 50th day*], and the
> exercises performed during those vigils... [*The customs demand*]
> no wine at all, nor any flesh, but water is their only drink, and
> the relish with their bread is salt and hyssop".[367]

Therapeutae means healer in Greek, and in the Aramaic the
word for healer is indeed "essene". When Yeshu was in Egypt
he would have kept this calendar when spending time with
the Therapeutae. What Philo tells us of this movement comes
from a treatise: de Vita Contemplativa (The Contemplative
Life) written around 30 AD. It may represent dietary customs
prevalent during the Essene equivalent of Lent.

> ..."They are Jewish recluses who reside in simple huts, at a short
> and suitable distance from one another. Each hut has a sacred
> chamber reserved for their sacred books by means of which

---

[366] 'The Encyclopedia Of Religion And Ethics', By Hastings, Therapeutae
[367] Church History, Book Ii,

religion and sound knowledge grow together into a perfect whole. After praying at dawn, they devote the day to meditation upon the Scriptures; these include writing or commentaries drawn up by the ancient founder of their sect…Prayers at sunset close the day. Such is the life in each hut. On the seventh day the various members meet for common worship; they arrange themselves according to age, sitting on the ground with the right hand between the chest and the chin, but the left tucked down along the flank. The senior recluse then delivers an address to which all listen in silence, merely nodding assent. A partition, ten or twelve feet high, separates the men from the women, so that the latter can hear the speaker without being seen by the male recluses.

…The seventh day is their day for relaxation. On the other days no one eats before sunset, and some go fasting almost entirely for three or even six days, in their contemplative raptures. But all use oil and on the seventh day all propitiate the mistresses hunger and thirst, which nature has set over mortal creatures; the diet is simply water and cheap bread, flavored with salt, and occasionally supplemented by hyssop.

…Once every seven weeks they assemble for their supreme festival, which the number 50 has had assigned to it, robed in white and with looks of serious joy. At a given sign from one of their leaders they arrange themselves in ranks, raising eyes and hands to heaven ('their hands because they are pure from unjust gains, being stained by no pretense of money-making') and praying for a blessing on the festival. Then, the senior members recline, in order of seniority, upon their cheap, rough couches; on the left side of the room the women also recline. The younger novices wait upon the older members, for the Therapeutae decline to be served by slaves; they deem any possession of servants whatever to be contrary to nature, which makes all alike free at birth. It is not a banquet of luxuries; no wine, only cold water, heated for those who are delicate; no meat-for the Therapeutae are vegetarians, living on nothing but bread and salt, with hyssop for the more delicate palates, the hyssop being added out of reverence for the holy table of offering in the sacred vestibule of the Temple, to signify that the Therapeutae are too humble to emulate the unleavened bread reserved for the priests. But before this Spartan meal is eaten, a quiet president. The rest listen in breathless silence; but, if the speaker does not make his meaning clear, they are allowed to indicate their perplexity by a slight movement of the head and a right-hand finger. When he is considered to have spoken long enough, all clap their hands three times. A hymn then follows, sometimes composed in honor of God by the singer either a new one which he has made himself, or some old one of the poets that were long ago. Each member has to sing a hymn in rotation, while the rest join in the chorus. Only after this religious service of an address and praise - does the banquet proceed.

...The final act of the festival is the famous 'all-night celebration' of a sacred singing dance by men and women in two choruses each headed by a chosen leader. Each of the choirs, the male and the female, begins by singing and dancing apart, partly in unison, partly in antiphonal measures of various metres, as if it were a Bacchic festival in which they had drunk deep of the divine love. Then, both unite to imitate the choral songs of Moses and Miryam at the Red Sea...It is a thrilling performance, this choric dance and exulting symphony: but the end and aim of it all is holiness...

...Such says Philo, is the method of life practiced by these true citizens of heaven and of the universe." ... [368]

Calendar Contention

Nazoreans had an ancient luni-solar calendar and almanac that would have influenced the rhythm of Yeshu's life from an early age. There was a huge controversy in later Christianity when the Church of Rome sought to abandon the original lunar dating system in favor of the Roman system.

---

[368] (From Therapeutae In Hastings Encyclopedia).

The writings of the "Apostle" Paul, rejected by the Nazoreans for their preponderance of bad advice and heretical doctrine, contain direction for abandoning this ancient Nazorean calendar system. Writing to gentile Romanized Christians, Paul says:

> "Let no man judge you for eating and drinking or in part of an holyday, or of the new Moon, or of the sabbaton ".

The Nazorean Way is characterized by a daily and weekly rhythm of spiritual events that contributes to the reshaping of ones consciousness. Nazorean communities are designed to follow certain symbolic spiritual schedules. These practices reflect ancient patterns of daily life that were supplanted in the west when Roman Christianity did away with most Nazorean customs.

Yeshu and other ancient Nazorean Essenes observed a fixed week along with a special liturgical calendar, or lunar almanac, based upon the dance of heavenly orbs. The name and number of seasons, of this ancient liturgical almanac has been preserved for us by the Aramaic speaking Syrian church. They called this special almanac a Shawui. The word means "a week of shawuahs" A Shawuah is any one of the 7 seasons within a Shawui year. This is not the same calendar used by modern Jews, but it has some similarities.

> "The Calendar is very peculiar. The year is divided into periods of about seven weeks each, called Shawu'i ..... [369]

Each of these seasons contains 7 weeks. At the end of the seven weeks there is a 50th day jubilee which overlaps with the first day of the next season. The observance of 50 day

---

[369] Catholic Encyclopedia, Under Syrian Rite

seasons is an ancient Nazorean custom which is partially adhered to, even in our day, among Catholic and Orthodox churches with roots in antiquity. Calendars containing 50 day seasons are called Pentecontad Calendars.

This original Nazorean lunar-solar calendar, which contained both fixed and lunar weeks, was almost completely supplanted by a Roman "planetary week" and calendar in 135 C.E. when the "Bishops of the Circumcision" (i.e. legitimate Nazorean successors to Yeshu-Miryai) were displaced from Jerusalem and Carmel. This began a three hundred year controversy concerning the true calendar and correct Sabbath:

> "This [calendar] controversy arose after the exodus of the bishops of the circumcision and has continued until our time." [370]

The groundwork for this supplanting of the true calendar, suggests the ancient historian Iranaeus, begun in Roman with a Bishop Sixtus (c.a. A.D. 116-c.a. 126). According to Irenaeus, Sixtus was the first to celebrate a Sunday Easter in Rome instead of the traditional Nisan 15 [full moon] date on the lunar [Shawui] calendar. This change from the luni-solar to a fixed solar calendar occurred in Rome during the repressive measures which were enacted against all Jewish customs and practices, including the lunar calendar, during Emperor Hadrian's reign. With the fall of the Nazorean headquarters in the Essene Temple at Jerusalem, this new Roman calendar quickly spread throughout "Christendom". This new calendar not only replaced yearly festival dates such as Passover, but also removed other moveable feasts from its calendar. Only Easter was loosely tied to the old luni-solar calendar by its observance on the first Sunday after the first full moon of spring.

---

[370] Epiphanius He4,6,4

Yeshu would have observed the seven week cycles of the liturgical year. Within these week of weeks would be found the various lunar months. The ancient Nazorean Aramaic names of the months which Yeshu used, as well as the harvests for those months, are:

Ambra (Aries/Nisan) - barley, peas, lentils
Taura (Taurus) – wheat, oats, peas, lentils
Silmia (Gemini) - chickpeas, grapes
Sartana (Cancer) - sesame, flax, millet, grapes
Arya (Leo) – figs, pomegranates, grapes, millet
Shumbulta (Wheat, Virgo) - figs, pomegranates, grapes, olives
Qaina (Libra) - olives
Arqba (Scorpio) -olives
Hatia (Mare, Sagittarius)
Gadia (Capricorn)
Daula (Aquarius)
Nuna (Pisces) [371]

Christian Calendar

The Christian calendar evolved over time from a mix between the Nazorean and the Roman. Over time the Roman became dominant. Justin Martyr was a non-Nazorean writer who wrote about 150 AD, describing Christian worship on a day of the sun. He says:

"...And on the day called Sunday, all who live in cities or in the country gather together to one place, and the memoirs of the apostles or the writings of the prophets are read, as long as time permits; then, when the reader has ceased, the president verbally instructs, and exhorts to the imitation of these good things. Then we all rise together and pray, and, as we before said, when our prayer is ended, bread and wine and water are brought, and the

---

[371] Spar Maluasia, Mandaean Book of the Zodiac.

president in like manner offers prayers and thanksgivings, according to his ability, and the people assent, saying Amen; and there is a distribution to each, and a participation of that over which thanks have been given, and to those who are absent a portion is sent by the deacons. And they who are well to do, and willing, give what each thinks fit; and what is collected is deposited with the president, who succors the orphans and widows and those who, through sickness or any other cause, are in want, and those who are in bonds and the strangers sojourning among us, and in a word takes care of all who are in need. But Sunday is the day on which we all hold our common assembly, because it is the first day on which God, having wrought a change in the darkness and matter, made the world; and Jesus Christ our Savior on the same day rose from the dead. For He was crucified on the day before that of Saturn; and on the day after that of Saturn, which is the 'day of the Sun', having appeared to His apostles and disciples, He taught them these things, which we have submitted to you also for your consideration."[372]

Note that this is "Christian worship", not Nazorean worship, and that "Sunday" may not refer to the present day of the sun in our modern fixed week calendar. One commentator on this passage writes:

"Undoubtedly, Justin was referring to the Temple calendar date for the 'cycle of the Sun', or 'Sunday', which should not be confused with the modern: Sunday - which came along later."[373]

The first Sunday Law was enacted by Emperor Constantine on March, 321 A.D.

"On the venerable Day of the Sun let the magistrates and people residing in cities rest, and let all workshops be closed. In the country, however, persons engaged in agriculture may freely

---

[372] Apology, 1, 67:1-3, 7; First Apology, 145 Ad, Ante-Nicene Fathers , Vol. 1, Pg. 186
[373] James D. Dwyer, Tracking the Day-of-the-Sun

and lawfully continue their pursuits; because it often happens that another day is not so suitable for grain-sowing or for vine-planting; lest by neglecting the proper moment for such operations the bounty of heaven should be lost. (Given the 7th day of March, Crispus and Constantine being consuls each of them for the second time [a.d. 321].) [374]

"This legislation by Constantine probably bore little relation to Christianity; it appears, on the contrary, that the emperor, in his capacity of Pontifex Maximus, was only adding the day of the Sun, the worship of which was then firmly established in the Roman Empire, to the other ferial days of the calendar:

"What began, however, as a pagan ordinance, ended as a Christian regulation; and a long series of imperial decrees, during the fourth, fifth, and sixth centuries, enjoined with increasing stringency abstinence from labour on Sunday."[375]

"The Church made a sacred day of Sunday ... largely because it was the weekly festival of the sun; for it was a definite Christian policy to take over the pagan festivals endeared to the people by tradition, and to give them a Christian significance."[376]

Sunday observance of Easter is a result of a strong, anti-Jewish movement which warred against all things Jewish and Nazorean, including the true calendar. This resulted in rejection of the Shawui and the acceptance of a non-Nazorean festival calendar based more on the planetary week than on the full moon.

"The social tension that existed between Jews and Christians, as well as the Roman anti-Jewish policy, greatly conditioned

[374] Codex Justinianus, Lib. 3, Tit. 12, 3; Trans. In Philip Schaff, History Of The Christian Church, Vol. 3 (5th Ed.; New York: Scribner, 1902), P. 380, Note 1.
[375] Hutton Webster, Rest Days, Pp. 122, 123, 270. Copyright 1916 By The Macmillan Company, New York.
[376] Arthur Weigall, The Paganism In Our Christianity, P. 145. Copyright 1928 By G. P. Putnam's Sons, New York.

Christians in their negative evaluation of significant Old
Testament institutions like the Sabbath." From Sabbath to
Sunday - [377]

"Let us have nothing in common with the detestable Jewish
crowd..."[378]

"Let us no longer keep the Sabbath after the Jewish [Nazorean]
manner . . . and not eating things prepared the day before, nor
using lukewarm drinks." [379]

Some "Christian" writers even stated that ancient institutions,
like the Sabbath, were actually a curse and a punishment
imposed upon Jews by an angry God. Although Nazoreans
did not keep the Jewish Sabbath on Saturday, they did keep a
Nazorean version on Sunday.

"It was by reason of your sins and the sins of your fathers that,
among other precepts, God imposed upon you the observance of
the Sabbath as a Mark . . . the purpose of this was that you and
only you might suffer the afflictions that are now justly yours! -
[380]

Pseudo-Cyprian - De Pashc Computus 243 A.D. has:

"We desire to show . . . that Christians need at no time . . . to
walk in blindness and stupidity behind the Jews as though they
did not know what was the day of the Passover."

"Having eliminated the Judaizing Quartodeciman tradition
[lunar calendar], repudiating even the Jewish computations,
making their own time calculations, since such dependence on
the Jews [Nazoreans] must have appeared humiliating." [381]

---

[377] Samuele Bacchiochi
[378] Eusebius, Life of Constatine
[379] Pseuso Ignatius, Epistle Magnesians
[380] Greek Justin Dialogue
[381] M. Righetti, Renowned Liturgist

Realizing the depth of animosity and hatred felt by early gentile Christians toward all Semite customs and people, one can easily see how the early Roman church was able to supplant original Nazorean leadership and customs by mixing them up with Jewish ones. By rewriting scripture and history, and by altering original customs and practices, the Roman Church was able to create a Christianity that bore only surface similarities to the original Nazorean religion taught by Yeshu. They took the original disdain which the Nazoreans had for Judaic traditions and applied it to the Nazoreans as well, lumping both Jew and Essene in one rejected group. Through centuries of careful editing and eradication of original documents and witnesses, this Roman Christianity was able to create the illusion of complete historical continuity with the early Nazorean Movement and with Judaism. Careful analysis of this claim, however, reveals that Roman Christianity is not the true preserver of the original tradition, nor were the Nazoreans or Yeshu Jewish.

˜ 11 ˜
GOSPEL OF JUDAS THOMAS

Judas Thomas Gospel

WE HAVE BEEN addressing the background and lifestyle of Yeshu in the previous chapters. We now turn to some of his teachings, but we shall avoid the New Testament gospels as hopelessly corrupt and turn instead to a much more pure gospel known as Thomas. The Gospel of Judas Thomas was written by Judas, the brother of Yeshu. It is noteworthy that this gospel is a sayings gospel only and it is devoid of the passion and nativity stories of the later Greek gospels. It contains sayings that the historians have quoted from the

Gospels used by Nazoreans and it is known that the later Manichaean Gnostics used this Gospel as well. There are 21 parallel saying that are found in both the Gnostic Thomas and the Biblical Mark. It has been convincingly shown by Biblical Professor Stevan Davies[382] that these 21 parallel sayings in Thomas are the inspiration for those found in the first biblical gospel of Mark from whence all other biblical gospels derived.

> "...the preponderance of evidence indicates that the Gospel of Thomas served as a source for the Gospel of Mark." [383]

This is important since Christians have always tried to portray Gnosticism as something inferior that came later and adulterated the orthodox position. The opposite is in fact true.

The difference between Thomas and the biblical Gospels is one of view. All major Christian denominations refuse to accept Thomas as scriptural. Mark and the others stress co-suffering with Christ, Thomas stresses co-understanding with Yeshu. Thomas was used by early Nazoreans, and also by later Manichaeans for just this reason. From a Gnostic perspective, only bible sayings that overlap with Thomas are to be fully trusted. Here is the complete text of this very important document that accurately portrays the original teachings of Yeshu to the lay members of the Nazorean faith.

Translation

> "These are the secret sayings which the living Yeshu spoke and which Didymos Judas Thomas wrote down.
> (1) And he said, "Whoever finds the interpretation of these sayings will not experience death."

---

[382] Mark's Use of the Gospel of Thomas by Stevan Davies, Prof. of Biblical Studies, The University of South Africa: Summer 1996, Part 1, also Gospel of Thomas Annotated & Explained by Stevan Davies
[383] Mark's Use of the Gospel of Thomas by Stevan Davies, Prof. of Biblical Studies, The University of South Africa: Summer 1996, Part 2

(2) Yeshu said, "Let him who seeks continue seeking until he finds. When he finds, he will become troubled. When he becomes troubled, he will be astonished, and he will rule over the All."

(3) Yeshu said, "If those who lead you say to you, 'See, the kingdom is in the sky,' then the birds of the sky will precede you. If they say to you, 'It is in the sea,' then the fish will precede you. Rather, the kingdom is inside of you, and it is outside of you. When you come to know yourselves, then you will become known, and you will realize that it is you who are the sons of the living father. But if you will not know yourselves, you dwell in poverty and it is you who are that poverty."

(4) Yeshu said, "The man old in days will not hesitate to ask a small child seven days old about the place of life, and he will live. For many who are first will become last, and they will become one and the same."

(5) Yeshu said, "Recognize what is in your sight, and that which is hidden from you will become plain to you . For there is nothing hidden which will not become manifest."

(6) His disciples questioned him and said to him, "Do you want us to fast? How shall we pray? Shall we give alms? What diet shall we observe?"

Yeshu said, "Do not tell lies, and do not do what you hate, for all things are plain in the sight of heaven. For nothing hidden will not become manifest, and nothing covered will remain without being uncovered."

(7) Yeshu said, "Blessed is the lion which becomes man when consumed by man; and cursed is the man whom the lion consumes, and the lion becomes man."

(8) And he said, "The man is like a wise fisherman who cast his net into the sea and drew it up from the sea full of small fish. Among them the wise fisherman found a fine large fish. He threw all the small fish back into the sea and chose the large fish without difficulty. Whoever has ears to hear, let him hear."

(9) Yeshu said, "Now the sower went out, took a handful (of seeds), and scattered them. Some fell on the road; the birds came and gathered them up. Others fell on the rock, did not take root in the soil, and did not produce ears. And others fell on thorns; they choked the seed(s) and worms ate them. And others fell on

the good soil and it produced good fruit: it bore sixty per measure and a hundred and twenty per measure."

(10) Yeshu said, "I have cast fire upon the world, and see, I am guarding it until it blazes."

(11) Yeshu said, "This heaven will pass away, and the one above it will pass away. The dead are not alive, and the living will not die. In the days when you consumed what is dead, you made it what is alive. When you come to dwell in the light, what will you do? On the day when you were one you became two. But when you become two, what will you do?"

(12) The disciples said to Yeshu, "We know that you will depart from us. Who is to be our leader?" Yeshu said to them, "Wherever you are, you are to go to James the righteous, for whose sake heaven and earth came into being."

(13) Yeshu said to his disciples, "Compare me to someone and tell me whom I am like."Simon Peter said to him, "You are like a righteous angel."

Matthew said to him, "You are like a wise philosopher."

Thomas said to him, "Master, my mouth is wholly incapable of saying whom you are like." Yeshu said, "I am not your master. Because you have drunk, you have become intoxicated from the bubbling spring which I have measured out." And he took him and withdrew and told him three things. When Thomas returned to his companions, they asked him, "What did Yeshu say to you?" Thomas said to them, "If I tell you one of the things which he told me, you will pick up stones and throw them at me; a fire will come out of the stones and burn you up."

(14) Yeshu said to them, "If you fast, you will give rise to sin for yourselves; and if you pray, you will be condemned; and if you give alms, you will do harm to your spirits. When you go into any land and walk about in the districts, if they receive you, eat what they will set before you, and heal the sick among them. For what goes into your mouth will not defile you, but that which issues from your mouth - it is that which will defile you."

(15) Yeshu said, "When you see one who was not born of woman, prostrate yourselves on your faces and worship him. That one is your father."

(16) Yeshu said, "Men think, perhaps, that it is peace which I have come to cast upon the world. They do not know that it is

dissension which I have come to cast upon the earth: fire, sword, and war. For there will be five in a house: three will be against two, and two against three, the father against the son, and the son against the father. And they will stand solitary."

(17) Yeshu said, "I shall give you what no eye has seen and what no ear has heard and what no hand has touched and what has never occurred to the human mind."

(18) The disciples said to Yeshu, "Tell us how our end will be."

Yeshu said, "Have you discovered, then, the beginning, that you look for the end? For where the beginning is, there will the end be. Blessed is he who will take his place in the beginning; he will know the end and will not experience death."

(19) Yeshu said, "Blessed is he who came into being before he came into being. If you become my disciples and listen to my words, these stones will minister to you. For there are five trees for you in Paradise which remain undisturbed summer and winter and whose leaves do not fall. Whoever becomes acquainted with them will not experience death."

(20) The disciples said to Yeshu, "Tell us what the kingdom of heaven is like."

He said to them, "It is like a mustard seed. It is the smallest of all seeds. But when it falls on tilled soil, it produces a great plant and becomes a shelter for birds of the sky."

(21) Mary said to Yeshu, "Whom are your disciples like?"

He said, "They are like children who have settled in a field which is not theirs. When the owners of the field come, they will say, 'Let us have back our field.' They (will) undress in their presence in order to let them have back their field and to give it back to them. Therefore I say, if the owner of a house knows that the thief is coming, he will begin his vigil before he comes and will not let him dig through into his house of his domain to carry away his goods. You, then, be on your guard against the world. Arm yourselves with great strength lest the robbers find a way to come to you, for the difficulty which you expect will (surely) materialize. Let there be among you a man of understanding. When the grain ripened, he came quickly with his sickle in his hand and reaped it. Whoever has ears to hear, let him hear."

(22) Yeshu saw infants being suckled. He said to his disciples, "These infants being suckled are like those who enter the kingdom."

They said to him, "Shall we then, as children, enter the kingdom?"

Yeshu said to them, "When you make the two one, and when you make the inside like the outside and the outside like the inside, and the above like the below, and when you make the male and the female one and the same, so that the male not be male nor the female female; and when you fashion eyes in the place of an eye, and a hand in place of a hand, and a foot in place of a foot, and a likeness in place of a likeness; then will you enter the kingdom."

(23) Yeshu said, "I shall choose you, one out of a thousand, and two out of ten thousand, and they shall stand as a single one."

(24) His disciples said to him, "Show us the place where you are, since it is necessary for us to seek it." He said to them, "Whoever has ears, let him hear. There is light within a man of light, and he lights up the whole world. If he does not shine, he is darkness."

(25) Yeshu said, "Love your brother like your soul, guard him like the pupil of your eye."

(26) Yeshu said, "You see the mote in your brother's eye, but you do not see the beam in your own eye. When you cast the beam out of your own eye, then you will see clearly to cast the mote from your brother's eye."

(27) Yeshu said, "If you do not fast as regards the world, you will not find the kingdom. If you do not observe the Sabbath as a Sabbath, you will not see the father."

(28) Yeshu said, "I took my place in the midst of the world, and I appeared to them in flesh. I found all of them intoxicated; I found none of them thirsty. And my soul became afflicted for the sons of men, because they are blind in their hearts and do not have sight; for empty they came into the world, and empty too they seek to leave the world. But for the moment they are intoxicated. When they shake off their wine, then they will repent."

(29) Yeshu said, "If the flesh came into being because of spirit, it is a wonder. But if spirit came into being because of the body, it

is a wonder of wonders. Indeed, I am amazed at how this great wealth has made its home in this poverty."

(30) Yeshu said, "Where there are three gods, they are gods. Where there are two or one, I am with him."

(31) Yeshu said, "No prophet is accepted in his own village; no physician heals those who know him."

(32) Yeshu said, "A city being built on a high mountain and fortified cannot fall, nor can it be hidden."

(33) Yeshu said, "Preach from your housetops that which you will hear in your ear. For no one lights a lamp and puts it under a bushel, nor does he put it in a hidden place, but rather he sets it on a lamp stand so that everyone who enters and leaves will see its light."

(34) Yeshu said, "If a blind man leads a blind man, they will both fall into a pit."

(35) Yeshu said, "It is not possible for anyone to enter the house of a strong man and take it by force unless he binds his hands; then he will (be able to) ransack his house."

(36) Yeshu said, "Do not be concerned from morning until evening and from evening until morning about what you will wear."

(37) His disciples said, "When will you become revealed to us and when shall we see you?" Yeshu said, "When you disrobe without being ashamed and take up your garments and place them under your feet like little children and tread on them, then will you see the son of the living one, and you will not be afraid"

(38) Yeshu said, "Many times have you desired to hear these words which I am saying to you, and you have no one else to hear them from. There will be days when you will look for me and will not find me."

(39) Yeshu said, "The Pharisees and the scribes have taken the keys of knowledge (gnosis) and hidden them. They themselves have not entered, nor have they allowed to enter those who wish to. You, however, be as wise as serpents and as innocent as doves."

(40) Yeshu said, "A grapevine has been planted outside of the father, but being unsound, it will be pulled up by its roots and destroyed."

(41) Yeshu said, "Whoever has something in his hand will receive more, and whoever has nothing will be deprived of even the little he has."

(42) Yeshu said, "Become passers-by."

(43) His disciples said to him, "Who are you, that you should say these things to us?" Yeshu said to them, "You do not realize who I am from what I say to you, but you have become like the Jews, for they (either) love the tree and hate its fruit (or) love the fruit and hate the tree."

(44) Yeshu said, "Whoever blasphemes against the father will be forgiven, and whoever blasphemes against the son will be forgiven, but whoever blasphemes against the holy spirit will not be forgiven either on earth or in heaven."

(45) Yeshu said, "Grapes are not harvested from thorns, nor are figs gathered from thistles, for they do not produce fruit. A good man brings forth good from his storehouse; an evil man brings forth evil things from his evil storehouse, which is in his heart, and says evil things. For out of the abundance of the heart he brings forth evil things."

(46) Yeshu said, "Among those born of women, from Adam until John the Baptist, there is no one so superior to John the Baptist that his eyes should not be lowered (before him). Yet I have said, whichever one of you comes to be a child will be acquainted with the kingdom and will become superior to John."

(47) Yeshu said, "It is impossible for a man to mount two horses or to stretch two bows. And it is impossible for a servant to serve two masters; otherwise, he will honor the one and treat the other contemptuously. No man drinks old wine and immediately desires to drink new wine. And new wine is not put into old wineskins, lest they burst; nor is old wine put into a new wineskin, lest it spoil it. An old patch is not sewn onto a new garment, because a tear would result."

(48) Yeshu said, "If two make peace with each other in this one house, they will say to the mountain, 'Move Away,' and it will move away."

(49) Yeshu said, "Blessed are the solitary and elect, for you will find the kingdom. For you are from it, and to it you will return."

(50) Yeshu said, "If they say to you, 'Where did you come from?', say to them, 'We came from the light, the place where the light

came into being on its own accord and established itself and became manifest through their image.' If they say to you, 'Is it you?', say, 'We are its children, we are the elect of the living father.' If they ask you, 'What is the sign of your father in you?', say to them, 'It is movement and repose.'"

(51) His disciples said to him, "When will the repose of the dead come about, and when will the new world come?" He said to them, "What you look forward to has already come, but you do not recognize it."

(52) His disciples said to him, "Twenty-four prophets spoke in Israel, and all of them spoke in you." He said to them, "You have omitted the one living in your presence and have spoken (only) of the dead."

(53) His disciples said to him, "Is circumcision beneficial or not?" He said to them, "If it were beneficial, their father would beget them already circumcised from their mother. Rather, the true circumcision in spirit has become completely profitable."

(54) Yeshu said, "Blessed are the poor, for yours is the kingdom of heaven."

(55) Yeshu said, "Whoever does not hate his father and his mother cannot become a discile to me. And whoever does not hate his brothers and sisters and take up his cross in my way will not be worthy of me."

(56) Yeshu said, "Whoever has come to understand the world has found (only) a corpse, and whoever has found a corpse is superior to the world."

(57) Yeshu said, "The kingdom of the father is like a man who had good seed. His enemy came by night and sowed weeds among the good seed. The man did not allow them to pull up the weeds; he said to them, 'I am afraid that you will go intending to pull up the weeds and pull up the wheat along with them.' For on the day of the harvest the weeds will be plainly visible, and they will be pulled up and burned."

(58) Yeshu said, "Blessed is the man who has suffered and found life."

(59) Yeshu said, "Take heed of the living one while you are alive, lest you die and seek to see him and be unable to do so."

(60) They saw a Samaritan carrying a lamb on his way to Judea. He said to his disciples, "That man is round about the lamb."

They said to him, "So that he may kill it and eat it." He said to them, "While it is alive, he will not eat it, but only when he has killed it and it has become a corpse." They said to him, "He cannot do so otherwise."

He said to them, "You too, look for a place for yourself within repose, lest you become a corpse and be eaten."

(61) Yeshu said, "Two will rest on a bed: the one will die, and the other will live."

Salome said, "Who are you, man, that you ... have come up on my couch and eaten from my table?"

Yeshu said to her, "I am he who exists from the undivided. I was given some of the things of my father."

Salome said, "I am Your disciple." Yeshu said to her, "Therefore I say, if he is undivided, he will be filled with light, but if he is divided, he will be filled with darkness."

(62) Yeshu said, "It is to those who are worthy of my mysteries that I tell my mysteries. Do not let your left (hand) know what your right (hand) is doing."

(63) Yeshu said, "There was a rich man who had much money. He said, 'I shall put my money to use so that I may sow, reap, plant, and fill my storehouse with produce, with the result that I shall lack nothing.' Such were his intentions, but that same night he died. Let him who has ears hear."

(64) Yeshu said, "A man had received visitors. And when he had prepared the dinner, he sent his servant to invite the guests.

He went to the first one and said to him, 'My master invites you.' He said, 'I have claims against some merchants. They are coming to me this evening. I must go and give them my orders. I ask to be excused from the dinner.' He went to another and said to him, 'My master has invited you.' He said to him, 'I have just bought a house and am required for the day. I shall not have any spare time.' He went to another and said to him, 'My master invites you.' He said to him, 'My friend is going to get married, and I am to prepare the banquet. I shall not be able to come. I ask to be excused from the dinner.' He went to another and said to him, 'My master invites you.' He said to him, 'I have just bought a farm, and I am on my way to collect the rent. I shall not be able to come. I ask to be excused.'

The servant returned and said to his master, 'Those whom you invited to the dinner have asked to be excused.' The master said to his servant, 'Go outside to the streets and bring back those whom you happen to meet, so that they may dine.' Businessmen and merchants will not enter the places of my father."

(65) He said, "There was a good man who owned a vineyard. He leased it to tenant farmers so that they might work it and he might collect the produce from them. He sent his servant so that the tenants might give him the produce of the vineyard. They seized his servant and beat him, all but killing him. The servant went back and told his master. The master said, 'Perhaps he did not recognize them.' He sent another servant. The tenants beat this one as well. Then the owner sent his son and said, 'Perhaps they will show respect to my son.' Because the tenants knew that it was he who was the heir to the vineyard, they seized him and killed him. Let him who has ears hear."

(66) Yeshu said, "Show me the stone which the builders have rejected. That one is the cornerstone."

(67) Yeshu said, "If one who knows the all still feels a personal deficiency, he is completely deficient."

(68) Yeshu said, "Blessed are you when you are hated and persecuted. Wherever you have been persecuted they will find no place."

(69) Yeshu said, "Blessed are they who have been persecuted within themselves. It is they who have truly come to know the father. Blessed are the hungry, for the belly of him who desires will be filled."

(70) Yeshu said, "That which you have will save you if you bring it forth from yourselves. That which you do not have within you will kill you if you do not have it within you."

(71) Yeshu said, "I shall destroy this house, and no one will be able to build it again."

(72) A man said to him, "Tell my brothers to divide my father's possessions with me." He said to him, "O man, who has made me a divider?"

He turned to his disciples and said to them, "I am not a divider, am I?"

(73) Yeshu said, "The harvest is great but the laborers are few. Beseech the Lord, therefore, to send out laborers to the harvest."

(74) He said, "O Lord, there are many around the drinking trough, but there is nothing in the cistern."

(75) Yeshu said, "Many are standing at the door, but it is the solitary who will enter the bridal chamber."

(76) Yeshu said, "The kingdom of the father is like a merchant who had a consignment of merchandise and who discovered a pearl. That merchant was shrewd. He sold the merchandise and bought the pearl alone for himself. You too, seek his unfailing and enduring treasure where no moth comes near to devour and no worm destroys."

(77) Yeshu said, "It is I who am the light which is above them all. It is I who am the all. From me did the all come forth, and unto me did the all extend. Split a piece of wood, and I am there. Lift up the stone, and you will find me there."

(78) Yeshu said, "Why have you come out into the desert? To see a reed shaken by the wind? And to see a man clothed in fine garments like your kings and your great men? Upon them are the fine garments, and they are unable to discern the truth."

(79) A woman from the crowd said to him, "Blessed are the womb which bore you and the breasts which nourished you."

He said to her, "Blessed are those who have heard the word of the father and have truly kept it. For there will be days when you will say, 'Blessed are the womb which has not conceived and the breasts which have not given milk.'"

(80) Yeshu said, "He who has recognized the world has found the body, but he who has found the body is superior to the world."

(81) Yeshu said, "Let him who has grown rich be king, and let him who possesses power renounce it."

(82) Yeshu said, "He who is near me is near the fire, and he who is far from me is far from the kingdom."

(83) Yeshu said, "The images are manifest to man, but the light in them remains concealed in the image of the light of the father. He will become manifest, but his image will remain concealed by his light."

(84) Yeshu said, "When you see your likeness, you rejoice. But when you see your images which came into being before you, and which neither die not become manifest, how much you will have to bear!"

(85) Yeshu said, "Adam came into being from a great power and a great wealth, but he did not become worthy of you. For had he been worthy, he would not have experienced death."

(86) Yeshu said, "The foxes have their holes and the birds have their nests, but the son of man has no place to lay his head and rest."

(87) Yeshu said, "Wretched is the body that is dependant upon a body, and wretched is the soul that is dependent on these two."

(88) Yeshu said, "The angels and the prophets will come to you and give to you those things you (already) have. And you too, give them those things which you have, and say to yourselves, 'When will they come and take what is theirs?'"

(89) Yeshu said, "Why do you wash the outside of the cup? Do you not realize that he who made the inside is the same one who made the outside?"

(90) Yeshu said, "Come unto me, for my yoke is easy and my lordship is mild, and you will find repose for yourselves."

(91) They said to him, "Tell us who you are so that we may believe in you."
He said to them, "You read the face of the sky and of the earth, but you have not recognized the one who is before you, and you do not know how to read this moment."

(92) Yeshu said, "Seek and you will find. Yet, what you asked me about in former times and which I did not tell you then, now I do desire to tell, but you do not inquire after it."

(93) Yeshu said, "Do not give what is holy to dogs, lest they throw them on the dung-heap. Do not throw the pearls to swine, lest they [...] it [...]."

(94) Yeshu said, "He who seeks will find, and he who knocks will be let in."

(95) Yeshu said, "If you have money, do not lend it at interest, but give it to one from whom you will not get it back."

(96) Yeshu said, "The kingdom of the father is like a certain woman. She took a little leaven, concealed it in some dough, and made it into large loaves. Let him who has ears hear."

(97) Yeshu said, "The kingdom of the father is like a certain woman who was carrying a jar full of meal. While she was walking on the road, still some distance from home, the handle of the jar broke and the meal emptied out behind her on the

road. She did not realize it; she had noticed no accident. When she reached her house, she set the jar down and found it empty."

(98) Yeshu said, "The kingdom of the father is like a certain man who wanted to kill a powerful man. In his own house he drew his sword and stuck it into the wall in order to find out whether his hand could carry through. Then he slew the powerful man."

(99) The disciples said to him, "Your brothers and your mother are standing outside." He said to them, "Those here who do the will of my father are my brothers and my mother. It is they who will enter the kingdom of my father."

(100) They showed Yeshu a gold coin and said to him, "Caesar's men demand taxes from us." He said to them, "Give Caesar what belongs to Caesar, give God what belongs to God, and give me what is mine."

(101) Yeshu said, "Whoever does not hate his father and his mother as I do cannot become a disciple to me. And whoever does not love his father and his mother as I do cannot become a disciple to me. For my mother [...], but my true mother gave me life."

(102) Yeshu said, "Woe to the Pharisees, for they are like a dog sleeping in the manger of oxen, for neither does he eat nor does he let the oxen eat."

(103) Yeshu said, "Fortunate is the man who knows where the brigands will enter, so that he may get up, muster his domain, and arm himself before they invade."

(104) They said to Yeshu, "Come, let us pray today and let us fast."

Yeshu said, "What is the sin that I have committed, or wherein have I been defeated? But when the bridegroom leaves the bridal chamber, then let them fast and pray."

(105) Yeshu said, "He who knows the father and the mother will be called the son of a harlot."

(106) Yeshu said, "When you make the two one, you will become the sons of man, and when you say, 'Mountain, move away,' it will move away."

(107) Yeshu said, "The kingdom is like a shepherd who had a hundred sheep. One of them, the largest, went astray. He left the ninety-nine sheep and looked for that one until he found it.

When he had gone to such trouble, he said to the sheep, 'I care for you more than the ninety-nine.'"

(108) Yeshu said, "He who will drink from my mouth will become like me. I myself shall become he, and the things that are hidden will be revealed to him."

(109) Yeshu said, "The kingdom is like a man who had a hidden treasure in his field without knowing it. And after he died, he left it to his son. The son did not know (about the treasure). He inherited the field and sold it. And the one who bought it went plowing and found the treasure. He began to lend money at interest to whomever he wished."

(110) Yeshu said, "Whoever finds the world and becomes rich, let him renounce the world."

(111) Yeshu said, "The heavens and the earth will be rolled up in your presence. And the one who lives from the living one will not see death." Does not Yeshu say, "Whoever finds himself is superior to the world?"

(112) Yeshu said, "Woe to the flesh that depends on the soul; woe to the soul that depends on the flesh."

(113) His disciples said to him, "When will the kingdom come?" Yeshu said, "It will not come by waiting for it. It will not be a matter of saying 'here it is' or 'there it is.' Rather, the kingdom of the father is spread out upon the earth, and men do not see it."

(114) Simon Peter said to him, "Let Mary leave us, for women are not worthy of life." Yeshu said, "I myself shall lead her in order to make her male, so that she too may become a living spirit resembling you males. For every woman who will make herself male will enter the kingdom of heaven."

The Gospel According to Thomas[384]

⁻ 12 ⁻
ⲘⲀⲚⲆⲀⲒⲤ ⲢⲀⲢⲀⲂⲖⲈⲤ

---

[384] Slightly altered translation (Jesus to Yeshu) by Thomas O. Lambdin, from James M. Robinson, ed., The Nag Hammadi Library

THE DRASHE DMALKE, or Discourses of Priestly Kings, contains many parables and teachings of Yeshu, Yuhana, Miryai and others from the Nazorean array of prophets and prophetesses. It contains the Sidra Dyahya or 16 chapters Book of John the Baptist. Within its 76 chapters are also many teachings and talks of Yeshu, although his name is not attached to them. When these are compared to the much shorter and less detailed parables in the Greco-Roman gospels, it is evident that the Greek New Testament version is dependent on hearsay reports of these original and longer Aramaic versions for their inspiration. Out of the many to choose from, we will give two of these Parables of Yeshu, that of the fisherman and shepherd.

Fisherman Parable

There are a few fish related parables in the New Testament gospels, the net and the fishes in John 21 and Luke 5, and the Apostles called fishers of men in Mark 1 and Matthew 4. Here we give the full and original version found in ancient Aramaic scrolls. It should be noted that Yeshu emphatically declares that he is a spiritual fisherman only, and never actually eats real fish. This is because his Nazorean sect was vegetarian:

> "In the Name of the Vast Vivification, may hallowed Light be glorified! A fisher am I, a fisher who is elect among fishers. A fisher am I who among the fishers is chosen, the chief of all catchers of fish. I know the shallows of the waters, the inner ... and the ...I fathom; I come to the net-grounds, to the shallows and all fishing spots, and search the marsh in the dark all over. My boat is not cut off from the others and I shall not be stopped in the night. I see: the fish in on the dike. I pressed forward on the way with a ... that was not of iron. I covered the ... which was for us an obstruction. Aside did I push the swimmers who hinder Life's way. On my head I set up a ... in whose shadow the fish sit. The fisher-trident which I have in my hand, is instead a

Margna (*staff*) select, a margna of pure water, at whose sight tremble the fishers. I sit in a boat of glory and come into this Tibil (*world*) of the fleeting. I come to the waters surface; thither to the surface of the water I drew, and I drew to the crossings surface. I come in a, ... in slow, steady course. The water by my boat is not ruffed, and no sound of my boat is heard. Before me stands Hibil; at my side Shitil of sweet name is to be seen, close by me, close in front of me, Anush sits and proclaims. They say: O Father, good fisher, shalam (*peace*)! O fisher of loveable name! Close by me, close near my boat, I hear the uproar of the fishers, the fishers who eat fish, and their stench rushes on me,- the uproar of the fishers and the uproar of their mongers who revile and curse one another. Everyone accuses the other, the buyer says to the fisher: Take back thy fish! They are stinking already, and no one wants to buy them off of me. Thou makest the catch far out at sea, so that loss falls on the buyer. Thereon speaks the fisher and makes the man, his customer, hear: A curse on thee, a curse on thy buyers, a curse on thy bell, a curse on thy boat for not filing up. Thou hast brought no salt and sprinkled it over thy fish which thou boughtest, so that the fish of thy boat will not be stinking and thou then canst sell for hard cash. Next, hast thou no meal and no dates brought, no salt ... hast thou brought. If then thou comest with empty hands, one who is of fair favor has no dealing with thee. Go, go, thou godless fellow, buy not from us to do business with thy fraudulent scales. Thou boldest them down to buy at false weight, then in selling keepest them up with thy elbow and gettest ten for five. Now does thy buying flee away, and thy buyer, and is as though it never had been. Thou dost complain of the ... of men and dost cherish no noble thought. When the chief fisher, the head of the race of the Living, the highest of all catchers of fish, heard this, he said to him: Bring me my ... hand me the squbra (*horn*), that I may make a call sound forth into the marsh, that I may warn the fish of the depths and scare away the foul-smelling birds that pursue after my fish. I will catch the great sidma, and tear off his wings on the spot. I will take from him ....And blow into my squbra. A true squbra is it, so that the water may not mix with pitch. Then the fishers heard the call, their heart fell down from his stay. One calls to the other and speaks to him: Go into thy inner ground.

For there is the call of the fisher, the fisher who eats no fish (*is a vegan*). His voice is not like that of a fisher, his squbra not like our squbra. His voice is not like our voice, his discourse not like to this world. But the fishers stand there; they seek not shelter in their inner ground. As the fishers stand there and are thinking it over, the fisher came swiftly upon them; he opened the cast-net, divided .. . . . He cast them bound into the .. . . . He tied them up with knots. They speak to him: Free us from our bonds, so that thy fish may not leap up to our bent. We catch not those who name thy Name. When the fishers thus spake to me, I smote them with a club made of iron. I bound their traders on the shore which lends not .. . . . . · I roped them with ropes of bast and broke up their ships ... I burnt up the whole of their netting and the.. . . . .which holds the nets together. I threw chains round them and hung them up aft on my ships stern. I made them take an oath, took from them their mystery, in order that they may not catch the good fish, that they may not steal them from me, stick them on a cane, hang them up, cut them in pieces and throw them into baskets with laurel and aloe. They are laid low and cannot rise up. The nets .. . . , and they no longer stab the fisher-trident into the Yardna (*Flowing*), They do not cut off ….and stand not in the river-lands and make not their catch in the shallows. They cast not the cast-net therein and therein not .. . . . and aloe. I spake to those who eat the . . . · of the fish whose name is eel. They eat the eel and the .. . . . , which stands upright on his forefeet. They eat the.....I bound them in the marshes of deception, and they were caught and were tied up. Water from the Ulai they drink not and know not the way to the Kshash River (*Styx*). I bound them fast in their ships, and threw out my ropes to the good ones. To them I speak: Draw your boat up here, so that it runs not into the dike. As the chief of the fish catchers thus spake, the fishers made answer unto him and said; Blessed be thee, O fisher, and blessed be thy boat and thy barque. How fair is thy cast-net, how fair the rope that is in it. Fair is thy cord and thy lacing, thou who art not like the fishers of this world. On thy meshes are no shell-fish, and thy trident catches no fish. Whence are thou come hither? Tell us, we will be thy hired servants? We will bake and stir about broth and bring it before thee. Eat, and the crumbs which fell from thy hand

these will we eat and therewith be filled. But I made answer
unto them: O ye fishers, who lap up your filth, no fisher arm I
who fishes for fish, and I was not formed for an eater of filth (*non
vegan*). A fisher am I of souls who bear witness to Life (*Living
Ones*). A poor fisher am I who calls to the souls, collects them
together and gives them instruction. He calls to them and bids
them come and gather together unto him. He says unto them: If
ye come, ye shall be saved from the foul-smelling birds. I will
save my friends, bring them on high and in my ship make them
stand upright. I will clothe them with vestures of glory and with
precious light mill enwrap them. I will put a crown of ether
upon them and what else for them the Greatness erects on their
head. Then sit they on thrones and in precious light do they
glisten. I bear them thither and raise them aloft; but ye Seven
shall stay here behind. The portion of filth and of filthy doings
shall be your portion. On the day when the Light ascends, the
darkness will return to his region. I and my disciples will ascend
and behold the Lights region. Life is transcendent and
victorious, and victorious are those that have gone forth!

In the Name of the all encompassing Animation, may hallowed
Light be glorified! A fisher am I of Great Life (*Living Ones*), a
fisher am I of the Mighty; a fisher am I of Great Life, an Envoy
whom Life has sent. They (*Living Ones*) spake unto me: Go, catch
fish who do not eat filth, fish who do not eat water-fennel and
reek not of foul-smelling fennel. They do not come nigh to
devour bad dates and get caught in the nets of the marsh. Life
knotted for me a noose and built for me a ship that fades not, a
ship whose wings are of glory, that sails along as in flight, and
from it the wings will not be torn off. Tis a well- furnished ship
and sails on in the heart of the heaven. Its ropes are ropes of
glory and a rudder of Truth is there on it. Habshabba (*first
weekday*) takes hold of the pole, Life's Son seized the rudder.
They draw thither to the Monastery and dispense Light among
the treasures. Thrones in Monasteries they set up, and long
drawn out come the Yardnas (*Flowing*) upon them. On the bow
are set lamps that in the wildest of tempests are not put out. All
ships that sight me, make obeisance submissively to me.
Submissively they make me obeisance and come to show their

devotion unto me. In the bows stands the fisher and delivers wondrous discourses. There are lamps there, whose wicks shift not hither and thither, and a . . .is not by him. He wears no ring of deception, and with white robes is he clad. He calls to the fish of the sea, and speaks to them: Give heed to yourselves in the world! Beware of the foul-smelling birds who are above you. If you give heed to yourselves, my brothers, I will for you be a succor, a succor and a support out of the regions of darkness unto Lights regions. Life is transcendent and victorious, and victorious are those that have gone forth!

In the Name of Ultimate Life, may hallowed Light be glorified! The fisher clad him with vestures of glory, and an axe hung from his shoulder ... and commotion of mischief and bell is not on the handle. When the fishers caught sight of the fisher, they came and gathered around him. Thou art, say they onto him, a... fisher, thou who hast caught no fish of the marsh. Thou hast not seen the ....in which the fish gather ....we will make thee familiar with the fishers; be our great partner and take a share as we do. Grant us a share in thy ship, and take thou a share in our ship. A bargain! Take from us as partner and grant us a share in thy ship. Grant us a share and we will give thee a share in what we possess. Join thy ship with ours and clothe thee in black as we do, so that, if thou boldest thy lantern on high, thou mayest find something, that the fish may not see thy glory and thy ship may take in fish. If thou dost give ear, thou shalt catch fish, throw them into thy ship and do business. If thou givest no ear to our discourse, thou shalt eat salt; but if thou doest our works, thou shalt eat oil and honey. Thou stirrest a broth, thou fillest a bowl and sharest it with all of the fishers. We appoint thee a head over all of us. The fishers gather together beside thee, the first follow behind thee; they will be thy slaves, and thou takest three shares of what falls to our share. Our father shall be thy servant and we mill call ourselves thy bondsmen. Our mother shall sit on thy couch and net nets, she shall be thy maid servant and knit for thee ropes of all kinds. She shall space out the floats of cedar and put the lead-sinkers into the meshes, meshes, meshes which are then more heavy than all of the world. She shall divide the water by means of the ropes , and when the fish run into them they shall be stopped. Then they know not the way that they seek, and have no understanding to turn back to their way. Like walls that collapse, they (*the-nets*) come and fall on the good. They do not let the fish rise, nor turn their face to the boulders which sink deep under the mud and shot them into...... ...... They collect them into heaps and shake them out of the.... There is there a ....into which the fish dash and are stopped. On the . . . . .of the . . . . . wattlework is set up between two machines. Nets are laid down and ... which are filled with bad dates as bait, which cease them to eat death. Woe to the fish who is blinded by them, whose eye sees not the Light. Wise are the fish who know them. They pass by all of the baits. The others repair thither and . .... and the nets will be for them there a lodging. One of a thousand sees it and of two thousand but two see it. His ... is closed, and a bell is hung on his side door, a bell that is forged in mischief and catches the whole of the world. There, is the water mingled with fennel .... the pegs of death. Woe to the fish who fall into them. When the fisher heard this, he stamped on the bow of the ship. The fisher stomped on the ships of the fishers; the fishers lie in the shallows close crowded together, tied up together like bundles of wheat, and cannot rise up. The reeds swish ... and the fish of the sea lie over the fishers. They snarl in the marsh and the water rings them round in his circle. Then loudly he spake with his voice. He discoursed with his voice sublime and spake to the catchers of fish: Off from me, ye foul-smelling fishers, ye fishers who mix poison. Begone, begone, catch fish who eat your own filth. Down with you to your ... and go to the end of the crossing. I am no fisher who catches fish and my fish are tested. They are not caught by the hook with bad dates, a food which fish do not eat. They fall not into the nets that are colored and turn not to the lamps of the Lie. They sink not down through the mud of the Water, and go not after the ... of deception. They divide not the water ....that shall fall on the good. If the fishers cast over them the cast-net they tear asunder the net and set themselves free. There will be no day in this world on which the fishers catch my fish. There will be no day in this world on which the dove loves the ravens. Accursed be ye, ye foul smelling birds, and accursed your nest, so that it may not be filled. Woe to your father Sirma: whose bed is in the reeds. Woe to thee, hungry Safna, whose wings do not dry in this world. Woe to thee foul smelling Sdagia thou who seest the fish and sighest for them. He shrieks and cries bitterly when he strikes for the fish and misses them. Woe to thee, Arbana ... those who haulest the fish out of the deep. Well for him who frees himself from the talons of those who catch fish. Well for him who frees himself from the men who are watchers of this world. Begone, begone with you ye planets, be of your own houses a portion. Water does not mix with pitch, and the Light is not reckoned as darkness. The perfect one's partner cannot be called your partner. The good one cannot belong to the wicked ones nor the bad to the good. Your ship cannot be tied up with mine, nor your ring be laid on my ring. There is the head of all of you: count yourselves unto his realm! This is your crass father stuck in the black mud. Your mother, who nets nets and heavy double machines have I beaten with the staff of (*living water*) and smashed a hole in her head. I lead on my friends, raise them on high in my ship and guide them past all the toll-collectors. I guide them through the passage of outrage the region where the fishes are taken. I make them escape the fish-eaters. But ye will come to an end in your dwellings. I and my friends of the Truth will have a place in Life's (*Living Ones*) Monastery. Into the height will I bear them on thrones surrounded with standards of glory. The Seven are vanquished and the Stranger stays victorious. The Man of righteousness put to the test was victorious and helped the whole of his race unto victory. Life is transcendent and victorious, and victorious are those that have gone forth!

In the Name of Vast Vitality, may hallowed Light be glorified! Tis the voice of the pure fisher who calls and instructs the fish of the sea, in the shallows. He speaks to them: Raise you up ... on the surface of the water, stand upright; then will your force be twice as great. Guard yourselves from the fishers who catch the fish and beat on the Yardna (*Flowing*). Shilmai and Nidbai curse them, and they depart and settle themselves down behind me a mile off. The fish curse their casting-net . . . . . . in their place. When the fisher thus spake warning all of the fish, when the fishers his voice heard, they came up and gathered around him.

They put themselves forward to ask of him questions, and knew·
not whence he came. Where wast thou, fisher they ask him, that
we heard not thy voice in the marsh? Thy ship is not like our
ship, and thy . . . . is not .... Thy ship is not tarred over with
pitch, and thou art not like the fishers of this world. The fishers
see him, become scarlet for shame and remain standing in their
places. They say to him: Whence comes these that thou dost fish
without finding? Thy ship is not like our ship; it shines by night
like the sun. Thy ship is perfected in aether, and wondrous
standards are unfurled above it. Our ship sails along in the
water, but thy ship between the waters. On reeds grumble at one
another and break into pieces. among them is the fish-trident of
wrath, on which . . . and . . are not. Thy ... o fisher, is such that
when the fish see it, they take themselves off. We have not yet
seen any fishers which are like unto thee. The mind wafts thy
ship on, the mast . . . . . for the fisher and a rudder that gleams in
the water shallows. On thy casting net is no cord, and have not
laid ... round it. There are no ... in it, which are a cunning device
against the fish of the ... Thou keepest thy cords, hast no clapper
and no hatchet. Thy net fishes not in the water and is not
coloured for catching fish. When the fishers thus spake, the
fisher made answer unto them: Have done, ye fishers and fishers
sons; off, get you gone from me! Off, go up to your village, the
ruins, Jerusalem. Ask about me of your father, who knows me,
ask of your mother, who is my maid-servant. Say to him: There
is a fisher in the boat, in which are four . . . There is a rudder,
and it stands and a mast .....and redemptions, they lay waste the
land of Jerusalem. When they heard this from the fisher who has
come hither, and understood, they spake to him: Have
compassion, forbearance and mercy on us and forgive us our
sins and transgressions. We are thy slaves, show thyself
indulgent towards us. We will look after thy fish that none of
them fails. We will be the servants of thy disciples, who name
thy Name in Truth. We will continue to look after all who name
thy Name. Life is transcendent and victorious, and victorious are
those that have gone forth![385]

---

[385] Sidra Dyahya (Book Of John)/Drashe Dmalke (Discourses Of Kings) 36-39

Shepherd Parable

Within the New Testament gospel of John 10:11-18 we find a parable of the shepherd. We quote it here for comparison with the longer more complete version found in writings passed down from the Nazoreans:

> "I am the good shepherd: the good shepherd giveth his life for the sheep. But he that is an hireling, and not the shepherd, whose own the sheep are not, seeth the wolf coming, and leaveth the sheep, and fleeth: and the wolf catcheth them, and scattereth the sheep. The hireling fleeth, because he is an hireling, and careth not for the sheep. I am the good shepherd, and know my sheep, and am known of mine. As the Father knoweth me, even so know I the Father: and I lay down my life for the sheep. And other sheep I have, which are not of this fold: them also I must bring, and they shall hear my voice; and there shall be one fold, and one shepherd. Therefore doth my Father love me, because I lay down my life, that I might take it again. No man taketh it from me, but I lay it down of myself. I have power to lay it down, and I have power to take it again. This commandment have I received of my Father.[386]

Now for the full and original version found in ancient Aramaic scrolls:

> "In the Name of Life's Grandeur, may hallowed Light be glorified! A Shepherd am I who loves his sheep; I watch over sheep and lambs. Round my neck I carry the sheep: and the sheep stray not from the hamlet. I do not carry them to the seashore, lest they see the turbulence of the water, and be afraid of the water, and so that they do not drink of that water if they are thirsty. I bear them away from the sea, and water them with the cup of my hand, until they have drank their fill. I bring them into the good fold, and they feed by my side. I brought them

---

[386] John 10:11-18

from the mouth of Frash-Ziwa, the radiant things of marvelous goodness from the mouth of Frash-Ziwa. I brought them myrtle, I brought them white sesame and I brought them bright banners. I cleansed them and washed them and made them to smell the sweet orders of Life. I placed around them a girdle, which the wolves tremble at the sight of. No wolf pounces into our fold; and they need not be alarmed by any fierce lion. Of the tempest they need not be frightened; and no thief can break in upon us. A thief breaks not into their fold; and of the knife they need not be anxious. When my sheep where quietly laid down and my head lay there on the threshold, a rift was rent in the height and thunder did thunder behind me. The clouds seized hold one of another, and unchained were the raging tempests. Rain poured down in sheets and hail that smites elephants low, hail that shatters the mountains. And the tempests unchain themselves in an hour. Seas burst forth; they flooded the whole of the world. There, under the water, no one escaped, once he sank from the height as into a gulf. The water swept off everyone who had no wings or no feet. He speeds on, and knows not he speeds; he goes, and knows not that he goes. Thereupon I sprang up and I entered the fold to bear my sheep forth from their place. I saw fully with my eyes, I saw the sea, I saw the fierce-raging tempest, I saw the storm-clouds that send forth no friendly greeting one to the other. Ten-thousand times ten-thousand dragons are in each single cloud. I weep for my sheep, and my sheep bleat for themselves. The little lambs are lamenting who cannot come out of the folds door. When then . . . . . . , I entered the house, I mounted up to the highest place, and I call to my sheep. To the sheep in my care do I call. I play the flute to them; I get them to hear, so that they come unto me. To them I play on my flute, and beat on my tambourine, leading them forth to the water. I call to them: My little sheep, little sheep, come! Rise up at my call, come, rise at my call; then will you escape the cloud-dragons! Come, come unto me, I am a shepherd whose ship is soon coming. My ship of glory is coming; and I come with it, and bring my sheep and lambs aboard it. Every one who gives ear to my Call and gives heed unto my voice, and who turns their gaze unto me, of that one I take hold with my hands and bring them unto me aboard my ship. But every lamb, male and female, that suffered themselves to be caught, the whirlpool carried away, the greedy water did swallow. Whoever gave no ear to my call, sank under. To the highest part of the vessel I went, the bows stand up with the bow-post. I say: How saddened am I for my sheep who have sunk under because of the mud. The whirlpool sucked them away from my reach, the swirling whirl of the water. How grieved am I for the rams whose fleece on their sides has dragged them down into the depths. How grieved am I for the lambs whose bellies have not yet been filled full of milk. Of a thousand, one I recovered; of a whole generation I found again only two. Happy are they who stood up in the water, and in whose ears no water has entered. Happy the great rams who have stamped with their feet. Happy the one who has escaped from the Seven (*planets*) and Twelve (*zodiac*), the sheep-stealers. Happy the one who has not couched down, has not lain down, has not loved to sleep deeply. Happy the one who in this defective age of Bisholm has endured to the end. Happy are they who free themselves from the snares of Ruha (*ignorance*), from the filth and the shame and the bondage that have no end. My chosen, whoever shall live at the end of this age of Nirig (*Mars*) for such a one let that ones own conscience be a support. That one will come and ascend up to the Radiant Dwelling, to the region whose sun never sets, and whose light-lamps never darken. Life is transcendent and victorious, and victorious are those that have gone forth! In the Name of Life's Greatness, may hallowed Light be glorified! A Treasure calls from without hither and speaks: Come, be for me a loving shepherd and watch me a thousand out of ten thousand. So then will I be a loving shepherd for thee and watch thee a thousand out of ten thousand. But how full is the world of vileness and sown full of thorns and of thistles! Come, be for me a loving shepherd and watch me a thousand out of ten thousand. I will bring thee then sandals of glory with them you can tread down the thorns and the thistles. Earth and heaven decay, but the sandals of glory decay not. Sun and moon decay, but the sandals of glory decay not. The stars and heavens zodiacal circle decay, but the sandals of glory decay not. The four winds of the world-house decay, but the sandals of glory decay not. Fruits and grapes and trees decay, but the sandals of glory decay not. All that is made and engendered decays, but the sandals of glory decay not. So then be for me a loving shepherd and watch me a thousand out of ten thousand. I will then be a loving shepherd for thee and watch thee a thousand out of ten thousand. But if a lion comes and carries one off, how am I to retrieve that one? If a thief comes and steals one away, how am I to retrieve that one? If one falls into the fire and is burnt, how am I to retrieve that one? If one falls into the water and drowns, how am I to retrieve that one? If one stays behind in the pen, how am I to retrieve that one? Nevertheless, come therefore, be for me a loving shepherd and watch me a thousand out of ten thousand. If a lion comes and carries off one, let that one go their way and fall prey to the lion. Let that one go their way and fall prey to the lion, in that they bow themselves down to the sun. If a wolf comes and carries off one let that one go their way and fall a prey to the wolf, in that they bow themselves down to the moon. If a thief comes and steals away one, then let that one go their way and fall a prey to the thief. Let that one go their way and fall a prey to the thief, in that they bow themselves down before Nigrig (*Mars*). If one falls into the fire and is burnt, let them go their way and fall a prey to the fire. Let that one go their way and fall a prey to the fire, in that they bow themselves dawn to the fire. If one falls into the mud and stays stuck there, then let them go their way and fall a prey to the mud. Let that one go their way and fall a prey to the mud, in that they bow themselves down to a false Messiah. If one falls into the water and drowns, then let them go their way and fall a prey to the sea. Let one go their way and fall a prey to the sea, in that they bow themselves down to the seas. If one stays behind in the cage, let them go their way and fall a prey to the cage-demon. Let him go their way and fall a prey to the cage-demon in that they bow themselves down to the idols. Come, be for me a loving shepherd and watch for me a thousand out of ten thousand. So will I then be for thee a loving shepherd and watch thee a thousand out of ten thousand. I will watch a thousand of thousands, yea of ten thousand those who adore Them.. . . . But some of them wander from me. I went up to the high mountains and went down into deep valleys. I went and found that one where they can Pasteur not. Of each single sheep I took hold with my right hand and on the scale did I lay him. A thousand among ten thousand have the right weight. Life is transcendent and victorious, and victorious are those that have gone forth![387]

⁻ 13 ⁻
INNER TEACHINGS

Gnostic Sayings

THERE ARE A HOST of sources for the saying of Yeshu outside of the questionable New Testament. Besides the Gospel of Thomas and passages in the Doctrine of Priestly Kings which we have already quoted, there are sayings in the Pistis Sophia, Brucianus Codex, Jesus Sutras found in a Dunhuang cave in China, and especially books like the Dialogue of the Savior and others from the Nag Hammadhi library. Here is an example from the Nag, called the Dialogue of the Savior, usually dated to the late first century by scholars.

Dialogue of the Savior

"Matthew said, "Lord, I long to see the place of eternal life; the place where there is no wickedness, but pure Light." The Lord replied, "Brother, you will never be able to see it in this life, not as long as you carry flesh around with you." Matthew said, "Lord, even if I cannot now see this place, let me know more about it." The Lord said, "Anyone who knows his true self has seen this place in every good work he has been given to do, and has come to experience a part of it through these good deeds."
Judas asked, "Tell me, Lord. What causes the earth to shake?" The Lord picked up a stone in his hand and asked, "What am I holding in my hand?" Judas said, "A stone." The Savior said to them, "That which supports this stone supports the earth and

---

[387] Sidra Dyahya (Book Of John)/Drashe Dmalke (Discourses Of Kings) 11,12

heavens. When the Word comes forth from the Greatness, it will come by the same force that supports the heavens and the earth. The earth does not move. If it were to move, it would surely fall. But it neither moves nor falls, in order that the First Word might not fail. After all, it was the First Word that established the world, caused it to be populated and inhaled fragrance from it. Likewise, sons of men who are established in the First Word do not move or fall. You are from the Greatness also. You exist for those whom in their hearts cry out for joy and truth. Even if the Greatness comes forth through you for these and is not received, the effort is not wasted, for the Word returns to its place. Whoever does not know this Word and its work knows nothing. If one does not stand in darkness, he will not be able to perceive light!"

"If someone doesn't know the meaning of fire, that person will burn in it, because he doesn't know how hot it is or where it came from. If someone doesn't know the origin of water, he knows nothing. What is the use of baptism if you doesn't understand the origin or meaning of the water? If someone doesn't understand how tornadoes came into existence and what their power is, he will blow away in one. If someone does not understand the origin or nature of the body that he carries with him, he will surely perish when the body does. Therefore, how will someone know the Father if he does not know the Son? If someone refuses to learn about the natures and origins of things, they remain unknowable secrets, although a person who doesn't know the origin of wickedness will practice it anyway! Whoever doesn't understand how he came will not know how to go. He will seem to know his way in this world, but will be utterly lost and humiliated."

Yeshu defines his doctrine as one of gnosis, of understanding the origin of things. Without gnosis, Yeshu tells us, even baptism is worthless: "What is the use of baptism if you don't understand the origin or meaning of the water?" Are there any baptized Christians in the world who understand the mystery, origin, and meaning of living water?

"Suddenly, Judas, Matthew, and Mary were transported in a vision to a place between heaven and earth. These disciple were perplexed by what they were experiencing. Despite their fears, they hoped that they might understand the mysteries before them as they felt Yeshu' hands upon them. Judas raised his eyes and saw a very high plateau above them and a deep abyss below. He said to Matthew, "Brother, we will never be able to escape this place by climbing up, for the way is much too steep. We can't go down into the abyss, for there is a tremendous fire there and other dreadful things!" At that moment a living Word in the form of a man came to them from above. Judas, amazed, asked the Living Word why it had come down. The Son of Man greeted the disciples and said, "A seed of power in heaven was imperfect, and was cast down to the abyss of the earth. The Greatness remembered it in love and sent the Word to it. The Word brought the imperfect seed up before the Greatness so that the First Word might not fail in his mission." The disciples were amazed at what they saw and heard. Although they could not understand what the Son was saying to them, they took all these things on faith. The one thing they concluded was that they could no longer entertain wicked ways.

Yeshu, as the Word (*Malala*), descends to rescue pearls that have lost their way. They are seeds, or progeny, of the Great Life who have descended to experience mortality, as Yeshu hath reasoned: "If one does not stand in darkness, he will not be able to perceive light!"

"Then the Savior said to his disciples, "Haven't I told you that with an audible cry and a flash of lightning the just will be taken up to the light?" Then all the disciples praised him and said, "Lord, before you made yourself known to us, who offered you praise? For all praise exists on your account. Or who is it that is able to bless you, since all blessings emanate from you?" Then, as they stood there, they saw two angels bringing a person with them in a great flash of lightning. A word came forth from the

Son of Man, saying, "Give them the garment that belongs to
them." And the small one became like the big one....

In the Pistis Sophia Yeshu explains that it is the mysteries
(*razia*) the endowments of power which these disciples have
already received, that allows one to ascend like an arrow or
flash of lightening to the throne of Abathur where a robe of
glory awaits.

> "Judas said, "Behold, those in power live above us and rule us."
> The Lord said, "It is you who will rule over them when you rid
> yourself of your jealousy. Only then will you be clothed in light
> and be worthy to enter the bridal suite."
> Judas asked, "How will our garments be brought to us?" Yeshu
> answered, "There are some appointed to provide them for you,
> and others to receive you. How else will one be able to enter the
> bridal chamber unless some provide appropriate garments and
> others receive? Remember that the bridal suite is a reward. The
> ones who know the path to their reward receive bridal garments,
> by which they leave this existence. It has been difficult even for
> me to endure it all."
> Mary said, "You speak these word in context with what you
> have told us about 'the wickedness of each day,' 'the laborer is
> worthy of his food,' and 'the disciple resembles his teacher.'" She
> spoke as a woman of complete understanding.

It is important that Miryai (Mary) is here called a woman of
complete understanding. As the spiritual partner and coregent
of Yeshu, she shines in her innate Buddha nature and
throughout this Dialogue she asks about as well as declares
the truth.

> "The disciples spoke, "How are we to know abundance from
> deprivation?" The Lord said, "You are from abundance and live
> in depravity. Behold! His light has poured down upon me!"
> Matthew asked, "Lord, how will the dead die and the living
> live?" The Lord answered, "Brother, you have asked me about

things that no one has before witnessed, nor has anyone asked but you. But I say to you, when the thing that keeps man alive is removed, he will be called 'dead.' When what is alive leaves what is dead, what is alive will be called upon."

Judas asked, "What else, but for the sake of truth, do people live and die?" The Lord answered, "Whatever is born of Truth doesn't die. Whatever is born of a woman will."

"Mary said, "Tell me, Lord, if I have come to this place to gain or lose." The Lord said, "You make it clear that you profit from the abundance of the Revealer."

Mary then said, "Is there a place, Lord, where there is no truth?" The Lord said, "The place where I am not." Mary finished by saying, "You are fearful and wonderful. Those who do not know you are losers indeed."

"Matthew asked, "When can we rest?" The Lord answered, "When you lay your burdens down." Matthew asked another question, "When does the insignificant join itself to the great?" Yeshu replied, "When you abandon unprofitable works, then you have laid down the burdens that keep you from unity and have found rest." Mary said, "I want to know all facts just as they are!" The Lord said, "Those that seek for eternal life will know all things. This knowledge is universal currency - far superior to gold and silver - those perishables that have misled so many."

"The disciples asked, "How shall we do our tasks perfectly?" The Lord said, "Be prepared for anything. Blessed is the one who has won the contest before it has even begun; who has seen sure victory before his eyes! When the fray is over, he emerges from the dust victorious neither by killing nor by being killed!"

"Judas asked, "Where does the path begin?" Yeshu answered, "It begins with love - love and goodness. If these were practices of your rulers in the beginning, wickedness would never have come into existence."

Yeshu here defines the beginning of the path in the self same manner as Mahayana Buddhism. The Beginning of the Essene

Nazorean Path is Love and Goodness. Without a desire to be loving and good, a person cannot begin to walk the Living Path of Yeshu and Miryam. We must plant within ourselves the seed of compassion and the wish for quick enlightenment (*bodhicitta*) so that we may more quickly end the suffering of all beings. Yeshu once said: "Be calm, be loving unto others, be gentle, be peaceful, be merciful, give tithes, help the poor and sick and distressed, be devoted to Deity, be righteous, be good that ye may receive the Mysteries of the Light and go on high into the Light Land." [388] Yeshu continues:

> "Matthew said, "Lord, you have spoken about the end of all things as though you were unconcerned!" The Lord said, "Matthew, you have understood most of what I have said to you and believed the rest by faith. Then if you know these things, they are yours to rest on; if not, then be concerned."
> They said to him, "Where are we going?" He replied, "Where you can reach."

Yeshu here stresses what he explains in such detail in the Pistis – that one rises only as high in the heavens as the initiations one has received.

> "Mary said, "Everything in place can thus be seen." The Lord said, "As I have told you, the one who sees, reveals!" Mary said, "I will say one thing to the Lord concerning the mystery of truth; that is, in truth we have taken our stand - we are transparent to the world."

Miryai shows forth her endowment here once again, begging the title of the work to be altered to 'The Dialogue of the Savior and Savioress'. The conversation turns once again the Rainbow Robe, that spiritual form that is given to the elect after they cast aside their garments of shame forever.

---

[388] Yeshu (Jesus) Pistis Sophia 102

"Judas said to Matthew, "Don't we want to know what sort of garment we will put on when we leave this decaying flesh?" The Lord heard them and said, "Those in temporal power wear garments of a temporary nature; such garments do not last forever. For children of truth like yourselves, your blessings of power remain when the flesh is stripped away!" Judas asked, "How is the spirit perceived?" Yeshu answered, "How do you perceive the sword?"

Mosque of Fatehpur Sikri

The mosque of Fatehpur Sikri preserves a Yeshu saying that is reminiscent of one spoken above in the Dialogue: "Yeshu replied, "When you abandon unprofitable works, then you have laid down the burdens that keep you from unity and have found rest." We quote it here for its beauty and the novelty of it appearing on a Mosque:

"Yeshu (peace be with him) has said, "The world is like a bridge. Pass over it, but do not settle down on it! He who hopes for an hour may hope for eternity! The world is but an hour: spend it in devotion, for the rest is of no worth." [389]

Oxyrhynchus Gospel

The Oxyrhynchus Gospel is a small fragment. Here is the total surviving scrap which emphasizes the difference between Nazorean and Jewish purity laws. For Jews, outward cleansing was the most important, for Nazoreans (who also ritually washed themselves daily and before temple entry) it was nevertheless understood that it was the inner man that must be washed, not just the outer flesh:

"Evil doers plan their evil works through crafty designs. Guard that you do not deserve the same fate as they! Evil doers not

[389] The mosque of Fatehpur Sikri (ca 1569).

only receive their just recompense in this life, but they must also suffer punishment and great torment after." He took his disciples to the place of purification, and he walked through the courts of the Temple of Jerusalem. Levi, a Pharisee, fell in with them and asked the Savior, "Who gave you and your followers permission to inspect this holy place and its holy utensils without having bathed and changed your clothing or even washing your feet? You are defiled, and have defiled this holy place and its utensils!" Not venturing to leave that place, the Savior spoke to Levi and said, "How is it with you, since you, too, are in the same Temple Court as we are? Are you then clean?" Levi said, "I am clean, because I washed in the pool of David by going down the one stair, through the water, and up the other stair, and I have put on clean, white clothing in the prescribed manner. Only after becoming clean have I ventured into this pure place and viewed its holy utensils." Then the Savior said to him, "Woe unto you unseeing blind man! So you have washed yourself in the water that was poured out from the same source where dogs and swine lie day after day. So you have scrubbed your skin to a chafe, just like prostitutes and erotic dancers do, making themselves up with rouge, oils, and perfumes in order to arouse men, looking so attractive, but being full of scorpions and vermin of every kind. You, who bathed with the swine, have dared to accused those who have been cleansed in the living water which falls from Heaven of being unclean? Woe to you and all like you!"[390]

Gospel of Philip

Discovered at Nag Hammadi but known before by quotations from Epiphanius (fourth century). Here are the verses from the much longer full text that preserve statements directly attributed to Yeshu. We begin with a statement about the stark division Yeshu sees between the spiritual world and the material concerns of life:

---

[390] Oxyrhynchus Gospel

"A disciple asked Yeshu to give him something belonging to the world. Yeshu told him, "Ask your mother and she will see that you have someone else's things."

Yeshu went into Levi's dye works. He took seventy-two different colors and mixed them in a vat. Afterward, the cloth in the vat came out all white. "Even so, the Son of Man has come as one who dyes," he said.

The disciples asked Yeshu, "Why do you love Mary [Magdalene] more than any of us?" The Savior answered them, "Why don't I love you as much as I love her? Who said that I loved her?

When a sighted person goes into a dark place with a blind person, they are both blind. When the light comes, the one who sees perceives it, but the blind man remains in darkness. The truth is that you are blind."

"I came to make all things new, as things above are new, and to make the outside things like the inside. I came to bring these things together in one place."

Yeshu here speaks of Dzogchen, the Great Perfection of the Bonpo Buddhists. He now goes on to speak of the Demiurge and different levels of Gods endorsed by all Gnostics, including the Nazoreans. Yeshu criticizes the up-down view as inferior to the inner-outer view and declares that the All-Good Father of All, whom Dzogchen calls Kuntuzangpo, is the outer of the outer that is also the inner of the inner.

"Some say that there is a heavenly man and one even above him. They call the former 'the lower one' and the latter, who knows all hidden things, 'the upper one.' This type of thinking is wrong. It would be more accurate for them to say, 'There is the inner and there is the outer. Then there is the one outside the outer.' For example, the mouthpieces of the Lord called the place of destruction 'the outer darkness' because there is no other greater darkness. Likewise, we pray to the 'outer one,' (known as the

Father, 'the one who is in secret'), from inside our own secret places. Yet, the Father, being the outer, is among us all at the same time and is the fullness of deity. So the Father is the one who they mean when they say, 'The man above.'"

"Some have entered the kingdom of heaven laughing, and have left laughing, as well."

Gospel of Thomas the Athlete

This writing is another from the Nag Hammadi Library found in 1945. We will quote it in its entirety inasmuch as it straightforwardly sets forth a very basic premise of Yeshu and the Nazorean cultus – that the flesh and its desires are the counterfeit opposite of the spiritual form and pure passion from above.

"You have heard it said, Everyone who seeks truth from the true Wisdom of God will grant himself wings to fly away from the lust that scorches men's spirits, as well as every spirit that the eye can see. Blessed is the wise one who has searched for the truth. When that one finds truth, he rests on it unafraid forever, undaunted by skeptics. It is useful and good to know the end. All things visible to men will dissolve, including men themselves. The vessel they call flesh will dissolve. Flesh will be dissolved to nothing. Those that have given up or otherwise denied the faith will count the flame as punishment for what they have renounced. The ordeal will make them finally realize that they are visible indeed and outside the invisible kingdom they once inhabited. Even those with a measure of spiritual insight will be scorched and perish, because their worldly concerns had overshadowed their first love. The dissolving of all things will happen unexpectedly. What will be left of men will appear to be shapeless ghosts unable to abandon their pain-filled corpses, dwelling forever in the dimness of the graveyard, their souls corrupted and ruined. Woe to you, godless ones, who have no hope, yet rely on a future that you have created for your own safety and security. Your future will never become reality! Woe to you, whose hope is set on your prison of flesh - you will surely die! How long will you be oblivious to the truth? How long will you suppose yourselves to be imperishable? Your hope is set on the world; your god is this life! Your blindness is ruining your chances by corrupting your souls.

Woe to you. The fire is already burning you up from within, and it is insatiable! Woe to you, for you are in the grip of an inward fire, which devours you openly, but secretly destroys your souls! Be prepared to meet your companions! Woe to you because of the wheels that grind in your minds."

Wheels that grind in the mind are slowed by meditation. We have records that Peter, who was taught his daily schedule by Yeshu, always rose hours before dawn and spent the dark hours of morning after waking from sleep and before formal prayers in meditation, contemplation, and spiritual learning. Peter also says: "I have customarily recalled to memory the sayings of my lord . . . so that by waking to them, going over and retracing each single one, I am able accurately to recall them." [391]

"Woe to you captives bound in dark caves! You laugh! In mad laughter you rejoice! You do not reflect on your dire circumstances nor understand that you are already in perdition: living in darkness and death! On the contrary, you are drunk on fire, and consumed by bitterness! Your minds are deranged from your inner burning; the poison is sweet, as are the blows of your adversaries! Darkness rises as sunlight to you, for you have traded your freedom for bondage! You have surrendered your minds to the folly of your ways - you meditate on smoke, thus your hearts are blackened from it! Light only exists within light. Any light you might have shone has been hidden in the haze - it enshadows you like a shroud! Consider whom you have believed! Don't you know that your confidence cannot be placed in those who share your desperate situation? That the baptism of the world is in dirty waters?"

---

[391] Rec. 2.1.6

Yeshu is referring here to Christian Baptisms that are not accomplished in flowing streams, rivers, and seas. Nazoreans taught that 8/9 of flowing fresh water was not living water. 100% of stagnant or stored water was considered turbid and not living. The living water was seen as the only thing that would quench the flame of death mentioned above.

> "That you are the victims of your own untimely whims? Woe to you who dwell in this error. Why can't you heed the light of the sun which observes all from the sky as it circles. Only light can free you from your enemies! Even the moon, with its lesser light, can judge you by observing the bodies left from your slaughtering!

Yeshu is referring to meat eaters when he mentions: "bodies left from your slaughtering!"

> "Woe to you sex perverts, who thrive on immoral and wanton acts with women! Woe to you, in the grips of the powers of your bodies! You are so afflicted! Woe to you, servants of the powers of demons! Woe to you who destroy your limbs in fire! Who is it that can quench the burning with refreshing dew? Who is it that can chase away the darkness that enshrouds you, enlighten your inner man, and cleanse the polluted baptismal waters with holy sunlight? Who is it that can hide the confusion that torments you? It is not too late! The light of the sun and the moon together with fresh air, holy spirit, clean earth and unpolluted water will give you a new fragrance if you allow it to be so!"

Yeshu speaks here of living earth, living water, living air, living fire, and Living Zephyr – the five light elements that Mani made so much of two centuries later.

> "For if the light does not shine on your bodies, they will dry up and die like weeds or grass. If the light shines on these, they become so strong that they grow to choke out the grapevine! But if the grapevine prevails, and shades the weeds and grasses, it alone inherits the land on which it is planted. Every place a

grapevine shades it dominates! We know grape arbors dominate all the land, bringing profit to the farmer, which pleases him greatly. He would have suffered great hardship on account of the worthless plants, until he would finally have to put forth the effort to uproot them! But the grapevine, because it was so nourished by the light, was able to remove them by choking them out. Thus the grapevine strengthens its dominion even more, as the remains of the weeds become as the soil, and provide mulch."

Nazorean initiates were always known as grapevines in the holy scrolls. Yeshu's point is that when the spirit is fed and dominates, it chokes out the darkness of the body and desire-soul (*napsha*).

"Blessed are you who know your stumbling-blocks, and flee alien things. Blessed are you who are reviled, and not respected because of the love that the Lord has for you. Blessed are you who weep and are held captive by the hopeless, for you will be released from every bondage. Watch and pray that you do not remain in the flesh, but that you come forth. For the flesh is a bondage of bitterness that brings much suffering and disgrace. When you leave the passion and suffering of your bodies, you will receive rest from the Good; you will reign with the King; you will be one with him and he with you from this time on and forever. Amen."

Book of Ieou

Here are a few selections from the heavily illustrated First Book of Yew, sometimes called a portion of the Brucianus Codex. The theme is the new man, born through ceremonial initiations and gnosis:

"The living Yeshu answered and said to his disciples: "Blessed is he who has crucified the world, and who has not the world to crucify him." The apostles answered with one voice, saying: "O Lord, teach us the way to crucify the world, that it may not crucify us, so that we are destroyed and loose our lives" The living Yeshu answered: "He who has crucified it is he who has found my word and has fulfilled it according to the will of him who has sent me."

"The life of my Father is this: that you receive your soul from the race of understanding mind, and that it ceases to be earthly and becomes understanding through that which I say to you in the course of my discourse, so that you fulfill it and are saved from the archon of this Aeon and his persecutions, to which there is no end. to send the earth to heaven is that he who hears the word of gnosis has ceased to have the understanding mind of man of earth, but has become a man of heaven. His understanding mind has ceased to be earthly, but it has become heavenly. Because of this you will be saved from the archon of this Aeon,…

And furthermore he who (is born) in the flesh of unrighteousness has no part in the Kingdom of my Father, and also he who me according to the flesh has no hope Kingdom of God the Father." The Apostles answered with one voice, they said: "Yeshu, O Lord, are we born of the flesh, and known thee according to the flesh? Tell us, O Lord, for we are troubled." The living Yeshu answered and said to his apostles: " I do not speak of the flesh in which you dwell, but the flesh of and non-understanding which exists in ignorance, which leads astray many from the …of my Father." [392]

A Johanian Gospel

A portion of a Gospel fragment of the school of John, and dated c150, has:

"Yeshu and his disciples were walking along the bank of the Jordan river. Yeshu quizzed his disciples, "Behold, a grain of wheat. When it is planted by nature, lying invisible beneath the

---

[392] Carl Schmidt, The Books of JEU and The Untitled Text in the Bruce Codex (Leiden: E. J. Brill, 1978).

earth, do we consider that time is well spent pondering its wealth?" And as they were pondering, perplexed by this strange question, Yeshu knelt and sowed a handful of wheat on the bank, watering it....[393]

˜ 14 ˜
death & ascension

Yeshu's Last Days

IN ANCIENT JEWISH records, B Sanhedrin 43a and 107b, we read that the Jews acknowledged Yeshu's royal parentage and that they warned him before crucifying him:

> "On the eve of the Passover Yeshu was hanged. For forty days before the execution took place, a herald went forth and cried, 'He is going forth to be stoned because he has practiced sorcery and enticed Israel to apostasy. Any one who can say anything in his favor, let him come forward and plead on his behalf.' But since nothing was brought forward in his favor he was hanged on the eve of the Passover! — Ulla retorted: 'Do you suppose that he was one for whom a defense could be made? Was he not an enticer, concerning whom Scripture says, neither shalt thou spare, neither shalt thou conceal him? With Yeshu however it was different, for he was connected with royalty."[394]

The Jews seem to take credit for crucifying Yeshu here, and this no doubt was the original truth of the matter before the alternative story emerged. According to the Mishna, in Jewish crucifixion a women were hung facing the cross, while men were crucified with their back to the cross.[395] This Jewish

---

[393] Gospel fragment is of the school of John, and dated c150.
[394] Babylonian Talmud: Tractate Sanhedrin Folio 43a
[395] M. Sanh. 6.4

crucifixion would have been with the consent and overseeing of Pilate however.

Dance of Life

According to biblical accounts, Yeshu went to the Mount of Olives on his last partially free night on Wednesday[396] the 5th of April, or Thursday the 6th, 30 AD: "They went to a place called Gethsemane".[397] This is the Aramaic Gat-shemanin, meaning "Oil Press". Egeria, writing about 382 CE, wrote that pilgrims going into Gethsemane were given candles "so that they can all see"[398] and in the six century Theodosius identified Gethsemane as a cave.[399] This cave still exists and is about 36 by 60 feet. It appears to have had an olive press in the first century, suggesting a nearby olive grove.

The Acts of John was greatly disliked by the "powers that be". These powers said in their Nicene Council of 787: "No one is to copy this book...we consider that it deserves to be consigned to the fire." This feared book detailed the last supper dance that took place in the Gethsemane cave and which is spoken of in Matthew: "When they had sung a hymn, they went out to the Mount of Olives." Although much of this Acts is contrived, the following dance sequence appears authentic:

> "Before Yeshu was arrested by the lawless Jews, whose lawgiver is the lawless serpent, he brought us together and said, "Before I am delivered to them, let us sing a hymn to the Father, and then go on to meet our destiny." We held hands at his bidding, and he

---

[396] "And so in the night when the fourth day of the week drew on, (Judas) betrayed our Lord to them. But they made the payment to Judas on the tenth of the month, on the second day of the week; wherefore they were accounted by God as though on the second day of the week they had seized Him, [[189]] because on the second of the week they had taken counsel to seize Him and put Him to death; and they accomplished their malice on the Friday..." Didascalia Apostolorum
[397] Mark 14:32
[398] Itinerarium 36.2
[399] De Situ Terae Sanctae 10

stood in the middle of our circle. "Answer Amen to me." He sang this hymn.

Glory be to thee, Father. Glory be to thee, Logos: Glory be to thee, Grace. --Amen. Glory be to thee, Spirit: Glory be to thee, Holy One: Glory be to thy Glory. --Amen. We praise thee, Father: We thank thee, Light: In whom darkness stays not. --Amen. And why we give thanks, I tell you: I will be saved, And I will save. --Amen. I will be loosed, And I will loose. --Amen. I will be wounded, And I will wound. --Amen. I will be born, And I will bear. --Amen. I will eat, And I will be eaten. --Amen. I will hear, And I will be heard. --Amen. I will be thought, Being wholly thought. --Amen. I will be washed, And I will wash. --Amen. Grace dances. I will pipe, Dance, all of you. --Amen. I will mourn, Beat you all your breasts. --Amen. The one Ogdoad sings praises with us. --Amen. The twelfth number dances on high. --Amen. To the Universe belongs the dancer. --Amen. He who does not dance does not know what happens. --Amen. I will flee, and I will be fled. --Amen. I will adorn, and I will be adorned. --Amen. I will be united, and I will unite. --Amen. I have no house, and I have houses. --Amen. I have no place, and I have places. --Amen. I have no temple and I have temples. --Amen. I am a lamp to you who see me. --Amen. I am a mirror to you who know me. --Amen. I am a door to you who knock on me. --Amen. I am a way to you the traveler. --Amen.

Now if you follow my dance, see yourself in Me who am speaking, And when you have seen what I do, keep silent about my mysteries. You who dance, consider what I do, for yours is This Passion of Man which I am to suffer. For you could by no means have understood what you suffer unless I was to you as the Word (*Malala*) sent by the Father. You who have seen what I suffer saw me as suffering yourself, and seeing it you did not stay, but were wholly moved. Being moved towards wisdom, you have me as a support; rest in me. Who I am, you shall know when I go forth. What I now am seen to be, that I am not; What I am you shall see when you come yourself. If you knew how to suffer you would be able not to suffer. Learn how to suffer and you shall be able not to suffer. What you do not know I myself will teach you. I am your Deity, not the Deity of the traitor. I will that there be prepared holy souls for me. Understand the word of wisdom!

As for me, If you would understand what I am: By the word "Malala" I was mocked at all things and I was not mocked at all. I leaped but do you understand the whole. And when you have understood it, then say, Glory be to thee, Father. Say again with me, Glory be to thee, Father, Glory be to thee, Word (*Malala*). Glory be to thee, Holy Spirit. --Amen. After the Lord had danced with us he left. We were like men amazed or fast asleep, and we ran away to and fro.[400]

Another section of this same Acts of John has:

"One time Yeshu took James, Peter, and I (John) to the mountain where he prayed, and we saw him in an indescribable light. Another time he bid us come up the mountain saying, "Come with me." When we arrived, he went a distance and began to pray. Since I knew he loved me, I quietly approached him from behind and stood looking at his back. Then I perceived in the spirit that he was not dressed in clothing, but stripped of his usual garments. As such, he did not look at all like a regular man. For his feet were very white, snow white, and the ground was lit up by them. And his head seemed to stretch upward to heaven. It so frightened me that I cried aloud. As he turned to answer my cry, I saw him once again as a small man. He grabbed my beard and pulled it saying, "John, do not be without your faith, but believe. Do not question the vision that you have seen." I said to him, "Lord, what have I done?" But I'm telling you, friends, that, for a month, I suffered nearly unbearable pain where he pulled at my beard. I even told him, "Lord, if your playful tug has caused me such pain, how much pain would I have had to bear if you had struck me?" He said to me, "Be concerned from now on not to tempt the untemptable one."

One time all the disciples were sleeping in a house in Gennesaret. I unwrapped my covers to see what Yeshu was doing. Yeshu said to me, "John, go back to sleep." I pretended to

---

400 The Acts of John

sleep, and after a while I saw another man like him descending and I heard him say to the Lord, "Yeshu, these men you have chosen still do not believe you." My Lord replied, "You are right; for they are men." [401]

Oath of Zatan

The Jews, angry at Miryai's abandonment of their cause and eventual conversion, had sworn an oath to crucify Yeshu and in the 31st year of his life they moved forward with that determination:

"We will slay them and make Miryai scorned in Jerusalem. A stake (cross) will we set up for the man who has ruined Miryai and led her away. There shall be no day in the world when a stranger (Gnostic) enters Jerusalem."[402]

Despite the biblical fanciful accounts, it can be argued that Yeshu may have suffered under the Jewish form of crucifixion, rather than the Roman.[403] Those not well studied might assume that only Romans practiced crucifixion, but the Jews were known to do it as well. Both Roman and Jewish custom required the criminal to carry the yoke to the place of execution. Unlike the Roman, the Jewish form began with a stoning which in most cases proved lethal. Jewish crucifixion stipulated that the person be hanged on a living tree and it is interesting that all Greek words describing the cross in the New Testament use the word that denotes living wood from a living tree. The fact that Yeshu was dead so quickly on the cross, to the surprise of Pilate[404], indicates some sort of trauma beforehand. Severe lashings with a Roman "cat of nine tails" could have done this as well as stoning, but Yeshu was more likely stoned and tortured after the Jewish fashion rather than

---

[401] The Acts of John
[402] Sidra Dyahya (Book Of John)/Drashe Dmalke (Discourses Of Kings)
[403] N.L. Kuehl (1997)
[404] Mark 15:43-44

the Roman. There were rare cases reported in Josephus in which a victim of flogging died during the process. This was much more common with stoning, however. When stoning someone to death, Jewish law insists that one say "his blood be upon us and our children." Matthew 27:25 reports that this was said at Yeshu's death. There is also a non biblical report of a stone hitting Yeshu's head. This would have been possible even if crucified by Romans, but is more likely a result of Sadducee crucifixion. It appears that Yeshu's crucifixion was viewed through a Jewish lens by Paul who referenced[405] Deuteronomy 21:23: "for anyone hung on a tree is under God's curse. From Islamic accounts[406] of now lost source material we read that the Jews actually crucified Yeshu under Roman auspice, after Pilate whipped him and gave him to them:

> "Herod said: "It is now night. Conduct him to prison." And they conducted him (there). The next day the Jews became importunate, seized him, proclaimed his infamy, tormented him, inflicting upon him various tortures, then at about the end of the day they whipped him and brought him to a melon-patch (mabtakha) and a vegetable garden (mabqala). There they crucified him and pierced him with lances in order that he should die quickly." [407]

The account of being hung on a tree in a garden is an ancient tradition that is closer to the truth than the Golgotha story that was created later.

Crucifixion

"'My God, my God, why oh Lord [have] thou abandoned me?'— He said these (words) on the cross. For he rent asunder the

---

[405] Galatians 3:13
[406] The Establishment Of Proofs For The Prophethood Of Our Master Mohammed'
[407] The Establishment Of Proofs For The Prophethood Of Our Master Mohammed'

[entire] place, having been begotten within the [Holy] Spirit by God."[408]

This is a quote from the Nazorean Psalm Book, called the Qulasta, not the Jewish Psalms of the Bible like so many Christians conclude. In the 75th Qulasta hymn it reads:

"Spirit lifted up her voice, she cried aloud and said: My Father, my father, why didst thou create me? My God, my God, My Allah, why hath thou set me so far off and cut me off and left me in the depths of the earth and in the nether glooms of darkness so that I have no strength to rise up thither?"

Although Yeshu was crucified, the story of the crucifixion within the Greek Bible cannot be trusted. This Nazorean attitude toward the Bible was expressed by Faustus, a Manichaean Bishop:

"We have proved again and again, the writings are not the production of Christ or of His apostles, but a compilation of rumours and beliefs, made, long after their departure, by some obscure semi-Jews, not in harmony even with one another, and published by them under the name of the apostles, or of those considered the followers of the apostles, so as to give the appearance of apostolic authority to all these blunders and falsehoods." [409]

Christianity teaches that their Jesus is the Christ because he shed his blood for sins. Nazoreanism taught that Yeshu is the Savior by light, not by blood. In the present Catholic and Protestant Bible it says:

"And taking bread, giving thanks, saying,' This is my body that is given for you. Do this in my remembrance. And the cup

---

408 Gospel of Philip 77
[409] Faustus, Contra Faustus Manicheun

> likewise after supper, saying: 'This cup is the new covenant in my blood that is poured out for you'." [410]

Yet this crucial blood verse is not in older texts like the 5th century Codex Bezae, and is found only as a footnote in the Revised Standard Version. It probably was not original to the Gospel of Luke and was added later as the idea of blood atonement gained ground. The phrase: "for you" occurs twice in this verse, and it, along with the word "remembrance" and "New Covenant", are found nowhere else in Luke-Acts, making it suspect. This apparent pericope is the only place where Luke seems to imply that Jesus died 'for your sins' or 'for you'." The true view of a Messiah is to see Him as a light bequeathing teacher, as Miryai here says in reference to herself:

> "Whosoever lets himself be enlightened through me and instructed, ascends and beholds the Light's region; who ever does not let himself be enlightened through me and instructed, is cut off and falls into the great End Sea."[411]

This principle also applies to Miryai's Yeshu.

Cross Mystery

Nazoreans understood the mystery of the cross to be the ritual of re-enactment of Adam and Havah Qadmon's descent into matter via the universal cross of light. This "mystery" was elaborated upon extensively by the third century prophet Mani. Here, however, we have it in the Acts of John:

> "Yeshu revealed the mystery of the cross. "One ready man must hear what I have to say, John.... For your sakes I sometimes call this mysterious 'cross of light' by various names, among them,

---

[410] Luke 22:19-20
[411] Miryai in the Book of John

the Word (*Malala*), the Son, the Father, the Spirit, Yeshu, the Christ, the Mind, the Door, the Way, the Bread, the Seed, the Resurrection, the Faith, and Grace. All these are part of the mystery, but given names for the sake of mankind. "But the true identity of the 'cross of light,' as it is known to itself and spoken to us, is the discernment of the nature of all things, the strengthening bulwark of stability from instability, and the harmonious application of wisdom, being wisdom in harmony. For unstable and transient things proceed from other convenient entities, such as principalities, powers, authorities, and demons with the accompanying demonic activities, the like of threats, inflamed passions, and devilish intentions. All these sprout from the inferior root of Satan and his nature. "This cross has united all things through the Word (*Malala*), then dispatched that which is unstable and inferior. But I do not speak of the cross made of wood that you will see when you descend from here; nor am I that man you on the cross, I who you can hear but not see. I was recognized for what I am not. That which I was recognized for was the subject of mean insults, the likes of them I did not deserve. I am the Lord of this place, and as my place of rest is not seen nor rightly spoken of, all the more will I not be seen or rightly spoken of. "Since the crowd around the cross is not united, then we perceive its inferior nature. Those who you saw on the cross are not united in him, for they had not yet been gathered together. When human nature is humbled and the masses come to me and obey me, the one who hears me will be united with me. That one will be changed, and become superior to the rest even as I am now superior. "For as long as you do not say that you belong to me, I am not what I am. If you listen to me, you will be like me, and I will be what I was, and we will be united - from me you become what I am! So ignore what the rest say, and despise the talk of those outside the mystery. Know only that I am with the Father entirely, and he is with me. "They will say I have suffered grievously, but I have not suffered at all. What you and the others perceived as suffering is to be called a mystery that has been revealed to you in my dance. For I have shown you that which you are; but what I am is known only to me. Allow me to be what I am and let me have that which is mine. What is yours you must see through me. Now you must see me not as I appear to your natural mind, but rather through your knowledge as my brother. "You have heard that I did suffer, but I did not. You heard that I did not suffer, yet I did. You have heard that I was pierced, yet I was not wounded; that I was hanged, yet I wasn't; that my blood flowed, yet it didn't. Those things that they say that I endured, I did not. But those things that they did not say I endured. I did! Now I will show you the mystery of what I really suffered, for I know that you will understand. Know me, then, as the torment of the Logos, the piercing of the Logos, the blood of the Logos, the wounding of the Logos, the nailing of the Logos, and the death of the Logos. I have thus discarded my manhood. In order to fully know the Deity, you must first know the Logos. Finally, know the man, and what he has suffered." [412]

Crucifixion Hymn

This Gnostic Crucifixion Hymn is of Manichaean origin:

"... Because of Satan the select were chosen by Jesus. He (Satan) wanted to break through the fiery waves, to burn the whole world with fire. The noble ruler (Jesus) changed his garment and appeared before Satan in his power. Then heaven and earth trembled, and Sammaèl plunged into the deep. The true interpreter (Jesus) as filled with pity because of the Light which the foe had devoured. He had raised it (the Light) up from the deep pit of death to that place of zeal from which it had descended. Honor to you, Son of Greatness, who has liberated your righteous ones. Protect, now, too, the Teacher Màr Zaku, the great keeper of your radiant herd. ... Awake, brethren, you chosen ones, on this day of the salvation of souls, the fourteenth day of the month of Mihr, on which Jesus, the Son of God, entered Parinirvana. Hearken, all you faithful: When the time for the perfection of the Son of Man had come, all the demons knew it. And the lord of the sinful doctrine ... covered himself in deceit. And the demons took counsel with each other. The

---

[412] The Acts of John

twelve thrones above were disturbed. Poison flowed down on the lower creation, upon the sons, and the chalice of death was prepared for him (Jesus). The Jews, the servants of the most high God, conceived of a deception ... They conspired against the Son of Man. They devised evil; in deception they brought forth false witnesses. Accursed Satan, who had always troubled the apostles, molested the herd of Christ. He turned the treacherous Iscariot into a steed, when the Most Beloved Jesus trusted the disciples. He (Judas) indicated him to the night-watchman by a kiss on his hand. He delivered the Son of God to the foes. He betrayed Truth. For the sake of a reward that the Jews gave, he offered up his own lord and teacher."

Death & Corpse Stories

Nisan 14, Yeshu's death date, is confirmed by a variety of sources, including the Manichaean and Jewish Talmud. Nisan 14 is the day before the full moon in the first lunar month of spring. It occurred in the 3790 year of the world, according to Jewish calendar reckoning. This lunar death date for Yeshu corresponds to shortly before 3 PM on Friday, the 7th of April, 30 AD, in the modern western calendar. Yeshu died at age 31 after public ally preaching for one year from the Passover of 29 AD to the Passover of 30 AD. Agobard, Bishop of Lyons, writing about 820-830 A.D., tells us of legends circulated among the Jews:

"For in the teachings of their elders they (the Jews) read: That Jesus was a youth held in esteem among them, who had for his teacher John the Baptist; that he had very many disciples, to one of whom he gave the name Cephas, that is Petra (Rock), because of the hardness and dullness of his understanding; that when the people were waiting for him on the feast-day, some of the youths of his company ran to meet him, crying unto him out of honour and respect, 'Hosanna, son of David'; that at last having been accused on many lying charges, he was cast into prison by the decree of Tiberius, because he had made his (T.'s) daughter (to whom he had promised the birth of a male child without [contact with] a man) conceive of a stone; that for this cause also he was hanged on a stake as an abominable sorcerer; whereon being smitten on the head with a rock and in this way slain, he was buried by a canal, and handed over to a certain Jew to guard; by night, however, he was carried away by a sudden overflowing of the canal, and though he was sought for twelve moons by the order of Pilate, he could never be found; that then Pilate made the following legal proclamation unto them: It is manifest, said he, that he has risen, as he promised, he who for envy was put to death by you, and neither in the grave nor in any other place is he found; for this cause, therefore, I decree that ye worship him; and he who will not do so, let him know that his lot will be in hell (in inferno). "Now all these things their elders have so garbled, and they themselves read them over and over again with such foolish stubbornness, that by such fictions the whole truth of the virtue and passion of Christ is made void, as though worship should not be shown Him as truly God, but is paid Him only because of the law of Pilate." [413]

A lot of source material on the life of Yeshu did not make it through the middle ages into the modern era. Scraps and fragments here and there were kept in various monasteries until they deteriorated beyond readability. Some of these were copied, some were not. Of the manuscripts that did survive sometimes only one or two of various versions endured. In light of this fact, we should not be too quick to dismiss later but still ancient sources who may have had source material at their disposal that we no longer possess. Here is an interesting piece that may fall into this category. Hrabanus Maurus, Archbishop of Mainz, wrote a book called "Contra Judaeos," in about 847 A.D. He writes that Yeshu's body was removed from the grave and dragged through the streets:

"They (the Jews) blaspheme because we believe on him whom the Law of God saith was hanged on a tree and cursed by God, .

---

[413] De Judaicis Superstitionibus

. . and [they declare] that on the protest and by direction of his teacher Joshua (i.e., J. ben Perachiah), he was taken down from the tree, and cast into a grave in a garden full of cabbages, so that their land should not be made impure . . .; they call him in their own tongue Ussum Hamizri, which means in Latin, Dissipator AEgyptius (the Egyptian Destroyer). . . . And they say that after he had been taken down from the tree, he was again taken out of the grave by their forebears, and was dragged by a rope through the whole city, and thus cast . . ., confessing that he was a godless one, and the son of a godless [fellow], that is of some Gentile or other whom they call Pandera, by whom they say the mother of the Lord was seduced, and thence he whom we believe on, born."

"And when the condemnation of Jeschu was proclaimed, and the time came to crucify him, and he saw the cross about the fourth hour of the day, he spake words of magic, flew away and sat himself upon Mount Carmel. R. Juda the gardener said to R. Joshua ben Perachiah: I will go after him and bring him back. He answered: Go, utter and pronounce the name of his Lord, that is the Schem ha-Mephoresch. He went and flew after him. When he would seize him, Jeschu spake words of magic, went into the cave of Elias, and shut the door. Juda the gardener came and said to the cave: Open, for I am God's messenger. It opened. Thereupon Jeschu made himself into a bird; R. Juda seized him by the hem of his garment and came before R. Joshua and the companions." [414]

This account is, of course, quite fanciful but certain allusions therein are of interest, such as the fact that Yeshu was associated with caves of Elijah on Carmel. The dragging of his body through the streets after internment is certainly plausible and may be the reason that no body was found there later by Miryai.

Nazorean Burials

---

[414] "The Touchstone" Of Schemtob Ibn Schaprut, The Fourteenth Century.

Nazorean burial customs, in accord with Gnostic philosophy, insist that the body is worthless after death, yet they do say that for three days the soul stays near it or connected to it before beginning its ascent toward heaven. They considered these first three days after death as a time when special precautions needed to be accomplished. These three days are not, however, three 24 hour periods, but three parcial or complete portions of three days. They placed water, a stone, and lit a candle near where the body died and kept it lit for three days. They wove silver and gold into the white clothing of the deceased, and tied it up in a special way. The body is buried facing north and a special wake meal called a Lofani is begun as soon as the body is placed in the earth and a Zidqa Brikha mass is said after burial as well. Sacred texts are also read constantly, and wet clay on the four corners of the burial site was impressed with a special iron seal and three rings are drawn in the earth with an iron knife. After three days the seals were removed, just as it says the seal on Jesus' tomb was removed after the third day. After the third day the soul begins a 45 day journey homeward. Special meals (*Lofani*) for the dead are eaten on the third, seventh, and forty fifth days.

The story of Yeshu being put in Yoseph of Arimathea's new tomb is substantiated by the Suddie Readings which have:

> "Yoseph has requested of Herod that he be allowed to take this body. And Herod sent him to Pilate who gave his permission. ...He told Yoseph that it was not his to give. Because he was slain by the Romans, it was theirs....and Pilate gives him permission to do this. And they take the body down and it is placed in the tomb"[415]

---

[415] Jesus and the Essenes, pg 256

These same readings speak also of seals, albeit different than the traditional Nazorean ones. These readings have the following account that differs greatly from the biblical one:

"You see, it is the custom of several days after, the body must again be anointed. And his mother and her cousin had come to do this. And it (the tomb) was again opened for this, with the guards being there. And they found that it was empty....the soldiers helped open the seal."[416]

Mass for the Dead

The original inspiration for the Catholic mass is the Nazorean Masqitha. Masqitha means rising up and it refers to assisting the soul in its flight homeward. There are seven variations of this sacred ceremony, each designed for special circumstances. It is a solemn ceremony performed by Priests in a temple. No observers are allowed. Miryai, James and the others did this for Yeshu after his death.

"Yeshu stands among us; he winks at us secretly and says, "Repent, so that I may forgive you your sins".[417]

The Nazorean Masqitha was misunderstood by those who became the Catholics. They have always been perplexed by the term "Mass", not knowing its true origins or Aramaic meaning. The Nazorean original Masqitha does indeed have wine and bread like the Catholic, but the whole rite and liturgy are totally different. In the secret ritual commentaries we are told that the Mystery of the Mother and the mystery of the Father are involved in the Masqitha. The Catholic version strove to eliminate the female mystery from their mutated form of this ancient ritual.

---

[416] Jesus and the Essenes, pg 258
[417] Fragment preserved in Manichaean texts

Resurrection Added

Yeshu once said:

"I am close to you, like clothing."[418]

For Nazoreans, the body was just like a set of clothes, to be discarded whenever too thread bear. The thought of resurrecting it and keeping it forever was ludicrous to the Essenic mind. In the earliest Codex Siniaticus and Codex Vaticanus, Mark's gospel ends at the tomb with no reference to resurrection. When Jerome wrote the Latin Vulgate in 383 AD, he made mention that twelve new verses on the resurrection, which had not been there in older copies, were now included in the copies of Mark given him to translate. Early Catholics like Origin and Clement seem to be unaware of the added verses but by Irenaeus' time in 185 AD they were known in some circles.[419] Bruce Metzger writes that four endings of the Gospel according to Mark 16:9-20 are current in the manuscripts:

"(1) The last twelve verses of the commonly received text of Mark are absent from the two oldest Greek manuscripts (⊚ and B), from the Old Latin codex Bobiensis (it k), the Sinaitic Syriac manuscript, about one hundred Armenian manuscripts, and the two oldest Georgian manuscripts (written A.D. 897 and A.D. 913). Clement of Alexandria and Origen show no knowledge of the existence of these verses; furthermore Eusebius and Jerome attest that the passage was absent from almost all Greek copies of Mark known to them. The original form of the Eusebian sections (drawn up by Ammonius) makes no provision for numbering sections of the text after 16:8. Not a few manuscripts which contain the passage have scribal notes stating that older

---

[418] Fragment preserved in Manichaean texts
[419] Irenaeus quotes Mark 16:19 in Against Heresies III:10:5-6, which was written c. 185;

Greek copies lack it, and in other witnesses the passage is marked with asterisks or obeli, the conventional signs used by copyists to indicate a spurious addition to a document. [420]

Another apparently unauthentic ending of Mark, as attested by some ancient manuscripts, was:

"But they reported briefly to Peter and those with him all that they had been told. And after this Jesus himself sent out by means of them, from east to west, the sacred and imperishable proclamation of eternal salvation."

Yet another version of the text was found by Freer in Egypt, which is thought to date from the 5th century:

"Afterward Jesus appeared to the eleven as they reclined at table and reproached them for their unbelief and hardness of heart, because they had not believed those who had seen him after he arose. The eleven made an excuse: "This age of lawlessness and unbelief is controlled by Satan, who, by means of unclean spirits, doesn't allow the truth to be known. So," they said to Christ, "reveal your righteousness now!" Christ replied to them, "The measure of Satan's years of power is filled up, although other fearful things draw nigh to those for whom I, because of their sin, was delivered to death, that they might turn back and not sin anymore so that they might inherit the imperishable, spiritual glory of righteousness in heaven."

These variant endings show the fluidity of the text that some think written in stone. The original ends with the women at the tomb thusly:

"And they went out quickly, and fled from the sepulchre; for they trembled and were amazed: neither *said they any thing to any man*; for they were afraid."

---

[420] Bruce Metzger, A Textual Commentary on the Greek New Testament, pages 122-126.

This seems to indicate that no one knew what happened to Yeshu's body. In the Gnostic Gospel of Philip we read:

> "Some are fearful lest they arise naked. Therefore they desire to arise in the flesh, and they do not know that those who wear the flesh are the denuded. Those [...] who are divested (of the flesh) are those who are clad (in the images).[421]

Nazoreanism, in contrast to Judeo-Christianity, teaches that the flesh is of the earth and shall not rise. Only the soul rises beyond the confines of the material sphere upon which the body was created. The resurrected form of Christ left a corpse behind, and this corpse was removed from where it had been placed before Miryai found the empty tomb. It did not rise but only rotted. Thus it is with all men and woman who rise before Abathur. The discarded rags wither whilst their eternal spirit soars. Those who cease to identify with their flesh and its cravings, even whilst enwrapped by it, are the ones who will wear the Rainbow Robe when their stinking skin garment is cast aside for more royal raiment. Ones image is their Dmuta form, their eternal counterpart to their physical form.

Nazirutha postulates a divine birth in a Light World for each legitimate Nazorean. This heavenly birth entailed a three fold soul/spirit housed in a fivefold spiritual body/form. The physical body we were born into in heaven consisted of the 5 light elements of that heavenly world. These 5 elements are fire, water, light, air and ether. When we fell from those perfect worlds (or if one prefers: "volunteered to descend into this darkened universe for experience"), our threefold soul fragmented into three diverse souls - Napsha, Ruha and Nishimta; and our bodily light form fragmented into five separate aggregates - Earth, Water, Fire, Air and Ether. This

---

[421] Gospel Of Philip 24

joint fragmentation of the souls and forms of the various beings of light, including Yeshu and Miryam the Primal Pair, is known collectively as the Light Cross or Living Soul.

> "(Paul claims that) 'flesh [and blood cannot] inherit the Sovereignty [of God].' What is this which shall not inherit? This which is upon us? Yet this is exactly what will inherit— that which belongs to Yeshu with his flesh and blood. Therefore he said: Whoever does not eat my flesh and drink my blood has no life within himself. What is his flesh?— it is the Logos. And his blood?— it is the Holy Spirit. Whoever has received these has food and drink and clothing. I disagree with those who say that flesh and blood shall not arise. Then (these) both are wrong: thou say that the flesh shall not arise, but tell me what will arise so that we may honour thee; thou say it is the spirit in the flesh and this light in the flesh, but this also is an incarnate saying. For whatever thou will say, thou do not speak apart from the flesh! It is necessary to arise in this flesh, as everything exists within it. [422]

Judeo-Christianity settled on the fabulous claim of physical resurrection, in direct contrast to statements in their own fabricated New Testament. They were not thorough enough to rid it of all original doctrines on the subject, hence Paul's claim that flesh would not enter heaven. Ziwane light sparks, the blood of Miryam and Yeshu spread out within vegan alms, is that with which the light robe is woven. Nazorean monastics, like their Manichaean counterparts later on, feasted upon the light of Christ hidden in vegan food and drink. These light particles were used to nourish the soul, unify it, and prepare basic elements for the creation of a spiritual bodily form for the future ascended Pearl soul. The flesh and blood that will rise is the ziwane flesh and blood of the Primal Pair, woven out of the five living elements, which returns to its source above.

---

[422] Gospel Of Philip 25

"In this world they who wear garments (of cloth) are more valuable than the garments. In the Sovereignty of the Heavens the garments (of imagery) are more valuable than those to whom they have been given by means of water and fire, which purify the entire place. [423]

Our soul survives longer than its clothing here in this eighth world, but in the Light Land the soul is covered with eternal flesh - the Rainbow Robe. Nazoreans taught that Yeshu was not resurrected physically, but spiritually in a Paranirvana.

"Awake, brethren, chosen ones, on this day of spiritual salvation, the 14th of the month of Mihr, when Jesus, the Son of God, entered into parinirvana.".[424]

"In Luke 24:6, Codex Bezae and most of the Old Latin texts do not have the phrase "He is not here, but has been raised". Apparently this phrase was another addition by a scribe to reinforce the physical resurrection theme."

"What is the good (of erecting a tomb)? The body is dirt and rubbish when once the soul has left it!"[425]

In the Pistis Sophia we read of Yeshu being reclothed in his original robe of light that he had left behind when he descended:

"It came to pass, through the command of that mystery, that there should be sent me my Light-vesture, which it had given me from the beginning, and which I had left behind in the last mystery, that is the four-and-twentieth mystery from within without,--those which are in the orders of the second space of the First Mystery. That Vesture then I left behind in the last mystery, until the time should be completed to put it on, and I

[423] Gospel Of Philip 26
[424] Parthian Manichaean Fragment M104 From Turfan
[425] From Mandaeans Of Iraq & Iran, Pg 184

should begin to discourse with the race of men and reveal unto them all from the beginning of the Truth to its completion, and discourse with them from the interiors of the interiors to the exteriors of the exteriors and from the exteriors of the exteriors to the interiors of the interiors. Rejoice then and exult and rejoice more and more greatly, for to you it is given that I speak first with you from the beginning of the Truth to its completion." [426]

There is a tradition that James took an oath not to eat until Yeshu arose from the dead. In Nazorean culture this is three days after the demise of the physical body. At this time a special meal for the dead is enacted to help the soul begin its Journey heavenward. Thus James is swearing to fast until he does the traditional Masqitha Rite that assists the Dead to Rise:

> "And when the Lord had given the linen cloth to the servant of the priest, he went to James and appeared to him. For James had sworn that he would not eat bread from that hour in which he had drunk the cup of the Lord until he should see him risen from among them that sleep. And shortly thereafter the Lord said: Bring a table and bread! And immediately it is added: he took the bread and blessed it and brake it and gave to James the Just and said to him: My brother, eat thy bread, for the Son of Man is risen from among them that sleep." [427]

Within the redacted remnants of early Nazorean texts, and within the relatively intact oral traditions of early Nazoreanism as preserved by the surviving Gnostic Mandaean sect of Iraq, we have preserved many original Nazorean and Gnostic teachings concerning the soul, its origins, and its fate after death. Included in these imperfect transmissions of early thought are teachings and practices relating to death, internment, and ascension of the soul, or souls, to heaven. These traditions reflect the traditions of

---

[426] Pistis Sophia 7
[427] Gosepl Of The Hebrews, (Jerome, De Viris Inlustribus 2

earliest Christianity BEFORE the tampering that occurred in later centuries by the Catholic school.

"What is the good (of erecting a tomb)? The body is dirt and rubbish when once the soul has left it!"[428]

"Awake, brethren, chosen ones, on this day of spiritual salvation, the 14th of the month of Mihr, when Jesus, the Son of God, entered into parinirvana.". [429]

Real Resurrection

In early Nazorean thought the Creation of Man was seen as a creation of dark beings working through evolution hundred of thousands of years ago. This is in accord with modern science and Darwinism. This is in stark contrast to the biblical school which asserts that their God created the human race in the Garden of Eden from dust just six thousand years ago. Because Gnostics did not believe in the divine origins of the human body, they saw no need of reclaiming that body after death. Roman Christianity reverenced the material world and form whereas Gnostics eschewed it and all material creation. This does not mean that the Gnostic disregarded the body; on the contrary, the purer Gnostic schools were very careful on their use and treatment of the human form. Even though they considered such a dim reflection of the purer non material robe of light worn in the heavens, earth bound Gnostics still treated their body respectfully.

Pure Gnostics survived upon a pure vegan diet and refused to let any form of flesh enter their mouths and defile them. The Manichaeans called this the seal of the tongue and it was taken most seriously. But when this human form, which they also

---

[428] From Mandaeans Of Iraq & Iran, Pg 184
[429] Parthian Manichaean Fragment M104 From Turfan

called the stinking stump, had reached the term of its use, it was buried in an unmarked grave. It was considered linked to the souls for three days, and so for that time period a certain respect was paid to it. Three concentric rings were drawn in the soil around the grave, and four impressions made in its four quarters by impressing a talisman seal into wet mud.

After three days these seals were broken and the grave ignored. At this point the soul began its journey through the purgatory realms. This journey was assisted by loved ones eating meals for these departed spirits, and doing a special Mass Ceremony, called a Masqitha in Aramaic, which was designed to help unite the different levels of the soul and prepare them to merge into a glorified light body called a Robe. This is similar to the Buddhist concept of the Rainbow Body, or Sambhogakaya body of the Buddha. The Pagra, or Stinking Stump of rotting flesh was never considered to be used again. This Nirmanakaya body of Yeshu was considered a temporary vehicle for the more real Sambhogakaya body of Yeshu-Ziwa, or Jesus the Splendorous. This relative disregard for the temporary physical form of Yeshu led to the accusations of the non Gnostic schools that the Manichaeans and other Gnostics denied the physical incarnation of Christ. They did not deny his Nirmanakaya body, but considered such irrelevant in comparison to his more glorious Sambhogakaya and Dharmakaya bodies.

The Nazorean's 45 day journey of the soul after death is encoded in our left Ginza and is also reflected in the later Bon tradition crystallized in the Tibetan Book of the Dead. These Tibetan teachings probably have their source in the Manichaean movement that dominated this region before Buddhism became entrenched there. This Manichaean movement continued the earlier Nazorean traditions of the fate of the soul and body at death.

In Nazorean teachings, the Napsha, Ruha and Nishimta souls must be purified and merged, and then enwrapped in a glorified Rainbow Robe called a Mana. This occurs at the Gates of the Light Land when Abathur, the Father of all Bodhisatvas, weighs the souls against that of Sethil and lets approximately one in a thousand enter in. All others are purged in purgatorial realms and sent back to earthly wombs for reincarnation.

Roman Christianity is founded on the supposed fact of the Resurrection of Jesus, Gnostic Christianity on a spiritual ascension. Without a physical resurrection most orthodox Christians would loose faith in Christ. It is one of the most, if not the most, important doctrines of the non Gnostic schools. It is of value to explore the plausibility and origins of this claim and compare such to the alternate Gnostic assertion of a spiritual "parinirvana".

Although Greek Orthodox and Eastern Christianity leans toward a spiritual rather than physical resurrection, as does Reformed Judaism, it is a fundamental assertion of Roman and Protestant Christianity that Jesus Christ had a special and supernatural birth, death and resurrection. All these events are interpreted physically, setting apart the earthly life of Jesus as special and unique from all others human beings and supposedly proving that the Christian God is willing to defy natural law for the sake of those who love Him and are willing to have unshakeable faith in this unlogical assertion. Many modern Christians feel that to question the physical resurrection is to question God and to set themselves outside of the arena of salvation. Blind faith in the ridiculous has always been demanded as a test of loyalty by the non Gnostic schools, whereas reasonable logical faith has been the hallmark of the Gnostic Nazorean schools, as Peter declared:

"Do not think that we say that these things are only to be received by faith, but also that they are to be asserted by reason. For indeed it is not safe to commit these things to bare faith without reason, since assuredly truth cannot be without reason." [430]

The supposed source of the physical resurrection doctrine is thought to be the Bible, but the earliest manuscripts of what scholars consider the earliest gospel, Mark, do not mention any appearances of Yeshu. All of the appearances in that gospel occur only in post-4th century manuscripts[431], although such is perhaps alluded to in the late 2nd century, in a passage of Irenaeus, though the text in question is also a late manuscript that could have been modified to match the Gospel that was in circulation centuries later.

These additions seem to have first appeared in Coptic manuscripts, and are then added to Greek versions a century or more later. These late additions shed doubt on whether earliest Christianity taught a physical resurrection at all. The references to Christ's resurrection in Paul's writings are also not supportive. For one, these appearances are not physical, but visionary: "All that appears is a light from heaven." [432] Paul also adamantly maintained that the Resurrection was spiritual, not a physical event when he says:

"a natural body is sown, a spiritual body is raised".[433]

This appears to have been the original teaching of Nazorean Christianity before Roman Christianity took over and altered things, including the ending of Mark. Paul even says that "flesh and blood cannot inherit the kingdom of God"[434],

---

[430] Chapter LXIX

[431] cf. The Greek New Testament, Fourth Revised Edition, p. 189, apparatus footnote 3

[432] phôs ek tou ouranou, 9.3; ek tou ouranou...phôs, 22.6; ouranothen...phôs, 26.13

[433] 1 Corinthians 15.44

[434] vv. 50

because flesh and blood is the perishable body, and we are resurrected as an imperishable body. It is thus apparent from a close reading of Paul that he does not believe in a physical resurrection involving flesh and blood, i.e a physical body, but rather in a spiritual ascension of the more spiritual parts of humankind.

> "The view expressed in the [Dead Sea] Scrolls accord in general with those attributed by Josephus (Antiq. XVIII.i.5; War II.viii.11) to the Essenes, with whom, indeed, the Qumran sectaries may be identical...They held that although bodies were perishable, souls endured and mounted upward, the good to the realm of bliss, the evil to be consigned to a place of torment. This view is expressed also in Wisd. Sol. 3:1ff.; 5:16; Jub. 25; while something of the same kind--though without the reference to ultimate judgment--appears in Eccl. 12:7 ('the dust returns to the earth as it was, and the spirit returns to God who gave it').[435]

It is sometimes said that no Jew would have believed in a spiritual resurrection and that the earliest Christians were Jews, but that is not true. Reformed Judaism has declared that the doctrine of physical resurrection does not have Biblical support and is rejected by them. The earliest Christians were of the sect of the Nazoreans who believed in a spiritual resurrection, not a physical one like the Pharisee sect. The later muddling of original Nazoreanism with Pharisee and Roman ideas departed radically from the original faith and teachings of Yeshu and Miryai. This radical departure is reflected in the modern Christian bible which does contains echoes of original Nazorean teachings, but on a whole is a forged document according to Gnostic teaching.

Many early Roman Christians even held to the doctrine of a spiritual rather than material resurrection. Origin, Jerome tells us, called those who believed in the physical resurrection

---

[435] Gaster

"simplices" (simpletons), "philosarcas" (flesh-lovers), and "innocentes et rusticos". Origin would no doubt not have been so outspoken if the doctrine of the material resurrection had been a universal belief in his day.

> "The vesture which First Life did give unto Adam, the man, the vesture which First Life did give unto Ram, the Man, the vesture which First Life did give unto Shurbai, the Man, the vesture First Life did give unto Shum bar Nuh (Shem son of Noah) has He given now unto thee. He hath given it thee, O Yahya, that thou mayest ascend, and with thee may those descend [. . . . . .] The house of the defect (thy body) will be left behind in the desert.[436]

> Everyone who shall be found sinless, will ascend unto thee, in the Region of Light, he who is not found sinless, will be called to account in the guard-houses. [437]

The Suddie readings explain the resurrection as being spiritual but not physical, and that only those with special abilities could see Yeshu after his death:

> "All who open themselves have this ability and could have seen him. Many did....Yes, but one who is . ... different. Who is more like one of the beings of light than having an earthly body. It is not one you could perhaps reach out and to touch., for your hand would pass through. [438]

Ascension

Regular Christians keep the Feast of the Ascension of Christ forty days after His resurrection. They base this on their flawed texts. The Sleeping Prophet more correctly has:

---

[436] Mandaean Text
[437] Mandaean Text
[438] Jesus and the Essenes, pg 259

"the time of the ascension, which was fifty days after the resurrection."

This is in harmony with the Shawui calendar, placing the "resurrection" at Passover, and the Ascension fifty days later on Pentecost.

⁻ 15 ⁻
POST RESURRECTION TEACHINGS

Apostle to the Apostles

YESHU'S TEACHINGS did not end with the death of his body. He continued to appear and communicate with those he had helped train, especially Miryai who became known as the Apostle of the Apostles. Many of his most important messages were communicated in this way through Miryai, James and others. In this chapter we will discuss some of these such as the full Gospel of Mary of Magdala because of its emphasis on the superior status of Miryai, and excerpts from the much longer Pistis Sophia because of its excellent explanation of the overall thrust of the mission of Yeshu, and a few verses from the Wisdom of Jesus Christ. From a Fragment preserved in Manichaean texts we learn that it is Miryai who replaces Yeshu at his death as the one who inspires the Apostles:

"Mary, Mary - know me but do not touch me. Stop the tears from flowing and know that I am your master. Only do not touch me, for I haven't seen my Father's face yet. Your God wasn't stolen from you, as your small thoughts lead you to believe. Your God did not die, but mastered death! I am not the gardener! I have given life and received life eternal. But I now appear to you because I have seen the tears in your eyes. Throw your sadness away from me to wandering orphans. Start rejoicing now and tell the eleven. You will find them gathered on

Jordan's bank. The traitor persuaded them to once again become fishermen as once they were and to lay down their nets that caught people to life! [439]

"Say to them, 'Rise up! Let's go! Your brother calls for you!' If they scorn brotherhood with me, tell them, 'Your master calls.' If they disagree with that, tell them, 'It is your Lord.' Use all your skill to bring the sheep in to the shepherd. If you see that they have lost their wits for grief, draw Simon Peter away and say to him, 'Remember what I spoke to you about privately on the Mount of Olives: I have something to say but no one to say it to.'[440]

Gospel of Mary Magdalene

The Gospel According to Mary Magdalene is part of a fifth century manuscript that exists now in Berlin. The original is much older. It is an unhampered with pure Gnostic document which we shall quote in full due to its shortness and its focus on the status of Miryai among the original disciples of Yeshu. The first six pages are missing and the surviving manuscript, after one fragmentary sentence, begins with:

"The Savior said, All nature, all formations, all creatures exist in and with one another, and they will be resolved again into their own roots. For the nature of matter is resolved into the roots of its own nature alone. He who has ears to hear, let him hear. Peter said to him, Since you have explained everything to us, tell us this also: What is the sin of the world? The Savior said There is no sin, but it is you who make sin when you do the things that are like the nature of adultery, which is called sin. That is why the Good came into your midst, to the essence of every nature in order to restore it to its root. Then He continued and said, That is why you become sick and die, for you are deprived of the one

---

[439] Fragment preserved in Manichaean texts
[440] Fragment preserved in Manichaean texts

who can heal you. He who has a mind to understand, let him
understand.

Matter gave birth to a passion that has no equal, which
proceeded from something contrary to nature. Then there arises
a disturbance in its whole body. That is why I said to you, Be of
good courage, and if you are discouraged be encouraged in the
presence of the different forms of nature. He who has ears to
hear, let him hear.

When the Blessed One had said this, He greeted them all, saying,
Peace be with you. Receive my peace unto yourselves. Beware
that no one lead you astray saying Lo here or lo there! For the
Son of Man is within you. Follow after Him! Those who seek
Him will find Him. Go then and preach the gospel of the
Kingdom. Do not lay down any rules beyond what I appointed
you, and do not give a law like the lawgiver lest you be
constrained by it. When He said this He departed.

But they were grieved. They wept greatly, saying, How shall we
go to the Gentiles and preach the gospel of the Kingdom of the
Son of Man? If they did not spare Him, how will they spare us?
Then Mary stood up, greeted them all, and said to her brethren,
Do not weep and do not grieve nor be irresolute, for His grace
will be entirely with you and will protect you. But rather, let us
praise His greatness, for He has prepared us and made us into
Men. When Mary said this, she turned their hearts to the Good,
and they began to discuss the words of the Savior.

Peter said to Mary, Sister we know that the Savior loved you
more than the rest of woman. Tell us the words of the Savior
which you remember which you know, but we do not, nor have
we heard them.

Mary answered and said, What is hidden from you I will
proclaim to you. And she began to speak to them these words: I,
she said, I saw the Lord in a vision and I said to Him, Lord I saw
you today in a vision. He answered and said to me, Blessed are
you that you did not waver at the sight of Me. For where the

mind is there is the treasure. I said to Him, Lord, how does he who sees the vision see it, through the soul or through the spirit? The Savior answered and said, He does not see through the soul (*ruha*) nor through the spirit (*nishimta*), but the mind (*mana*) that is between the two that is what sees the vision.

There are four pages missing here in the surviving manuscript, at which point the narrative begins again with a description of the soul ascending through the hostile lower heavens after death:

"And desire said, I did not see you descending, but now I see you ascending. Why do you lie since you belong to me? The soul answered and said, I saw you. You did not see me nor recognize me. I served you as a garment and you did not know me. When it said this, it (the soul) went away rejoicing greatly. Again it came to the third power, which is called ignorance. The power questioned the soul, saying, Where are you going? In wickedness are you bound. But you are bound; do not judge! And the soul said, Why do you judge me, although I have not judged? I was bound, though I have not bound. I was not recognized. But I have recognized that the All is being dissolved, both the earthly things and the heavenly. When the soul had overcome the third power, it went upwards and saw the fourth power, which took seven forms. The first form is darkness, the second desire, the third ignorance, the fourth is the excitement of death, the fifth is the kingdom of the flesh, the sixth is the foolish wisdom of flesh, the seventh is the wrathful wisdom. These are the seven powers of wrath. They asked the soul, Whence do you come slayer of men, or where are you going, conqueror of space? The soul answered and said, What binds me has been slain, and what turns me about has been overcome, and my desire has been ended, and ignorance has died. In a Aeon I was released from a world, and in a Type from a type, and from the fetter of oblivion which is transient. From this time on will I attain to the rest of the time, of the season, of the Aeon, in silence."

At this point we learn the reaction of the Apostles to Miryai's teachings. Andrew and Peter are skeptical, and Peter displays male chauvinism before being put in his place by Levi. Peter's chauvinism and jealousy of Miryai also arises in the Gospel of Thomas text, as well as the Pistis Sophia, betraying a Jewish background for this apostle. Men raised in the Nazorean faith would not likely have such chauvinistic tendencies due to the strong reverence for the Goddess and acceptance of female priests.

> "When Mary had said this, she fell silent, since it was to this point that the Savior had spoken with her. But Andrew answered and said to the brethren, Say what you wish to say about what she has said. I at least do not believe that the Savior said this. For certainly these teachings are strange ideas. Peter answered and spoke concerning these same things. He questioned them about the Savior: Did He really speak privately with a woman and not openly to us? Are we to turn about and all listen to her? Did He prefer her to us? Then Mary wept and said to Peter, My brother Peter, what do you think? Do you think that I have thought this up myself in my heart, or that I am lying about the Savior? Levi answered and said to Peter, Peter you have always been hot tempered. Now I see you contending against the woman like the adversaries. But if the Savior made her worthy, who are you indeed to reject her? Surely the Savior knows her very well. That is why He loved her more than us. Rather let us be ashamed and put on the perfect Man, and separate as He commanded us and preach the gospel, not laying down any other rule or other law beyond what the Savior said. And when they heard this they began to go forth to proclaim and to preach.[441]

Peter's jealous question: "Did He really speak privately with a woman and not openly to us? Are we to turn about and all listen to her? Did He prefer her to us?" is answered by Levi who says: "Surely the Savior knows her very well. That is why

---

[441] The Gospel According to Mary

He loved her more than us." Thus ends this short but important document that clearly sets forth the preeminence of Miryai as the Apostle to the Apostles as shown forth in her opening statement to her disciples:

> "Do not weep and do not grieve nor be irresolute, for His grace will be entirely with you and will protect you. But rather, let us praise His greatness, for He has prepared us and made us into Men. When Mary said this, she turned their hearts to the Good, and they began to discuss the words of the Savior."

Wisdom of Yeshu

We now look to the Sophia (Wisdom) of Jesus Christ, from the Nag, in which the "secret of the holy plan" of Yeshu is alluded to:

> "After he rose from the dead, his twelve disciples and seven women continued to be his followers, and went to Galilee onto the mountain called "Divination and Joy". When they gathered together and were perplexed about the underlying reality of the universe and the plan, and the holy providence, and the power of the authorities, and about everything the Savior is doing with them in the secret of the holy plan, the Savior appeared - not in his previous form, but in the invisible spirit. And his likeness resembles a great angel of light. But his resemblance I must not describe. No mortal flesh could endure it, but only pure, perfect flesh, like that which he taught us about on the mountain called "Of the Olives" in Galilee.

Yeshu's disciples are here described as trying to make sense out of the root teachings of their master. They are not musing over doctrines considered important by the Christians, like atonement, going to church, repenting, etc. They are concerned with very Gnostic matters like the underlining structure and pattern of the universe, of our entrapment here, and of Yeshu's program to assist pearls in escaping from the clutches of their flesh and the dominion of the fallen gods who reign in the lower spheres.

> "And he said: "Peace be to you, My peace I give you!" And they all marveled and were afraid. The Savior laughed and said to them: "What are you thinking about? Are you perplexed? What are you searching for?" Philip said: "For the underlying reality of the universe and the plan." The Savior said to them: "I want you to know that all men are born on earth from the foundation of the world until now, being dust, while they have inquired about God, who he is and what he is like, have not found him. Now the wisest among them have speculated from the ordering of the world and (its) movement. But their speculation has not reached the truth. For it is said that the ordering is directed in three ways, by all the philosophers, (and) hence they do not agree. For some of them say about the world that it is directed by itself. Others, that it is providence (that directs it). Others, that it is fate. But it is none of these. Again, of the three voices I have just mentioned, none is close to the truth, and (they are) from man. But I, who came from Infinite Light, I am here - for I know him (Light) - that I might speak to you about the precise nature of the truth. For whatever is from itself is a polluted life; it is self-made. Providence has no wisdom in it. And fate does not discern. But to you it is given to know; and whoever is worthy of knowledge will receive (it), whoever has not been begotten by the sowing of unclean rubbing but by First Who Was Sent, for he is an immortal in the midst of mortal men."

Yeshu's "Secret of the Holy Plan" is reserved for those born again in living waters – the immortal race of Nazoreans. These are they that function and make decisions from a purely spiritual perspective on life. Those still under the dominion and strong influence of their physical forms which were conceived by "unclean rubbing" are not to be made privy to it. For Yeshu, there were unclean and clean conceptions, an unclean body and a pure spiritual form, and a tainted worldview and a spiritual worldview as in Buddhism which Yeshu was very familiar with in both its Jain and Bonpo forms.

Yeshu goes on to describe the All Good Father and Mother of Light in great detail, and then describes the descent of spiritual beings into the world:

"Again, his disciples said: "Tell us clearly how they came down from the invisibilities, from the immortal to the world that dies?" The perfect Savior said: "Son of Man consented with Sophia, his consort, and revealed a great androgynous light. His male name is designated 'Savior, Begetter of All Things'. His female name is designated 'All-Begettress Sophia'. Some call her 'Pistis'.

"All who come into the world, like a drop from the Light, are sent by him to the world of Almighty, that they might be guarded by him. And the bond of his forgetfulness bound him by the will of Sophia, that the matter might be revealed through it to the whole world in poverty, concerning his (Almighty's) arrogance and blindness and the ignorance that he was named. But I came from the places above by the will of the great Light, (I) who escaped from that bond; I have cut off the work of the robbers; I have awakened that drop that was sent from Sophia, that it might bear much fruit through me, and be perfected and not again be defective, but be joined through me, the Great Savior, that his glory might be revealed, so that Sophia might also be justified in regard to that defect, that her sons might not again become defective but might attain honor and glory and go up to their Father, and know the words of the masculine Light."
442

Yeshu is explaining how he and Miryam sent Gnostic souls like drops into the world until he, Yeshu, could awaken them, free them, and teach them to ascend back to the light once more. The remainder of the text explains the occurrences in the lower heavens that led to the creation of humanity.

Pistis Sophia

---

442 Translated by Douglas M. Parrott

The lengthy Askew codex, containing the Pistis Sophia, was acquired by the British Museum in 1795, having been previously acquired by a Dr. Askew from an unknown source. It has heavy Manichaean overtones and many beautiful and important teachings despite its apparent alterations and interpolations over time. Here is a small sample of the text, the opening lines of Book Three, which perfectly introduces the purpose, teachings, mysteries, method, and salvatory plan of Yeshu:

> "Yeshu continued again in the discourse and said unto his disciples: "When I shall have gone into the Light, then herald it unto the whole world and say unto them: Cease not to seek day and night and remit not yourselves until ye find the mysteries of the Light-kingdom, which will purify you and make you into refined light and lead you into the Light-kingdom.

> "Say unto them: Renounce the whole world and the whole matter therein and all its care and all its sins, in a word all its associations which are in it, that ye may be worthy of the mysteries of the Light and be saved from all the chastisements which are in the judgments.[443]

After listing 32 renouncings that each disciple is required to accomplish in order to escape certain punishments, the text continues with ten positive affirmations which could be called Yeshu's Ten Commandments:

> "Say rather to the men of the world: Be calm, that ye may receive the mysteries of the Light and go on high into the Light-kingdom. "Say unto them: Be ye loving-unto-men, that ye may be worthy of the mysteries of the Light and go on high into the Light-kingdom. "Say unto them: Be ye gentle, that ye may receive the mysteries of the Light and go on high into the Light-kingdom. "Say unto them: Be ye peaceful, that ye may receive

[443] The Pistis Sophia

the mysteries of the Light and go on high into the Light-kingdom. "Say unto them: Be ye merciful, that ye may receive the mysteries of the Light and go on high into the Light-kingdom. "Say unto them: Give ye alms, that ye may receive the mysteries of the Light and go on high into the Light-kingdom. "Say unto them: Minister unto the poor and the sick and distressed, that ye may receive the mysteries of the Light and go on high into the Light-kingdom.

"Say unto them: Be ye loving-unto-God, that ye may receive the mysteries of the Light and go on high into the Light-kingdom. "Say unto them: Be ye righteous, that ye may receive the mysteries [of the Light] and go on high into the Light-kingdom. "Say unto them: Be good, that ye may receive the mysteries [of the Light] and go on high into the Light-kingdom.

After listing these Ten Commandments and reiterating the need to renounce the world and its ways, Yeshu sets forth the most important facet of his work – the giving of "mysteries" or rituals of redemption. These Mysteries (*raza*) are the major thrust of the Nazorean Way.

"Say unto them: Renounce all, that ye may receive the mysteries of the Light and go on high into the Light-kingdom. These are all the boundaries of the ways for those who are worthy of the mysteries of the Light. "Unto, such, therefore, who have renounced in this renunciation, give the mysteries of the Light and hide them not from them at all, even though they are sinners and they have been in all the sins and all the iniquities of the world, all of which I have recounted unto you, in order that they may turn and repent and be in the submission which I have just recounted unto you. Give unto them the mysteries of the Light-kingdom and hide them not from them at all; for it is because of sinfulness that I have brought the mysteries into the world, that I may forgive all their sins which they have committed from the beginning on. For this cause have I said unto you aforetime: 'I am not come to call the righteous.' Now, therefore, I have brought the mysteries that [their] sins may be forgiven for every

one and they be received into the Light-kingdom. For the
mysteries are the gift of the First Mystery, that he may wipe out
the sins and iniquities of all sinners." [444]

After receiving their commission to perform rituals in behalf
of sincere souls, Miryai asks about the details of carrying out
this task. She is told that those who receive the rituals but
continue to sin will have to undergo reincarnation again on
earth until they get it right. Yeshu is emphatic that only those
souls who have received the proper initiations and are true to
them will inherit the Light Land:

> "If on the contrary he hath sinned once or twice or thrice, then
> will he be cast back into the world again according to the type of
> the sins which he hath committed, the type of which I will tell
> you when I shall have told you the expansion of the universe."
> But amen, amen, I say unto you: Even if a righteous man hath
> committed no sins at all, he cannot possibly be brought into the
> Light-kingdom, because the sign of the kingdom of the mysteries
> is not with him. In a word, it is impossible to bring souls into the
> Light without the mysteries of the Light-kingdom." [445]

The absolute necessity of receiving the elaborate array of
Nazorean rites of passage is emphasized throughout the 390
Coptic pages of the Pistis Sophia. This emphasis cannot be
underestimated when seeking a clear understanding of the
teachings of Yeshu. This ritual emphasis is not noticeable in
the Gospel of Thomas, for instance, because this is a different
type of document addressed to a different audience. The Pistis
Sophia is a priest and priestess text that explains the real inner
workings of the Nazorean way. Most of the Aramaic texts that
have come down to us from the ancient Nazoreans, via their
Mandaean remnants, are of this priestly type. They detail how
to perform numerous Gnostic rituals and delve into the type

---

[444] The Pistis Sophia
[445] The Pistis Sophia, 3:103

and symbolic meaning of each facet of the rite and liturgy. Having touched lightly on the ritual emphasis of the Nazorean teachings of Yeshu, we will now turn to the public presentation of the Way as presented by Peter to the masses. These teachings are in stark contrast to the deeper teachings for Lay Nazoreans living in spiritual communities, and for Priests and Priestesses living more of a monastic type of lifestyle focused on ritual work.

- 16 -
PETER IN RECOGNITIONS

Yeshu & Peter

UNLIKE THE PREVIOUS post resurrection apparitional teachings, the teachings of Yeshu found in the Clementine works are a direct result of Peter remembering Yeshu's words when he was alive, and sharing some of them with the crowds who had previously listened to the teachings of Peter's adversary. Peter presents Yeshu as the True Prophet. The figure of Yeshu as the True Prophet presented by Peter in the Clementine Homilies and Recognitions is vastly different from the one put forth by the Roman Christians in their Greek gospels where Jesus is presented as a Greco-Roman God. Peter also comes across as a different more astute person than the degraded version of him found in the Greek gospels. After reading Peter's words in these works, it is apparent how malicious the writers of the Greek gospels were when they portrayed all the original disciples in such a poor light.

These two Clementine books are universally accepted in scholarly circles as recensions of an earlier book called Preachings of Peter:

"The entire literature is of Jewish-Christian, or Ebionitic, origin. The position accorded to "James, the Lord's brother," in all the writings, is a clear indication of this; so is the silence respecting the Apostle Paul... the literature has been connected with the Ebionite sect called the Elkesaites."[446]

In the Preachings of Peter it is thought that the original opponent of Peter was not Simon, but Paul. In them Peter teaches that Yeshu, the True Prophet, reincarnates from time to time to teach humankind the truth. Peter does not teach the divinity of Jesus, or blood atonement, and he is against celibacy, quick conversions, faith without reason, and meat eating. He advocates initiatory immersions, daily baptisms, and ritual washing after sex and abstinence during menstruation, few possessions and a vegan diet. These are foundational principles of the Nazorean faith that all converts were expected to fully embrace. These principles are not emphasized in the sayings of Yeshu since he was addressing a crowd who already habitually observed this lifestyle to perfection. Only when the message is shared abroad with outsiders does Peter find the need to talk of them. Yet Peter not only alludes to these beginning principles, but in response to the teachings of Simon or Paul, also speaks of deeper matters as well. The ancient translator of this work, who died in 410, tells us that it contained many deeper doctrines that he has omitted:

"There are also in both collections some dissertations concerning the Unbegotten God and the Begotten, and on some other subjects, which, to say nothing more, are beyond our comprehension. These, therefore, as being beyond our powers, I have chosen to reserve for others, rather than to produce in an imperfect state.[447]

---

446 Introductory Notice To Pseudo-Clementine Literature By Professor M. B. Riddle, D.D.
447 Rufinus, Presbyter Of Aquileia; His Preface To Clement's Book Of Recognitions. To Bishop Gaudentius.

Although most references to diverse levels of Gods were left out by the translator as he has said, there are a few fragments, such as Peter saying:

> "And, indeed, if there is another above the Creator (Demiurge), he will welcome me, since he is good..."

In a Roman Christian "profession of faith" appended to an ancient copy of the Clementine Recognitions was found the following curse:

> "I anathematize the Nazoreans, the stubborn ones, who deny that the law of sacrifices was given by Moses, who abstain from eating living things, and who never offer sacrifice. I anathematize the Osseans, the blindest of all men who use other scriptures than the Law." [448]

This Roman Christian denouncement clearly sets forth what Peter in the Clementine literature boldly preaches and which the Christians boldly denigrate.

Teachings of Yeshu

That which Peter boldly preaches represents the true teachings of Yeshu. Peter tells us that he is faithfully remembering the things Yeshu taught him and teaches that the Torah, or Pentateuch, did not originate with Moses who is said to have written nothing. Peter says, in Yeshu's name, that those who wrote the Torah later introduced many false teachings. Peter teaches that animal sacrifices are a later false addition to the original Law and that other similar interpolations occurred which were only rectified with the coming of Yeshu.

---

[448] From p. 54, The Essene Odyssey by Hugh Schonfield, Element Books, Ltd. Longmead, Shaftesbury, Dorset, 1984. P. 87. Quoted from page 398, The Conflict of the Church and Synagogue, by James Parkes, London: The Soncino Press, Five Gower Street, 1934.

The Clementine teachings also expound the doctrine of opposites in a way that is reminiscent of the Book of Yetzirah and the Cabala. All things separate and go in opposite directions, unite, separate, and finally unite again. Heaven is contrasted with earth, sun with moon, life with death, Peter with Simon, etc. On the earth the weaker darker principle is said to always precede the better and because of this Peter says he has come after the false prophet Simon to set matters strait. These teachings originated with Yeshu and the Nazoreans who were before him and are not new doctrines being made up by Peter. The Clementine teachings are quite extensive and we will quote only a very few passages that illustrate their doctrinal diversity from the Greek gospel teachings. Included in this Clementine literature is an authentic letter from Peter to James.

Epistle of Peter to James

In the Clementine Homilies we have a letter of Peter to Yeshu's brother which tells us, among other things, that the Roman Christians were beginning to pervert the original gospel and the sacred scriptures of the Nazoreans needed to be withheld from them. This letter, in many ways, is the key to understanding how original Nazorean and Greek Christianity split, and where the Bible came from, and so we quote it in full. It also confirms the fact that James, and not Peter, was the head of the early Nazoreans contrary to later Catholic wishful doctrine:

"Peter to James, the lord and bishop of the holy Church, under the Father of all, through Jesus Christ, wishes peace always. Knowing, my brother, your eager desire after that which is for the advantage of us all, I beg and beseech you not to communicate to any one of the Gentiles the books of my preachings which I sent to you, nor to any one of our own tribe before trial; but if any one has been proved and found worthy, then to commit them to him, after the manner in which Moses delivered his books to the Seventy who succeeded to his chair. Wherefore also the fruit of that caution appears even till now. For his countrymen keep the same rule of monarchy and polity everywhere, being unable in any way to think otherwise, or to be led out of the way of the much-indicating Scriptures. For, according to the rule delivered to them, they endeavour to correct the discordances of the Scriptures, if any one, haply not knowing the traditions, is confounded at the various utterances of the prophets. Wherefore they charge no one to teach, unless he has first learned how the Scriptures must be used. And thus they have amongst them one God, one law, one hope.

In order, therefore, that the like may also happen to those among us as to these Seventy, give the books of my preachings to our brethren, with the like mystery of initiation, that they may indoctrinate those who wish to take part in teaching; for if it be not so done, our word of truth will be rent into many opinions. And this I know, not as being a prophet, but as already seeing the beginning of this very evil. For some from among the Gentiles have rejected my legal preaching, attaching themselves to certain lawless and trifling preaching of the man who is my enemy.

And these things some have attempted while I am still alive, to transform my words by certain various interpretations, in order to the dissolution of the law; as though I also myself were of such a mind, but did not freely proclaim it, which God forbid! For such a thing were to act in opposition to the law of God which was spoken by Moses, and was borne witness to by our Lord in respect of its eternal continuance; for thus he spoke: "The heavens and the earth shall pass away, but one jot or one tittle shall in no wise pass from the law." And this He has said, that all things might come to pass. But these men, professing, I know not how, to know my mind, undertake to explain my words, which they have heard of me, more intelligently than I who spoke them, telling their catechumens that this is my meaning, which indeed I never thought of. But if, while I am still alive, they dare thus to misrepresent me, how much more will those who shall come after me dare to do so!

Therefore, that no such thing may happen, for this end I have prayed and besought you not to communicate the books of my preaching which I have sent you to any one, whether of our own nation or of another nation, before trial; but if any one, having been tested, has been found worthy, then to hand them over to him, according to the initiation of Moses, by which he delivered his books to the Seventy who succeeded to his chair; in order that thus they may keep the faith, and everywhere deliver the rule of truth, explaining all things after our tradition; lest being themselves dragged down by ignorance, being drawn into error by conjectures after their mind, they bring others into the like pit of destruction.

Now the things that seemed good to me, I have fairly pointed out to you; and what seems good to you, do you, my lord, becomingly perform. Farewell.

Therefore James, having read the epistle, sent for the elders; and having read it to them, said: "Our Peter has strictly and becomingly charged us concerning the establishing of the truth, that we should not communicate the books of his preachings, which have been sent to us, to any one at random, but to one who is good and religious, and who wishes to teach, and who is circumcised, and faithful. And these are not all to be committed to him at once; that, if he be found injudicious in the first, the others may not be entrusted to him. "Wherefore let him be proved not less than six years. And then according to the initiation of Moses, he that is to deliver the books should bring him to a river or a fountain, which is living water, where the regeneration of the righteous takes place, and should make him, not swear -- for that is not lawful -- but to stand by the water and adjure, as we ourselves, when we were regenerated, were made to do for the sake of not sinning. "And let him say: 'I take to witness heaven, earth, water, in which all things are comprehended, and in addition to all these, that, air also which pervades all things, and without which I cannot breathe, that I

shall always be obedient to him who gives me the books of the
preachings; and those same books which he may give me, I shall
not communicate to any one in any way, either by writing them,
or giving them in writing, or giving them to a writer, either
myself or by another, or through any other initiation, or trick, or
method, or by keeping them carelessly, or placing them before
any one, or granting him permission to see them, or in any way
or manner whatsoever communicating them to another; unless I
shall ascertain one to be worthy, as I myself have been judged, or
even more so, and that after a probation of not less than six
years; but to one who is religious and good, chosen to teach, as I
have received them, so I will commit them, doing these things
also according to the will of my bishop. "'But otherwise, though
he were my son or my brother, or my friend, or otherwise in any
way pertaining to me by kindred, if he be unworthy, that I will
not vouchsafe the favor to him, as is not meet; and I shall neither
be terrified by plot nor mollified by gifts. But if even it should
ever seem to me that the books of the preachings given to me are
not true, I shall not so communicate them, but shall give them
back. And when I go abroad, I shall carry them with me,
whatever of them I happen to possess. But if I be not minded to
carry them about with me, I shall not suffer them to be in my
house, but shall deposit them with my bishop, having the same
faith, and setting out from the same persons as myself. But if it
befall me to be sick, and in expectation of death, and if I be
childless, I shall act in the same manner. But if I die having a son
who is not worthy, or not yet capable, I shall act in the same
manner. For I shall deposit them with my bishop, in order that if
my son, when he grows up, be worthy of the trust, he may give
them to him as his father's bequest, according to the terms of this
engagement.

"'And that I shall thus do, I again call to witness heaven, earth,
water, in which all things are enveloped, and in addition to all
these, the all-pervading air, without which I cannot breathe, that
I shall always be obedient to him who giveth me these books of
the preachings, and shall observe in all things as I have engaged,
or even something more. To me, therefore, keeping this
covenant, there shall be a part with the holy ones; but to me

doing anything contrary to what I have covenanted, may the universe be hostile to me, and the all-pervading ether, and the God who is over all, to whom none is superior, than whom none is greater. But if even I should come to the acknowledgment of another God, I now swear by him also, be he or be he not, that I shall not do otherwise. And in addition to all these things, if I shall lie, I shall be accursed living and dying, and shall be punished with everlasting punishment.' "And after this, let him partake of bread and salt with him who commits them to him."

James having thus spoken, the elders were in an agony of terror. Therefore James, perceiving that they were greatly afraid, said: "Hear me, brethren and fellow-servants. If we should give the books to all indiscriminately, and they should be corrupted by any daring men, or be perverted by interpretations, as you have heard that some have already done, it will remain even for those who really seek the truth, always to wander in error. Wherefore it is better that they should be with us, and that we should communicate them with all the fore-mentioned care to those who wish to live piously, and to save others. But if any one, after taking this adjuration, shall act otherwise, he shall with good reason incur eternal punishment. For why should not he who is the cause of the destruction of others not be destroyed himself?" The elders, therefore, being pleased with the sentiments of James exclaimed, "Blessed be He who, as foreseeing all things, has graciously appointed thee as our bishop; "and when they had said this, we all rose up, and prayed to the Father and God of all, to whom be glory for ever. Amen." [449]

Peter Withholds Texts

In the above letter Peter expresses his wish that none of the writings of the Nazoreans be given to the Roman Christians lest they pervert and change them.

---

[449] Recognitions of Clement

"I beg and beseech you not to communicate to any one of the Gentiles the books of my preachings which I sent to you, nor to any one of our own tribe before trial; [450]

The reason Peter gives for this has to do with the new religion which "the man who is my enemy", presumably Paul, is making up:

"For some from among the Gentiles have rejected my legal preaching, attaching themselves to certain lawless and trifling preaching of the man who is my enemy. [451]

Peter seemed to know beforehand that Roman Christianity would eventually fabricate a whole range of texts and documents to distort the original message of Yeshu.

"And these things some have attempted while I am still alive, to transform my words by certain various interpretations.... But if, while I am still alive, they dare thus to misrepresent me, how much more will those who shall come after me dare to do so! [452]

James responds favorably to Peter's request, and sets a six year trial, as well as solemn oaths of secrecy, upon all who are given copies of the sacred Nazorean scrolls. This edict is only meaningful if James, as head of the Nazoreans, is in control of all sacred scrolls of the Order. This implies that no one was authorized on their own to write and publish scriptures without first submitting them to James for the approval of the higher enclaves of the Order. This forced those unwilling to cooperate with James and his edicts to work on hearsay and conjecture when writing unauthorized texts, rather than on actual source documents containing words of Yeshu had amongst the Nazoreans. The non Nazoreans who wrote or

---

[450] Recognitions of Clement
[451] Recognitions of Clement
[452] Recognitions of Clement

expanded the New Testament Gospels were in just such a situation. Not only were they bereft of authorized source documents, they also were lacking the benefit of competent first hand witnesses to edit and second check their writings.

Pride

Peter, commenting on the pride of the Jews and the future Christians, explains why it is fair that they be kept from the secrets of the truth:

> "'Thou hast concealed these things from the wise, and hast revealed them to sucking babes.' Now the word 'Thou hast concealed' implies that they had once been known to them; for the key of the kingdom of heaven, that is, the knowledge of the secrets, lay with them. [453]

> "And do not say He acted impiously towards the wise in hiding these things from them. Far be such a supposition from us. For He did not act impiously; but since they hid the knowledge of the kingdom, and neither themselves entered nor allowed those who wished to enter, on this account, and justly, inasmuch as they hid the ways from those who wished, were in like manner the secrets hidden from them, in order that they themselves might experience what they had done to others, and with what measure they had measured, an equal measure might be meted out to them. For to him who is worthy to know, is due that which he does not know; but from him who is not worthy, even should he seem to have any thing it is taken away, even if he be wise in other matters; and it is given to the worthy, even should they be babes as far as the times of their discipleship are concerned."[454]

> "Wherefore it is that He says, 'For say not that the way has been hid from me.' But by the way is meant the mode of life; for

---

[453] Homily, Chapter XV
[454] Homily, Chapter XVIII

Moses says, 'Behold, I have set before thy face the way of life and the way of death.' And the Teacher spoke in harmony with this: 'Enter ye through the strait and narrow way, through which ye shall enter into life.' And somewhere else, when one asked Him, 'What shall I do to inherit eternal life?' He pointed out to him the commandments of the law.[455]

"And Peter said: "We remember that our Lord and Teacher, commanding us, said, 'Keep the mysteries for me and the sons of my house.' Wherefore also He explained to His disciples privately the mysteries of the kingdom of heaven. But to you who do battle with us, and examine into nothing else but our statements, whether they be true or false, it would be impious to state the hidden truths." [456]

"Remember these things, therefore; for I must not state such things to all, but only to those who are found after trial most trustworthy. Nor ought we rashly to maintain such assertions towards each other, nor ought ye to dare to speak as if you were accurately acquainted with the discovery of secret truths, but you ought simply to reflect over them in silence; for in stating, perchance, that a matter is so, he who says it will err, and he will suffer punishment for having dared to speak even to himself what has been honoured with silence." [457]

Moon Cycles & Marriage

Peter, verifying the Nazorean use of a lunar calendar and almanac, explains that there are certain times of the lunar month when intimacy is not advised:

"Because men, following their own pleasure in all things, cohabit without observing the proper times; and thus the deposition of seed, taking place unseasonably, naturally produces a multitude of evils. For they ought to reflect, that as a season has been fixed

---

[455] Homily, Chapter XVIII, Chapter XVII.
[456] Homily, Chapter XIX, Chapter XX.
[457] Homily xx, Chapter VIII.

suitable for planting and sowing, so days have been appointed
as appropriate for cohabitation, which are carefully to be
observed. Accordingly some one well instructed in the doctrines
taught by Moses, finding fault with the people for their sins,
called them sons of the new moons and the sabbaths. Yet in the
beginning of the world then lived long, and had no diseases. But
when through carelessness they neglected the observation of the
proper times, then the sons in succession cohabiting through
ignorance at times when they ought not, place their children
under innumerable afflictions." [458]

And he adds: "... it is better not to have intercourse with a
woman in her separation, but purified and washed. And also
after copulation it is proper to wash." [459]

Peter on the Bible

Yeshu taught that some good was to be found in the Jewish
texts, but much evil as well:

"Then Peter said: "If, therefore, some of the Scriptures arc true
and some false, with good reason said our Master, ' Be ye good
money-changers,' inasmuch as in the Scriptures there are some
true sayings and some spurious. And to those who err by reason
of the false scriptures He fitly showed the cause of their error,
saying, 'Ye do therefore err, not knowing the true things of the
Scriptures; for this reason ye are ignorant also of the power of
God.'" Then said I: "You have spoken very excellently. [460]

Nazoreans taught that the true law was Kabballistic and oral,
and not written down:

"For the Scriptures have had joined to them many falsehoods
against God on this account. The prophet Moses having by the

---

[458] Homily, Chapter XIX
[459] Ante-Nicene Fathers, Vol VIII: Pseudo-Clementine Literature, Chapter XXX
[460] Homily II

order of God delivered the law, with the explanations, to certain chosen men, some seventy in number, in order that they also might instruct such of the people as chose, after a little the written law had added to it certain falsehoods contrary to the law of God, who made the heaven and the earth, and all things in them; the wicked one having dared to work this for some righteous purpose." [461]

"The law of God was given by Moses, without writing, to seventy wise men, to be handed down, that the government might be carried on by succession. But after that Moses was taken up, it was written by some one, but not by Moses. [462]

This happened in the days of Ezra when someone named Tavish forged the Jewish Torah. Apparently, it was the Nazorean policy not to talk about the corruptions too openly to those who might have their faith shaken by such a revelation. This reticence resulted in much confusion among the Roman Christians later:

"Simon, therefore, as I learn, intends to come into public, and to speak of those chapters against God that are added to the Scriptures, for the sake of temptation, that he may seduce as many wretched ones as he can from the love of God. For we do not wish to say in public that these chapters are added to the Bible, since we should thereby perplex the unlearned multitudes, and so accomplish the purpose of this wicked Simon." [463]

"For they not having yet the power of discerning, would flee from us as impious; or, as if not only the blasphemous chapters were false, they would even withdraw from the word. Wherefore we are under a necessity of assenting to the false chapters, and putting questions in return to him concerning them, to draw him into a strait, and to give in private an explanation of the chapters that are spoken against God to the

---

[461] Homily II
[462] Homily III, Chapter XLVII
[463] Homily II

well-disposed after a trial of their faith; and of this there is but
one way, and that a brief one. It is this." [464]

Peter explains that the Nazoreans have knowledge of the bible
"books which are able to deceive" and are not easily led astray
like the Roman Christians.

"And with us, indeed, who have had handed down from our
forefathers the worship of the God who made all things, and also
the mystery of the books which are able to deceive, he will not
prevail; but with those from amongst the Gentiles who have the
polytheistic fancy bred in them, and who know not the
falsehoods of the Scriptures, he will prevail much." [465]

Discernment

Peter and the other Apostles are often shown confused and
bewildered in the New Testament. This apparently was a ploy
of the Pauline School to discredit them. In the Homilies Peter
tells us:

"Whenever we did not understand anything of what had been
said by Him,--a thing which rarely happened,--inquired of Him
privately, that nothing said by Him might be unintelligible to
us," [466]

Peter warns us:

"Wherefore every man who wishes to be saved must become, as
the Teacher said, a judge of the books written to try us. For thus
He spake: 'Become experienced bankers.' Now the need of
bankers arises from the circumstance that the spurious is mixed
up with the genuine." [467]

---

[464] Homily II
[465] Homily III
[466] Homily XVII.
[467] Homily XVIII

Peter also tells us that Yeshu taught to seek after that which is hidden:

> "'I am the gate of life; he who entereth through me entereth into life,' there being no other teaching able to save. Wherefore also He cried, and said, 'Come unto me, all who labour,' that is, who are seeking the truth, and not finding it; and again, 'My sheep hear my voice;' and elsewhere, 'Seek and find,' since the truth does not lie on the surface." [468]

> "Peter said: "It is because my discourses are not charms, so that every one that hears them must without hesitation believe them. The fact that some believe, and others do not, points out to the intelligent the freedom of the will." [469]

> "Do not think that we say that these things are only to be received by faith, but also that they are to be asserted by reason. For indeed it is not safe to commit these things to bare faith without reason, since assuredly truth cannot be without reason." [470]

Law of Opposites

Peter here speaks of the "ziwa" and the "noorah", the yin and yang of the Nazoreans:

> "Peter said: "Listen, therefore, to the truth of the harmony in regard to the evil one. God appointed two kingdoms, and established two ages, determining that the present world should be given to the evil one, because it is small, and passes quickly away; but He promised to preserve for the good one the age to come, as it will be great and eternal. Man, therefore, He created with free-will, and possessing the capability of inclining to whatever actions he wishes. And his body consists of three parts,

---

[468] Homily II.
[469] Homily XX
[470] Chapter LXIX

deriving its origin from the female; for it has lust, anger, and grief, and what is consequent on these. But the spirit not being uniform, but consisting of three parts, derives its origin from the male; and it is capable of reasoning, knowledge, and fear, and what is consequent on these. And each of these triads has one root, so that man is a compound of two mixtures, the female and the male. Wherefore also two ways have been laid before him-- those of obedience and disobedience to law; and two kingdoms, have been established,--the one called the kingdom of heaven, and the other the kingdom of those who are now kings upon earth. Also two kings have been appointed, of whom the one is selected to rule by law over the present and transitory world, and his composition is such that he rejoices in the destruction of the wicked. But the other and good one, who is the King of the age to come, loves the whole nature of man; but not being able to have boldness in the present world, he counsels what is advantageous, like one who tries to conceal who he really is." [471]

"For the universal and earthly soul, which enters on account of all kinds of food, being taken to excess by over-much food, is itself united to the spirit, as being cognate, which is the soul of man; and the material part of the food being united to the body, is left as a dreadful poison to it. Wherefore in all respects moderation is excellent." [472]

Oral Law of Moses

Peter here sums up the oral Nazorean version of the Law of Moses taught him by Yeshu:

""And this is the service He has appointed: To worship Him only, and trust only in the Prophet of Truth, and to be baptized for the remission of sins, and thus by this pure baptism to be born again unto God by saving water; to abstain from the table of devils, that is, from food offered to idols, from dead carcasses,

---

[471] Homily XX
[472] Homily IXX

from animals which have been suffocated or caught by wild beasts, and from blood; not to live any longer impurely; to wash after intercourse; that the women on their part should keep the law of purification; that all should be sober-minded, given to good works, refraining from wrongdoing, looking for eternal life from the all-powerful God, and asking with prayer and continual supplication that they may win it." [473]

"Many forms of worship, then, having passed away in the world, we come, bringing to you, as good merchantmen, the worship that has been handed down to us from our fathers, and preserved; showing you, as it were, the seeds of plants, and placing them under your judgment and in your power. Choose that which seems good unto you. If, therefore, ye choose our wares, not only shall ye be able to escape demons, and the sufferings which are inflicted by demons, but yourselves also putting them to flight, and having them reduced to make supplication to you, shall for ever enjoy future blessings. [474]

Warnings of Heresy

"For there will be, as the Lord said, false apostles, false prophets, heresies, desires for supremacy..." [475]

"Thus, we cannot infer with absolute certainty that the man who has seen visions, and dreams, and apparitions, is undoubtedly pious." [476]

"He would not have wished this to be given through the left hand to those on the right hand, exactly as the man who receives anything from a robber is himself guilty." [477]

---

[473] Homily II
[474] Homily IXX
[475] Homily XVI
[476] Homily XVII.
[477] Homily XVIII.

These warning ironically even found there way into the very texts of the group being warned against:

> "Now we beseech you, brethren, by the coming of our Lord Jesus Christ, and by our gathering together unto him, that ye be not soon shaken in mind, or be troubled, neither by spirit, nor by word, nor by letter as from us, as that the day of the Lord is at hand. Let no man deceive you by any means: for that day shall not come, except there come a falling away first, and that man of sin be revealed, the son of perdition." [478]

There are many other wonderful teachings in the Recognitions and Homilies of Clement, too numerous to go over here, and so we move on to certain Islamic sources on the life and teachings of Yeshu.

˜ 17 ˜
ISLAMIC SOURCES

WE WILL NOW introduce a very important document preserved through Islamic channels. Within an Arabic manuscript from the 10th century there are over 60 folios on the origins of Christianity. Some of these folios seem to contain older non-Moslem and probable Nazorean material from the fifth century or earlier. It is evident from the text that 'Abd al-Jabbar has only slightly edited, or interpolated a few of his own comments, on much older Nazorean like legends and material. The name of the work is Tathbit Dala'il Nubuwwat Sayyidina Mahammad (The Establishment of Proofs for the Prophethood of Our Master Mohammed') by 'Abd al-Jabbar.

Pines published the material in his "The Jewish Christians of the Early Centuries of Christianity according to a New

---

[478] II Thessalonians 2:1-3

Source". Pines felt that the Moslem author was quoting from very ancient Jewish Christian sources. He commented:

> "It is virtually certain that it was written in Syriac. It is also clear that its author or authors had some connection with the region of Harran (and perhaps also with the district of Mosul)."[479]

We know that there were Syrian speaking Nazorean remnants in these areas and it is unusual that any of their historical records survived. This makes these fragments priceless. References to early Nasarene beliefs and practices are extremely rare in western literature. The few we find in Epiphanius' unsympathetic Panarion and other such "Christian" propaganda literature represent the "party line" against the original Essene Nasarene Way.

The Christian movement was relatively thorough, even ruthless, in destroying all original documents and indicators of its true origins. The only things we are given to know are what they wanted us to know. Farther east, in the Islam world, their influence was not so strong and perhaps not so thorough. It appears as if some original documents, traditions and legends have survived in this 10th century Mu'tazilite Islamic literature.

Whatever the tradition represented by this text, it is evident that they shared the Ebionite belief in the corruption of the Pauline branch of Christianity. Here are some excerpts translated from The Establishment of Proofs for the Prophethood of Our Master Mohammed' by Shlomo Pines:

Proofs of Mohamed

[479] The Jewish Christians Of The Early Centuries Of Christianity According To A New Source", By Pines

'He (Yeshu) and his companions behaved constantly in this manner, until he left this world. He said to his companions: "Act as you have seen me act, instruct people in accordance with instructions I have given you, and be for them what I have been for you." His companions behaved constantly in this manner and in accordance with this. And so did those who (came) after the first generation of his companions, and (also) those who came long after (the second generation). Then they began to make changes and alterations, (to introduce) innovations into the religion (al-din), to seek dominion (ri'asa), to make friends with people by (indulging) their passions, to (try) to circumvent the Jews and to satisfy the anger (which) they (felt) against the latter, even if (in doing so) they (had) to abandon the religion. This is clear from the Gospels which are with them and to which they refer and from their book, known as the Book of Praxeis (Acts). It is (written) there: A group (qawm) of Christians left Jerusalem (bayt al-maqdis) and came to Antioch and other towns of Syria (al-Sham). [480]

Paul's Roman associations are now explained:

"The Romans (al-Rum) reigned over them. The Christians (used to) complain to the Romans about the Jews, showed them their own weakness and appealed to their pity. And the Romans did pity them. This (used) to happen frequently. And the Romans said to the Christians: "Between us and the Jews there is a pact which (obliges us) not to change their religious laws (adyan). But if you would abandon their laws and separate yourselves from them, praying as we do (while facing) the East, eating (the things) we eat, and regarding as permissible that which we consider as such, we should help you and make you powerful, and the Jews would find no way (to harm you). On the contrary, you would be more powerful than they." [481]

Paul's Romanized converts are asked to eat a non vegan diet like the Romans, to abandon other Nazorean laws, and to

---

[480] The Jewish Christians Of The Early Centuries Of Christianity According To A New Source", By Pines
[481] The Jewish Christians Of The Early Centuries Of Christianity According To A New Source", By Pines

separate off from the Nazoreans in Palestine. Their acceptance of these conditions is the beginning of western Christianity.

> "The Christians answered: "We will do this." (And the Romans) said: "Go, fetch your companions, and bring your Book (*kitab*)." (The Christians) went to their companions, informed them of (what had taken place) between them and the Romans and said to them: "Bring the Gospel (*al-injil*), and stand up so that we should go to them." But these (companions) said to them: "You have done ill. We are not permitted (to let) the Romans pollute the Gospel. (71b) In giving a favorable answer to the Romans, you have accordingly departed from the religion. We are (therefore) no longer permitted to associate with you; on the contrary, we are obliged to declare that there is nothing in common between us and you;" and they prevented their (taking possession of) the Gospel or gaining access to it. [482]

Here we have the Nazorean account of Paul's converts making their pact with Rome and of how the Nazoreans successfully kept the pure Gospel of the Nazoreans from them and excommunicated them from their fellowship. The Roman Christians now sought the help of Rome to force the Nazoreans to deliver up their texts, but they fled to northern Syria where they were persecuted further:

> In consequence a violent quarrel (broke out) between (the two groups). Those (mentioned in the first place) went back to the Romans and said to them: "Help us against these companions of ours before (helping us) against the Jews, and take away from them on our behalf our Book (*kitab*)." Thereupon (the companions of whom they had spoken) fled the country. And the Romans wrote concerning them to their governors in the districts of Mosul and in the Jazirat al-'Arab. Accordingly, a search was made for them; some (qawm) were caught and burned, others (qawm) were killed. [483]

[482] The Jewish Christians Of The Early Centuries Of Christianity According To A New Source", By Pines
[483] The Jewish Christians Of The Early Centuries Of Christianity According To A New Source", By Pines

Deprived of original authentic eye witness accounts of the life of Yeshu, the Roman Christians were forced to make up their gospels that are now so widely accepted in Christendom. We are told that they based these new fables on the Old Testament stories and on hearsay and tidbits of true sayings remembered from association with true Nazoreans. They also say that "a great part of what was in the original" Nazorean gospel was left out of these new texts even though some knew the truth:

"(As for) those who had given a favorable answer to the Romans they came together and took counsel as to how to replace the Gospel, seeing that it was lost to them. (Thus) the opinion that a Gospel should be composed (*yunshi'u*) was established among them. They said: "the Torah (consists) only of (narratives concerning) the births of the prophets and of the histories (*tawarikh*) of their lives. We are going to construct (*nabni*) a Gospel according to this (pattern).

Everyone among us is going to call to mind that which he remembers of the words (*ajfar*) of the Gospel and of (the things) about which the Christians talked among themselves (when speaking) of Christ." Accordingly, some people (*qawm*) wrote a Gospel. After (them) came others (*qawm*) (who) wrote (another) Gospel. (In this manner) a certain number of Gospels were written. (However) a great part of what was (contained) in the original was missing in them. There were among them (men), one after another, who knew many things that were contained in the true Gospel (*al-injil al-xahih.*), but with a view to establishing their dominion (*ri'asa*), they refrained from communicating them. In all this there was no mention of the cross or of the crucifix.

According to them there were eighty Gospels. However, their (number) constantly diminished and became less, until (only) four Gospels were left which are due to four individuals (*nafar*). Every one of them composed in his time a Gospel. Then another came after him, saw that (the Gospel composed by his predecessor) was imperfect, and composed another which according to him was more correct (*axahh*), nearer to correction (*al-xihha*) than the Gospel of the others. Then there is not among these a Gospel (written) in the language of Christ, which was spoken by him and his companions (*axhab*), namely the Hebrew (*al-`ibraniyya*) language, which is that of Abraham (*Ibrahim*), the Friend (*khalil*) of God and of the other prophets, (the language) which was spoken by them and in which the Books of God were revealed to them and to the other Children of Israel, and in which God addressed them. [484]

We are further told that the original versions did not contain a crucifixion story, which suggests that this was added much later. We are also told that these made up Greek gospels purposely avoided using Aramaic so that they would not be compared with the original authentic Nazorean texts. This was a ruse to gain power and influence outside of and away from the Nazorean center in Aramaic speaking Palestine:

"(For) they have abandoned (*taraka*) (this language). Learned men (*al-`ulama'*) said to them: "Community of Christians, give up the Hebrew language, which is the language of Christ and the prophets (who were) before him, peace be upon them, (72a) and (adopt) other languages." Thus there is no Christian who (in observing) a religious obligation recites these Gospels in the Hebrew language: he does not do so out of ruse (using) a stratagem, in order to avoid (public) shame.

Therefore people said to them: The giving-up (the language: *al-`ud-l `anha*) occurred because your first masters (*axhabukum al-aw-walun*) aimed at deception in their writings (*maqalat*) using such stratagems as quotations from counterfeit authorities in the lies which they composed, and concealing these stratagems. They did this because they sought to obtain domination (*ri'asa*). For at that time the Hebrews (*al-`ibraniyya*) were people of the Book and men of knowledge. Accordingly, these individuals (*nafar*) altered (*ghayyara*) the language or rather gave it up altogether, in order that the men of knowledge should not grasp

---

[484] The Jewish Christians Of The Early Centuries Of Christianity According To A New Source", By Pines

quickly their teaching and their objectives. (For if they had done
so these individuals) would have been disgraced before having
been (able) to consolidate their teaching and their (objectives)
would not have been fulfilled. Accordingly, they gave up
(Hebrew and took up) numerous other languages which had not
been spoken by Christ and his companions. (Those who speak
these languages) are not people of the Book and have no
knowledge concerning God's books and commandments. Such
were the Romans (al-Rum), the Syrians, the Persians, the
Armenians and other foreigners. This was done by means of
deception and ruse by this small group of people who (wanted)
to hide their infamy and to reach the goal of their wishes in their
aspiration for dominion (which was to be won) through (the
instrumentality of) religion.

If this were not so they would have used the language of
Abraham, of his children and of Christ, through whom the
edifice had been constructed and to whom the books had been
revealed. In establishing a proof (meant) for the Children of
Israel and the unbelievers among the Jews (al-yahud) it would
have been better that a call be made to them in their own tongue
(lisan) and a discussion engaged with them in their language
(lugha), which they would not have been able to refuse. Know
this; it is a great principle. [485]

The well informed 'Abd al-Jabbar comments on the fake
nature of the Greek gospels and explains that very little of
what Yeshu actually said or did is contained in them. He
writes:

"Know may God have mercy upon you-that these three sects do
not believe that God revealed to Christ in one way or another a
Gospel or a book. Rather, according to them, Christ created the
prophets, revealed to them the books and sent to them angels.
However, they have with them Gospels composed by four
individuals, each one of whom wrote a Gospel. After (one of
them) came (another) who was not satisfied with (his

---

[485] The Jewish Christians Of The Early Centuries Of Christianity According To A New Source", By Pines

predecessor's) Gospel and held that his own Gospel was better. (These Gospels) agree in certain places and disagree (72b) in others; in some of them (there are passages) which are not (found) in the other. There are tales concerning people-men and women-from among the Jews, the Romans, and other (nations, who) said this and did that. There are many absurdities, (many) false and stupid things and many obvious lies and manifest contradictions. It was this which people have thoroughly studied and set apart. However, a person who reads it becomes aware of this if he examines it carefully. Something-but little-of the sayings, the precepts of Christ and information concerning him is also to be found there.

As for the four Gospels: one of them was composed by John (*Yuhanna*) and another by Matthew. Then, after these two came Mark (*M.r.q.s.*) who was not satisfied with their two Gospels. Then, after these came Luke (Luqa), who was not satisfied with these Evangels and composed (still) another one. Each one of them was of the opinion (*wa-kana `inda kull wahid min ha`ula'*) that the man who had composed a Gospel before him, had given a correct account of (certain) things and had distorted (*akhalla*) others, and that another (Gospel) would be more deserving of recognition and more correct. For if his predecessor had succeeded in giving a correct account, there would have been no need for him to compose another, different from that of his predecessor.

None of these four Gospels is a commentary upon another (Gospel); (it is not a case of) someone who coming after (someone else) comments upon his predecessor's book, giving first an account of what the latter had said, and then (proposing) a commentary. Know this: (he who composed a Gospel) did this, because another man had fallen short of success (*qaxxara*) (at his task). [486]

Next 'Abd al-Jabbar hits upon a very important facet of Christendom – its erroneous belief that original disciples of

[486] The Jewish Christians Of The Early Centuries Of Christianity According To A New Source", By Pines

Yeshu wrote the Gospels. He writes of the absurdity of this and goes on to say that these Greek Gospels are of no value to anyone and that "they have abandoned the religion of Christ and turned towards the religious doctrines of the Romans":

> "These (Christian) sects are of the opinion that these four (Evangelists) were companions and disciples of Christ. But they do not know, having no information (on the subject), who they were. On this (point) they can (merely) make a claim. For Luke mentions in his Gospel that he had never seen Christ. Addressing (the man) for whom he composed his Gospel---he is the last of the four (Evangelists)--- he says: "I knew your desire of good, of knowledge and of instruction (*al-adab*), and I composed this Gospel because I knew this and because I was close to those who had served and seen the Word (*al-kalima*)." Thus he says clearly in the first place that he did not see the Word---they signify by this word Christ; thereupon he claims to have seen people) who had seen Christ. But his having seen them is a (mere) assertion (on his part). If he had been someone deserving of trust, he would not have-in view of the (kind of) information (which was at his disposal)---composed anything at all. In spite of this he mentions that his Gospel is preferable to those of the others.

> (73a) If the Christians would consider these things, they would know that the Gospels which are with them are of no profit to them, and that the knowledge claimed (on their behalf) by their masters and the authors (of the Gospels) is not (found) in them, and that on this point) things are just as we have said---it is a well-known (fact) which is referred to here (namely the fact that they have abandoned the religion of Christ and turned towards) the religious doctrines of the Romans, prizing and (seeking to obtain) in haste the profits which could be derived from their domination and their riches.'

> They called upon the people (to obey) the law (*al-sunna*) of the Torah, to forbid offering sacrifices to those who have not the necessary qualifications (*laysa min ahliha*) (to practice)

circumcision, to observe the Sabbath, to prohibit pork and other things (forbidden) by the Torah. These things were regarded as burdensome by the Gentiles and they took little notice (of the exhortations). [487]

We now have an account of the Jerusalem council in 44 AD in which James laid down laws governing gentile converts. 'Abd al-Jabbar speaks of a book, probably the biblical Acts of the Apostles, which describes concession made to the lax gentile converts. 'Abd al-Jabbar does not seem fully aware that the account in Acts was not historical, but a contrived piece of propaganda put forth by the Christians to cover up the fact that James would not concede to their demands:

> "Thereupon, the Christians of Jerusalem forgathered to take counsel as to the stratagems which were to be employed with regard to the Gentiles in order (to make) the latter respond and obey them. They were of the opinion that it was necessary to mix with the Gentiles, to make them concessions (*rukhs*), to descend to (the level of) their erroneous beliefs, to eat (a portion) of the sacrifices they offer, to adopt their customs and to approve of their way (of life). And they composed a book on this.'[488]

'Abd al-Jabbar here speaks of the miracles attributed to Christ, saying that the original disciples never claimed such of him. He tells of how Christians in his day were still making up such things about their leaders:

> "As for the prodigies and miracles which as the Christians claim (were worked) by him, all this is baseless. He himself did not claim (to have worked) them. Nor is there in his time or in the generation which followed any disciple who claimed (that Jesus had worked miracles). This was first claimed only a very long time (*ba`d... al azman wa'l-ahqab*) after his death and after the death of his (direct) disciples; similarly the Christians have

---

[487] The Jewish Christians Of The Early Centuries Of Christianity According To A New Source", By Pines
[488] The Jewish Christians Of The Early Centuries Of Christianity According To A New Source", By Pines

claimed that the Jew Paul (Bul.s al-yahudi) (has worked miracles and this) in spite of his being known for his tricks (*hiyal*), his lying (*kadhb*) and his baseness; they have done the same for George (*J.urj.s*) and for Father Mark, and they do the same at all times with regard to their monks and nuns. All this is baseless.'
489

These next verses we quote from the Proofs of 'Abd al-Jabbar are from a Gospel that reads very differently than any known text. 'Abd al-Jabbar is obviously quoting from a lost work no longer available. If not the Nazorean Gospel itself, then a similar one circulating in Nazorean territory of northern Syria must be the source:

"(65a) 'When the Gospels speak of him who was killed and crucified and of the crucifixion they say: On the Thursday of Passover, the Jews went to Herod (*Hayridhs*), a companion of Pilate (*Filats*) the king of the Romans, and said to him: "There is a man here, one of us, who has corrupted and led astray our brethren. We stipulate accordingly with regard to you that you should give us power over (the man) whose way is (as described) so that we should carry out our judgment on him." Accordingly, Herod said to his auxiliaries: "Go with them, and bring their opponent (here)." Thereupon the auxiliaries went forth with the Jews and came to the gate of that government house. The Jews turned to the auxiliaries an asked them: "Do you know our opponent?" They said: "No. The Jews said: "Neither do we know him. However, come with us. We shall not fail to find somebody who will show him to us." Accordingly they went, and Judas Iscariot met them. He was one [53] of the intimates and followers of Christ, one of his greatest disciples, one of the Twelve. He said to them: "Do you search for Jesus the Nasarene (*Ishu` al-nasiri*)?" They said: "Yes." He said:
"What shall I get from you, if I show him to you?" One of the Jews wanted to give him monies which he had with him, counted thirty pieces and said: "They are yours." Judas said to

---

them: "As you know, he is my friend, and I would be ashamed to say: that one, that's he. However, be with me and look at (the man) to whom I shall give my hand and whose head I shall kiss. Take hold of him as soon as my hand will let go his and lead him away."

There was a great (crowd) of people in Jerusalem where, (coming) from all places, they gathered to celebrate that feast. Judas Iscariot took the hand of a man, kissed his head, (65b) and as soon as his hand let go that of (the other), he plunged into the crowd. Then the Jews and the auxiliaries seized (the man). He said to them: "What do you want from me?" and felt a poignant anguish. They answered him: "The government wants you." He said: "What have I to do with the government?" And they led him away and made him come before Herod. But the man's reason had flown because of his fear and anguish. He wept and had no self-control. Having become aware of his fear, Herod pitied him and said: "Let him be." He asked him to come nearer, made him sit down and tried to make him feel at ease. Thanks to him (the man) became calm. Herod said to him: "What do you say with regard to the claim (about which they speak), namely that you are the Christ, king of the Children of Israel? Have you said this, or appealed to the people on this subject?" He denied that he had said or claimed this. In spite of this, his perturbation was not quieted, although Herod tried to tranquillize him. Herod said to him: "Remember what is yours and try [54] to convince (people) if it is really yours." He did not want to make him deny (the thing). For it was not (the man) who had said it; they, and not he, had said it, and they had wronged him through what they had claimed and said with regard to him.

Accordingly Herod said to the Jews: "I do not see that he agrees with you, that he says what you claim. I only see that you attribute to him utterances (that were not his) and that you wrong him. There is a basin and water for me to wash my hand in (so that it should be innocent) of this man's blood."

(Then) Pilate the great king of the Romans addressed Herod. He said to him: "Information has come to me that the Jews have had an opponent of theirs, a man of education (*adab*) and knowledge, conducted before you for judgment. Give him over to me, so that I should probe him and see what is the matter with him." And

Herod gave him over to Pilate. Thus (the man) who was (still) in a state of perturbation, fear and anguish, was brought before Pilate. The king tried to tranquillize him and asked him as to what the Jews had asserted with regard to him, namely that he was the Christ. He denied having said this. (Pilate however) did not cease asking him and trying to make him feel at ease, so that he should give an explanation about himself and that (Pilate) should hear from him a witty saying (adab) or a precept. However, he could not allay the perturbation, fear, anguish, the weeping and the sobbing (of the man) and he sent him back to Herod, saying to the latter: "I have found in this man nothing that has been ascribed to him. There is nothing good in him. "And he explained this (by referring) to the man's deficiency (66a) and ignorance. Herod said: "It is now night. Conduct him to prison." And they conducted him (there). The next day the Jews became importunate, seized him, proclaimed his infamy, tormented him, inflicting upon him various tortures, then at about the end of the day they whipped him and brought him to a melon-patch (mabtakha) and a vegetable garden (mabqala). There they crucified him and pierced him with lances in order that he should die quickly. As for him, crucified upon a piece of wood as he was, he did not cease crying out as loudly as he could: "My God, why did you abandon me, my God, why did you forsake me" until he died.

Then Judas Iscariot met the Jews and said to them: "What did you do with the man you seized yesterday?" They said: "We have crucified him." Judas was amazed at this, and thought (the thing) hardly credible (istab'ada). But they said to him: "We have done it. If you want to know it (for sure), go to a certain melon-patch." He went there, and when he saw him, he said: "He is an innocent man." He insulted the Jews, got out the thirty pieces which they had given him as a reward and threw them in their face. And he went to his (own) house and strangled himself.' [490]

This account varies greatly from those found in the New Testament gospels. Jews seize Yeshu, not Roman soldiers, and Herod washes his hands, not Pilate, which makes more sense

---

[490] The Jewish Christians Of The Early Centuries Of Christianity According To A New Source", By Pines

since he kept some Jewish customs. It also says that the Jews crucified Yeshu, not the Romans. Next 'Abd al-Jabbar speaks of assertions made by both Jews and Christians that he knows, and again, the material is different from that found in any known biblical or non biblical text:

> (56b) 'Both the Christians and the Jews assert that Pilate (Filat.s) the Roman, king of the Romans, seized Christ, because the Jews had maligned him, and delivered him up to them. They led him away upon an ass, with his face turned towards the ass' hind quarters, put upon his head a crown of thorns and went around in order to [58] make an example out of his punishment. They beat him from behind, attacked him from before and said to him in mockery: "King of the Children of Israel, who has done this to you?" Being thirsty because of the fatigue and the distress which afflicted him, he humbled himself and said to them: "Give me water to drink." And they took a bitter tree, pressed out its juice, put into it vinegar and gave this to him to drink. He took it (57a), thinking that it was water, tasted it, and when he perceived that it was bitter, spat it out. They for their part, made him inhale this drink (or according to another possible interpretation: "forced him to drink it") and tortured him one whole day and one whole night. When the next day came---it was a Friday, the one which they call Good Friday they asked Pilate to have him whipped; which he did. Thereupon, they got hold of him, crucified him and pierced him with lances, while he, being crucified upon a piece of wood, did not cease from crying: "My God, why did you abandon me? My God, why did you forsake me?" until he died. (Then) they brought him down and buried him.'[491]

'Abd al-Jabbar's lost source tells us that the Jews actually crucified Yeshu under Roman auspice, after Pilate whipped him and gave him to them. The source now says that Yeshu's three brothers were at the cross with their mother, which again is a very different account from the New Testament fables:

---

[491] The Jewish Christians Of The Early Centuries Of Christianity According To A New Source", By Pines

(95a) 'It is (said) in their Gospels and in their narratives (*akhbar*) that, when Christ was crucified, his mother Maryam came to him with her sons James (*Ya'qub*), Simon (*Sham'un*) and Judah (*Yahudha*), and they stood before him. And he, (while attached) to the piece of wood, said to her: "Take your sons, and go away (*insarifi*)."'[492]

'Abd al-Jabbar's lost source now confirms that it was in agreement with the general position of the Ebionite and other Aramaic followers of Yeshu who maintained that Yoseph was Yeshu's actual father and that some sort of Sabbath observance was valid:

(94a) '(According) to their prevalent (traditions)... people thought that Jesus was a son of Joseph up to the time when John baptized him in the Jordan and the voice came from the heaven "This is my son in whom my soul rejoices." '[493]

(67a) '(It is said) there: Maryam al-Majdalaniyya and the other Maryam refrained from sending (*ba'tha*) perfume to our master (*lisayyidina*) the Christ on a Sabbath day because of the commandment (*sunna*) with regard to the observance of the Sabbath.'

'Abd al-Jabbar is definitely quoting from a lost gospel for he says "It is said there". These last couple of quotes sound closer to what one finds in the New Testament, but they are nevertheless different:

(47a) 'They say: When John (*Yuhanna*) baptized him in the Jordan the gates of heaven were opened and the Father cried out: "This is my son and my beloved (*habibi*) in whom my soul rejoices." '

---

[492] The Jewish Christians Of The Early Centuries Of Christianity According To A New Source", By Pines
[493] The Jewish Christians Of The Early Centuries Of Christianity According To A New Source", By Pines

(67b) '(It is said) there: He said to the Children of Israel: "O' serpents, children of vipers, you profess the Scripture, and you do not understand. You wash the outside of the vessel, and its inside is full of filth. You seek on land and on sea, in the plain and in the mountain, a disciple, and when you find one, you teach him your ways, so that he becomes worse than you. You have not entered yourselves the Kingdom, and you have not let (other) people enter the Kingdom of Heaven---since you have not entered (it)." [494]

These accounts, since it originated in Syria where the eye witnesses to the events fled, is more credible than the Greco-Roman gospels which were penned by those who worked on hearsay and legend only. They also present a more logical series of events than does the New Testament which has serious contradictions and absurdities within it.

- 18 -
The SEVERING

Saul/Paul

THE RISE OF Paul's "Churchanity" fulfilled Yeshu's prophecy of "false apostles, false prophets, heresies, and desires for supremacy". It began when Romanized converts to Nazoreanism decided to change the original teachings of Yeshu to fit their own needs and lifestyles. They were able to do this quite effectively since their founder, Paul, had been in major disagreement with many basic Nazorean principles. Modern Christianity is Paul based and has arisen out of this original watering down of the true Teachings of Christ, mingled with those of Judaism and the Roman Mystery Cults.

---

[494] The Establishment Of Proofs For The Prophethood Of Our Master Mohammed'

Miryai, Peter, James and John preserved the true teachings of
Yeshu the Nazorean after his death. Paul did not. Paul was
seen by Yeshu's Nazoreans as the opponent and not the
apostle of Historic Christianity. They felt he used the name of
Christ, but little else from earliest Nazorean Christianity. He
rejected the goodness that was at the core of their Nazorean
motto: "Good is the Good to the Good".

Thus the early Nazoreans, Ebionites, Gnostics, and Elchasaites
taught that the New Testament is a false fabrication of Paul's
school and the stories therein were based only loosely on the
historical personage of Yeshu. They were seen to be full of
subtle propaganda against the true lineage of light. And in
turn, later heresiologists of Paul's school characterized the true
Nazorean branch as heretic Gnostics. Through their pact with
Rome they were able to complete the takeover started so many
years before by their founder Paul. In Paul's new "feel good"
religion few spiritual practices were required and Nazorean
culture and diet were abandoned.

"Saint" Saul's Schism

In Paul's own account of his conversion he declares his
independence from the Jerusalem church:

> "Immediately, I conferred not with the flesh and blood; neither
> went I up to Jerusalem to them who were Apostles before me;
> but I went away into Arabia." He adds: "I made known to you,
> brethren, as touching the gospel which was preached by me, that
> it is not after man. For neither did I receive it from man, nor was
> I taught it, save through revelation of the Christ revealed
> within."

What gospel was this? Not the same one that Peter, James, and
John got from Yeshu! Why was it necessary for Paul to get his
revelation from the "Lord"? Paul implies that this was

necessary because the original disciples were too ignorant and too Jewish. Why then did Yeshu choose them to begin with? The only plausible answer is that Paul did not want to be trained, or was not allowed to be trained, in the Nazorean faith by the legitimate successors of Christ - James and the Jerusalem Church, but instead wished to start his own faith based only loosely on the teachings of Jesus.

Rejection of James

Paul began creating his own converts to his own religion, warning them to reject Peter, James, and John: those "pre-eminent apostles," whom he calls "false prophets, deceitful workers, and ministers of Satan", who came among them to preach "another Jesus" whom he did not preach, and a different gospel from that which they had received from him. To the Galatians he says:

> "If any man preacheth unto you any gospel other than that which ye received, let him be damned;"

Or let him be cursed. He was speaking of the Jerusalem church, of course, which had already rejected him as an Apostle.

> "Those who are called Ebionites . . . repudiate the Apostle Paul, maintaining that he was an apostate from the law."[495]

The "law" Paul was against was the oral law of Yeshu and Moses - the law of the original Judean church. Paul's side of the story is given in the New Testament Book of Acts. The Nazoreans version of the Acts of the Apostles is preserved in the Clementine Homilies and Clementine Recognitions. In these one finds the true Peter represented, and Paul called "the

---

[495] Irenaeus, Adversus Haereses (Against Heresies), 180 A.D.)

man who is my enemy"[496] In these texts Peter speaks against blind faith of Paul who said "a man is justified by faith without the deeds of the law"[497]. Peter said:

> "Do not think that we say that these things are only to be received by faith, but also that they are to be asserted by reason. For indeed it is not safe to commit these things to bare faith without reason, since assuredly truth cannot be without reason."[498]

Paul's New Church

Paul's new religion was an amalgamation of the Mystery Religions of Rome, his own interpretation of fake Jewish Scriptures, and his own take on the meaning of Christ. His goal was the replacement of the 3 Pillars of Nazoreanism - Peter, James and John, with a fourth pillar - himself. This switch was bolstered up by the Epistles of Paul and Acts wherein Paul is made the champion of the faith and the original disciples are cast in the light of ignorant fisherman filled with doubt, fear and prejudice against outsiders. Paul preached against the Law of Yeshu and his brother James whom Paul had rejected:

> "Therefore we conclude that a man is justified by faith without the deeds of the law"[499].

He taught that you could do anything you wanted, just so long as you had "faith" in being saved by a divine redeemer. Yeshu never taught salvation by faith, nor did his successors James or Miryai. They taught development of character through spiritual service, rituals, discipline, faith, and gaining

---

[496] Letter Of Peter To James
[497] Rom.3:28
[498] Recognitions of Clement, Chapter LXIX.—Faith and Reason.
[499] Rom.3:28

of gnosis. This was their "law", not the Jewish Torah that some of the ignorant ones have postulated. Paul says:

> "I went up [to Jerusalem] by revelation and communicated unto them that gospel which I preached among the gentiles..."[500].

If this was the same gospel Peter, James, and John were preaching, what need was there of explaining it to the elders at Jerusalem? This was the Jerusalem Council, which was held in about A. D. 45. There is no indication that Paul's new religion found any favor in Jerusalem. In Paul's accounts it sounds like James okayed Paul to work among the gentiles just so long as he collected tithes for the poor and sent them to the Nazoreans and avoided certain unclean meats. In reality the vegetarian restrictions that James and the other Nazoreans insisted upon for the gentiles were too much for Paul to incorporate into his congregations. He went his own way and started his own religion with the help of Rome. Paul tried to keep some loose ties to the Jerusalem church by collecting donations during famine times, but he operated independently of James and taught a very different gospel that was rejected by the vegan Nazoreans. Because his school won the propaganda war they were able to rewrite history their way.

Paul's Pact

We know from the Letter of Peter to James that the Nazorean's refused to share their scriptures with Paul, forcing his school to create their own made up "New Testament":

> "And this I know, not as being a prophet, but as already seeing the beginning of this very evil. For some from among the Gentiles have rejected my legal preaching, attaching themselves to certain lawless and trifling preaching of the man who is my

---

[500] Gal.2:2

enemy. . . Therefore, that no such thing may happen, for this end
I have prayed and besought you not to communicate the books
of my preaching which I have sent you to any one, whether of
our own nation or of another nation, before trial..."[501]

Our other source for these events, the ancient Arabic text we
quoted previously, says:

"The Romans reigned over them. The Christians used to
complain to the Romans about the Judeans, showed them their
own weakness and appealed to their pity. And the Romans did
pity them. This used to happen frequently. And the Romans said
to the Christians: "Between us and the Judeans there is a pact
which obliges us not to change their religious laws. But if you
would abandon their laws and separate yourselves from them,
praying as we do while facing the East, eating the things we eat,
and regarding as permissible that which we consider as such, we
should help you and make you powerful, and the Judeans
would find no way to harm you, On the contrary, you would be
more powerful than they. The Christians answered: "We will do
this." And the Romans said: "Go, fetch your companions, and
bring your Book .

"The Christians went to their companions, informed them of
what had taken place between them and the Romans and said to
them: "Bring the Gospel, and stand up so that we should go to
them." But these companions said to them: "You have done ill.
We are not permitted to let the Romans pollute the Gospel. In
giving a favorable answer to the Romans, you have accordingly
departed from the religion. We are therefore no longer permitted
to associate with you; on the contrary, we are obliged to declare
that there is nothing in common between us and you;" and they
prevented their taking possession of the Gospel or gaining access
to it. In consequence a violent quarrel broke out between the two
groups."[502]

---

[501] Letter Of Peter To James
[502] The Establishment Of Proofs . . . By 'Abd Al-Jabbar

Continued integration of Paul's Christians with Rome persisted until its Emperor Constantine eventually invited 1800 Greco-Roman Christian bishops to attend a Council at Nicea. Only about 300 from this Pauline heresy came despite an all expenses paid invitation. Another 1500 or so refused. No true Gnostic bishops were invited or attended. This was on purpose. Paul's pact should have been with James, but instead, he forged his alliances with Rome. As for the Nazoreans, they too kept there distance from the Christians:

> "In giving a favorable answer to the Romans, you have accordingly departed from the religion. We are (therefore) no longer permitted to associate with you; on the contrary, we are obliged to declare that there is nothing in common between us and you." [503]

Controversy & Exile

In the Pauline Book of Acts, which was not acknowledged by the original Nazoreans, a version of the supposed compromise between Paul and James is set forth. It makes it sound like James accepted Paul's innovations when this was not the case. In the Clementine literature we have a more accurate portrayal of the rules set forth by James for the Gentiles. Peter sums these up as:

> "And the things which are well-pleasing to God are these: to pray to Him, to ask from Him, recognizing that He is the giver of all things, and gives with discriminating law; to abstain from the table of devils, not to taste dead flesh, not to touch blood; to be washed from all pollution; and the rest in one word,--as the God-fearing Jews have heard, do you also hear, and be of one mind in many bodies; let each man be minded to do to his neighbor those good things he wishes for himself. And you may all find out

---

[503] The Establishment Of Proofs For The Prophethood Of Our Master Mohammed'

what is good, by holding some such conversation as the following with yourselves: You would not like to be murdered; do not murder another man: you would not like your wife to be seduced by another; do not you commit adultery: you would not like any of your things to be stolen from you; steal nothing from another. And so understanding by yourselves what is reasonable, and doing it, you will become dear to God, and will obtain healing; otherwise in the life which now is your bodies will be tormented, and in that which is to come your souls will be punished." [504]

These Jamesian edicts are often reworded or poorly translated to make it sound like James was only proscribing against eating road kill, but the above statement of Peter is very clear when it says: "not to taste dead flesh". This was a major point of contention between the converts of Paul and the vegetarian Nazoreans of Yeshu. Roman Christianity has tended to interpret these rules, such as not eating at the table of demons, as some sort of law against eating animals sacrificed at pagan temples. Yet the Clementine teachings of Peter are very clear that the table of demons is any table where meat is served. This is not something the Nazoreans were prepared to compromise on for it lay at the very foundation of their faith in a way that those who eat meat can seldom grasp.

Paul's Success

Paul was very successful with his new religion. His success, however, seemed to be at least partially rooted in the fact that he relaxed so many rules and also because he knew so many people in power.

"There are materials in the New Testament, early Church literature, Rabbinic literature, and Josephus which point to some

---

[504] Clementine Homily 7, Chapter 4

connection between Paul and so-called "Herodians." These materials provide valuable insight into problems related to Paul's origins, his Roman citizenship, the power he conspicuously wields in Jerusalem when still a young man, and the "Herodian" thrust of his doctrines (and as a consequence those of the New Testament) envisioning a community in which both Greeks and Jews would enjoy equal promises and privileges.[505]

Paul Challenges Peter

Peter explained in his teachings that appeared in the Clementine literature that he could and would not eat at a common table with meat eaters:

> "I wish you to know, O woman, the course of life involved in our religion. We worship one God, who made the world which you see; and we keep His law, which has for its chief injunctions to worship Him alone, and to hallow His name, and to honour our parents, and to be chaste, and to live piously. In addition to this, we do not live with all indiscriminately; nor do we take our food from the same table as Gentiles, inasmuch as we cannot eat along with them, because they live impurely. But when we have persuaded them to have true thoughts, and to follow a right course of action, and have baptized them with a thrice blessed invocation, then we dwell with them. For not even if it were our father, or mother, or wife, or child, or brother, or any other one having a claim by nature on our affection, can we venture to take our meals with him; for our religion compels us to make a distinction."

We can partially understand this oral Law by those who opposed it, like Paul. In Colossians he encourages his followers to reject this Law reaffirmed by Christ to his disciples. Paul calls this Law the "commandments and

---

doctrines of men". He particularly is opposed to Yeshu's admonitions to observe a plant based diet, avoidance of drunkenness, observe lunar festivals, and keep daily prayer to various gods and goddesses, etc. Paul writes:

> "Let no man therefore judge you in meat, or in drink, or in respect of an holyday, or of the new moon, or of the sabbath [days]....voluntary humility and worshipping of angels..." [506]

Of course Paul and his fellow Christians were being legitimately judged for exactly these things by those who knew what Yeshu had taught and were trying to preserve such.

Paul Breaks Away

There is a false tradition in Christianity that the differences between Peter and Paul in Antioch were worked out, and that they worked together to establish the Roman church. This is the impression the Pauline authors wished to convey. This did not occur and Roman church history was rewritten later to show otherwise. The truth of the matter is that Paul's position on James, as expressed in his book of Galatians, was "let him be damned;" [507] and the Nazorean position on Paul was "that he was an apostate from the law."[508] Once Paul had succeeded in amassing a large and powerful enough following to defy Peter and the James, he did so. His conflict with Peter in Antioch caused his long time companion Barnabas to abandon him and come over to the side of Peter and James. From this point onward Paul was on his own. It is amazing that the propaganda of his school was able to so successfully convince his future followers that there was an unbroken continuity

[506] Colossians
[507] Galatians 1:9
[508] Irenaeus, Adversus Haereses (Against Heresies), 180 A.D.)

between their church and Yeshu, as well as the original followers of Yeshu in Palestine.

Two Groups

Originally there was only one type of "Christ disciple" - the Essene Nazorean family and followers of Yeshu and Miryai. They had a very strong and unique "Essene" culture. They also had their own set of scriptures, different from the Old and New Testament canon we know today. This original Nazorean Family had various levels and degrees of initiation and purification associated with it. Those on the outer probationary levels retained many of their former customs and beliefs, including gentile and Jewish ones, while those initiated into deeper levels became well versed in deeper Essene doctrines.

It appears that these early Nazarenes were a Christ centered expression of the ancient Nazarites and a continuation of the ancient Essene Nazoreans spoken of by Epiphanius, although Epiphanius himself is reluctant to admit this fact. It is also probable that these New Testament Nazarenes accepted both gentile and Pharisee Jews, along with many of their customs and varied beliefs, into the outer fringes of their society. When fully integrated they became Mandai, or Gnostics. Those who continued to progress became Nazoreans, or initiates and keepers of the mysteries.

Being the most viable and growing sect of their time, these Nazoreans and their break off groups eventually became the melting pots, especially after the fall of Jerusalem in 68 A.D., for a wide array of converts from all seven of the ancient Jewish sects, several Samaritan sects, numerous Gnostic and Pythagorean groups, as well as converted and semi-converted Roman and Greek pagans.

Eventually a second and third type of "Christ disciple" evolved
from the teachings of Paul - the gentile Christians and the
Jewish Christians. This second and third type tended to be
non-Jewish and Pharisee Jewish, and were eventually
disconnected with the original followers of the Messiah. They
tended to have Roman, Pharisee or Hellenic backgrounds and
they tended to put great trust in the writings and doctrines of
either Paul on the one hand, or the false Torah and Pharisee
customs on the other. Their descendants did not like the
original Nazoreans very much and preferred a different non-
Essene culture and non-Nazorean approach to their spiritual
matters.

The more numerous gentile Christians set about redefining the
mission and role of Yeshu the Messiah, recasting Him in the
light of their Greek and Roman dying and resurrecting god
myths. The Nazoreans, or "Jewish-Christians" as some of them
were eventually called by the Romanized Christians, did not
appreciate this distortion of their Teachers of Righteousness.
These Nazoreans did not initially accept the writings and
doctrines of Paul, nor did they take much account of the
Gospels which found their way into the New Testament bible.
Instead, they used the Gospel of Hebrews which denied,
among other things, the Roman version of the virgin birth.

Modern theological studies suggest that the New Testament's
two letters of Peter, the second speaking unconvincingly of
'our brother Paul...so dear to us',[509] were most likely forged in
Peter's name by some pro-Pauline writer, and that other letters
attributed to Paul, notably the Pastorals, were fabricated to
create a false impression of harmony with Peter and James.
Recent computer tests have clearly confirmed what theological
scholars have long suspected, that whoever wrote Paul's

---

[509] 2 Peter 3:15

letters to Timothy and Titus was not the person, Paul, who wrote Galatians, Romans and Corinthians.

This original group of Nazorean disciples had firsthand knowledge of what Yeshu and Miryai had taught and stood for, and were holding to the original vision which focused on purity laws, study of hidden gnosis, and reception of purifying rituals of redemption. The non-Nazorean "Jewish-Christians" and the "Gentile Christians", on the other hand, did not have or want the firsthand knowledge possessed by the original Nazoreans, but instead preferred creating their own myths concerning the Christ and using only a few distorted rites only loosely based on the original Nazorean ones. This led to conflict and eventual persecution of the Nazoreans. The more powerful and numerous gentile Christians of the Paul School eventually removed most vestiges of the original Nazorean Way from their gentile gospel, and what little was left of the original Nazorean Way was only partially preserved by the monastic orders which slowly began to arise as the Nazoreans were persecuted into extinction.

When they rewrote history, it appears that these Christians associated the original Essene-Nasorene disciples and their descendents with the semi-converted Pharisee Nazarenes and their remnants, referring to both groups as "Jewish Christians", casting them in the light of narrow minded Pharisee Jews and weak willed vegetarians incapable of fully accepting their Christ.

Christians eventually cultivated great hostility toward the original Judean Nazoreans, as we can read from John Chrysostom, the Patriarch of Constantinople:

"Jews are the most worthless of men - they are lecherous, greedy, rapacious - they are perfidious murderers of Christians, they worship the devil, their religion is a sickness ... The Jews are the odious assassins of Christ and for killing god there is no expiation, no indulgence, no pardon. Christians may never cease vengeance. The Jews must live in servitude forever. It is incumbent on all Christians to hate the Jews."

These true Essene Nazoreans would, in turn, not accept the gentile's "Christ", or the gentile "New Testament", because they knew both had been tampered with, altered and remade in the image of the Roman Gods.

A later non Nazorean group called "Nazarenes" was spoken of by Epiphanius as being totally Jewish and accepting of the Torah and other practices rejected by earlier Nazoreans. These were not the Gnostic Nazoreans and were probably a remnant of Jewish converts to Paul's Christianity who never fully gave up their old beliefs and customs when becoming outer level Roman Christians. Epiphanius himself admits that in the beginning all followers of Jesus, even non-Jewish ones, were called Nazoreans. In the same light, the eventually dominant Roman Church were probably descended from only partially converted gentiles on the outer fringes of the original Nazorean Way who never sloughed off their Hellenistic customs in favor of the full Nazorean-Essene lifestyle and were taught by Paul to ignore all Nazorean customs and laws.

Eventually the true Essene Nazorean remnants gravitated to Elchasaite and various other monastic orders in Upper Egypt, Babylon and elsewhere. In these monastic worlds they were able to preserve some of their original traditions, but often were forced to compromise on many issues as they came under the dominion of the growing Pauline form of

Christianity centered in Rome. The uncompromising Pharisee-like Nazarenes faded from history as their monastic cousins blended more completely with the Rome centered new Christianity.

It is important to understand that the Nazorean's "jewishness" is not the Jewish ness which modern people associate with Judaism. Modern Rabbinic Judaism is an evolvement of the Pharisee sect of ancient Judea, which is itself a form of the ancient Pharisee, or Persian belief. Nazoreans were from the Essene Nazorean Sect of Carmel. They did not accept the Old Testament, the Jerusalem Temple, the animal sacrifices, or even the celebration of Passover as we know of it today. They, therefore, are not correctly understood by the modern label of "Jew". The ancient Nazoreans were more akin to the Osseaen sect, which may be partially understood by studying the documents and historian reports, such as Josephus and Philo, on the Essenes.

ˉ 19 ˉ
FAITHFULNESS & CONTINUITY

Scribing Memoirs

SIMULTANEOUS WITH the Paulite's bible the Nazorean preserved the true traditions taught by Yeshu and the true scrolls of light, including the original Nazorean Gospel that the Christians had been unsuccessful at acquiring from the Nazoreans. The Nazoreans had many books, some open ones reserved for lay Gnostics (*mandai*) and some for secret initiates only. In addition, public preachers like Peter were presenting a watered down introduction into the faith of the Nazoreans to non Nazorean audiences. In The Apocryphon of James from the Nag Hammadhi library we read of the Nazorean tradition of passing about these various types of books:

> "... the twelve disciples were all sitting together and recalling what the Savior had said to each one of them, whether in secret or openly, and putting it in books - But I was writing that which was in my book - lo, the Savior appeared ...[510]

In this same text we read more of the scribing tradition and of the various levels of security needed to access certain scrolls:

> "Since you asked that I send you a secret book which was revealed to me and Peter by the Lord, I could not turn you away or gainsay you; but I have written it in the Hebrew (i.e. Aramaic-Syriac) alphabet and sent it to you, and you alone. But since you are a minister of the salvation of the saints, endeavor earnestly and take care not to rehearse this text to many - this that the Savior did not wish to tell to all of us, his twelve disciples. But blessed will they be who will be saved through the faith of this discourse. I also sent you, ten months ago, another secret book which the Savior had revealed to me. Under the circumstances, however, regard that one as revealed to me, James; but this one ... [511]

These comments betray an intricate level of initiation and varied levels of texts and scrolls. What found their way into the New Testament did not even qualify as beginner texts. They were hopelessly adulterated to the point of promoting another religion altogether – the religion of Rome not Carmel.

Manichaean Scribes

One of the main duties of a Nazorean priestess or priest was to copy scared texts under the watchful eye of those who held

---

[510] The Apocryphon Of James
[511] The Apocryphon Of James

the responsibility for their limited dissemination. There are at least 32 Priestess scribes recorded in the colophons at the end of ancient Nazorean scrolls preserved by the Mandaeans. This tradition survived through the centuries. It is also evident in the third century expression of Nazoreanism called Manichaeanism. Priests in Mani's system were excused from agricultural labor so that they could concentrate fully on the production of scriptures and sermons. Within a very labor intensive agricultural culture this arrangement allowed the few Electi more time to produce more written copies of sacred scripture. One scholar has said:

> "The high quality of execution of both the miniatures and the calligraphy of the Manichaean texts attests to an active scribal tradition in Turfan and this finds expression in what can only be termed a group-self-portrait of Manichaean Electi performing scribal duties. Seated in two rows in front of two Trees of Life, they are shown to be engaged in their craft with intense expressions. Two of the figures hold a pen in each hand - one perhaps for copying in black ink and the other for red as many of the extant Manichaean text fragments are two-toned. As Manichaeism was a religion of the book, the Manichaeans took their scribal duties very seriously. A monk is required in a Sogdian confessional to ask for forgiveness for having neglected his calligraphy, for hating or despising it and for having damaged or injured a brush, a writing board, a piece of silk or' paper."[512]

We know the Manichaean electi of the Manichaean monasteries were directly responsible for the creation of many scrolls and indirectly responsible for the production of much produce through their management of Oblates. There also exist certain repentance's for Manichaean monastic scribes who built up resentment toward their scribal art.

---

[512] Manichaeism In Central Asia And China By Samuel Lieu

In the Kitāb al-ḥayawān, al-Ǧahiẓ related the following account of the great care these later Nazoreans "Righteous Ones (*Tzadiks*) put into their scribal art:

"Ibrāhīm asSindī once said to me: "I wish the Zandiks [i.e. the Manichaeans] were not so intent on spending good money on clean white paper and for the use of shining black ink and that they would not put such great value on calligraphy und would encourage the calligraphers less; because indeed no paper that I ever saw is comparable to the paper of their books and no calligraphy with that which is used therein." I replied to Ibrāhīm: "When the Manichaeans go to great lengths for the decoration of their holy books it is the same as when the Christians do it for their churches". [513]

These Manichaean scribes were carrying on a tradition once observed by Yeshu himself.

Ginza Rba

When Epiphanius wrote of the Nasaraeans, he said:

"But they hold that the scriptures of the Pentateuch were not written by Moses, and maintain that they have others."

One of these "others" that the Nasaraeans had was the Ginza Rba, or Great Treasury. The Ginza Rba is the Nazorean equivalent of the Jewish Old Testament and contains 618 pages when translated from Aramaic. Unlike the Jewish Old Testament, it is not an account of earthly affairs. The Ginza Rba focuses on the spiritual worlds and the affairs that occurred there, the spiritual wars, creation of worlds, etc. The Ginza has a left and a right side, one for the dead and the other for the living. The Opening verse of the 62 chaptered

---

[513] (Translation Of A Quote From K. Keßler: Mani. Forschungen Über Die Manichäische Religion. Berlin 1889, S. 366

Right side of the Ginza Rba, the Great Treasury or Bible of ancient Nazoreans and Essenes, has:

"Great is thy name, my Lord I mention your name with pure heart, thou Lord of all worlds; blessed and Holy thy name my Lord, the High the mighty, king of worlds of Sublime Light, whose power is infinite thou, the brilliant and the inexhaustible Light. God, you, the Merciful, the compassionate, and the Forgiving the saviour of all believers and the supporter of all good people. Thou art the wise, the omnipotent that knows everything. Thou art capable of doing every thing; Lord of all worlds of Light, the high, middle and lower worlds. Thou art of the respectful Face, which cannot be seen; thou art the only God who has no partner and no equal in his Power. Any one who trusts in you will never be disappointed; any one who depends on you; will never be humiliated, Lord of all angels, without His presence, there is no existence; without Him, nothing could exist, He is Eternal without beginning and an end."

Nazorean Book of the Dead

The left side of the Great Treasure (*Ginza Rba*), or Great Book (*Sidra Rabba*), is a Nazorean Book of the Dead. The "Ginza Left" consists of 3 Books totaling 94 Chapters and concerns itself solely with the fate of the soul after death. It was preserved due to the scribal wisdom of the ancient Nazorean Priestess Lama who made a copy of it before 270 AD.

It consists of 3 separate tractates, or sections, that deal with the ascent of the soul upward into the higher heavens. This text is associated with the Last Rites ceremony of the Nazorean Essenes which is called the "N'girta", or "Letter". It begins by explaining how the Great Life decided that it was time for the thousand year old Adam to die and return home to heaven. The Angel of Death was dispatched, but Adam refused to go with him for he had become attached to the earth and its affairs and associations. Adam pleads that his son Seth be taken in his stead, and the Great Life agreed, since They approved of such self-sacrificing for the sake of another. After Seth's ascension into heaven, Adam becomes jealous of the spiritual experiences which Seth enjoyed, and begs to ascend also. The text continues with descriptions of the heavenly journey through various worlds and purgatories, and the eventual return to the highest heaven. This ascent includes interrogations by hostile guards at each of the seven dark heavens of this world.

These hymns from the Book of the Dead have traditionally been read by Nazoreans after the death of one of its members. They are beautiful and inspiring and take into account the natural reluctance of humans to leave behind their bodies and friends at death. It would have been read by Miryai after the death of Yeshu during the first three days. The text is 174 pages in length. It begins thusly:

"Praised by my Lord with an open heart! In the names of the great, lofty, foreign Life which stands above all struggles, illuminators of garments of those who honor their father their, the Master of Greatness. First Part: Praised be Life, and the righteous, and the brethren Hibil, Shitil and Anush –
The Life decided death to envelop the thousand year old Adam and sends Saurel, the Angel of Death, to him to call his soul. Adam weeps and moans and begs that instead of him, he will fetch the soul of Sethil, saying: First let the green grain be eaten, and then the ears. Saurel presents such to the First Life, who agrees with Sethil's soul being reaped instead, and sends Saurel to him. Sethil first sends the Angel of Death back to Adam, whom he leaves again, returns and convinces him and cast off the body. He beholds the Light Land, and through his prayer the eyes and other senses of Adam are opened. Now Adam also wants to go to that world, but he is, however, repulsed by Sethil. Sethil is then lifted into the height and is welcomed and called by the Uthra-Buddhas and the Living Ones. Who are the

mountains that move not, and the water heights that are not changes, which shook not, nor created, and whose body has not its garb created? The Great Life is a mountain that moveth not, and water-Heights that change not, which quaked not, nor cried, and whose body is not in a garment created." [514]

Gospels of Nazoreans

The Nasaraeans had other books as well, including accounts of Yeshu's life and words. We have previously quoted a portion of these as found in the fragments preserved by 'Abd al-Jabbar. There are four gospels mentioned by various Pauline historians – the Gospel of the Nazoreans, the Gospel of the Hebrews, and the Egyptian Gospel, and the Gospel of the Ebionites. Not to mention Matthew's original Aramaic sayings scroll mentioned by Papias.[515] Scholars are in disagreement as to whether these were one and the same book, or three or four separate books. Only a few quotes from each survive. Jerome, who translated the Vulgate Bible for the Roman Christians, also translated a Gospel of the Nazoreans from Aramaic. His translation has not survived. Jerome wrote:

"In the Gospel which the Nazoreans and Ebionites use which I have lately translated into Greek from the Hebrew and which is called by many people the original of Matthew..." [516]

The Gospel of the Nazoreans was quoted by Ignatius in 98 A.D. and so was written prior to this date and was associated with the early eye witness Nazoreans. The Stichometry of Nicephorus assigns 2,200 lines, 300 less than Matthew, to a Gospel of the Nazoreans. This may have been the original Gnostic Gospel or an alternate non-Gnostic Book of Matthew

---

[514] Nazorean Book of the Dead, Ginza Rba
[515] Appendix two contains 72 sayings attributed to Jesus extracted from the New Testament Gospels. These may have some relationship to Matthew's Aramaic sayings document.
[516] Jerome; On Matt. 12:13

used by Hellenistic Jewish Christians. The original Gospel according to the Nazoreans was a Gnostic, not a Christian text, used by the original disciples of Yeshu and Miryai. It was useless outside of Nazorean circles so all originals were burned by the orthodox.

In the Panarion of Epiphanius of Salamis, excerpts of a Gospel of the Nazoreans, which promoted vegetarianism, are preserved:

> "I am come to do away with sacrifices, and if you cease not sacrificing, the wrath of God will not cease from you."[517]

> But they abandon the proper sequence of the words and pervert the saying, as is plain to all from the readings attached, and have let the disciples say: "Where will you have us prepare the Passover?" And him to answer to that: "Do I desire with desire at this Passover to eat flesh with you?" [518]

Only a few fragments survive from what is called the Gospel of the Hebrews. It may, or may not, be the same as the gospel quoted above. This gospel was said to have been held in high regard by Jewish Christians, as reported by Eusebius. From 'The History of the Church' we have this quote from the gospel of the Hebrews:

> "When the Lord ascended from the water, the whole fount of the Holy Spirit descended and rested upon him, and said to him, "My son, in all the prophets I was waiting for you, that you might come, and that I might rest in you. For you are my rest; and you are my firstborn son, `who reigns forever." [519]

The Gospel of the Egyptians no longer exists, unless it lies unrecognized, or buried and undiscovered somewhere. Egypt

---

[517] Epiphanius, Panarion 30.16,4-5
[518] Epiphanius, Panarion 30.22,4
[519] Jerome, Commentary On Isaiah11:2

was predominantly Gnostic for the first few centuries of the Christian era, and so the Gospel used there might have been the original Gnostic Gospel of the Nazoreans. Orthodox Rome backed Christianity only came to prominence in Egypt with the rise of one Demetrius, the Roman bishop of Alexandria from 189 to 231 A series of passages from Clement of Alexandria is our chief source of knowledge concerning the Gospel of the Egyptians. The second and third of these quoted verses are also represented in the Gospel of Thomas. The existing quotes are as follows:

> "Whence it is with reason that after the Word had told about the End, Salome saith: Until when shall men continue to die? and it is advisedly that the Lord makes an answer: So long as women bear children. Salome: for when she had said, 'I have done well, then, in not bearing children?' the Lord answers and says: Every plant eat thou, but that which hath bitterness eat not. [520]

> When Salome inquired when the things concerning which she asked should be known, the Lord said: When ye have trampled on the garment of shame, and when the two become one and the male with the female is neither male nor female.[521]

> For the Lord himself being asked by some one when his kingdom should come, said: When the two shall be one, and the outside (that which is without) as the inside (that which is within), and the male with the female neither male nor female.) [522]

> The Lord said to Salome when she inquired: How long shall death prevail? 'As long as ye women bear children', not because life is evil, and the creation evil: but as showing the sequence of nature: for in all cases birth is followed by decay.[523]

---

[520] Clem. Alex. Strom. Iii. 9. 64, 66.
[521] Iii. 13. 92, also Thomas 37
[522] Second Epistle Of Clement, also Thomas 22
[523] Iii. 6. 45.

"And when the Saviour says to Salome that there shall be death as long as women bear children, he did not say it as abusing birth, for that is necessary for the salvation of believers. [524]

(The Naassenes) say that the soul is very hard to find and to perceive; for it does not continue in the same fashion or shape or in one emotion so that one can either describe it or comprehend its essence. And they have these various changes of the soul, set forth in the Gospel entitled according to the Egyptians.[525]

It should be noted that in Nazirutha, the world of the lay person is called the world of the female; and the reality of the Priesthood (*Tarmidaya*) is called the world of the male. When a female becomes a priestess, it is said that she leaves the female world and enters the male. Had the Nazoreans been gender prejudice, they would not have worshipped a Goddess and allowed priestesses. Use of male and female is their equivalent to the Chinese yin and yang and should not be misunderstood when reading ancient quotes.

It is possible that the Gospel of the Egyptians quoted above was the Secret Gospel of Mark mentioned by Clement, since we know that the Carpocracian version of this text had a lot to do with Salome, just like our quotes above.

"Moreover, the followers of the Egyptian Gnostic Carpocrates derived the origin of their teaching from Salome" [526]

An Alexandrian female leader of the Carpocracians named Marcellina taught Gnosticism in Rome around 150 A. D. She claimed to have received secret teaching from Mary, Salome, and Martha. These are three of the four woman heirs of

---

[524] Excerpts From Theodotus, 67
[525] Hippolytus Against Heresies, V. 7.
[526] So Celsus according to Origen Against Celsus 5.62.

Yeshu's Gnosis mentioned in the Apocalypse of James from the Nag:

> "When you speak these words of this perception, encourage these four: Salome and Mariam and Martha and Arsinoe ..."

It appears that Clement of Alexandria sought to distance himself from these Gnostics in favor of the orthodox camp which had been gaining ground in Alexandria since 180 AD. This camp would eventually disown him for retaining too many Gnostic ideas in his belief system. Clement wrote:

> "Celsus knows, moreover, certain Marcellians, so called from Marcellina, and Harpocratians from Salome, and others who derive their name from Mariamme, and others again from Martha...."[527]

Despite the growing power of Rome and its false form of Christianity, the true Nazorean Gnostics continued onward, preserving the true tradition of Yeshu with great sincerity and purpose.

> "He (*Yeshu*) and his companions behaved constantly in this manner, until he left this world. He said to his companions: "Act as you have seen me act, instruct people in accordance with instructions I have given you, and be for them what I have been for you." His companions behaved constantly in this manner and in accordance with this. And so did those who came after the first generation of his companions, and also those who came long after."[528]

James as Successor

---

[527] Origen, Against Celsus, Bk. V, 62, 63
[528] The Establishment Of Proofs . . . By 'Abd Al-Jabbar

Just before Yeshu was crucified, He was asked who would be His successor as head of the Nazorean Way:

> "The Disciples say to Yeshu: We know that thou shall go away from us. Who is it that shall be Rabbi over us? Yeshu says to them: In the place that you have come, you shall go to James the Righteous, for whose sake the sky and earth come to be. " [529]

This tradition is in stark contrast to the Roman Catholic which promotes Peter into this position, yet the most ancient Christian historians, such as Eusebius tell us:

> "To James the Just, and John and Peter, the Lord after his resurrection imparted knowledge. These imparted it to the rest of the Apostles, and the rest of the Apostles to the seventy, of whom Barnabas was one."[530]

Although in the interests of Roman supremacy the primacy of James was dropped in the West from the time of Irenaeus onward, it was continued in the East for a time, however. In the Clementine Recognitions and Homilies Peter insists that no teacher or prophet is to be believed unless he has been certified by James.

> "Wherefore observe the greatest caution, that you believe no teacher, unless he bring from Jerusalem the testimonial of James the Lord's brother, or of whosoever may come after him. For no one, unless he has gone up thither, and there has been approved as a fit and faithful teacher for preaching the word of Christ,- unless, I say, he brings a testimonial thence, is by any means to be received. But let neither prophet nor apostle be looked for by you at this time, besides us. For there is one true Prophet, whose words we twelve apostles preach; for He is the accepted year of God, having us apostles as His twelve months. [531]

[529] Gospel Of Thomas, 12
[530] Eusebius Eh 2:1, 4
[531] Recognitions of Clement 4:35

"Wherefore, above all, remember to shun apostle or teacher or prophet who does not first accurately compare his preaching with *that of* James, who was called the brother of my Lord, and to whom was entrusted to administer the church of the Hebrews in Jerusalem,-and that even though he come to you with witnesses. [532]

In the epistle to James attached to the Homilies Peter transmits the books of his preaching (Kerygmata Petrou) to James for safekeeping. Hippolytus, in describing the Gnostic Naassenes, speaks of:

"the heads of the very many discourses which they say James the brother of the Lord handed down to Mariamme."[533]

Now we understand this Mariamme to be Mariamme of Magdala, or Miryai the Maiden of Light and James' coregent after the demise of Yeshu. With James, she was in charge of what texts were written and which were to be published. All the Greek gospels appear to have arisen without her stamp of approval.

Appearance to Miryai

The legend of the appearance of Yeshu first to Miryai, or Mary Magdalene, cannot be discounted. It is the type of event that the Patriarchal minded Roman Christian "church fathers" would not have made up. The testimony of a woman was not considered reliable or admissible in those times, and was an embarrassment for all Non Nazorean Christians. Just who and when Yeshu appeared to certain individuals was considered validation for their holding office and jurisdiction in the early

---

[532] Homilees of Clement 1135
[533] Refutation Of All Heresies V:7

church. This is why Paul made so much of his vision. He used it to try to side step having to bow to the authority of James. It was to James and Miryai, however, that Yeshu passed on his authority. His appearance first to Miryai, and then to James, establish these two as the legitimate successors to Yeshu. In the Cayce material Mary Magdalene is said to have died twenty two years after Yeshu, at about age 45. This puts her death a decade before that of James in 62 AD.

James' Oath

There is a tradition that James took an oath not to eat until Yeshu arose from the dead. In Nazorean culture this is three days after the demise of the physical body. At this time a special meal for the dead is enacted to help the soul begin its Journey heavenward. Thus James is swearing to fast until he does the traditional Masqitha Rite that assists the Dead to Rise:

> "And when the Lord had given the linen cloth to the servant of the priest, he went to James and appeared to him. For James had sworn that he would not eat bread from that hour in which he had drunk the cup of the Lord until he should see him risen from among them that sleep. And shortly thereafter the Lord said: Bring a table and bread! And immediately it is added: he took the bread and blessed it and brake it and gave to James the Just and said to him: My brother, eat thy bread, for the Son of Man is risen from among them that sleep."[534]

Yuhana's wife Anhar talked of taking a similar oath when Yuhana died:

> "Yahya opened his mouth and spake to Anhar in Jerusalem If I leave the world, tell me, what wilt thou do after me? I will not eat and will not drink, she answered him, until I see thee again.

---

[534] Gospel Of The Hebrews, Jerome, De Viris Inlustribus 2

Priority of James

In I Corinthians 15:7, it is recorded that Jesus appeared to his brother James after the resurrection. The leadership role held by James is explained as the first Bishop of the Jerusalem church by Eusebius and other second century writers.

While James was Bishop of the Jerusalem congregation, two important Councils of church leaders were held under his direction. These are recorded in Acts 15, which as Hervé Ponsot has noted seems to combine two different meetings in one account. The first of these Councils appears to have met in 37 C.E. at the beginning of Paul's missionary travels. The focus of its concern was the question of the necessity of requiring Gentile converts to adopt the Jewish custom of circumcision. The second Council occurred around 52 or 53 C.E. after the controversy at Antioch about whether vegan members of the church should be allowed to share meals with Gentile meat eaters. Peter and Paul, who played central roles in this controversy, may not have been present at the Council itself.

The last reference to the Jerusalem church in the Christian scriptures is the reference to Paul's visit there in 57 C.E. At this time, James was still the Bishop of the Hebrew congregation there. Not many years after this, Peter, Paul, and James were martyred. Little is known of the first two deaths. Eusebius records only that "in his [Nero's] time Paul was beheaded in Rome and Peter was likewise crucified". [535] Clement of Rome is accredited with writing:

> "Let us set before our eyes the good apostles: Peter, who because of unrighteous jealously suffered not one or two but many trials,

---

[535] Eusebius, Eh 2:25

and having thus given his testimony went to the glorious place
which was his due. Through jealously and strife Paul showed
the way to the prize of endurance; seven times he was in bonds,
he was exiled, he was stoned, he was a herald both in the East
and in the West, he gained the noble fame of his life, he taught
righteousness to all the world, and when he had reached the
limits [literally, "pillars"] of the West he gave his testimony
before the rulers, and thus passed from the world and was taken
up into the Holy Place, -- the greatest example of endurance."[536]

The Pseudo Clementine Recognitions tells us a little of James's
role as Bishop of the Jerusalem church.

> "He received reports (I:66; cf. II:73), engaged in disputations
> (I:66-69), sent letters of authorization with official representatives
> (IV:35), and even gave specific tasks to Peter (I:72). James is
> referred to as "chief of the bishops" and is described counterpart
> to "Caiaphas . . . the chief of the priests." His leadership role,
> even over the apostles, is also described in Acts 21:17-22:23
> where he is the one who articulates the rules to be followed by
> non Jewish converts. He first enjoins Paul to disabuse Jewish
> followers of his rumored abandonment of the Law by
> participating in and paying for the ritual purification of four
> men who have been observing a Nazarite vow, and continues by
> declaring, "But as for the Gentiles who have become believers,
> we have sent a letter with our judgment that they should abstain
> from what has been sacrificed to idols and from blood and from
> what is strangled [i.e., meat from animals that had not been
> ritually slaughtered with a knife as required by the Law] and
> from fornication" (Acts 21:25)." [537]

Death of James

James the Righteous, holy brother of Yeshu, was very popular
with the Aramaic speaking community of Nazoreans and also

---

[536] The Epistle Of Clement, 5
[537] An Anthropologist Looks at the Judeo-Christian Scriptures

the larger Jewish people as a whole. According to Eusebius, he was widely known in the Jewish community as "Righteous and Oblias, meaning "bulwark of the people"." Under his influence the Nazorean movement grew until his death in 63 C.E, as Hegesippus goes on to say:

"Some of the seven sects, therefore, of the people, mentioned by me above in my commentaries, asked him what was the door to Y'shua? and he answered: "That he was the Saviour." From which, some believed that Y'shua is the Messiah. But the aforementioned heresies did not believe either a resurrection, or that he was coming to give to every one according to his works; as many however, as did believe, did so on account of James. As there were many therefore of the rulers that believed, there arose a tumult among the Jews, Scribes and Pharisees, saying that there was danger, that the people would now expect Y'shua as the Messiah. They came therefore together, and said to James: "We entreat you, restrain the people, who are led astray after Y'shua, as if he were the Messiah. We entreat you to persuade all that are coming to the feast of the Passover rightly concerning Y'shua; for we all have confidence in you. For we and all the people hear the testimony that you are just, and you respect not persons. Persuade therefore the people not to be led astray by Y'shua, for we and all the people have great confidence in you. Stand therefore upon a wing of the Temple, that you may be conspicuous on high, and your words may be easily heard by all the people; for all the tribes have come together on account of the Passover, with some of the Gentiles also. The aforesaid Scribes and Pharisees, therefore, placed James upon a wing of the Temple, and cried out to him: "Oh you just man, whom we ought all to believe, since the people are led astray after Y'shua that was crucified, declare to us what is the door to Y'shua that was crucified." And he answered with a loud voice, "Why do you ask me respecting Y'shua the Son of Man? He is now sitting in the heavens, on the right hand of Great Power, and is about to come on the clouds of heaven." (Ps. 110:1 & Dan. 7:13). And as many were confirmed, and glorified in this testimony of James, and said, Hosanna to the son of David, these same priests and

Pharisees said to one another: "We have done badly in affording such testimony to Y'shua, but let us go up and cast him down, that they may dread to believe in him." And they cried out: "Oh, oh, the Just himself is deceived," and they fulfilled that which is written in Isaiah: Let us take away the just, because he is offensive to us; wherefore they shall eat the fruit of their doings [Is. 3:10]. "Going up therefore, they cast down the just man, saying to one another: "Let us stone James the Just." And they began to stone him, as he did not die immediately when cast down; but turning round, he knelt down saying, "I entreat you, O Lord God and Father, forgive them, for they know not what they do." Thus they were stoning him, when one of the priests of the sons of Recheb, a son of the Rechabites, spoken of by Jeremiah the prophet, cried out saying: "Cease, what are you doing? Justus is praying for you." And one of them, a fuller, beat out the brains of Justus with the club that he used to beat out clothes. Thus he suffered martyrdom, and they buried him on the spot where his tombstone is still remaining, by the Temple. He became a faithful witness, both to the Jews and the Greeks, that Y'shua is the Messiah. Immediately after this, Vespian invaded and took Judea. [538]

Josephus also records the death of Yeshu's brother James the Just this way:

"Festus was now dead, and Albinus was but upon the road; so he [the High Priest Ananus] assembled the sanhedrin of the judges, and brought before them the brother of Y'shua, who was called Messiah, whose name was James, and some others, [or some of his companions;] and when he had formed an accusation against them as breakers of the law, he delivered them to be stoned: but as for those who seemed the most equitable of the citizens, and such as were the most uneasy at the breach of the laws, they disliked what was done. (Josephus, Antiquities 20:9:1)

---

[538] Hegesippus as quoted by Eusebius, Ecclesiastical History 2:23

According to Eusebius, his version of Josephus's works contained the following in relation to the destruction of Jerusalem and the Temple in 70 C.E.:

> "These things happened to the Jews to avenge James the Just, who was brother of him that is called the Messiah, and whom the Jews had slain, not withstanding his pre-eminent justice." [539]

After the rise of Rome in the affairs of Greek speaking Christians, the roll of James was diminished and obscured and that of Peter was accentuated. This was felt necessary by them because the lineages of James were too Gnostic.

Flight to Pella

Eusibius, in the fourth century, is the first to explicitly mention the exodus:

> "The whole body, however, of the church at Jerusalem, having been commanded by a divine revelation, given to men of approved piety there before the war, removed from the city, and dwelt at a certain town beyond the Jordan, called Pella. Here those that believed in Christ, having removed from Jerusalem, as if holy men had entirely abandoned the royal city itself, and the whole land of Judea; the divine justice, for their crimes against Christ and his apostles finally overtook them, totally destroying the whole generation of these evildoers form the earth."[540]

It is also was recorded by Flavius Josephus the following:

> "Moreover, at that feast which we call Pentecost as the priests were going by night into the inner court of the temple...they said that, in the first place, they felt a quaking and heard a sound as of a multitude saying, 'Let us remove hence.'" [541]

---

[539] Josephus quoted by Eusebius; Eccl. Hist. 2:23
[540] Eusebius, bk. 3, ch. 5
[541] Josephus, Wars, bk. VI, ch. v, sec. 3; Whiston 1957:825

The region of Decapolis had been made semi-autonomous by the Romans, and Jewish rebels in the great war had destroyed cities there, including Pella. When the Nazoreans fled Judea and arrived at Pella, they found few people still there. They settled in and made it one of their homes. It was at Pella that the Ebionites first emerged as a separate sect. By the third century, non Nazorean Christian churches are found there, indicating that the Nazoreans eventually moved on to other locales.

Jewish Cursings

All Nazoreans probably fled to Pella during the war, but afterward some migrated to other areas where Jews were active. After a couple decades the Jews felt a need to condemn these Nazoreans once again. The Talmud explains that in 90 CE,

> "Our Rabbis taught: Simeon ha-Pakuli arranged the eighteen benedictions in order before Rabban Gamaliel in Jabneh. Said Rabban Gamaliel {Rabban Gamaliel II, the Nasi', or leader of the rabbis) to the Sages: 'Can any one among you frame a benediction relating to the Minim [sects]?' Samuel the Lesser arose and composed it."[542]

This "blessing" was added into the Eighteen Benedictions that were spoken by Jewish congregations during their worship at synagogues. The modern "amida" no longer has a direct curse of the Nazoreans, but the older Cairo Genizah version reads this way:

> "For the renegades let there be no hope, and may the arrogant kingdom soon be rooted out in our days, and the Nazoreans and

---

[542] b.Berakot 29a

the Minim perish as in a moment and be blotted out from the book of life and with the righteous may they not be inscribed. Blessed are you, O Lord, who humbles the arrogant. [543]

This curse upon them in formal synagogue worship, composed by Samuel the Lesser, was not to ferret out covert Nazoreans hiding amongst the ranks who would be afraid to utter the curse upon themselves, but was simply an expression of the deep hate and resentment the Jewish congregations had for all things Nazorean. It was their response to the growing success they felt the Nazoreans were experiencing. Thus we have Epiphanius reporting around 370 AD that:

"Not only do Jewish people have a hatred of them; they even stand up at dawn, at midday, and toward evening, three times a day when they recite their prayers in the synagogues, and curse and anathemize them. Three times a day they say, "G-d curse the Nazoreans." For they harbor an extra grudge against them, if you please, because despite their Jewishness, they proclaim that Y'shua is Messiah. . ." [544]

This hatred toward the Nazoreans by the Jews would soon be expressed equally as vehemently by the growing Roman Christians.

Shimeon Takes Over

The Catholics have their supposed successors to the "chair of Peter" in Rome that are supposed to be the popes of the church. In reality, James sat in the original chair, not Peter, and was succeeded in his role as Archbishop, or Ganzibra of Jerusalem, by his half brother and cousin Shimeon bar

---

[543] Old copy of the Birkat haMinim found at the Cairo Genizah
[544] Epiphanius Panarion 29

Miryam. After James and spouses came Shimeon bar Miryam and spouses on the Jerusalem chair:

> "After the martyrdom of James and the capture of Jerusalem which instantly followed, there is a firm tradition that those of the apostles and disciples of the Lord who were still alive assembled from all parts together with those who, humanly speaking, were kinsmen of the Lord--for most of them were still living and they all took counsel together concerning whom they should judge worthy to succeed James and to the unanimous tested approval it was decided that Symeon son of the Clopas, mentioned in the gospel narrative, was worthy to occupy the throne [i.e., the position of Bishop] of the Jerusalem see. He was, so it is said, a cousin of the savior, for Hegesippus relates that Clopas was the brother of Joseph"[545]

Symeon could have been both the brother and cousin of Yeshu:

> "Cousin marriages were legal under the Mosaic law, as was polygamy. That was why men could be brothers and cousins at the same time. Their father and mother may have been cousins, or their father may have married sisters.[546]

With the murder of Simeon comes the end of the Desposyni reign of the three great brothers: "Yaqif (James), Beni-Amin (Yeshu), and Shumel (Samuel/Shimeon)." Those three that did "assemble on Mount Carmel." [547]

In other sources we are told that Miryai was the successor to James. Hippolytus, in describing the Gnostic Naassenes, speaks of:

---

[545] Eusebius, Ecclesiastical History. 3.11.1
[546] Salome: Matron Saint Of Midwives
[547] Sidra Dyahya (Book Of John)/Drashe Dmalke (Discourses Of Kings) 26

"the heads of the very many discourses which they say James the brother of the Lord handed down to Mariamme."[548]

Mariamme, as receptor of the secret scrolls possessed by James, was his essential heir and the head of the Nazoreans. We know that Salome was also a head of the Nazoreans since the Egyptian Gnostics looked to her for the source of their lineage:

"Moreover, the followers of the Egyptian Gnostic Carpocrates derived the origin of their teaching from Salome" [549]

This was in accord with the command of Yeshu that James should pass on his keys to Marriamme, Martha, Salome and Arsinoe.

Ebionite Nazoreans

Ebionites, from Hebrew; Ebyonim, "the poor ones", were a designation of the Nazorean sect after the death of James. They are first reported in the Pella area where the Nazoreans fled after the death of James. There have seldom been a richer people on earth than the Ebionites. They possessed vast treasuries of truth, secret scrolls, and hidden Mysteries. Outwardly, however, they were individually poor like their Buddhist monk cousins who had consecrated all their wealth to the monastery.

Few writings of the Ebionites have survived. The Recognitions of Clement and the Clementine Homilies are regarded by general scholarly consensus as largely or entirely Jewish-Christian, and specifically Ebionite, in origin. The main source for our knowledge of the literature and ideas of the Ebionites

---

[548] Refutation Of All Heresies V:7
[549] So Celsus according to Origen Against Celsus 5.62.

comes from brief quotations from their writings by orthodox Christian theologians such as Irenaeus, Hippolytus, Tertullian, and Epiphanius of Salamis, who erroneously considered the Ebionites to be heretics. The most complete of these comes from Epiphanius of Salamis, who wrote his "Panarion" in the fourth century, denouncing 80 heretical sects, among them the Ebionites, described in Panarion 30.

Epiphanius wrote in his Panarion 16:9 that some Ebionites maintained that Paul was a Greek who pretended conversion to Sadducean Judaism in order to marry the High Priest's daughter, and then apostatized when she rejected him.

All these sources within mainstream Christianity agree that the Ebionites denied the divinity of the earthly Jesus' body, the doctrine of the Trinity, the Virgin Birth and the death of Jesus as atonement for the Original Sin. Epiphanius describes them as opposing animal sacrifice and as vegetarians. All these are in harmony with the teachings of the Gnostic Nazoreans.

Epiphanius quotes their gospel as ascribing the words to Jesus, "I have come to destroy the sacrifices"[550], and as ascribing to Jesus rejection of the Passover meat. [551]This is in agreement with numerous passages found in the Recognitions and Homilies. [552]

According to Irenaeus, in Against Heresy (ca. 180-199 CE), the Ebionites were strict adherents of the Law of Moses. This of course was the Nazorean oral Law, not the dark Jewish one:

> "Those who are called Ebionites agree that the world was made by God; but their opinions with respect to the Lord are similar to those of Cerinthus and Carpocrates. They use the Gospel

---

[550] Panarion 30.16.5
[551] Panarion 30.22.4
[552] Recognitions 1.36, 1.54, Homilies 3.45, 7.4, 7.8

according to Matthew only, the Gospel of the Ebionites, and repudiate the Apostle Paul, maintaining that he was an apostate from the law. As to the prophetical writings, they endeavor to expound them in a somewhat singular manner: they practice circumcision, persevere in the observance of those customs which are enjoined by the law, and are so Judaic in their style of life, that they even adore Jerusalem as if it were the house of God" [553]

Circumcision and adoration of Jerusalem are not in harmony with Gnostic Nazoreanism. The Ebionites also held the view that Yeshu was fully human and that he became the Son of God only at his baptism by John the Baptist. Jerome cited the Hebrews account of the baptism is described in this way:

"According to the Gospel written in Hebrew speech, which the Nazoreans read, the whole fount of the Holy Spirit shall descend upon him. . . Further in the Gospel which we have just mentioned we find the following written: And it came to pass when the Lord was come up out of the water, the whole fount of the Holy Spirit descended upon him and rested on him and said to him: My Son, in all the prophets was I waiting for thee that thou shouldest come and I might rest in thee. For thou art my rest; thou art my first-begotten Son that reignest for ever." [554]

Epiphanius also quotes from the Gospel According to the Hebrews' account of Yeshu's baptism:

"And after much is said in the Gospel it continues: "After the people had been baptized Jesus also came and was baptized by John. And when he ascended from the water the heavens opened and he saw the Holy Spirit in the form of a dove descending and coming to him. And a voice from heaven said: 'Thou art my beloved Son, in thee I am well pleased,' and next: 'This day I have generated thee.' And suddenly a great light

---

[553] (Against Herersies, Book I, Chapter 26, Paragraph 2
[554] Jerome, In Is. 11,2

shone about that place. When John saw it, they say, he said to him: 'Who art thou Lord?' And again a voice came from heaven which said to him: 'This is my beloved Son, in whom I am well pleased.' After this, it says, John fell down before him and said: 'I pray thee, Lord, baptize thou me.' But he withstood him and said: 'Let it be, since so it is necessary that everything will be fulfilled'.[555]

Ebionites may have derived their name from this beautiful Aramaic Gnostic Psalm, called the Ebionite, or Poor One:

"A poor one am I, who has come out of the celestial fruits. A stranger to the world, who comes out of the distance. A Poor man am I, to whom Great Life gave ear, a Stranger to this world, whom the Light-treasures made world-strange. They brought me out of the abode of the good ones; ah me! in the wicked ones' dwelling they made me to dwell. Ah me! they made me to dwell in the wicked ones' dwelling, which is filled full of nothing but evil. It is filled full of nothing but evil, filled full of the fire which consumes. I would not and will not dwell in the dwelling of naughtiness. With my power and with my enlightening I dwelt in the dwelling of naughtiness. With my enlightening and my praise-giving I kept myself stranger to this world. I stood among them as a child who has not a father, As a child who has not a father, as a fruit who has not a tender. I hear the voice of the Seven, who whisper in secret and say: Whence is this Stranger man, whose discourse is not like to our discourse? I listened not to their discourse; then were they full of wicked anger against me. Life, who gave ear to my call, a Messenger sent forth to meet me. He sent me a gentle Treasure, an armored, well-armored Man. With his pure voice he makes proclamation, as the Treasures make in the House of Perfection. He speaks Poor one, from anguish and fear be thou free Say not: I stand here alone. For thy. sake, 0 Poor, this firmament was outspread, Was this firmament spread out, and stars were pictured upon it. For thy sake, 0 Poor, this firm land came into existence, Came into existence this firm land, the condensing took form, fell into the

---

water. For thy sake came the sun, for thy sake the moon was revealed. For thy sake, 0 Poor, came the Seven, and the Twelve are hither descended. Thou Poor one! On thy right rests glory, on thy left rest [light-] lamps. Hold steadfast in thy security, until thy measure has been completed. When thy measure has been completed, I will myself come to thee. I will bring thee vestures of glory, so that the worlds will long for them, desireful. I will bring thee a pure, excellent head-dress, abundant in infinite light. I will set thee free from the wicked, from the sinners will I deliver thee. I will make thee dwell in thy shekinah free thee into the region unsullied." I hear the voice of the Seven, who whisper in secret and speak: "Blessed is he who is to the Poor one a father, who is unto the Fruit a tender. Hail to him whom Great Life knows, woe to him whom Great Life knows not." Hail to him whom Great Life knew, who has kept himself stranger to this world, The world of the defect, in which the Planets are seated. They sit on thrones of rebellion and drill their works with the scourge. For gold and for silver are they disquiet, and strife they cast into the world. Disquiet are they and therein cast strife; therefore will they go hence and seethe in the fire. The wicked shall seethe, and their pomp shall vanish and come to an end. But I with my offspring and kindred shall ascend and see the Light's region, The region whose sun never sets, and whose light-lamps never darken-That region, the state [of the Blessed), whereto your souls are called and invited. And so are our good brothers' souls, and the souls of our faithful sisters. 'Life is exalted and is victorious1 and victorious is the One who has come hither."[556]

It is probable that Epiphanius is mistaken as to the Ebionites practicing physical circumcision and adoring Jerusalem since Epiphanius is writing from hearsay about this sect several centuries later. This is likely since the Nazorean and Ebionite observance of the oral Gnostic Law of Moses was usually misunderstood by the Greco Romans who lumped them together with the circumcising Jews of Palestine. The

---

[556] The Canonical Prayerbook of the Mandaeans (Leiden: Brill, 1959). ES Drower

Nazoreans did indeed practice what they called spiritual circumcision which had nothing to do with removing the foreskin of the penis. The term Ebionite seems to be a designation of Gnostic Nazoreans after their migration as a body northward into Syria and before they were known as Elchasaites after 100 AD.

Elchasai

Around 100 AD, according to Epiphanius in his Panarion, there lived an Ossaean prophet, by the name of Elchasai, who was married, and was accepted by both the Ossaeans and the Nasaraeans as a prophet. He "introduced" the "oaths" to the substances of salt, water, earth, bread, heaven, aether, and wind; with seven "witnesses": sky, water, holy spirits, angels of prayer, the olive, salt, and earth. Elchasai came to prominence among the Nazoreans, and became their leader, at the time of the death of Simeon the brother of Yeshu. Elchasai and his brother Yexai would have been from a younger generation than Yeshu, James, and Simeon who had all been siblings as well as leaders of the Nazoreans from 30 AD to 100 AD. Epiphanius quotes from the "Book of Elchasai" as follows:

> "My sons, go not to the image of the fire, for ye err; for this image is error. Thou seest it [the fire], he says, very near, yet is it from afar. Go not to its image; but go rather to the voice of the water!" [557]

This appears a warning to stay far from the animal sacrifices of the Jews and ever close to the mystical immersion of the Essenes. Some say that:

---

[557] Haer.," Xix. 3

"In 1415 the Church of Rome took an extraordinary step to destroy all knowledge of two second century Jewish books that it said contained the true name of Jesus Christ. The Antipope Benedict XIII firstly singled out for condemnation a secret Latin treatise called "Mar Yesu" and then issued instructions to destroy all copies of the book of Elchasai. The Rabbinic fraternity once held the destroyed manuscripts with great reverence for they were comprehensive original records reporting the life of Rabbi Jesus."[558]

G. R. S. Mead, in 1903, claimed that Elchasai was the Holy Ghost and Yexai was Yeshu:

"I, therefore, conclude with no rash confidence, that Elchasai, the Hidden Power, was in reality one of the many names of the Sophia or Wisdom, the Holy Ghost, the mystic sister or spouse (the Shakti as Brahmanical mysticism calls it) of the Masculine One, the Christ. And this is borne out by the main apocalyptic fragment of the Book which has survived among the few quotations made by Hippolytus and Epiphanius, and which is in the form of a vision of the Christ and Sophia as of two immense beings, reaching from earth to highest heaven, of which the mystic dimensions are given, just as in the diagram of the Heavenly Man, as portrayed in the apocalypse of Marcus. But we have not yet done with the matter, for Epiphanius tells us that Elchasai, who, as we have seen, he takes for a man, and a dangerous and blasphemous heretic to boot, had a brother called Iexaios ("Haer.," xix. 1), and in another place ("Haer.," liii. 1), he further informs us that the Sampsaeans said they possessed another book, which they regarded with very great reverence, namely, the "Book of Iexai," the brother of Elchasai. [559]

Mead is not correct, however, for the later Gnostic prophet Mani, who grew up in Elchasai's sect reading Elchasai's books, spoke of him being a man other than Yeshu:

---

[558] Bible Fraud' By Tony Bushby
[559] Did Jesus Live 100 B.C.? By G. R. S. Mead

"For Elchasai, the founder of your Law, points this out: when he was going to bathe in the waters, a image of a man appeared to him from the source of the waters, saying to him: "Is it not enough that your animals injure me, but do you yourself also mistreat me without reason and profane my waters ?" So Elchasai marveled and) said to it: "Fornication, defilement, and impurity of the world are thrown into you and you do not refuse (them), but are you grieved with me?" It said to him: "Granting that all these have not recognized me (as to) who I am, you, who say that you are a servant and righteous, why have you not guarded my honor? And then Elchasai was upset and did not bathe in the waters." [560]

The affect of this Book of Elchasai should not be under estimated.

Elchasai and Yexai's Books

Epiphanius tells us that the "Sampsaeans"[561] said they possessed another book, which they regarded with very great reverence, namely, the "Book of Yexai," the brother of Elchasai." [562] This book is not known to have survived, at least under this title. Part of Elchasai's book has probably survived in the second part of "The Great Revelation", an early Nazorean text redacted about 640 A.D. by a Mandaean named Rumuia. In the "Tafsir Pagra", or "Explanation of the Body" the giant mystical body of Adam Qadmon is discussed in some length.

Hyppolitus, in his Refutation of all Heresies writes negatively on the Elchasaites and the vision of 96 mile high Yeshu and Miryam contained therein. The practices of the Elchasaites

---

[560] Concerning The Origin Of His Body
[561] Probably a corruption of the Aramaic name for Baptists.
[562] Did Jesus Live 100 B.C.? By G. R. S. Mead

were learned from Yeshu, so we will quote in full that which
remains of his book:

> "The doctrine of this Callistus having been noised abroad
> throughout the entire world, a cunning man, and full of
> desperation, one called Alcibiades, dwelling in Apamea, a city of
> Syria, examined carefully into this business. And considering
> himself a more formidable character, and more ingenious in
> such tricks, than Callistus, he repaired to Rome; and he brought
> some book, alleging that a certain just man, Elchasai, had
> received this from Serae, a town of Parthia, and that he gave it to
> one called Sobiai. [563]

This negative diatribe is Hyppolitus' attempt to discredit the
person who brought the Book of Elchasai to Rome, but he was
no doubt a faithful Elchasaite and Nazorean. Sobiai was a
disciple of Elchasai, and Mani mentions him in his writings:

> "Again he (Mani) points out that Sabbaios, the Baptist, was
> carrying vegetables to the elder of the city. And immediately
> that produce said to him: "Are you not righteous? Are you not
> pure? Why do you carry us away to the fornicators?" Thus
> Sabbaios was upset on account of what he heard and returned
> the vegetables." [564]

He next tells us of Yeshu and Miryam in their cosmic
dimensions:

> "And the contents of this volume, he alleged, had been revealed
> by an angel whose height was 24 schoenoi, which make 96 miles,
> and whose breadth is 4 schoenoi, and from shoulder to shoulder
> 6 schoenoi; and the tracks of his feet extend to the length of three
> and a half schoenoi, which are equal to fourteen miles, while the
> breadth is one schoenos and a half, and the height half a
> schoenos. And he alleges that also there is a female with him,

---

[563] Hyppolitus The Refutation Of All Heresies Book lx Xi. Precepts Of Elxai.
[564] Concerning The Origin Of His Body

whose measurement, he says, is according to the standards already mentioned. And he asserts that the male (angel) is Son of God, but that the female is called Holy Spirit. By detailing these prodigies he imagines that he confounds fools, while at the same time he utters the following sentence: "that there was preached unto men a new remission of sins in the third year of Trajan's reign."

And Elchasai determines the nature of baptism, and even this I shall explain. He alleges, as to those who have been involved in every description of lasciviousness, and filthiness, and in acts of wickedness, if only any of them be a believer, that he determines that such a one, on being converted, and obeying the book, and believing its contents, should by baptism receive remission of sins. Elchasai, however, ventured to continue these knaveries, taking occasion from the aforesaid tenet of which Callistus stood forward as a champion. For, perceiving that many were delighted at this sort of promise, he considered that he could opportunely make the attempt just alluded to. And notwithstanding we offered resistance to this, and did not permit many for any length of time to become victims of the delusion. For we carried conviction to the people, when we affirmed that this was the operation of a spurious spirit, and the invention of a heart inflated with pride, and that this one like a wolf had risen up against many wandering sheep, which Callistus, by his arts of deception, had scattered abroad. But since we have commenced, we shall not be silent as regards the opinions of this man. And, in the first place, we shall expose his life, and we shall prove that his supposed discipline is a mere pretence. And next, I shall adduce the principal heads of his assertions, in order that the reader, looking fixedly on the treatises of this (Elchasai), may be made aware what and what sort is the heresy which has been audaciously attempted by this man. [565]

Hyppolitus continues his negative innuendoes and goes on to tell us that the Elchasaites did not accept the virgin birth myth

---

[565] Hyppolitus The Refutation Of All Heresies Book Ix Xi. Precepts Of Elxai.

and understood Yeshu to have many incarnations on earth. He confuses the Elchasaite propensity to observe a simple Gnostic Law of Moses and spiritual circumcision with that of the dark law and foreskin cutting practices of the Jews:

> "This Elchasai puts forward as a decoy a polity (authorized in the) Law, alleging that believers ought to be circumcised and live according to the Law, (while at the same time) he forcibly rends certain fragments from the aforesaid heresies. And he asserts that Christ was born a man in the same way as common to all, and that Christ was not for the first time an earth when born of a virgin, but that both previously and that frequently again He had been born and would be born. Christ would thus appear and exist among us from time to time, undergoing alterations of birth, and having his soul transferred from body to body. Now Elchasai adopted that tenet of Pythagoras to which I have already alluded. But the Elchasaites have reached such an altitude of pride, that even they affirm themselves to be endued with a power of foretelling futurity, using as a starting-point, obviously, the measures and numbers of the aforesaid Pythagorean art. These also devote themselves to the tenets of mathematicians, and astrologers, and magicians, as if they were true. And they resort to these, so as to confuse silly people, thus led to suppose that the heretics participate in a doctrine of power. And they teach certain incantations and formularies for those who have been bitten by dogs, and possessed of demons, and seized with other diseases; and we shall not be silent respecting even such practices of these heretics. Having then sufficiently explained their principles, and the causes of their presumptuous attempts, I shall pass on to give an account of their writings, through which my readers will become acquainted with both the trifling and godless efforts of these Elchasaites. [566]

Hyppolitus affirms for us the Nazorean use of astrology, numerology, and other occult arts which were practiced

---

[566] Hyppolitus The Refutation Of All Heresies Book Ix Xi. Precepts Of Elxai.

before, during, and after Yeshu in all Nazorean circles. He next tells us that the Elchasaites called seven elements to witness their renewal through living water. This too was an ancient Nazorean practice, for even James' letter to Peter affirms that at baptism initiates were made to adjure: 'I take to witness heaven, earth, water, in which all things are comprehended, and in addition to all these, that, air also which pervades all things, and without which I cannot breathe, that I shall always be obedient to him who gives me the books of the preachings". Hyppolitus' account continues:

"To those, then, that have been orally instructed by him, he dispenses baptism in this manner, addressing to his dupes some such words as the following: "If, therefore, (my) children, one shall have intercourse with any sort of animal whatsoever, or a male, or a sister, or a daughter, or hath committed adultery, or been guilty of fornication, and is desirous of obtaining remission of sins, from the moment that he hearkens to this book let him be baptized a second time in the name of the Great and Most High God, and in the name of His Son, the Mighty King. And by baptism let him be purified and cleansed, and let him adjure for himself those seven witnesses that have been described in this book--the heaven, and the water, and the holy spirits, and the angels of prayer, and the oil, and the salt, and the earth." These constitute the astonishing mysteries of Elchasai, those ineffable and potent secrets which he delivers to deserving disciples. And with these that lawless one is not satisfied, but in the presence of two and three witnesses he puts the seal to his own wicked practices. Again expressing himself thus: "Again I say, O adulterers and adulteresses, and false prophets, if you are desirous of being converted, that your sins may be forgiven you, as soon as ever you hearken unto this book, and be baptized a second time along with your garments, shall peace be yours, and your portion with the just." But since we have stated that these resort to incantations for those bitten by dogs and for other mishaps, we shall explain these. Now Elchasai uses the following formulary: "If a dog rabid and furious, in which inheres a spirit of destruction, bite any man, or woman, or youth, or girl, or may worry or touch them, in the same hour let such a one run with all their wearing apparel, and go down to a river or to a fountain wherever there is a deep spot. Let (him or her) be dipped with all their wearing apparel, and offer supplication to the Great and Most High God in faith of heart, and then let him thus adjure the seven witnesses described in this book: 'Behold, I call to witness the heaven and the water, and the holy spirits, and the angels of prayer, and the oil, and the salt, and the earth. I testify by these seven witnesses that no more shall I sin, nor commit adultery, nor steal, nor be guilty of injustice, nor be covetous, nor be actuated by hatred, nor be scornful, nor shall I take pleasure in any wicked deeds.' Having uttered, therefore, these words, let such a one be baptized with the entire of his wearing apparel in the name of the Mighty and Most High God." [567]

Hyppolitus tells us that the Elchasaites practiced secrecy, multiple baptisms observed according to auspicious astrological times, as indeed the Mandaean remnants of the Elchasaites have preserved. Hyppolitus continues to mock and deride, and says further:

"But in very many other respects he talks folly, inculcating the use of these sentences also for those afflicted with consumption, and that they should be dipped in cold water forty times during seven days and he prescribes similar treatment for those possessed of devils. Oh inimitable wisdom and incantations gorged with powers! Who will not be astonished at such and such force of words? But since we have stated that they also bring into requisition astrological deceit, we shall prove this from their own formularies; for Elchasai speaks thus: "There exist wicked stars of impiety. This declaration has been now made by us, O ye pious ones and disciples: beware of the power of the days of the sovereignty of these stars, and engage not in the commencement of any undertaking during the ruling days of these. And baptize not man or woman during the days of the

---

[567] Hyppolitus The Refutation Of All Heresies Book Ix Xi. Precepts Of Elxai.

power of these stars, when the moon, (emerging) from among them, courses the sky, and travels along with them. Beware of the very day up to that on which the moon passes out from these stars, and then baptize and enter on every beginning of your works. But, moreover, honour the day of the Sabbath, since that day is one of those during which prevails (the power) of these stars. Take care, however, not to commence your works the third day from a Sabbath, since when three years of the reign of the emperor Trojan are again completed from the time that he subjected the Parthians to his own sway,--when, I say, three years have been completed, war rages between the impious angels of the northern constellations; and on this account all kingdoms of impiety are in a state of confusion." [568]

Inasmuch as (Elchasai) considers, then, that it would be an insult to reason that these mighty and ineffable mysteries should be trampled under foot, or that they should be committed to many, he advises that as valuable pearls they should be preserved, expressing himself thus: "Do not recite this account to all men, and guard carefully these precepts, because all men are not faithful, nor are all women straightforward." [569]

In his later summary of the followers of Elchasai, Hyppolitus says the Elchasaites also taught the multiple reincarnation of Yeshu:

"But certain others, introducing as it were some novel tenet, appropriated parts of their system from all heresies, and procured a strange volume, which bore on the title page the name of one Elchasai. These, in like manner, acknowledge that the principles of the universe were originated by the Deity. They do not, however, confess that there is but one Christ, but that there is one that is superior to the rest, and that He is transfused into many bodies frequently, and was now in Jesus. And, in like manner, these heretics maintain that at one time Christ was begotten of God, and at another time became the Spirit, and at

---

[568] Hyppolitus The Refutation Of All Heresies Book Ix Xi. Precepts Of Elxai
[569] Hyppolitus The Refutation Of All Heresies Book Ix Xi. Precepts Of Elxai.

another time was born of a virgin, and at another time not so. And they affirm that likewise this Jesus afterwards was continually being transfused into bodies, and was manifested in many (different bodies) at different times. And they resort to incantations and baptisms in their confession of elements. And they occupy themselves with bustling activity in regard of astrological and mathematical science, and of the arts of sorcery. But also they allege themselves to have powers of prescience."[570]

These Elchasaites represented the legitimate successors to original true Christianity. Mani's birth into their religion was no accident, even though he was destined to transform it into something entirely new. From these Elchasaites Mani no doubt learned of the concept of a Gnostic Savior figure, reincarnation, the importance of a vegetarian diet, the use of purification rituals, occult arts like healing, astrology, numerology, and Qabbalah - all of which carry over into reformed Elchasaitism, or Manichaeanism.

Nazoreans in Alexandria

There is little doubt that fully established Essene Nazorean communities existed in Egypt during the first few centuries of the Christian era. Noticeable presence of Roman Christianity is particularly lacking in Egypt. It appears that for the first few centuries Yeshu believing Egypt was almost entirely Gnostic, A strong Manichaean presence was also found in Egypt during the late third century and afterward. Certain renowned Gnostic teachers, such as Valentinius in the second century, were also associated with Alexandria.

Valentinus was born in Phrebonis in Upper Egypt about 100 AD and educated in nearby Alexandria. There he became a

---

[570] Hyppolitus The Refutation Of All Heresies Book Ix Xi. Precepts Of Elxai.

disciple of the Gnostic-Christian teacher Theudas who had been a disciple of Paul. He claimed that Theudas taught him secret wisdom that Paul had taught privately to his inner circle. Valentinus, however, was not one who followed the path of Paul. Like many early Christian mystics, Valentinus claimed that that he had a vision of the risen Christ. Following his vision, he began his career as an Apostle of Light and a Caller of Life at Alexandria around 120AD. His esoteric theology quickly attracted a large following in Egypt and Syria. In 136 AD, he went to Rome after stopping briefly in Cyprus. At Rome he quickly rose to prominence and was widely respected for his eloquence. He was so well regarded in the Roman church that in 143 AD he was a candidate for the office of bishop. It seems likely he refused the position. He continued to teach in Rome for at least ten more years. Valentinians are best known for their system of 30 Aeons.

Mani

Nazoreans and Ossaeans resettled in northern Syria, Edessa, Harran, Inner Harran. They also migrated down the Euphrates to settle in Basra and other places along the lower Tigris and Euphrates. The marshes around Basra were known to have many Elchasaites living there. Mani, predicted by Yeshu, was raised in one of these coed Elchasaite monasteries near Basra.

The enlightened master Mar Mani, peace be upon him, entered the world on April 14, 216 A.D. (Iyar 9, 3976) He was born in a little village in southern Iraq, along the Euphrates River. In his own native tongue Mani means "spirit" or "vessel" and Hayya means "living", and so Mani-Hayya's name means the "Living Spirit" or the "Vessel of Life". Mani claimed to be the restorer and synthesizer of Gnostic Nazorean Christianity, Zurvan Zoroasterism, and Mahayana Buddhism. He created a worldwide vegan church which synthesized original

Nazorean Christianity, Zarathustrianism and Buddhism and which profoundly influenced the Buddhist, Tibetan, Taoist, and Sufi traditions.

Mani died on February 26, 277 AD if his death date is correctly 6 Adar, 4037).[571]

Mani's teachings have profoundly enriched the Nazorean Way. He came to be regarded by his Christian disciples as the Paraclete, by his Persian followers as the Zoroastrian redeemer Saoshyant, and by his Buddhist adherents as the Avatar Maitreya. He is known to have invented a lyre like instrument, upon which the priests of the Manichaean communities played, and which got adopted broadly into other circles. He was reputed to have been a gifted artist, physician, astrologer and a miracle-worker. He personally illuminated and illustrated many of his original scriptures.

Historical Manichaeanism began on Sunday, 20 March, A.D. 242 (Nisan 2, 4002). It was a vibrant continuation of the ancient Nazorean Essene current vivified by Yeshu and Miryai. The Religion of Mani eventually grew into an Eastern and a Western branch, and gave birth to many subgroups such as the Mazdakians and the Mihrites in the east, and the Cathars and Bogomils in the west. During Mani's lifetime he sent out many missionaries, beginning with Adda and Patteg to Rome and Alexandria, and Mar Ammo to India and the East. The "Religion of Light" expanded rapidly in the West, in Africa, Spain, France, North Italy, the Balkans, where it survived for a thousand years. It grew even more rapidly in Mesopotamia, Babylonia, Turkestan, Northern India, Western China, and Tibet. By 1000 A.D. the bulk of the Tibetan land was said to have been Manichaeans.

---

[571] Some accounts put it 3 years earlier in 274, giving 2 veAdar, 4034 as a death date.

Mani's teaching may be summed up by his declaration he
made to the Elchasaites:

> "Therefore, make an inspection of yourselves as to what your
> purity really is. For it is impossible - to purify your bodies
> entirely--for each day the body is disturbed and comes to rest
> through the excretions of feces from it--so that the action comes
> about without a commandment from the Savior. The purity,
> then, which was spoken about, is that which comes through
> knowledge, a separation of light from darkness, of death from
> life, of living waters from turbid, so that you may know that
> each is . . . one another and . . . .the commandments of the Savior,
> so that . . . might redeem the soul from annihilation and
> destruction. This is in truth the genuine purity, which you were
> commended to do; but you departed from it and began to bathe,
> and have held on to the purification of the body, (a thing) most
> defiled and fashioned through foulness; through it (i.e., foulness)
> it (the body) was coagulated and having been founded came into
> existence.' [572]

More information on Mani's metaphysics can be had in the
third volume to this series, entitled: "Buddha-Messiahs,
Vol. III: Mani, Christian Buddha and Taoist Sage".

Later Successors

After the rise of Elchasai and Mani the influence of the
Desposyni are still heard of. They did not disappear
immediately after the demise of Simeon, as is attested by
Hegessipus's statement that the grandsons of Judas were still
"leaders of the churches" during the reign of Domitian.
Nevertheless, with the rapid spread of Christianity throughout
the empire and its eventual appointment by Constantine as the

---

[572] Concerning The Origin Of His Body

official religion of the empire, Palestinian "Christianity" found itself marginalized and cursed more and more in western Roman Christianity. By the beginning of the fourth century, neither the Bishop of Jerusalem nor the Desposyni in general played any important role in the political developments of the west that led Constantine to recognize Sylvester, the non Desposyni Bishop of Rome, as holding the position of leadership among the bishops of the Christian religion.

It is interesting to note that in 318 C.E. a delegation of Palestinian Desposyni who presided over branches of the church met with the new Pope in Rome at the Lateran Palace and urged him to recognize the preeminence of Jerusalem, return to the custom of the payment of tithes to the church at Jerusalem, and to replace Greek bishops with ones selected from the Desposyni. Sylvester, having the support of the Roman government to back his status as the primary bishop, was not disposed to subordinate himself to the Jewish Christians of Palestine and declined their requests. "The emperor provided sea transport as far as Ostia for eight of them and then they rode on donkeys to Rome and the Lateran where Sylvester now lived in splendor. They wore rough woolen clothes, with leather boots and hats. The conversation was in Greek as they spoke Aramaic and had no Latin, and Sylvester spoke no Aramaic."[573]

Thereafter, Palestinian Christianity plays no influential role in the history of the Gentile Christian church and for all intents and purposes, it is a different religion all together. Yet the Nazorean faith, the only true form of Yeshu's religion, quietly carried on. Eusubius lists the successor to Symeon as Justus and says that all of the bishops of Jerusalem were Desposyni, or relatives of Yeshu, until 135 AD. After this date Elchasaites continued to flourish along the Euphrates and in 216 A.D was

---

[573] Roman Catholic historian Malachi Martin

born Mani the Paraclete who revitalized Yeshu's Gnosticism for another thousand years.

ˉ 20 ˉ
ҺEARSAY & ҺERESY

Ꝑaul's ҺERESY Ꝑredicted

THE IMPORTANT TEXT, the Apocalypse of Peter from the Nag Hammadi library, speaks of a falling away from original Nazorean Christianity. This is important because if there was a full falling away, then no church claiming to go all the way back to early Christianity can be a true church! This not only discredits Roman Catholicism and Eastern orthodox Traditions, but also all other reformation and protestant sects which simply reformed a portion of these older traditions. The text begins:

> "As the Savior was sitting in the temple in the three hundredth (year) of the covenant and the agreement of the tenth pillar[574], and being satisfied with the number of the living, incorruptible Majesty, he said to me . . . . I have told you that these (people) are blind and deaf. Now then, listen to the things which they are

---

[574] This is most likely a reference to King Asoka (239-23 B.C.), the third emperor of the Mauryan dynasty of India. He came to the throne in 264 BC., approximately 300 years before the public ministry and death of Yeshu (Jesus, circe 35 A.D.). Asoka renounced war, became a Buddhist and erected ten pillars inscribed with his edicts, one of which said: "Here (in my domain) no living beings are to be slaughtered or offered in sacrifice." If vegetarian non sacrificing Nazoreans like Yeshu and Peter wished to date their activities with reference to a worldly power, it makes some sense that they would choose a worldly power like Ashoka who was in harmony with their ideals and ethics. In that day and age there was not a universal system of dating, as exists in the modern world. Time was kept via reference to the reigns of various kings. Nazoreans would not have been keen on dating their documents with the reigns of the corrupt Jewish kings. They would have preferred to invoke the rule of a more benevolent ruler such as Asoka. They would have known about Ashoka from their own travels to India and from Ashoka's missionaries which he sent all over the then known world, including Egypt, Israel, and Syria. Asoka even created at least two inscriptions in the Nazoreans native tongue - Aramaic. One of these is in both Greek and Aramaic at the old city of Kandahar in southern Afghanistan and would have been known to the Nazorean Essenes since Kandahar dominated the southern route from India to the areas farther west.

telling you in a mystery, and guard them, Do not tell them to the sons of this age. For they shall blaspheme you in these ages since they are ignorant of you, but they will praise you in knowledge. For many will accept our teaching in the beginning. And they will turn from them again by the will of the Father of their error, because they have done what he wanted."[575]

The Savior warns Peter that their teachings are about to be corrupted by those who love death rather than Life. Yeshu warns that they shall begin to trust in the name of a dead man, perhaps referring to Pauline Christianity's trust in the name of Jesus which is here distinguished from the name of Yeshu the Living One.

"And he will reveal them in his judgment, i.e., the servants of the Word. But those who became mingled with these shall become their prisoners, since they are without perception. And the guileless, good, pure one they push to the worker of death, and to the kingdom of those who praise Christ in a restoration. And they praise the men of the propagation of falsehood, those who will come after you. And they will cleave to the name of a dead man, thinking that they will become pure. But they will become greatly defiled and they will fall into a name of error, and into the hand of an evil, cunning man and a manifold dogma, and they will be ruled without law.[576]

The alteration of the Nazorean culture is in full accord with ancient Nazorean beliefs:

"He (Yeshu) and his companions behaved constantly in this manner, until he left this world. He said to his companions: "Act as you have seen me act, instruct people in accordance with instructions I have given you, and be for them what I have been for you." His companions behaved constantly in this manner and in accordance with this. And so did those who came after the

---

[575] Apocalypse Of Peter
[576] Apocalypse Of Peter

first generation of his companions, and also those who came long after. Then they began to make changes and alterations, to introduce innovations into the religion, to seek dominion, to make friends with people by indulging their passions, to try to circumvent the Judeans and to satisfy the anger which they felt against the latter, even if in doing so they had to abandon the religion. This is clear from the Gospels which are with them and to which they refer and from their book, known as the Book of Acts. It is written there: A group of Christians left Jerusalem and came to Antioch and other towns of Syria." [577]

Roman Christianity has gained the ascendancy in western culture as the one and only version of Christianity, but anciently there was another equally viable interpretation of Christ and His Teachings. The pre Christ polar opposition between Judaism and Nazoreanism was reflected after Christ by the polarity between Pauline and Gnostic (Nazorean) Christianity.

This original group of Nazorean disciples had firsthand knowledge of what Yeshu and Miryai had taught and stood for, and were holding to the original vision. The non-Nazorean "Jewish-Christians", or Roman Christians, and the "Gentile Christians", on the other hand, did not have or want the firsthand knowledge possessed by the original Nazoreans, but instead preferred creating their own myths concerning the Christ. This led to conflict and eventual persecution of the Nazoreans. The more powerful and numerous gentile Christians eventually removed most vestiges of the original Nazorean Way from their gentile version, and what little was left of the original Nazorean Way was only partially preserved by the monastic orders which slowly began to arise as the Nazoreans were persecuted into extinction. These monastic orders were highly Judaized by their use of Jewish Psalms. Those of Egypt had quite a time competing with the Gnostic

---

monastic orders who used the Manichaean Psalms. So many defections occurred to the Gnostics because of the superiority of their psalms over those of the Christians. Anthony, alive in 305 AD, was known for forbidding his monks to have any contact with Manichaeans since so many of them were being converted by the Manichaean Psalms which are so much more beautiful and inspiring than the poorer and meaner Jewish Christian Psalms.

Due to rapid growth and a general "Diaspora" dispersion due to persecution and other factors, original Nazoreans quickly divided into numerous and varied factions and groups. The small central core of original Yeshu-Miryai disciples, attempting to live a pure Essene communal life, were quickly outnumbered by vast conversions from non-essene circles. These gentile converts, with their Roman and Greek customs and lifestyles, eventually rejected the original Nazorean Way in favor of their own adaptation and revision of the original Gospel. When they gained political power after 135 A.D. they rewrote history and altered their previously forged New Testament in a manner fitting their own divergent views and lifestyles, rendering their religion as only a shadow of its original parent. They successfully destroyed, or drastically altered, most of the original writings and customs of the earliest disciples. This fulfilled a prophecy that the Times of the Gentiles would hold sway until an eventual resurgence and return of the true Israelite Essene Nazorean Ebionite Way. The resultant tradition became Pauline, or Roman Christianity. The following quote from the Proofs on the pact between the Pauline School of Christianity and the Roman Government and culture is in full accord with ancient Nazorean beliefs:

> "The Romans reigned over them. The Christians used to complain to the Romans about the Judeans, showed them their own weakness and appealed to their pity. And the Romans did pity them. This used to happen frequently. And the Romans said

to the Christians: "Between us and the Judeans there is a pact which obliges us not to change their religious laws. But if you would abandon their laws and separate yourselves from them, praying as we do while facing the East, eating the things we eat, and regarding as permissible that which we consider as such, we should help you and make you powerful, and the Judeans would find no way to harm you, On the contrary, you would be more powerful than they. The Christians answered: "We will do this."" 578

The Saviour continues and speaks of the seed of darkness, the non Gnostics, who fail to comprehend the light but which nevertheless claim to possess its true religion:

"For some of them will blaspheme the truth and proclaim evil teaching. And they will say evil things against each other. Some will be named: (those) who stand in (the) strength of the archons, of a man and a naked woman who is manifold and subject to much suffering. And those who say these things will ask about dreams. And if they say that a dream came from a demon worthy of their error, then they shall be given perdition instead of incorruption. For evil cannot produce good fruit. For the place from which each of them is produces that which is like itself; for not every soul is of the truth, nor of immortality. For every soul of these ages has death assigned to it in our view, because it is always a slave, since it is created for its desires and their eternal destruction, in which they are and from which they are. They love the creatures of the matter which came forth with them. But the immortal souls are not like these, O Peter. But indeed, as long as the hour is not yet come, it (the immortal soul) shall resemble a mortal one. But it shall not reveal its nature, that it alone is the immortal one, and thinks about immortality, having faith, and desiring to renounce these things. For people do not gather figs from thorns or from thorn trees, if they are wise, nor grapes from thistles. For, on the one hand, that which is always becoming is in that from which it is, being from what is not good, which becomes destruction for it and death. But that

---

578 The Establishment of Proofs . . . by 'Abd al-Jabbar

which comes to be in the Eternal One is in the One of the life and the immortality of the life which they resemble. Therefore all that which exists not will dissolve into what exists not. For deaf and blind ones join only with their own kind." [579]

The Saviour warns Peter further:

"But others shall change from evil words and misleading mysteries. Some who do not understand mystery speak of things which they do not understand, but they will boast that the mystery of the truth is theirs alone. And in haughtiness they shall grasp at pride, to envy the immortal soul which has become a pledge. For every authority, rule, and power of the aeons wishes to be with these in the creation of the world, in order that those who are not, having been forgotten by those that are, may praise them, though they have not been saved, nor have they been brought to the Way by them, always wishing that they may become imperishable ones. For if the immortal soul receives power in an intellectual spirit -. But immediately they join with one of those who misled them." [580]

The Saviour warns Peter further of the non Gnostics who shall come and set up a false counterfeit religion, condemn dualism, and charge money for their false teachings, and create much negative karma. Yeshu also speaks of someone creating an imitation religion, someone named Hermes which is a title for the "apostle" Paul in the new Testament and also the Greek name for the planet Mercury on which the Nazorean tradition would blame the false teachings of false Christianity on: "The third is Nbti (Mercury/Hermes), the false messiah which is a distortion the original worship." [581]

"But many others, who oppose the truth and are the messengers of error, will set up their error and their law against these pure

[579] Apocalypse of Peter
[580] Apocalypse of Peter
[581] Ginza Rba 1

thoughts of mine, as looking out from one (perspective) thinking that good and evil are from one (source). They do business in my word. And they will propagate harsh fate (karma). The race of immortal souls will go in it in vain, until my Parousia (coming). For they shall come out of them - and my forgiveness of their transgressions, into which they fell through their adversaries, whose ransom I got from the slavery in which they were, to give them freedom that they may create an imitation remnant in the name of a dead man, who is Hermas, of the first-born of unrighteousness, in order that the light which exists may not believed by the little ones. But those of this sort are the workers who will be cast into the outer darkness, away from the sons of light. For neither will they enter, nor do they permit those who are going up to their approval for their release. [582]

Yeshu here seems to prophecy of false ascetics, both monk orders and nun orders, saying:

"And still others of them who suffer think that they will perfect the wisdom of the brotherhood which really exists, which is the spiritual fellowship of those united in communion, through which the wedding of incorruptibility shall be revealed. The kindred race of the sisterhood will appear as an imitation. These are the ones who oppress their brothers, saying to them, "Through this our God has pity, since salvation comes to us through this," not knowing the punishment of those who are made glad by those who have done this thing to the little ones whom they saw, (and) whom they took prisoner." [583]

Here Yeshu speaks of the false priesthood that arose outside of the Nazorean tradition in Pauline Christianity, a dead lineage still adhered to by Rome and its break offs:

"And there shall be others of those who are outside our number who name themselves bishop and also deacons, as if they have

---

[582] Apocalypse of Peter
[583] Apocalypse of Peter

received their authority from God. They bend themselves under the judgment of the leaders. Those people are dry canals."

But I said " I am afraid because of what you have told me, that indeed little (ones) are, in our view, the counterfeit ones, indeed, that there are multitudes that will mislead other multitudes of living ones, and destroy them among themselves. And when they speak your name they will be believed." [584]

This reminds one of the passages in the Doctrine of Kings 30:

"The Yardna (Path) in which Messiah Paulis ("Apostle" Paul) was baptized have I made into a "cesspool" (dead religion).

The bread which Messiah Paulis (Pauline Christians) receive have I made into "sacrament" (false sacrament). The drink which Messiah Paulis receives, have I made into a "supper" (false eucharist). The headband which Messiah Paulis receives, have I made into a "priesthood" (priestcraft). The staff which Messiah Paulis receives, have I made into a "dung-stick" (Bishop's Crosier). Gnosis of Life (Yeshu Messiah) speaks: Let me warn you, my brothers, let me warn you, my beloved! Let me warn you, my brothers, against the [....]who are like unto the cross. They lay it on the walls; then stand there and bow down to the woodblock. Let me warn you, my brothers, of the god (Roman theology), which the carpenters have joined together. If the carpenter has joined together the god, who then has joined together the carpenter?"

Yeshu then sums up, speaking of the duration of this darkness until a restoration comes through the reincarnation and efforts of the "never-aging one" who is to come, saying:

"The Saviour said, "For a time determined for them in proportion to their error they will rule over the little ones. And after the completion of the error, the never-aging one of the immortal understanding shall become young, and they (the little ones) shall rule over those who are their rulers. The root of their

[584] Apocalypse of Peter

error he shall pluck out, and he shall put it to shame so that it shall be manifest in all the impudence which it has assumed to itself. And such ones shall become unchangeable, O Peter. Come therefore, let us go on with the completion of the will of the incorruptible Father. For behold, those who will bring them judgment are coming, and they will put them to shame. But me they cannot touch. And you, O Peter, shall stand in their midst. Do not be afraid because of your cowardice. Their minds shall be closed, for the invisible one has opposed them. . . . When he (Jesus) had said these things, he (Peter) came to himself." [585]

Paul's Bible

From accounts of attitudes of Christ's followers in Judea, and later Manichaean sources we know that early true followers of Yeshu did not accept the Pauline School's New Testament as authentic. The Gnostic Manichaean's said:

"We have proved again and again, the writings are not the production of Christ or of His apostles, but a compilation of rumors and beliefs, made, long after their departure, by some obscure semi-Jews, not in harmony even with one another, and published by them under the name of the apostles, or of those considered the followers of the apostles, so as to give the appearance of apostolic authority to all these blunders and falsehoods."[586]

These writings of Paul's do not mention much of Jesus or of James and Peter except in a negative light. Paul tells us a few things about Yeshu, but not much. The Acts and Gospels produced later by his school mention Peter and James only in negative condescending terms, and present a made-up miracle Christ whose words are distorted and his acts fantasized. Paul

---

[585] Apocalypse of Peter
[586] Faustus, Contra Faustus Manicheun

openly opposed all the original followers of Yeshu, especially Peter, as he says in Galatians:

"But when Peter was come to Antioch, I withstood him to the face, because he was to be blamed" [587]

Paul's New Scripture

During the first few years, the Pauline Christianity School just used the epistles of Paul. After having their request to get the Nazorean scriptures rejected, they were forced to produce their own. They eventually made up the New Testament:

"As for those who had given a favorable answer to the Romans they came together and took counsel as to how to replace the Gospel, seeing that it was lost to them. Thus the opinion that a Gospel should be composed was established among them. They said: "the Torah consists only of narratives concerning the births of the prophets and of the histories of their lives. We are going to construct a Gospel according to this pattern. Everyone among us is going to call to mind that which he remembers of the words of the Gospel and of the things about which the Christians talked among themselves when speaking of Christ."

Recycling Bible Stories

Nazoreans after Yeshu had their own set of scriptures, but the Roman Christians did not. All they had was an unauthorized private short letter recounting some of the public words of Peter and Barnabas. So, according to their plan articulated in the "Proofs", they created their own gospel stories by expanding this letter based on Elijah myths only slightly reworked. One writer has written:

[587] Gal.2:11

"The early Christians drew upon the one source that they held to be infallible - the Old Testament. They felt quite justified in taking stories from the Old Testament and applying them to Jesus. After all, they knew that the Old Testament was full of coded 'prophecies' and that they could, if they examined them cleverly enough, work out what Jesus must have done. They certainly never needed to ask eyewitnesses what happened. Why should they, when they had a written record, in the Old Testament, of Jesus's life? All they had to do was tidy up a few of the miracle stories, exaggerate the numbers and they had ready-made miracles for Jesus to have done. Rewriting old books to create new books is a well-known Biblical technique. The books of Chronicles were pieced together from the books of Kings. It is no surprise that this process continued into New Testament times. It wasn't just Old Testament stories that were reworked. Of the 661 verses in Mark's Gospel, Matthew used 607 of them."[588]

The extent to which they fashioned their gospels after the Torah pattern is amazing. They used the Elijah-Elisha stories the most, only slightly revamping them and changing a word here and there.

"Accordingly, some people wrote a Gospel. After them came others who wrote another Gospel. In this manner a certain number of Gospels were written. However a great part of what was contained in the original was missing in them. There were among them men, one after another, who knew many things that were contained in the true Gospel, but with a view to establishing their dominion, they refrained from communicating them. In all this there was no mention of the cross or of the crucifix. According to them there were eighty Gospels. However, their number constantly diminished and became less, until only four Gospels were left which are due to four individuals. Every one of them composed in his time a Gospel. Then another came after him, saw that the Gospel composed by his predecessor was imperfect, and composed another which according to him was more correct, nearer to correction than the Gospel of the others. . . . .These sects are of the opinion that these four Evangelists were companions and disciples of Christ. But they do not know, having no information on the subject, who they were. On this point they can merely make a claim."[589]

Betrayal of Peter's Trust

As we mentioned before, Peter was very explicit that his teachings, and indeed all the scriptures and scrolls of the Nazoreans, be kept back from the non Nazorean branches of Christianity which were already corrupting, changing and altering the texts and message. Peter and James had entered into an agreement that prohibited anyone from self publishing their version of the life of Yeshu. Implicit in this agreement was the fact that James would have to okay all texts, as well as those they were given to. Among these were true Nazoreans scrolls like the Gospel of Thomas and of the Nazoreans which had been approved by James and Miryai and which were being circulated within appropriate circles.

The first Greek gospel to be written was a rudimentary Mark around 59 AD. This was not a text validated by the Nazorean central leadership. Earliest Mark was apparently written as a letter with Barnabas and Peter's collaboration, then expanded a bit and circulated privately amongst a few. This would have been near the end of Peter's life, some 22 years after Peter's request to James to keep back the more secret sacred scrolls from the uninitiated. During these two decades Peter would have been asked to recount, over and over again, what details he could remember of the acts and sayings of Yeshu so many years before. These comments would have been repeated, sometimes inaccurately, and added to by other stories from

---

[589] The Establishment Of Proofs . . . By 'Abd Al-Jabbar

other sources, creating a hodge podge of tales and accounts of Yeshu. It is understandable that near the end of his life, Peter would not condemn a private unpublished account of his own version of events. Peter did not have the will or authority to authorize their publication, however. After James and Peter's death in the 60's, these notes were greatly expanded, perhaps without the approval of those who had replaced James as administrative head of the Order. They were circulated about and influenced other unauthorized texts based upon them. From early Mark came later editions of Mark as well as the book of Luke and all the others. Their unauthorized evolution into the present Biblical accounts was one of the things that Peter did not want to happen. Peter had apparently tolerated the existence of Mark's notes being shared with a few. He would not have authorized its publishing or its expansion and altering to become what it now is. Papias, the bishop of Hierapolis A.D. 140, wrote in his last work:

> "The Elder said this also: Mark, who became Peter's interpreter, wrote accurately, though not in order, all that he remembered of the things said or done by the Lord. For he had neither heard the Lord nor been one of his followers, but afterwards, as I said, he had followed Peter, who used to compose his discourses with a view to the needs of his hearers, but not as though he were drawing up a connected account of the Lord's sayings. So Mark made no mistake in thus recording some things just as he remembered them. For he was careful of this one thing, to omit none of the things he had heard and to make no untrue statements therein."[590]

So this first biblical "gospel", upon which all the others are based, was written by someone who "had neither heard the Lord nor been one of his followers". Papias, when defending his scribal tradition, stresses that Mark didn't add or take anything away from Peter's words, but this is most certainly

---
[590] Exegesis Of The Lord's Oracles

false in regards to later editions of the book. Papias is probably making this claim because already those who knew the truth are questioning the exaggerations and fables of the text which was embellished again and again and so different from the true accounts by the true Nazorean sect. This continual revision and revamping of the sacred scrolls was one of the reasons why Peter had warned against their dissemination among the ignorant masses.

> "Our Peter has strictly and becomingly charged us concerning the establishing of the truth, that we should not communicate the books of his preachings, which have been sent to us, to any one at random, but to one who is good and religious, and who wishes to teach, and who is circumcised, and faithful. And these are not all to be committed to him at once; that, if he be found injudicious in the first, the others may not be entrusted to him. Wherefore let him be proved not less than six years.[591]

Near the end of Peter's life, Clement of Alexandria tells us more of these private notes of Mark. We are told that Peter tolerated such once he discovered it:

> "But again in those very books Clement presented a tradition of the original elders about the disposition of the gospels, in the following manner: He said that those gospels with genealogies were openly published, but Mark had this procedure: when Peter was in Rome preaching in public the word and proclaiming the gospel by the spirit, those present, who were many, entreated Mark, as one who followed him for a long time and remembered what was said, to record what was spoken; but after he composed the gospels, he shared it with anyone who wanted it; when Peter found out about it, he did not actively discourage or encourage it; but John, last, aware that the physical facts were disclosed in the gospels, urged by friends, and inspired by the Spirit, composed a spiritual gospel."[592]

---

[591] Epistle of Peter to James, Homilees of Clement
[592] Hypotyposeis apud Eusebius, Hist. eccl. 6.14.5-7

Clement testifies that Mark's text was initially distributed to a limited number of people without the awareness or endorsement of Peter or James. This means it was not an authorized text. Since it originally contained only notes of Peter's public speeches, it was tolerated in private circulation but not sanctioned. It did not contain the more serious and esoteric teachings which Peter gave to initiates and which James had agreed to keep secret. This privately circulated document penned by Mark was later used to create Luke which was circulated publicly, but again, probably without endorsement and approval of James' successor. A later expanded version of Mark was redacted and published and was used to create Matthew as well as John. None of these must have been sanctioned since we are told that the Nazorean Ebionites under James did not use any of them! Had the Nazorean leadership endorsed these projects, the Nazoreans would have embraced them. Even if unendorsed, if they had turned out wonderfully, they would have been reluctantly accepted anyway. The fact that Ebionites continued to reject them is good cause to dismiss them as erroneous.

> "These men thought that it was necessary to reject all the epistles of the apostle, whom they called an apostate from the Law and they used only the so-called Gospel of the Hebrews making little account of the others."[593]

These biblical gospels totally miss the point of what Yeshu taught and stood for. They are of little use to those who are truly seeking after the kingdom of light. But because so many consider them the definitive word on the truth, we will delve into them a bit more.

Mark First Draft

---

[593] Eusebius, Ecclesiastical History, 3.27.4.

An ancient prologue to Mark from the late second century says:

> "...Mark declared, who is called 'stumb-fingered' because he had short fingers in comparison with the size of the rest of his body. He was Peter's interpreter. After the death of Peter himself he wrote down this same gospel in the regions of Italy."[594]

According to Cayce:

> "Mark was first dictated greatly by Peter. And this in those periods just before Peter was carried to Rome. " [595]

This would have been proto-Mark, or *"Ur-Markus"*, written down in Rome and passed about privately before being later expanded and edited many times, as were the others, before becoming the texts known in the orthodox New Testament. Helmut Koester argued that Matthew and Luke used the first version of proto Mark, which was revised into Secret Mark, which in turn was edited to form the extant Mark.[596] This seems highly likely. In the Proofs we are told that all the early drafts of the gospels did not contain an account of the cross or crucifixion:

> "In all this there was no mention of the cross or of the crucifix."
> [597]

The proofs also say that the early versions did not contain miracles stories:

---

[594] The Anti-Marcionite Prologue To Mark (A.D. 160-180)
[595] Cayce Reading 1598-2
[596] H. Koester, "History and Development of Mark's Gospel (From Mark to Secret Mark and 'Canonical Mark')"
[597] The Establishment Of Proofs For The Prophethood Of Our Master Mohammed'

"As for the prodigies and miracles which as the Christians claim (were worked) by him, all this is baseless. He himself did not claim (to have worked) them. Nor is there in his time or in the generation which followed any disciple who claimed (that Jesus had worked miracles). This was first claimed only a very long time (ba'd... al azman wa'l-ahqab) after his death and after the death of his (direct) disciples; similarly the Christians have claimed that the Jew Paul (Bul.s al-yahudi) (has worked miracles and this) in spite of his being known for his tricks (hiyal), his lying (kadhb) and his baseness; they have done the same for George (J.urj.s) and for Father Mark, and they do the same at all times with regard to their monks and nuns. All this is baseless.'" [598]

Besides the crucifixion and later resurrection ending to Mark, there are other sections that were added, including most of a large section running from 6:45 through to 8:22. This is called the "Bethsaida Section" and did not exist in Mark when Luke copied from it. Part of this Bethsaida section deals with John the Baptist's death. Like so many of the pericopes in Mark's gospel, it appears to be almost entirely borrowed from the Old Testament and should be totally rejected. Here is the story from Mark of John the Baptist's head on a platter – a rewrite from the Book of Esther and various rabbinical texts.

Book of Esther	Gospel of Mark
Vashti, wife of the Persian King, is granddaughter of Nebuchadnezzar	Herodias, wife of Herod, is granddaughter of Herod the Great
Vashti is commanded to appear before the Court wearing her crown (seen by later Jews as wearing only the crown). In Talmud Megillah 12B she is to appear only wearing royal crown	(Herodias' daughter dances lasciviously before Herod)
Esther marries the King of Persians, displacing Vashti	Herod has taken his brother's wife as his own, setting aside his own wife
Haman suggests Vashti be killed	(Herodias suggests John be killed)

[598] The Jewish Christians Of The Early Centuries Of Christianity According To A New Source", By Pines

(Midrash)	
Vashti's head is brought before the King on a platter (Midrash)	(John's head is brought before Herod on a platter)
Esther wants to stop Haman from destroying the Jews	Herodias wants John dead for criticizing her marriage
The enemy of Esther, Haman, is the king's favorite.	Herodias' enemy, John, is thought to be a "righteous and holy man" by Herod, who "kept him safe" and "heard him gladly."
Haman goes home to get the advice of Zeresh his wife and his friends (twice)	(Herodias' daughter asks her mother what to ask for.)
Esther and the King are at a banquet arranged by her for herself and Haman	Herod on his birthday gave a banquet for his courtiers and officers and the leading men of Galilee.
"And it was so, when the king saw Esther the queen standing in the court, that she obtained favor in his sight; and the king held out to Esther the golden sceptre that was in his hand. So Esther drew near, and touched the top of the sceptre."	"For when Herodias' daughter came in and danced, she pleased Herod and his guests"
"And the king said to Esther' Whatever thy petition, it shall be granted thee; and whatever thy request,"	the king said to the girl, "Ask me for whatever you wish, and I will grant it."
"...even to the half of the kingdom, it shall be performed.'	23: And he vowed to her, "Whatever you ask me, I will give you, even half of my kingdom."
Vashti makes the King lose face in front of his court by refusing his command to appear before his courtiers, naked.	Herod is forced to keep his promise to the daughter to prevent a loss of face in front of his court.

This rewrite is not something Peter would have dictated to Mark, but a later addition in accord with the Proofs contention that people wanted a Torah patterned story book to read:

"One of his most important arguments is that the so-called "Bethsaida Section" of Mark is an interpolation by a later redactor. For Koester, one strong signal of wrongess lies in the fact that nothing in this section is reproduced in Luke, who copied Mark. Koester (1990) argues that although it is possible that Luke's copy of Mark was simply missing some pages, certain features of the Bethsaida Section differentiate it from the rest of the Gospel of Mark….. Koester argues that Matthew knew an expanded version of Mark that had the Bethsaida section, while Luke did not."[599]

According to Clement, Mark himself continued to add things to the original account.

"But when Peter died a martyr, Mark came over to Alexandria, bringing both his own notes and those of Peter, from which he transferred to his former book the things suitable to whatever makes for progress toward knowledge. Thus he composed a more spiritual Gospel for the use of those who were being perfected.[600]

Mark had not asked for permission to write down proto-Mark when Peter was alive and Peter did not endorse it once it came to his knowledge. After Peter's death Mark continued to write texts. It is out of character for the Peter of the Clementine Homilies to have endorsed much of what is now in the Biblical Mark and it would be a mistake to see the modern Mark as authorized by the Nazorean leadership under James. Cayce said of Mark:

"And the first account which was written by anyone – that remains as an account-was written by him under the direction of the person to whom was given the Keys of the Kingdom….And he was the first compiler of a letter which later became the gospel known as Mark, in the writing of which he collaborated with Peter and Barnabas….This was written in the year 59, when he was thirty four years old….

---

[599] http://users2.ev1.net/%7Eturton/GMark/GMark06.html#6X
[600] From The Letters Of The Most Holy Clement, The Author Of The Stromateis. To Theodore.

This was the first of the written words respecting the acts, life and deeds of the Master. ...There had been some distribution of writings, which had been carried to the various groups, before Mark's was accepted. This was also before Matthew's was given, for it was written about ten to eighteen years later." [601]

The distribution of writings to the various groups before Mark was probably the Gospel of Thomas and perhaps even a similar short list of less than 72 Aramaic sayings of Yeshu compiled by Matthew. Cayce's statement may mean that Mark came ten to eighteen years after the earlier distribution of these Matthew or Thomas saying of Yeshu. Cayce says that Mark's was the first account, not of the words of Yeshu, but of the acts and deeds of Yeshu. After Codex Siniaticus was discovered and serious textual criticism ensued, scholars have universally agreed that Mark was written first among the Greek Gospels. From one or more of its varied versions the others came.

Mark Dependent on Thomas

The dependency of the first Greek gospel of Mark on the Aramaic Gnostic Thomas has been successfully argued by Stevan Davies.[602]

"And what we have is a collection of sayings attributed to Jesus called the Gospel of Thomas, and reasons to think that Mark used it, and adapted it, and sought to refute elements of it. Consideration of the sheer number of Thomas sayings used by Mark, and the evident Markan adaptation of specifically Thomasine elements such as the juxtaposition of sayings 65 and

---

[601] Cayce Reading 452
[602] Mark's Use of the Gospel of Thomas by Stevan Davies, Prof. of Biblical Studies, The University of South Africa: Summer 1996

66 and the story crucial to the Thomas gospel that validates the primacy of Thomas himself should lend credence to the idea. [603]

The use of Gnostic Thomas in the creation of Mark is an important point because it shows the primacy of the Gnostic worldview and indicates that what later became "orthodoxy" began as a heretic movement altering and borrowing from the original Nazorean tradition.

> "Perhaps -- I repeat, *perhaps* -- certain manifestations of Christian life that the authors of the church renounce as "heresies" originally had not been such at all, but, at least here and there, were the only form of the new religion -- that is, for those regions they were simply "Christianity." [604]

Mark's expanded Secret Gospel may have influenced, or even been, the Gnostic Gospel utilized later by the Nazoreans and Ebionites. If so it would have had to have been validated and issued under the jurisdiction of the reigning Rishama of the Nazoreans, Shimion or his successors.

ℏisτoʀicaℓ Auτhenτiciτy

Origen (*c*182–*c* 251) was a renowned early Roman Church theologian and scholar from Alexandria. He revived, in 203, the catechetical school at Alexandria, whose last teacher, Clement of Alexandria, was apparently driven out by the persecution. He was eventually excommunicated[605] by his Roman Church in 553. He understood well the unhistorical nature of the Biblical texts:

---

[603] Mark's Use of the Gospel of Thomas, Stevan Davies

[604] Orthodoxy And Heresy In Earliest Christianity, By Walter Bauer

[605] "If anyone does not anathematize Arius, Eunomius, Macedonius, Apollinaris, Nestorius, Eutyches and Origen, as well as their impious writings, as also all other heretics already condemned and anathematized by the Holy Catholic and Apostolic Church, and by the aforesaid four Holy Synods and [if anyone does not equally anathematize] all those who have held and hold or who in their impiety persist in holding to the end the same opinion as those heretics just mentioned: let him be anathema."

"Scripture interweaves the imaginative with the historical, sometimes introducing what is utterly impossible, sometimes what is possible but never occurred. Sometimes it is only a few words, not literally true, which have been inserted; sometimes the insertions are of greater length. [606]

Origen was the greatest of the ancient biblical scholars. It is unfortunate that these words of his were not emblazoned on the cover of ever bible book that Rome ever printed.

˗ 21 ˗
BIBLE EVOLUTION

Mark Revised

THE ORIGINAL NOTES of Mark were revised and rewritten a number of times, bringing the text ever closer to the modern version. One writer has said:

"In the story that emerged, the Gospel of Mark, essentially, the author composites more than fifty 'micro-stories' (mainly healings and miracles, of the type told of Apollonius), sandwiched between a put-down of John the Baptist (whose followers were serious rivals to the early proto-Christians) and a dying-saviour sequence (of the kind then being officially promoted for the dead Antinous. [607]

Clement, head of the Alexandrian catechetical school around 200 C.E., referred to three versions of the Gospel of Mark circulating during the second century CE:

---

[606] The Philocalia of Origen, 1:16
[607] Kenneth Humphreys

- A short version of Mark for simple minded and new Christians.
- A long version "....for those more advancing in gnosis in Clement's circle of Christians.
- "A long version" used by Salome honoring Egyptian Gnostics which includes sexual passages condemned by Clement.

To these we would add an edited redaction of the long Christian version which exists in modern bibles.

Clement of Alexandria, or Titus Flavius Clemens, succeeded Pantaenus as head of an Alexandrian "school of oral instruction" about AD 190. This school, an official institution of the Catholic "Church", was founded in the later half of the second century in Alexandria, Egypt. Lectures were given to which pagan hearers were admitted, with separate advanced teachings to Christians. Apparently there was also an elite group that used even more secret material like Secret Mark. Clement had prepared himself to head this ancient "School of the Prophets" by traveling from place to place seeking higher instruction. Starting at Athens, he attached himself to different masters; to a Greek in Ionia, another in Magna Graecia, a third of Coele-Syria, and finally to Pantaenus in Alexandria. He says the instructed Christian is the perfect Christian, or "the true Gnostic" who has insight into "the Great Mysteries" and who leads a life of unalterable calm. Despite Clement's zeal for the Roman Catholic faith, Pope Gelasius condemned him for his belief in reincarnation and other matters, saying: "they are in no case to be received among us." Clement represents a middle ground between true Nazoreanism and later Roman Christianity. He was aware of several texts of Mark and the Carpocratian version of the same which he condemned in his letter may have been the original authentic account that had been redacted down to become a text Clement's orthodox school could accept. Both the Carpocratians and the Clementites claimed to be the true successors to the secret tradition. Both claimed to be the legitimate heirs to secret documents like Secret Mark. Since the versions used by these two groups differed, each thought the other had altered the texts. Clement claims it was Carpocrates in his preserved letter. If we had a preserved letter from the Carpocrates school, it would claim that it was Clement's school who did the stealing and altering, not the Gnostic one. Clement's orthodox Christian school now disowns Clement and his claims to a secret text from Mark.

The Discovery

In 1958, Morton Smith found this authentic correspondence written by Clement of Alexandria at the Mar Saba monastery near Jerusalem. The letter is on a Secret Gospel of Mark, and is a fragment found in the Mar Saba monastery library in 1958. It is a surviving section of one of 21 of Clement's letters mentioned by John of Damascus who resided at Mar Saba from 716 to 749. The monastery, 12 miles southeast of Jerusalem in the same canyon as Qumran, site of the Dead Sea Scroll discovery, was founded in the fifth century. It had a devastating fire in its treasury cave in the early seventeen hundreds which smoldered for weeks, leaving many ancient manuscripts and letters in fragmentary condition. This fragment of Clement's letter, found handwritten in the back of the monastery's 1646 edition of the letters of Ignatius of Antioch, was perhaps recorded from one of these charred fragments sometime after 1750 AD.

The Secret Gospel of Mark

Clement explains the origins of both biblical Mark and Secret Mark:

> "As for Mark, then, during Peter's stay in Rome he wrote an account of the Lord's doings, not, however, declaring all of them, nor yet hinting at the secret ones, but selecting what he thought most useful for increasing the faith of those who were being instructed. But when Peter died a martyr, Mark came over to Alexandria, bringing both his own notes and those of Peter, from which he transferred to his former book the things suitable to whatever makes for progress toward knowledge. Thus he composed a more spiritual Gospel for the use of those who were being perfected.[608]

Cayce also stated that Mark assisted Barnabas in setting up churches in northern Africa, in Alexandria. To cover up the existence of this secret version of Mark, Clement suggests lying:

> To them, therefore, as I said above, one must never give way; nor, when they put forward their falsifications, should one concede that the secret Gospel is by Mark, but should even deny it on oath. For, "Not all true things are to be said to all men".[609]

Nazoreans would not have tolerated lying as Clement suggests. Here are the two additional passages from Secret Mark mentioned in the letter. The first fragment is to be found between Mark 10:34 and 10:35:

> "And they came into Bethany and a certain woman whose brother had died was there. And, coming, she knelt down before Jesus and said to him, "Son of David, have mercy on me". But the disciples rebuked her. And Jesus got angry with them and went off with her into the garden where the tomb was. Right away there was a loud cry from inside the tomb. Then Jesus rolled

---

[608] From The Letters Of The Most Holy Clement, The Author Of The Stromateis. To Theodore.
[609] From The Letters Of The Most Holy Clement, The Author Of The Stromateis. To Theodore.

away the stone from in front of the tomb. He went in where the youth was and stretched forth his hand and raised him up. The youth, looking upon him, loved him and began to beg him to be with him. They left the tomb and went to the young man's house, for he was rich. Six days later, Jesus gave him instructions of what to do and in the evening the youth came to him, wearing nothing but a linen cloth over his naked body. He remained with him that night, for Jesus taught him the mystery of the Kingdom of God. And when Jesus woke up, he returned to the other side of the Jordan.

The second fragment is to be found between Mark 10:46a and 10:46b:

"And the sister of the young man whom Jesus loved was there, along with his mother and Salome, but Jesus did not receive them.

What is more interesting than the actual content of the passages are Clement's comments about them and the gospel from whence they came. This letter proves beyond a shadow of a doubt that early Roman Christianity, at least its Alexandria expression, had a secret higher level within it. As it evolved further and farther away from its original Nazorean mother, it became increasingly hostile to all such traditions. Here is what remains of Clement of Alexandria's letter in full, followed by a few comments.

Clement To Theodore

1 "The Letter Attributed to Clement To Theodore.

2 You did well in silencing the unspeakable teachings of the Carpocrations. For these are "wandering stars" referred to in the prophecy, who wander from the narrow road of the commandments into a boundless abyss of the carnal and bodily sins.

3 For, priding themselves in knowledge, as they say, "of the deep things of Satan, they do not know that they are casting themselves away into "the netherworld of the darkness" of falseness, and boasting that they are free, they have become slaves of servile desires.

4 Such are to be opposed in all ways and altogether. For, even if they should say something true, one who loves the truth should not, even so, agree with them.

5 For not all true (things) are the truth, nor should that truth which seems true according to human opinions be preferred to the true truth, that according to the faith.

6 Now of the they keep saying about the divinely inspired gospel according to Mark, some are altogether falsifications, and others, even if they do contain some truth, nevertheless are not reported truly.

7 For the truth, being mixed with inventions, is falsified, so that, as the saying, even the salt loses its savor.

8 Mark, then, during Peter's stay in Rome he wrote the Lord's doings, not, however, declaring all, nor yet hinting at the secret, but selecting those he thought most useful for increasing the faith of those who were being instructed.

9 But when Peter died as a martyr, Mark came over to Alexandria, bringing both his own notes and those of Peter, from which he transferred to his former book the things suitable to whatever makes for progress toward gnosis.

10 He composed a more spiritual gospel for the use of those who were being perfected.

11 Nevertheless, he yet did not divulge the things not to be uttered, nor did he write down the hierophantic teaching of the Lord, but to the stories already written he added yet others.

12 And, moreover, brought in certain sayings of which he knew the interpretation would, as a mystagogue, lead the hearers into the innermost sanctuary of that truth hidden by seven.

13 Thus, in sum, he prearranged matters, neither grudgingly nor incautiously, in my opinion, and, dying, he left his composition to the church in Alexandria, where it even yet is most carefully guarded, being read only to those who are being initiated into the great mysteries.

14 But since the foul demons are always devising destruction for the race of men, Carpocrates, instructed by them and using deceitful arts, so enslaved a certain presbyter of the church in Alexandria that he got from him a copy of the secret gospel, which he both interpreted according to his blasphemous and carnal doctrine and, moreover, polluted, mixing with the spotless and holy words utterly shameless lies.

15 From this mixture is drawn off the teaching of the Carpocratians.

16 To them, therefore, as I said above, one must never give way, nor, when they put forward their falsifications, should one concede that the secret gospel is by Mark, but should even deny it on oath.

17 for, "not all truth is to be said to all men."

18 For this the wisdom of God, through Solomon, advises, "answer the fool from his folly," teaching that the light of the truth should be hidden from those who are mentally blind.

19 Again it says, "from him who has not shall be taken away," and, "let the fool walk in darkness."

20 But we are "children of light," having been illuminated by "the dayspring" of the spirit of the Lord "from on high," and "where the spirit of the Lord is," it says, "there is liberty," for "all things are pure to the pure."

21 To you, therefore, I shall not hesitate to answer the you have asked, refuting the falsifications by the very words of the gospel.

22 For example, after "and they were in the road going up to Jerusalem," and what follows, until "after three days he shall arise,"[610] brings the following word for word:

23 "And they come into Bethany, and a certain woman, whose brother had died, was there.

24 And, coming, she prostrated herself before Jesus and says to him, "son of David, have mercy on me."

25 But the disciples rebuked her.

26 and Jesus, being angered, went off with her into the garden where the tomb was, and straightway a great cry was heard from the tomb.

---

[610] Biblical Mark 10:32-34

27 And going near Jesus rolled away the stone from the door of the tomb.

28 And straightway, going in where the youth was, he stretched forth his hand and raised him, seizing his hand.

29 But the youth, looking upon him, loved him and began to beseech him that he might be with him.

30 and going out of the tomb they came into the house of the youth, for he was rich.

31 and after six days Jesus told him what to do and in the evening the youth comes to him, wearing a linen cloth over nakedness.

32 and he remained with him that night, for Jesus taught him the mystery of the kingdom of God.

33 and thence, arising, he returned to the other side of the Jordan."

34 after these follows the text, "and James and John come to him," and all that section.

35 but "naked with naked" and the other things about which you wrote are not found.

36 and after the: "and he comes into Jericho," adds only, "and the sister of the youth whom Jesus loved and his mother and Salome were there, and Jesus did not receive them."

37 but the many other which you wrote both seem to be and are falsifications.

38 now the true explanation and that which accords with the true philosophy...

Some have sought to read into the "naked with naked" an endorsement of homosexuality, but this seems forced since it says "naked", not "naked man". One scholar writes:

"BTW, the 'naked to naked' passage is sometimes forced to serve the 'homosexual theory', but there are major problems with this: (1) the phrase does NOT occur in the 'young man' section at all (!); and (2) we know the Cx were sexually promiscuous *heterosexually* (sharing wives)-- this addition is more likely to have served THAT dogmatic agenda rather than some unknown and undocumented homosexual praxis." [611]

The early Christians did not like the Gnostic Carpocratians any more than they liked the Gnostic Nazorean tradition of Yeshu. Irenaeus Of Lyons, in his Adversus Haereses, explains his take on the Doctrines Of Carpocrates:

> 1. Carpocrates, again, and his followers maintain that the world and the things which are therein were created by angels greatly inferior to the unbegotten Father. They also hold that Jesus was the son of Joseph, and was just like other men, with the exception that he differed from them in this respect, that inasmuch as his soul was steadfast and pure, he perfectly remembered those things which he had witnessed within the sphere of the unbegotten God. On this account, a power descended upon him from the Father, that by means of it he might escape from the creators of the world; and they say that it, after passing through them all, and remaining in all points free, ascended again to him, and to the powers, which in the same way embraced like things to itself. They further declare, that the soul of Jesus, although educated in the practices of the Jews, regarded these with contempt, and that for this reason he was endowed with faculties, by means of which he destroyed those passions which dwelt in men as a punishment [for their sins].
>
> 2. The soul, therefore, which is like that of Christ can despise those rulers who were the creators of the world, and, in like manner, receives power for accomplishing the same results. This idea has raised them to such a pitch of pride, that some of them declare themselves similar to Jesus; while others, still more mighty, maintain that they are superior to his disciples, such as Peter and Paul, and the rest of the apostles, whom they consider to be in no respect inferior to Jesus. For their souls, descending from the same sphere as his, and therefore despising in like manner the creators of the world, are deemed worthy of the same power, and again depart to the same place. But if any one

---

[611] Glenn Miller, October 18, 1999

shall have despised the things in this world more than he did, he thus proves himself superior to him.

3. They practice also magical arts and incantations; philters, also, and love-potions; and have recourse to familiar spirits, dream-sending demons, and other abominations, declaring that they possess power to rule over, even now, the princes and formers of this world; and not only them, but also all things that are in it. These men, even as the Gentiles, have been sent forth by Satan to bring dishonor upon the Church, so that, in one way or another, men hearing the things which they speak, and imagining that we all are such as they, may turn away their ears from the preaching of the truth; or, again, seeing the things they practice, may speak evil of us all, who have in fact no fellowship with them, either in doctrine or in morals, or in our daily conduct. But they lead a licentious life, and, to conceal their impious doctrines, they abuse the name [of Christ], as a means of hiding their wickedness; so that "their condemnation is just," when they receive from God a recompense suited to their works.

4. So unbridled is their madness, that they declare they have in their power all things which are irreligious and impious, and are at liberty to practice them; for they maintain that things are evil or good, simply in virtue of human opinion. They deem it necessary, therefore, that by means of transmigration from body to body, souls should have experience of every kind of life as well as every kind of action (unless, indeed, by a single incarnation, one may be able to prevent any need for others, by once for all, and with equal completeness, doing all those things which we dare not either speak or hear of, nay, which we must not even conceive in our thoughts, nor think credible, if any such thing is mooted among those persons who are our fellow-citizens), in order that, as their writings express it, their souls, having made trial of every kind of life, may, at their departure, not be wanting in any particular. It is necessary to insist upon this, lest, on account of some one thing being still wanting to their deliverance, they should be compelled once more to become incarnate. They affirm that for this reason Jesus spoke the following parable:-"Whilst thou art with thine adversary in the way, give all diligence, that thou mayest be delivered from him, lest he give thee up to the judge, and the judge surrender

thee to the officer, and he cast thee into prison. Verily, I say unto thee, thou shalt not go out thence until thou pay the very last farthing." They also declare the "adversary" is one of those angels who are in the world, whom they call the Devil, maintaining that he was formed for this purpose, that he might lead those souls which have perished from the world to the Supreme Ruler. They describe him also as being chief among the makers of the world, and maintain that he delivers such souls [as have been mentioned] to another angel, who ministers to him, that he may shut them up in other bodies; for they declare that the body is "the prison." Again, they interpret these expressions, "Thou shalt not go out thence until thou pay the very last farthing," as meaning that no one can escape from the power of those angels who made the world, but that he must pass from body to body, until he has experience of every kind of action which can be practiced in this world, and when nothing is longer wanting to him, then his liberated soul should soar upwards to that God who is above the angels, the makers of the world. In this way also all souls are saved, whether their own which, guarding against all delay, participate in all sorts of actions during one incarnation, or those, again, who, by passing from body to body, are set free, on fulfilling and accomplishing what is requisite in every form of life into which they are sent, so that at length they shall no longer be shut in the body.

5. And thus, if ungodly, unlawful, and forbidden actions are committed among them, I can no longer find ground for believing them to be such. And in their writings we read as follows, the interpretation which they give [of their views], declaring that Jesus spoke in a mystery to His disciples and apostles privately, and that they requested and obtained permission to hand down the things thus taught them, to others who should be worthy and believing. We are saved, indeed, by means of faith and love; but all other things, while in their nature indifferent, are reckoned by the opinion of men-some good and some evil, there being nothing really evil by nature.

6. Others of them employ outward marks, branding their disciples inside the lobe of the right ear. From among these also arose Marcellina, who came to Rome under [the episcopate of] Anicetus, and, holding these doctrines, she led multitudes

astray. They style themselves Gnostics. They also possess
images, some of them painted, and others formed from different
kinds of material; while they maintain that a likeness of Christ
was made by Pilate at that time when Jesus lived among them.
They crown these images, and set them up along with the
images of the philosophers of the world that is to say, with the
images of Pythagoras, and Plato, and Aristotle, and the rest.
They have also other modes of honoring these images, after the
same manner of the Gentiles." [612]

There is nothing un-Nazorean about any of the practices or
beliefs that Irenaeus accuses the Carpocrates of, including
their belief in reincarnation and karma. Clement adds to this
list, however, by writing:

"But the followers of Carpocrates and Epiphanes think that
wives should be common property." [613]

This statement does not mean that everyone was a spouse, and
therefore a sexual partner, of everyone else. It refers to the
Gnostic practice of polygyny and polyandry which allows for
a man or woman to marry more than one person at a time.
Clement quotes one of their texts written by a seventeen year
old which elaborates on the rationale of their polygamist
philosophy:

"The righteousness of God is a kind of universal fairness and
equality. There is equality in the heaven which is stretched out in
all directions and contains the entire earth in its circle. The night
reveals equally all the stars. The light of the sun, which is the
cause of the daytime and the father of light, God pours out from
above upon the earth in equal measure on all who have power to
see. For all see alike. There is no distinction between rich and
poor, people and governor, stupid and clever, female and male,
free men and slaves. Even the irrational animals are not

[612] Irenaeus Of Lyons, Adversus Haereses, Book I, Chapter Xxv, The Doctrines Of Carpocrates
[613] Clement of Alexandria, Stromata, Book III, II

accorded any different treatment; but in just the same way God pours out from above sunlight equally upon all the animals. He establishes his righteousness to both good and bad by seeing that none is able to get more than his share and to deprive his neighbor, so that he has twice the light his neighbor has. The sun causes food to grow for all living beings alike; the universal righteousness is given to all equally. In this respect there is no difference between the entire species of oxen and any individual oxen, between the species of pigs and particular pigs, between the species of sheep and particular sheep, and so on with all the rest. In them the universality of God's fairness is manifest. Furthermore all plants of whatever sort are sown equally in the earth. Common nourishment grows for all beasts which feed on the earth's produce; to all it is alike. It is regulated by no law, but rather is harmoniously available to all through the gift of him who gives it and makes it to grow.

"And for birth there is no written law (for otherwise it would have been transcribed). All beings beget and give birth alike, having received by God's righteousness an innate equality. The Creator and Father of all with his own righteousness appointed this, just as he gave equally the eye to all to enable them to see. He did not make a distinction between female and male, rational and irrational, nor between anything and anything else at all; rather he shared out sight equally and universally. It was given to all alike by a single command. As the laws (he says) could not punish men who were ignorant of them, they taught men that they were transgressors. But the laws, by pre-supposing the existence of private property, cut up and destroyed the universal equality decreed by the divine law." As he does not understand the words of the apostle where he says "Through the law I knew sin," he says that the idea of Mine and Thine came into existence through the laws so that the earth and money were no longer put to common use. And so also with marriage. "For God has made vines for all to use in common, since they are not protected against sparrows and a thief; and similarly corn and the other fruits. But the abolition, contrary to divine law, of community of use and equality begat the thief of domestic animals and fruits.

He brought female to be with male and in the same way united all animals. He thus showed righteousness to be a universal

fairness and equality .But those who have been born in this way
have denied the universality which is the corollary of their birth
and say, 'Let him who has taken one woman keep her,' whereas
all alike can have her, just as the other animals do."

"Consequently one must understand the saying 'Thou shalt not
covet' as if the lawgiver was making a jest, to which he added
the even more comic words 'thy neighbor's goods'. For he
himself who gave the desire to sustain the race orders that it is to
be suppressed, though he removes it from no other animals. And
by the words 'thy neighbor's wife' he says something even more
ludicrous, since he forces what should be common property to
be treated as a private possession." [614]

Epiphanius of Salamis says that Carpocrates taught his
followers to perform every obscenity and every sinful act,
saying that unless one proceeds through all of them, and
fulfils the will of all demons and angels, he cannot mount to
the highest heaven. If he is correct in this, then they had
strayed from the true Gnostic path of always doing good and
virtuous works. He, however, probably misunderstood or
misrepresented their teaching on past life karma to vilify and
slander a rival group. Epiphanius, Irenaeus and the rest of
their gang had few scruples when it came to bearing false
witness against Gnostics and their accusations must be taken
with a grain of salt. They were quick to falsely accuse Gnostics
of all types of sexual sins. Gnostics viewed sexuality from a
different vantage from the orthodox, but they were not
deviates.

Many of the Carpocratian's beliefs were based upon solid
Gnostic tradition, and the text of Secret Mark which
apparently had teachings of Yeshu on this subject. Clement
may have had problems with these teachings, but his main

---

[614] Concerning Righteousness, Epiphanies, Clement of Alexandria, Stromata, Book III, CHAPTER II

problem with the Carpocrates is their claim to secret apostolic Gnostic authority. They represent a rival sect to Clement and he wants them censured in any manner possible. He is even willing to lie to discredit them. Irenaeus of Lyons has written that the Caprocrations had a commentary on the secret sayings of Yeshu. Included in these commentaries must have been their interpretation of this secret gospel of Mark, referred to above.

It is interesting that Clement himself represents a transitional stage between the original true Gnosis of Nazoreanism and later Catholic Christianity. He is too orthodox Christian to be considered part of the original pure Nazorean faith, but too Gnostic to be accepted by the later Catholic orthodoxy. Hence Pope Gelasius said that his numerous writings "are in no case to be received among us." Mark, however, was probably quite deeply initiated into Nazirutha and much that he added to his original gospel draft was probably accurate. His full text was better suited to Gnostic use than Christian. After Mark's death it appears that his Christian followers edited out many Gnostic features of his Secret Mark, added many of their own ideas and miracle stories, and published the text as the Gospel of Mark that we know today.

Implications of Clement's Letter

Clement in his letter says that proto-Mark was a partial and incomplete account put together by Mark for novices not yet ready for the real truth. Apparently Clement was aware of how flawed Mark was. If Clement realized this, he was not ready to admit it to the Christian masses who he felt needed faith promoting works of fiction to inspire them. This was not the Gnostic way, but it was Clement's way. We know from other writings of Clement that he felt, as did true Gnostics, that there was three types of Christians, and that the lowest were superstitious and incapable of receiving deeper truth. Unfortunately for Clement, this stratum of Christianity overwhelmed all others. When they eventually became dominant, they even kicked Clement out of their ranks for being too Gnostic.

We are told by Clement that the exoteric Mark written for the outer church was added to in Alexandria in order to form a more complete and proper text more suitable for those being initiated into inner church circles. Clement here reassures Theodore that these inner truths are legitimate apostolic tradition who have their source in Peter and who have crystallized into a secret text via Mark and Peter's esoteric notes. Of course modern Mark is not a legitimate and authorized text, but Secret Mark may have been before Clement's group watered it down and fluffed it up.

The secret gospel is said by Clement to be for those on a deeper level than ordinary Christians, yet still not the deepest level. Clement is again speaking as one halfway between the true Nazorean faith and the developing false. He is part of a secret inner order of Christianity that is still below and outside of the true tradition. He refers to stories as if he knew them to be fables and myths. We here see evidence of a deliberate scheme of a multi-leveled ancient initiation and indoctrination where the most promising of the outer church are presented with certain mysteries, which if they utilize properly, will qualify them for initiation into an even deeper church or level. Clement is not concerned with how factual the stories in Mark and Secret Mark are, only in their affect on Christians. Mark was meant to inspire faith among simple minded ignorant people, and indeed it does. Secret Mark was meant to wean people from the common perception and introduce them to new ways of thinking and behaving. Secret Mark, as a companion text to the other Mark, was designed to undo the harm done by the first false version. When Secret Mark went out of use, there was no check and balance on the fantasies of the public version. Secret Mark was for Clement a remedy for the problems created by public Mark. He used it as a catalyst for change. Clement appears to value these texts for their psychological affect on people rather than their supposed historical veracity. It is evident that the Carpocratians are using Secret Mark to introduce candidates of their inner circle into their doctrine of community of wives. Clement denies using the text for this purpose, but admits that it is being used by his group to introduce some form of higher mystery which he does not divulge.

To find historical reference to secret Greater Mysteries in ancient proto-Christianity, especially when found in the writings of such early writers like Clement, opens a Pandora's box of confusion for ordinary Christians basing their faith on the false assumption that their faith alone will save them. The great mysteries of the true lineage are deeper enshroudment ceremonies given to those having graduated from the lesser mysteries. Even the concept of lesser mysteries is a stumbling block to most of modern Christianity which bases their spiritual program not on mysteries, a Greek word anciently meaning priesthood or ceremonial allegorical plays, but on mere feeling or prayer. The Pistis Sophia text that speaks much of these greater and lesser mysterions could never be appreciated by the mainstream Christian, for its implications demand deeper commitment.

Clement here supports the multi-leveled scheme set up by Mark, by which thinking Christians can be separated off from lower superstitious Christianity, like cream from milk, via graduation exams based on intuitive use of secret sayings. Clement is claiming that his school represented the legitimate line from Yeshu, not the Gnostic Carpocrations. He accuses them of stealing the text. It is of course more likely that Clement's school acquired it from the Gnostics.

Counterfeit Nazoreanism

There were isolated pockets of Greco-Roman influenced churches spread over the entire Mediterranean basin in the first few centuries after the Yeshu, being propagated by Paul and others. Within this loosely knit confederation of growing Christian communities existed some souls aware of deeper gnosis, such as Clement. Their loyalties were not to the Nazoreans, however. They used their deeper knowledge to attempt to set up their own counterfeit Nazoreanism devoid of those elements that they did not like. Their efforts were only partially successful, however, for it was not long before mainstream Christianity purged itself of these deeper elements and excommunicated anyone who promoted them. The geographical and communication limitations and lack of central organization in early Christianity delayed this purge. Once fully organized and centralized, this organization ruthlessly reduced its rivals. Their Paul the apostate apostle spoke of various levels of the original Nazoreans when he wrote:

"Howbeit we speak wisdom among them that are perfect."[615]

"And I, brethren, could not speak unto you as unto spiritual, but as unto carnal, as unto babes in Christ. I have fed you with milk, and not with meat; for hitherto you were not able, neither yet now are you able." [616]

---

[615] First Corinthians 2:6
[616] First Corinthians 3:1-2

Quoting from Paul, Clement revels in his esoteric knowledge. Here in his letter we have a hint that Clement understands that many of the secrets of his higher mysteries contradict the outer presentation of Christianity that he is also involved in. Because he rejects the Gnostic position, and because of his own public promotion of another orientation, he deems it proprietous to deny the existence of such things as Secret Mark, even under oath. Too much credit would be given to Clement's scruples if we assumed this dishonest attitude of his arose from strict vows of silence and secrecy he encountered in his own initiatory endeavors. His attitude was more likely due to the fact that he knew his school's claim to Apostolic authority going back to Mark and his secret Text was fabricated. His reluctance to admit that the Gnostics had true deeper texts was probably a result of his awareness that they had a good claim to being the true heirs to such, so good in fact that if their claims were known publicly they might cause many to go over to their side. By agreeing to speak of such hidden things to Theodore, we may surmise that Clement feared a complete Carprocratian takeover of the community to which Theodore must have resided in at the reception of this letter. Hence his insistence on deception and denial.

The sexual innuendoes associated with Yeshu mentioned in Clement's letter were problematic for the early Christians. There were too many Gnostic groups in too many places making similar claims to such a tradition passing down from Yeshu himself. This was a huge problem for the early Christian churches who sought to promote a non sexual orientation. This view goes back to Paul who stood in opposition to the Nazoreans who were against celibacy:

"They didn't take the vows of celibacy! Not to have children during those periods was considered to be ones not thought of by God!" [617]

As for Paul's celibacy, it is written in the Cayce readings:

"owing to the teachings of Paul concerning the interests of those who were as leaders or the head of the churches, and from which grew in many quarters the commanding or demanding of celibacy as a prerequisite for the activities as a bishop or leader." [618]

The story in Secret Mark appears to be a partial account of an ancient ordination, which in Nazorean circles, entailed seven days of preparation, staying up throughout the night for instruction, and a baptism at the end. During such ordination, the officiating Rabai was mandated to teach the mysteries of the kingdom to the candidate all through the night without slumber. There were others who assisted in this vigil as well. Certain secret formulas and texts were revealed. Certain marriage ceremonies also had similar proceedings, including double baptisms, and if this is a distorted account of a Nazorean wedding then naked with naked would have resulted, but not between Yeshu and the young man, for this was not the Nazorean way. The Jews, in their proselyte baptism, insisted upon nudity to such an extent that "a ring on the finger, a band confining the hair, or anything that in the least degree broke the continuity of contact with the water, was held to invalidate the act". [619] The early Catholic Church Fathers also spoke of nudity in their early Christian baptisms. Cyril of Jerusalem, born about 315AD, in his twentieth Catechetical Lecture, wrote:

---

617 Text Of Reading 2175-6
618 Text Of Reading 1468-3
619 C. Taylor, The Teaching of the Twelve Apostles, Cambridge, 1886, pp. 51, 52

"those things, which were done by you in the inner chamber, were symbolical. As soon, then, as ye entered, ye put off your tunic; and this was an image of putting off the old man with his deeds. Having stripped yourselves, ye were naked; in this also imitating Christ, who was stripped naked on the Cross, and by His nakedness put off from Himself the principalities and powers, and openly triumphed over them on the tree. . . . Then, when ye were stripped, ye were anointed with exorcised oil, from the very hairs of your head to your feet, and were made partakers of the good olive-tree, Jesus Christ."

Yeshu, Miryai and other disciples traveled in groups. They constantly performed ritualistic initiations during their travels, including many forms of baptism and marriage, including nude baptisms and consummated polygamous unions. According to Cayce, this lifestyle was also characterized "and indicated in the lack of celibacy." [620] These facts explain Secret Mark's inclusion of "naked with naked". During Priesthood initiation, many initiators were involved and multiple baptisms and anointings occurred.

Clement maintained that naked with naked (*gymnon gymnō*[621]) was not part of the original expanded Markian text being used by the elite of Alexandrian Christianity, but an addition made by the Caprocrations to further their own ideas. Clement may have been lying to Theodore, thinking him not ready for the practices of Clement's inner circle. He has certainly admitted his belief in doing so when it suits his purpose. More likely, however, is that the text of Secret Mark that Clement had had been edited and did not have the controversial verses that he disliked. The "naked with naked" could have been an oral tradition attached to the text which the Carpocrations included as a marginal note, but it probably was in the

---

620 Text Of Reading 2067-11
621 gymnon means naked, not naked man as some have translated it. There is no man (άντρας) in the verse.

original penned by Mark. Whether it was there in the original Secret Mark or not, it is important to note that both Mark, and Secret Mark, used by the school of Clement had been tampered with extensively before being released in private or to the public in the form of the known Greek Gospels. Tampering was not a Gnostic trait, but a Christian one.

"Morton Smith, followed by Crossan, Koester, and others, has argued that the *Secret Gospel of Mark* was a source of canonical Mark's narrative. This seems correct since otherwise meaningless fragments, like the young man fleeing naked in canonical Mark, only make sense in the context of the full story as told in Secret Mark.

Marcion's Luke

Alexandrian circles were trying to develop an inner and an outer Christianity, just like the Gnostic pattern, by use of secret texts and rituals. They could not use the pure Gnostic texts since they denied many of their tenets, such as sacred sexuality, and so they were forced to mutilate and alter those texts for their own ends. Other pockets of Pauline Christianity sought to develop their own unique expression of Paul's religion based loosely on some elements of Nazoreanism mixed with Greco-Roman ideas. The pocket of Paulites that came up with the book of Luke rewrote the now lost shorter Mark to accomplish this, and created Acts to promote Paul's version of history. Cayce says of Luke:

> "Luke was written by Lucius rather than Luke, though a companion with Luke during those activities of Paul – and written of course, unto those of the faith under the Roman influence. Not to the Roman peoples, but to the provinces ruled by the Romans. And it was from those sources that the very

changes were made as to the differences in that given by Mark and Matthew." [622]

Through textual analysis it can be proved that Luke came from a rewriting of an early form of Mark. According to the sources of the Proofs, it was published as the last of the four Greek accounts. According to the Christian heresiologists, the Gnostic Marcion deleted all references to Jewish scriptures in his edited version of Luke. Marcion may have had an early copy of Luke before these additions were added. The Manichaeans claimed later that all biblical references found in the Gospels were added later. From the Proofs we know that the miracles were added later as well. There may have been some accounts of Yeshu healing various people, by faith or otherwise, since this was an area of expertise of the original Nazoreans, but walking on water and other such things were certainly added later on and are an adulteration of the original pure tradition. Miracle mongering was not a trait of the Gnostikoi, but rather, the seeking of divine understanding as in Vajrayana Buddhism.

Matthew

"The next was Matthew, written by the one whose name it bears. As for the specific reasons – to those who were scattered into the upper portions of Palestine and through Laodicea. This was written something like thirty-three to thirty-four years later than Mark, and while this body that wrote same was in exile." [623]

33 to 34 years after Mark gives a date of about 93 AD, which fits well with modern views on Matthew's date. This work seems to be a rewrite of expanded Mark for the sake of

---

[622] Cayce Reading 1598-2
[623] Cayce Reading 1598-2

Hellenistic Jews who had been partially converted to Paul's Roman form of Christianity.

> "Matthew prefaces Mark with the genealogy and the story of the birth and early childhood of Jesus, and supplements it with an account of the resurrection of Jesus and his apparition to his disciples."[624]

There is a Shem Tov version that is slightly variant from the biblical version. Neither of these versions are Papias' original Aramaic gospel of which he writes:

> "Matthew put together the oracles [of the Lord] in the Hebrew language, and each one interpreted them as best he could." [625]

These oracles, or sayings[626], had more to do with the Gospel of Thomas and would not have been acceptable to the Roman Christians who put together the biblical Matthew. Most contemporary scholars, based on analysis of the Greek in the Gospel of Matthew and use of sources such as the Greek Gospel of Mark, conclude that the New Testament Book of Matthew was written originally in Greek and is not a translation from Hebrew or Aramaic.

> "Plagiarist 'Matthew' plundered Old Testament scripture for almost every chapter of his novel."[627]

John's Four Drafts

---

[624] Geza Vermes (The Changing Faces of Jesus, p161

[625] Volume I of The Ante-Nicene Fathers

[626] Appendix two contains 72 sayings attributed to Jesus extracted from the New Testament Gospels. These may have some relationship to Matthew's Aramaic sayings document.

627 Kenneth Humphreys

The Gospel of John's first draft had a sequence of events exactly the same as the "gospel of Mark" that inspired it. One scholar writes of its first draft:

> "It was written around 75-80C.E. when Mark's gospel (GMark) was known in the community. This gospel was very COHERENT, with the material drawn from GMark considerably embellished. There are many clues pointing to the fact the author knew about GMark but was not aware of the other synoptic gospels.

> "What is remarkable about the original version, made up of nine "blocks" of the final gospel (about 65% of it altogether), is that all the parts fit well with each other, requiring no additional wording to link them (but some, of the awkward kind, will be inserted for the later versions). The gospel ended then at Jn20:10, after the 'empty tomb' segment (as in Mk16:8, the original end of GMark), when "... the disciples went away again to their own homes", as "prophesied" in Mk14:27-28 & Jn16:32 "... you will be scattered, each to his own home, and will leave Me alone". [628]

Gospel of John second rewriting:

> 2.2 Alterations after GLuke was known: Considerable additions and some relocations were done after Luke's gospel got known in the community. These changes were made in at least two phases. All inclusions then can be related to passages in GLuke. The overall result was a rather disjointed gospel, with Jesus' ministry extended to at least two years (from one year and a few weeks), including more visits to Jerusalem (from two to four). The end of the gospel was then pushed back to Jn20:23, in order to include a brief post-mortem appearance to the disciples, as the one in Lk24:36-49 right before the ascension (24:50-51). . [629]

Gospel of John third rewriting:

---

[628] John's Gospel, From Original To Canonical
[629] John's Gospel, From Original To Canonical

2.3 Alterations after 'Acts' was known: A few additions were made after 'Acts' appeared. Here, all inserted items have parallel notions occurring in 'Acts' (but NOT in GLuke).

The ending was again extended, this time up to Jn20:31, with a second post-mortem appearance to the disciples, one week later, as "allowed" by the "forty days" of 'Acts' (1:3) before the ascension (1:9). .[630]

Gospel of John fourth rewriting:

2.4 Additions after the "beloved disciple" died: Finally, the "epilogue" (Jn21:1-25ff), widely considered to be an appendix, was added on at the end. Furthermore, some notes, likely first written in the margin, were inserted in the body of the text, either at that time or earlier. The gospel was finished then (97-105?).

There is little evidence to support the view the author(s) of the gospel used (or even knew about) GMatthew. [631]

Cayce also spoke of the Gospel of John, saying it had multiple authors and that sections were compiled some 50 years after the crucifixion which would have been around 81 AD.:

"John was written by several; not by the John who was the Beloved, but the John who represented, or was the scribe for, John The Beloved – and, as much of the same, was written much later. Portions of it were written some fifty years after the Crucifixion." [632]

This would refer to the first draft of John before the later alterations ending around 100 AD. In Irenaeus' surviving works, the author of the 4th gospel and 'Revelation' is often called simply John. Not until Origen (203-250C.E.) do we hear

---

[630] John's Gospel, From Original To Canonical
[631] John's Gospel, From Original To Canonical
[632] Cayce Reading 1598-2

of this John being the son of Zebedee. All these modern Gospels are far removed from the original truth. They should not be trusted.

Gradual Reworkings

Nazoreans, knowing that the Roman Christian gospels were not pure when they were written, were no doubt aghast as they saw them slowly altered more and more over the centuries to provide better ammunition against true believers. As Roman Christian theology evolved, they altered their texts to keep up with the changes. One example of the numerous occurrences of alteration is Luke 22:43-44 ' which now reads:

> "And being in an agony, he prayed more earnestly, and his sweat became like great drops of blood falling down upon the ground'.

These words are not in the quote of the text by Clement around 200AD, or in P69, P75 of the 3rd century, nor Codex Alexandrinus, Codex Vaticanus of the 4th century, or Codex Washingtonensis from the 5th century. These words are, however, in many other manuscripts including Sinaiticus from the 4th century. They are quoted by Justin around AD 130 in his attacks against Gnostics[633]; by Irenaeus around 170 AD[634]; and by Hippolytus around 190 AD[635]. These alterations to Luke must have occurred before 130 AD in order for Justin to use them against certain Gnostics. Other reworkings abound as well, this being but one small sample.

The final selection of the four gospels was declared by Irenaeus, Gentile bishop of Lyons, France around 180:

---

[633] Dialogue With Trypho, 103
[634] Against Heresy 3,22,2
[635] Against Noetus, 18

"It is not possible that the Gospels can be either more or fewer in number than they are. For, since there are four zones of the world in which we live, and four principal winds, while the Church is scattered throughout all the world, and the "pillar and ground" of the Church is the Gospel and the spirit of life; it is fitting that she should have four pillars, breathing out immortality on every side, and vivifying men afresh."[636]

In the same chapter he introduced an author for each one of the four: Matthew, Luke, Mark and John. The Proofs have it right when they declare:

"These (Christian) sects are of the opinion that these four (Evangelists) were companions and disciples of Christ. But they do not know, having no information (on the subject), who they were. On this (point) they can (merely) make a claim. [637]

Summary of Gospels

The so called Gospels of the Bible could not have been written in their present form by Semites who were the original witnesses, for they all have very overt anti-Semitic diatribes imbedded in them. They were written in Greek which was the language of the Roman Christians before Gregory the Great.

"The local church of Rome had begun as a Greek-speaking body; the majority of its members were Greek-speaking Levantines living in the foreign quarters of the city. But it began to use Latin in its liturgy, probably in the latter half of the second century, as the faith spread among the Latin-speaking inhabitants; though the use of Greek went on side by side with Latin down to the fourth-perhaps even the fifth century.[638]

---

[636] Irenaeus, "Against Heresies", Iii, 11, 8
[637] The Establishment Of Proofs . . . By 'Abd Al-Jabbar
[638] Benjamin D. Williams

Manichaean bishop Faustus, about 400 A.D., sums up the Aramaic speaking world's view of the Greek Gospels:

> "We have proved again and again, the writings are not the production of Christ or of His apostles, but a compilation of rumors and beliefs, made, long after their departure, by some obscure semi-Jews, not in harmony even with one another, and published by them under the name of the apostles, or of those considered the followers of the apostles, so as to give the appearance of apostolic authority to all these blunders and falsehoods."[639]

Fake Epistles of Paul

Tertullian (160-225) wrote about his fellow Roman Christians forging letters of Paul such as the 'Acts of Paul' and the unauthentic epistle 3 Corinthians:

> "in Asia, the presbyter who composed that writing, as if he were augmenting Paul's fame from his own store, after being convicted, and confessing that he had done it from love of Paul, was removed from his office"[640]

Irenaeus Polarization

Irenaeus was a student of Polycarp, who was supposedly a student of St. John the Apostle (actually John the Elder who probably wrote the Gospel of John.) Irenaeus lived ca. 120-202 C.E. Polycarp had at least one Gnostic student as well, but Irenaeus chose the non Gnostic path and became a bitter opponent of all things Gnostic. He wrote anti-Gnostic writings that drew a clear line of separation between the two schools. Some have said:

---

[639] Faustus, Contra Faustus Manicheun
[640] On Baptism 17

"What Irenaeus achieved . . . was not only the intended refutation, but the lasting polarization of Christian fronts"[641]

Irenaeus engages in overt ridicule against the true lineage, which demonstrates the confidence and feeling of superiority that his school was beginning to feel by his time. Irenaeus cleverly labels the true Gnostics as heretics, and his own false school as the true preserver of the original tradition. To achieve this Irenaeus quotes his opponents out of context and couched within his own ridiculing comments, and makes false claims to an Apostolic Authority for his school and his tradition. Later elements of Pauline Churchanity will take this theme and elaborate on it, rewriting history to reflect their desire for legitimacy, and employing the might of Rome and the Emperor Constantine to enforce it.

Constantine's Bible

In the year 331 AD, six years after the Council of Nicea, Constantine ordered that 50 copies of the bible be prepared at a scriptorium run by Eusebius. Those bibles included the Old Testament and, for the first time, the New Testament. Two of the 331 AD fifty bibles have survived. One of them has been kept at the Vatican at least since 1475 AD, when it first appeared on their catalog list. It is called the Codex Vaticanus. In 1844, Constantin von Tischendorf discovered another of the fifty 331 AD bibles in a monastery at Mount Sinai and it is called the Codex Siniaticus. Both Codex Vaticanus and Codex Siniaticus omit the ending of the Mark gospel describing the resurrection of Christ as well as the ascension of Christ into heaven found in modern bibles. These were added after 331 AD.

---

[641] Gerard Vallee

A harmony of the Gospels was accredited to Tatian, an Assyrian and the disciple of Justin Martyr, about A.D. 170, and was widely used in Syria. Ephraem's commentary on the Diatessaron proves its existence early on, before his death in 373 AD. Tatian, or Titianus, probably did not write his Harmony but inherited at least some of it from his teacher Justin. Scholars are inclined to make Tatian's to be the earliest Syriac translation of the Greek Gospels. It contains material of the four distinct Greek Gospels rewritten as a continuous narrative only 72% as long as the combined originals. It left out only 56 verses of the canonical Gospels, most of which are from the two genealogies of Jesus and the pericope of the adulteress in John 7:53 - 8:11. It resolved some contradictions in the Greek gospels.

The Harmony was replaced amongst gentile Christians of Syria by the Aramaic Peshitto in the fifth century. The earliest manuscript of this Syriac text is dated A.D. 464. The name 'Diatessaron' is Greek for 'through four'; the Syriac name for this gospel harmony is 'Ewangeliyôn Damhalltê' ('Gospel of the Mixed'). The Peshitto is just an Aramaic translation of the Greek gospels and therefore is not an authentic source for the real Yeshu.

The harmony of the Gospels, as well as the Peshita, are not good sources for the words and events of Yeshu. They are both based ultimately on the unauthorized Gospel of Mark and its rewrites. True Yeshu history is more appropriately found in the better of those texts labeled as Gnostic.

Irenaeus promoted the four present biblical Gospels as the only reliable ones for Christians. He invested a lot of time in condemning all others. His efforts resulted in the Roman Church condemning all other gospels. In 367 Athanasius, a

Pauline Bishop of Alexandria and great admirer of Irenaeus, issued a proclamation listing the 27 texts that now make up the New Testament. In this same edict he demanded the destruction of all other texts, including those in the Nag Hammadhi library which was buried at that time in conformity to his ignorant insistence. These were found in 1945 and are a great treasury of truth.

Faustus on the Bible

All Nazorean Essenes have traditionally looked with great suspicion on the authenticity of the Old and New Testaments. This ancient position on the Bible was summed up by the Manichaean bishop Faustus about 400 A.D.:

> "You say, that if we believe the Gospel, we must believe everything that is written in it. Why, then, since you believe the Old Testament, do you not believe all that is found in any part of it? Instead of that, you cull out only the prophecies telling of a future King of the Jews, for you suppose this to be Jesus, along with a few precepts of common morality, such as, Thou shalt not kill, Thou shalt not commit adultery; and all the rest you pass over, thinking of the other things as Paul thought of the things which he held to be dung. Why, then, should it seem strange or singular in me that I select from the New Testament whatever is purest, and helpful for my salvation, while I set aside the interpolations of your predecessors, which impair its dignity and grace?
>
> If there are parts of the Testament of the Father which we are not bound to observe (for you attribute the Jewish law to the Father, and it is well known that many things in it shock you, and make you ashamed, so that in heart you no longer regard it as free from corruption, though, as you believe, the Father Himself partly wrote it for you with His own finger while part was written by Moses, who was faithful and trustworthy, the Testament of the Son must be equally liable to corruption, and

may equally well contain objectionable things; especially as it is allowed not to have been written by the Son Himself, nor by His apostles, but long after, by some unknown men, who, lest they should be suspected of writing of things they knew nothing of, gave to their books the names of the apostles, or of those who were thought to have followed the apostles, declaring the contents to be according to these originals. In this, I think, they do grievous wrong to the disciples of Christ, by quoting their authority for the discordant and contradictory statements in these writings, saying that it was according to them that they wrote the Gospels, which are so full of errors and discrepancies, both in facts and in opinions, that they can be harmonized neither with themselves nor with one another. This is nothing else than to slander good men, and to bring the charge of dissension on the brotherhood of the disciples. In reading the Gospels, the clear intention of our heart perceives the errors, and, to avoid all injustice, we accept whatever is useful, in the way of building up our faith, and promoting the glory of the Lord Christ, and of the Almighty God, His Father, while we reject the rest as unbecoming the majesty of God and Christ, and inconsistent with our belief.

To return to what I said of your not accepting everything in the Old Testament. You do not admit carnal circumcision, though that is what is written;(1) nor resting from all occupation on the Sabbath, though that is enjoined;(2) and instead of propitiating God, as Moses recommends, by offerings and sacrifices, you cast these things aside as utterly out of keeping with Christian worship, and as having nothing at all to recommend them. In some cases, however, you make a division, and while you accept one part, you reject the other. Thus, in the Passover, which is also the annual feast of the Old Testament, while it is written that in this observance you must slay a lamb to be eaten in the evening, and that you must abstain from leaven for seven days, and be content with unleavened bread and bitter herbs,(3) you accept the feast, but pay no attention to the rules for its observance. It is the same with the feast of Pentecost, or seven weeks, and the accompaniment of a certain kind and number of sacrifices which Moses enjoins:(4) you observe the feast, but you condemn the propitiatory rites, which are part of it, because they are not in harmony with Christianity. As regards the command to abstain from Gentile food, you are zealous believers in the uncleanness of things offered to idols, and of what has died of itself; but you are not so ready to believe the prohibition of swine's flesh, and hares, and conies, and mullets, and cuttle-fish, and all the fish that you have a relish for, although Moses pronounces them all unclean.

I do not suppose. that you will consent, or even listen, to such things as that a father-in-law should lie with his daughter-in-law, as Judah did; or a father with his daughters, like Lot; or prophets with harlots, like Hosea; or that a husband should sell his wife for a night to her lover, like Abraham; or that a man should marry two sisters, like Jacob; or that the rulers of the people and the men you consider as most inspired should keep their mistresses by hundreds and thousands; or, according to the provision made in Deuteronomy about wives, that the wife of one brother, if he dies without children, should marry the surviving brother, and that he should raise up seed from her instead of his brother; and that if the man refuses to do this, the fair plaintiff should bring her case before the elders, that the brother may be called and admonished to perform this religious duty; and that, if he persists in his refusal, he must not go unpunished, but the woman must loose his shoe from his right foot, and strike him in the face, and send him away, spat upon and accursed, to perpetuate the reproach in his family.(5) These, and such as these, are the examples and precepts of the Old Testament. If they are good, why do you not practice them? If they are bad, why do you not condemn the Old Testament, in which they are found? But if you think that these are spurious interpolations, that is precisely what we think of the New Testament. You have no right to claim from us an acknowledgment for the New Testament which you yourselves do not make for the Old.

Since you hold to the divine authorship of the Old as well as of the New Testament, it would surely be more consistent and more becoming, as you do not obey its precepts, to confess that it has been corrupted by improper additions, than to treat it so contemptuously, if it is genuine and uncorrupted. Accordingly, my explanation of your neglect of the requirements of the Old Testament has always been, and still is, that you are either wise enough to reject them as spurious, or that you have the boldness and irreverence to disregard them if they are true. At any rate, when you would oblige me to believe everything contained in the documents of the New Testament because I receive the Testament itself, you should consider that, though you profess to receive the Old Testament, you in your heart disbelieve many things in it. Thus, you do not admit as true or authoritative the declaration of the Old Testament, that every one that hangeth on a tree is accursed, for this would apply to Jesus; or that every man is accursed who does not raise up seed in Israel, for that would include all of both sexes devoted to God; or that whoever is not circumcised in the flesh of his foreskin will be cut off from among his people, for that would apply to all Christians; or that whoever breaks the Sabbath must be stoned to death; or that no mercy should be shown to the man who breaks a single precept of the Old Testament. If you really believe these things as certainly enjoined by God, you would, in the time of Christ, have been the first to assail Him, and you would now have no quarrel with the Jews, who, in persecuting Christ with heart and soul, acted in obedience to their own God.

I am aware that instead of boldly pronouncing these passages spurious, you make out that these things were required of the Jews till the coming of Jesus; and that now that He is come, according, as you say, to the predictions of this Old Testament, He Himself teaches what we should receive, and what we should set aside as obsolete. Whether the prophets predicted the coming of Jesus we shall see presently. Meanwhile, I need say no more than that if Jesus, after being predicted in the Old Testament, now subjects it to this sweeping criticism, and teaches us to receive a few things and to throw over many things, in the same way the Paraclete who is promised in the New Testament teaches us what part of it to receive, and what to reject; as Jesus Himself says in the Gospel, when promising the Paraclete, "He shall guide you into all truth, and shall teach you all things, and bring all things to your remembrance." So then, with the help of the Paraclete, we may take the same liberties with the New Testament as Jesus enables you to take with the

Old, unless you suppose that the Testament of the Son is of greater value than that of the Father, if it is really the Father's; so that while many parts of the one are to be condemned, the other must be exempted from all disapproval; and that, too, when we know, as I said before, that it was not written by Christ or by His apostles.

Hence, as you receive nothing in the Old Testament except the prophecies and the common precepts of practical morality, which we quoted above, while you set aside circumcision, and sacrifices, and the Sabbath and its observance, and the feast of unleavened bread, why should not we receive nothing in the New Testament but what we find said in honor and praise of the majesty of the Son, either by Himself or by His apostles, with the proviso, in the case of the apostles, that it was said by them after reaching perfection, and when no longer in unbelief; while we take no notice of the rest, which, if said at the time, was the utterance of ignorance or inexperience, or, if not, was added by crafty opponents with a malicious intention, or was stated by the writers without due consideration, and so handed down as authentic? Take as examples, the shameful birth of Jesus from a woman, His being circumcised like the Jews, His offering sacrifice like the Gentiles, His being baptized in a humiliating manner, His being led about by the devil in the wilderness, and His being tempted by him in the most distressing way. With these exceptions, besides whatever has been inserted under the pretence of being a quotation from the Old Testament, we believe the whole, especially the mystic nailing to the cross, emblematic of the wounds of the soul in its passion; as also the sound moral precepts of Jesus, and His parables, and the whole of His immortal discourse, which sets forth especially the distinction of the two natures, and therefore must undoubtedly be His. There is, then, no reason for your thinking it obligatory in me to believe all the contents of the Gospels; for you, as has been proved, take so dainty a sip from the Old Testament, that you hardly, so to speak, wet your lips with it." [642]

---

[642] Faustus, Contra Faustus Manicheun

ˉ 22 ˉ
mystery of the kingdom

finding the kingdom

YESHU TAUGHT THE MYSTERY of the Kingdom of Heaven,
the *"Razia dMalakut"*. This was a reign of righteousness and
purity that orthodox Christians put off into the distant future
but which Yeshu demanded be established here and now in
one's heart, mind, view, and flesh. Yeshu once referred to it as
the "Secret of the Holy Plan". When "His disciples said to him,
"When will the kingdom come? Yeshu said":

> "It will not come by waiting for it. It will not be a matter of
> saying 'here it is' or 'there it is.' Rather, the kingdom of the father
> is spread out upon the earth, and men do not see it." [643]

He also warned not to look for it in heaven, or the sky, at some
vague future point:

> "Yeshu said, "If those who lead you say to you, 'See, the
> kingdom is in the sky,' then the birds of the sky will precede
> you. If they say to you, 'It is in the sea,' then the fish will precede
> you. Rather, the kingdom is inside of you, and it is outside of
> you. When you come to know yourselves, then you will become
> known, and you will realize that it is you who are the sons of the
> living father. But if you will not know yourselves, you dwell in
> poverty and it is you who are that poverty." [644]

Yeshu laid down the non dual nature of entrance into this
realm when he uttered:

> "When you make the two into one, and when you make the
> inner like the outer and the outer like the inner, and the upper

---

[643] Thomas 113
[644] Thomas 1-3

like the lower, and when you make male and female into a single
one, so that the male will not be male nor the female be female,
when you make eyes in place of an eye, a hand in place of a
hand, a foot in place of a foot, an image in place of an image,
then you will enter." [645]

He warned that the transition from worldly consciousness to
kingdom consciousness was fraught with inner turmoil and
transformation:

"Yeshu said, "Let him who seeks continue seeking until he finds.
When he finds, he will become troubled. When he becomes
troubled, he will be astonished, and he will rule over the All." [646]

Entering the Stream

Yeshu was once asked by Judas:

""Tell me, Lord, what is the beginning of the Path." He said,
"Love and Goodness." [647]

The commencement of the Path of Yeshu is Compassion and
Goodness. Without a desire to be loving and kind, a person
cannot begin to walk the Living Path taught by the Nazorean
Buddha Messiah. He taught that we must plant within
ourselves the seed of compassion and the wish for quick
enlightenment so that we may more quickly end the suffering
of all light entrapped in matter. Yeshu taught that anything
other than a vegan lifestyle compromises goodness because it
causes distress and death of innocent creatures. This was part
of the Nazorean tradition that Yeshu grew up with and he
taught such until his death. This foundation of goodness was
continuously stressed in Yeshu's program. After basic

---

[645] Thomas 1
[646] Thomas 2
647 The Dialogue of the Savior, Nag Hammadi

goodness was developed, a greater degree of goodness was called for. This greater goodness was dependent on an awakened alert mind and heart. Early Gnostic Christians called this awakened mind the "Light Mind of Christ". In the east it is called Bodhicitta, which also means "an enlightened mind" or "heart". Bodhicitta is both Wisdom and Compassion in balance. Yeshu taught a balancing of these two virtues. Unlike mainstream Christianity which entices its followers to do good with the promise of a reward in heaven, Yeshu Miryai and Mani stressed doing good for goods sake alone.

Yeshu's Call to Oneness

So what did Yeshu mean when he cried:

> "Blessed are the solitary and elect, for you will find the kingdom. For you are from it, and to it you will return." [648]

He was not teaching that you entered it alone and by yourself, like a hermit, but that you entered into it when you became one with other righteous ones, or elect, and saw, felt and acted with one heart, one mind, and one body. This is, once again, the concept of the "Living Soul" that we mentioned in the earlier chapters. This is the unity of sparks that fly off from Adam Kadmon and which are gathered up again through Havah Kadmon, like Isis collected the scattered limbs of Osiris toward his resurrection. This collecting cannot completely happen unless a group of like hearted souls unite as one in a coed monastic setting. Without the rules and principles of Yeshu's Holy Order, all attempts to live as one with others only lead to chaos. Yeshu brought souls into this unity by stages, through enlightening and transforming Gates, or ritual mystery passages. The eternal laws behind these stages were

---

[648] Thomas 49

the reason Yeshu said that no one could enter the kingdom without the mysteries, or rites of passage.

> "But truly, truly, I say unto you: Even if a righteous man hath committed no sins at all, he cannot possibly be brought into the Light-kingdom, because the sign of the kingdom of the mysteries is not with him. In a word, it is impossible to bring souls into the Light without the rituals of the Light-kingdom." [649]

Yeshu taught that being within the Kingdom of Light was a state of mind and heart, and was something that developed by stages within one until a sudden flash of enlightenment occurred. In the Gospel of Thomas we have reference to it developing like a mustard seed, or like leaven within a loaf. Yeshu taught his disciples the techniques that allowed this seed which he planted to develop and mature. This is what Yeshu's lineage of Salome was referring to when it is said:

> "And in their writings we read as follows, the interpretation which they give [of their views], declaring that Jesus spoke in a mystery to His disciples and apostles privately, and that they requested and obtained permission to hand down the things thus taught them, to others who should be worthy and believing. "[650]

Yeshu's Yoga

Yeshu, according to the Sleeping Prophet Readings, taught meditation techniques to his disciples. These were the same "Great Perfection" practices observed by the Dzogchen practitioners that Yeshu would have interacted with in his eastern travels. In Dzogchen:

---

[649] The Pistis Sophia, 3:103
[650] Irenaeus Of Lyons, Adversus Haereses, Book I, Chapter Xxv, The Doctrines Of Carpocrates

"Our ultimate nature is said to be pure, self-existing, all-encompassing awareness. This 'intrinsic awareness' has no form of its own and yet is capable of perceiving, experiencing, reflecting, or expressing all form. It does so without being affected by those forms in any ultimate, permanent way. The analogy given by Dzogchen masters is that one's nature is like a mirror which reflects with complete openness but is not affected by the reflections, or a crystal ball which takes on the colour of the material on which it is placed without itself being changed. Other evocative phrases used by masters describe it as an 'effulgence', an 'all-pervading fullness' or as 'space that is aware'. When an individual is able to maintain the rdzogs chen state continually, he or she no longer experiences dukkha, i.e., feelings of discontent, tension and anxiety in everyday life." [651]

Yeshu's teacher Judy was also knowledgeable in these matters according to Cayce:

"Judy came into contact with the Medes, Persians and Indians as a result of the commerce with those countries, as well as the influences of Saneid, Brahma and Buddha" [652]

Yeshu's disciple Mani also taught meditation:

"In this sinful time, the pure denavar (monk) should sit down in pious meditation and should turn away from sin and develop what is good." [653]

Outside of Nazorean circles these meditative exercises were foreign to many in the Middle East who did not have the extensive education and experience of Yeshu and other developed Nazorean initiates. Of one Ullen, Cayce spoke:

---

651 Dzogchen, From Wikipedia, the free encyclopedia
652 Cayce Reading 1472
653 Mani to Mar Ammo called Sweet Teaching of the Sinless

"However, confusion resulted to some extent because of the differences in the practices of the Arabs, and that which was taught by the Apostles. This was particularly so when visions, dreams, and the use of quiet moments became a part of the teachings....Yet much can be learned from the lessons learned then, which manifest as urges. This particularly refers to the innate urges for meditation on spiritual and inspirational matters" [654]

Of another, Cayce spoke to one once known anciently as Susane:

"She can help her present physical condition by deep meditation, as she learned in that experience, and as it was given by Him [Yeshu] to all. Each should turn within and trust wholly in the power of God." [655]

It would be a mistake to view Yeshu as a Palestinian national attempting to introduce some form of Buddhism or Hinduism to his native land. The teachings of Yeshu were unique unto himself, despite certain affinities to some portions of the Tao, Savaite, Mahayana, Bonpo, Zarathustrian, Cha'an, Pythagorian and Jewish philosophies. The full range and depth of these unique teachings of Yeshu are perhaps best approached through an in depth study of Manichaean philosophy, which is something we will address in the third volume of this series.

Removing Obstacles of Enlightenment

It is easy to misunderstand what the message and meaning of Yeshu's Kingdom was and is. The principles and practices of the lifestyle that accompanies that Kingdom are not the Kingdom. Often these practices and customs are only tools to

[654] Cayce Reading 1431
[655] Cayce Reading 1179

remove some obstacle or intruding reality that cause a disconnect with the reality Yeshu sought to reveal. Some of these are mental and soul residues from former lives lived imperfectly. These karmic residues need to be removed before the Pearl can return to his or her original self. Epiphanius of Salamis' serious misunderstanding that the followers of Salome taught sinning as the means to heaven betrays the orthodox ignorance of the laws of karma taught by Yeshu. Yeshu taught that we humans have passed through all levels of degradation, but that in this life we must undo all the past by exceptional purity. He also taught that part of that purity was no longer viewing life as a disconnected individual but instead merging into unity with others of like mind and heart. Yeshu taught that this unity was not possible as long as his deeper disciples kept barriers to oneness erected between them. One of the most serious of these barriers was the concept of individual private property. Separate goods make for separate souls, and Yeshu came to undo the bonds that separate one part of the Living Soul from another part. Early Nazoreans understood this and attempted to live in that unity as much as possible. Echoes of this unified lifestyle can be found even in the orthodox Book of Acts:

> "The multitude of those who believed were of one heart and soul. Not one of them claimed that anything of the things which he possessed was his own, but they had all things in common." 656

It is interesting that it says "all things in common", not all material possessions in common. The New Testament reference to appointment of seven deacons was a facet of this situation that dealt primarily with the material goods side of this oneness. Cayce supports this tradition when he speaks of

---

656 Biblical Book of Acts 4:32

the appointment of souls to manage the community of goods among the Nazoreans:

> "That was when all of their material belongings had been turned over to the disciples, or Apostles." [657]

This was not a novel system, for even the Community Rule from Qumran insisted that new members of the Yahad would have:

> "... his property and earnings shall be handed over to the Bursar"

The process of consecration for Nazoreans, like that of the sect described in the Community Rule, would have been gradual.

> "Then when he has completed one year within the Community, the Congregation shall deliberate his case with regard to his understanding and observance of the Law. And if it be his destiny, according to the judgment of the Priests and the multitude of the men of their Covenant, to enter the company of the Community, his property and earnings shall be handed over to the Bursar of the Congregation who shall register it to his account and shall not spend it for the Congregation. . . . But when the second year has passed, he shall be examined, and if it be his destiny, according to the judgment of the Congregation, to enter the Community, then he shall be inscribed among his brethren in the order of his rank for the Law, and for justice, and for the pure Meal; his property shall be merged and he shall offer his counsel and judgment to the Community."[658]

Having "all things in common" meant then something very different than it would now mean to many. Middle class and even many "poor" in more affluent countries have dozens, if not hundreds, of clothes, not to mention televisions,

---

[657] Cayce Reading 1468
[658] Rule of the Community (1QS) VI.

electronics, cars, bikes, watches, and other personal items. Cupboards full of kitchenware, closets full of junk, garages and storage sheds full of yard equipment, sporting goods, Christmas decorations, etc.. In contrast, a common Galilean of Yeshu's day might have one or two sets of linen clothes, reed sandals, a wooden comb, and perhaps a wooden bowl and spoon. The literate, like the Nazoreans, might have had a scroll or two. Land owning families might have a simple adobe shelter or two, some cooking and storage jars, an oil lamp, baskets, a few simple tools, as well as a small orchard with olives, dates and figs, and a small vineyard and field. Since so many were landless, affiliation with a communal orientated group like the Nazoreans meant that you could share in the labor and harvests of Nazorean orchard, vineyards, and fields. Communal kitchens and shelters made survival in a hostile land much easier. Organized group economics ensured that there was enough to go around, as well as a surplus for trading and to assist non Nazorean poor of the land.

Some Things In Common

In the Community Rule we read:

> "They shall eat in common and pray in common and deliberate in common."[659]

The orthodox Christians have consoled themselves that they have abided by this principle in their monasteries, but they have not lived the full unity of Yeshu's "kingdom". Christian monasteries may deny personal possessions and personal will to their monks or nuns, but they have not created the real unity of soul that Yeshu spoke of. For the unity put forth by Yeshu also entailed the unity of man and woman:

---

[659] Rule of the Community (1QS) VI.

"Yeshu said to them, "When you make the two one, and when you make the inside like the outside and the outside like the inside, and the above like the below, and when you make the male and the female one and the same, so that the male not be male nor the female female; and when you fashion eyes in the place of an eye, and a hand in place of a hand, and a foot in place of a foot, and a likeness in place of a likeness; then will you enter the kingdom." [660]

Yeshu was talking about something other than male female physical union, but he was also talking about this physical union as a manifestation of the other union he referred to. Celibate Christian monasteries do not have the "the male with the female, neither male nor female." as taught by Yeshu in the Nazorean Gospel of the Egyptians:

"For the Lord himself being asked by some one when his kingdom should come, said: When the two shall be one, and the outside (that which is without) as the inside (that which is within), and the male with the female neither male nor female. [661]

In the Cayce writings these matters are hinted at as well. When asked to describe Judy's home life as well as her Essene activities, the reticent Cayce replied that modern people are not open minded enough to grasp the lifestyle lived by Yeshu, Judy and other advanced Essenes:

"(Q) Please describe Judy's home life as well as her Essene activities. (A) That as might be the description of an individual who had set self aside as a channel for such activities. These are very hard to be understood from the material mind, or from the material understanding or concept, especially in this period of consciousness. For, then man walked close with God. When there were those preparations - it is possible in the present, but

---

[660] Thomas 22
[661] Second Epistle Of Clement, also Thomas 22

not ACCEPTABLE. .... This did not prevent her from being, then, a material person, nor one with the faculties and desires for material associations - as indicated in the lack of celibacy. Is this indicated in any condition in the book, or man's relationship to God? Nowhere is this indicated!" [662]

So what uncelibate lifestyle could Judy and other high level Essenes have been living that would be so unacceptable to the modern mind? The answer lies in teachings of Yeshu and Salome:

> "But the followers of Carpocrates and Epiphanes think that wives should be common property." [663]

Few things could be more unacceptable to the modern materialistic worldview, especially to those whose erroneous Christian indoctrination taught them that Jesus was celibate and considered all sexuality evil. In light of this, it is not surprising that the Gnosis behind Cayce's utterances was reluctant to say much about Judy's lifestyle except that such was presently too unacceptable to even speak of. Times have changed, and although viewing Yeshu as engaging in spiritual sexuality is still taboo in many orthodox circles, much of the world finds such information refreshing.

All the Gnostics were accused of these non celibate practices by the celibate loving, but not observing, Roman Christians. Not more than a small minority of these Christians were in fact celibate, and only a minority of those in supposed monogamous relationships were totally true to that ideal. It is a well known fact that infidelity statistics are always high in monogamous subscribing cultures. Gnostic Monastics eradicated much infidelity and adultery, as well as thievery

---

[662] Cayce Reading 2067-11
[663] Clement of Alexandria, Stromata, Book III, II

and a host of other crimes by the very nature of their communal system. Roman Christians found it useful to characterize their Gnostic rivals as sexually promiscuous, but these Gnostics were probably having no more intimacy than their Christian counterparts, but more honestly. Christians kept their sexual lives more private, more secretive, more in the dark, and separate from their spiritual lives. Gnostics could not do this, for they sought to spiritually infuse all facets of their life, even the intimate ones. The growing Catholic Church never fully came to grips with the fact that most of these Gnostics received their traditions through direct transmission from the earliest disciples and relatives of Yeshu, who were themselves Gnostic and themselves upholders of these heavenly mandated but presently unacceptable teachings.

Misuse of Higher Law

It should be noted that Yeshu, and Mani after him, never taught his ordinary followers to engage in these more advanced activities, nor did he allow his deeper disciples to abuse these principles for personal lust or aggrandizement. Yeshu never taught promiscuity, adultery, or any other deceitful or out of control expression of sexuality. What Yeshu taught was that his most serious adult disciples, after great preparation and instruction, should become one Living Soul and no longer act as separate disconnected individuals. He taught them that private possessions were contradictory to such as state of unity. He also taught that private bodies and private spouses were contradictory as well, but only after a certain quite advance point in his program. One soul in many bodies makes each of those bodies bound to one another - all members of one body. To have gone outside that body and been intimate with someone outside the "kingdom" was considered adultery, and Yeshu taught against such misapplication of his higher teachings:

> "Indeed, every act of sexual intercourse which has occurred between those unlike one another is adultery." [664]

An uninitiated person who takes it upon themselves to implement any of these principles of unity outside of a Holy Order makes a grave mistake. Even if all parties are in agreement, such will bring only disunity, not unity, if attempted outside the bounds of the rigid rules of Yeshu's Monastic Ordination. Awareness of these practices among Yeshu's inner circle should not become an excuse to go behind another's back and betray their trust in order to engage in some sort of quasi-spiritual affair. Yeshu was very much against hurting and alienating others, especially for selfish reasons. Such acts create karma that takes lifetimes to undo and is a foolish misapplication of higher truth.

Temperance

The early Gnostics did not engage in orgies or forced relationships between everyone in their Holy Orders. What they did allow was the possibility for more than one disciplined relationship at a time. A selfless priest might have, within any given year, occasional circumspect physical relationships with one or two priestesses who themselves might be intimate with one or two other priests during that same year. Everyone was not being intimate with everyone else, but everyone was linked to everyone else through someone they themselves were one with. As in the human body, the arm is not necessarily touching the leg, but both are linked together by the common torso between them. Yeshu taught "all things in common" only for those who had

---

[664] Gospel of Philip

renounced all, joined his coed monasteries, and advanced therein enough to handle such dangerous fire. He referred to this when he said:

> "He who is near me is near the fire, and he who is far from me is far from the kingdom." [665]

No soul was allowed to practice or promote such teachings without being initiated into the level of light where such things could be lived purely. To attempt to live such outside the confines of a very special and limited arena was to invoke all manner of difficulties problems for all involved. That is why such secrecy was involved concerning them:

> "Listen! The tantric mysteries are said to be secret. Not because the Tantra is immoral but because it is closed. Closed to the narrow-minded adherents of lesser paths." -Yeshe Tsogyel

Secrecy

Nazoreans and Essenes were always a secretive people. They did not openly reveal all levels of their society to outsiders. Even insiders were tried for a number of years before having deeper doctrines revealed to them. Speaking of the Essenes, Josephus says:

> "They are not allowed to keep any secrets from other members of the sect; but they are warned to reveal nothing to outsiders, even under the pain of death. They are not allowed to alter the 'books of the sect, and must keep all the information secret, especially the names of the angels." [666]

This Essene attitude toward secrets was partially a result of their attempt to be respectful toward the intimate side of their

---

[665] Gospel of Thomas 82
[666] Josephus, writing about the death of Antigonus in 103 B.C.

Gods and Goddesses, as expressed in their ancient texts. The ancient Nazoreans understood that the Gods and Goddesses created the universe thru a sexual act and they saw each personal intimacy as a divine requirement and reenactment of this ancient cosmic drama. The Nazoreans use the Date Palm tree as a symbol of the male and the Wellspring as a symbol of the female. They thought it unbecoming to discuss such things in public. These are explained openly only in their most secret scrolls:

"Explanation of the cosmic pair is confined to the secret scrolls. The Diwan Malkuta 'laita explains bluntly that the Date-palm is a phallic symbol, and sexual metaphors and images employed by initiates are protected by special oaths of silence." [667]

A warning and call to strict secrecy concerning these things is found in one secret Mandaean book:

"And be careful, be careful, three hundred and sixty times be careful, as I have warned you, in explanation of the Wellspring and Palmtree and [of] 'When I arose to My feet and when (as yet) I had created no Companion for Myself.' [668]

Another verse within secret Mandaean literature describes the cosmic union of the Datepalm and Wellspring, saying that through it both plants (offspring) and physical worlds are created:

"I am Mara-d-Rabutha [Lord of Greatness], Father of 'uthras; and the Wellspring is my Spouse. Praised is the great 'zlat for She is the wellspring of light: she is my Spouse, [mine], your Father, Mara-d-Rabutha.... Praised be Treasure-of-Life, Mother of all worlds, She from whom the upper, middle and lower worlds emanated, for she is my Spouse, [the spouse of] Mara-d-Rabutha, since her name is Nasirutha....

---

[667] The Secret Adam by Drower, p 10
[668] Diwan Malkuta 'laita, lines 331

And He took a Spouse for Himself and created plants (children) and created worlds." [669]

Yeshu spoke of the day, our day, when the secrecy behind the mystery of Wellspring and Datepalm would be revealed, and the long buried truth of Yeshu's Kingdom would be raised:

> "For there is nothing hidden that will not be revealed. And there is nothing buried that will not be raised." [670]

These controversial teachings were preserved amongst all legitimate branches of Nazoreanism. They were lived before Yeshu on Carmel, and after him these principles were promulgated by his closest disciples like Mary, Martha and Salome. They existed secretly in the Manichaean era of Nazoreanism among the Manichaean elect, and even became a national movement for about 30 years in sixth century Iran when Mazdak succeeded in converting the king and most of the entire country to a vegetarian society with common goods and women. By 528 AD a massacre of Mazdak and most of his followers reversed this novel social order. Some of these Mazdakian practices and practitioners survived in remote areas for centuries, but eventually were absorbed by Central Asian Buddhism[671] which also has similar teachings in many of its branches. As an example, here is a passage from a secret text of the Bonpo's of Central Asia:

> "With a pure vow as precondition the important thing is a worthy mate as virtuous companion . . . Ravishing and gently spoken, yet like the meanest servant . . . eschewing evil acts and exerting herself in the ten good acts . . . observing pure conduct and living in chastity . . . "

---

[669] Alp Trisar Suialia ("A Thousand and Twelve Questions"), p.11
[670] Gospel of Thomas 5
[671] Mazdak, From Wikipedia, the free encyclopedia

"The instructions and the secret practice must be concealed and kept secret. Such is the description of the mate for the realization of enlightenment. Having thus received the inspired teachings from the sages, the brethren and their sworn maidens gather together and seek for a secret place as the site of their practice, a site such as one which was used in former times."[672]

Rumors of the Manichaean practice of such tantric mysteries can even be found in the Mandaean Ginza:

"Then I explain to you, my disciples, that there is yet another Gate (Sect) that derives from Msiha (Messiah). They are called "Zandiqi" (Saints) and "Mar dMani"(of Lord Mani). They sow seeds in concealment ...." [673]

They are also found amongst ex Manichaean Christians like Augustine:

"Moreover, when you are so eager in your desire to prevent the soul from being confined in flesh by conjugal intercourse, and so eager in asserting that the soul is set free from seed by the food of the saints, do you not sanction, unhappy beings, the suspicion entertained about you? . . . And as your followers cannot bring these seeds to you for purification, who will not suspect that you make this purification secretly among yourselves, and hide it from your followers, in case they should leave you?" [674]

It is perhaps noteworthy to notice that Manichaean monks and nuns lived together in the same location, and not separate as did Catholic monastics, as is proven by the following:

"When the Lords (monks/electi) and the Ladies (nuns, electae) take meals at the monastery, or go out when they are invited,

[672] The Way of the Primordial Shen
[673] Ginza Right 9:1
[674] Morals of the Manichaean's, chapter 18, by Augustine

they should each be brought two cups or bowls with water . . .
"[675]

This alone would have made many Catholics conclude that the Manichaean monastics were sexually active. This general Catholic attitude is summed up by a famous Catholic monk St. Bernard who said that "for men and women to live together without having sexual relations was a greater miracle than raising the dead." Tantric sexual behavior among monastics is consistent with Bon and Nyingma traditions from Tibet and is not out of harmony with their strong spiritual focus and higher monastic morals. Cayce warned that sacred sexuality has oft been misunderstood and misused:

> "Hence we have found throughout the ages, so oft the times when conception of truth became rampant with free-love, with the desecration of those things that brought to these in the beginning that of the KNOWLEDGE of their existence, as to that that may be termed - and betimes became - the MORAL, or morality OF a people. [676]

Misunderstandings

It is easy to misconstrue what such a life without traditional boundaries would entail. It is unnatural for all within a group to share the same level of attraction and interact equally. Within close knit social groups unfettered by strict boundaries, only limited intimacy ensures. For example, in a large group of unmarried college students, relationships with any of the opposite sex are possible, but in reality, individuals develop closeness with only one or two at a time, and some with no one at all. Even when it is possible in a society or group, everyone is never intimate with everyone else. Occasionally in some circles an off balance promiscuous person will seek to

---

[675] charter of a Manichaean monastery in Kocho
[676] Text Of Reading 364-6

develop a series of shallow relationships, but the more grounded will not.

It is very common in western society for married people to have affairs. A candid review of cultures that have a monogamous ideal leads one to conclude that it is not human nature to remain monogamous like the goose and the wolf. Yet humans are not by nature as promiscuous as chimpanzees either. Ancient religious societies, like the Nazoreans and Tibetans, that allowed more than one mate should not be seen as an untempered troop of chimpanzees. Nazorean society was certainly sober and temperate in their connections. Well rounded souls within these ancient Holy Orders were not driven by selfish lust or desires to make sexual conquests, but rather, were motivated by a desire to serve others. The form of this service varies in both type and intensity with various spiritual comrades within their social group. The Divine speaking through Cayce promised that when done correctly goodness could indeed come from association of kindred flesh:

> "Yet this same feeling, this same exaltation that comes from association of kindred bodies - that have their lives consecrated in a purposefulness, that makes for the ability of retaining those of the essence of creation in every virile body - can be made to become the fires that light truth, love, hope, patience, peace, harmony; for they are EVER the key to those influences that fire the imaginations of those that are gifted in ANY form of depicting the high emotions of human experience, whether it be in the one or the other fields, and hence is judged by those that may not be able, or through desire submit themselves - as did Amilius and I to those ELEMENTS, through the forces in the life as about them. [677]

Cayce once answered the following question:

---

[677] Text Of Reading 364-6

"Is the destiny of woman's body to return to the rib of man, out of which it was created? If so, how; and what is meant by "the rib?" (A) With this ye touch upon delicate subjects, upon which MUCH might be said respecting the necessity of that UNION of influences or forces that are divided in the earth in sex, in which all must become what? As He gave in answer to the question, "Whose wife will she be?" In the heavenly kingdom ye are neither married nor given in marriage; neither is there any such thing as sex; ye become as ONE - in the union of that from which, OF which, ye have been the portion from the beginning!" [678]

In the Gospel of Philip we read:

"When Eve was still with Adam, death did not exist. When she was separated from him, death came into being. If he enters again and attains his former self, death will be no more. "

In both the Cayce Readings and Philip we are led to understand that the disunity of separation into male and female is a disconnect from the oneness we once enjoyed above. Sex is a two-edged tool to recover the oneness. Once there is oneness, sex is not possible since sex implies union of opposites. When Yeshu was asked "whose wife shall she be?" he replied that she would not be the personal property of any one man. This is what he meant when he said that there was no marriage in the kingdom of heaven. He meant no nuclear families coexist in the unity of the Bridal Chamber.

Mainstream Christianity, following Paul's lead, is forced to condemn these truths and all who would observe them such as modern and ancient Gnostics. Mainstream Christianity knows of only two types of sexuality. Dirty depraved selfish sexuality, and tolerated but still deplored monogamous

---

[678] Text Of Reading 262-86

marital sexuality. When faced with sacred sexuality, they categorize such as the first depraved form. They cannot conceive of those "fires that light truth, love, hope, patience, peace, harmony...". It is impossible for mainstream Christianity to be the true heirs of the message of Yeshu, for they have squelched these fires of creativity and beauty and created a boring monotonous tradition far removed from the virile life filled Gnostic view of Yeshu the Nazorean. Yeshu once said: "By their fruits ye shall know them."[679]

New Temple Orders

Yeshu's birth was a result of a carefully executed plan involving a eugenics practicing Temple Cultus:

> "In the preparation for the coming of the Son of man, there were those during those periods who joined in their efforts to consecrate their lives, their bodies, for a service; for a channel through which activities might be had for the perfecting, as it were, of the material channel through which such an expression of the Creative Forces might come into the earth. See? [Essenes] There were, then, twelve maidens in the temple, or of the ORDER of the temple, who were dedicated for such preparation.[680]

The need of this Temple Cultus was not a first century phenomena, for in its replication lies the hope of the incarnation of many great messengers sent from above. The living of this program, whether in a grand temple or small household monastery, leads to a certain purity of life that is not obtained in any other way. For the pure prodigy of such a program is only one of its benefits. An even greater benefit is the selflessness and purity that arises among those that seek to

---

[679] Mt. 12.33
[680] Text Of Reading 649-2

be channels for light beings from above. The men who live such a life become holy. They become as pure as the:

> "...HOLY women who had dedicated their lives, their bodies, their purposes, their aims, to those changed teachings between John the forerunner and the Master, Jesus. [681]

Yeshu taught a deeper level of commitment than did Yuhana, a commitment to a coed Holy Order. Yeshu taught of Hiya, the Living God, and of the dedication and consecration required to return to Them in the heavens above. Yeshu taught that one's life must conform to the principles and practices set forth from above, and that one must even dedicate their bodies to such. Hence the admonition given through the Cayce conduit:

> "He gives His blessings on those who dedicate their lives and their bodies and their hearts to the service of a living God!"[682]

Holy souls in our day are still called to the self same Gospel preached by Yeshu - the same spiritual program that demands that souls "dedicate our lives and our bodies and our hearts to the service of a living God!" This pure dedication of the flesh and its desires to the Living God is typified by the mother of Yeshu: Cayce uttered:

> "Were this turned to that period when this desire, then, becomes consecrated in that accomplished again in the virgin body of the mother of the SON of man, we see this is then crystallized into that, that even that of the flesh may be - with the proper concept, proper desire in all its purity - consecrated to the LIVING forces as manifest by the ability in that body so brought into being, as to make a way of escape for the ERRING man. [683]

---

[681] Text Of Reading 540-4
[682] Text Of Reading 620-1
[683] Text Of Reading 364-6

Future Souls

The continual need of a Temple Order to bring pure souls into
the world was spoken of by the Sleeping Seer when he said:

> "First, then: There is soon to come into the world a body; one of
> our own number here that to many has been a representative of
> a sect, of a thought, of a philosophy, of a group, yet one beloved
> of all men in all places where the universality of God in the earth
> has been proclaimed, where the oneness of the Father as God is
> known and is consciously magnified in the activities of
> individuals that proclaim the acceptable day of the Lord. Hence
> that one John, the beloved in the earth - his name shall be John,
> and also at the place where he met face to face. When, where, is
> to be this one? In the hearts and minds of those that have set
> themselves in that position that they become a channel through
> which spiritual, mental and material things become one in the
> purpose and desires of that physical body! "[684]

A Temple Order is never designed to bring but one soul into
the earth, and then go defunct, for many must come and work
as one for the benefit of future generations. Each new
generation builds on the holiness of the previous one until a
true crescendo of righteousness is born in the earth. Then the
Acceptable Year of the Lord can be lived in its purity once
again.

> "Who shall proclaim the acceptable year of the Lord in him that
> has been born in the earth in America? Those from that land
> where there has been the regeneration, not only of the body but
> the mind and the spirit of men, THEY shall come and declare
> that John Peniel is giving to the world the new ORDER of things.
> Not that these that have been proclaimed have been refused, but
> that they are made PLAIN in the minds of men, that they may
> know the truth and the truth, the life, the light, will make them
> free. I have declared this, that has been delivered unto me to give

---

[684] Text Of Reading 3976-15

unto you, ye that sit here and that hear and that see a light breaking in the east, and have heard, have seen thine weaknesses and thine faultfindings, and know that He will make thy paths straight if ye will but live that YE KNOW this day - then may the next step, the next word, be declared unto thee." [685]

The Readings make it plain that the restoration of the ancient Nazorean Temple Order of Carmel will happen in America.

Transcendence

As for the Kingdom of Heaven that Yeshu taught, it is not found just in having all things in common. Having all things in common does not make one pure or enlightened. Not having all things in common does present an obstacle, however, in becoming totally pure and enlightened. A degree of righteousness and illumination is indeed possible whilst clinging to private possessions, companions, and certain levels of exclusivity in social, mental and physical arenas. This was achieved before and after Yeshu on the lower levels of the Nazorean and Essenes Orders and in certain other religions. Great holiness even ensued within celibate enclaves of certain Rechabite Essene groups and enclaves of eastern adepts, but the great and holy purity of the great and holy plan of Yeshu required more. It required an intensity of unity on the level of the Living Soul that could not be maintained under normal earthly constraints. Only by full initiation into the Mysteries of the First Mystery was such perfection possible. The environment where such occurs does have certain hallmarks. It is vegan, for harming the creatures of the earth creates a subtle disharmony within the soul that can not be overcome by other exercises. It has self sustaining agricultural endeavors that allow the Cross of Light to be redeemed through organic alms. It holds goods in common, for the hording clinging

---

[685] Text Of Reading 3976-15

tendency in the fearful chakras of humankind is easily activated. It does not possess people, either as servant, slaves or spouses. It walks to the rhythm of a luni-solar calendar with fixed fasts and feasts. It possesses and uses ancient Gnostic texts to illuminate the mind. It utilizes mind controlling meditation as a bridge to the primordial purity and certain periods of daily prayer to laud the pure ones above. And perhaps most importantly, it bequeaths the liberating Mysteries of the Messiah, the rituals of redemption, that give one the authority to move from one level to another and to live deeper law. All these things are but a small part of a Holy Order that dwells within and about a Holy Temple dedicated to Yeshu and Miryam, the Messiahs of man. The constraints of this book do not allow a full disclosure of the enlightening system of Nazirutha taught by Yeshu, but more details concerning it can be found in the second and third volume to this series, entitled: "Buddha-Messiahs, Vol. II: Miryai, the Mysteries of Mary Magdalene" and "Buddha-Messiahs, Vol. III: Mani, Christian Buddha and Taoist Sage". Those convinced of the truth of Yeshu's program, but who find themselves living outside of a Holy Order, can still do much to progress. One may master ancient Gnostic texts that illuminate the mind. One can practice mind controlling meditation, and one can keep four periods of daily prayer to laud the pure ones above. One may also practice ancient washing and purification rites, even though full baptism cannot be done without finding an authorized Tarmidaya. One can also practice a form of consecration by sending a tithe of earnings to a Nazorean Temple for common use by its Order. All these things are within the grasp of anyone and will prepare the soul to move forward to the next degree of dedication when it becomes wise.

Motivation

In the Gnostic tradition, all souls must be judged after death. If they are pure and lived truth to its fullness, they are robed in glory and allowed to enter the light land. Ancient Gnostics found it useful to project themselves forward in time to this judgment and to imagine being asked by Abathur of the Scales, if they lived with all their heart the fullness of the truth they knew on earth? They knew that if they were aware of deeper truths but chose not to live up to those ideals because they were too scarred, too selfish, or because that opportunity seemed too small, humble, or unimpressive, that the Keeper of the Gate of Light would not let them pass. They knew that he accepted no excuses from those who knew in their heart the truth, but chose another path. The reader may decide for themselves the usefulness of their line of self questioning, remembering the words of the Oracle:

> "Know that He will make thy paths straight if ye will but live that YE KNOW this day - then may the next step, the next word, be declared unto thee." [686]

Unlike Islam and Christianity, Gnosticism did not threaten people with harsh judgment and hell fire. Gnostics expected to pay for their own karma by being reborn on earth. Their hope was to escape this fate by being so pure that they would be allowed into the highest heaven.

Eternal Cycles

Through numerous incarnations and appearances Yeshu and Miryam have established the truth upon the earth, creating spiritual cultures such as the Nazorean and Manichaean which

---

[686] Text Of Reading 3976-15

supported and taught sincere souls how to overcome the allures of the world and abide in perfection. In almost every incarnation they taught the importance of constant involvement in purifying rituals and mysteries coupled with study and service work. They utilized astrology, numerology, and reincarnation to help them overcome the temptations and hardships of the world. They revealed spiritual texts of great purity which were always reservedly kept from the masses. And they offered a purified viewpoint, a holy "dzogchen" outlook which allowed an awakened one to live in the Kingdom of Heaven here and now.

Modern Christianity and its bible have not faithfully recorded the authentic sayings or acts of Yeshu, and are a perverse Roman distortion of his original message. The original and authentic message of the Gnostic Yeshu is available for those who sincerely search for it. One of the first Yeshu sayings encountered in such a search are those found in the beginning of the Gospel of Thomas:

> "Let one who seeks not cease seeking until they find, and when they find they will be troubled..."

Why troubled? Because one will discover that many cherished beliefs are wrong and must be discarded in favor of what may seem like strange ideas taught by the Gnostic Yeshu. Those who pass through this psychological readjustment phase are promised great things:

> "Yeshu said, "Let him who seeks continue seeking until he finds. When he finds, he will become troubled. When he becomes troubled, he will be astonished, and he will rule over the All." [687]

---

[687] Gospel of Thomas 2

epilogue

In the modern era one may look long and hard and still fail to find a viable expression of Gnostic Christianity that conforms to the original authentic Nazorean paradigm. In the perusal of the past it appears that such opportunities abounded, but in reality a fullness of truth was always a grail quest fraught with many counterfeits. In our era, as in all eras, there are repositories of gnosis, enclaves of light, doorways to the beyond that avail themselves to the sincere and relentless seeker. "Let her who seeks, not cease seeking until she finds!"[688]

Peace to All . . .

---

[688] Yeshu, Gospel of Thomas 1

APPENÒIX 1
SOURCE ÒOCUCDENTS

Despite this campaign to destroy all Gnostics and their literature, many great Gnostic writings have resurfaced in the last few years. Among these primary source documents used in this book are Mandaic texts preserved by the Mandaeans of southern Iraq and Iran (1586 pages total), the 1153 page Nag Hammadhi Library, 389 page Pistis Sophia, and 275 page Books of Yeu from Upper Egypt. The Manichaean texts from upper Egypt, found in 1930, contain over 3500 badly preserved pages which still remain untranslated for the most part. About 343 pages of Manichaean texts from Turfan, China have also been found and partially translated. There are also the Jesus Sutras found in the sealed cave of Dunhuang. In addition to these, information drawn from the Spiritual readings of Edgar Cayce and Suddie is available. There is also valuable information sandwiched between derogatory comments in the major Heresiologist works of Clement, Irenaeus, Eusibius, Epiphanius, and others.

Ancient Aramaic Scrolls

"Asafar Malwasha" – Book of the Zodiac
Diwan of the First Life (Book of Souls) 72 pages
Baptism of Hibil Ziwa 66 pages
Shishlam Rba Scroll (Coronation of Shislam Rba 37 pages)
"Qulasta" 316 pages
Greater First World 53 pages
Lesser First World 35 pages
Nazorean Book of the Dead (Ginza Rba left)174 pages
"Diwan Abathur" – Scrolls of Abathur 37 pages
1012 Questions - Haran Gawaitha/Great Revelation 181 pages
"Ginza" - The Treasure (Ginza Rba right) 422 pages
Drashe Dmalke (Discourses of Kings) or Sidra Dyahya (Book Of John the Baptist) 244 pages

Copтic Naɣ ɦammadhi

Codex I (The Jung Codex) The Prayer of the Apostle Paul
Codex I (The Jung Codex) The Apocryphon of James:
Codex I (The Jung Codex) Gospel of Truth
Codex I (The Jung Codex) The Treatise on the Resurrection
Codex I (The Jung Codex) The Tripartite Tractate
Codex II The Apocryphon of John (long version)
Codex II Gospel of Philip
Codex II Gospel of Thomas
Codex II The Hypostasis of the Archons
Codex II On the Origin of the World
Codex II The Exegesis on the Soul
Codex II The Book of Thomas the Contender
Codex III The Apocryphon of John (short version)
Codex III The Gospel of the Egyptians
Codex III Eugnostos the Blessed*
Codex III The Sophia of Jesus Christ
Codex III The Dialogue of the Savior
Codex IV The Apocryphon of John (long version)
Codex IV The Gospel of the Egyptians
Codex V Eugnostos the Blessed
Codex V The Apocalypse of Paul
Codex V The (First) Apocalypse of James
Codex V The (Second) Apocalypse of James
Codex V The Apocalypse of Adam
Codex VI The Acts of Peter and the Twelve Apostles
Codex VI The Thunder, Perfect Mind
Codex VI Authoritative Teaching
Codex VI The Concept of Our Great Power
Codex VI Plato, Republic 588A-589B
Codex VI The Discourse on the Eighth and Ninth
Codex VI The Prayer of Thanksgiving
Codex VI Asclepius 21-29
Codex VI (Codex XIII) Trimorphic Protennoia
Codex VI (Codex XIII) On the Origin of the World
Codex VI (Berlin Codex) Gospel of Mary

Codex VI Acts of Peter
Codex VII The Paraphrase of Shem
Codex VII The Second Treatise of the Great Seth
Codex VII The Apocalypse of Peter
Codex VII The Teachings of Silvanus
Codex VII The Three Steles of Seth
Codex VIII Zostrianos
Codex VIII The Letter of Peter to Philip
Codex IX Melchizedek
Codex IX The Thought of Norea
Codex IX The Testimony of Truth
Codex X Marsanes
Codex XI The Interpretation of Knowledge
Codex XI A Valentinian Exposition
Codex XI 2a.On the Anointing;; 2b. On the Baptism A; 2c. On the Baptism B; 2d. On the Eucharist A; 2e. On the Eucharist B
Codex XI Allogenes
Codex XI Hypsiphrone
Codex XII The Sentences of Sextus
Codex XII The Gospel of Truth

Berlin Papyrus 8502

The Gospel according to Mary
The Apocryphon of John
The Wisdom of Jesus Christ
The Act of Peter

Jesus Sutras

Sutra of the Teachings of the World-Honored One Translated 641 CE.
Sutra of Cause, Effect, and Salvation (First Treatise on Oneness of Heaven).
Sutra of the Teachings of the World-Honored One (Origins)
Sutra of Jesus Christ. Translated around 645.
Da Qin Liturgy of Taking Refuge in the Three. Translated 720 CE.
Let Us Praise (Invocation of the Dharma Kings and Sacred Sutras)

The Sutra of Returning to Your Original Nature. Translated c. 780–790

Major Manichaean

The Kephalaia
Manichaean Psalm Book
Cologne Mani Codex
Pistis Sophia
Turfan Texts

Other

Secret Gospel of Mark
Clement Recognitions
Clement Homilies
The Books of Jeu and the Untitled Text in the Brucianus Codex
Cayce Regression Readings
Suddie Regression Readings

Polemical

Irenaeus of Lyon: Against All Heresies
Tertullian: Against All Heresy, et al
Origen: Contra Celsum
Hippolytus: Refutations of all Heresies
Clement of Alexandria: Stromata,
Augustine: Contra Epistolam Fundamenti Manichaei,
Contra Faustum Manichaeum, et al
Chrysostom, Homily Against Marcionists and Manichaeans
Jerome, Letter to Pammachius Against John of Jerusalem, et al
Ephraim: To Hypatius Against Mani, Marcion, and Bardaisan

APPENDIX 2
Suspect Sayings

Here are the seventy-two sayings of Yeshu gleaned from the New Testament, most of which are authentic saying of Yeshu while others were perhaps only attributed to him later on. They are grouped into saying about entering the kingdom, about the mission of the kingdom, about the coming kingdom, and about the obstacles to the kingdom:

Entering the Kingdom

1 Blessed are the poor, for theirs is the kingdom of God. Blessed are the hungry, for they shall be satisfied. Blessed are those who mourn, for they shall be comforted. Blessed are the meek, for they shall inherit the earth. Blessed are the merciful, for they shall obtain mercy. Blessed are the pure in heart, for they shall see God. Blessed are you when people insult you and persecute you and say all sorts of evil against you on account of the Son of Man. Rejoice and be glad for your reward will be great in heaven, for so they persecuted the prophets who were before you.

2 Salt is good; but if salt has lost its saltiness, what use is it? It is no longer fit for the earth or the dunghill, but is thrown out and trodden underfoot.

3 No one after lighting a lamp puts it under a measuring bowl, but on a lamp stand, and it gives light to all in the house.

4 It is easier for heaven and earth to pass away than for one stroke in a letter of the law to be dropped.

5 While you are going on the way with your accuser, try to get away from him, lest the accuser hand you over to the judge, and the judge to the guard, and the guard throw you into prison. I tell you, you will not get out of there until you have paid the last penny.

6 If your right hand is causing your downfall, cut it off and throw it away; it is better that you lose one of your members than that your whole body go into hell. And if your right eye is

causing your downfall, pluck it out and throw it away; it is better for you to enter the kingdom of God with one eye than with two eyes to be thrown into hell.

7 Any man who divorces his wife and marries another commits adultery, and he who marries a woman divorced from her husband commits adultery.

8 If anyone strikes you on one cheek, offer him the other as well; and if anyone wants to take you to court to get your shirt, let him have your coat as well. Give to anyone who begs from you, and from one who borrows, do not ask to get back what is yours. Love your enemies and pray for those who persecute you, so that you may become sons of your Father, for he makes the sun rise on the evil and on the good, and sends rain on the just and on the unjust. For if you love those who love you, what reward do you have? Do not even the tax collectors do the same? And if you lend to those from whom you expect repayment, what reward do you have? Do not even the Gentiles do the same? So be compassionate, just as your Father is compassionate.

9 Can a blind man lead a blind man? Will they not both fall into a pit?

10 A disciple is not above his teacher. It is enough for the disciple to be like his teacher.

11 Unless you change and become like children, you will never enter the kingdom of God.

12 It is easier for a camel to go through the eye of a needle than for a rich man to enter the kingdom of God.

13 Why do you see the speck that is in your brother's eye, but do not notice the log that is in your own eye? How can you say to your brother: "Let me take the speck out of your eye", when there is a log in your own eye? You hypocrite! First take the log out of your own eye, and then you will see clearly to take the speck out of your brother's eye.

14 Do not judge, and you will not be judged. For as you judge others, so you will be judged, and the measure you give will be the measure you get back.

15 Do not give your rings to the dogs, and do not throw your pearls to the pigs, lest they trample them underfoot and turn to attack you.

16 Enter by the narrow gate. For the gate is wide and the way is easy that leads to destruction, and those who enter through it are many. But the gate is narrow and the way is hard that leads to life, and those who enter through it are few.

17 Beware of false prophets, who come to you in sheep's clothing but inwardly are ravenous wolves. You will know them by their fruits. Are grapes gathered from thorns, or figs from thistles? Every sound tree bears good fruit, but the rotten tree bears evil fruit.

18 The good person out of good treasure produces good things, and the evil person out of evil treasure produces evil things. For out of the abundance of the heart the mouth speaks.

19 Ask, and you will receive; seek, and you will find; knock, and the door will be opened to you. For everyone who asks, receives; and whoever seeks, finds; and to the one who knocks, the door will be opened. Which person among you, if your son asks you for a fish, will give him a snake? Or if he asks for an egg, will give him a scorpion? So if you who are evil know how to give good gifts to your children, how much more will your Father in heaven give good things to those who ask him?

20 Just as you want people to do to you, so you should do to them.

21 Not everyone who says to me: "Master, Master" will enter the kingdom of God, but whoever does the will of my Father in heaven. On that day many will say to me: "We ate and drank with you, and you taught in our streets". But I will say to them: "I never knew you; depart from me you evildoers".

22 Everyone who hears my words and does them, is like a man who built his house on rock. The rain came down, the floods rose, the winds blew and battered that house; but it did not fall because it had been founded on rock. And everyone who hears these words of mine and does not do them, is like a man who built his house on sand. The rain came down, the floods rose, the winds blew and battered that house; and immediately it collapsed, and it fell with a great crash.

Mission of the Kingdom

1 A man said to him: "I will follow you wherever you go". And Jesus said to him: "Foxes have dens, and birds of the sky have nests, but the Son of Man has nowhere to lay his head". To another he said: "Follow me". But he said: "Master, first let me go and bury my father". But he said to him: "Let the dead bury their own dead; but as for you, go and proclaim the kingdom of God".
2 Whoever gives even a cup of cold water to one of these little ones because he is a disciple, will by no means lose his reward.
3 The harvest is plentiful, but the workers are few, so ask the Lord of the harvest to send out workers into his harvest.
4 Go nowhere among the Gentiles, and do not enter any Samaritan town, but go rather to the lost sheep of the house of Israel. Preach as you go saying: "The kingdom of God is getting near". Carry no money, no bag, no sandals, nor a staff, and greet no one on the way. Whatever house you enter, first say: "Peace to this house". And if a son of peace is there, your peace shall rest upon him; but if not, it shall return to you. And stay in the same house, eating and drinking whatever they provide, for the worker deserves his pay. But if you enter a town and they do not receive you, as you leave shake the dust from your feet as a testimony against them. I tell you, it will be more tolerable on that day for Sodom than for that town.
5 Look, I am sending you out like sheep among wolves; so be wary as snakes and innocent as doves.
6 You will be hated by all for my name's sake. But he who endures to the end will be saved.
7 When they persecute you in one town, flee to the next; for you will not have gone through all the towns of Israel before the Son of Man comes.
8 When they hand you over to the synagogues, do not worry about how you are to answer or what you are to say, for it will be given to you at that time what to say.
9 Nothing is hidden that will not be made known, or secret that will not come to light. What I say to you in the dark, speak in the light; and what you hear whispered in the inner rooms, proclaim on the housetops. Do not be afraid of those who can kill the body but cannot kill the soul. Rather fear the one who is able to destroy both body and soul in hell. Are not five sparrows sold for two pennies? Yet not one of them will fall to the ground

without your Father's consent. Moreover even the hairs of your head have all been counted. So do not be afraid; you are worth more than many sparrows. And I tell you, everyone who acknowledges me in front of others, the Son of Man also will acknowledge in front of the angels of God; but whoever disowns me in front of others, will be disowned in front of the angels of God.

10 Do you think that I have come to bring peace on earth? I did not come to bring peace but a sword. For I have come to set a man against his father, and a daughter against her mother, and a daughter-in-law against her mother-in-law.

11 Whoever does not hate his father and mother cannot be my disciple. Whoever does not hate his son and daughter cannot be my disciple. And whoever does not take up his cross and follow me cannot be my disciple.

12 Whoever wants to save his life will lose it, but whoever loses his life for my sake will save it.

13 Whoever welcomes you welcomes me, and whoever welcomes me welcomes him who sent me.

14 Whoever is not with me is against me, and whoever does not gather with me scatters.

Coming of the Kingdom

1 In praying do not go babbling on as the Gentiles do, for they think they will be heard for their many words. Pray then like this: "Father, may your name be honoured, may your kingdom come. Give us this day our daily bread; and forgive us our sins, as we also have forgiven those who have wronged us; and do not bring us to the time of trial".

2 Many are called, but few are chosen.

3 The eye is the lamp of the body. So if your eye is healthy, your whole body will be full of light. But if your eye is not healthy, your whole body will be full of darkness. So if the light within you is darkness, how great must be the darkness.

4 Give to Caesar what belongs to Caesar, and to God what belongs to God.

5 It is an evil generation which seeks a sign. But no sign will be given to it except the sign of Jonah. For as Jonah became a sign to

the men of Nineveh, so the Son of Man will be to this generation. The queen of the South will arise at the judgment with this generation and condemn it. For she came from the ends of the earth to hear the wisdom of Solomon, and look, something greater than Solomon is here. The men of Nineveh will arise at the judgment with this generation and condemn it. For they repented at the preaching of Jonah, and look, something greater than Jonah is here.

6 Blessed are the eyes which see what you are seeing. For I tell you, many prophets and kings desired to see what you see, and did not see it; and to hear what you hear, and did not hear it.

7 A woman said to him: "Blessed is the womb that bore you, and the breasts that you sucked!" But he said: "Blessed rather are those who hear the word of God and comply with it."

8 If your brother wrongs you, rebuke him, and if he repents, you must forgive him. And if one day he wrongs you seven times, you must forgive him seven times.

9 Occasions for stumbling are bound to come, but woe to him by whom they come. It would be better for him if a millstone were hung round his neck and he were thrown into the sea, than that he should cause the downfall of one of these little ones.

10 You know that among the Gentiles their so-called rulers lord it over them, and their great men exercise authority over them. It shall not be so among you, but whoever would be great among you must be your servant, and whoever would be first among you must be your slave.

11 Everyone who exalts himself will be humbled, and whoever humbles himself will be exalted.

12 Among those standing here there are some who will not taste death before they see the kingdom of God come with power.

13 When you see a cloud rising in the west, you say at once: "A shower is coming"; and so it happens. And when you see the south wind blowing, you say: "There will be scorching heat"; and it happens. You hypocrites! You know how to interpret the appearance of the earth and the sky; so why do you not know how to interpret the present time?

14 What is the kingdom of God like, and to what should I compare it? It is like a mustard seed which a man took and sowed in the earth. It grew and became a tree, and the birds of

the sky made nests in its branches. To what should I compare the kingdom of God? It is like yeast which a woman took and hid in three measures of flour until it was fully fermented.

15 What man among you having a hundred sheep, if he loses one of them, does not leave the ninety-nine in the hills and go after the one which is lost? And when he finds it, I tell you that he rejoices more over that one sheep than over the ninety-nine that did not go astray. Or what woman having ten silver coins, if she loses one coin, does not light the lamp and sweep the house and search until she finds it? And when she finds it, she calls together her friends and neighbors saying: "Rejoice with me, for I've found the coin which I had lost".

16 Nobody can serve two masters; for either he will hate the one and love the other, or he will be devoted to the one and despise the other. You cannot serve God and wealth.

17 If you had faith like a mustard seed, you could say to this mulberry tree: "Be rooted up and planted in the sea", and it would obey you.

18 Do not store up for yourselves treasure on earth, where moths consume, and where thieves break in and steal. But store up for yourselves treasure in heaven, where no thief comes near, and no moth destroys. For where your treasure is, there will your heart be also.

19 Therefore I tell you, do not worry about your life, what you will eat, or about your body, what you will wear. Is not life more than food, and the body more than clothing? Consider the ravens; they neither sow nor reap nor gather into barns, and yet God feeds them. Are you not worth more than the birds? And which of you by worrying can add one hour to your span of life? Consider the lilies, how they grow; they neither toil nor spin; yet I tell you, even Solomon in all his glory was not clothed like one of these. But if God so clothes the grass in the field, which is alive today and tomorrow is thrown on the stove, how much more will he clothe you, people of little faith! And do not be anxious saying: "What shall we eat?" or "What shall we drink?" or "What shall we wear?", for it is the Gentiles who strive for all these things, and your Father knows that you need them. But instead seek his kingdom, and all these things will be given to you as well.

20 For to everyone who has will be given, but from the one who does not have, even what he has will be taken away.

21 When his kingdom comes, and the Son of Man is seated on his glorious throne, you who have followed me will likewise sit on twelve thrones, judging the twelve tribes of Israel.

22 Those who are last will be first, and the first will be last.

Obstacles to the Kingdom

1 Woe to you, lawyers; for you shut the kingdom of God against men; neither entering yourselves, nor allowing those who would enter to go in.

2 Woe to you, Pharisees; for you clean the outside of the cup and of the plate, but leave the inside full of greed and self-indulgence. You blind Pharisee! First clean the inside of the cup, so that the outside also may become clean.

3 Woe to you, Pharisees; for you tithe mint and dill and cumin; but you have overlooked justice and mercy and faithfulness. These you ought to have done, without neglecting the others. You blind guides, straining out a gnat and swallowing a camel!

4 Woe to you, Pharisees; for you love to have the place of honour at banquets, and the best seats in the synagogues, and to be greeted with respect in the marketplaces.

5 Woe to you, Pharisees; for you are like indistinct tombs, and people walk over them without knowing it.

6 Woe to you, lawyers; for you bind burdens and load them on people's shoulders, but you yourselves are unwilling to lift a finger to ease them.

7 Woe to you, scribes and Pharisees; for you build the tombs of the prophets. And you say: "If we had lived in the days of our ancestors, we would not have taken part with them in shedding the blood of the prophets". Thus you testify against yourselves that you are descendants of those who murdered the prophets. So then, fill up the measure of your ancestors! Therefore I send you prophets and sages, some of whom you will kill, and some you will persecute from town to town, so that you may be charged with the blood of all the prophets shed on earth, from the blood of Abel to the blood of Zechariah, who was murdered

between the sanctuary and the altar. Yes, I tell you, all this will be charged to this generation.

8 Many false prophets will arise, and will lead many astray.

9 If they say to you: "Look, he is in the wilderness", do not go out. If they say: "Look, he is in the inner rooms", do not follow.

10 For as the lightning comes from the east, and lights up the sky as far as the west, so will the Son of Man be in his day.

11 Where the corpse is, there the vultures will gather.

12 As it was in the days of Noah, so it will be in the days of the Son of Man. For as in those days they were eating and drinking, marrying and being given in marriage, until the day that Noah entered the ark, and the flood came and swept them all away, that is how it will be on the day when the Son of Man comes.

13 Then there will be two men in the field; one will be taken, and the other left. Two women will be grinding at the mill; one will be taken, and the other left.

14 Keep awake, then, for you do not know on what day your Lord will come. Be sure of this: if the householder had known at what time of night the thief was coming, he would have stayed awake and not let his house be broken into. So you also must be ready, for the Son of Man is coming at an hour you do not expect. [689]

APPENDIX 3
PSEUDO WORKS

There are a lot of writings that claim to be original sayings, teachings, and history of Yeshu, but which fall far short of meeting basic criteria for authentic acts and sayings. Several could be considered "inspirational" despite being unhistorical. Among these we would include the Bible.

Channeled Works

---

689 Source: English language reconstruction of Papias' LOGIA by Ron Price

A plethora of modern works claiming to reveal the hidden years of Christ are being published. These are a few older channeled works on Yeshu which we would mention, and one new one. Most of these erroneously claim a historical document is behind their text.

The Unknown Life of Jesus Christ by Nicolas Notovitch
The Gospel of the Holy Twelve by G. J. R. Ouseley
The Essene Gospel of Peace by Edmund Bordeaux Szekeley
The Aquarian Gospel, by Levi H. Dowling
The Mystical Life of Jesus by H. Spencer Lewis
The Archko volume, by W.D.Mahan
The Crucifixion Of Jesus, By An Eyewitness, published in 1880.
Confessions of Pilate by B. Shehadi, in New South Wales, in 1893
The Letter Of Benan, by Ernst Edler von der Planitz,, 1910
The Twenty-Ninth Chapter Of Acts, published in London in 1871
The Letter Of Jesus Christ, a 1917 anonymous writing
Letters of Pontius Pilate, published in 1928 by W. P. Crozier.
The Gnostic Gospel of Saint Bartholomew appeared in May of 2005
Gospel of Judas, first translated in 2006
Ghazali Sayings by Shaykh Ahmad Darwish

The Unknown Life of Jesus

The Unknown Life of Jesus Christ was published by Nicolas Notovitch late in the nineteenth century. Notovitch claimed that while recovering from a broken leg in a monastery in Himis, Tibet, he discovered a secret account of Jesus' travels to Tibet in a work called *Saint Issa*. Research found that the book was not catalogued in Tibetan libraries and the year his book was published, an English visitor wrote: "Yesterday we were at the great Himis monastery . . . There is not a single word of truth in the whole story!"[690] The next year, a professor read part of Notovitch's book to the head lama who responded: "Lies, lies, lies, nothing but lies!" After these reports Notovitch recanted and admitted he had never been to Himis monastery. He then began saying he had found the story of Issa in untitled fragments at various locations. Due to this inconsistency, it appears that this work is not a historical document.

The Gospel of the Holy 12

G. J. R. Ouseley published vegetarian promoting "*The Gospel of the Holy Twelve.*" in the late nineteenth century. It has also been re-issued with the name "*The Humane Gospel of Jesus.*" and "*The Nazorean Gospel*". In some editions there are claims that it is a translation of an ancient text found in a Tibet monastery, but some have a preface that explains its real origins as a channeled work:

> "Their "Gospel of the Holy Twelve" was communicated to the Editors, in numerous fragments at different times, by Emmanuel Swedenborg, Anna Kingsford, Edward Maitland, and a priest of the former century, giving his name as Placidus, of the Franciscan Order, afterwards a Carmelite. By them it was translated from the original, and given to the Editors in the flesh, to be supplemented in their proper places, where indicated, from the "Four Gospels" (A. V.) revised where necessary by the same. To this explanation, the Editors cannot add, nor from it take away. By the Divine Spirit was the Gospel communicated to the four above mentioned, and by them translated, and given to the writers; not in séance rooms (where too often resort the idle, the frivolous and the curious, attracting spirits similar to themselves, rather than the good), but "in dreams and visions of the night," and by direct guidance, has God instructed them by chosen

---

[690] Edgar J. Goodspeed, Strange New Gospels,

instruments; and now they give it to the world, that some may be wiser unto Salvation, while those who reject it, remain in their blindness, till they will to see.[691]

The Essene Gospel of Peace

The Essene Gospel of Peace by Edmund Bordeaux Szekeley and Lawrence Purcell Weaver was first published by them in 1937 with the title *The Gospel of Peace by the disciple John.*, In 1937 he states the text was only an eighth of the total Aramaic text from the first century; but in 1977 Szekeley dropped his co-author and changed this to a third of the total of a third century text.

In 1937 a copy came into the hands of Johnny Lovewisdom who later reworked and reword the text to a degree. He lived as a hermit in the mountain Crater Lake, Quilotoa, in Ecuador and published his version of the text under the title: *The Buddhist Essene Gospel of Jesus.* It contained an appendix pushing a raw foods diet: *Special Appendix: Diet of the Essene Jesus and The Healing Transition Diet.* Szekeley also promoted an all raw diet.

Many modern exponents of the raw food diet claim that the ancient Essenes were raw foodists. The association of raw food with Essenes is the product of one interpretation of Szekely's and Lovewisdom's writings. We can not find any historical justification for the ancient Essenes or Nazoreans being raw foodists and are leery of accepting the Essene Gospel of Peace as an ancient document since such is unsubstantiated, despite its poetic beauty.

Szekeley claims to have found original manuscripts of his Gospel in various locations, including the Vatican Library, the

---

[691] "Explanatory Preface" From An Early Twentieth Century Edition Published In London.

Royal Archives of the Hapsburgs in Vienna, and the monastery at Monte Cassino. Szekeley claims to have seen Hebrew, Aramaic, and Old Slavonic versions of the manuscript. He writes:

> "The content of this book represents only about a third of the complete manuscripts which exist in Aramaic in the archives of the Vatican and in old Slavonic in the Royal Archives of the Hapsburgs (now the property of the Austrian Government). We owe the existence of these two versions to the Nestorian priests who, under pressure of the advancing hordes of Genghis Khan, were forced to flee from the East towards the West, bearing all their ancient scriptures and ikons with them. The ancient Aramaic texts date from the third century after Christ, while the old Slavonic version is a literal translation of the former."

Careful research into these various claims have not supported his allegation. Per Beskow, writing in Strange Tales About Jesus, states that when he asked the National Library of Vienna about the Old Slavonic text, the reply was sent that "there is no such text, that a number of people have made inquiries about the text, and the general opinion was that Szekeley made it up."

A similar negative answer came from the Vatican as follows: "Dear Sir, Thank you for your letter of 25th May inquiring about Edmond Bordeaux Szekeley. This author's book is known to me and I can assert categorically that no such manuscript of an Aramaic Gospel is possessed by the Vatican Archives. Moreover, Szekeley's name has not been found in the card index of scholars admitted to the Archives."

Also, the Monte Cassino monastery was destroyed by being bombed during the Second World War. Szekeley knew this and made no mention of the Hebrew fragments found at Monte Cassino until after this destruction when he knew such could not be verified. There was once quite a lot of pressure for Szekely to substantiate his claims and he promised to one day write out the discovery of the Gospels for his detractors. When this work eventually was published, it was quite disappointing. His account of the discovery of the Essene Gospel of Peace had little. if any, information about the actual manuscript he claimed to have found. Instead, it was an account of his own spiritual search and experiences. No description of the text was forthcoming, its size, condition, place of origin, or any hard details. Instead, one finds only a vague reference to having found such in the Vatican library.

Thus one should be dubious of accepting his works as authentic historical documents since they cannot stand up to this criteria, although they are seen as valuable inspirational works helpful in inspiring one to return to a natural lifestyle. There is a great gulf between historical and inspirational works, however.

A careful reading of the historical authors on the Essenes, such as Josephus, betrays no reference to raw food. In fact, these accounts speak of cooked bread being set before the Essenes by Bakers at their common meal.

"And after this purification is over, they every one meet together in an apartment of their own, into which it is not permitted to any of another sect to enter; while they go, after a pure manner, into the dining room, as into a certain holy temple, and quietly set themselves down; upon which the baker lays them loaves in order; the cook also brings a single plate of one sort of food, and sets it before every one of them; but a priest says grace before meat; and it is unlawful for any one to taste of the food before grace be said." (Josephus on the Jewish sects, Wars of the Jews Book II Chapter 8)

Most raw foodists lean heavily on the writings of Szekely to substantiate their lifestyle. Many also believe Ouseley's *Gospel of the Holy Twelve*. This is a psuedipigraphic text, however, and not a historical document as he himself stated:

The closest historical verification for a raw food diet would be within the oral legends of the Mandaeans, as recorded by E.S. Drower in her studies of this remnant of the ancient Nazorean Essenes. She records that Mandaean Priests, during certain feasting periods, are supposed to eat raw fruits and vegetables along with cooked bread. She reports that they no longer observe this type of temporary raw produce fast and think no great thing of it. Such may indicate an ancient tradition of fasting on raw produce but not raw bread. The Greek Orthodox tradition also preserves a custom of xerophagy, or the eating of dry, uncooked foods, as a type of fasting. This tradition may go back to ancient Nazorean times as well, but it is significant that these are types of fasts, not types of lifestyle and perpetual diet.

The Aquarian Gospel

The Aquarian Gospel, by "Levi," is a work by Levi H. Dowling who lived from 1844 to 1911. The work, first published in 1972, claims that Jesus lived in India and was initiated in Egypt. It admits to being a channeled work and has little of import in regards to the true Nazorean Way of Yeshu.

The Mystical Life of Jesus

In *The Mystical Life of Jesus* by H. Spencer Lewis Yeshu is depicted as a celibate gentile, conceived of an aryan virgin, who survived the crucifixion. These ideas are not in harmony with ancient Nazorean understandings.

The Archko Volume

The Archko volume, by W.D.Mahan was first published in 1884 under the title "The Archaeological and the Historical Writings of the Sanhedrin and Talmuds of the Jews...". Its first edition contained a flagrant plagarization from the 1880 novel Ben Hur called 'Eli and the Story of the Magi'. [692] This was dropped in latter editions. The work has been discredited.

Protevangelium of James

The *Protevangelium of James* is a highly Catholicized infancy gospel which may have preserved a few tidbits of original Nazorean tradition, but overall has little value in recovering the historical Yeshu. In it the mother of John the Baptist is said to hide her son from Herod in a mountain cave. The Protevangelium of James also speaks of the perpetual virginity of the mother of Yeshu and James. This is of course a Catholic gloss and has nothing at all to do with the facts. Its mentioning in this second century text is its first known occurrence in writing. Yet even at the end of this century Catholic writers like Tertullian (c160-221AD) are still writing that Mary had her children normally and that the brothers of Yeshu are his real and full brothers. A little later Origin (185-254 AD) speaks of having read a writing of James, perhaps this Protevangelium, for he declares that Yeshu was not a man, but something divine. He also says that the brothers of Jesus were the sons of Joseph from another wife whom he had married before Mary. The Protevangelium of James also speaks of Mary having been a weaver of veils in the temple, and of her parents giving a third of their earning to the poor, a third to the temple, and a third they lived on. These may be echoes of true events since our Cayce source says Mary indeed lived in the Carmel

---

[692] Edgar J. Goodspeed, Strange New Gospels,

Temple and it was indeed a Nazorean custom to donate much, if not all, of ones earnings to toward the good of others. As a whole, however, the Protevangelium of James is worthless, being written by uniformed foreigners and not the brother of Yeshu as claimed.

Gnostic Gospel of Saint Bartholomew

The *Gnostic Gospel of Saint Bartholomew* appeared in May of 2005. It claimed to be a modern translation of an ancient text by an American branch of an underground European Cathar organization. They claim to have had it for 900 years and that it has been tested to be from the first few centuries AD. The newly published text appears to be a modern reworking of the apocryphal Gospel of Saint Bartholomew. Although it contains some elements in harmony with original Nazoreanism, such as the co-messiahship of Mary Magdalene, it also contains elements that conflict with Yeshu's teachings.

The Gospel of Judas

The *Gospel of Judas* is a Gnostic gospel which was translated in 2006. Most of it is not in harmony with true events surrounding Yeshu, but it does contain a true summary and a slightly better translation of the longer cosmology of the Apocryphon of John from the Nag.

"Yeshu said, "Come , that I may teach you about secrets no person has ever seen. For there exists a great and boundless realm, whose extent no generation of angels has seen, in which there is a great invisible Spirit, which no eye of an angel has ever seen, no thought of the heart has ever comprehended, and it was never called by any name. "And a luminous cloud appeared there. He said, 'Let an angel come into being as my attendant.' "A great angel, the enlightened divine Self-Generated, emerged from the cloud. Because of him, four other angels came into

being from another cloud, and they became attendants for the
angelic Self-Generated. The Self-Generated said, 'Let ... come
into being ... ,' and it came into being ... . And he created the
first luminary to reign over him. He said, 'Let angels come into
being to serve him,' and myriads without number came into
being. He said, 'Let an enlightened Aeon come into being,' and
he came into being. He created the second luminary to reign
over him, together with myriads of angels without number, to
offer service. That is how he created the rest of the enlightened
aeons. He made them reign over them, and he created for them
myriads of angels without number, to assist them. "Adamas was
in the first luminous cloud that no angel has ever seen among all
those called 'God.' He ... that ... the image ... and after the
likeness of this angel. He made the incorruptible generation of
Seth appear ... the twelve ... the twenty-four ... . He made
seventy-two luminaries appear in the incorruptible generation,
in accordance with the will of the Spirit. The seventy-two
luminaries themselves made three hundred sixty luminaries
appear in the incorruptible generation, in accordance with the
will of the Spirit, that their number should be five for each. "The
twelve aeons of the twelve luminaries constitute their father,
with six heavens for each Aeon, so that there are seventy-two
heavens for the seventy-two luminaries, and for each of them
five firmaments, for a total of three hundred sixty firmaments ...
. They were given authority and a great host of angels without
number, for glory and adoration, and after that also virgin
spirits, for glory and adoration of all the aeons and the heavens
and their firmaments. "The multitude of those immortals is
called the cosmos— that is, perdition—by the Father and the
seventy-two luminaries who are with the Self-Generated and his
seventy-two aeons. In him the first human appeared with his
incorruptible powers. And the Aeon that appeared with his
generation, the Aeon in whom are the cloud of knowledge and
the angel, is called El. ... Aeon ... after that ... said, 'Let twelve
angels come into being to rule over chaos and the underworld .'
And look, from the cloud there appeared an angel whose face
flashed with fire and whose appearance was defiled with blood.
His name was Nebro, which means 'rebel'; others call him
Yaldabaoth. Another angel, Saklas, also came from the cloud. So

Nebro created six angels—as well as Saklas—to be assistants, and these produced twelve angels in the heavens, with each one receiving a portion in the heavens. "The twelve rulers spoke with the twelve angels: 'Let each of you ... and let them ... generation —*one line lost*— angels': The first is Seth, who is called Christ. The second is Harmathoth, who is ... . The third is Galila. The fourth is Yobel. The fifth is Adonaios. These are the five who ruled over the underworld, and first of all over chaos. "Then Saklas said to his angels, 'Let us create a human being after the likeness and after the image.' They fashioned Adam and his wife Eve, who is called, in the cloud, Zoe. For by this name all the generations seek the man, and each of them calls the woman by these names." [693]

The Ghazali Sayings

The *Ghazali Sayings* are 83 pithy sayings translated from Aramaic into Arabic by al-Ghazali who was born in 1058 A.D. in Khorasan, Iran. And died in 1111 AD. There is an English translation of his sayings by Shaykh Ahmad Darwish. Ghazali was a sufi mystic who upheld an ascetic wandering type of ideal, and the sayings he has collected in the name of Jesus are more of this tone than of the original Nazoreanism that Yeshu lived. Some of the sayings may be authentic, but for the most part they betray a Path other than the Nazorean one of Yeshu.

APPENDIX 4
CELIBATE ESSENES

Several of the ancient historians describe a branch of the Essenes that appear to have honored celibacy and to have lived in small, often all male, monasteries in the desert. Yeshu was not of this persuasion, being a member of the Nazorean Essenes who honored and insisted upon marriage for all. We

---

[693] Gospel of Judas

are also told that that the Ossaeans, which would have once included these celibate honoring branches, accepted Elchasai as a prophet in circa 101 AD. We are also told that Elchasai insisted on marriage for all. We can therefore assume that any openness to celibacy dissipated among Essene remnants during his prophetic career, its only continuation being amongst the later Roman Christian monastics who insisted upon celibacy for their monasteries. These later Roman Christian monasteries seemed to have borrowed many ideas from these Essene like celibate communities, but their spiritual foundation was laid on the Old and New Testaments which were never at the core of any Essene community, celibate or married.

Philo on Essenes

A first hand report concerning celibate Essenes come from the Jewish philosopher of the Egyptian dispersion, Philo of Alexandria, who lived between 30 B.C. and 40 A.D. His writings about the Essenes comes from two works, 'Quod omnis probus Fiber sit' and 'Apologia pro Judais.' The second work was lost but quotes are preserved in Eusebius' 'Praeparatio Evangilica.' Philo's account:

> "The Essenes live in a number of towns in Judea, and also in many villages and in large groups. They do not enlist by race, but by volunteers who have a zeal for righteousness and an ardent love of men. For this reason there are no young children among the Essenes. Not even adolescents or young men. Instead they are men of old or ripe years who have learned how to control their bodily passions. They possess nothing of their own, not house, field, slave nor flocks, nor anything which feeds and procures wealth. They live together in brotherhoods, and eat in common together. Everything they do is for the common good of the group. They work at many different jobs and attack their work with amazing zeal and dedication, working from before

sunrise to almost sunset without complaint, but in obvious exhilaration. Their exercise is their work. Indeed, they believe their own training to be more agreeable to body and soul, and more lasting, than athletic games, since their exercises remain fitted to their age, even when the body no longer possesses its full strength. They are farmers and shepherds and beekeepers and craftsmen in diverse trades. They share the same way of life, the same table, even the same tastes; all of them loving frugality and hating luxury as a plague for both body and soul. Not only do they share a common table, but common clothes as well. What belongs to one belongs to all. Available to all of them are thick coats for winter and inexpensive light tunics for summer. Seeing it as an obstacle to communal life, they have banned marriage."

Therapeuts of Egypt

Philo graphically described the usage of a seven-weeks calendar (with fiftieth day) among the Therapeutae and Therapeutridae of Egypt whom Epiphanius later reports to be Nazoreans. Therapeutae means healer, and in the Aramaic the word for healer is "essene". When Yeshu was in Egypt he may have kept this calendar with the Therapeutae. This second account of Philo comes from a treatise: de Vita Contemplativa (The Contemplative Life) written around 30 AD. It probably represents dietary customs prevalent during the Nazorean equivalent of Lent. Philo, in his De Vita Contemplativa writes:

"Having mentioned the Essenes, who in all respects selected for their admiration and for their especial adoption the practical course of life, and who excel in all, or what perhaps may be a less unpopular and invidious thing to say, in most of its parts, I will now proceed, in the regular order of my subject, to speak of those who have embraced the speculative life, ... Now the lifestyle of these philosophers is at once displayed from the appellation given to them; for with strict regard to etymology, they are called Therapeutae and Therapeutrides, either because they profess an art of medicine more excellent than that in general use in cities (for that only heals bodies, but the other heals souls which are under the mastery of terrible and almost incurable diseases, which pleasures and appetites, fears and griefs, and covetousness, and follies, and injustice, and all the rest of the innumerable multitude of other passions and vices, have inflicted upon them), or else because they have been instructed by nature and the sacred laws to serve the living God, who is superior to the good, and more simple than the one, and more ancient than the monad; with whom, however, who is there of those who profess piety that we can possibly compare? . . . . But the therapeutic race, being continually taught to see without interruption, may well aim at obtaining a sight of the living God, and may pass by the sun, which is visible to the outward sense, and never leave this order which conducts to perfect happiness.

But they who apply themselves to this kind of service, not because they are influenced to do so by custom, nor by the advice or recommendation of any particular persons, but because they are carried away by a certain heavenly love, give way to enthusiasm, behaving like so many revelers in bacchanalian or corybantian mysteries, until they see the object which they have been earnestly desiring.

Then, because of their anxious desire for an immortal and blessed existence, thinking that their mortal life has already come to an end, they leave their possessions to their sons or daughters, or perhaps to other relations, giving them up their inheritance with willing cheerfulness; and those who know no relations give their property to their companions or friends, for it followed of necessity that those who have acquired the wealth which sees, as if ready prepared for them, should be willing to surrender that wealth which is blind to those who themselves also are still blind in their minds.

. . . . but they take up their abode outside of walls, or gardens, or solitary lands, seeking for a desert place, not because of any ill-natured misanthropy to which they have learnt to devote themselves, but because of the associations with people of wholly dissimilar dispositions to which they would otherwise be compelled, and which they know to be unprofitable and mischievous.

Now this race may be found in many places, for it was fitting that both Greece and the country of the barbarians should partake of whatever is perfectly good; and there is the greatest number of such men in Egypt, in every one of the districts, or nomoi as they are called, and especially around Alexandria; and from all quarters those who are the best of these therapeutae proceed on their pilgrimage to some most suitable place as if it were their country, which is beyond the Mareotic lake, lying in a somewhat level plain a little raised above the rest, being suitable for their purpose by reason of its safety and also of the fine temperature of the air.

For the houses built in the fields and the villages which surround it on all sides give it safety; and the admirable temperature of the air proceeds from the continual breezes which come from the lake which falls into the sea, and also from the sea itself in the neighborhood, the breezes from the sea being light, and those which proceed from the lake which falls into the sea being heavy, the mixture of which produces a most healthy atmosphere.

But the houses of these men thus congregated together are very plain, just giving shelter in respect of the two things most important to be provided against, the heat of the sun, and the cold from the open air; and they did not live near to one another as men do in cities, for immediate neighborhood to others would be a troublesome and unpleasant thing to men who have conceived an admiration for, and have determined to devote themselves to, solitude; and, on the other hand, they did not live very far from one another on account of the fellowship which they desire to cultivate, and because of the desirableness of being able to assist one another if they should be attacked by robbers.

And in every house there is a sacred shrine which is called the holy place, and the monastery in which they retire by themselves and perform all the mysteries of a holy life, bringing in nothing, neither meat, nor drink, nor anything else which is indispensable towards supplying the necessities of the body, but studying in that place the laws and the sacred oracles of God enunciated by the holy prophets, and hymns, and psalms, and all kinds of other things by reason of which knowledge and piety are increased and brought to perfection.

Therefore they always retain an imperishable recollection of God, so that not even in their dreams is any other object ever presented to their eyes except the beauty of the divine virtues and of the divine powers. Therefore many persons speak in their sleep, divulging and publishing the celebrated doctrines of the sacred philosophy.

And they are accustomed to pray twice every day, at morning and at evening; when the sun is rising entreating God that the happiness of the coming day may be real happiness, so that their minds may be filled with heavenly light, and when the sun is setting they pray that their soul, being entirely lightened and relieved of the burden of the outward senses, and of the appropriate object of these outward senses, may be able to trace out truth existing in its own consistory and council chamber. And the interval between morning and evening is by them devoted wholly to meditation on and to practice of virtue, for they take up the sacred writings and philosophize concerning them, investigating the allegories of their national philosophy, since they look upon their literal expressions as symbols of some secret meaning of nature, intended to be conveyed in those figurative expressions.

They have also writings of ancient men, who having been the founders of one sect or another have left behind them many memorials of the allegorical system of writing and explanation, whom they take as a kind of model, and imitate the general fashion of their sect; so that they do not occupy themselves solely in contemplation, but they likewise compose psalms and hymns to God in every kind of metre and melody imaginable, which they of necessity arrange in more dignified rhythm.

Therefore, during six days, each of these individuals, retiring into solitude by himself, philosophizes by himself in one of the places called monasteries, never going outside the threshold of the outer court, and indeed never even looking out. But on the seventh day they all come together as if to meet in a sacred assembly, and they sit down in order according to their ages with all becoming gravity, keeping their hands inside their garments, having their right hand between their chest and their dress, and the left hand down by their side, close to their flank; and then the eldest of them who has the most profound learning in their doctrines, comes forward and speaks with steadfast look and with steadfast voice, with great powers of reasoning, and great prudence, not making an exhibition of his oratorical powers like the rhetoricians of old, or the sophists of the present day, but investigating with great pains, and explaining with minute accuracy the precise meaning of the laws, which sits, not indeed at the tips of their ears, but penetrates through their hearing into the soul, and remains there lastingly; and all the rest listen in silence to the praises which he bestows upon the law, showing their assent only by nods of the head, or the eager look of the eyes.

And this common holy place to which they all come together on the seventh day is a twofold circuit, being separated partly into the apartment of the men, and partly into a chamber for the women, for women also, in accordance with the usual fashion there, form a part of the audience, having the same feelings of admiration as the men, and having adopted the same sect with equal deliberation and decision; and the wall which is between the houses rises from the ground three or four cubits upwards, like a battlement, and the upper portion rises upwards to the roof without any opening, on two accounts; first of all, in order that the modesty which is so becoming to the female sex may be preserved, and secondly, that the women may be easily able to comprehend what is said being seated within earshot, since there is then nothing which can possibly intercept the voice of him who is speaking. And these expounders of the law, having first of all laid down temperance as a sort of foundation for the soul to rest upon, proceed to build up other virtues on this foundation, and no one of them may take any meat or drink before the setting of the sun, since they judge that the work of philosophizing is one which is worthy of the light, but that the care for the necessities of the body is suitable only to darkness, on which account they appropriate the day to the one occupation, and a brief portion of the night to the other; and some men, in whom there is implanted a more fervent desire of knowledge, can endure to cherish a recollection of their food for three days without even tasting it, and some men are so delighted, and enjoy themselves so exceedingly when regaled by wisdom which supplies them with her doctrines in all possible wealth and abundance, that they can even hold out twice as great a length of time, and will scarcely at the end of six days taste even necessary food, being accustomed, as they say that grasshoppers are, to feed on air, their song, as I imagine, making their scarcity tolerable to them. And they, looking upon the seventh day as one of perfect holiness and a most complete festival, have thought it worthy of a most especial honor, and on it, after taking due care of their soul, they tend their bodies also, giving them, just as they do to their cattle, a complete rest from their continual labors; and they eat nothing of a costly character, but plain bread and a seasoning of salt, which the more luxurious of them to further season with hyssop; and their drink is water from the spring; for they oppose those feelings which nature has made mistresses of the human race, namely, hunger and thirst, giving them nothing to flatter or humor them, but only such useful things as it is not possible to exist without. On this account they eat only so far as not to be hungry, and they drink just enough to escape from thirst, avoiding all satiety, as an enemy of and a plotter against both soul and body.

And there are two kinds of covering, one raiment and the other a house: we have already spoken of their houses, that they are not decorated with any ornaments, but run up in a hurry, being only made to answer such purposes as are absolutely necessary; and in like manner their raiment is of the most ordinary description, just stout enough to ward off cold and heat, being a cloak of some shaggy hide for winter, and a thin mantle or linen shawl in the summer; for in short they practice entire simplicity, looking upon falsehood as the foundation of pride, but truth as the origin of simplicity, and upon truth and falsehood as standing in the light of fountains, for from falsehood proceeds every variety of evil and wickedness, and from truth there flows every imaginable abundance of good things both human and divine. I wish also to speak of their common assemblies, and their very cheerful meetings at convivial parties, setting them in opposition and contrast to the banquets of others, ...

But since the entertainments of the greatest celebrity are full of such trifling and folly, bearing conviction in themselves, if any one should think fit not to regard vague opinion and the character which has been commonly handed down concerning them as feasts which have gone off with the most eminent success, I will oppose to them the entertainments of those persons who have devoted their whole life and themselves to the knowledge and contemplation of the affairs of nature in accordance with the most sacred admonitions and precepts of the prophet Moses. In the first place, these men assemble at the end of seven weeks, venerating not only the simple week of seven days, but also its multiplied power, for they know it to be pure and always virgin; and it is a prelude and a kind of fore feast of the greatest feast, which is assigned to the number fifty, the most holy and natural of numbers, being compounded of the power of the right-angled triangle, which is the principle of the origination and condition of the whole. Therefore when they come together clothed in white garments, and joyful with the most exceeding gravity, when some one of the ephemereutae (for that is the appellation which they are accustomed to give to those who are employed in such ministrations), before they sit down to meat standing in order in a row, and raising their eyes and their hands to heaven, the one because they have learnt to fix their attention on what is worthy looking at, and the other because they are free from the reproach of all impure gain, being never polluted under any pretence whatever by any description of criminality which can arise from any means taken to procure advantage, they pray to God that the entertainment may be acceptable, and welcome, and pleasing; and after having offered up these prayers the elders sit down to meat, still observing the order in which they were previously arranged, for they do not look on those as elders who are advanced in years and very ancient, but in some cases they esteem those as very young men, if they have attached themselves to this sect only lately, but those whom they call elders are those who from their earliest infancy have grown up and arrived at maturity in the speculative portion of philosophy, which is the most beautiful and most divine part of it.

And the women also share in this feast, the greater part of whom, though old, are virgins in respect of their purity (not indeed through necessity, as some of the priestesses among the Greeks are, who have been compelled to preserve their chastity more than they would have done of their own accord), but out of an admiration for and love of wisdom, with which they are desirous to pass their lives, on account of which they are indifferent to the pleasures of the body, desiring not a mortal but an immortal offspring, which the soul that is attached to God is alone able to produce by itself and from itself, the Father having sown in it rays of light appreciable only by the intellect, by means of which it will be able to perceive the doctrines of wisdom.

And the order in which they sit down to meat is a divided one, the men sitting on the right hand and the women apart from them on the left; and in case any one by chance suspects that cushions, if not very costly ones, still at all events of a tolerably soft substance, are prepared for men who are well born and well bred, and contemplators of philosophy, he must know that they have nothing but rugs of the coarsest materials, cheap mats of the most ordinary kind of the papyrus of the land, piled up on the ground and projecting a little near the elbow, so that the feasters may lean upon them, for they relax in a slight degree the Lacedaemonian rigor of life, and at all times and in all places they practice a liberal, gentlemanlike kind of frugality, hating the allurements of pleasure with all their might.

And they do not use the ministrations of slaves, looking upon the possession of servants or slaves to be a thing absolutely and wholly contrary to nature, for nature has created all men free, but the injustice and covetousness of some men who prefer inequality, that cause of all evil, having subdued some, has given to the more powerful authority over those who are weaker. Accordingly in this sacred entertainment there is, as I have said, no slave, but free men minister to the guests, performing the offices of servants, not under compulsion, nor in obedience to any imperious commands, but of their own voluntary free will, with all eagerness and promptitude anticipating all orders, for they are not any chance free men who are appointed to perform these duties, but young men who are selected from their order with all possible care on account of their excellence, acting as virtuous and wellborn youths ought to act who are eager to attain to the perfection of virtue, and who, like legitimate sons, with affectionate rivalry minister to their fathers and mothers, thinking their common parents more closely connected with them than those who are related by blood, since in truth to men of right principles there is nothing more nearly akin than virtue; and they come in to perform their service ungirdled, and with their tunics let down, in order that nothing which bears any resemblance to a slavish appearance may be introduced into this festival.

I know well that some persons will laugh when they hear this, but they who laugh will be those who do things worthy of weeping and lamentation. And in those days wine is not introduced, but only the clearest water; cold water for the generality, and hot water for those old men who are accustomed to a luxurious life. And the table, too, bears nothing which has blood, but there is placed upon it bread for food and salt for seasoning, to which also hyssop is sometimes added as an extra sauce for the sake of those who are delicate in their eating, for just as right reason commands the priest to offer up sober sacrifices, so also these men are commanded to live sober lives, for wine is the medicine of folly, and costly seasonings and sauces excite desire, which is the most insatiable of all beasts.

These, then, are the first circumstances of the feast; but after the guests have sat down to the table in the order which I have been describing, and when those who minister to them are all standing around in order, ready to wait upon them, and when there is nothing to drink, the one [who presides] will speak, [after a general silence has been achieved -- one might ask when there is not silence,] but [now] even more so than before -- so that no one ventures to mutter, or even to breathe at all hard, and then he searches out some passage in the sacred writings, or explains some difficulty which is proposed by some one else, without any thoughts of display on his own part, for he is not aiming at reputation for cleverness and eloquence, but is only desirous to see some points more accurately, and is content when he has thus seen them himself not to bear ill will to others, who, even if they did not perceive the truth with equal acuteness, have at all events an equal desire of learning. And he, indeed, follows a slower method of instruction, dwelling on and lingering over his explanations with repetitions, in order to imprint his conceptions deep in the minds of his hearers, for as the understanding of his hearers is not able to keep up with the interpretation of one who goes on fluently, without stopping to take breath, it gets behind-hand, and fails to comprehend what is said; but the hearers, fixing their eyes and attention upon the speaker, remain in one and the same position listening attentively, indicating their attention and comprehension by their nods and looks, and the praise which they are inclined to bestow on the speaker by the cheerfulness and gentle manner in which they follow him with their eyes and with the fore-finger of the right hand. And the young men who are standing around attend to this explanation no less than the guests themselves who are sitting at meat.

And these explanations of the sacred writings are delivered by mystic expressions in allegories, for the whole of the law appears to these men to resemble a living animal, and its express commandments seem to be the body, and the invisible meaning concealed under and lying beneath the plain words resembles the soul, in which the rational soul begins most excellently to contemplate what belongs to itself, as in a mirror, beholding in these very words the exceeding beauty of the sentiments, and unfolding and explaining the symbols, and bringing the secret meaning naked to the light to all who are able by the light of a slight intimation to perceive what is unseen by what is visible.

When, therefore, the president appears to have spoken at sufficient length, and to have carried out his intentions adequately, so that his explanation has gone on felicitously and fluently through his own acuteness, and the hearing of the others has been profitable, applause arises from them all as of men rejoicing together at what they have seen and heard; and then some one rising up sings a hymn which has been made in honor of God, either such as he has composed himself, or some ancient one of some old poet, for they have left behind them many poems and songs in trimetre iambics, and in psalms of thanksgiving and in hymns, and songs at the time of libation, and at the altar, and in regular order, and in choruses, admirably measured out in various and well diversified strophes. And after him then others also arise in their ranks, in becoming order, while every one else listens in decent silence, except when it is proper for them to take up the burden of the song, and to join in at the end; for then they all, both men and women, join in the hymn.

And when each individual has finished his psalm, then the young men bring in the table which was mentioned a little while ago, on which was placed that most holy food, the leavened bread, with a seasoning of salt, with which hyssop is mingled, out of reverence for the sacred table, which lies thus in the holy outer temple; for on this table are placed loaves and salt without seasoning, and the bread is unleavened, and the salt unmixed with anything else, for it was becoming that the simplest and purest things should be allotted to the most excellent portion of the priests, as a reward for their ministrations, and that the others should admire similar things, but should abstain from the loaves, in order that those who are the more excellent person may have the precedence.

And after the feast they celebrate the sacred festival during the whole night; and this nocturnal festival is celebrated in the following manner: they all stand up together, and in the middle of the entertainment two choruses are formed at first, the one of men and the other of women, and for each chorus there is a leader and chief selected, who is the most honorable and most excellent of the band. Then they sing hymns which have been composed in honor of God in many metres and tunes, at one time all singing together, and at another moving their hands and dancing in corresponding harmony, and uttering in an inspired manner songs of thanksgiving, and at another time regular odes, and performing all necessary strophes and antistrophes. Then, when each chorus of the men and each chorus of the women has feasted separately by itself, like persons in the bacchanalian revels, drinking the pure wine of the love of God, they join together, and the two become one chorus, an imitation of that one which, in old time, was established by the Red Sea, on account of the wondrous works which were displayed there; for, by the commandment of God, the sea became to one party the cause of safety, and to the other that of utter destruction; for it being burst asunder, and dragged back by a violent reflux, and being built up on each side as if there were a solid wall, the space in the midst was widened, and cut into a level and dry road, along which the people passed over to the opposite land, being conducted onwards to higher ground; then, when the sea returned and ran back to its former channel, and was poured out from both sides, on what had just before been dry ground, those of the enemy who pursued were overwhelmed and perished. When the Israelites saw and experienced this great miracle, which was an event beyond all description, beyond all imagination, and beyond all hope, both men and women together, under the influence of divine inspiration, becoming all one chorus, sang hymns of thanksgiving to God the Savior, Moses the prophet leading the men, and Miryam the prophetess leading the women. Now the chorus of Therapeutae and Therapeutrides [i.e. male and female] being formed, as far as possible on this model, makes a most harmonious concert, and a truly musical symphony, the shrill voices of the women mingling with the deep-toned voices of the men. The ideas were beautiful, the expressions beautiful, and the chorus-singers were beautiful; and the end of ideas, and expressions, and chorus singers, was piety; therefore, being intoxicated all night till the morning with this beautiful intoxication, without feeling their heads heavy or closing their eyes for sleep, but being even more awake than when they came to the feast, as to their eyes and their whole bodies, and standing there till morning, when they saw the sun rising they raised their hands to heaven, imploring tranquility and truth, and acuteness of understanding. And after their prayers they each retired to their own separate abodes, with the intention of again practicing the usual philosophy to which they had been wont to devote themselves. This then is what I have to say of those who are called Therapeutae, who have devoted themselves to the contemplation of nature, and who have lived in it and in the soul alone, being citizens of heaven and of the world, and very acceptable to the Father and Creator of the universe because of their virtue, which has procured them his love as their most appropriate reward, which far surpasses all the gifts of fortune, and conducts them to the very summit and perfection of happiness."[694]

Josephus on Essenes

This reference to celibate Essenes comes from Flavius Josephus writing about the death of Antigonus in 103 B.C. Josephus relates that the Essenes had an uncanny ability to successfully predict future events, and that the death of Antigonus at the hands of his brother, Aristobulus, ruler of Judea, had been accurately forecast by an Essene named Judas. Josephus states that Judas was an Essene born and bred, indicating that he had been born into the movement at least a few decades earlier. On this occasion, according to Josephus, Judas was sitting in or near the Jerusalem temple with a number or his pupils, showing that he was an Essene teacher of the Law and that he

---

[694] Philo Judaeus, Alexandria, Egypt, 30 A.D

was able to speak his views apparently quite freely in Jerusalem at the end of the second century B.C.

"The sect of the Essenes maintain that Fate governs all things, and that nothing can befall man contrary to its determination and will. These men live the same kind of life which among the Greeks has been ordered by Pythagoras."

"The Essenes are Jews by race, but are more closely united among themselves by mutual affection, and by their efforts to cultivate a particularly saintly life. They renounce pleasure as an evil, and regard continence and resistance to passions as a virtue. They disdain marriage for themselves, being content to adopt the children of others at a tender age in order to instruct them. They do not abolish marriage, but are convinced women are all licentious and incapable of fidelity to one man. They despise riches. When they enter the sect, they must surrender all of their money and possessions into the common fund, to be put at the disposal of everyone; one single property for the whole group. Therefore neither the humiliation of poverty nor the pride of possession is to be seen anywhere among them. They regard oil as a defilement, and should any of them be involuntarily anointed, he wipes his body clean. They make a point of having their skin dry and of always being clothed in white garments. In their various communal offices, the administrators are elected and appointed without distinction offices. They are not just in one town only, but in every town several of them form a colony. They welcome members from out of town as coequal brothers, and even though perfect strangers, as though they were intimate friends. For this reason they carry nothing with them ashen they travel: they are, however, armed against brigands. They do not change their garments or shoes until they have completely worn out. They neither buy nor sell anything among themselves. They give to each other freely and feel no need to repay anything in exchange. Before sunrise they recite certain ancestral prayers to the sun as though entreating it to rise. They work until about 11 A.M. when they put on ritual loincloths and bathe for purification. Then they enter a communal hall, where no one else is allowed, and eat only one bowlful of food for each man, together with their loaves of bread. They eat in silence.

Afterwards they lay aside their sacred garment and go back to work until the evening. At evening they partake dinner in the same manner. During meals they are sober and quiet and their silence seems a great mystery to people outside. Their food and drink are so measured out that they are satisfied but no more. They see bodily pleasure as sinful. On the whole they do nothing unless ordered by their superiors, but two things they are allowed to do on their own discretion: to help those 'worthy of help', and to offer food to the needy. They are not allowed, however, to help members of their own families without permission from superiors. They are very careful not to exhibit their anger, carefully controlling such outbursts. They are very loyal and are peacemakers. They refuse to swear oaths, believing every word they speak to be stronger than an oath. They are scrupulous students of the ancient literature. They are ardent students in the healing of diseases, of the roots offering protection, and of the properties of stones. Those desiring to enter the sect are not allowed immediate entrance. They are made to wait outside for a period of one year. During this time each postulant is given a hatchet, a loincloth and a white garment. The hatchet is used for cleanliness in stooling for digging and covering up the hole. Having proved his continence during the first year he draws closer to the way of life and participates in the purificatory baths at a higher degree, but he is not yet admitted into intimacy. His character is tested another two years and if he proves worthy he is received into the company permanently.

They are sworn to love truth and to pursue liars. They must never steal. They are not allowed to keep any secrets from other members of the sect; but they are warned to reveal nothing to outsiders, even under the pain of death. They are not allowed to alter the 'books of the sect, and must keep all the information secret, especially the names of the angels. The name of the Lawgiver, after God, is a matter of great veneration to them; if anyone blasphemed the name of the Lawgiver he was sentenced to death. Those members convicted of grave faults are expelled from the order. In matters of judgment Essene leaders are very exact and impartial. Their decisions are irrevocable. They are so scrupulous in matters pertaining to the Sabbath day that they refuse even to go to stool on that day, They always give way to the opinion of the majority, and they make it their duty to obey their elders. They are divided into four lots according to the duration of their discipline, and the juniors are so inferior to their elders that if the latter touch them, they wash themselves as though they had been in contact with a stranger. They despise danger: they triumph over pain by the heroism of their convictions, and consider death, if it comes with glory, to be better than the preservation of life. They died in great glory amidst terrible torture in the war against the Romans. They believe that their souls are immortal, but that their bodies are corruptible. They believe the soul is trapped in the body and is freed with death. They believe that there is a place 'across the ocean' where just souls gather, a place reserved for the immortal souls of the just. The souls of the wicked, however, are relegated to a dark pit, shaken by storms and full of unending chastisement. Some of the Essenes became expert in forecasting the future."

Pliny on Essenes

The Roman writer, Pliny the Elder, who died in 79 A.D., also wrote of celibate Essenes in his 'Natural History':

"To the west (of the Dead Sea) the Essenes have put the necessary distance between themselves and the insalubrious shore. They are a people unique of its kind and admirable beyond all others in the whole world; without women and renouncing love entirely, without money and having for company only palm trees. Owing to the throng of newcomers, this people is daily reborn in equal number; indeed, those whom, wearied by the fluctuations of fortune, life leads to adopt their customs, stream in in great numbers. Thus, unbelievable though this may seem, for thousands of centuries a people has existed which is eternal yet into which no one is born: so fruitful for them is the repentance which others feel for their past lives!"

INDEX

CPSIA information can be obtained
at www.ICGtesting.com
Printed in the USA
FSHW021943291118
54134FS